Here's what readers are saying about Randy Alcorn's novels:

"I have just finished reading Randy Alcorn's new novel. *Deception* is the same high quality as Randy's related novels *Deadline* and *Dominion*. All three are page-turners.... Randy is a gifted writer. I strongly recommend that you read his books."
CHUCK NORRIS, SIX-TIME WORLD KARATE CHAMPION, INTERNATIONAL FILM AND TELEVISION STAR, AND CREATOR OF THE WORLD COMBAT LEAGUE AND THE KICKSTART FOUNDATION

"Randy Alcorn's *Deception* is a fiction thriller that delivers. It was as engaging to me as books by Crichton or Clancy. I really resonated with the main character, Ollie Chandler. He tells it like it is, with sarcasm and humor. I'm sure glad Randy can't paint, or I'd be in big trouble!"
RON DICIANNI, AWARD-WINNING ARTIST AND AUTHOR OF *BEYOND WORDS*

"Randy Alcorn is amazing. He's one of my all-time favorite authors."
KAREN KINGSBURY, BESTSELLING AUTHOR OF THE REDEMPTION SERIES AND THE FIRSTBORN SERIES

"With humor, verve, and his usual attention to detail, Randy Alcorn has crafted a detective story that grips on page one and doesn't let go. Ollie Chandler won my admiration and Mike Hammer, aka "Mulch," won my heart as *Deception* explored the nature of man, the deceit of evil, and the breadth of eternity. Not to be missed."
ANGELA HUNT, AUTHOR OF *UNCHARTED*

"Alcorn has written a novel that combines the suspense of John Grisham and the theological pondering of C. S. Lewis."
NEW MAN MAGAZINE FOR *DEADLINE*

"[*Deadline*] is for clear thinkers who enjoy a good argument. There can be no mistaking—and there should be no ignoring—the vital message of this book."
FRANK PERETTI, BESTSELLING AUTHOR OF *THIS PRESENT DARKNESS*

"Randy Alcorn has hit it out of the park. *Deadline* is riveting. Motivating. Intriguing. Provocative. And it's for the mystery lovers too. Many books feed the mind. Some feed the heart. *Deadline* nourishes both."
STU WEBER, AUTHOR OF *TENDER WARRIOR*

"My hat is off to Randy Alcorn for his novel *Dominion*. Wow, what a book. It was a great read, and entertaining, fascinating, and educational as well. I enjoyed it immensely and learned from it too, and what could be better than that? We need more of such books."
DOUGLAS GRESHAM, AUTHOR OF *LENTEN LANDS: MY CHILDHOOD WITH JOY DAVIDMAN AND C. S. LEWIS* AND *JACK'S LIFE: THE LIFE STORY OF C. S. LEWI*; CO-PRODUCER, *THE LION, THE WITCH AND THE WARDROBE*

"Alcorn's writing remains top-notch, and he fills the pages with enough tension to cause ulcers."
BOOKSTORE JOURNAL FOR *DOMINION*

"Astonishing book."
THE LAMPLIGHTER FOR *DOMINION*

"*Dominion* is a murder mystery in the best tradition of the genre—but it is written with a steely-edged factualness that is nothing short of haunting."
WORLD MAGAZINE

"This is one of those rare books that I (a woman) enthusiastically recommend to men but am confident women will enjoy as well… Alcorn takes the reader on a suspense-filled journey between heaven and earth, into the depths of darkness itself."
THE RIVENDELL REPORT FOR *DEADLINE*

DECEPTION

a novel

RANDY
ALCORN

Multnomah Books

DECEPTION
published by Multnomah Books
A division of Random House, Inc.

© 2007 by Eternal Perspective Ministries
International Standard Book Number: 1-59052-616-3

Cover design by the DesignWorks Group, Inc.
Cover image by Steve Gardner, www.shootpw.com
Interior design and typeset by Pamela McGrew

Unless otherwise indicated, Scripture quotations are from:
The Holy Bible, New International Version
© 1973, 1984 by International Bible Society,
used by permission of Zondervan Publishing House

Multnomah is a trademark of Multnomah Books,
and is registered in the U.S. Patent and Trademark Office.
The colophon is a trademark of Multnomah Books.

Printed in the United States of America.

For information:
MULTNOMAH BOOKS
12265 Oracle Boulevard, Suite 200
Colorado Springs, CO 80921

Library of Congress Cataloging-in-Publication Data
Alcorn, Randy C.
    Deception : a novel / Randy Alcorn.
      p. cm.
    ISBN 1-59052-616-3
    I. Title.
PS3551.L292D45 2007
813'.54—dc22

                                        2006039133

07 08 09 10 11 12 13 14 — 10 9 8 7 6 5 4 3 2 1 0

OTHER BOOKS BY RANDY ALCORN

FICTION:

Deadline
Dominion
Edge of Eternity
Lord Foulgrin's Letters
The Ishbane Conspiracy (with Angela and Karina Alcorn)
Safely Home
Wait Until Then

NONFICTION:

50 Days of Heaven
Heaven for Kids
Heaven
The Law of Rewards
The Purity Principle
Why Pro-Life?
The Grace and Truth Paradox
The Treasure Principle
In Light of Eternity
Money, Possessions, and Eternity
Pro-Life Answers to Pro-Choice Arguments
Sexual Temptation
Women Under Stress (with Nanci Alcorn)
Christians in the Wake of the Sexual Revolution

To Diane Meyer
Who lived with us as a teenager when our girls were small
and will always be a sister and daughter to us.
We marvel at the great things God has done in your life, Di.
We're among your greatest admirers. You've said for years that you wanted me to
write a spin-off from *Deadline* and *Dominion*.
Nanci and I can't think of anyone we'd rather dedicate it to than you.

ACKNOWLEDGMENTS

My heartfelt thanks to Doreen Button, who looked over the manuscript in detail and made suggestions at critical points, all the way through proofreading.

Thanks to my friend and skilled editor Rod Morris for our partnership on yet another project. Thanks also to Julee Schwarzburg for her graciousness, attention to detail, and editorial input, as well as to Jennifer Barrow, for her outstanding copyediting. And to Rebekah Nafziger and Adrienne Spain for proofreading, and Pamela McGrew for typesetting.

Thanks to Kevin Marks and Doug Gabbert, for your encouragement and patience with this project. And to Sharon Znachko, for all your work and your kind words…thanks, sis.

I'm grateful to all those who have been part of the Multnomah family—including my friend Jay Echternach—and to my dedicated partners at WaterBrook who will help get this book into people's hands. And to the booksellers, without whom it wouldn't matter that I write books.

Thanks to the DesignWorks Group and especially to Tim Green for his great work on the *Deception* cover, as well as the new covers for *Deadline* and *Dominion*. (And thanks to Lawrence and Robin Green, who get some credit for Tim.)

Thanks to the staff of Eternal Perspective Ministries, who do so much for me and who put up with a lot while I was buried in this project. Specifically, thanks to my assistants, Kathy Norquist and Linda Jeffries; my secretary, Bonnie Hiestand; and our bookkeeper and diligent proofreader, Janet Albers. Bonnie in particular spent many hours deciphering my handwritten changes when I was reading the book aloud.

Thanks to Diane Meyer for her interest in a spin-off book from *Deadline* and *Dominion* and her encouragement after reading an early draft. Also for her great job on the study questions. And to all the readers who've written me about those books, published in 1994 and 1996, who asked me to write another, not expecting to wait this long.

Thanks to our dear friend Sue Keels, for coming up with the title *Deception* while we were brainstorming during a glorious vacation. Thanks also to my buddy Steve Keels, Sue's husband, who regularly made helpful comments, such as "Aren't you done with that book yet?"

Special thanks to Detective Sergeant Tom Nelson, who helped me years ago with *Deadline* and *Dominion* and who cheerfully answered many questions over many months concerning *Deception*. Thanks also to my friends Jim Seymour, police officer, and Darrell MacKay, arson investigator, for your helpful insights.

Thanks to Sarah Ballenger for her research on various questions. And to Amy Campbell for entering my manuscript changes on short notice, while trying not to let it spoil the book for her.

Thanks to Tony and Martha Cimmarrusti, Carlos and Gena Norris, Stu Weber, Carol Hardin, Ken and Joni Tada, Sarah Thebarge, and our Sunday night football group, for comments they made that contributed to this book though they didn't know it. Thanks to Dave Stout for introducing me years ago to one of Ollie's mottoes.

Thank you, Frank and Myrna Eisenzimmer and Randy and Sue Monnes, for offering me places to write that proved to be great sanctuaries. And to our EPM Prayer Partners, whose prayers as I wrote this book may prove to be the single greatest human contribution to it.

Heartfelt thanks to my wife and best friend, Nanci, whose encouraging comments on the manuscript kept me going in rough times and who thoughtfully gave me permission to go back to work many times when neither of us wanted me to.

Thanks to my precious daughters, Karina and Angela, who made valuable comments on the prologue, and to my wonderful sons, Dan Franklin and Dan Stump, whose lives and interactions contributed to portions of the book. Thanks to Angie also for the medical insights. Thanks to our grandsons, Jake, Ty, and Matt, endless sources of delight when I came in from my office needing a joy transfusion.

I also want to acknowledge Rex Stout, creator of the Nero Wolfe mysteries, written in the 1930s to 1960s. Ollie, my viewpoint character, admires Nero Wolfe and Archie Goodwin. Now and then I've put into Ollie's mouth some of Stout's expressions, a tribute to him. I couldn't give Stout credit each time, nor can I remember all I've absorbed from many pleasant hours reading his books. So I credit him here for what are probably several dozen of his phrases or ideas scattered throughout this book.

Finally and most importantly, thank You, my Lord Jesus, for sustaining me through this project, which was delayed by innumerable unanticipated events in order to conform to Your perfect timing. I pray above all that You are pleased by it and will use it as You see fit.

"Those who seek my life set their traps,
those who would harm me talk of my ruin;
all day long they plot deception."
PSALM 38:12

"Messin' with me's like wearin' cheese underwear down rat alley."
OLLIE CHANDLER

Prologue

"I fear that if the matter is beyond humanity it is certainly beyond me."
SHERLOCK HOLMES,
THE ADVENTURES OF THE DEVIL'S FOOT

IN A DARK ROOM punctured by a bare hundred-watt bulb, two newspaper clippings on the card table appeared whitish gray, four others dim and yellow. Agile fingers arranged them chronologically so the handiwork could be better displayed.

Should they be placed in a scrapbook? What if they were found? Of all places, surely no one would try to break into this one. The world's full of stupid people, but not that stupid.

Most of the people in the clippings had been stupid. But over the years, one by one, they'd been abruptly liberated of their stupidity. And the world had been liberated of them.

A penciled list of names dropped to the table, by the playing cards, next to the clippings.

It was time for another stupid person to go away.

But which one?

The liberator brooded thirty minutes, forearm bulging, squeezing hard a small object.

Finally, one name rose to the top.

The mastermind wrote the name down, then covered it with the ace of spades.

"My eyes have been trained to examine faces and not their trimmings. It is the first quality of a criminal investigator that he should see through a disguise."
SHERLOCK HOLMES, *THE HOUND OF THE BASKERVILLES*

WEDNESDAY, NOVEMBER 6

MY CHEST POUNDING like a dryer load of army boots, I knocked the noisemaker off its cradle, then groped for it in the darkness. Three enormous red digits— 2:59—assaulted my eyes.

"Hello?" The voice on the phone was deep and croaky. "Detective Ollie Chandler?"

I nodded my head, admitting it.

"Chandler?"

"Yeah."

"You didn't answer your cell." His voice was a hacksaw cutting a rain gutter. "You awake?"

"No. But…you may as well finish the job."

"In bed?"

"Mowin' the lawn. Who died?"

I've been waiting all my life for good news from a 3:00 a.m. phone call. It's been a wait of Chicago Cubs proportions.

Many imagine that middle-of-the-night phone calls mean someone's been killed. I don't imagine it. It's true.

Jake Woods tells me there's a God in charge of the universe. I'm not convinced. But if there is, I'd appreciate it if He'd schedule murders during day shift.

"Victim's Jimmy Ross," Sergeant Jim Seymour said. I pictured him sitting home in his underwear. Not a pretty picture.

"Drug dealer."

I didn't shed a tear. They say cops are cynical. To me drug dealers are a waste of protoplasm. They should be shot, injected, then put on the electric chair at a low setting.

"Officer Sayson's the patrol," Sergeant Seymour said. "1760 Southeast Clinton, apartment 34." I scratched it down in the dark, postponing those first daggers of light.

As I hung up, I sensed a presence in the dark room and reached toward the nightstand for my Smith and Wesson 340 revolver. I saw the whites of two eyes three feet away. My hand clenched the revolver. Suddenly I recognized the sympathetic eyes of Mike Hammer, my bullmastiff, who spends his nights getting in and out of my bed, licking my toes to reassure me he's back.

Slowly I withdrew my hand from the gun, not wanting to send the wrong message to my bullie.

What was wrong with me? How could I forget Mike Hammer, my roommate and best friend? I shuddered, remembering five years ago, when I drew the gun on Sharon when she came back to bed after taking Advil.

The problem with morning is that it comes before my first cup of coffee. I stumbled toward the kitchen, fingertips on the hallway wall, stubbing my toe on the exercise bike Sharon bought me. I've used it twice in four years. I keep it around to maintain the illusion that it's making me healthy. Since this helps me justify the next cheeseburger, it's worth every penny she paid.

I keep water in my top-of-the-line Mr. Coffee, poured to the ten-cup mark, with Starbucks French roast always waiting. In my quest for maximum darkness, I load the filter to the top. Whether it's 7:00 a.m. or 3:00 a.m., I can throw the switch and, even though the world's going to hell in a handbasket, coffee's brewing…so there's hope.

I leaned against the fridge and pulled the pot off the burner every few ounces to get what was there. I'd mainline it if I could. Sharon told me maybe I should drink less coffee now that Juan Valdez named his donkey after me.

Trying to remember whether I'd had three hours of sleep or two, I put Mike Hammer—I call him Mulch for short—out the back door to do his business. Every morning he acts like it's his first time, a privilege he's been waiting for all his life. After two minutes outside for him and six more ounces of coffee for me, Mulch blew open the door to get his biscuit.

I abandoned Mr. Coffee and headed for the bathroom. I put my face two inches from the showerhead and let the water pummel me.

Presumably I dressed, poured the last of the coffee into my thirty-ounce mug, and said good-bye to two of my favorite people—Mulch and Mr. Coffee. Mulch licked my face. I wiped off Mulch-slobber and tossed the paper towel at the sink, coming up short. I slowly shut the front door, watching Mulch shred the paper towel—his reward whenever I miss.

"You're in charge while I'm gone."

Mulch loves it when I say that.

It was early November but felt like late December. Like a polar bear on ice, I negotiated the slick walk to my white Ford Taurus. I dropped into the driver's seat and kicked aside a Big Gulp cup and a Burger King bag, which expelled the scent of French fries like a perfume spray bottle. I must have been on a stakeout the night before. Maybe two nights before. Eventually I'd remember.

You shouldn't assume I was conscious during all this. A detective establishes his routine so he can do it in his sleep. You wake up on the way, more at each stoplight. By the time you really need consciousness, it's usually there. You just hope it doesn't arrive at the scene after you do.

It was dripping cold. I drew the window half down to double-team with the coffee. Every few blocks I stuck my face out—I learned this from Mulch—and gulped a quick fix of wet oxygen. Then I pulled in my frozen face and warmed it with the coffee. It's a ritual, like those Scandahoovean men who go back and forth from ice baths to saunas.

The Portland night, nearly uninhabited, smelled of frosty rain on asphalt. It reminded me of working the beat, night shift. One year I saw no daylight between November and February. From what I heard, I didn't miss much.

When you're on the "up team"—on call for the next murder—getting yanked from the netherworld in the middle of the night comes with the territory. It's the only thing easier now since Sharon died: I don't have to worry about her worrying about me.

I turned onto Burnside, next to Max, the light-rail tracks, where there's only one lane. Occasionally people don't understand that what I'm doing is more important than what they're doing. The moron in front of me—only the fourth car I'd seen—just sat there in his lowrider Acura Integra, figuring that since it's 3:23 a.m., he can chat with someone on the curb, even after the light's turned green.

My Taurus is a slicktop—unmarked. Cop on the inside, civilian on the outside. Usually that's handy. Not this time. I honked. Nothing.

I honked again. Then I reached to my right and typed in the license number on my mobile data computer. I honked a third time.

The bozo charged out of his car, yelling and swearing. When he was two feet from my window, I pulled my Glock 19 and pointed it at his face.

"Get out of my way. *Now.*"

He froze, with the fixated expression of a man wetting his pants. He scuttled back to his car sideways, like a crab, and hopped in, banging his head on the door frame. He turned his key with a garbage-disposal grind, forgetting he'd left the car running. He screeched through the now-red light.

I flipped on my flashing red and blue grill-mounted strobes. He edged to the right, and I passed with an inch clearance. My computer screen flashed. I lowered my passenger window and shouted, "Have a nice day, Nathan Roberts!"

Okay, maybe when he approached my car I should have identified myself as a cop. But many people assume that if you're a cop you won't shoot them. I didn't want Nathan to labor under this assumption.

Having been a cop for thirty years, I find that you can get most of what you want with a kind word. But sometimes, as Al Capone put it, you can get more of what you want with a kind word and a gun.

"Sayson?" I spoke into the car phone. "Chandler. Homicide. On my way. 1760 Southeast Clinton? Apartments?"

"Greenbridge Arms. Third floor, four doors left off the elevator. Apartment 34's sealed. My partner's checking on neighbors. Dozen people heard the shots. One possible witness."

"Be there in five."

When I'm on the up team, anybody who kills somebody does it on my watch. That means they're messin' with me. And messin' with me's like wearin' cheese underwear down rat alley.

I pulled up to the Greenbridge Arms, studying the four-story brick building. I settled next to one of three patrol cars in a no parking zone, beside a van labeled KAGN.

Four criminals rushed me, armed with notepads, pens, electronic gadgets, and cameras. Crips and Bloods have a name. So do these—journalists.

"What can you tell us, Detective Chandler?" The *Oregon Tribune* reporter brandished her notepad, poison pen ready to scribble.

"Nothing. If you check your notes, you'll see I just arrived."

"They're denying us entrance to the apartments."

"Good for them." This was standard procedure, but reporters—thinking they're royalty—are outraged when they aren't allowed to trample a crime scene.

"Victim's name's Jimmy Ross, apartment 34. Right?"

Apparently someone on police radio had slipped up and said the victim's name. "There's a victim?"

"We called neighbors, and they confirmed it was Jimmy Ross. True?"

"Why would I tell you?"

"What's the harm? We heard it on the radio. We just want you to confirm it."

"Don't hold your breath."

"We're just doing our job."

"You're getting in the way of me doing *my* job. Monitor your own calls."

"Cops don't own the airwaves. The public deserves to know what's going on."

I turned away as her photographer took a photo. He grabbed the sleeve of my trench coat. I yanked it back. I turned toward him. His camera flash did that dagger thing in my eyes.

"Out of my face!"

I saw the red light of a television news camera right behind him. Images of my anger management class assaulted me. I'd sworn I'd never subject myself to that again.

I smiled and waved to the camera. "Just kidding! Actually, I want to thank you folks for coming. I wish I had time for tea and crumpets, but we have a crime to solve and people's lives to protect, so if it doesn't inconvenience you, I'll be going up to the crime scene now. Enjoy."

The *Tribune* and TV reporters and their cameramen followed me to the front door of the apartments, where Officer Brandon Gentry opened the door for me. He and I nodded at each other, two professionals trying to beat off the vultures. I wondered if he was an anger management alumnus. They should give us a secret hand signal. I signed his log sheet and wrote down the time: 3:39 a.m.

The TV cameraman pushed open the front door and did a quick sweep with his video. As I stepped in the elevator, I said, "Officer Gentry, there's a van illegally parked. I think it has the letters KAGN on it. Would you please write a parking citation?"

The door closed and I tried not to ponder how the media, especially the *Tribune*, had been my judge, jury, and nearly my executioner fifteen years before. I needed to switch gears to the job at hand. At least I was awake.

The elevator was old, with a bad case of asthma. As I got out on the third floor, I popped in a stick of Black Jack gum—my crime scene entrance ritual.

I headed up the hall to the left and saw a cop, midtwenties, poised like a jackal guarding pharaoh's tomb.

"Sayson?"

He nodded, too eagerly. Academy written all over him, Officer Sayson exuded a Secret Service alertness. If he lives long enough, eventually it'll give way to the fear of dying on duty and leaving behind kids and the wife he's promised not to forsake. Eagerness to jump into the middle of a dangerous situation is inversely proportionate to age. Twenty years ago I was chasing armed fugitives down back alleys, by myself. Now my first thought is to call for SWAT teams, armored cars, helicopters, guided missiles, or stealth bombers—whatever's available.

I'm a Vietnam vet. Someone watching my back means everything. Officer Sayson was protecting my crime scene; he was my new best friend.

Entering apartment 34, I stepped from hallway to crime scene. There, sprawled in a death pose, was Jimmy Ross, two shots to the head. Physical evidence all over the place, with a bonus: a sealed Ziploc bag of Ecstasy and a half-spilled sack of meth. No need for a lab report to tell me what was what.

Sayson introduced me to the apartment manager, who assured me Ross lived alone. No wife, live-in girlfriend, brother, cousin, friend, or roommate. Sayson consulted two neighbors who'd noticed lots of coming and going. The manager appeared shocked, as if he'd never suspected one of his renters was a drug dealer. Go figure.

Since most murders are done by family members, that's where you look first. Domestic arguments normally begin in the living room, where weapons are limited. They migrate to the kitchen, where weapons abound, or the bedroom, where there's a gun, which has a way of ending fights. This argument had stayed in the living room. No sign the killer had been anywhere else—only between the door and body. Didn't fit the domestic murder profile.

Sayson told me the paramedic who'd come twenty minutes ago had pronounced Jimmy Ross dead. I looked at what used to be the man. He was dead all right.

The medical examiner, Carlton Hatch—I'd seen him at a dozen other homicides—showed up ten minutes after I did. Most MEs ask you to call them when you want the body removed, after the crime scene's clean and detailed. Unless time of death is unknown, the ME may not arrive until three or four hours later. Not Hatch. Every time I've worked with him, he's come immediately, like an autograph hound to an NFL team hotel.

Hatch is a number two pencil, head pink and bald like an eraser. He carries a man-purse and wears a nicely fitted suit beneath a poorly fitted face. His pointy chin isn't a good match for his pale, bloated cheeks. Too much chlorine in his gene pool.

I gazed down at my Wal-Mart jacket over my flannel shirt spotted with yesterday's bacon and cheese omelet. I considered my rumpled slacks, pockets holding Tuesday's Taco Bell receipt and a packet of hot sauce. Then I looked again at the ME's tailored suit.

"Tuxedo at the dry cleaners?" I asked him.

His smile came quick and left quicker. This guy should be home watching *Quincy* reruns. I wanted to be home sleeping it off or watching Jack Bauer interrogate a terrorist.

"Blood spattered here." Hatch pointed to the wall. "Isn't that interesting?"

I nodded, though it wasn't. I prefer the CSI techs, who quietly collect evidence, report to me, and let me interpret it. The ME's specialty is the state of the body: cause and time of death. I like it when people stick to their specialties.

"Probable cause of death gunshots to the head," he said slowly, as if he had drawn on years of training to come up with this. Any kindergartner could have told me the same.

"Another splatter here. Don't you find that interesting?"

"Isn't that what you'd expect with two head shots at close range?" I asked.

"Still, it's interesting."

"As interesting as last month's cricket scores," I said.

Two CSIs in forensic bunny suits arrived. One vacuumed; the other photographed. They collected blood samples, carpet fibers, and anything possibly containing DNA fragments. I sketched the scene on a yellow pad. I supplemented with dozens of photos on my Olympus digital camera. Nice change from the Polaroids we used to take.

"Chandler?" The loud voice startled everybody. Barging in the door was my partner, Manny Domast, wiry, short, and high-strung, like one of those yippy dogs who starts the day with five cappuccinos.

"You look terrible," he said.

Manny's grumpy at 10:00 a.m. At 3:48 a.m. the difference isn't noticeable.

"What we got?" he asked.

"It's interesting," I said, eyeing the ME, who chose that moment to formally declare that Ross had died one to two hours ago. Good estimate, since the gunshots eighty minutes ago woke up all tenants except the hard rock fans.

After CSI went over Ross's cell phone, I checked its directory, jotted down the numbers of the last five incoming and outgoing calls. Manny listened to messages. He contacted two of the callers, a middle-of-the-night fishing expedition. Meanwhile, I talked with the wide-eyed ponytailed witness in apartment 36.

She'd been walking up and down the hallway at 2:30 a.m.

"Why?" I asked.

"I had rats in my legs." She gave a detailed description of a tall black guy with lots of hair and red sweatpants who'd been in the hallway five minutes before she heard the shots. He'd scared her. She pretended not to look at him.

Within twenty minutes, Manny and I determined it was a case of a drug dealer blown away by his competitor. A turf dispute. We found one bullet embedded in the floor, probably the second shot. Apparently the other bullet hadn't exited. Fingerprints with slight blood traces were on the doorknob. But there was no indication that the killer had touched the victim, so it seemed likely the blood was the killer's, though what made him bleed wasn't obvious. Perhaps a small pre-existing wound that reopened without him knowing it? DNA tests wouldn't be back for months, but I called headquarters to see if we could get the lab to do a rush on the three good fingerprints collected.

Murder is never convenient, but solving a murder can be routine. This one had routine written all over it. The only thing missing was the killer's name, Social Security card, and a confession written in lipstick on the bathroom mirror.

While Manny canvassed the apartments, I went to the hallway's end and stepped outside onto a rickety fire escape. I opened my mouth wide, gulping life.

It seemed so easy. A good description and fingerprints and DNA.

That's when I should have suspected something was wrong.

Napoleon said—I heard this on the History Channel while eating Cheetos with Mulch—that every campaign has ten minutes in which the battle's won or lost. Sometimes investigations are that way. Looking back, the ten minutes in which I botched that investigation were right when everything fell together perfectly.

I got a call from precinct saying an anonymous tipster had heard Lincoln Caldwell boast of offing another drug dealer. By 6:00 a.m., we found tall, big-haired Lincoln Caldwell, asleep in his room, red sweatpants hanging on his bedpost. His gun, in the top dresser drawer, had been recently fired. As I looked at the four rounds left in it, I didn't need ballistics to convince me that the gun would prove a perfect match for the rounds that killed Ross. His cell phone confirmed he'd called Ross six hours earlier.

He denied it all, naturally. They always do. We arrested him and hauled him in.

I felt like a crossword puzzle champion holding a puzzle any kid could solve. I'm a Sherlock Holmes fan. I like to follow bread crumbs, not six baguettes leading me to someone standing twelve feet away who hands me a business card saying "Lincoln Caldwell, Murderer."

Still, I couldn't argue with the bottom line. Two drug dealers for the price of one. One dead, the other off the streets for however long the court decides. Never long enough for me.

Sometimes the bad guys help out the good guys by doing what we can't—blowing each other away. Kill a killer and you may save a half dozen lives. Kill a drug dealer and you may save a couple dozen. That's what cops say to each other off the record. And cop-to-cop is always off the record.

I once cracked a case based on my discovery that one Monday morning a woman had broken her routine by ordering a grande white chocolate mocha. Remarkable for one reason: Every weekday for five years she'd gone to the same coffee shop and ordered a tall skinny latte. Something had to account for her celebratory mood. I checked on her because her husband had died of "natural causes" on Saturday. The white mocha tipped me off that she might have contributed to those natural causes.

It took me a whole baseball season to prove it, but by the time the Yankees took the field for the first game of the World Series, I'd got her. No prize. No bonus. No street named after me. No letters of gratitude from husbands whose wives were on the verge of ordering their first white chocolate mochas. But that's okay. I don't do it for the thanks. I do it because justice is my job, my one contribution to a world that is truly—and I mean big time—a mess.

I'm saying this because the devil's in the details. Jimmy Ross's murder didn't require turning over rocks. Everything that mattered fell into place. Even if we never identified the tipster, when they processed the fingerprints and the weapon and the blood DNA, it would be a trifecta, a perfect triangle of independent evidence. Together they were irrefutable. The case was open and shut. Lincoln Caldwell was our man.

I spent more time on the paperwork than investigating. When two and two make four, you don't try to refigure it six different ways to see if it comes out three or five. You tie a bow around it, give it to the district attorney, and move on. You hoist a beer or two and watch a football game and tell yourself that even though you're no Mother Teresa, you've done something that mattered. Case closed.

Of my 204 murder cases, I've solved 177. That's 87 percent. The rest, cold cases, still burn deep in my gut. Every year or two, sometimes on vacation, I solve one of those oldies in my quest to raise my batting average to .900. Of course, if I ever make that, I'll want more.

I sent a man to jail for a double murder he didn't commit. Bradford Downs. I know his face well. Two credible witnesses offered convincing testimony to back up compelling physical evidence. He claimed innocence, but his record made that hard to believe. After ten years of appeals, he was executed by lethal injection.

Turns out the witnesses were the real killers. We'd never have known if the one dying hadn't confessed and offered proof…three years after an innocent man was put to death.

Maybe there is something as bad as murder and getting away with it—being murdered for a murder you didn't commit. Since I put him away, that makes me an accessory to murder.

Bradford Downs's face wouldn't be my first choice to fill the back of my eyelids when the lights go out, but some nights there he is.

So why am I telling you this? Because I didn't realize that morning at Jimmy Ross's apartment that nothing was as it appeared. That case was open and shut all right…open and shut on a dead-wrong conclusion. And I fell for the setup. That makes me mad. It makes me even madder that it was only fate or circumstances or luck or providence—whichever you believe in doesn't matter to me—that made me realize it.

Portland homicide has five teams, so Manny and I get every fifth murder. It was our next murder, the one fourteen days later, that pulled the rug out from under me. Eventually it woke me to a shocking truth that forever revised the story of Jimmy Ross and Lincoln Caldwell.

That second murder turned me, my job, and my friendships upside down. It shook all the change out of my pockets. It threatened to bring down a police department, end my career, and place me inside a white chalk outline, with some other homicide detective trying to figure out who murdered me.

Not one of those 204 cases prepared me for that next murder, where sinister eyes, hidden in the shadows of a violated house, gazed out at me through a broken window. It was the most unconventional and baffling case I've ever worked.

If that's not enough, my investigation threatened to end the lives of people I cared about.

And, ultimately, that's exactly what it did.

*"Watson here will tell you that I never can resist
a touch of the dramatic."*
SHERLOCK HOLMES, *THE NAVAL TREATY*

MONDAY, NOVEMBER 18

IN THE MORNINGS I go fishing.

By the side of my bed.

For clean clothes.

I seldom catch much.

This morning, though, I made a great find. Buried under Tuesday's blue shirt
was my favorite flannel, also blue. It was a good omen.

On mornings when I don't have to rush, I flip on the coffee, grab two oat-nut
English muffins, and follow Mulch onto the back porch, where my toaster is. I
toast those suckers until they're carbon-based life forms. Then I smother them
with butter and a thin slice of Limburger cheese. Years ago Sharon banned the
toaster to the back porch, far from smoke detectors.

My next ritual, on lazy mornings, is to quick-fry a couple of eggs and three
bacons for Mulch. If I don't have time to stop at Lou's Diner, I join Mulch with
three eggs and four bacons of my own, splitting the fourth with him. The high-
light for Mulch and me is when we get a double yolk.

I stabbed an egg covered with Tabasco sauce. If there's a God, thinking up
food was one of His best moves. So were dogs. Some of the best friends I've ever
had were dogs. If I manage not to die soon, I may be good for a couple more. I'm
considering Nero, for Nero Wolfe, my favorite detective. Or Archie, for Archie
Goodwin, Nero Wolfe's legman.

The more people I've met, the more I've come to appreciate my dog. After
Sharon died, Mulch was developing male pattern baldness. I was afraid he'd con-
tracted some fatal dog disease, so I stopped giving him beer and bacon for a couple
of weeks. That just made him grouchy. Then one day, running my hand over his
head, I noticed a wad of fur between my fingers. I realized I'd been petting him
within an inch of his life.

And you know what? He would gladly have become a bald bullie for me.
That's more love than I've known from anybody. Beside Jake Woods, my best
human friend. And Sharon, of course. Without Sharon I don't hang out or play

cards or see movies with couples anymore. When I'm with them, I can't stop thinking about her. It's like the hole your tongue keeps going to when you've lost a tooth.

One fall day four years ago I was walking Mulch at Laurelhurst Park, where you can let your dog off-leash in a designated area. I unhooked him early. He went after a squirrel. I chased him. Rounding a big fir, I saw Mulch, who'd forgotten the squirrel, beeline to a park bench. He trotted right up to a guy in a business suit, whose back was to me, and hiked his leg on him. For a moment the guy didn't notice, then he looked down and swore at my dog, kicking his rear.

Then I saw the man's face. It was Edward Lennox, the brand new chief of police, talking with Portland's mayor, the distinguished Garrison Branch. I stayed behind the tree and whistled. Mulch ran around it, passing me. I chased him through some rhodies, and we both slipped down into a thick grassy area piled with old leaves, where he licked my face mercilessly. That's when I nicknamed him Mulch.

We walked back to our car the long way. I took Mulch to Burgerville and bought him a Tillamook cheeseburger. Got one for myself to keep him company and gave him the last gulp of my blackberry shake.

In the years since, as Chief Lennox has led our police force, I've come to realize that Mulch, from the beginning, was an extraordinary judge of character. Lennox has been chief of police five years. In dog years, that's thirty-five, but it feels like more. For most Portland cops, his reign has been a long, cold winter.

By the time I read the paper and took Mulch for a walk and changed the oil in my Taurus, it was lunchtime. Mulch's stomach growled. I checked the cupboard. Hiding behind the Ovaltine were the cans of Dinty Moore beef stew and SpaghettiOs. Sharon was wine, shrimp salad, Perrier, and asparagus. I'm beer, pizza, cream soda, and SpaghettiOs.

Not a day goes by when I don't wish she were here to give me a hard time about SpaghettiOs.

An hour later I crossed the Hawthorne Bridge, turned left on First, and pulled into the parking garage on my right, opening the gate with my precinct key card. I parked, then walked to the northwest corner, crossed Madison to the north, then Second Street to the west and entered the Justice Center, home of the Portland Police Bureau. I veered to the elevators. The uniformed officer nodded. Since most of this building is a jail, with a 676-inmate capacity, his job's more important than it appears.

The elevator gives only five options for the sixteen floors. Floors 2 and 3 are courtrooms, 4 to 11 jail floors, accessible only by authorized personnel.

Twelfth floor's intelligence, identification, juvenile, and narcotics. Thirteenth floor's the DA's office and Internal Affairs, where for six months I spent more time than I care to remember. They'd gotten bad information from the *Tribune* and went after my scalp.

I pushed fourteen for detective division. It has only one place the general public can go—the reception desk, with a thick bulletproof window and no door that opens from the outside. All the detectives hang their hats here, everyone from robbery and pawnshop details to homicide.

I hadn't even made it through security before Mitzie called, "Chief needs to see you."

"Let me get settled first."

"His assistant said it's urgent."

"Does that mean I'll have to wait one hour instead of two?"

I went to my workstation and looked out the huge windows, soaking in the panoramic view of Portland. It all seemed so tranquil from up there. So ordered and peaceful. Years ago it was just a bunch of buildings to me. Now it's more than that. Feels like nothing should escape your sight up here. Ironic that such a grand view is from homicide. My job takes me lower to the ground, where things aren't so lofty and inspiring.

I retraced my steps to the elevator and pushed floor 15, home of the chief of police's office and the media room. If any chief ever wanted to be near media, it was Lennox.

After passing through security, I was escorted into the waiting area outside the chief's office. It brought back memories of when a cop could walk right through the chief's open door. Now who'd want to?

I saw on the walls three paintings, two of which were classical, with people centuries old wearing funny hats and looking serene. The other was vague and surreal, the type I saw in a gallery that Sharon made me go to in retaliation for pretending I had the flu so I could watch a play-off game and miss her family gathering. They were paintings you had to develop a taste for. I was still at the gag reflex stage.

The chief's assistant, Mona, fifty-five trying to look thirty-five, marched toward me. Her perfume arrived three seconds before she did. Her aide, twenty-five trying to look thirty-five, walked eighteen inches behind her, leaning forward to hear every word.

"Sit," Mona said. "Chief Lennox will be with you soon. He's on an important phone call."

I started to sit in a chair facing away from the chief's office.

"No," Mona said, waving her hand, propelling the perfume toward me like nerve gas. "There, on the couch. Chief Lennox prefers people to sit on the couch. But you *must* take off that raincoat."

"It's a trench coat. Columbo wore a raincoat. Sam Spade wore a trench coat…and a fedora." I waved my hat at her.

Her assistant looked curious, but Mona Estée Lauder, lip curled, looked at me like I was an idiot.

"Humphrey Bogart in *The Maltese Falcon*? Raincoats are to trench coats what a minivan is to a sports car." I posed dramatically, like a fashion model on the runway. "Notice the ten buttons, epaulets, shoulder straps, and D rings. In the inside pocket we have—"

"It's wet and it stinks. Keep it off the couch." Mona marched off, her assistant smiling back at me. The younger woman was too new to realize she didn't need to be cordial with working stiffs who put away bad guys. She could save her smiles for journalists and the public.

I sat down, still wearing the coat. I gazed across the corridor into the inner sanctum—throne room of the King of Police.

A long man with a big jaw threw his voice at the speaker phone on his desk, leaning toward it, bawling it out. He was gangly and mechanical. Yet his voice was smooth and commanding, a radio voice, the kind that comes in handy for banana republic dictators and Eastern European tyrants.

"That's not going to cut it," Lennox said. "Those dogs won't bark." A few minutes later I heard, "He's dumb as a post."

The chief's king of clichés. *What next,* I wondered? *Soft as a baby's bottom?*

His office, I knew from prior visits, was the size of a tennis court, his private bathroom big enough for Ping-Pong.

On the coffee table in front of me were a number of magazines, including the *New Yorker*, with its stupid highbrow comics, and *Architectural Digest*. No cop, gun, or sports magazines. Four news and two home decor periodicals.

Next to me was a lamp stand with an eight-by-ten photo of the chief, his wife, and presumably his teenage daughter. What it was doing out here I didn't know, but maybe it was a statement: "All this is my turf."

I studied the photo of the Lennox family. The chief looked noble, refined, confident—right down to the perfect triangle of the handkerchief folded in his suit coat pocket. He looked far better in the picture than in real life. Maybe somebody had altered his face in Photoshop. Or maybe it was his makeup.

His wife, prim as her husband, had the smile of a woman who's looked at more cameras than books. The teenager had too many rings in her face. Beneath the hardware she was pretty but looked miserable. Her face screamed, "Let me out of this picture!" If I had that much metal in my skin, I'd feel lousy too.

If this is the picture they chose, I'd hate to see the rejects.

It made me think of Kendra, my younger daughter. When she was a little girl, she couldn't get enough of me. That all stopped as a teenager. She's thirty now and lives in Beaverton, on Portland's west side. Fourteen miles away. Might as well be Neptune, which as far as I know is still a planet.

When she turned fourteen, Kendra became an explosive compound of hormones and acne, replete with habitual eye-rolling and a terminal case of protruding lip. At fifteen, she was a walking melodrama. She lived in two modes: despondency and rampage. Whichever she was currently in, I always longed for the other. I lost her at sixteen. I was told it was just a phase, that she'd come back. She never did.

This couch had known a thousand posteriors, and so far it had spent forty minutes getting to know mine. This was Lennox World, and I was but a bit player in it. He strutted around his office, in front of the framed awards, trophies, and VIP photographs visible from the hall. One with Clinton, one with Bush. He had his bases covered.

Why the open door? He had to have an audience. People kept passing by, glancing into the inner sanctum. They could remark at the dinner table, "I saw the chief of police today. He smiled at me."

I crossed and uncrossed my legs, trying to invent a new way of doing it. Why was I here? Students get called to the principal for two reasons. One I've seen in a Hallmark commercial but never experienced: The boss wants to congratulate you. The second reason: You're in trouble. That one I know. I felt like a fly called to meet with the spider.

Ten feet away, Lennox's voice rose, dripping with disdain. Apparently some minion was daring to question him. "There's no way that's going to happen. Learn to live with it. No pain, no gain. Am I clear on that point?"

He had little hair but plenty of jaw, which is more important in police work. I'm talking Jay Leno jaw. And teeth that had more man-hours invested in them than the Hoover Dam. Why not? Teeth are a politician's greatest asset, and the chief was a PR man. He'd grinned his way to the top.

Our police department doesn't exist merely as an arm of law and justice. We exist to further the chief's reputation, make him look good, and allow Portland to be a stepping-stone toward his lifelong dream of being Chicago chief of police.

At that moment, two cameramen and a television reporter walked by. They slowed outside the chief's office. He smiled broadly and waved to them. One of the cameramen gave him an "okay if I shoot?" look. The chief nodded and smiled warmly, oblivious to the poor sap on the other end of the phone.

"He's really a fun guy," the reporter said.

There isn't a cop I know who'd call him a fun guy.

While peering in at Lennox, I caught sight of his full-length mirror. A cop with a full-length mirror? I wondered how many hours he'd watched himself, practicing looking natural.

I saw my face in the lower corner of the mirror. I stuck out my tongue. Then I held up my hand, moving thumb and fingers together in a yakety-yak. The chief turned and looked at me. I went seamlessly into a wave, smiling at him.

Anyway I hoped it was seamless.

The chief emphatically hung up and walked toward his door.

I looked at my watch. I'd been sitting fifty-three minutes.

"Sorry for the wait," he said, not sounding sorry. "It was important."

"So I was told."

He didn't offer his hand, which was fine with me since shaking it would have required touching him.

"Time gets away from you in a job like this."

"No problem. I'm just working a murder investigation. No need to hurry on my account."

The chief looked me over like you do a bad piece of fruit. "I'm the chief of police. I have many important responsibilities."

We stared at each other to see who would blink. I stared at his mostly bald head. Despite his Mexico vacations and tanning booth visits, it had a gray pall. The slight sheen reminded me of a steelhead fresh out of the river. I saw slight streaks of makeup, a big joke among the cops. The chief lived for his photo ops.

I looked at his eyes, the color of last week's barbecue coals. Like a propane stove, they could be turned off and on. Right now they were off. "You're still wearing that raincoat."

"Trench coat."

"You wear it to defy me, don't you?"

"I wear it because the classic detectives wore it. It helps create the mood, the mindset."

"You look like an oddball."

"Maybe Sam Spade and Philip Marlowe looked like oddballs, but they did their job. I do mine."

"This isn't a novel. This is the real world."

"We're all inspired by different things." I gestured at his artwork, none of which inspired me.

"All right, Chandler…I know we have some history. We need to get on the same team, lock arms." He invited me into his office with a sweeping gesture, like I was entering the home of the pope, Vince Lombardi, or Chuck Norris.

"Sit down," he said, shutting the door. "I'm going to tell you the unvarnished truth. These are challenging times. We need to set aside our differences for the greater good."

I knew whose greater good he meant. Still, I sensed a conciliatory tone. *What's up with that?*

"I have an idea I want to bounce off you."

Lennox didn't bounce ideas off you; he dumped them on you. Something was up.

"I told you to sit down," he said.

"I've got a back spasm. Been sitting too long."

"Sit down."

I'm three inches taller than the chief, and he doesn't like looking up at me. I stretched myself on tiptoes for about five seconds, then sat.

"What's that smell?" He leaned down, two feet from my face.

I ran through the options: coffee, beer, smoke from Rosie O'Grady's pub, Limburger cheese on my morning muffin, Jade East, English Leather Lime. Since I hadn't worn the last two since I was a junior higher, I finally said, "My gum? Black Jack?"

"It smells terrible. And it leaves a black film on your teeth."

"That's licorice."

"I've been looking through your file," he said. "Before I took over, you were cited for 'inappropriate levity.' Do you recall why?"

"It would be hard to pinpoint."

"During Christmas season you answered your phone, 'Ho, ho, ho…homicide.'"

"Oh yeah."

"And what is the public supposed to think? We take our work seriously here, Detective."

"I thought it was an internal line. Another cop."

"That doesn't make it right. We need to set examples for each other. And don't you agree we need to give the public a good impression?"

"I agree that we need to do our jobs."

"And you don't consider leaving a good impression part of your job?"

The sweat on his forehead was building.

"Sometimes we're pulling double shifts, haven't slept for a day and a half. What we do is serious. A little humor helps."

"Appropriate humor."

"Yes, sir." I don't know if my voice conveyed respect. If it did, it was lying.

"You're a rule bender, Chandler," he said, saying the word like Jack Bauer would say *terrorist*.

"I'm a risk taker. I do what it takes to get my job done."

"Policies govern how you can do your job."

"Some policies keep me from doing my job."

"So you ignore them?"

"I try to figure out how I can fulfill them and still catch the bad guys."

"That has to change."

"If it does, fewer bad guys will get caught."

His face turned cherry. I knew he was about to explode into a lecture I'd heard before. But he didn't. That unnerved me.

"Why are you telling me this now, sir? What's going on?"

He took a file folder and scanned neatly typed notes. He took a deep breath. "The *Oregon Tribune* and the police department have a long history of tense relations."

"You mean we hate each other's guts?"

"You'll be glad to know, Detective Chandler, that you have the opportunity to help mend fences."

"I do?"

"You know Raylon Berkley?"

"The *Tribune* publisher? Sure. He's an idiot."

"He's brilliant. And a potential ally to our cause."

"What cause would that be?"

"The cause of…this police department. What we stand for. Justice."

"What did I miss? What happened to make an enemy an ally?"

"Raylon has never been our enemy. The media's job is to press hard, ask the difficult questions, hold us accountable."

"And lie about us?"

"You're talking about your situation fifteen years ago?"

"Berkley was there then. He never struck me as an ally."

"He doesn't write the stories."

"No, but he pays to have them written, then makes the bucks when they're sold."

"Actually, the *Tribune* has lost money the last two years."

"That's what I hear. You have no idea how many sleepless nights it's caused me."

He lifted still another file folder that showed rubber band marks. "You feel the *Tribune* accused you of police brutality."

"It's more than a feeling."

"The investigation cleared you."

"Sure. But our neighbors, my wife's coworkers, and my kids' friends will always think I beat up that guy unnecessarily, and I did it because of his skin color. I used force against him because he was acting violently and putting people at risk."

"So you said."

"So I said because it's true."

"You're going to have to get beyond your stereotype of Raylon Berkley."

"Why? Is he a new homicide sergeant?"

"Look, Chandler, the last two years haven't just been bad for the *Tribune*. They've been bad for the Portland Police."

I agreed, though I would have taken it back five years, to the day he became chief, not long before Mulch introduced himself to his pant leg.

He picked up a clipboard that held what looked like a dozen pages of handwritten notes. "We've had a series of shootings, two where officers were found liable for the deaths of innocent citizens."

"The *Tribune* found them liable."

"In one case they were right."

"Okay. Blalock was a jerk and deserved to be busted. I'm all for that. I hate dirty cops. But what about Collins? Sure, he's back on the streets, but nobody trusts him. You can't do your job when everybody thinks you strong-armed a store owner and destroyed his shop."

"It looked bad."

"And who made it look bad, before all the facts came in, before the two witnesses came forward who saw the store owner pull his gun on the cop? The *Tribune* and the news stations. Collins's life will never be the same. Trust me. People still think I'm a racist and brutalized some helpless guy."

"My point is, our problems with police behavior and the fund-raiser and the embezzlement…it's hurt our image."

"So? Where are we going here?" I squirmed, feeling like I was wearing a wool sweater with no undershirt.

"Raylon Berkley and I have had lunch a half dozen times the last two months. We've come up with a plan we believe can be good for both of us. Something that will bolster the public's understanding of our department and at the same time increase sales of the *Tribune*. Raylon has taken it to their directors, and I've taken it to our advisory council. Everybody's on board."

"What board are they on?"

"You have to remember that PR is everything."

"Everything? What about justice?"

"Well, yes, justice, naturally. But you can't have justice without good public relations. Anyway, in order to be on the same team with the *Tribune*, in order for them to see us as we are, we need to spend time together, see each other at work, get to know each other."

"Like…dating?"

"A crude analogy," he said. "But there's truth in it."

"Look, I've got murders to solve. Are you going to tell me what's going on here?"

He shook like a volcano about to erupt.

Instead, he calmly said, "We have a plan. A *Tribune* reporter will cover a murder case, working alongside one of our homicide detective teams, start to finish. They'll be there from crime scene to lab, interviews, every aspect of the investigation. The reporter will write it up for the public—" he raised his hand when he saw my face—"leaving out anything that could compromise the investigation. Two days a week an article will be written, allowing the readers of the *Trib* to follow the investigation."

"Tell me you're kidding."

"Look at the success of *COPS*. It shows people what we really do. People love it. Just like they love *CSI*."

"Right, and they expect cases to be solved like they are on *CSI*. And juries now demand *CSI*-type evidence to prove guilt when it normally doesn't work that way. And people who watch *COPS* figure out ways to outsmart the system."

"But people have gained a much greater understanding of our work. It's helped our image. We need it here in Portland. I had a few conditions, of course, and so did Raylon. All but one of his conditions were reasonable."

"I think it's a big mistake. But you don't need my permission."

"I certainly don't."

"So again I ask, why am I here?"

The barbecue coals in his eye sockets flamed on. Lenox slammed down his clipboard on his desk, three inches from my fingers. "Because Raylon Berkley's condition is that his reporter has to work with *you*."

"**I'M NOT ASKING YOU**," the chief said, wagging his finger at me. "This isn't a democracy."

"There's no way I can do my job with a journalist in my pocket. Ridiculous!"

"It's not your call, Detective."

"What about Jack Glissan or Brandon Phillips? They're perfect. Veterans. Punctual. Look good in suits. They're fit. Hair's nice, everything the public likes."

"For once we agree," Lennox said. "That's what I told Raylon. But no, he said, 'I want Ollie Chandler.'"

"Had he been drinking?"

"I couldn't believe it either," the chief said. "Why choose a velvet Elvis when you can have a Monet?"

"I have a velvet Elvis hanging in my garage. Who's Mohnay?"

He nodded, as if proving a point.

"So why does Berkley want me?"

"He said it's because you're colorful and interesting and you have a history."

"I'm good-looking and brilliant too, but Glissan or Phillips are still better choices."

He stood, face red, waving his hands like a conductor. "I think the real reason was stated—the exact words were, 'Chandler can act like a moron.' I think he hopes you will."

"I'll bet you stuck up for me when he said that."

"He didn't say it. *I* did. You're a fish out of water. And your career direction…you're up a creek without a paddle."

"One day my ship will come in. You can't judge a book by its cover."

"Raylon thinks the handwriting's on the wall. When you mess up, readership increases. After all, idiots can be interesting."

You're an idiot and you're not interesting, I said.

Okay, I didn't *say* it, but I thought it. And that's why I'm putting it in italics. (I'm hoping eventually to turn this into a detective novel. I figure any idiot can write one of those.)

"Well, if *you* don't want me to do it, and *I* don't want to do it, why are we even talking about it?"

"Because…we're that desperate." He sighed and plopped into his chair.

"We?"

"Our future's at stake."

"Do you mean your future?" Chicago was on his mind.

"The future of the police department!"

"Are they considering dismantling the department and having the city run by gangs and vigilantes? Because I'm thinking that may not work too well. Didn't work in Chicago."

"It's signed, sealed, and delivered. You're going to do it. Unless you want to turn in your badge and find a job in mall security."

With three hours' sleep and eight cups of coffee, I had one nerve left and the chief was getting on it. I stood and walked to the door.

"Malls have their upsides. There's a pet store. Caramel corn. Starbucks. Hot Dog on a Stick. Beats the lousy vending machines in detective division."

I walked out the door, right past Mona and her cute little lapdog, who pretended they weren't eavesdropping. The chief followed me. I turned and said, "Chicago winters are rough anyway. As we speak, it's probably raining cats and dogs."

I rarely leave the Justice Center until after rush hour. But I had to escape.

I went out of my way to gaze on the cornerstone inscribed with Martin Luther King's words: "Injustice anywhere is a threat to justice everywhere." Ironic that he spoke those words while locked up in a place like this. It burned me that injustice still worms its way inside the building that bears those words.

I crossed the Morrison Bridge, got on I-84 east, then exited early and pulled into a 7-Eleven on Halsey. Bought a six-pack of Bud, then drove to a Minit Mart two miles down Stark Street and bought another six-pack. When you're a cop, you have to be careful. Somebody might think you have a drinking problem.

My last stop was Taco Bell, where I ordered a bean burrito, two chicken chalupas, and a steak gordita. I turned on the car radio and in forty seconds heard about a kidnapping, arson, and an escaped child molester. I punched it off.

I walked in my front door, and Mulch did the doggy dance of joy. I let him out onto my splintery back deck, catching the faint smell of burnt English muffins, gazing at my measly yellowish lawn and its unspread pile of moldy bark dust, by the rotting elm tree.

I grabbed two beers and poured one into Mulch's bowl. He lapped it up. Then

I popped in a *24* DVD and settled onto the couch. I handed Mulch a chalupa. He inhaled it in three seconds.

When Nero Wolfe, master detective, wants a beer, he presses a button and Fritz comes in with a tray. I don't have a Fritz. Or a Theodore to tend the orchids. Or an Archie to do my legwork. All I've got is Mulch. But I wouldn't trade him even for Fritz, Theodore, and Archie.

I love Nero Wolfe and Jack Bauer and Chuck Norris. They're my escape from a world that doesn't make sense, a world I find myself liking less every day.

I pressed the remote and watched Jack Bauer save the country despite the bureaucrats. Justice prevails. It's a nice thought. After the fifth beer it's almost believable.

If there is a God, I wonder if He gets as tired of this world as I do.

TUESDAY, NOVEMBER 19, 6:30 A.M.

My shaky, headache-riddled memories of the night before included *Walker, Texas Ranger* roundhouse kicking a gang of thugs into tomorrow and Jack Bauer chopping a bad guy's hand off to save the city from a nuclear bomb. Or something.

They say that when the boogeyman goes to sleep, he checks his closet for Chuck Norris. Superman wears Chuck Norris pajamas. Chuck Norris doesn't sleep; he waits.

That's why I like Chuck Norris and Jack Bauer. They do what the rest of us can't. Hey, they can get McDonald's breakfast after ten thirty. They scare the crud out of bad guys, and they give us hope that maybe in the end good will beat out evil.

I also remembered my conversation with the chief, reason enough to drink myself into unconsciousness. At least I'd made it all the way to bed this time.

I sipped coffee to pull myself back into the world I'd checked out of twelve hours ago. Beer pulls me out; coffee pulls me back. A bungee cord effect.

I pulled three case files out of my briefcase. The Jimmy Ross murder was on top. It had been so easy, but a few things about it niggled at me, like a carpenter ant munching wood siding.

Let it go. Why was that case still bugging me?

I stood on Justice Center floor 14, the detective floor, at the watercooler, watching bubbles rise. The sun coming through the windows of Portland Homicide was suddenly eclipsed. I looked up. Hovering over me was a human planetoid.

"Clarence Abernathy," I said. I stepped back so as not to be sucked in by his gravity. "Big as life. Bigger."

"Hello, Detective."

I suppose we both felt awkward, like guys who should be friends by now but aren't. We see each other once a week, at Lou's, for lunch with Jake. Never anywhere else. Clarence and I get along only if Jake's there. Without him, our chemistry goes bad.

He wore a meticulous black suit, maroon tie, and dress shoes, looking like a CEO or corporate attorney. His clothes appear permanently ironed. He's a columnist for the *Oregon Tribune*, where most of the reporters dress like war protestors. But Abernathy always looks like he's come from the tailor.

His back's half an acre. There's so much of the man you're tempted to stare. He's no more than thirty pounds overweight—not bad for a guy who maybe hit three hundred pounds at fifteen.

"I haven't been here since…since Dani…" He peered out the huge windows overlooking Portland, his voice sounding like distant thunder. I remembered that night we'd met, at his sister's house, forty minutes after she'd been murdered.

"You're wondering why I'm here." His words were clean and precise, like a Shakespearean actor. He gave me a half smile.

"Being a detective, I think I just figured it out. Are you the chosen one?"

"When I heard Berkley cut a deal with your chief and wanted someone assigned to you, I volunteered. I figured I'd rescue you from my colleagues."

"Am I supposed to feel relieved that I'm ending up with you rather than one of those arrogant journalists who thinks he knows everything?"

"It could be worse. I could be one of those arrogant cops who thinks he knows everything. Besides, I figured I was the only one who could get past your…idiosyncrasies."

"Never underestimate a reporter's ability to overestimate his ability."

"They call us journalists now."

"Yeah, and they call drug addicts chemically dependent. Doesn't Berkley know we're friends? I mean, as much as a cop and a *journalist* can be friends."

"Berkley knows your reputation. So he wanted to assign you a woman or a minority."

"Are you the woman or the minority?"

"You're a pain, Chandler. What was I thinking?"

Clarence sounded like a disgruntled bull. I like that sound, so I make a point of pushing his buttons. Jake is our buffer, managing to keep us civil. It'd been years since I'd gone one-on-one with Clarence.

"C'mon, sit down," I said. "Give the sun a chance to shine. So you think we're going to be partners?"

"Not partners. Two guys doing their jobs. I'll be happy if we don't kill each other."

"Can we lower our sights to something more realistic? Like, we'll kill each other, but quickly and with minimal suffering?"

"I assume your chief made the decision without you?"

"Quit calling him *my* chief. I've been sideswiped. Berkley and Lennox are a couple of big egos. And they're using us."

"Your chief isn't keen on you either. Berkley said he called you King of the Idiots."

"He actually said King of the Idiots?"

"Don't take it personally."

"Like his opinion matters to me. King's not bad. Beats Queen. Or Jack. Actually, you're lucky, Abernathy. Not many journalists get to see a mastermind at work. Watson wrote up Sherlock Holmes. Every Holmes needs a Watson."

"I'm not your Watson. Anyway, here's the deal. The moment you get notified of a murder, you're to call me. Immediately. You give me the address, and you're not supposed to do anything until I get there. I need to see everything as the case unfolds."

"You're already taking charge?"

"My job is to observe and communicate how you do your work, start to finish."

"Just you, right, and just day-shift hours?"

"You haven't seen the agreement? Check your e-mail. You know how to open an attachment, right? It says you must include me in any actions taken on the case. If it intrudes too much into my private life, I make that call, but most of the time I'll join you. Nights too."

"What if having a journalist around intrudes into my *professional* life?"

"That would be a problem…if your opinion mattered."

"It'll just be you? Not one of those nitwits like Kost or Button?"

"Kost's no nitwit. No comment on Button. Anyway, when it comes to the murder, Carp will be on call too. You remember Lynn Carpenter?"

"The photographer who helped us on your sister's case?"

"You liked her didn't you?"

"She was okay. Considering she's…one of you. But at the *crime scene*? We've got professionals taking pictures."

"Carp's a professional."

"I meant a *real* professional. Police department. I can't let a newspaper—"

"Read your e-mail. The agreement says pictures can be taken, but before anything's published you'll see it. You'll be asked to approve. If we disagree, we say so and your chief makes the call."

Clarence pulled out one of those miniature computer doohickeys and poked at it with a magic wand.

"So," he said, "how long before we'll be working a case?"

"We try not to put murders on the calendar anymore. It was nice for planning vacations, but it looked suspicious."

"Approximately."

"Do I appear to be all-knowing?"

"Not remotely."

I sighed. "Manny and I get every fifth murder. There've been, let's see, three murders since Jimmy Ross, you know, the dude Lincoln Caldwell blew away? Doyle and Suda are working on the guy who went over the bridge last night. Glissan and Barrows are next. Murder rate's been unusual. We're already on deck."

"So what's your best guess? Based on averages."

"Block out everything from now until next month, and you should have it covered. Or if you want things to move quicker, kill somebody yourself."

"I'm considering it," he said.

I didn't like the way he looked at me. He scribbled something and handed me a business card. It was neat and professional. "That's my cell number."

"Got it already." I waved my phone at him.

"Now you have it in your wallet. If your cell dies, you can still find a phone and call me. Don't forget. I need to be there from the beginning."

Apparently I told my face I was unhappy.

"It could be worse," Clarence said. "We could be television. Cameras and bright lights."

"That's next. After that, they'll film the murders live." I shook my head. "I'm telling you, Abernathy, the detectives are going to think this is a sellout. That *I'm* a sellout."

"Berkley said your chief's the one who suggested it."

"You're saying '*your* chief' on purpose, aren't you?"

I walked away. This is usually a good move when you feel like decking somebody.

THURSDAY, NOVEMBER 21

There was a time in my life when I would have been sound asleep at 3:07 a.m. without assistance. That time passed when lightning struck two years ago, and somebody yanked Sharon from my life.

Since then I've had to use sleeping pills, or my preferred pharmaceutical, Budweiser. I'd been on a bender at Rosie O'Grady's pub the night before, so when the phone rang at 3:07, I wasn't sure if I'd gone to bed three hours or twenty minutes ago.

"Chandler?" the raspy voice said. "It's me."

Why do people say "It's me"? What's the alternative—demon possession?

"Who's you?"

"Lieutenant Mike Petersen."

I saw his image rising from the ashes of my torched mind: built like an oak, but with rougher bark, mosslike hair coming out his ears.

"Hang on a second." He was whispering, which meant he was trying not to wake his wife. "Okay. There's been an incident." If you drive a bus, an incident is a fender bender or two passengers squabbling over a seat. If you're a cop, incidents involve bombs, attacks, crashes, and mayhem. When you're a homicide detective, incidents are murders.

"One body. 2230 Southeast Oak. House is green with—"

"Yellow tape and cop cars out front?" I said, legs heavy as sandbags. Wading through the darkness and feeling cold kitchen tile against my bare feet, I flipped Mr. Coffee. "Who's patrol?"

"Officers Dorsey…and Guerino."

"Do I know them?"

"If I were you, I could answer that."

"Grumpy, Lieutenant?"

"You know what time it is?"

"3:11?"

"My grandkids are spending the night. I'm in the hallway." He gave me Dorsey's number.

"Got it. Go back to bed."

"Don't forget to call your shadow."

"Huh?"

"The *Tribune* reporter. What's his name? The big black guy who used to do sports."

My gut squirmed like a fish tossed on the bank. "Abernathy."

"Chief said to make sure you call Abernathy. I'll call Manny. Longer trip for him. Wait for Abernathy before you go in. That's what the chief said. You're calling him?"

"Got it."

I hung up and started to call Abernathy. I stopped. I emptied into my giant Seahawks mug the first eight ounces from the coffeepot. Nice and black. I go through bags of coffee like they're paper towels.

What was that? Something in my driveway. Sounded like a car door latching. I reached for the nearest gun, the Ruger P-97 in the cupboard, behind two coffee mugs.

I went to the front window and looked at the driveway. Nothing. I snuck out into the garage, opened the door, and followed my Ruger. I studied my car. Okay. Came around to the front porch. Okay. I realized only then how cold it was, especially on my legs. I wasn't wearing pants.

In case someone was watching, I posed like Dirty Harry, lacking only a .357 Magnum, shoes, and pants. I backed into the garage and shut the door.

I replaced the P-97 in the cupboard, took the Browning in the Seahorse waterproof case out of the medicine cabinet, set it in the soap dish, and took my shower. I threw on the least offensive clothes lying by the bed and tucked a tie in my jacket pocket. I pulled on a dark blue stocking cap and put my black Sam Spade fedora over it. I grabbed my cell phone and headed to the car. As I pulled out, I punched numbers.

"Dorsey."

"Ollie Chandler, homicide. On my way. What we got?"

"Scene's pretty clean, but the vic's a mess. Something went sideways here, Detective. He—"

"All I need to know. Be there in ten. Keep everybody out, okay?"

I prefer not to hear crime scene descriptions over the phone. I like to rely on my own eyes. I want to see what I see, not what somebody else says I should see. I'd get patrol's report after my own wheels were turning.

As I drove, I noticed something in the passenger seat. A box. It said Wally's Donuts. In it was a single glazed donut, with telltale signs that it'd recently had five companions.

There were three reasons I didn't eat it. One, I didn't remember buying those donuts. Two, I didn't remember going to Wally's Donuts. Three, I didn't remember ever *hearing* of Wally's Donuts.

The last six months, when I come home late from Rosie O'Grady's, there's a lot I don't remember. But donuts from a place I'd never heard of? It wasn't like me to have eaten five donuts. If I'd bought these, I would've eaten all six. Or given the last one to Mulch. Could I have been drunk enough to leave a donut in the car?

What's going on? The donut wasn't my only issue. Why did they call me? Manny and I aren't the up team. We're on deck. *Aren't we?* But then, if I couldn't remember buying a box of donuts…

My plan was to call Abernathy once I arrived at the scene. I'd still be in the car, so I could tell him I hadn't entered yet. That would give me a head start. I'd be holding the cards when he got there.

At the scene were a dozen people, two in bathrobes covered by coats. Crime scenes are magnets. Fortunately, at 3:30 a.m. not as many gawkers are available, and most journalists are sleeping in their crypts, or doing whatever vampires do when they're not sucking blood.

My biggest concern was the swarm of uniforms. It looked like the Policemen's Ball. That always makes me nervous. The greater the numbers, the greater the potential for contaminated evidence. Cops, firemen, paramedics, all kinds of trained and helpful people can trample a scene and destroy or bury evidence.

I saw two EMTs smoking cigarettes outside the ambulance across the street. That always means somebody's dead.

Two civilian cars in the driveway, patrol car at the curb. On the porch, two cops were having an animated exchange with somebody.

I reached into my trench coat's inner pocket for my Black Jack gum. Nothing. I patted it down. No Black Jack? Bad luck. I dialed Abernathy's cell number. One ring.

"Yeah?"

"It's Chandler. Sorry to get you up."

"I *am* up."

"Just got a call, Eeyore. There's been a murder."

"No kidding."

I stepped out of the car. "The address is—"

"2230 Southeast Oak."

On the porch, one officer was looking at me, the other was eyeing the big guy in suit and tie, who was pointing at the house numbers with his cell phone, glaring at me.

"Oh, boy."

I approached, identified myself to the uniforms, then looked up at the shall-we-say tense face of Clarence Abernathy.

"So you 'just' got a call?"

"It was at 3:07. Only twenty minutes ago."

He looked at his watch. "Twenty-six minutes ago. Twenty-two minutes ago *I* got a call."

"The lieutenant?"

"He said you'd call me, but just in case…"

Light shone on our faces from the video camera of a bozo named Jordan who comes to murder scenes and sells footage to two of the TV stations.

"Hey, Jordan, we're having a private conversation here. Mind turning that off?" Jordan didn't say anything. He kept filming.

"Shaq here wanted us to let him in," Dorsey said. "Can you believe that?"

"Yeah," I said. "It's just like him."

It was a cold night. Abernathy had steam rising from his forehead, like it was the fourth quarter in a long, icy drive up Lambeau Field.

"We had an agreement," Clarence said.

"I kept it. I didn't enter the crime scene before calling you. I still haven't entered the crime scene."

"That's why people don't trust cops. You're liars."

I saw Guerino's hand lower a few millimeters toward his pistol. It was a flinch, but I notice things.

Jordan stepped over the yellow tape onto the lawn. I wanted to put a couple of Glock holes through his camera, but I figured that might win me a return trip to anger management.

Officer Guerino shouldered up by Dorsey and gave Abernathy a hard stare, which he apparently thought was intimidating. But staring a man in the Adam's apple, or craning your neck so he's looking down your nostrils, does not intimidate.

"You need coffee," I said to Clarence. "Here's my thermos. Leave some for me."

He eyed the thermos like it harbored an Ebola culture.

"Look," I said, "you want to stand here and fight while the body gets cold? We could sit on the lawn and play pinochle. You and Guerino can be partners."

Abernathy stared at Guerino. Finally the cop blinked.

"Or how 'bout I go in the door and do my job?"

"Your job was to call me."

"I called you. Want to watch me work? Fine. Otherwise, quit whining and go back to bed."

"You crossed me and you lied," Abernathy said. "I won't forget it."

"Does this mean," I said, tapping my fingers on the yellow crime scene tape, "that the honeymoon's over?"

"My mind rebels at stagnation. Give me problems, give me work, give me the most abstruse cryptogram, or the most intricate analysis, and I am in my own proper atmosphere."
SHERLOCK HOLMES, *THE SIGN OF FOUR*

THURSDAY, NOVEMBER 21, 3:45 A.M.

I PULLED ON LATEX GLOVES and foot covers, then handed a pair of each to Abernathy.

"Never take these off. Got it? Take them off for one second, and you're on the other side of the yellow tape."

His hands didn't fit the one-size-fits-all. He grumbled but wrestled them on, short of his wrists.

"Crime scene contamination's our worst enemy. Somebody visits her cousin and discovers he's been murdered. She picks up the phone and calls 911. She's handled the phone, the doorknob, possibly the victim. All contamination."

He was taking notes now, so I figured I was forgiven. This was my chance to shine in the newspaper I hated.

"The 911 operator tells her don't touch anything else; wait outside for the cops. She might still use the toilet, wash her hands, get a glass of water, pick up her cousin's picture, and make three more phone calls."

Clarence tried to read his handwriting and glared at the gloves.

"Here's where I take my first mental photograph of the crime scene. Ready?"

I turned the corner into the living room. After hundreds of homicides, I've learned that what I first see is the image that stays with me. What struck me this time was a smell—the coppery scent of blood that hadn't dried.

As I looked at the face of the victim, something crawled across the nape of my neck—it felt like a big spider with wet feet.

I recognized the man on the floor. He was a professor at Portland State University. I'd sat in on one of his classes years ago—I was trying to remember exactly when and why since I never attended there. I hadn't seen him since...or had I? Actually, it felt like I'd seen him more recently. But where?

His face was a color it shouldn't have been. I don't mean he looked dead. I mean he didn't look like a dead person is supposed to look. His skin had a hint of blue, but not the shade of asphyxiation.

And yet...around his neck was a rope, bright blue with red flecks in it. The rope was three feet long, and the excess beyond the noose was too short to hang from anything. The end was cut smooth, barely fraying. I stared at the knot, which raised a host of knot-making memories from my childhood. Though it was tied snugly, his neck and throat showed no signs it had been tighter, no signs he'd been hung. I looked above me at an undisturbed ceiling.

The source of the smell was a wound in his chest. Given the shirt fabric, it appeared to be two shots, close together, over the heart. His shirt was soaked.

Multiple causes of death on one body?

I'd never been in this house. *Why did it seem familiar?* It was as if I'd been here in a dream. A recent dream. I tried to shake off the déjà vu.

The victim's clothes swallowed him. I remembered him as bigger in that classroom. Death had shrunk him 20 percent. I studied his dark eyes, open and vacant. They looked like manholes over hell.

I used to stare at stiffs without taking death personally. Lately it's been different. I've been pondering that the death rate is 100 percent, and I'm not going to be the exception. I wonder…does everyone slip into a dreamless sleep? Part of me hopes so. Hell scares me. Heaven scares me almost as much.

Suddenly I realized I was holding hands with a dead man. I dropped it. I looked up, hoping Abernathy wasn't watching. He was.

The victim's wallet was stuffed in his right front pocket. I examined his driver's license and another picture ID.

"Professor William Palatine," I said. A tech informed me Palatine had taught at PSU for many years.

"What do you call those outfits?" Clarence asked, pointing at two criminalists.

"Bunny suits. The technical name is biohazard coveralls. Protects them from contact with body fluids. And protects the evidence from them."

Already one criminalist was on his hands and knees fussing with carpet fiber.

"Why's he that color?" I asked.

"What color?" the criminalist said, reluctantly turning from fiber, his first love, to flesh.

"Bluish."

He shrugged. "You're the detective."

"I'm the detective who's asking the criminalist why he's that color."

He looked around the room as if, having no opinion of his own, he wanted to borrow one. "ME'll run a tox."

I pointed to the computer. "Check the keyboard for prints?"

He looked at me as if the question didn't deserve an answer. One thing I've learned in decades of detective work: I'd rather get dirty looks now than find out later that somebody messed up.

"We'll get the bullets first," he said.

"How many?"

"Two through his chest. Presumably in the floor."

"He was on the floor like this when shot?"

"Looks like it."

"Seen the bedroom?" It was Officer Guerino.

I followed his pointing finger to the hallway leading to the back left of the house. The bedroom was mostly neat and tidy, bed made, drawers shut, light lemon smell. But the outside window had been broken.

I looked it over. Entry point? Break-in? No. Not a big enough hole in the glass. And too jagged. No blood evident. Anyone coming in this way would have taken a couple more whacks at it and cleared the jagged glass before entering. They probably knocked it in, then decided on another entry.

I stared out the fractured window into the darkness. A single streetlight was blocked by a tall maple still holding a third of its leaves. Then I realized what wasn't lying at my feet: broken glass.

"What are you seeing?" Abernathy sounded like Darth Vader with a head cold.

"The glass didn't fall inside." I shone my flashlight on the carpet to make sure I wasn't contaminating evidence.

"So?"

"So it has to be outside." I stepped forward carefully and looked out the window, following the beam.

"There." I pointed outside to broken glass on the ground.

"This wasn't an attempted break-in. It was an attempted break-*out*."

"Who?"

"Palatine? Hard to imagine the killer breaking the window from the inside. Why risk waking the neighbors?"

"Why wouldn't he unlock the window and pull it up? There's room to crawl out. Not for you or me, but he's not that big."

"Maybe he was running and panicked, threw himself at the window. If so, fibers from his clothes may show up on the glass." I knelt down. "There's a shoe impression here in the carpet. And a slight mud residue. And there's a little glass too. I see five shards. Sometimes there's a bounce-back when glass bends out and comes back before breaking.

I went to the closet and took out a right dress shoe, then brought it over and put it by the mark. I looked inside. "Professor wore a size 8. This print is about size 10. It's pointed toward the window. Why would a killer look out a broken window visible from the front of the house? It's like he stood right here, peering into the darkness."

I stepped back and took a couple dozen pictures with my Olympus Stylus 500. First of the shoe impression, then the rest of the room.

"Why so many pictures?" Clarence asked.

"No downside. It has a one-gig memory card, so I can take over five hundred high-resolution photos. These are the only shots we'll get of an undisturbed crime scene."

I pulled a yellow pad from my trench coat and started sketching the room, the window, everything.

"Pictures aren't enough?"

"I make my own record. Photographs are no substitute for what you see in real time. Plus it impresses the scene on your memory. Later, when you view the pictures, they stimulate a three-dimensional image in your mind. If I don't sketch, it's not as clear."

I walked back into the living room, confirming that CSI would record the shoe print and collect the shards on the bedroom carpet. They assured me they would. I leaned over the body and manipulated the ankles. Pressed on the stomach. Tried to turn the head. Locked. Stomach was tying up, but extremities moved well.

"Medical examiner's going to say time of death was four hours ago."

"Oh, is he now?" a new voice asked. I turned to see the number two pencil in a suit, carrying his man-purse.

"Carlton Hatch—the Johnny-on-the-spot medical examiner. Two cases in a row!"

"Interesting," he said, nodding at the body.

I said to Clarence, "Dr. Hatch will be your only competition for best dressed at a murder scene."

I've never met a criminalist, medical examiner, or coroner like the ones on TV, who appear to have given up careers in modeling to pursue a love of dead bodies. Most of the real ones look like Hatch but dress like street people.

"Interesting," Hatch said. "I'm sure you noticed the skin. Something's in the bloodstream."

"Poison?"

Clarence's phone rang. He stepped away.

"We may have a couple different causes of death to choose from," Hatch said. "What's primary and what's secondary? The rope has nothing to do with it." He carefully pulled back the unbuttoned shirt and pointed to Palatine's shoulder. "Needle marks."

"Drugs?"

"Insulin, probably. He's diabetic according to his chain."

I reached for the silver metallic tag and fingered it in my gloved hand. Framed by red medical symbols, including snakes, it said, "Medical Warning: Insulin Dependent Diabetic."

"Interesting," Hatch said. "No needle marks in his stomach."

I went to the refrigerator and poked around, finding an insulin bottle next to the orange juice.

"Clarence, you're diabetic, aren't you?"

He nodded as he shut his phone.

"Wear one of these medical IDs?"

"For the first year. Now it's sitting in a drawer."

"The professor was diabetic. Dr. Hatch thinks he injected something. Or somebody did. Maybe a poison. Help me lift him."

Clarence looked like he was ready to put in for a new assignment. We lifted the right side, Hatch supervising and warning caution. Nothing underneath. We lifted the left and found a needle underneath. I picked it up.

"Like your insulin syringes?" I asked Clarence.

"No. It looks like the older style I used ten or fifteen years ago."

Hatch studied it. "The residue's blue, while insulin is either clear or milky. It's 100 ccs."

Clarence reached in his coat pocket and pulled out a little black packet. He unzipped it and produced a small white plastic syringe with an orange cap.

"That's 50 ccs," Hatch said, like a mechanic looking at a spark plug.

I resumed sketching the floor plan, drawing in body location, furniture, telephone, computer. I took out a measuring tape and stretched it from body to walls, three directions.

I heard commotion at the front door. Clarence's cell phone rang again.

"Carp's at the front door," he said. "They won't let her in."

"They won't let a newspaper photographer into a *crime scene*? What's wrong with those cops?"

I walked to the front door. Lynn Carpenter stood there, camera in hand, *Tribune* ID hanging from her neck, like it said FBI or CTU or something. Guerino's arm stretched out in front of her.

"Can you believe this?" Dorsey asked.

"A newspaper photographer!" Guerino said.

"I hate to be the one to say it, boys. Let her in."

"A *reporter* and a *photographer* inside a crime scene?"

"Next year they'll be selling Cracker Jacks and letting in the general public," I said. "Ten dollars a head. Box seats for forty bucks. Touch the corpse for a hundred. Then they'll be auctioning crime scene memorabilia on eBay."

"This is wrong," Guerino moaned.

"Tell me about it." I handed gloves and foot covers to Carp. "Keep 'em on."

"Nice to see you too, Detective," she said.

I felt slightly bad considering she'd been a big help on Clarence's sister's case ten years ago.

"I'm Ollie, your tour guide."

I extended my hand, glove touching glove. Her face melted into a smile. I can be a real charmer with the ladies. Carp had changed since I'd last seen her. She'd been a quiet tomboy; now she was warmer and more feminine. Age had softened her. I liked it.

With most of the team staring at her, I cleared my throat and said, "I got an e-mail from Chief Lennox." I looked at Clarence. "It even had an attachment. The deal is that the *Oregon Tribune*—our beloved newspaper, so cherished by this police department—can take pictures of this crime scene. They can't print any photo without department clearance. Can't divulge sensitive information. They won't jeopardize our investigation. Anyway, that's what they tell me. If they get in your way, respectfully Taser them or beat them senseless with a nightstick."

There were a number of chuckles, including Carp's. None from Abernathy.

Carp's camera started flashing. Clarence was looking over my shoulder like a three-hundred-pound gargoyle. I walked to the professor's desk, turning my best side to the camera.

"Walk me through procedure," Clarence said.

"Yes, sir," I said. "I've written Ollie's Rules of Investigation. I'll give you a copy. Ninety-two of them. The first ten are never touch anything. Number 11 is protect the scene. Number 12 is write everything down. Number 13 is don't trust what anybody else writes down. Number 14 is don't trust anyone who says they didn't touch anything, especially if they keep insisting on it."

"What were you doing with the measuring tape?"

"Triangulating body location. An inch here and there can make all the difference."

I went to the front door and asked Dorsey, "Witnesses?"

"Nobody. The people we've talked to came when they saw the patrol cars or got a wake-up call from the media. Some are from those apartments."

He pointed at a two-story building the next street over, where most of the blinds were closed. I saw one television on, and in the next apartment, barely visible, someone with elbows pointed outward, which made me think they might be holding binoculars.

"Nobody we've talked with on this street saw anything—except somebody noticed two vagrants who often wander over here from their settlement three streets down."

"Who made the 911 call?"

He shrugged. "Want me to check?"

"Manny'll handle it. Talk to the rubbernecks?" I pointed to the dozen people on the other side of a police tape, including three kids who should've been in bed.

"We've focused on protecting the scene."

"Good choice." I turned back to Clarence. "Once I finish here, we'll canvass for witnesses, take written statements."

"These guys collecting stuff in the bags—are they called CSIs? Or criminologists?"

"Criminologists aren't evidence collectors, they're experts in why criminals commit crimes. What you know as CSIs are what we call criminalists. They're crime scene techs, evidence collectors. They make sketches, usually a detailed drawing later. They're more artistic than detectives."

He peered at my sketch on the yellow pad. "I hope so. Keisha drew better than that in first grade. Where do they take the bags?"

"Evidence locker. They maintain a chain of custody. If we have a particular lab request, we ask. Otherwise, they check for fingerprints, DNA traces, et cetera. Then they search for a match." I looked up at him. "Can I do my job now?"

"Part of your job is helping me do mine."

"Yeah. The attachment."

Carlton Hatch loudly pronounced death. Everybody else stifled their smirks.

"What's the medical examiner's role?" Clarence asked.

"He's the ranking official at the crime scene, even over the lead detective. Which is why I don't like him showing up early. Generally, they estimate cause of death and time of death, then go over the results of the autopsy. Then revise as needed. They usually show up on the scene later. Not Carlton Hatch."

"Chandler!"

Manny Domast exploded into the room. There are advantages to having a thirty-six-year-old partner who's a former gangbanger. He's street savvy, shrewd, bold. A pit bull.

He's also sixty-grit sandpaper.

"What took you so long?" I asked.

"We weren't the up team, man. What happened?"

"Not sure. Maybe a sick detective or two deaths in one night? Somehow we got bumped up to the top."

"That's crazy, man. Maria's pulling a shift at the hospital. I had to get the kids dressed and into the car. Who wants to take three kids under five in the middle of the night?"

"Detective Domast," said James Earl Jones, or someone borrowing his voice. "It's been a long time."

Manny twirled to look straight into the knot in Clarence Abernathy's tie.

"It's just gettin' worse," Manny said.

"You read your e-mail, right?" I asked. "And the attachment?"

"Where'd you find him this time of night?" Manny said. "Jazzy's Barbecue?"

"We've been investigating," Clarence said, "while you were fighting chickens behind Taco Bell."

"Whoa, hold it," I said. "Look, you guys don't like each other, and I don't like either of you. But we've got a job to do. Manny, meet Lynn Carpenter, *Tribune* photographer."

Carp extended her hand. Manny didn't.

"*Photographer?*"

"I thought the same. Before I realized how the public good would be served with crime scene photos."

"But that'll compromise—"

"Supposedly that's not going to happen."

"It's all in the attachment," Clarence said. Not sweetly.

I asked a criminalist, "Those chairs clean? The table?" I looked at Clarence and Manny. "Sit down, both of you."

Neither budged.

"Sit!"

Clarence sat. Manny pulled up a chair on the opposite side.

"Let's get you up to speed, Manny." We did.

Manny and Clarence and I once drove to a baseball game in Seattle, with Obadiah, Clarence's dad, the best man I've ever known. Obadiah's presence had made them civil. It was a long time ago. Obadiah Abernathy's magic was gone.

Manny gave Clarence one last hundred-yard stare, from two feet away, then went to the bedroom to examine the broken window.

"Manny's got an attitude," I said to Carp. "In time, he grows on you." *Like mildew.*

I stood beside the professor's desk looking at two piles of papers, one with a red C on the top, the other unmarked.

"Philosophy 102," I read. "Ethics."

"May I touch them?" Clarence asked.

"As long as your gloves are on. Careful."

Clarence shuffled through them. "Mostly Cs and Bs. A few Ds. Not a single A. Either he's a tough grader or he was in a bad mood."

"Or his students are dunderheads," Carp said.

Dunderheads? I liked it. She was winning me over.

"Interesting," Dr. Hatch said, pointing at the computer monitor.

"One thing at a time." I flipped through the stacks. "Fifteen graded. Five to go."

Next to the papers were seven piles of playing cards, faceup, with other cards staggered below them.

"Solitaire?" Abernathy asked.

"I've seen murders over poker, never solitaire. But it gives us the victim's frame of mind, doesn't it?"

"What do you mean?"

"He'd stopped grading papers. If he was playing solitaire, he was bored, wanting to kill time."

"Or taking a break from the papers," Manny said, reappearing. "Rewarding himself."

"Or he might have been distracted from his work," I said. "Knew something was looming. Nervous. Expecting someone? Check out the last card facing up, by the main deck. What do you see, Abernathy?"

"The ace of spades."

"Anything strike you as strange?"

"No."

"It hasn't been played."

"So?"

"Look, he's got two aces played above, diamonds and clubs, with a two and a three on it. With this kind of solitaire, when you flip an ace you play it then build on it. It's a no-brainer. You don't leave it sitting there like that. You make your play. Unless you're interrupted."

"Meaning what?"

"He stopped midstream. When someone came to the door, if that's what happened, he was playing solitaire, not grading papers."

I noticed a criminalist poised over the professor's body, shining a flashlight.

"What you seeing?" I asked.

"A strand of hair," he said. "Not the professor's."

"Perfect," I said. "Bag it."

"Mind if I move that lamp?" Carp asked.

"Don't touch anything," I said. "I'll do it."

"About three inches back from the screen," Carp said.

"Hey, I'm here to serve you *Trib* folks. Can I order you a pizza?"

"Double pepperoni, double cheese," Carp said, smiling.

I froze. "Who told you that?"

"Told me what?"

"My favorite pizza. Double pepperoni, double cheese."

"That's my favorite pizza," Carp said. "Always has been."

It was one of those magical moments. If it had been a movie, the music would have changed. Lynn Carpenter was speaking my love language.

"I'll search the desk," I said, eyeing Carp. "Manny, you want to grill the rubbernecks?"

"Nobody's done that?" He was out the door, pulling out pad and pen, a warrior looking for a war.

In the professor's oak desk, I discovered paper clips, rubber bands, a roll of peppermint BreathSavers, an unopened Snickers bar, reading glasses, three blue and four black Pilot G2 gel pens, three phone numbers without names, a Matt Hasselbeck rookie card, and a Shaun Alexander MVP card. Plus a nearly empty 8.45-ounce bottle of Pelikan fountain pen ink, royal blue.

I showed the ink bottle to Clarence.

"They still make fountain pens?" he asked.

"I just realized," Carp said, pointing to a corkboard covered with pictures, including a newspaper clipping. "I know this man. I took that picture. He was receiving the Rotary Club community service award." She scanned the article. "For his 'investment in the lives of young people.' It goes to one college professor each year."

"When was it taken?" I asked.

"June, I think." She stepped closer. "Yeah. The June 13 edition. So I took it June 12."

"What was he like?"

"Seemed a bit…taken with himself."

"Yeah," I said, stepping in close beside her to view the picture. "Some men can be real jerks. Not every man's humble and sensitive like me."

She nodded knowingly.

"What've you found, Chandler?" Another familiar voice. I turned.

"*Suda*? What are you doing here?"

Kim Suda's one of our two female homicide detectives. She's all female and all detective, petite but powerful, with a fifth degree black belt in Tae Kwon Do. She was wearing a stylish maroon coat.

"I live six blocks from here. I couldn't sleep, so I took a drive. Heard about it on the monitor and figured I'd check it out."

"You don't get enough murders?"

"Professional hazard. Architects look at buildings; I check out murders. You've never dropped by someone else's crime scene?"

Truth was, I had. Three times.

"It's getting to be a rock concert in here," I said. "Make yourself useful…get that patrol out; then tell me if you see something helpful."

"You got it, boss." Within ten seconds she had her hand on the arm of a uniformed officer. Smiling sweetly, she led him out the door.

"Who's she?" Clarence asked.

"Kim Suda. Homicide detective. Been in the department five years. Chris Doyle's her partner."

"Strange time to drop by."

"We detectives are strange people."

Clarence nodded, more vigorously than necessary.

I saw Suda and Carpenter watching each other. No smiles. Two attractive females suspicious of each other? Both wanting to impress me?

Once upon a time I thought I understood women.

What an idiot.

Clarence and Carp drifted from me, walking around the room talking and picture-taking.

I munched on the Snickers bar. It had been checked for prints. No sense letting it rot in the evidence room.

"Carp's going outside to take pictures of the neighborhood," Abernathy announced. "Eventually we'll want to use one or two for a feature. Will they let her back in?"

"Got your ticket stub?" I asked her.

"Thought maybe you'd stamp my hand."

"Once we start doing general admissions we'll have to do that. Tell Guerino and Dorsey I said they should let you back in. Let me know if they give you problems."

She smiled again. I'm not used to all these smiles at murder scenes. I looked at her, heart aflutter. She'd had me at double cheese.

I walked over to the far end of the couch, against the wall. I noticed crumbs on the ground. Big crumbs.

"What's this?" I asked the criminalist.

"Figured you'd want to see it as is before we vacuumed."

"What do you make of it?"

"Crumbs," he said.

"What kind?"

"Graham cracker?"

I looked closely. Someone had sat on the couch eating.

On my hands and knees, I looked over every inch of the coffee table. It was clean except for two identical circular stains two feet apart. They looked recent, slight moisture still evident. I took close-up photos of both stains, jotting down which picture corresponded to which stain. Then I took a wide-angle of the coffee table in relation to the couch, noting the location of the crumbs.

"You can bag the crumbs," I told the tech. "Need them all?"

"Nope. Maybe a third."

I reached down and picked up three big crumbs. I went to my briefcase and took out a water bottle to get the taste of Snickers off my palate. I put the yellow-brownish crumbs in my mouth.

"Not graham cracker," I said. "Granola bar. The crunchy type, not chewy. With a nut component. Maybe almond. Or hazelnut."

"They could use your mouth in the crime lab."

I went to the kitchen sink and found what I was looking for: two glasses, one with a residue of white wine.

"Test this," I said to the criminalist. "Fingerprints and DNA."

I searched for a wine bottle. Nothing in the fridge, garbage, or on the counter.

"I want to know what kind of wine."

Two empty bottles of Budweiser sat on the counter to the left of the sink. "At least he drank a good beer," I said.

"Bag them?"

"Why not?"

Ten minutes later I was back on the floor, hunting more crumbs (being a specialist in food particles), when I noticed something by the corner of the right front leg of the couch, six inches from the north wall. It was blue and black. I scooted over, stared at it in disbelief, then picked it up.

"What are you doing?" Kim Suda's voice sounded accusing, but her voice usually does.

I snapped my neck around. "Nothing." I heard the nerves in my voice. Had she seen what I picked up? I hid it in my hand and stood.

"What are *you* doing, Suda? It's my crime scene."

"You sound like you did it."

"If I'd done it, it would've been between nine and five."

"What's in your hand?"

"Nothing. What's in your brain?"

"Find something?" the tech asked.

"Nada," I said, putting my hand in my coat pocket while my body ran interference. "Just a shadow. Bathroom done?"

"Good to go. Nothing big. Hair samples with his brush. Follicles, presumably his. I left the toothbrushes for you to see. Two of them. We'll take them for saliva."

I walked to the bathroom. One Sonicare electric toothbrush, plugged into the charger. The other was a Colgate, old and frayed. Clarence joined me.

"Excuse me," I said to Clarence. "I have some business."

I locked the bathroom door. I heard my heart pound as I took out the piece of paper. I stared at it. It was a gum wrapper.

Black Jack.

I left the bathroom, preoccupied with my discovery, but determined to finish my job undistracted and figure out the gum wrapper later.

I examined the professor's closet, filled with shirts, Dockers, sport coats and ties, and a dozen pairs of shoes. Men shouldn't have that many shoes. On the left side of the closet was a red plastic storage box turned catawampus and with a crack in it, like something heavy had been on it. Everything else was neat and tidy, remarkably unlike my closet.

I checked the spare bedroom, mainly used for storage. Nothing stood out. But I took pictures anyway in hopes that eventually the house would yield its secrets to me. Clarence and Carpenter periodically crowded me, nearly stepping on my heels. I was winsomely gracious, especially to the double cheese pizza girl.

When I returned to the living room, the professor was still dead.

I began to systematically examine the photographs on the wall. Vacations in Hawaii and Mexico and the Caribbean, judging by the locals. In one he was speaking behind the lectern in an academic environment. In several he was wearing robes and regalia.

"The peacock displays his feathers," I said. "Graduation?"

Clarence nodded and pointed. "That one's a formal lectureship."

I looked at a couple of hanging frames that displayed academic degrees. Doctorate from Princeton.

I was about to examine the photos on the mantel when Dr. Hatch spoke.

"Interesting," he said, staring again at the computer screen. It reminded me I'd been distracted from the desk twenty minutes ago when Suda appeared. I hadn't made my way back.

"Mouse is on the left side," Clarence said. "He was lefthanded?"

Hatch was leaning over the desk, staring at the screen, his hand to the left of the monitor, inches from the mouse.

"Don't touch it," I said.

"Relax," the criminalist chimed in from the dining room table. "It was wiped clean."

"Then somebody used it."

"Besides the professor?" Clarence asked. "How do you know?"

"Do you wipe prints off your mouse?"

I picked up the reading glasses sitting on the desk and read aloud the words on the screen. "I, Dr. William Palatine, do not deserve to live. I've crossed boundaries and forfeited my life. I admit my arrogance. I deserve judgement. I should be cast into a deep sea with a millstone around my neck."

"A suicide note?" Clarence asked.

"Ever hear a suicide note that sounds like that? What's the millstone mean?"

Everybody looked at each other and shrugged.

"It's from the Bible," Clarence said. "Millstones were large rocks used to grind grain. They might weigh a couple hundred pounds. Jesus said if anyone hurt one of His children, he'd be better off cast into the sea with a millstone around his neck."

"The professor probably didn't type it, but if he did, it's a forced confession," Manny said. "I say the guy threatened to kill him if he didn't type it. Or the killer typed it himself. Either way, the words are the killer's."

"What's your next move," Clarence whispered, "now that you ate the victim's candy bar?"

"That won't show up in an article, will it?"

"Depends on whether you start keeping your word."

"Excuse me while I play solitaire. Okay if I handle the cards?" I asked the criminalist.

"Carefully. Gloves can smudge prints."

I picked up the ace of spades by the edges.

There were seven columns of cards. A deck was facedown, and next to it, faceup, was a small stack. Knowing I had a dozen photos, I took the ace of spades and played it. I started flipping up every third card carefully, by the edges.

"You're finishing a dead man's game of solitaire?" Clarence asked.

"Not only was the ace up, he had two good plays after that. Game definitely wasn't over. Like I said, he was interrupted."

Hatch cleared his throat.

"Time of death?" I asked.

"That's going to be tough," Hatch said. "May depend on what was injected and how it would likely affect rigor mortis."

"Your best guess?"

"Ten thirty to midnight."

I wanted a smaller window than ninety minutes. Hopefully someone heard the shots. I pressed the phone's message button. "No messages."

"It's digital, so it has a magnetized erase," Manny said. "No recovery."

I pressed Play Greeting.

A tenor voice spoke, as if from another world: *"This is Dr. William Palatine.*

Nietzsche said, 'All things are subject to interpretation; whichever interpretation prevails at a given time is a function of power and not truth.' Leave a message."

After a moment of silence and profound meditation, Manny mumbled, "What a jerk."

"He was a philosophy professor," I said. "Apparently he wanted everyone to know it."

"A student might be impressed," Suda said. "Anybody else would be annoyed."

"An answering machine greeting is self-expression," I said. "Like bumper stickers. They say something about the man."

"Right," Manny said. "They say he's an arrogant son of a—"

I held up my hand. "With the press here, we might want to guard our observations about the deceased."

"Let's find out who the professor called last."

"The philosophy hotline?" Manny said. Manny's not an Ivy Leaguer.

I pressed redial and waited. A voice started speaking. The words were clear enough but the voice sounded like someone gargling gravel.

"After the tone, leave your name, number, and the location of the money. I'll get back to you as soon as it's safe for you to come out of hiding."

I stared at the phone. Then at the redial button.

"Voice mail? Answering machine?" Manny asked.

I nodded.

"And?"

I disconnected, then pressed redial, hoping I'd heard wrong. I listened again, then hung up.

"What was the message?" Clarence asked. "Whose number is it?"

"It's...mine."

5

"Scotland Yard feels lonely without me,
and it causes an unhealthy excitement among
the criminal classes."
SHERLOCK HOLMES, *THE DISAPPEARANCE OF LADY*
FRANCES CARFAX

"YOU DIDN'T DIAL your number by habit?" Manny asked.

"I couldn't have."

"Why not?"

"For one thing, it's not my habit. I never call myself. If I want to talk to myself, I just start talking. I'm always right there. Besides, I'd know I wasn't home."

"You sure you pressed redial?"

"Positive."

"But…you didn't know the professor, right?" Clarence asked.

"No."

"Never met him?" Suda asked.

"Not exactly. I sat in the back, visiting one of his classes years ago."

"Why?" Manny asked.

"I don't remember."

"Why would you be his last call?" Clarence asked.

I was on the wrong side of the questions. It didn't feel good.

"Maybe it was about a murder," Suda said. "Like thinking he was going to be the victim?"

"He'd just call the police. Not me."

"Unless he had a personal reason," Abernathy said.

"Like what?"

"Did the professor leave you a message?" Suda asked.

"Not sure if I checked my messages last night."

The truth was, I didn't even remember coming home last night. I'd been at Rosie O'Grady's, but after that…it was like a dream of a dream.

"So," Clarence said, "retrieve your messages and find out."

"I will when I get home."

"You don't know how to retrieve your messages remotely?" Clarence asked.

"Just call your number, put in your code, and listen to your messages," Manny said. His tone suggested I had the IQ of a split-leaf philodendron.

"I don't know any code."

Manny phoned my number and pressed buttons. "Usually a preset code." He disconnected and tried three combinations. "Nothin'," he said, looking disgusted.

"Anyone I want to hear from calls me on my cell." No one seemed to buy it.

"Take over," I told Manny. "Make sure the place is sealed. Goin' home to check messages."

"I'll follow you," Clarence said.

"No."

"It's part of the investigation."

"Manny needs you here." I didn't look up, but I felt their glares hitting me from both sides.

"Go through the professor's speed dial options," I told Manny. "Contact those he called most. See what they know."

"I'll get phone company records," Manny said. As I left the room he called, "And read the stupid manual about retrieving messages."

Clarence and I walked out the door right into the hands of the media standing in front of the crowd of neighbors.

"Clarence? What're you doing here?" one reporter said. "This is my assignment."

"Guess nobody told night beat I'd be handling the case," Clarence said. "Sorry. It's a couple of features a week. Guess you still need to report the news."

"Why were you inside? They never let us inside."

I started my car. The whiny reporter stood right there, a foot from the car, even though he could see I couldn't back up. Occasionally journalists block your car like they're that protester in Tiananmen Square who stopped the tanks. I edged the car, just touching him. He backed off a few inches until I bumped him again. Then I popped the car in neutral and gunned it, motor screaming. He jumped to the side, falling into bushes.

That dude in Tiananmen Square never flinched.

I unlocked the front door. Mulch was all over me. When he saw Clarence, his lip twitched.

"Big guy's with me," I reassured him.

Clarence put out his hand. Mulch sniffed it, licked it, then started investigating his pant leg and constructing a mental image of Clarence's dog.

"Okay, Mulch, we're here to check messages. Looks like we've got two." I punched the button.

"*11:17 p.m. Ollie, it's Brandon Phillips. Saw you forty minutes ago, pulling out of Rosie O'Grady's. You were headed west, away from home. You looked kind of…well, your driving was a little…anyway, thought I should check up on you. Hoped you'd turned around and made it home by now. Later.*"

"Who's Brandon Phillips?" Clarence asked.

"One of the homicide detectives."

"Who's Rosie?"

"Let's hear the other message."

This time I played my voice first. It sounded like the guy in an old Western who'd had been cut down after the lynching started and was hoarse the rest of his life. I've never smoked, but when restaurants had smoking sections, on hearing my voice they took me straight there. My voice didn't get this way because a thug smashed my Adam's apple with a crowbar (though that did happen once). It's been this way since the summer between sixth and seventh grade. Some guys wake up with a golden bass voice; I woke up with a cement truck in my throat.

After my voice, we waited for the professor's. "*11:37 p.m.*" Five seconds of nothing. No sound, except faint breathing, as if waiting for me to pick up. I played it again, turning out the lights to focus on the sound. Yeah. Breathing.

"You weren't home at 11:37?"

"Maybe not. Or I'd gone to bed. Or I was home but didn't check messages."

"That's pretty vague."

"You accusing me of something?"

"Why would I accuse you?" Clarence asked. "Just wondering why you don't remember. You answered the phone when the lieutenant called about the murder, right?"

I held up my cell. "Everything comes through this. Unless they can't get me; then they call the home number."

"Apparently the professor didn't have your cell number."

"I'd like to know how he had my home number. It's unlisted."

"What do we do now?"

"You do whatever reporters do," I said. "I'm going to sit down, have coffee, and Mulch and I are going to think this through."

"You want to cancel lunch with Jake?"

"We have to eat anyway. And it's Jake's turn to buy. Lunch isn't for six hours. I'm not canceling yet."

Clarence took off, eager to start writing, even though I warned him he couldn't say much.

Manny would make sure the crime scene was preserved. Before returning, I wanted to look over my notes. With sugarless gum in his drawer, the professor didn't strike me as a Black Jack kind of guy. His toothy grin in the photos on the mantel and the walls suggested he got his teeth polished. People who speak in public for a living don't film up their teeth with Black Jack. We Black Jack chewers are an elite group, and if we took a vote, based on his teeth, we'd kick the professor off

Black Jack Island. I bump into a Black Jack chewer once in a blue moon. There's instant camaraderie, partly because it defies all reason, like being a Raiders fan.

So what was a Black Jack wrapper doing at the professor's? And why couldn't I remember coming home? And what was with Wally's Donuts?

I plugged in my camera and downloaded my photos into my notebook computer. I went through them one by one, enlarging some. Whenever I found myself wanting a better angle, I jotted a note for when I returned.

I sat in my old brown recliner, the one Sharon special ordered and we picked up at Clemmer's Furniture, east of Gresham. I reached out and touched the horizontal eight-by-ten photo on the table next to the chair, taken ten months before Sharon died. It was of all the Portland homicide detectives and their spouses, so there were about seventeen of us in the picture, including three unmarrieds. It happened to be the best picture of Sharon and me anywhere. I should ask a computer nerd to do one of those Photoshop things so the picture would just be me and Sharon, maybe on a beach in Hawaii, though that wouldn't work since I was in coat and tie and she was wearing her favorite black dress. I still have that dress in the closet. Sometimes I take it out to remember her scent.

My mind went back to the crime scene. I was searching it, comparing sketch with pictures, romancing it, asking it to whisper secrets in my ear.

I heard the ring tone of the phone at CTU headquarters, where Jack Bauer works. It was my cell. "Manny" showed in the display.

"Jack Bauer," I answered.

"I sealed the crime scene. Body's been taken away."

"Where you standing?"

"By the front door, about to lock up."

"Look into the room, turn immediately to your left, and walk five feet. See that miniature bookshelf that's maybe three feet high?"

"Yeah?"

"There's a greenish book, hardcover, on top."

"How do you know—?"

"I have a photographic memory for crime scenes."

"You're in Photoshop."

"What's the book called?"

"It's by…some honcho named Bertrand Russell. Title's *Why I Am Not a Christian*."

"No kidding? Okay, leave it right there. Going fishing for witnesses?"

"Yeah. Those second-floor apartments on the next street have a clear view of the house. You?"

"Studying the scene."

"It's right here."

"You know my methods, Watson."

"Watson was a gringo."

I studied the pictures and read my notes. I printed out six photos. Next thing I knew, it was 9:15. I called Clarence and told him I was returning to the scene. I gave White's Market beef to Mulch, with a dab of Sweet Baby Ray's barbecue sauce. Then I was out the door.

I scanned titles on Palatine's bookshelves, ignoring those by German men with long last names. My eyes landed on Sherlock Holmes. I opened it up. The spine cracked, and its first few pages stuck together. Didn't take a skilled detective to figure out it was a gift Professor Smart Guy never opened. Too bad, since it beat to blazes everything else on his shelves.

When Abernathy arrived, I pointed to the Holmes book. "Watson showed Holmes to the world. Your words will immortalize me—until the afternoon, when people put the *Tribune* on the bottom of the birdcage."

"If you end up looking good, which is unlikely, you'll frame the article. If you look bad, you'll blame me and trash it. I was a sports columnist, remember? The guys who whined about my criticisms loved my praise."

"When you feature my brilliance, I'll tack it on my wall."

"You'll have to show your brilliance first."

"I have."

"I must have blinked. You didn't even know how to retrieve phone messages. And you ate a dead man's Snickers bar."

"Not going to let it drop, are you?" I leaned against the bookcase. "You want brilliance? I'll show you something I learned from Nero Wolfe and Archie Goodwin."

"You haven't told me who they are, and I'm not going to look it up."

"Nero Wolfe was the last of the great detectives. Always stayed in his old brownstone on West Thirty-fifth Street in New York. He weighed a seventh of a ton—like you only a lot shorter. He was a gourmet. Kept ten thousand orchids. Sent Archie Goodwin out to do his investigating, bringing back the facts so Wolfe could apply his brain and solve the crime."

"He wasn't real?"

"It's fiction, okay, but to me he's real. As real as you and me and Mulch and Lou's onion ring platter. Forty-seven books, written by Rex Stout. Classics. Stout was the best. Hemingway was a hack."

"So what did you learn from them that can help us?"

"Archie Goodwin once paged through every book on a shelf."

"*All* of them?" He looked at the professor's books.

"There're just a couple hundred. People can stick something important between the pages. Notes. Letters. Business cards. Then they forget them, and eventually they're back on the shelves. Hidden evidence."

"Needle in a haystack."

"We can do it in an hour or two. The point is to flip pages, not read."

After some intellectual yawners, I came to The Adventures of Huckleberry Finn. I fingered it and inhaled the smell of old pages. My grandfather used to do that, when books were few enough to instill reverence. I'd picked up the book-sniffing habit and never lost it, though it seems wasted on the slick mass-produced stuff.

Clarence and I paged through Plato. René Descartes. John Locke. Some woman named René with a mustache. Voltaire. Rousseau. Adam Smith. Kant. Nietzsche. Francis Bacon (Mulch's favorite philosopher).

"Here's a phone number inside the back cover of Karl Marx," Clarence said.

"Think it's Marx's home number?" I asked.

No response.

"Who was your favorite Marx brother? Mine was Harpo."

Still no response. I jotted down the number.

Five minutes later, Clarence said, "Here's a travel book for Maui. Same thing—phone number inside the back cover."

"We've got a pattern now. Look for it."

I remembered the green book. I went over to the small bookcase and picked up *Why I Am Not a Christian.* I slipped it in my briefcase.

We found a few more phone numbers in the backs of books—strangely, not one of them with a name.

I turned and looked around at all the mementos and photos taped, pinned, and hung on the wall. "There's lots of visual evidence in this room. It's cluttered...hard to see what's really here. I'm going to call in some eyes." I punched 2 on my cell phone, for the department.

"Mitzie? Ollie. I'm going to drop by some case notes before lunch. If you can type them this afternoon, I'd appreciate it. Hey, who's hanging around the donuts? Cimmatoni? No thanks. Anyone else? Yeah, Phillips is fine."

When Phillips came to the phone, I said, "You busy?"

"Always."

"I'm in the first twenty-four hours of this case. Could use your eyes. 2230 Southeast Oak."

"Want me to bring Cimma?"

"Uh, no...this is more up your alley. Just need one pair of eyes. Yours."

"Okay. Give me fifteen."

I sat in front of the computer. They'd removed the hard drive and taken the keyboard for computer forensics, but the monitor was still there.

"Something's wrong. Didn't think about it last night. The professor was just a couple inches shorter than me, wasn't he? This chair's way too high. If they want to use the keyboard, tall people lower the seat and short people raise it, right? Sit in this chair."

Clarence looked ridiculous, the keyboard way too low.

"How tall would someone be who'd put a chair at this setting?" I asked.

"Five foot? A woman?"

"Or a fourth grader? A jockey?" I knelt, looking at the metal rod on the chair adjustment. "See the marks? That's the normal position, the professor's setting. What does that tell you?"

"Someone else used it."

"Palatine was grading. Played solitaire. Then someone adjusted the chair. You don't do that unless you're sitting a while. If it's just a minute, why bother? I say they did it to type the confession."

"Then wouldn't their prints show up on the keyboard?"

"We'll see when tests come back." I walked toward the fireplace.

"Look at the photos on the mantel," I said. "What do you see?"

Clarence moved in for a closer look. "Mediocre quality pictures in cheap stand-up frames."

"How many?"

"Nine."

"Four on one side and five on the other," I said. "Now, look at all the picture groupings on the wall. Everything's balanced, symmetrical. So why the imbalance on the mantel?"

I stepped up onto the hearth to get a closer look. "Yeah. The dust tells the tale."

"What tale?" Clarence got on his tiptoes and could see the top without climbing.

"The four pictures on this side…they've been moved to equal spacing. But there were five pictures, just like on the other side. One picture's been taken. Someone didn't want us to notice, so he filled in the spaces."

"Why?"

"Because he thought if we noticed a photo was missing, it might incriminate him."

"How?"

"Don't know. But if it wouldn't, why cover it up? Why not just snatch the picture and forget it? He took that photo for a reason—it was important to him. But it was also important to him that we didn't notice."

"So far you've got him carrying away a wine bottle and a five-by-seven picture frame."

"There's a reason for every action. This brings us one step closer to the killer."

"Anybody home?"

Brandon Phillips is that ageless sort who looked old in his twenties when I met him and now in his forties looks young. He was a Golden Gloves boxer, rugged, leathery face like a mountain climber. Broad shoulders, big chest. And fit? I could see him offering his water to Sherpas climbing Everest as he passed them.

I introduced Phillips to Clarence and said, "I humbly request your observations on my crime scene. And thanks for not dropping by uninvited, like Suda did last night."

Phillips cleared his throat. Though we were standing right in front of the mantel, with me leaning against the brick, he walked immediately to the other end of the room. "Lots of books. Computer's nice. Wide-screen. Flat. He buys over the Internet."

"How do you know?"

"It's a Dell. I've seen that model on the website. You can only get it online. It's not available in stores…not in Portland anyway."

"See?" I said to Clarence. "You never know what you'll get from a detective."

Phillips walked around making other observations. Nothing particularly helpful.

"What about at this end? What do you see?" I pointed toward the mantel and the photos.

"Lots of pictures." Phillips coughed. He cleared his throat and rubbed his face.

"You okay?"

"I need the bathroom." He walked quickly around the corner and I heard the door shut.

"What's with him?" Clarence asked.

I shrugged. He came back five minutes later.

"Anything wrong?" I asked.

"Allergies. I'm fine."

"So, what do you see on this mantel?"

"He's no photographer."

"Yeah, but proud of his work. Nine photos up there, huh?" I pointed to the mantel.

"Hang on. I have to call Cimma." Phillips stepped into the other room, and I heard his muffled voice. A minute later he reappeared. "Cimma needs me."

"I didn't think Cimma needed anybody."

"One more witness on our case. Cimma wants me to see if I can catch him before lunch. Sorry."

Fifteen seconds later Phillips was gone. I looked at Clarence and shrugged.

I swung by detective division at eleven to drop off case notes for Mitzie to type. I was fortunate to find one of the precious few police only parking spaces on Second Street, just south of Madison, a stone's throw from the Justice Center. I was back in my car ten minutes later because though Lou's Diner is only five blocks away, the midday sky was dark, threatening rain. It looked like it had been rubbed hard with gray finger paint. It made me thirsty.

I got to Lou's early enough to think through the case before Jake and Clarence arrived. And have a couple of beers. Lou's is "The Diner Time Forgot." The jukebox was playing "Surfin' USA." Archie, Betty, and Veronica could have been sitting in the next booth. I'd be Jughead, since I play his part, downing the cheeseburgers.

I love old diners, but nothing compares to this one. Lou's son Rory keeps the place sparkling, unlike Ralph's Diner on Ankeny, where you need a crowbar to remove syrup bottles from the lazy Susan.

Three years ago, Jake, Clarence, and I started meeting at Lou's on Thursdays for lunch. We all work downtown, so we rarely miss, and work in a second lunch during the week whenever we can. We shoot the breeze about lots of things, but sometimes Jake gets us talking about…well, spiritual stuff. Once they tried to get me to read something called *The Purpose-Driven Life*. I told them I already had a purpose-driven life. Justice—hunting down criminals in a Clint Eastwood, Chuck Norris, Jack Bauer sort of way. I don't see religion as a solution, but a problem. My job is to hunt down the bad guys God lets get away. Jake said maybe I'm serving God's ends and He's using me to get the bad guys. Whatever.

We can hardly have lunch without the afterlife intruding into the conversation. But I don't want to die trusting that God will make things okay. I want to make them okay right here, right now. Is that so much to ask? If I can make things right, I do. So if God can make things right, why doesn't He?

These are not popular questions to ask Christians. Jake and Clarence listen and nod and say they understand my questions, that they too once struggled with such things. But I must have faith, I must trust, I must believe, and all will be better. Well, sorry, but I just *don't*. And most of the time, frankly, I don't want to.

Sometimes these guys are stubborn and opinionated. I feel like they're taking the moral high ground, like the rest of us aren't good enough for them. I guess I'm saying ours is a complicated friendship.

I looked at my watch. 11:52. I waved to Rory and pulled out my wallet. "This is for my beers."

"I can just put it on your bill," he said.

"Jake's turn to buy. And take my bottles and the glass, would you?"

"I brewed your dark Italian roast extra bold. You'll love it."

"You're a good man, Rory. If you ever get murdered, I'll go after the guy. That's a promise."

"*Grazie*, Mr. Ollie."

Okay, I feel guilty for what I said about Jake and Clarence. Because there's another side, and I guess it's why I keep meeting them for lunch. The conversations sometimes bug me, but they make me think. Occasionally they're downright interesting. And yes, Jake asked my permission, and I've agreed to talk about the Bible now and then. These guys aren't total morons, and they have hope. I admit that it seems a naive and baseless hope. And yet…there's a certain comfort in being around people who really believe—deep in their gut—that one day things will be better than they are now.

It seems like if you become a Christian, everything's supposed to be great, right? You live happily ever after because you go to heaven, and that makes up for life's miseries. Never mind that people—like my Sharon—suffer and die, and murderers get away. After all, there's pie in the sky by and by.

Sorry, but I'd rather have my pie here and now. Speaking of which, I'd noticed that huckleberry was Lou's pie of the day.

My phone rang. Manny again.

"You need to listen to the 911 call about the professor."

"Who called? A neighbor?"

"Didn't identify himself. Came from a cell phone, but wasn't traceable. It was an old one without GPS. Dispatch sent us an audio file."

"I'm going back to the scene after lunch. Then I'll swing by the office and listen to the call."

Jake appeared that moment, smiled broadly, shook my hand with a vise grip, and sat down. We traded small talk, exchanging theories on the Seahawks. Pretty soon we were laughing.

Clarence arrived and sat next to Jake. It's a big booth, but their side was suddenly full.

Nobody had to look at the menu. Rory came over and asked, "The usual?" Everyone nodded. Lou's serves a mean cheeseburger.

"Okay," Jake said. "Last week we said we'd read the first eight chapters of the book of John. How'd we do?"

"I had a busy week," I said. "Couldn't squeeze it in."

"Five minutes a day or one reading of half an hour? Come on. That's just a sit-com."

"I like sitcoms better."

"John 8 relates to your work as a detective."

"How's that?"

Jake opened his Bible, full of underlines. "Jesus says, 'If you hold to my teaching, you are really my disciples. Then you will know the truth, and the truth will set you free.' He says the truth will set us free from lies."

"Whose truth we talkin' about?"

"*The* truth. He says we're slaves, but 'if the Son sets you free, you will be free indeed.' He's talking about freedom from deception."

"Every day I sift through the lies people tell," I said. "I dig for the truth all the time."

"I'm grateful you do, Ollie. We all benefit from your work. Now check out what Jesus says about Satan in the next verse: 'He was a murderer from the beginning, not holding to the truth, for there is no truth in him. When he lies, he speaks his native language, for he is a liar and the father of lies.' So Satan is a murderer, and he lies to cover up his murders. That should interest a homicide detective."

"The devil must be a good liar," I said.

"The best," Jake said. "Lying is his native language."

"The truth challenges our assumptions," Clarence said. "It's more comfortable just to believe the lies. We fall for lies because we're wired that way."

"In my work, deception is fatal."

"Jesus said the truth sets us free," Jake said. "In an investigation, once you see through the lies, when you discover the truth, don't you feel free?"

"It's an adrenaline rush. Nothing like it."

"Well, then, we'll pray that God will help you see the truth. To see through the lies."

"What do you mean?"

"In your investigation. The Palatine case."

"Okay. I guess your prayers can't hurt."

"Who knows?" Jake said with a cocky smile. "Since it's the God of all truth and the Enemy of all deception that we're praying to, our prayers may even help."

"Fine," I said. "Fine" is what Jack Bauer and Chloe say whenever they don't like a situation, such as having to cooperate with terrorists.

I escaped by going over to the jukebox, a vintage Rock-Ola straight from the sixties boasting "Stereo" in ostentatious letters, like they'd split the atom. Three songs for a quarter, just like the old days. Rory told me he'd added new selections. I spotted one and selected C3: "Bridge over Troubled Water."

"Wow," Jake said. "Takes me back to Nam."

I nodded. As we listened, Jake and I relived memories half a world away and almost a lifetime ago. Clarence was probably thinking of his brother who died in Nam. I found myself sitting in the Mekong Delta with Neal Crane, a Mississippi farm boy, and listening to Simon and Garfunkel in the evening, when it cooled down to the midnineties.

I heard Neal's twang as he said, "What's up, bro?" and backslapped me with his big right arm. Neal and I would talk about friendlies and hostiles, about Old Miss football, about our dreams after the war, maybe living near each other and raising our families. Two months later Neal stepped on a land mine. He was gone.

Rory waded into our sea of Garfunkel-induced melancholy to bring us burgers and onion rings. That quickly we were back at Lou's, jibing and laughing again.

Jake and Clarence turned down dessert, but it didn't keep them from hefty bites of my huckleberry pie with French vanilla ice cream. Clarence took some extra insulin. I sipped my coffee. The pot Rory brewed for me was nice and dark, which is why I always go over the top and give him a 10 percent tip.

"Okay if I talk about the investigation?" I asked, noting the closest people were sitting three booths away. "Off the record?"

They nodded. I got up and put quarters in the jukebox to get cover from the Four Seasons, Turtles, and Monkees. There's a speaker over our booth that projects into the room but allows us to hear each other.

I told Jake about the solitaire game and the ace of spades.

"At first I thought it proved he was interrupted. He was about to play the ace, but something happened—phone rang, somebody came to the door, he heard a noise outside, whatever. But now I don't buy it. Interrupted before you turn it over? Sure. But after you see the ace? Nah. Phone rings, teakettle whistles, someone comes to the door, maybe you stop turning cards. But once you turn up an ace, you play it instantly, before anything else."

"You make it sound like a science," Clarence said.

"I was testing it last night. You see an ace, you play it, in a heartbeat."

"Yet there it sat," Clarence said. "So what's your point?"

"Somebody else placed it, not Palatine. Probably the murderer. Pulled it out of the deck after he killed the professor."

"You're sure?"

"Somebody sat down in front of the cards and messed with them…and maybe turned to type that stuff on the computer too. And why the ace of spades? Random? I don't think so."

"Isn't it the death card?" Jake asked.

"Exactly. Symbolism."

"But who kills someone, then sits around fiddling with cards?" Jake said. "Why risk being caught?"

"Maybe he was relishing what he'd done," I said. "But he was unusually comfortable at a murder scene. Why wasn't he more afraid of being caught? Consider the time involved with the rope, typing, messing with playing cards."

"It's like he was waiting for something," Jake said.

"Waiting for him to die?" Clarence asked.

"And when he'd waited long enough, he put the bullets in his chest. Then there's the wineglasses."

"Wineglasses?" Clarence asked.

"In the sink. You were off with Carp when I found them. Two wineglasses with a white wine residue. Couldn't see fingerprints."

"What do you think it means?"

"Maybe the professor had a guest earlier, came and went before the murder. But why wipe prints off the glasses? Could be the murderer was his guest. If they're drinking together, he knows him."

"Then he'd have good reason to wipe the glasses," Jake said. "His anyway."

"But where's the wine bottle? Not in the house. Not in the trash. Nowhere. Manny searched, and he's good. Looks like the killer took it. Why? Why take the risk of carrying a wine bottle from a murder scene if you don't want to be noticed and might need to run?"

We sat there quietly. No takers.

"I've got questions too," Clarence said. "Like, why didn't the neighbors hear the gunshots?"

"Could've had a silencer," I said. "Then the shots aren't much louder than a cough. Not enough to wake someone. If it was an apartment in the still of the night maybe, but not in a house next door or across the street."

Sherlock Holmes smoked while contemplating evidence and occasionally listened to himself play the violin. We sipped Rory's dark Italian coffee. And listened to the Rock-Ola spin a 45, "It Ain't Me, Babe."

"Ollie Chandler doesn't understand, does he?"

"Even Jake and Clarence don't fully understand."

"Yes, but they know the One who knows all. And therefore they have a framework to understand what Ollie can't."

"And yet he seeks the truth, doesn't he?"

"He seeks one kind of truth. The kind that leads to the incrimination and capture of others. He seeks truth that will expose them and justify himself. But does he seek truth that would expose himself?"

"Does any man seek such truth unless the King empowers him?"

"There's always much to be learned from watching them, isn't there?"

"Yes. Just as there was much to be learned from watching us when we walked that world."

I drove toward the professor's house, preoccupied. Suddenly I realized I'd gone three blocks too far. It was an unfamiliar part of town. I turned around at the next driveway, circling quickly by a little hole-in-the-wall with an old beat-up sign. It said "Wally's Donuts." I braked and swung back into the parking lot, popping the car into park before it stopped, lurching. I looked at the donut box still sitting in the passenger seat.

Wally's Donuts.

The guy didn't speak English, but after I showed him my badge, he got me on the phone with Big Wally himself, who said he'd closed the place up at ten thirty last night, but they have a Wednesday night special on donuts in the dozen and half dozen boxes, and they probably sold six hundred donuts to eighty different people, and he's bad with faces, and it's all cash, no credit or debit cards, so no records.

Back in my car, I stared at a donut and a box. I closed my eyes and walked through the scattered events of the night before, moving the jigsaw pieces around, trying to make them fall into place.

They wouldn't.

6

THURSDAY, NOVEMBER 21, 1:30 P.M.

TAPED TO MY DASHBOARD are the words of Detective Hercule Poirot: "It is the brain, the little gray cells, on which one must rely. One must seek the truth within—not without."

I was searching inside myself, looking for the truth. I was pondering the professor but also thinking, inexplicably, of Jimmy Ross and Lincoln Caldwell. That irritated me.

As a detective, sometimes you sense something's wrong, but you don't know what. Something was wrong on my old case, and plenty was wrong on my new one. My little gray cells were telling me that.

When I arrived back at the crime scene, I decided to call in more eyes to help me see what I was missing.

"Jack? You're in Lloyd Center area, right? How's your case going?"

"All done but the paperwork. Guy shot his wife's boyfriend. He confessed. Open and shut. I hear we both got called to murders the same night. Yours as easy as ours?"

"I don't think so. We're back at the house of the professor who lost his tenure last night. I need a second opinion."

"Noel's with me."

"Bring him."

After I gave Jack the address, Clarence—pen and pad in hand—asked, "More detectives? Is it normal to do all this consulting?"

"Never did it in the old days. But they've changed policy. We've had too many cases where something important was missed that other guys would've noticed. Someone who knows electrical work, plumbing, music, or art will pick up on things another detective misses. Phillips knows his Dell computers. Probably makes no difference, but it could. So we help each other out. It's fun to get called to a scene where you don't have to do the grunt work. You can just look around and throw out your ideas like you're a character in a murder mystery."

↔

I heard the sound of heavy shoes. Next thing I knew, one of those shoes stepped on my foot.

"That's inappropriate behavior," I told Noel Barrows.

Noel's a good golfer, but it's all in his arms and wrists. His feet are klutzy.

"Sorry." Noel smiled like a schoolboy.

Okay, he's a likable klutz. Especially likable at a poker game, where he's as excited by a good hand as a little girl at her birthday party. He doesn't know the meaning of a poker face. Which is why we always invite him back.

Jack shook my hand, then saw Clarence, who you don't have to be a detective to notice. "Clarence Abernathy, right?"

He nodded.

"Jack Glissan. My partner's Noel Barrows. I used to love your column."

"Used to?" I heard the smile in my voice.

"You're still a great writer. I just read you more when you did sports."

"Jack started as a detective back when they solved crimes the old-fashioned way," I said. "Killing a chicken and examining its entrails."

"Twenty years ago this month, on November 4," Jack said, "Ollie and I started our three-year partnership as detectives." He paused. "It was the worst three years of my life."

I laughed. "He's joking," I said to Clarence. "He loved me as a partner."

Jack shook his head, deadpan.

"They assigned you to Ollie, Clarence?" Jack asked. "What'd you do to deserve that kind of punishment?"

"That's what I've been asking myself."

"Jack's got lots of candles on his cake," I said, "but the frosting's still moist. And they say Abernathy's okay too, once you get used to him. I haven't gotten used to him. Okay, guys, look around the room. Tell me what you see."

"Guy was playing cards with somebody?" Jack walked over to the table by the computer. "No, looks like solitaire. They're running prints on the cards, obviously. Was the computer on?"

"Yeah. Interesting message typed in." I handed him a printout of the supposed confession.

"Sound like something he'd write?"

"No," I said.

"The killer wrote it?"

"Maybe."

Jack pointed to the two piles of student papers. "Gonna read 'em?"

"Think it's worth it?"

"Probably not. But you never know."

I looked at Clarence. "You have to sift through lots of rocks and mud to find the gold."

He jotted it down. Maybe I'd have to read the *Tribune* after all.

I played the professor's message machine, with the Nietzsche quote. Jack raised his eyebrows and Noel grinned.

"What a piece of work," Jack said. "Guess I shouldn't speak ill of the dead, but…"

"Pretentious, wasn't he?" I said. "Any advice?"

"Check students' grades," Jack said. "Who'd the professor fail last semester that kept him from graduating or made him lose a scholarship or go on drugs or take up shoplifting? Anybody with an ax to grind."

"It's all about motive," I said to Clarence. I pointed the guys toward the mantel. "Check out the pictures."

Jack looked them over. "He's in half of these himself, mostly with students. Look, he's ten years younger in this picture. Maybe five years in this one. And that one looks recent, judging by the gray hairs. It's like he never took his pictures down. He only added. Check out that bulletin board. He's got pictures tacked on pictures. There must be a hundred of them."

"One hundred nineteen," I said. "Lots of them are group photos, so there's got to be five hundred people in these, mostly students. Guess he hadn't heard about photo albums. The place is neat and tidy, except for these pictures. Looks like a third of them were taken right here. Apparently he handed off his camera so he could be in them. Wanted to remind himself how handsome he was."

"And how young and attractive his students are," Clarence said.

Jack studied the pictures closely. "Did he have family?"

"Father's deceased, mother's in a rest home. Brother's a doctor. Manny checked into him. They fight a lot."

"Brothers do that," Clarence said.

Jack and Noel nodded. So did I. I haven't talked with my brother for two years.

Noel kept staring at the mantel. "Something's fishy," he finally said. He paused, looking side to side like we were under FBI surveillance. He whispered, as if a high-powered eavesdropping device were pointed at us. "Something's really fishy."

"Am I supposed to ask, 'What's fishy?' Noel, or are you going to tap it out on my foot in Morse code?"

"I'm telling you, it's fishy."

"You're telling me nothing. Telling is when you get to the part after 'it's fishy.'"

Noel turned and said, "Okay, I'll tell you."

"Good," I said. "I was just about to do a Jack Bauer and hook you up to battery cables."

"Don't you love that show? Remember the one where Tony shoots the—"

"Shut up and tell me what's fishy!"

"Somebody removed a picture," Noel said. "See, there's four on this side and five on that side." He climbed on the hearth and pointed to the top of the mantel. "Look at the dust. They've been moved recently. I don't think the dead guy did it, because everything else is…arranged just right."

"Symmetrical," I said.

"Couldn't there have been an odd number of pictures to start with?" Clarence asked.

"He'd have put one in the middle," Jack said.

Jack put his arm around Noel, twenty-five years his junior. "Good catch. Let him focus and he earns his paycheck."

"If we find that picture," I said, "I bet we'll solve this crime."

"There's a possible witness here at those apartments with the view of Oak Street," Manny told me on the phone. "She saw something, but she's a case. Maybe you can charm her. She's your type. Second floor. 205. Name's Rebecca Butler."

Twenty minutes later Clarence and I were standing outside apartment 205. Painted lime green, the hallway was a fake clean with the smell of heavy chemicals that sterilize dirt without removing it. Four decades of cumulative neglect.

I knocked.

"Who's it?" a woman's voice shouted.

"Detective Ollie Chandler. Police."

"That spic send you?" Still shouting.

"Officer Domast? He's my partner."

"Too bad for you," she said, now peering through the fish-eye. "Don't look like a cop. Why should I believe you're a cop? Show me a donut."

"Crack the door, and I'll show you my badge."

"After you tie me up and rob me. Hold it up to the peephole."

I held up my badge.

"Move it to the right. No the other way. No, not that close. You're dumb enough to be a cop."

Finally the dead bolt snapped back, but the door didn't open.

I waited.

"You didn't open the door," I called, not letting my voice in on my attitude.

"You can't open a door yourself? It's not much harder than pickin' up a donut." Two donut cracks and we weren't even in the door.

"We can come in?"

"It's unlocked," she called. "I'm watching my soaps."

We walked into a living room that looked like it had thrown up on itself.

She was sitting, curled up in a seventies recliner, wearing sweatpants and a mustard-stained undersized T-shirt that showed way more than I wanted to see. She was surrounded by a bag of Lay's potato chips and a jumbo bag of Cheetos, a liter of Pepsi plus two empties, and stained paper plates.

Her eyes were close-set, squinty and molelike, as if she hadn't seen the sun for a year. Her age was a difficult call. Forty-five? People don't age as much when they don't see the sun. Cheetos and Lay's probably help the skin too with all that oil. Like her apartment building, she was showing forty years of cumulative neglect. If she'd been painted lime green, it would have been a perfect match.

She didn't look up until the commercial, ten seconds after we entered.

"I'm Ollie. This is—"

"Who's the black guy?"

"Clarence. He's studying to be a cop when he grows up. Pretend he's not here. He's used to it."

"Can you dunk it?" she asked him.

"I used to be able to," Clarence said.

"Too fat now, huh?"

He said nothing, but his eyes spoke volumes. Forgoing handwritten notes, he flipped open his PDA, stylus in hand.

"I thought you people could dunk it even when you're old and fat. Hey, do you know Stevie Wonder?"

"Not personally."

"I like his music. Tell him for me, would you? 'Tutti Frutti's my favorite."

"That was Little Richard," Clarence said.

"And 'Hit the Road Jack.'"

"Ray Charles."

"You know them, too?"

"Yeah. Stevie, Richard, Ray, and I meet for chitlins and cornbread every Friday night."

Not bad, I nodded to Clarence. "Mrs. Butler, could you—"

"I'm not a Mrs. My no-good husband left me."

"Ms. Butler, could—"

"I'm not one of those either."

"Miss Butler—"

"Do I look like I'm nineteen?"

"No," I said. "You certainly don't."

"What's that supposed to mean?"

"Only that you are a youthful yet mature woman. May I call you Rebecca?"

"Friends call me Becky."

"All right, Becky, did you—"

"We're not friends."

"Okay...did you see a man come out of the professor's house last night?"

"Who's the professor?"

"The man who lives in the house where you told my partner—"

"The spic?"

"We prefer to call him Hispanic. You told my partner you saw a man come out of the professor's house."

"Whatever."

"What did he look like?"

"The spic? Short and wiry. Burr under his saddle."

"No. I mean the man coming out the professor's door...the man you saw. What did he look like?"

"Like Abraham Lincoln," she said.

Now we were getting somewhere. Abe Lincoln wouldn't blend into a crowd. "Tall?" I asked.

"No. Medium. About my brother's size."

"How tall's your brother?"

"I'm not on trial here. Neither's my brother."

"You mentioned your brother. I've not had the privilege of meeting him."

"It's no privilege."

"Is he six feet tall?"

"Who?"

"Your brother."

"You're still on my brother?"

"I'll get off your brother as soon as you answer my question. Is he six feet tall?"

"My brother? You crazy?"

"Look, ma'am, I've never seen your brother. I can't begin to guess how tall he is. I'm assuming you *have* seen him. Could you just take a guess?"

"Six inches taller than me."

"How tall are you?" She was still sitting, like she'd been poured into the recliner.

"You going to ask me how much I weigh, too?"

"Only if you tell me your brother weighs forty pounds more than you."

She glared at me.

"Could you stand, please?"

"I've been up and down all day, answering the phone and the door and trying to fix the antenna for my soaps, and now you're asking me to stand?"

My face, if it was following orders, looked earnest and sympathetic. "I've got all day, but I don't want you to miss your soaps. How about you stand just for a second then answer a few more questions, and we'll leave you alone?"

She stood slowly, but it didn't take long for her to get straight.

Five-foot-one, at most.

"Then your brother's about five seven?"

"You tell me."

"If he were my brother, I would."

"Don't get smart with me, Kojak."

She aimed a frown at me, and when I wouldn't let it land, she aimed it at Clarence. It landed.

"I'm not getting smart," I said. "You'll know when I get smart. So was he thin?"

"He used to be, but he's been laid off and watches lots of TV. Loves the soaps and *Oprah* and *Dr. Phil*. He's put on fifty pounds."

"Who are you talking about?"

"My brother!" She looked at me like I was a finalist on *American Idiot*.

"Let's forget about your brother, okay?"

"It's about time. I told you he has nothing to do with this. He's written bad checks and spent time in the pokey, but he's no killer. And for sure he doesn't know any professors."

"I'll bet he doesn't. How about the man who was at the professor's door? Was he thin?"

"Nope. Pudgy. Like you."

Clarence looked up from his PDA. He folded the lid.

I paused, putting my tongue between my teeth to keep them from locking. "Did I miss an episode?"

"Whatcha mean?" she asked.

"I mean…in what way did this man remind you of Abraham Lincoln?"

"He had a beard!" she said, with a look that confirmed I wasn't merely a finalist for *American Idiot*, but had been crowned.

"Lots of hair?"

"He was bald."

I stared at her, giving the words time to go through my universal translator. It wasn't working. "Bald…like Abraham Lincoln?"

"Don't know if Lincoln was bald. He always wore a hat."

"Not when he bathed."

"What are you, a pervert?"

"No, ma'am. So, you're saying he was short, mostly bald, pudgy, and looked like Abraham Lincoln? I'm glad to hear he had a beard."

"*Of course* he had a beard. How could he look like Lincoln and not have a beard?"

"Black?"

"Nope. I told you, he was a white guy."

"Do you think he could dunk it?" I couldn't resist. It was worth it to see Abernathy. "What I meant is was his *beard* black?"

"Not many blacks in this building," she said.

"How fortunate for them," Clarence muttered.

"I repeat—was his beard black?"

"No way. This guy was…maybe Swedish. A pale face. What's that other country that's part of Sweden?"

"Norway?"

"Yeah, he looked sort of like one of those cow milkers with their red barns. Yellow hair. Funny accents. Go out naked in the freezing water."

"You heard his voice?"

"How could I hear his voice? He was across the street, and *Law & Order* was on. It was during the last commercial."

I jotted it down. That put it around 10:50.

"You said he was bald, but he had yellow hair?"

"Yeah. The part that wasn't bald was blond. You know, like what's-his-name, the football announcer…Terry Bradshaw? The guy that played for the Cowboys?"

"Steelers. He played for the Pittsburgh Steelers."

"Did not."

"Did too. So the beard was blond?"

"Grayish. Salt-and-pepper. But more salt than pepper. More like Lawry's seasoned salt. You know, sort of orangish."

"An orange beard?"

"Just a tint of orange, that's all I'm saying."

"What was he wearing?"

"Jeans. Coat. Shoes. I dunno. Plus the stocking cap."

"Stocking cap?"

"Yeah. It was black. Or green. Could've been blue. Hard to tell it was so dark out."

I paused, sorting it through. "If he had on a stocking cap, how do you know he was bald…and blond?"

"Look, don't try to make this my problem. I didn't kill Dr. Einstein."

Sometimes you keep fishing; sometimes you just cut bait and walk.

"We'll be going now," I said. "We have business elsewhere."

She waved her hand, grabbed the remote, and turned up the volume.

"Where's our business?" Clarence asked as we shut the door behind us.

"On planet earth."

He scrunched his face. "Maybe you cops earn your pay after all."

"I may be King of the Idiots," I said, "but my kingdom is vast, and my subjects are everywhere."

THURSDAY, NOVEMBER 21, 6:30 P.M.

WE HAD THREE more interviews after Rebecca Butler, but hers turned out to be the most productive. At least we got a time, 10:50 p.m., when a man, the Abraham Lincoln clone, came to the front door. Maybe. If it was the right night. And right program. And right commercial break. And right house…Dr. Einstein's.

I headed home in thick traffic on a stormy afternoon, dark clouds pressing on the car tops. Driving was slow, and radio didn't interest me. When I'm caught in traffic on a rainy day, sometimes my car becomes a cocoon, and I'm transferred back to childhood. Thoughts from long ago resurfaced. Those led me into a series of reflections, somewhat random, but related at their core.

My grandmother was a Baptist, and she took it out on the rest of us. She told me God was watching. He was out to get me when I did something bad. This meant He was out to get me seventy times a day. Grandma's favorite phrase was "the day of reckoning." Since she believed that most of what I wanted was sinful, I knew I'd be toast on the day of reckoning. It scared me. That was her point. Drive the fear of God into me.

It had a side effect she didn't intend.

God reading my mind and spying on me and wanting to skewer me made Him seem petty. Like He had nothing better to do than wait until I thought or did something wrong…which, trust me, would never be a long wait.

My options were to disbelieve in Him. Or give up trying to please Him. Or live with constant guilt because I wasn't the kind of person He—and my grandmother—wanted me to be. I've never been a big fan of helpless, self-flagellating guilt, so I turned away from "spiritual things" to "worldly things." I liked cars, sports, girls, and everything else that sends a guy to hell.

Jake Woods assures me that not all Baptists are like my grandmother. I have no plans to find out.

I'm not religious, but that doesn't mean I don't care about whether things are right. I care about that more than anything.

If I told you "Justice is my middle name," it might surprise you that I mean it literally. My given name is Oliver Justice Chandler. My middle name came from my mother's grandfather, Justice Elwin Carlson, a bricklayer. His father had lived in Justice, Illinois. He was named after a town, not a virtue. But the name Justice shaped me.

As a kid, I wasn't wild about Oliver, but I was proud of my middle name. My favorite comic book? *The Brave and the Bold*, featuring the Justice League of America. My favorite Justice Leaguer? Green Lantern, test pilot Hal Jordan, given the ring of power by a dying alien. I dreamed about the Justice League, about flying in with my green cape and rescuing people and making things right. I wore a green ring to bed every night for five years. I'd take my flashlight under my covers and read comics way past midnight, waking up with my face on the pages.

At age ten, I recited Green Lantern's words a bazillion times a day. Fifty years later, as Mulch would testify if he could, the words still roll off my tongue: "In brightest day, in darkest night, no evil shall escape my sight. Let those who worship evil's might, beware my power…Green Lantern's light!"

Hal Jordan's closest friend was Green Arrow, real name Oliver Queen, so my first name made the big time too. But Green Arrow's powers weren't great enough for me—I wanted to protect the solar system, Green Lantern style. As far back as I can remember, this passion for justice fueled me.

I didn't feel like waiting until some far-off day of reckoning. When guys ganged up on somebody, I went after them. I figured, if you can do the reckoning today, why wait? Green Lantern wouldn't.

As the years went on, my little boy's naïveté gave way to the cruel facts of life. I sort of believed in God when I was a kid, but it didn't hold up. When you once had faith and no longer do, I suppose it's like a woman carrying a dead baby. The sight of live babies becomes painful. Maybe that's why Jake and Clarence bother me sometimes. But I guess I never had a faith of my own. It was my grandmother's, foisted upon me like a backpack loaded with stones, strapped to me till I was big enough to cast it off.

In the months before she died, Sharon ended up believing like the Christians. I saw the peace it gave her, but you know what—people find peace believing in Krishna or the Dalai Lama or Oprah or chocolate or multilevel marketing.

I don't doubt Geneva Abernathy's or Janet Woods's sincerity—I'll always be grateful for the care they gave Sharon when she was dying. But I sort of think they took advantage of my wife. She needed encouragement. But Christianity? I thought we were doing okay without it. I was there for her. I felt like they were saying, and she was saying, she needed someone else.

Before I lost her to death, I'd already lost her to Jesus.

↔

The dark was already two hours old when I turned up the street to the old brown-stone, 151st and Yamhill. It's actually a single-story ranch house, built in 1968. But I call it "the old brownstone" because that's what Archie Goodwin named the three-level house in New York City where he lived with Nero Wolfe, detective genius.

The moment I turned the corner onto Yamhill, I slowed to a crawl. The living room light of the old brownstone was on, as it should have been. But the light in my office, which I keep on through the dark winter, wasn't.

Any normal person would assume the bulb had burned out. But I'm a cop. I parked roadside, sixty feet from my house. I approached the house like a black cat. A cat with Daddy Glock in one paw and Baby Glock strapped to his ankle.

I ducked under the bedroom window and moved across the front porch, then slowly turned the front doorknob. Locked, as I'd left it. I inserted the key and qui-etly opened the door. A loud noise followed, then a jumping movement, straight at me.

"Hello, boy," I whispered. "You don't have company, do you?"

Something in Mulch's eyes kept my guard up. When your dog greets you the same way every day, you know when something's different. I walked back to my office, which years ago had been Kendra's bedroom. The door was shut. But I never shut that door. The office has a western exposure, and Mulch likes to bask in the afternoon sunlight, which is why I leave the blinds open…and the door.

I entered and looked at the office window, seeing the back side of my security sticker that warns you a SWAT team, two Black Hawks, Vin Diesel, and Force 10 from Navarone will appear if you even think about intruding. I'm too cheap to actually pay for the service, but the stickers were three for a buck, and there's no monthly charge.

Window was unlocked. I'd opened it yesterday for fresh air, but surely I'd relocked it. I always do.

I examined the floor for footprints. Nothing.

I poked the barrel of my Glock into the mirrored sliding closet door and pushed it open slowly. I got it open a foot, then yanked. It slammed against the far side. Mulch barked up a storm, then jumped and grabbed a coat sleeve, pulling it to the ground.

It was an old army surplus coat I'd used for hunting a few times. Mulch taught it a lesson it won't soon forget.

I checked the rest of the house systematically. Everything appeared secure. My Browning was in the middle cabinet. I reached below the bathroom sink, behind the Lysol, and checked my Kimber Gold Math .45. Since kids never visit the old brownstone, I'd hidden it there, figuring if under fire I'd be on the ground, so it was a good place for it. I breathed easier, knowing all my babies were sleeping peacefully.

I went back to the office to see if the desk lamp bulb was burned out. I turned the switch. Light.

Had I forgotten to leave it on? Maybe. But turning it on was as routine as making coffee. And the door closed? I turned on the hallway light. Scratch marks all over the door. Fresh? I could see grooved varnish. I put a sheet of printer paper under Mulch's front right paw. I ran my hand over the paw and several brown flecks dropped to the paper. Perfect match. He'd been trying to get in the door.

Was he going after an intruder?

I looked at his worried eyes. "Talk to me, boy. Tell me what happened here."

I don't know where instinct comes from. I've heard about whale language and saw a film about how bees convey information to each other. And read a book about a gorilla named Sema who used sign language to communicate abstract concepts. I'm telling you, animals are smart. Generally you can trust them more than people. But when it comes to extracting detailed information from dogs, it's not easy.

Mulch looked at me with such earnestness that for a split second I thought he was going to spill it. If there's a world where dogs talk, I'd like to live there. But tonight Mulch's lips were sealed.

I grabbed a bag of carrots. I don't eat them, but Mulch does. Once he finishes his meat, I've seen him go for carrots and corn before apple pie. He even likes broccoli and cauliflower, especially with a dab of gravy. This came in handy when Sharon was on a crusade to feed me vegetables. I'd shovel them under the table to Mulch. In biology this is called a symbiotic relationship. It means everybody's happy.

We had Dinty Moore beef stew with Jiffy cornbread muffins, which always soothes him. I made a fire and pulled my recliner toward it, then turned on Rex Stout's *Over My Dead Body*. I lined up my Budweisers while Nero Wolfe and Archie Goodwin came into my living room, read by Michael Pritchard, who seems like an old friend now. Mulch usually lies on the right side of my recliner, where I reach down to stroke him. This time he crawled up on my lap. He's a lot of dog. But then, I've got a lot of lap.

With my left hand, I reached to the inside back flap of the recliner and felt for the duct tape, and under it the 9 mm SIG-Sauer P226. I looked at the coffee table, two feet from my elevated slippers, at the three-year-old Family Circle magazine. It was Sharon's. I could never bring myself to throw it out. Next to Sharon's magazine lay one of my best old friends besides Mulch, Jake Woods, and Mr. Coffee…Daddy Glock.

Nothing like a cozy Oregon night in the old brownstone.

Manny and I sat at our adjoining workstations, forty feet into homicide detail, to the right of the aisle. Conference rooms and offices are to the left. My desk reaches to the windows. Manny's desktop has pictures of his wife and kids and is otherwise squeaky clean. I have a few snapshots of Sharon, oases in the midst of a hopeless desert of papers, some from cases closed three months ago. It only takes me ten minutes to clear off my desk, but requires an empty drawer to stuff it all into. No drawers were currently empty.

Manny and I had been discussing the case for over an hour, disagreeing in our interpretations of the evidence whenever possible. When Clarence showed up, Manny disappeared.

"It's confirmed," I told Clarence. "The killer used the professor's keyboard."

"Fingerprints?"

"Nope."

"Then how do you know?"

"Because no prints. They were wiped clean."

Out of the blue, Clarence asked, "How's Kendra?"

He'd taken me by surprise. He nodded at the picture where she and Sharon were hugging.

"Your daughter."

"I know who she is."

"I haven't seen her for years," Clarence said. "Not since…Sharon's funeral."

"Haven't seen much of her myself. She's…I don't know. Something's wrong with our chemistry. One of us needs our fuse box rewired. Kendra's granola. Hates anything you have to plug in, unless it's a computer, a microwave, or a hair dryer. She says the advancements of civilization have ruined the environment. She used to tell me how air conditioners are killing us. Then we had that hot summer, and she got an air conditioner at Costco. I made the mistake of mentioning it."

"Do you call her?"

"I saw her every few months after Sharon died. Then it was only on Thanksgiving and Christmas. Then Thanksgiving was so awkward she started making excuses about Christmas. Everything I say irritates her."

"You? Irritating?"

"Once when she came over she had a bumper sticker on her car that said, 'Meat is murder.' So I said, 'If meat is murder, I'm a serial killer.' That's how our night started."

"Still no word from Andrea?"

Just hearing her name felt like a punch in the gut. I told Clarence I needed to take a walk. I took the elevator to ground level and walked the streets around the Justice Center. The clean rain fell lightly on my eyelashes, an occasional drop hanging on for dear life before plunging to the pavement. Just when I thought I'd adjusted to the cold, a gust of wind rushed up Madison to quick-freeze my lashes, winter reminding me that it had a lot more to dish out and it would do it in its own sweet time.

The good thing about winters is they're always followed by spring. You remember what it was two months ago, and you reassure yourself with what it will be like two months from now.

Andrea's my older daughter. Always troubled. Only her mom could keep her stable. And after Sharon died, Andrea floundered. Six months later she disappeared. No forwarding address. I've made a hundred calls. Friends say she's never contacted them. She ran away as a kid, and she's run away as an adult. I keep thinking she'll come back, that one day I'll get a call. Hasn't happened.

I walked the concrete maze, taking Madison to Second, then to Jefferson, around the Federal Building. I stared into cracks only to periodically look up into drips of rain. As I walked, I pondered fatherhood.

Children are terrorists. They work you over with sleep deprivation. They make you say and do things you're not responsible for, like promising that if they'll go back to sleep you'll buy them a yacht when they turn six.

I feel like I no longer have children. All that links us is genetic material and the hole in my heart. Andrea's out of reach. Maybe I could take a few months off and hunt her down. But then what? She didn't want anything to do with me. Obviously that hasn't changed.

As for Kendra, it's even harder. I call her periodically, but I've learned to have a stiff drink first. It's brutal.

Kendra lives twenty minutes away, but there's a thousand light-years between us.

I went into fatherhood an ignoramus, and I emerged twenty-five years later not knowing how to go back and unscramble the eggs. I'd been determined to be Ward Cleaver. Instead I became my father—there, but barely. My daughters have never forgiven my absence.

Neither have I.

I remember the spring, summer, and fall with my daughters, before the cold hardness of winter settled in. But the winter had been so long now, so many years I'd nearly given up hope that spring would ever come, that our relationships might someday thaw.

The last night we'd had a discussion, the night I was telling Clarence about, Kendra told me I was modern and she was postmodern. I said I knew Post Toasties, but please explain postmodern. She said modern meant I believed in truth, absolute rights and wrongs. She explained that enlightened postmoderns, such as herself, realize there's no such thing as truth or moral absolutes. I said, "So criminals are postmodern, right?" She said I was a dinosaur. I thought about how much money I'd spent to send her to Portland State, where she could learn to be a moron, whereas she could have skipped college entirely and become a moron for nothing.

I might have even said something to that effect. If I did, it was not well-received.

That night Kendra slammed the door and didn't look back. I watched her drive off in her meat-is-murder-mobile and knew the cold war was on. That same night I said good-bye to five months of sobriety. I haven't come back yet. Haven't even been to a meeting.

Life makes outrageous promises. It seldom delivers. Just thinking about it, walking downtown in the eye-numbing Oregon air, made me thirsty again.

An hour later Clarence and I drove to the professor's house to meet Manny and walk the neighborhood. We got out at the corner of 22nd and Oak. Manny saw us as he approached from Pine, following his scowl.

"Tell us where to go," I said, though I wouldn't recommend putting it that way to Manny.

"What took you? We're way behind. Here's a list of apartments I've covered in the big complex," he said, pointing. "I'm canvassing all houses within a two-block perimeter. If I find a Dumpster or anyplace good for a toss, I'll cover it."

"Want company?"

"We'll cover more ground working alone."

"Clarence comes with me," I said. It saves time to let Manny do what he wants. As long as he's still on the waiting list for that personality transplant, it's easier for everyone that he works alone.

Manny was halfway across the street when he called back, "Listened to the 911 yet?"

I shook my head.

"Check it out!"

We walked in the door of the Franklin Terrace apartments. No sign of a manager. We climbed to the second floor, starting a couple doors down from Rebecca Butler, where I knew other apartments had a view of the professor's house. When we came to the first number not on Manny's list, I knocked.

"We just knock on doors?" Clarence whispered.

"Unless you have a better idea," I said. "If you do, send a memo to the whole department. Include an attachment."

A tall pale guy with frazzled hair and a greasy ponytail opened the door, looking out suspiciously.

"Police," I said. "Mind if we come in?"

The guy mumbled something that wasn't "stay out," so we entered. The smell of burned cocaine and aged meat was in the air. Drug paraphernalia lay on the table. He wasn't bothering to cover up.

I walked to the window. "See that house across Oak, the gray one?"

He looked, but I wasn't sure he saw. His eyes said, "Nobody's home."

I pointed at the weather-beaten Colt on the table.

"That yours?"

He hesitated, apparently trying to think of the best answer as opposed to the true one. Nothing came out.

I picked up the gun with a paper towel and smelled it. Not fired recently. I opened the chamber. Not loaded. I don't like loaded weapons nearby when I'm with someone I don't know—or my sister-in-law.

"Did you see or hear anything over there last night?"

No head motion detectable.

"Gunshot?"

He shook his head, barely.

"What's your name?"

Nothing. I'd have to avoid the hard questions.

"That your wallet sitting there?"

Slight nod, or maybe it was the breeze and his head was loose.

"Can you show me your ID?"

His head bobbed, but his body didn't move.

"Open it please," I said.

"Go ahead."

"Only because you're telling me to," I said, looking at Clarence like he might have to testify. I checked. "Nice meeting you, Ryan Moffat." I handed his driver's license to Clarence.

"Take down the info, Watson. Tell you what, Mr. Moffat, we'll come back later. Meanwhile, get some sleep. Just say no to drugs a couple of days. Have some coffee when you get up. You drink coffee? It's a legal drug. You should try it. We'll talk more when your brain returns, if you still have one. Okay?"

He nodded. Clarence finished scribbling. I backed out the door, something I learned to do years ago after I got a surprise steak knife between my shoulder blades, courtesy of a guy I'd thought was comatose.

After the door closed, Clarence asked, "Why didn't you take his gun?"

"Second amendment."

"You think it's his?"

"Maybe not, but no time for the paperwork. Wasn't the right caliber for our murder."

"Drugs were sitting right there."

"And did you notice the three DVD players and half dozen car stereos in original boxes? No? How about the dozen Fleetwood Mac: Greatest Hits CDs still in their wrappers? When he's not breaking into cars and houses, he's shoplifting. It all supports his habit."

"And…you're letting him get away with it?"

"Let's set aside the issue of whether he really invited us in so I could confiscate illegal items in plain sight without a warrant. Do you know how many hours it would take to arrest him? How many depositions and court appearances and answering his lawyer's insinuations that I planted it to set up his model-citizen client, who, if we keep him out of jail, will probably discover the cure for Hodgkin's disease? I'm telling you, it's not worth it."

"But you can't just turn the other way."

"I saw three people jaywalking earlier."

"It's not the same."

"You live in an idealistic world."

"This is Mr. Justice-Is-My-Middle-Name talking?"

"If I started arresting people for the little stuff, I'd never solve a murder. I'm looking for murderers, not addicts and burglars. I'd enforce the laws against small crimes if the system didn't punish me for it. And if criminals got more than a judge's stern look."

We walked to the next door. I lifted my hand to knock.

"I'm not carrying a gun," Clarence said, eyeing a creepy-looking resident staring at us.

"Relax. If you need one, most of these apartments have a couple of guns stashed. Statistically you have a much greater chance of being killed by a family member or friend than a stranger."

"That's comforting. I'll have to remember to have strangers over for Christmas and not turn my back on Geneva and the kids."

"You're really nervous, aren't you?"

"These tenants are mostly white. They see a big black guy at the door, and it's scary. People can get nervous, and nervous people can be violent."

"You're right. You could get killed. But that's a chance I'm willing to take."

"Very funny."

"I thought you were a Christian…aren't you ready for heaven? Isn't that what you're always talking about?"

"I may be ready for heaven, but that doesn't mean I have a death wish!"

"You could always explain in your article that you were afraid to interview witnesses."

"I wouldn't be if I were a white guy wearing a badge and carrying a gun."

"Yeah, yeah," I said. "Chicken," I whispered.

"What did you say?"

"I said I'm thinking of a chicken sandwich for lunch. Getting tired of Whoppers."

The interviews were going nowhere when Manny called.

"I found a gun."

"Where?"

"In a Dumpster by Lone Fir Cemetery, Twenty-third and Stark. Across from Central Catholic High School. No serial number."

"Wine bottle?"

"No. And I sifted everything."

"Glad it was you. Clarence couldn't fit in a Dumpster. Sure it's our gun?"

"It's a Taurus Millennium Pro, 9 mm, recently fired. Two or three blocks from Palatine's. Nobody would ditch a decent piece like this unless it was hot. You could get a couple hundred bucks for it easy. Lucky a Dumpster-diver didn't see it."

"It's been wiped clean?"

"I think I see a couple of prints, but hard to say."

"Tell forensics to put a rush on it."

"Like always."

After seven short interviews that yielded nothing, Clarence and I settled at Burger King for a late lunch. I wanted something else, but I'd inadvertently committed myself to a chicken sandwich.

"We haven't come up with much today," Clarence said.

"Remember how I said it's like panning for gold?"

"And you don't know in advance what's mud and rocks and what's gold."

"Exactly. The more you see and hear, the more questions you ask, the wider you throw your net, the better your chances. It's like casting a line when you're not catching anything. It seems pointless—but you can't catch a fish without doing it. Any cast has better chances than no cast. Eventually you get a bite. Other apartments have a good view of Palatine's house. There's another guy Manny wants us to follow up on. Beats scraping stuff off the bottom of Dumpsters. Let's go back and pan for gold."

We visited apartments; then I phoned the lab, called people who knew the professor, and tracked down a half dozen items on the Internet. I got home at 7:00 p.m., let out Mulch, and gave him a couple of Purina Beggin' Strips, bacon and cheese. Took a little bite myself. Not that bad, but too salty. Mulch and I wrestled.

My couch is so clean you could eat off it—in fact, I often do. While I cooked a DiGiorno pizza, I put on my extra-large gray hooded Barlow Bruins sweatshirt—a gift from Sharon's niece five years ago—stepped into my Emu slippers, tossed a pillow on the couch and put my feet on the coffee table, then grabbed the remote.

When you live by yourself long enough, you begin to think the world's a stage. You're the lead, and the people around you are actors in supporting roles. Sometimes, like when they deliver mail or fry you a steak, they make your life more convenient. Sometimes, like when they cut into your lane or foist a journalist on your investigation—or tell you that someone looked like Abraham Lincoln except that he was short, pudgy, blond, bald, and wearing a stocking cap—they don't.

If the stuff about me being the lead sounds insightful, it's because it came from Sharon. If my calling is to take down the bad guys, hers was to remind me it wasn't all about me. I needed that reminder. I wish she could come back and remind me again. I wish she could come back for any reason.

I've turned her into a saint: Saint Sharon of Calcuttafornia and her sisters of charity. I never liked Saint Sharon's sisters, but that's another story. (I never saw their endearing qualities, hidden beneath their bitter exteriors, because, being a man, I just didn't get it. Men never do.) Sharon was from Venus and I was from Mars, and her sisters were from somewhere on the dark side of Pluto, no offense to the dog. (And I don't care if people say it's no longer a planet. For all I know, scientists on Pluto took a vote and decided Earth's no longer a planet.)

Sharon wasn't perfect, but I don't remember the specifics of her imperfection. I would have taken a bullet for her any day. What I took instead was a nuclear blast in my face the day she died. Or maybe it was the next morning when I woke up without her beside me, when I got up to go visit her in the hospital, trying to shake that bad dream about her dying, then realized it hadn't been a dream.

The fallout continues, like the ash that dropped on us from Mount St. Helens for weeks back in 1980. My throat's ash dry.

Occasionally I see the sun, but mostly I live under the mushroom cloud.

A homicide detective is something between an atheist and a monk. Since Sharon died, I've been closer to atheist. Yet sometimes when I least expect it, a flash of light, a face in a crowd, the feel of a breeze, the smell of the air, make me suddenly feel like she's alive. That's when for fleeting moments I feel like that medieval monk detective I watch on PBS, Brother Cadfael. Sometimes he drinks wine, and I wonder, after the show's over, if he doesn't drink a lot more.

I went to the fridge and this time bypassed the Bud and reached for the

Gewürztraminer, which I like but can't pronounce. I raised a toast to Sharon, and then to Brother Cadfael, and then to Mulch and his predecessor, Philip Marlowe, two of history's greatest dogs. Thirty minutes later the wine was gone. I hoped I'd soon follow.

The darkness felt thick enough to lean on. I leaned, but it didn't hold me up. The next thing I knew it was midnight, three hours since Mulch had stolen the last pizza bone from my plate. I dragged myself to bed.

"Give him peace, Lord," she said.

"I offer him peace," the One beside her said. "So far he hasn't chosen to receive it. I don't force My peace on anyone."

"It's hard for Ollie," she said.

"I know. I made him." He smiled.

"You didn't make him so stubborn. He got that way on his own."

"With the help of a world that isn't what it was meant to be…and forces that deceive him."

"Will he accept Your offer? You know the answer."

"Yes, I know. But I wouldn't impose upon you such weighty knowledge. You're too small for it, little one." He put His arm around her. "He calls you Saint Sharon."

She smiled. "I wasn't as great as he remembers me."

"No. But much that he remembers is truer than he realizes. You did become a saint there. You had moments, even days, of greatness, especially as you lay in that bed, walking with Me when you could no longer walk on your legs."

"You were so faithful to me, Lord. Every day. Sometimes I doubted it. Now that I'm here with You, I wonder why I doubted."

"It's not an easy world to live in. I lived there too, you know. It's not the Eden I made, nor is it the new earth I will make. It's the in-between world, the isthmus between heaven and hell."

"For most of my life, I never saw that."

"But you came to see it. And now you see it much more. Ollie's right. You are Saint Sharon. And one day you will be Queen Sharon. You shall rule a city."

"I can hardly believe that."

"If you, being here and looking into My eyes, can hardly believe what I tell you, then is it surprising that Ollie, being there and without Me, finds it impossible to believe?"

"It is impossible to believe without You, isn't it?"

"That doesn't mean exactly what you think it means. But the words are true enough."

"Please draw him to Yourself, would You, Lord?"

"I will do what I will do. But it may prove more difficult than you imagine."

"Nothing's too hard for You."

"I mean that it will be hard for him. But some things were hard for Me too."

Sharon saw the terrible scars on His hands. She bowed her head and whispered, "Thank You."

I woke at 6:00 a.m., realizing I still hadn't listened to that 911. I went to my home computer to access precinct e-mail.

The e-mail accompanying the recording, from dispatch, said, "Unusually short call. From cell phone, no GPS. Somebody was driving. You can hear traffic."

I opened the audio file and watched the colorful sound wave depictions on my screen. The voice sounded muffled, like someone had wrapped a washcloth around the phone.

"You better send somebody to the professor's house at 2230 Southeast Oak Street. Something fishy's going on."

I played it three times.

Something *fishy?*

"Each fact is suggestive in itself. Together they have a cumulative force."
SHERLOCK HOLMES, *THE ADVENTURE OF THE BRUCE-PARTINGTON PLANS*

SATURDAY, NOVEMBER 23

I STOPPED AT LOU'S for breakfast and my fourth and fifth cups of coffee. I did something I never do—I actually bought a *Tribune*, which killed me, but it was too early to get somebody's castoff. Knowing this was the day, I eagerly searched for Clarence's article. Found it on B1 just as Bill Haley and the Comets promised they'd rock around the clock till broad daylight.

After some opening remarks about the nature of his investigative articles and the ground rules, he wrote this:

> Detective Ollie Chandler is a brilliant and quick-witted homicide detective with exceptional deductive skills and street smarts. He's a police department legend for his offbeat methods that solve crimes and coax confessions.
>
> But, sources tell me, Chandler's a risk taker and rule bender who drives his procedure-conscious superiors crazy. If not for his success rate, he'd have been squeezed out of the department years ago, wisecracking his way as a security guard at Clackamas Town Center, raiding cheese and sausage samples at Hickory Farms.
>
> Ollie Chandler is unorthodox and pit-bull determined. He's also cynical, like most homicide detectives, and at times can be hard-boiled. He hates the *Tribune* and says he doesn't read it, but why do I believe he's going to be reading this column?

I put the paper down and looked around Lou's to see if anybody was watching. The coast was clear. I started reading again.

> My assignment is to tell it like it is. This won't be a PR job for the Portland Police, but it won't be an attack piece either. Truth is, Chandler and I got off to a rocky start when he failed to honor our agreement to call me the moment he was assigned to a murder. I told him he reinforced the image of cops who don't keep their commitments. People like me have as hard a time trusting cops as he has trusting journalists.

Chandler appears to be a competent and thorough investigator, once you put on your wise-guy filter to get past his mask—I think it's a mask—of Columbo-type incompetence. He lacks the skills to remotely retrieve a message from his own answering machine, and I can only deduce that his VCR is flashing 12:00 as I write. But he isn't paid to be high-tech.

Time will tell whether he's on the right track to solving this murder. Detective Chandler assures me he'll live up to his reputation for brilliance. If I don't see it myself, I'm sure he'll point it out to me so I can inform my readers…you folks with poor enough taste to read the *Oregon Tribune*.

I parked my car on Jackson Street in North Portland, where Clarence lives in his sister's old house. I knocked on the front door. When he answered, I held up the newspaper.

"This was out of bounds."

"The part about you being competent and thorough?"

"The answering machine part. And the VCR. And me not keeping a commitment. Cheap shots."

Clarence stepped out on the front porch, a place that held bad memories for us both. I could still see the placement of the shells from the automatic weapon that had killed his sister ten feet from where we stood.

"The cheap shot," Clarence said, "was you not following through on a commitment, *not* my pointing out that you didn't. I'm going to tell the truth. You do good, you'll look good. Act like a jerk, you'll look like a jerk in print. It's up to you. I'm not going to coddle you."

"Watson didn't make Sherlock Holmes look bad."

"He showed he was a drug addict, for crying out loud!" Clarence raised his left arm, and his oven-mitt hand nearly hit the porch ceiling. "You need thicker skin."

"The part about the answering machine could compromise my investigation."

"No one knows what I'm talking about. No one's asked. If they do, I'll just say I left you a message, which I did. And you didn't know how to retrieve it, which you didn't."

"The murderer will know."

"So? You trying to impress him?"

"You compromise this investigation, we're tearing up that e-mail attachment. I'll resign before I let the *Tribune* help a killer slip away."

"If a killer slips away, it won't be because of me. You're capable of bungling your own case."

We traded stares. I exchanged hellos with Geneva. Clarence and I didn't exchange good-byes.

Three hours later, Manny and I stood again in the professor's living room. Unfortunately, Clarence felt like he had to be there too.

"Can you absolutely eliminate suicide?" Clarence asked.

"Yeah," Manny said. "You can put a noose around your neck, inject yourself with poison, and even shoot yourself in the chest. But only once. The second shot's tough. But he was nearly dead before the shots anyway. Which makes both shots a problem."

"So he could have injected himself before someone else shot him," Clarence said. "If he were going to kill himself, did he maybe *want* to suffer?"

"Penance?" I asked. "Doesn't fit Palatine's profile. Neither does suicide." I waved my hand at all the pictures. "He was too infatuated with himself."

"He'd been grading papers," Manny said. "Who grades papers as his final act on earth?"

"I've seen lots of suicides," I said. "This is murder. We have to assume that everything means something. So why the noose? Why bother with suggestions of suicide when it's so obvious it wasn't? Either our perp's an idiot or he thinks I'm an idiot."

"Could be both," Manny said. "And could be right in both cases. He's playin' with us."

"Or trying to send a message."

The greasy, unshaven man peeked out his door, past the chain, at Clarence and me.

"Paul Frederick?" I showed him my badge. He studied it, moving his reading glasses up and down.

"I'm with homicide. My partner's Manny Domast. Stopped by earlier. Asked me to follow up."

Frederick unlatched the chain and put a butcher knife on the kitchen counter. Clarence ogled it.

Midfifties, Frederick had a crossword puzzle smile like a hockey player who couldn't afford dental work. His eyes were droopy, disinterested. His hair went everywhere—Einstein with a perm in a wind tunnel. This was where the similarity to Einstein ended. He wore what may have been pajamas and looked like he'd been dragged through a hedge by a mule team.

"He's a jerk."

"Who?"

"Your partner."

"Yes. However, being a jerk is not a prosecutable crime." I walked to the window and pointed down to the professor's house. "Good view. What'd you see and hear? If you answer, I won't send my partner back to ask you."

"You wouldn't…would you?"

"Answer me and maybe I won't." Manny makes good cop/bad cop easy.

Frederick moved to a sagging card table with a cage on it. Inside was a golden teddy bear hamster poised by his wheel, stroking his whiskers and appearing to have an IQ twenty points higher than his caregiver.

"I'm not answering."

"Too bad," I said. "See my other partner here? I could leave the two of you alone. He'll eat your hamster like it was a tater tot."

Clarence covered his face. I couldn't look at him.

Frederick stepped between me and his hamster. Voice squeaking, he asked, "You threatening us?"

"I wouldn't put it that way."

"You better not hurt Brent," he said to Clarence.

"Your hamster's named Brent?" I asked.

He nodded.

"If you love Brent, you'll answer my questions."

He looked at me long and hard, then took a comb out of his pocket and ran it over Brent, who squealed with delight. Finally he said, "A guy knocked on the door. I could see the professor inside look through the peephole."

"How'd you know he was a professor?"

"Read the newspaper."

I pointed at Palatine's house. "You saw him through the living room window? Blinds were up?"

"Down but open. You know, so I could see the professor—there's a bright light over his computer. I saw the guy on the other side of the door, under the porch light, same time."

I walked out onto his paint-peeled deck. He followed me, keeping an eye on Clarence and Brent. "Quite a view."

"Professor was sitting by his computer, reading or something."

I noticed binoculars hanging from a lawn chair.

"Then what?"

"The guy at the door gave him something. Then the professor let him in. They stood and talked."

"What happened next? Don't leave out the details."

He wrinkled his nose. "I don't have time for this."

He walked to the sink and reached underneath. As I pulled my Glock from its shoulder holster, he pulled out a handful of hamster food. Brent had the munchies.

I pointed at the binoculars. "I see your days are busy. You can take a little time now or a lot later…at the police station…with my partner Manny. We can bring in a subpoena, all kinds of court orders. Clarence can be Brent's sitter. But he has to be fed every couple hours. Clarence, I mean. Your choice."

He lowered his eyes, such as they were, to keep me from looking into his brain, such as it was.

"What you want to know?"

"How long between the time this visitor went in and the time he left?"

"Forty minutes? An hour?"

"I don't know. That's why I'm asking you."

"Forty minutes."

"What else did you see?"

"Nothin'."

"There a reason you seem reluctant to offer information?"

"You accusing me of something?"

"I don't know. You guilty of something?"

"I didn't do anything." Suddenly his face softened, and his voice went limp. "You have to believe me."

"Actually, I *don't* have to believe you. Look, Mr. Frederick, both of us want this to be over. I'm sure Clarence and Brent want it to be over. You have your binoculars. Earlier you said the guy at the door gave him something. What?"

Frederick stared at us, like we were conspirators. "How should I know what he gave him?"

"Because you're the witness. Witnesses witness things. How big was it?"

"I was clear up here."

"The binoculars bring you seven times closer. Just take a guess at the size and shape."

"Maybe it was a picture."

"A picture?"

"He unfolded it. Maybe someone lost his dog."

"His dog?"

"Somebody came to my door with a picture of their dog."

"That same day?"

"No. Months ago."

"What did he look like?"

"Just a little black dog. A mutt, maybe some terrier in him."

"I mean the person holding up the…picture or whatever."

"She was maybe forty years old."

"The person at the professor's door?"

"No. The woman showing me the picture of her dog."

"I'm talking about the guy across the street, at the professor's house, Wednesday night. The one you said was holding something up for the professor. What did he look like? White? Black? Hispanic? Asian?"

He nodded.

"Which you nodding at?"

"White maybe."

"Size?"

"Looked sort of big. Maybe heavy."

"Hair color?"

"Couldn't see it. Maybe a gray sweatshirt, with the hood up. Or…wearing a stocking cap, I think."

"What color was the cap?"

"Dark blue."

Finally two points of agreement. I was tempted to ask if he looked like Abraham Lincoln. I also thought if we have a lineup, it would be great to have a Lincoln look-alike to see the expression on Rebecca "my friends call me Becky" Butler's face.

"If we end up with a suspect, we'll get back to you to identify him."

Suddenly his eyes lit up and his shoulders straightened. "One of those police lineups where you pick out the guy?"

"Would you like that?"

"Yeah. That's cool."

"We're all about cool. What happened next, after he gave him the little poster or showed it to him, and he let him in the door?"

"Don't know."

"You must've kept watching."

"Not when he closed the blinds."

"The professor closed the blinds?"

"The other guy."

"Didn't you get a clear look at him then?"

"I was watching the professor."

"How'd he look?"

"Surprised. I was looking at his surprised face when he disappeared."

"Disappeared?"

"Behind the blinds. One second he was there, the next he vanished. Poof."

"You call 911?"

"Why? People shut the blinds so people don't spy on them. I shut my blinds. You never know, a pervert might be spying on you."

"Yeah," Clarence said.

"It's not like I saw a murder or something."

"You may not have seen it, but it happened."

We went over details, trying to fasten down the times.

"All right, Mr. Frederick, we'll be in touch. Think of anything else, here's my cell number."

As we walked to his door, he stood between Brent and Clarence. He pulled out a piece of newspaper lining the bottom of the hamster cage and replaced it with a page from today's *Tribune*. I'm not kidding—it was page B-1.

"Enjoy, Brent," I said, as we went out the door. "Brent's about to bury your byline," I said to Clarence.

"Don't use me to threaten people."

"I'll use anything and anybody to get the job done. You don't like it, shadow the paperboy. You see Brent quiver when he looked at you?"

"At least you got something from this Frederick character."

"He didn't want to help until we came to the lineup. Suddenly he sees himself on TV. Now he's civic-minded." I shook my head. "Whatever it takes."

"He acted guilty, didn't he?"

"Ask somebody a question and if they're guilty, they always assume you're accusing them. Ask a guilty woman, 'How well did you know Bob Smith?' and she hears, 'I know all about your affair with Bob Smith.' Frederick's guilty all right. But of what? Voyeurism? Tax evasion? Welfare fraud? Claiming Brent as a dependent? Everybody's guilty of something. It's probably not the professor's murder. But once we feed him some suspect photos, who knows? He might hand us the killer."

Clarence and I picked up drinks to go at a Seattle's Best. I treated myself to the special, a Butterfinger mocha. He had a skinny latte. No wonder he's such a grouch.

We were back downtown in homicide detail, at the Justice Center, reports laid out in front of us.

"Lab confirms bedroom window was broken from the inside," I said. "Most of the glass was on the outside. But, like I pointed out, some thin shards fell inside. CSI vacuumed the carpet and found more. No blood, skin fragments, or DNA. No fingerprints. But when they tried to put together all the fragments, the ones from the floor and the ones outside, some were missing. That could mean they're stuck in the bottom of someone's shoes."

"The killer's?"

"Hopefully. But here's the zinger. You know what I said about crime scene contamination? Well, remember that long strand of hair with that nice root on the professor's body? We got a rush job on it. Guess whose hair?"

"No clue."

"Kim Suda's! Can you believe it? Hairnets should be mandatory. She crashes my scene, and then she's careless enough to drop hair on the dead guy!"

"I've got a general question about murder investigations," Clarence said. "For my articles. Once you come up with suspects, how do you choose the most likely?"

"Study them. Find out their background and habits, patterns and prejudices. People are predictable. A certain kind of personality exposed to a certain kind of circumstances responds with a certain attitude and behavior…including murder."

"Sounds deterministic, doesn't it?"

"I'll look it up and let you know."

"Not everything's easily explained. Sometimes we deceive ourselves. Sometimes people deceive us."

"I'm a professional observer. A student of human nature. Everybody can be explained."

"You got to know my daddy pretty well, didn't you?"

"In such a short time, yeah, I did."

"You remember his background, the shame and humiliation, that he couldn't take his family to eat in most restaurants, that he had to use a different restroom and drinking fountain. You remember how the cops tortured him in that Mississippi jail?"

"Wish I could forget."

"So, given your philosophy of human behavior, how do you explain my daddy? How do you explain the man that he was?"

I sat there pondering the question and fighting the lump in my throat. "Your daddy was the finest man I ever met. And…to tell you the truth, I can't explain the way he was."

I sat there waiting for him to tell me it was God who touched his heart, Jesus who gave him the power to forgive.

But he didn't say it. He just sat there. All the responses I was ready to give were stuck in my ammo box. And the longer they stayed there, the weaker they looked. I thought about that old man, who played in the Negro Leagues. He knew Satchel Paige, can you imagine that? Jackie Robinson, Hank Aaron, Willie Mays—he knew them all.

The corners of my eyes got hot and wet when I thought about that sheriff and his deputy and how they beat and tortured Obadiah Abernathy. I'd dreamed of getting my hands on them. I wouldn't use a baseball bat or a fork on them like they used on him. I'd want to feel my fingers around their throats. I wouldn't kill them maybe, but I'd make them wish they were dead.

Obadiah Abernathy—I never detected an ounce of bitterness. He'd been dead years now. Other than that day to and from Seattle for a Mariners game and a couple of fishing trips, I never spent more than three hours with him. Yet he became more of a daddy to me than my father had in fifty years.

But Mr. Abernathy's gone now. He left a big space.

"Ollie?" The voice was out of place.

"Jake? What are you doing here?" I looked around to confirm that I was still in homicide.

"When we were at Lou's, I forgot to give you something from Carly."

As he put the white envelope in my hand, I cleared my throat. "I meant to ask you…how is Carly?"

"Not so good. Her immune system's getting weaker, and she keeps catching stuff. Pneumonia twice. Infections all the time."

"I'm sorry," I said.

"She's in good spirits though. She's an amazing girl."

"Yeah."

"She asks me about her Uncle Ollie."

"I've been thinking of dropping by."

"It would mean a lot to her."

Quick as that, Jake was gone. I opened the card. It was a white dog wearing four red sneakers, camera close to his snout. I laughed. Inside it said, "Saw this and thought of you, Uncle Ollie. I love you and miss you. Carly."

I drew my sleeve across my face and stood up. Not sure why I stood up, except that I wanted to do something.

I see dead people. A lot. But I can't stand to see a young woman like Carly waste away. The last few months, my coward's way of not seeing her die has been not to see her at all.

How do you find hope in a world where men like Obadiah Abernathy and girls like Carly Woods suffer and die?

Clarence ran off to his daughter's volleyball game. I dropped by a stop 'n' rob to get two corn dogs and a thirty-two-ouncer. I sat in the parking lot guessing which customers were criminals and what crimes they'd committed. This is how cops while away time. But mainly, I thought about the Palatine case. I didn't like what I was thinking.

I went back to the Justice Center, to the evidence room, and put in a request to check out something that had been processed. The clerk documented this in the chain of custody records. I walked out with a blue rope, still in its evidence bag, inside a plain plastic WinCo sack.

I drove to George's Marine Supply, between downtown and my home, one of two big nautical stores I know of. George was in. I showed him my credentials and handed him the three feet of rope, which CSI had cut through the noose while leaving the knot intact, since knots can be valuable evidence.

George examined the rope like Tiger Woods examines a driver.

"Bowline knot," he said.

I nodded.

After a long pause, George said, "Polyester, three-millimeter fiber. A Marlow. Comes in four colors, all obnoxiously bright. There's a fluorescent pink, a purple, and a greenish yellow. Then this here blue, with the red woven into it. It has a low-stretch polyester core with high-tenacity, good for tie-downs and control lines. It's smooth to minimize friction through blocks and leads."

"You carry it?"

"Used to but stopped three years ago. People want white and brown and conservative colors. I think David Strickland still carries it, over at Strickland's Sail Shop on Eighty-second. I've got a Marlow catalog. Want me to look it up?"

Within two minutes he produced a page with the four rope colors he'd described. He had an extra catalog, so he tore out the page and gave it to me.

"Tell David Strickland hi from George."

I waved my thanks and sat in the driver's seat for ten minutes, picking up a few scraps of corn dog with my fingertips and thinking. I swore, louder than I meant to.

I wasn't going to Strickland's Sail Shop.

A pessimist has many pleasant surprises, an optimist many disappointments. Pessimism is safer. After years of optimism that didn't pan out, I find life less difficult when I keep my expectations low.

But some days things go just right—beautifully, perfectly, to the point that I'm tempted to revert to optimism. You want to bottle those days and just break out into a big grin.

This wasn't one of those days.

Jake Woods and Clarence Abernathy were probably winding down their afternoons with their families, looking forward to sitting around a campfire singing

"Kum Bay Yah" and counting their blessings.

Me, I counted roadblocks, annoyances, and uncertainties. I contemplated the meaning of the gnawing suspicion that had come over me at George's Marine Supply. A suspicion I didn't dare verbalize to anyone.

So I made my way to Rosie O'Grady's Irish pub, where they water the drinks like geraniums, but if you buy them by the bottle you can still get the real stuff. I was there by four thirty, several hours earlier than usual.

My pessimism had nothing to do with my nagging suspicions and certainly nothing to do with not knowing where my older daughter is or even if she's alive and not seeing my other daughter for nearly a year. Nothing to do with Kendra changing her plans and not showing up last Christmas and not inviting me over on my birthday, or hers. Nothing to do with the fact that I'd left two messages inviting her to come with me to Thanksgiving at Jake's place, which was five days away and counting down. I hadn't heard from her and didn't expect to.

Rosie's was heavy with the smell of tap beer and fried grease.

"Hey, here comes the man. He's early today. Must've gotten his quota of jay-walkers."

Not wearing a uniform saves me from these lines where I'm not known, but not at Rosie's.

"Hide your pipe bomb. It's the fuzz."

This is a guy from the sixties who never stopped smoking pot long enough to realize we're no longer called the fuzz.

Some NASCAR wannabe named Mikey, dressed in a Jimmie Johnson T-shirt and hat and wearing a Lowe's team jacket, stood up putting his hands in the air. "I didn't do it!" he called, breaking into uproarious laughter.

Sometimes even sober people do that when cops walk into a room. They think it's original and hugely funny.

In the years I was on patrol, no one ever said anything brilliant when I pulled them over. But in their memories, people are dazzlingly clever.

Mikey isn't done yet: "So I says to the cop, 'I can't reach my license unless you hold my beer and my cell phone.'"

Another goofball chimes in: "Thank you, sir. The last officer only gave me a warning, too!" It falls flat. No laughter. He's banished to the audience. Mikey is now king of Comedy Central, on stage by himself, a legend in his own mind.

"So this cop says to me, 'Sir, your eyes look red. Have you been drinking?' So I says, 'Officer, your eyes look glazed. Have you been eating donuts?'"

Pretty soon everybody's putting in their two cents, shelling out their cop stories.

I picked up my beer and moved to the far end of the bar, resisting the temptation to head-butt somebody onto the pool table.

Billy the bartender approached, supposing I must need a new beer after the long walk. He was right. His face was a doughy pool of flesh in the eerie light of the Michelob neon. There were shreds of red peanut skins between his teeth.

To some guys, a bartender's like a priest or therapist. To me, he's just a pharmacist with a limited inventory. Sometimes I talk with Billy. Not tonight.

The guys three stools away suddenly got louder. They're funny drunks. I'm a quiet drunk. Funny drunks think everything's hilarious. They're Seinfeld, only he got the breaks and they didn't. Being such accomplished humorists apparently makes them feel better about the affair their wife's having or that their kids are doing drugs while they pour their miserable lives away at Rosie's.

I ask for another beer and point to where I'm about to vanish, then walk into the cool darkness to a small table where no one will be tempted to sit by me. In the safety of the darkness I pull out what I keep stashed in my trench coat's inner pocket: orange foam earplugs. I put on my black fedora to make me feel Bogart-like, sitting in the shadows.

Sometimes I just sit there and think about Sharon. I drink to stop thinking about her, but as I drink I think about her more. Sometimes, just for a second, I fall under a spell that she's home waiting for me. And Kendra's a little girl who adores her daddy. What am I doing here with these drunken bums and the bartender with peanut skins on his teeth when they're waiting for me at home?

So I stand, stagger a little, and remember Sharon's dead. And Kendra's lost. Then I sit down again. Next thing I know it's half-past Cinderella, and somehow I'm home, falling into bed. Most times I don't recall hitting the mattress. I wake up and wonder where I am. These days I seem to lose two or three hours routinely.

It's now 5:15, morning after my latest binge. I wake up to the cranial jackhammer. Seeing me bonding with Mr. Coffee, Mulch already has bacon fantasies, but my thoughts are limited to French roast, my drug of choice.

As the little gray cells start to wake up, I contemplate the jerks in the bar, trying to remember what they really said and what I really said and rehearsing what I should have said and indulging my fantasy of taking them all out with a series of head butts.

Wouldn't have been worth the paperwork. And then there's anger management…

After two eighteen-ounce cups of French roast, the sun still wasn't threatening to rise. I lacked sufficient fuel for takeoff, so I cooked a round of bacon and eggs, with blackened English muffins. I decided to do what I'd been dreading since leaving George's Marine Supply yesterday afternoon. I knew what I'd find when I looked in my garage, but I still hoped I was wrong.

I stepped onto the back porch, Mulch at my feet, but I felt dizzy and needed to sit. I thought about sitting on my grandfather's back porch and him teaching me to tie knots, including the bowline. I didn't know Grandpa well, but those knots he taught me were more than I ever got from my father. Dad threw me a ball once. He got mad when I threw it back too low. Said he wasn't going to waste his time with a kid who couldn't even toss a baseball.

I pulled myself up, leaning on Mulch, and opened the door to a pitch-black garage. I turned on the wimpy overhead light. The hundred-watt bulb was fifteen feet up, nearly worthless, barely enough to illuminate the velvet Elvis I bought roadside in Arizona twenty years ago as an anniversary gift for Sharon. I grabbed a flashlight and looked on the shelves, past toolboxes, hoses, and transmission fluid. I pointed the light up to the storage platform behind me, built to take advantage of the dead space. It was full of boxes of junk Sharon had asked me to toss. Miscellaneous sailing paraphernalia reminded me how, after Sharon died, I bought that used sailboat. I'd been out in it three lousy times in two years. Finally sold it.

I stopped rummaging and shone the flashlight around the garage. I passed Elvis and held the beam on an old blue plastic box by two studded snow tires. I stood over it, hands shaking.

I opened the box, pushed aside a block and tackle, some lures and line, and found a couple of ropes.

I pulled one of them out, laid it on the cement floor, pushed back Mulch, and aimed the flashlight. The rope's end had been cut neatly by something sharp. Stretching it out, I guessed that three feet had been cut off, recently, since even in a dusty garage the cut fiber was still sparkling clean.

The rope was bright blue, with a red weave. Polyester with three-millimeter fibers. A Marlow.

I'd bought it three years ago at Strickland's Sail Shop.

"I do not think there are any insuperable difficulties. Still, it is an error to argue in front of your data. You find yourself insensibly twisting them round to fit your theories."
SHERLOCK HOLMES, *THE ADVENTURE OF WISTERIA LODGE*

SUNDAY, NOVEMBER 24

MY IDEA OF FUN is not discovering that the rope around the neck of a murder victim is mine. I sipped coffee at my kitchen table, pondering it.

Finally, I picked up that thought and set it on a shelf, making room on my mind's tabletop to spread out Professor William Palatine. Who was he? And what made me think I was supposed to already know?

By all accounts, Palatine was brilliant, accomplished, and occasionally charming. He was popular among the students—especially intellectuals and females. Female intellectuals? They were crazy about him. Even so, I wouldn't want to trade places with William Palatine. Not sure how much Teacher of the Year and a Princeton diploma means when you're alive, but I'm pretty sure I know how much they matter when you're dead.

In the absence of determinative evidence, you have to know the victim to figure out the most likely person to have killed him. That's why I had to get to know Professor Palatine. Especially since the last phone call he ever made was to me.

Had I been home that night, maybe Palatine and I would have chatted. Or maybe he would've said, "There's a man with a gun; he's 5' 10", carrying a box and wearing a Pizza Hut jacket. The name on the jacket is Reggie."

Jake tells me death's not a hole, but a doorway—that dead people are now alive on the other side. He said that about Sharon. I hope he's right. For her sake anyway. I don't know what I hope about me. Or the professor.

I'm a trained observer of the real world. I know nothing about what lies beyond the senses. This much I do know…when a man is lying on his living room floor with a few gallons of his blood soaked into a blue carpet that's now dark purple, he is not mostly dead, but as Miracle Max said in *The Princess Bride*, "he's all dead."

Solving a murder is a final gift to the deceased. Whether they know about this gift, or whether they can ever know anything again, is a matter of debate, a debate Jake and Clarence love to engage me in.

If Palatine has a soul and there's a God, then it's God's job to judge his soul. Even though I have the distinct feeling I wouldn't have liked him, when it comes to the crimes against his body, if anyone's going to get him justice, it's me.

That's what I do. I get justice for the dead.

After moving from the kitchen to my office, down the hall past the bathroom, I opened up files of photocopied letters Palatine had sent. Many of them appeared to be love letters, saying how his heart was pierced and he felt a fire within and how he hated to be separated from her, blah, blah, blah. Yet not one of the letters addressed a woman by name. If I'd written love letters to Sharon, I'd have put her name on them.

And why make the photocopies? What was his future use for them?

The professor's signature was there on other documents in his files. It was fancy and borderline illegible. Only the *W* and the *P* were clear—except the *Dr.*, which was prominent and unmistakable.

I spent the next hour reading various things written by him in school papers, as well as two introductions online from when he was a visiting lecturer in the ivied halls of academia.

I read again the printout of his supposed "I deserve to die" confession on the computer screen.

I went to the shelf and got down my *Webster's* dictionary. I looked up the word *judgement*.

I stayed home all afternoon, making phone calls, trying to reconstruct Palatine.

Manny and I are both on T-Mobile, for the free minutes, since we can exchange a dozen calls a day. In the last three hours this was call six.

"You know his stupid habit of not putting a name with the number?" Manny asked. "I've been calling all the numbers on papers in his desk. A real estate agent, plumber, and computer tech. A student named Brandy who said she had no idea why he had her phone number. He'd never called. But there was another number. A private detective."

"No kidding? Who?"

"Ray Eagle."

"Wait…the guy who helped us with Abernathy's sister's case? Why would the professor have his number?"

"Ray Eagle," Manny said, clearly irritated, "says to give you this message: 'If Ollie Chandler wants to know why the professor called me, I'll meet him at the precinct tomorrow morning.' He said he read Abernathy's article on the investigation, so he's invited too."

I heard the slow burn in Manny's voice.

"Can you join us?"

"No. I've got work to do. Trying to solve a murder."

Mulch got restless and talked me into a 9:00 p.m. walk. As we headed toward a nearby greenway, a light, cool rain blew into my face, and a thought hit me like a bolt out of nowhere.

What if that call to me from the professor's house wasn't made by him? What if it was made by the last person there after he died?

MONDAY, NOVEMBER 25

Before leaving for work, I saw Saturday's newspaper on the recycle pile. It inspired me to pull out the VCR manual. I put on my reading glasses and found the page about setting the clock. I didn't manage to set the correct time, but at least I stopped it from flashing. I raised a Budweiser in victory when it turned to 12:01.

You never know when some smart-aleck journalist might drop by.

Ray Eagle, short and athletic looking, wearing wire-rimmed glasses, Levis, and an OSU baseball cap, met Clarence and me at the Justice Center. I refreshed my memory before he came. He'd been a Detroit cop fifteen years, five as a detective before moving back to Portland.

After we took five minutes to catch up, I asked, "So what was the professor doing with your number?"

"Palatine called me twice. He wouldn't identify himself. Caller ID gave me nothing. I had the next call traced."

"How?" I asked.

"Friends in the right places," he said. "I used to be a cop, remember? Anyway, he called from his home, not the college. He said he'd gotten some threats, but they were oblique."

"He used the word *oblique*?"

"Yeah. I checked it online five seconds after he said it to make sure I knew what it meant."

"It's a college professor word," I said. "They throw it out there to impress you. Journalists do the same."

"People like you are why we write at a sixth-grade level," Clarence said.

"If I were one of your readers, I'd be insulted."

"If you were one of our readers, you'd be informed."

"You guys need a counselor," Ray said, raising his hands.

"What was the threat about?" I asked.

"He'd been getting phone calls every week, near midnight. The caller implied that Palatine was going to be held accountable for how he'd wronged someone. I think he knew what it was about but didn't tell me."

"Why'd he call you?"

Ray took off his glasses and cleaned them on his shirt. "Somebody recommended me. I told him if he thought his life was being threatened he should call the police. He didn't want to. His second call was Tuesday morning, thirty-six hours before he was killed. When I heard about the murder, I wished I'd done more. Maybe I should've called the cops."

"Why didn't you call us after the murder?"

"Cops don't like PIs sticking their noses in. I figured you'd be calling me. Sure enough, you did."

After Ray Eagle left, I drove the five minutes to the PSU library, by the Park Blocks. It would have been a fresh but drippy half mile walk. Showing my badge to a wide-eyed librarian, I requested the videos of the professor's lectures, which I'd learned existed from a previous call. He carried three videos and escorted me to a private viewing room with an uncomfortable metal chair.

I'd asked computer forensics to send me all Palatine's lecture notes. With a keyword search, I'd located the notes corresponding to these exact lectures and had them with me. Two were the same presentation from his Philosophy 102: Ethics class, given in back-to-back sessions. I watched both sessions to see what I could learn about him. What struck me was how he would roll his eyes up, as if searching for a word. Then suddenly he'd come up with it, when it was right there in front of him in his notes and he'd said the same thing in the previous class, also rolling back his eyes and searching for that same perfect phrase.

In other words, Palatine was the south end of a northbound horse.

He spoke about the dominance in literature and philosophy of dead white males. Never mind that he was a white male. And dead to boot.

He talked about the naïveté of believing in moral absolutes. Listening to the professor, and the student comments that mirrored him, reminded me that many educated people believe there's no such thing as right and wrong. And that many educated people, therefore, are stupid.

Why would I be a cop if there wasn't right and wrong? Steal their skateboard, stereo, or spouse, and suddenly they believe in moral absolutes.

I'm no church boy, but the Christians have it right on this one. When you deal every day with crimes against people, you can't stomach all this waffling on right and wrong. As I listened to the lectures, it struck me as odd how much money people are willing to pay to be taught ethics by people who don't believe in ethics.

It ticks me off that all of us are paying the price for raising a generation that doesn't know the difference between right and wrong

But what would I know? I'm no college graduate. I'm just a working stiff, trying to keep the next person from being mugged or raped or murdered by people who—guess what—don't believe in moral absolutes.

Jake called me about football at my place that night. He assured me that many philosophy teachers these days believe in moral absolutes, and Palatine was a throwback to moral relativism. Well, okay, but do universities offer students their money back when the philosophies they learned there ruin their lives…and other people's?

The professor's lectures were as heavy on ego as they were light on morals. After the fourth video, I was surprised someone hadn't killed him years ago. And dumped him and his smart-aleck philosophy-quoting answering machine into the Willamette River.

For the third and final time I absolutely ruled out suicide. Could a gun, in a recoil back on the finger, fire a second time? Maybe. Could a man put a noose around his neck and put a gun to his chest? Sure. But after watching Palatine's lectures, I decided I'd never seen a man with less self-loathing. If he killed himself, he'd have done it the easiest way, mourning humanity's loss of himself.

After leaving the PSU library and entering the real world, I pulled up the collar of my trench coat, pulled down my wool fedora, and leaned into the icy rain to my car eighty feet away. I thought of my cousin Harvey in San Diego. Maybe I should move there. If I did, I'd stay away from Harvey. But the weather sounded great.

I went to the old brownstone for lunch and worked through the afternoon. Sarge knows I work well at home, so he gives me a long leash. I changed into sweatpants and sweatshirt, sat down at the kitchen table, threw away the mail, heated Nalley chili, smothered it in cheddar cheese and chopped onion, and sat back with a box of Ritz crackers, thinking step by step through the crime.

After getting a second glass of milk, I found myself staring at the message on my fridge: "Examine the evidence. Then follow wherever it leads."

Monday night football, usually at Jake's, was at the brownstone tonight. I scanned the house, put in some elbow grease, and ten minutes later the place was spotless.

Clarence came at five thirty to show me a draft of his next article. I told him to strike a couple of sentences that said too much.

"You'll notice my VCR clock isn't blinking," I said nonchalantly.

"It's three hours fast," he said.

"It was made on the East Coast."

Jake joined us, the pizza arrived, and one of those great kickers named Jason set a football on the tee.

During halftime my cell rang.

"No kidding? You're sure?" I hung up, staring at nothing.

"What?" Jake asked.

"The Franklin Terrace apartments."

"What happened?" Clarence asked.

"Our binocular-gazing hamster-loving Mr. Paul Frederick…the guy who told us the man at the professor's door might've been wearing a stocking cap and looking for his lost dog?"

"How could I forget him?"

"They say he had an accident thirty minutes ago. He fell off his second-story deck. He's dead."

10

MONDAY, NOVEMBER 25, 8:45 P.M.

WE TURNED OFF FOOTBALL. Sitting there in my living room, Clarence and I told Jake about Frederick and what he saw at the professor's through his binoculars.

"Are you going to Frederick's to check it out?" Clarence asked.

"It's Karl and Tommi's case. I have to let them sort things out first."

"Frederick actually fell?"

"Yeah," I said. "After he was pushed. Gravity'll do that."

"Why would somebody kill him?" Jake asked.

"Because they knew he saw something."

"But how would they know?"

"My question exactly. Did someone tail us to the apartments to see who we were interviewing? I keep thinking about those narrow apartment hallways with their creaky steps and floorboards. How could somebody follow us without us seeing him?"

"But we talked with maybe ten people," Clarence said. "Manny talked with more, didn't he? They haven't been killed. Why single out Frederick?"

"He'd seen the guy at the professor's from a distance. Did the killer have eagle eyes? Did he spot him up there with the binoculars? Or was it something Frederick told us that made him worth killing? Or something he *might* tell us but hadn't yet? But how could anyone know?"

Clarence shook his head, saying something about how short life is.

"Frederick left a handwritten will," I said.

"He did?"

"Yeah. He designated you as Brent's legal guardian."

"Who's Brent?" Jake asked.

"Forget it," Clarence said.

"This guy Frederick getting killed," I said. "It's another example of why I don't believe in God."

"You believe in free choice?" Jake asked.

"Yeah."

"Doesn't free choice demand the freedom to choose evil?"

"Not if it causes this much suffering."

"How much suffering is acceptable? Can you have real choices without consequences, both good and bad?"

I shrugged.

"Isn't it inconsistent," Clarence piped in, "to say it's good for God to give us free choice, but then say He shouldn't allow evil consequences from evil choices?"

"You can't have it both ways," Jake said.

These guys were a regular tag team.

"I've made some bad choices," I said. "If I had it to do over again, I'd have been there for my daughters. But if God's all-powerful, couldn't He have made me do it right in the first place?"

"*Made* you do it right?" Jake asked. "What do you want, for God to make us all into Stepford wives?"

"I always thought the Stepford wives were kinda cute."

"If I were to offer to make things okay in your life, but to do it I had to take away your ability to choose, would you take me up on it? Ask me to make all your decisions for you?"

"Then it would be your life, not mine," I said.

"Exactly. So how can you expect God to give us free choice, then fault Him because He did? What could He do to make you happy?"

"Give me Sharon back."

Jake nodded. "He went so far as to give His life on the cross and conquer death in His resurrection so that you and Sharon and everybody who accepts His gift could be together forever."

"So you say. I've looked at Christianity, and I don't like what I see."

"You don't like love, grace, forgiveness, justice, feeding the hungry and caring for the sick? You know where hospitals came from? Christians. Atheists and agnostics aren't behind prison reform. They're not the ones who got slavery outlawed. It was Christians."

"Don't forget the Crusades and inquisitions and all the killjoys, like my grandmother. If I were to judge Christ by some Christians I know, He'd look pretty bad."

"I agree," Jake said. (I hate it when he says that. It throws me off.) "So why don't you judge Christ by Himself instead of by others?"

"Christians are just into rules and dos and don'ts."

"Some are," Jake said. "But I can't think of anything more pointless than Christianity without Christ. And nothing more exciting than knowing Jesus and following Him."

"Pardon me for not agreeing."

"You don't need my pardon," Jake said. "But you're my friend, and friends tell each other the truth. I'm asking you, Ollie, take your focus off the church and off Christians you've known, and just look at Jesus. Read the Gospel of John, and judge Him by what He said and did, not by everybody who claims His name. Who did He claim to be? Investigate. Then make up your own mind about Him. And stop assuming things are as they appear."

"In other words," Clarence said, "practice what you preach."

It was time to change the subject. I pulled out my yellow notepad. "Here's my verse for the day. It's from Dashiell Hammett's *The Continental Op*. He says, 'In the case of a murder it is possible sometimes to take a shortcut to the end of the trail, by first finding the motive.'"

"How do you find that shortcut?" Jake asked.

"By figuring out who benefits from Palatine's death. Someone's trying to come out ahead. Possible motives? Money. Power. Romance. Business. Revenge. Self-preservation. Justice. Somebody thinks the murder makes perfect sense. They think they'll sleep better knowing he's dead. It's 99 percent motive. Remember that *Purpose Driven Life* study you guys tried to con me into?"

"Yeah," Jake said. "We were hoping to bilk you out of your mansion in the Caribbean."

"Well, let me tell you about the purpose driven murder. There's always a purpose, always a motive. Find it and you have the killer. But to find the killer you must know the victim. That's why I listened to the professor's lectures and why I'm becoming a student of philosophy. That's why I'm reading Bertrand Russell." Okay, I'd read eight pages. "Which reminds me, has somebody written *Nietzsche for Dummies*?"

"So what are the possible motives?" Clarence asked.

"Nothing unusual about the professor's finances. Doesn't appear to have been a big gambler. Manny called his attorney about the will. Has no kids. Divorced. Looks like it goes to his brother, a wealthy doctor."

"Romance?" Jake asked.

"Possibly. Hell knows no fury like a woman scorned. Isn't that in the Bible?"

"Nice try," Jake said.

"What about a student?" Clarence asked.

"Maybe a student was humiliated by the professor. Manny says last term three students were caught plagiarizing papers from the Internet. Palatine flunked them. Manny'll pay them a visit."

Clarence was taking notes.

"The question with murder," I said, "is always this—*who's better off* because this person is dead? Better off in body, mind, or bank account? A victim's abused wife is better off. A victim's girlfriend's husband is better off because he's eliminated the competition and gotten revenge. Whose life's easier because Palatine's gone? Or rather, who might imagine his life would be easier? Because murder complicates his life in ways he never imagined."

"Your sins will find you out," Jake said.

"A man reaps what he sows," Clarence said.

After a pause, I cleared my throat and said, "A rolling stone gathers no moss?"

11:00 Monday night, Mulch and I kicked back on the couch. I was still pondering Frederick's murder. Suddenly, I thought of something he'd said to us. A mental picture formed. Why hadn't it dawned on me before?

If I was right, it would explain how the killer might have known what Frederick said to us. And why, knowing that, he might kill him. The two fit, like gun and holster.

I thought it through backward and forward. Usually I fear that I won't discover the truth. This was one of the few times I'd been afraid I *had* discovered it.

My nerves were like worms on a fishhook.

The one thing that keeps me from drinking at night is the need to stay sharp to figure out a case. But this time, if my mind was catching the right scent, the last thing I wanted to do was stay sharp. I didn't want to go where the evidence was leading me.

I had to say yes either to the train of thought or to the six-pack.

It was an easy choice.

11

TUESDAY, NOVEMBER 26, 8:00 A.M.

I WOKE UP with a hippopotamus sitting on my head. The fact that it was invisible unnerved me.

By the time I got to the office the hippo was the size of a rock badger—not overwhelming, just annoying. At nine, crime lab said the toxicology report was ready. Clarence joined me.

"It's bizarre," the tech said, handing me his report. "Somebody injected this guy with over twelve ounces of ink. Pelikan ink, royal blue, same stuff in the bottle, only more. Maybe he found extra bottles. Or brought his own. He used that syringe you found at the scene."

"Injection was where we saw the marks in his shoulder?"

"Yeah."

"Why so many?"

"You know how many injections from a 100-cc needle it takes to make twelve ounces?" he asked. "Do the math."

Clarence closed his eyes, mumbling something about thirty cubic centimeters in an ounce. "Even with that big syringe, at least four shots. Could've been a half dozen."

"That's a break for us. The killer wouldn't do that without a specific reason. You don't just notice a couple of ink bottles in a drawer and say, 'Hey, I'll kill him with fountain pen ink.' It's too bizarre and time-consuming."

"Maybe a sadist wanted him to die slowly."

"In the killer's mind it made perfect sense. It wasn't random."

The first seventy-two hours after a murder are critical. Unfortunately, it had been six days. Clarence couldn't make lunch, so it was Jake and me at Lou's.

I took the six steps to the Rock-Ola, which reminds me of the robot in *Lost in Space*, and pressed B9, "Mr. Tambourine Man."

As we waited for burger baskets, I said, "Okay, it's not suicide. Not the work of a serial killer. I mean, we aren't finding other people injected with ink with nooses around their necks. And it's not a hired killer."

"Why not?" Jake asked.

"Too messy. All those unnecessary garnishes. Somebody's trying to make a statement. To mock us or to tell us something. A professional killer would be in and out in two minutes. This guy hung around, maybe forty minutes. It wasn't business. It was personal."

"I don't understand why the killer would leave all that evidence," Jake said. "The insulin, the syringe, the ink, the injections, the rope, the gun. Why bother?"

"Right. And don't forget the crumbs and the wineglasses," I said. "Why not just whack the guy and leave? My theory is, he's trying to overwhelm us with evidence. It's brilliant. There's enough evidence that we can't tell what's real and what's phony."

"What do you mean?" Jake asked, squeezing a lemon slice in his Diet Coke.

"The chair, for instance. Normally you'd say this was a short person. But maybe it's a tall person making it appear that a short person adjusted the chair."

"Or maybe it really *is* a short person."

"Exactly. That's the problem. Suppose the killer tripped up and left some real evidence. How would we distinguish that from the contrived evidence? At first I thought somebody wanted to be caught. Now I think they're smart enough to know there're always some bread crumbs. So they've crumbled a whole loaf and spread it out. How do you find the real bread crumbs—or know when you've found them?"

"Whoever your killer is," Jake said, "he seems to know enough about investigations to realize how to mess one up."

"Yeah." Jake didn't know how close to home he was hitting.

My phone gave me its "missed a call" ring. The message was Manny saying, "Ballistics confirmed murder weapon's the Taurus."

"Good news," I told Jake. "The Dumpster gun's the murder weapon. Now we wait to see about fingerprints."

I took a celebratory bite of cheeseburger. I'm telling you, Rory's a master. Emeril's got nothing on him but a TV show.

"There's something else," I said, wiping my mouth. "I don't think the professor called me that night."

"But…I thought you said he did."

"His phone was used to call my number. That doesn't mean he was the caller."

"You're thinking it was…?"

"The killer," I said.

"How would the killer know your number?"

"Same way as the professor. There are ways to get unlisted numbers."

"But why call you? The killer wouldn't know you'd be investigating the case. Even *you* didn't know, right?"

"And if he was going to call me, why linger at the murder scene to do it?" I picked up a printout. "I've been going over the confession. Listen: 'I, Dr. William Palatine, do not deserve to live. I've crossed boundaries and forfeited my life. I admit my arrogance. I deserve judgement. I should be cast into a deep sea with a millstone around my neck.'"

"First time I've heard that," Jake said. "Weird."

"The prints were wiped off the keyboard, so Palatine didn't write it. Probably the killer. But here's the best part. Up to now, I've had to deal with a ninety-minute window for time of death. Computer forensics told me this afternoon that the file wasn't saved by the user, but it was autosaved."

"So?"

"The automatic file recovery was set to save every five minutes, whenever a change had been made. It backed up last at 11:40. That means the killer was still there, typing, after 11:35. And I got my phone message at 11:37. I say he was wrapping things up. He'd just finished off Palatine or was about to. Once he fires those two shots, he's got to get out of the house. Time of death was probably 11:30 to 11:40. Given the multiple injections and everything else, I don't see how it could have been before, say, 11:20. A ten- or twenty-minute spread's worlds better than ninety."

"What time did that woman say she saw the professor let the guy in?"

"Becky Butler pinpointed the commercial break that put it about 10:50 p.m. So the guy was in the house with him at least forty-five minutes."

"Isn't that an awfully long time?" Jake asked.

"Yeah. The killer wasn't in a hurry. And I want to know why."

It was twenty minutes out of my way, but after leaving Lou's I decided to swing by Dea's In and Out in Gresham for an orange malt. I listened to a Nero Wolfe audio, *Murder by the Book.* Sometimes I hear something I can use in my investigation.

But I was distracted, mulling over the case. I was looking for a crumb, a trace, a scrap of a hint. Anything. I was trying to discredit my unsettling hunch, unsuccessfully.

I'd attempted five times to contact the professor's brother, the doctor. I turned off Nero Wolfe and pulled to the side of the road as we finally connected.

"You've heard my messages?" I asked. "I need to meet with you as soon as possible."

"The next three days are impossible," Dr. Warner Palatine said. "I've got a few minutes now while they transport a patient. Then I scrub in for an emergency surgery."

"Let's get started." The orange malt could wait. "I have the impression you and your brother weren't real close."

"We saw each other Thanksgiving, Christmas, birthdays. Two years ago we spent a week together at Sunriver. It wasn't fun. What? Thirty ccs? No way. I told you twenty." I heard muffled voices.

"Doctor?"

"Sorry. I'm back."

"So did you talk to your brother on the phone?"

"I used to, but I got tired of his stupid answering machine. Did you know every week he'd have a quote from a different philosopher? Even when we were kids, he was a show-off."

"How old was he when he became a diabetic?"

"Who?"

"Your brother."

"What are you talking about? Bill wasn't a diabetic."

"But…he was insulin-dependent."

"No way…unless it happened in the last month, and that's impossible. Too old for type 1."

"But he was wearing one of those ID tags on a chain. Plus, a needle and insulin in the fridge."

"Speaking of chains, somebody's yanking yours, detective. The one thing Bill talked to me about was his medical condition, enlarged prostate and all. He'd call me to double-check his doctor's advice. He was taking Diovan for high blood pressure."

"Yeah, we found it in the medicine cabinet."

"I've been his free medical consultant for twenty years. No co-pay. Type 1, insulin-dependent? No way. I'd know about it. Look, I've got to get to surgery."

I pulled the file from my beat-up briefcase and searched my crime scene notes. Then I called the evidence room.

"I need information right now on a piece of bagged evidence. It's on the Palatine murder, November 20. Last Wednesday. It's the medical ID chain that was around his neck. I need to know exactly what it says."

I sat there feeling dumb for not checking his medical records. But what's the point of faking a medical condition on a dead man?

"Okay," said the tech. "On the back side it says 'MedIDs.' On the front side, in a red imprint, it says 'Insulin-Dependent Diabetic.' And under that it says 'See wallet card.'"

"Is his wallet still bagged?"

"It's here."

"Can you check for a wallet card?"

"Isn't this your job? You want me to interview witnesses, too?"

"Just check, would you?"

"He's got his health insurance card. The rest is credit cards, a coffee card, and a few pictures. That's it. There's no medical card."

I contacted Palatine's primary physician, assured him of my credentials, and he confirmed that Palatine wasn't diabetic.

I left a message for Manny and called Clarence to fill him in.

"So if the professor wasn't a diabetic," I said, "where'd the insulin bottle come from? And whose chain was hanging around his neck?"

TUESDAY, NOVEMBER 26, 3:00 P.M.

I VISITED Paul Frederick's apartment, with Detectives Karl Baylor and Tommi Elam as my tour guides but found nothing helpful. The neighbors testified that Frederick would hang over the edge of his deck, spying on people with his binoculars. He'd often do it at night. This time he'd leaned too far.

Yeah, right.

As I waited for the elevator on the ground floor of the Justice Center, Clarence walked in the front door. I held the elevator for him and prepared him for our appointment by saying, "You can learn a lot about someone by studying their computer." We exited on floor 14, entered detective division, and this time turned right, away from my workstation, to computer forensics. There we met Detective Julia Stager.

"The professor visited plenty of raunchy websites," Stager said. "He thought he'd erased them, but we can pull up everything. Keep that in mind, gentlemen. There's no such thing as a private moment."

She handed me the list.

"Palatine searched for the kinds of things you'd expect a philosophy teacher to search for. And he also entered lots of names to search for phone numbers. Ninety percent of them were women's. Sometimes he reverse searched, entering phone numbers to try to identify the name."

"Someone he contacted might've had a motive," I said. "Or a boyfriend."

"Or husband or brother," Clarence said. "Or father."

"Given his indiscretions, he made some enemies."

"The sites marked were in his favorites folder," Stager said. "Here's an unlikely one."

"Bill's Fountain Pen Page?" I asked.

"Yeah, and two sites about collecting fountain pens."

Manny had told me he'd found a dozen fountain pens in Palatine's office at the college and even more at his home, in a shoe box. Plus those three I'd found in his desk.

"Not many people use fountain pens anymore, do they?" Clarence asked.

"The professor did. Which means I've developed a keen interest in fountain pens."

WEDNESDAY, NOVEMBER 27

The next morning I asked Clarence to meet me at Lou's at 7:30 a.m. before sitting in on his first detectives' meeting at nine.

Before the pancakes and western omelets were served, and after Clarence had rolled his eyes at "Puff the Magic Dragon" and put in a request for the Supremes, I said, "There's something you need to hear before you come to the meeting. I've been thinking about Paul Frederick. You know how he said the man at the door gave the professor something or was holding something up for him to look at, like a little poster?"

"Yeah?"

"I think he was showing him ID."

"What kind of ID?"

"Well, who shows ID to gain entrance?"

"Cops?"

"Or FBI. Arson investigators. Someone associated with law enforcement. Not that long of a list."

"Are you saying...the killer could be a cop?"

"Killers can be anybody with a motive, and cops have motives just like everybody else. If the guy was holding up ID and it persuaded the professor to let him in the door, it could've been a cop. Let's go back to our original question of why someone would kill Frederick," I said, as "Puff" gave way to "My World Is Empty Without You."

"If he thought Frederick told us something incriminating. Or that he could?"

"Right. But what puzzled us is how would he know what he said to us?"

"He wouldn't. It was just you, me, and him. Unless...a bugging device?"

"I considered that. But how would he know to plant one in the first place? How else could he find out?"

Clarence shrugged.

"Didn't you take notes?"

"Sure, but nobody saw them. You playing 'blame the journalist' again?"

"You're certain your editor didn't see them? Carp? A custodian looking on your desk?"

"I keep them in my briefcase. It's with me at all times." Clarence pointed to his black leather case, which looked like it had come off the assembly line that morning.

"Do you take it with you when go to the bathroom?"

"Of course not."

"Does it have a lock?"

"Yes. But—"

"You don't use it, do you?"

"No reason to."

"Unless you're carrying eyewitness testimony in a murder case."

"You think someone at the *Trib* is the murderer?"

"No reason they couldn't be. I'll grant you it's unlikely. Unfortunately, there's another possibility."

"What?"

"I took notes too."

"What did you do with them?"

"What I always do. Gave them to Mitzie in the secretarial pool so she could type them for me."

"You think the typist is a killer?"

"This typist is sixty-four years old and weighs a hundred pounds. But someone could see it on her desk when she steps away. People pass by her desk all the time."

"Not people off the street," Clarence said. "It's pretty high security."

"I've thought about it. We've got custodians. Maintenance staff. Secretaries. And of course…cops."

"You think…?"

"Mitzie types it into the system. She saves the file on the server. She e-mails it to me. And to top it off she gives me a hard copy. That's how I like it. My notes of the Frederick interview might have sat for hours on Mitzie's desk. But even if she typed them right away, one of the detectives could've accessed the file or hard copy."

"But…one of the detectives?"

"Why not? Someone knows Frederick saw some things. They kill him to shut him up or keep him from remembering something critical. Dead men don't pick you out in a lineup."

"That's a serious accusation," Clarence said, leaning forward.

I got up and pressed a few more rose-colored buttons, invoking the artistry of Herman's Hermits and the Dave Clark Five.

We no longer had to whisper once we were under the melodious strains of "I'm 'Enery the Eighth, I yam, 'Enery the Eighth, I yam, I yam."

"It's a hypothesis. Unfortunately, it's holding up. Think about how much time this guy spent at the crime scene. Who would take that risk? But if a guy had his police monitor on, he'd know exactly when dispatch called for patrol. He could be out of the house in a heartbeat. Hey, even if he was found at the scene, he could tell patrol he heard it on his monitor and was nearby, so he came to check it out. If you're a cop, you can do that."

"But—"

"Consider the phone call to my house from the professor's. My home phone's unlisted, but all the homicide detectives have it. He uses official ID to get Palatine's door open. He has access to the information Frederick gave us and knows he might ID him. He can enter Frederick's apartment the same way we did—by showing his badge. Only a handful of people could've read my notes and learned what Frederick told us. And most of them are homicide detectives."

"You really believe one of the detectives killed Professor Palatine?"

Hearing Clarence say it made it seem more real. More frightening.

"You have no clue how badly I want to be wrong."

Clarence and I walked single file through detective division, since no aisle is wide enough to accommodate us side by side.

"Team meeting's once a week," I said. "We update each other on our cases. Compare notes. Helps to have a fresh perspective."

"We do that at the *Trib* sometimes. Call in other reporters and pick each other's brains."

"That must be slim pickin's."

When we walked into the conference room, Detectives Brandon Phillips, Kim Suda, and Chris Doyle were already there. They were huddled, but the moment we entered, Doyle stood and headed for the coffee.

Tommi Elam walked in behind us, smacking her bubble gum louder than any forty-two-year-old should. Tommi's chin and nose don't quite match, but it's a good chin and a good nose. She's not beautiful, but she's cute. A little sister type. She's big sister to her partner, Karl, who's ten years younger. Her gum cracking reminds me of a gangster's girlfriend in a B movie. But she's the most likable person in homicide.

Tommi walked toward Clarence. Heavy makeup surrounded her left eye, which was puffy and bloodshot. The lower eyelid showed underlying red and purple. I'd noticed this late last week. If it was still this bad, I'd hate to have seen it when it happened.

"I'm Tommi Elam," she said to Clarence, sticking out her hand like she was chairperson of the homicide Welcome Wagon.

"Clarence Abernathy."

"The columnist. That's what I thought! That piece you wrote on volunteerism in the inner city?"

"Yes?"

"It was excellent."

"Thanks. I appreciate that."

"It's great to have you here, Clarence. Let me know if I can do anything for you." Tommi sat in front.

"She's a compulsive liar," I whispered to Clarence. "She's in therapy."

He gave me his look. ❙

"Here comes Karl Baylor, Tommi's partner," I said. "I'm sure he'll introduce himself to you. He's a Christian, so you two might understand each other."

"Clarence Abernathy, right?" Baylor said, smiling broadly. Ten seconds into the conversation he was calling Clarence "brother," in the Christian sense I suppose, since Baylor's white as I am. This guy pushes my buttons. He should either have something done to his teeth or stop smiling so much. He always has to let people know he's a Christian.

"Don't we have the greatest view of the city from up here?" Baylor gushed like a tour guide.

His voice irritates me. It's like his diaphragm needs a larger outlet than his throat affords. It's always spurting out words in loud, spasmodic bursts of dogmatism.

"Welcome to the inner sanctum, Clarence." It was Jack Glissan, offering his hand. He waved to Noel, his partner, over by the concessions. "I'll have a Sprite."

"Sure," Noel said, then looked at Clarence and me. "Get you guys a soda?"

"I'm good," Clarence said.

"Coke," I said.

"Coca-Cola?"

I nodded, smiling at the blend of personalities that make up our homicide department. I felt guilty for suspecting them.

Manny walked through the doorway, looking for a seat by himself. He took the second seat from Bryce Cimmatoni, which guaranteed the seat between them wouldn't get taken. Who sits between two megagrouches?

Sergeant Jim Seymour stood behind the flimsy wooden podium. Things started to quiet.

"What's he doing here?" Doyle asked, pointing at Clarence.

"You've probably heard," Sarge said, "Clarence Abernathy is observing the William Palatine murder investigation. Part of the arrangement Chief Lennox made with the *Tribune* is for Abernathy to attend this meeting, but only while it's pertinent to that case."

"Great," said Suda, with a fake good-natured tone.

"Yippee," said Phillips, not bothering to fake the tone.

Tommi grinned and rolled her eyes at Clarence, like "this is the sort of stuff we have to put up with every day." Her makeup under her tender left eye was wearing off.

"No offense," I whispered to Clarence, "but cops are as fond of the media as a Frenchman is fond of deodorant."

"So we'll start with the Palatine case. Chandler?"

I handed out notes, summarized what we'd found, the limited lab results, witness interviews, the options we were considering. Naturally, I didn't say what I was *really* thinking about the killer's identity.

"Manny and I are open," I said. "Suggestions?"

"It's obvious," said a face grooved by time and trouble. Cimmatoni's jaw is so solid it doesn't move when he talks. He looks as if he could bite off a steel rod like a pepperoni stick. His voice is huge, the sort ancient orators must have used to speak on hillsides to a thousand people. Too bad Cimmatoni usually says nothing worth listening to.

"What's obvious?" I asked.

"It was a transient. A street person."

"We know what a transient is," I said. "Didn't you say the same thing when the priest was murdered by that CEO?" That got two chortles, a guffaw, and a giggle.

"Transients are your default murderers, aren't they, Cimma?" Doyle asked.

"Half our unsolved crimes are probably transients. Could be a gang member, but they're too obvious. Probably four dozen transients with digs within a quarter-mile of that house. I'll lay two to one on a transient."

"I'll put down twenty bucks," I said.

He looked like he didn't believe me, but I didn't take it personally. He hadn't believed anybody for a couple of decades.

Phillips was looking over the notes I'd handed out. "Why'd he turn blue?"

"The killer injected him repeatedly with ink," I said. There was a low whistle and some grimaces. "Summary of the toxicology report's on page three. Blue fountain pen ink."

"Traceable?"

"We're working on it."

"The noose?" Sarge asked.

"A special rope sold in nautical supply stores, used mostly for tying boats. But unless it's a recent purchase, or he used a credit card or made a cash purchase in a store where there's a security camera…"

"Once you get a suspect," Doyle said, "take his picture to boating stores."

"A suspect would be nice," I said.

"Transient," Cimmatoni muttered.

"Rope important or just a diversion?" Suda asked.

"You tell me," I said. "And here's one. Talked to his brother, who's a doctor. Palatine wore a medical chain identifying him as an insulin-dependent diabetic. Insulin bottle in the fridge. Needles in the drawer. But the professor wasn't a diabetic."

"Plus the only needle marks were in his shoulder," Clarence said. "Diabetics don't take injections there."

The silence was deafening. Outsiders never came to these meetings. That an outsider would speak was unthinkable. That the speaking outsider was a journalist was strike three.

"Why don't you take over the investigation?" Manny mumbled. "We'll write your useless columns."

"I didn't know you could write," Clarence said.

Manny's usual scowl cranked up a notch.

"People leave evidence because they're hurried," I said, "or careless, or want to be caught. Doesn't seem like he was in a hurry. But why the noose? Injection? Fountain pen ink? Insulin bottle? Needle? What does it all mean?"

"The noose suggests suicide," Karl Baylor said.

"Or execution," Cimmatoni said.

Until then, that thought hadn't crossed my mind. Two miles to the north of us, in Washington, they still hang people. Only by the condemned prisoner's request, so it's rare, but it happens. This fit the note on the computer screen and other indications that the professor had been brought to justice. But what had he done to warrant execution? If we knew, it would point to the killer.

"It doesn't have to make sense," Cimmatoni said. "Killers aren't brainiacs."

"Even when it doesn't appear to make sense, it does," I said, "if you're in the head of the killer."

"Yeah, and to be in his head it helps if you *are* the killer."

I stared at Cimmatoni. Why had he said that?

"Okay," Sarge said, "we've had more murders in the last four weeks than in the previous three months. Everybody has an open case, so we've got lots of ground to cover. Suda and Doyle, you're next. Mr. Abernathy, you're excused."

Clarence put his notepad in his briefcase and snuck out. I waved bye-bye to him, kissing the air, feeling a little smug that at least we weren't letting the *Trib* in on everything.

It seemed a long wait between breakfast with Clarence at Lou's and lunch at New York Burrito by the Federal Building, across from the Justice Center.

The only downside was that Manny was with me, and he's not a happy eater.

He made a face at his burrito. I don't mean he showed displeasure by raising his eyebrow. I mean he made an actual face. Manny's eating skills are remarkably similar to his people skills.

My partner doesn't just have a lot of issues; he's got the whole subscription.

Personality aside, however, in most respects Manny's a good partner. He's efficient, hard-nosed, and lock-jawed determined. If he catches a scent, that dog'll hunt. And he knows how to turn the thumbscrews, especially with the young and cocky. He'd make Jack Bauer proud. The world's full of personality—I don't need that in a partner.

Right now I was contemplating how to tell Manny what I was thinking about the killer being a detective.

"I don't like Abernathy coming to our meeting," he said, turning his displeasure from the burrito to me. "And I don't like him working on our case."

"Neither do I. But he's a decent guy. Almost a friend."

Manny stopped chewing and stared me down.

"Speaking loosely. In the broadest sense of *friend*. But he's a journalist. Now, if he were his father, it'd be a pleasure to have him around."

"His father was his only good feature," Manny said. "Too bad he's gone for good."

"Gone for good?"

"Yeah. Dead. You know what dead means, right?"

"It comes up now and then in this business."

"Dead is dead."

"Some say people still live after they die," I said. "That they just go somewhere else."

"Yeah, and some say we were made by aliens and at night they take us up on their ships and perform experiments."

"And that proves there's no life after death?"

"You turning religious on me?"

"No." I said it too quickly, hearing my defensiveness and wondering how I'd suddenly fallen on the other side of the argument. "You sound like Nietzsche."

"You looked up Nietzsche, didn't you?" Manny asked. "You didn't know jack about Nietzsche, and you looked him up."

"Nietzsche schmietzsche," I said, as Manny swallowed his last bite, leaving half a dead burrito, and headed out the door.

This was the deepest philosophical discussion Manny and I've ever had. It bothered me to hear him say what I'd thought myself, that Obadiah Abernathy no longer existed. Something inside, buried deep, told me this couldn't be true. And if it were, the universe was just a cruel joke.

I consoled myself with the remnants of Manny's burrito.

↔

I'd left my notebook in the office, but I jotted down my thoughts on a New York Burrito sack. It wasn't the Gettysburg Address, but it was a piece of work: \

1. The killer planned the murder methodically, including the bizarre elements with the noose and the ink injections. He may have stayed forty-five minutes at the crime scene.
2. The killer knew how long it would take the cops to get there. He might have had a police monitor.
3. The killer took unnecessary measures that might make him vulnerable, like he was daring a detective to catch him. He took the time and trouble to put on the noose, inject the ink, and remove items, at least a photo and a wine bottle.
4. The killer—almost certainly—knew the private number of a homicide detective and called him from the scene.
5. The killer believes he knows investigative procedures well enough to get around them. He may take pride in his ability to outwit homicide detectives.

Seeing it in black and white was disturbing. I wanted to add a sixth point, but I wasn't sure I could. "The killer—possibly—planted incriminating evidence at the scene, including a Black Jack wrapper and a rope belonging to me. And he may have planted a donut in my car."

But if he used my rope and planted my wrapper and Wally's donut and called me from the scene, he was setting me up. Did he believe I was going to investigate the case? Or was he expecting it to be someone else, knowing that whoever did would find the evidence against me and I might be tagged with a homicide?

But something bothered me more. I couldn't remember the night of the murder. It was just…not there in my mind. Had I come home from Rosie's? Or had I gone to the professor's house?

Strange how anxiety over a blackout due to drinking can make you want to drink more.

13

"The plot thickens."
SHERLOCK HOLMES, *A STUDY IN SCARLET*

WEDNESDAY, NOVEMBER 27, 1:30 P.M.

A JOURNEY OF A THOUSAND MILES begins with a single step.

Falling down a flight of stairs begins the same way.

The step my little gray cells had taken—that the murderer was one of our own detectives—was that kind of step.

As I walked slowly back to the Justice Center, under a thick cloud cover, I marveled at how that awful thought, on its face inconceivable, had walked right in the back door of my mind, taken off its shoes, and thrown itself on my cerebral couch. And like my cousin from South Carolina who showed up twenty years ago with a backpack and a pet boa, it showed no signs of leaving.

We're the fraternity of detectives. It's a brotherhood, including Tommi and Kim, who are brothers with different shapes and higher voices. Comrades in arms, for crying out loud. Even Cimma.

Like my platoon in Nam. We didn't all like each other, but we'd die for each other. We watched each others' backs. That's what cops do. That's what the brotherhood does.

And I was going after one of them?

"I wish you were here, Sharon," I said aloud, looking up but seeing no crack in the clouds. "I need you. I need to talk with you."

"I know, Ollie. I know. But there's someone you need a lot more than me. He can do for you far more than I ever could. Talk to Him. Turn to Him. I love you. More importantly, He loves you."

In the conference room near our work area, I walked Manny through my written points on the burrito sack.

"That's ridiculous. Your prime suspect is one of *us*?"

"Why is it ridiculous? Because you know them? Killers are always known by people. They always work with somebody. Everybody goes on TV when it all comes out and says he was a nice guy and washed their car and made them cookies and they had no clue."

"There's no way."

"Okay," I said. "If you were going to kill somebody, how would you do it?"

"I have to fight for time to go to my son's T-ball games," Manny said. "I don't have time to stage a murder."

"But if you *did* stage a murder, you'd be successful, wouldn't you?"

"You tryin' to say somethin' to me?" He stood, fists clenched tight, as if he were a gang member again and I was calling him out.

"My point is, if anybody's going to know how to pull off a murder and not get caught, it's a homicide detective, right? Any of us could do it."

He went to the door. "I'm going back to the professor's hood. I say somebody saw something. And about your theory?"

"Yeah?"

"You're losin' it."

Was I?

A homicide detective would know what *not* to do—all the things we catch people on. If I were going to kill somebody, I'd plan it so nobody would catch me.

If I was sober, that is.

I headed to Sergeant Jim Seymour's office. I took a breath and walked in. His office is well-organized, and he must have a dozen pictures of his wife and four kids, in everything from baseball to band.

"What's with that?" he asked, pointing at the sack in my hand.

I read him the burrito bag. After I'd made my case for the murderer being a detective, Sarge kept blinking at me like maybe I'd disappear after one more blink.

"I don't know what else to think," I said. "It's a hunch, but it's based on evidence. I have to consider it."

"We've got ten homicide detectives. You going to check their alibis? Let's say five of them were home alone or with their wives, then what? You'll suspect that their wives, or Tommi's husband, may be lying. Where's this going to take us? Who're you going to eliminate? Manny?"

"How can I?"

"Did you say that to his face?"

"No."

"I wouldn't recommend it. What about Jack? You going after him?"

"Sure. Everybody. Jack'll understand."

"Right. I'm sure the whole team will be dripping with sympathy."

"Look, means and opportunity come easily for us, don't they? It's all about motive. So can't homicide detectives have a motive to kill someone?"

"Sure, but…not this crew. Don't you know them better than that, Ollie? You still read your murder mysteries, don't you?"

"Yeah."

"Me too. What if you read that the prime suspects in a murder mystery were a bunch of homicide detectives?"

"Well, in a book I might think it was…lame."

"That's what I think."

"Okay, in a novel I'd never make ten homicide detectives the murder suspects. The author would be an idiot to even try it. But this is the real world."

"You said ten suspects. You mean *nine,* right? Unless you're suspecting yourself."

"Hey, it could be eleven. You have access to everything. If the evidence leads me to you, what should I do?"

"Investigate me," Sarge said. "Clear me or keep me on the suspect list."

"Then that's what I have to do with everybody."

I took the elevator down two floors to criminalist detail. The receptionist confirmed Phil Oref was there. I signed in, and she buzzed me through the security door.

As I went down the hall I saw a technician making tool marks on wood to see what they looked like, then glanced into ballistics, where they were testing guns. While the state crime lab has lots of scientists, criminalists are sworn officers, so you get to know them cop-to-cop. Sometimes you can ask a favor.

I shook Phil's hand, and we talked about the case for a few minutes.

"Know when we'll get the fingerprints on the Dumpster gun, the murder weapon? We need them pronto."

"You need everything pronto. Bates is on those. He's way behind."

"It's urgent!"

"Like always. Something else on your mind, Detective?"

"I have a confession to make," I said. "Keep it confidential?"

"Long as it's not murder."

"Last week, at the professor's house, the murder scene…you remember?"

"Be a while before I forget that one."

"Anyway, I got this terrible itch on my palm."

Phil held up his hands like stopping traffic. "You're not going to tell me you took off a glove?"

"Just for a second. Right then I saw something on the floor, by the couch, and instinct kicked in…I picked it up."

He whistled. "You contaminated evidence."

I produced the sealed bag.

"Gum wrapper? *Black Jack?* I didn't know they still made this stuff."

"They didn't for a long time."

"What was that other one, you know, um…?"

"Beemans?"

"No."

"Clove?"

"Yeah. They still make Clove?"

"You're talking to an expert. Every three years they produce Clove and Black Jack and Beemans too. I stock up on Black Jack."

"You're chewing it right now, aren't you? I can smell it. You sure it didn't just fall out of your pocket at the professor's?"

"That's what I've been wondering."

The truth is, I knew I had no gum that night. No way it fell out of my pocket. But this isn't something you tell the criminalist.

"What you want?"

"I know these wrappers can hold a print." I nodded toward the bag.

"Usually inside the wrapper, the white part. You want me to run it for you outside the system, that it? Don't want it officially entered as evidence?"

"As long as it just shows my print, either I contaminated it or just dropped it. But if someone else's print comes up…"

"Okay, Detective, I won't tell on you. We all make mistakes. Even Mr. Have-you-checked-the-keyboard-for-prints? I probably won't even tell anyone you ate the corpse's Snickers bar."

"You said you checked it for prints. It was unopened, so no saliva. Why waste it?"

"There've got to be rules against eating evidence. I should ask the chief. You not only contaminated evidence; you removed it from the crime scene. You're a piece of work, Chandler."

"You remember that journalist, Abernathy? If I'd told people what happened, it'd be in the paper, and we'd all look bad."

"You'd look bad."

"Not just me. CSI team had been all over the part of the room where I found the wrapper. I shouldn't have picked it up, but that never would've been an issue if you guys had done your job."

"I don't believe you."

"If I dropped it, okay, you're clear. But if it was already there, you guys should have seen it. While we're at it, I could mention how on the Danny Stump case you forgot to take prints from the orange juice glass, and on the Eric Wood case you knocked the houseplant on the bloodstained carpet."

"It was 3:00 a.m. I was tired!"

"It's *always* 3:00 a.m., Phil. We're always tired. Anyway, check out the gum wrapper for me. And get it back to me directly. ASAP."

"You guys always want it yesterday."

"Today would be fine."

"Tomorrow's Thanksgiving. After that, we'll see."

"Remember, this is just between us, okay?"

When I returned at three, Clarence was at my workstation, looking over the crime scene notes and lab reports.

"Insulin bottles have an expiration date on them," he said without saying hello. "What's the date on that bottle you found in the professor's fridge?"

I called the evidence room, and five minutes later Wanda had the bag and said, "Let's see, expiration date is…wow."

"What?"

"It expired in June…nine and a half years ago."

When I told Clarence he said, "You can use it a few months after expiration. A year's pushing it. Nearly ten years? Nobody'd keep it that long."

"Nice catch, Abernathy. There has to be a reason somebody held on to it. Could've been found in a drawer that hadn't been cleared out for years. But once you find it, why keep it? Why not toss it?"

"You know how I said that big syringe reminded me of the ones I used to have? I'll bet it's as old as the insulin."

"We figure out where that insulin and needle came from," I said, "and why someone held on to them ten years…and why they'd bring them to the murder scene and leave them there…we're in business!"

"Guess what," Sergeant Seymour said, leaning down over my desk, where I could see the hairs climbing out his ears. "The chief wants to meet with you, me, the lieutenant, and the captain."

"I talked to you, what, two hours ago? Word travels quickly."

"You know the drill. If it affects the larger police force, I have to take it to the lieutenant. He took it to the captain, and you know who he took it to. Now the four of us get to have a meeting. Thanks for messing up everybody's day before Thanksgiving!"

"Chief's office?"

"He's coming here. Fifteen minutes."

"But I was supposed to—"

"Doesn't matter. Drop it. You think the rest of us were doing crossword puzzles?"

Fifteen minutes later, Sarge called me into a conference room. Immediately in front of me sat Lieutenant Taylor Nicks, a bead of sweat on his forehead, which gravity was toying with. To my right was Captain Justin Swiridoff, expressionless. To my left was Chief Edward Lennox, in a suit worth more than the combined value of all clothing I'd bought in the last five years.

"What do you think you're doing?" Lennox asked.

Sergeant Seymour gestured for me to sit. I examined the chair. It didn't have straps and electrical wiring, so I sat.

"I'm doing what I always do. I'm going where the evidence points. I don't know how to do detective work any other way."

"You'd better learn another way," Lennox said. "You realize what you'd do to this department if you send the message that *one of our own* killed a popular college professor?"

"What difference would it make if he was a college professor or a plumber or a homeless guy? And why does it matter if he was popular?"

"You're trying to goad me. My point is you can't just go off, head over heels, like a chicken with its head cut off. We just can't afford more bad publicity. And the worst publicity I can imagine is acting as if one of our own murdered someone!"

"Nobody's *acting as if*. It's a working hypothesis. If it turns out to be wrong, I'll be thrilled. I'm just saying that's where the evidence seems to point." I stood up, stretched my torso, then sat back down when I saw the looks. "Doctors, lawyers, accountants, teachers, and grocery clerks have all killed people. Why not a homicide detective? Who'd be better at it? The more murders you've worked on, the more you know about murder. And how you can get away with it."

"Inconceivable," Lennox said. Captain Swiridoff nodded vigorously. Lieutenant Nicks nodded moderately. Sarge nodded slightly. The higher in the chain of command, the greater the head movement.

"Why is it inconceivable?"

"How can you even ask that question?" Lennox rubbed his moist gray forehead, swirling his makeup. "Captain? Lieutenant? Sergeant? Can you tell this man why it's just *unthinkable*?"

"We have good people here," Swiridoff said. "Our detectives solve murders; they don't commit them. Chief's right. The public would eat us alive if we tagged a detective."

"Wouldn't they eat us alive," I asked, "if we looked the other way because we knew he was one of us?"

"Lieutenant?" Lennox's voice sounded whiny.

"The evidence can be interpreted different ways," Nicks said. "There's no proof it's one of the detectives. We should operate on the assumption it's *not*. Trace down all the other leads first. Naturally, everything's complicated by your friend Abernathy working with you."

"It wasn't my idea." I stared at Lennox, whose lower teeth were moving out and back against his upper lip.

"If the newspaper gets an inkling of what you're thinking," Swiridoff said, "it could tear apart the department."

"You…haven't said anything to Abernathy, have you?" Lennox asked, his face drained of blood.

I thought of how I'd unveiled my suspicions to Abernathy, shocking him with the prospect that a detective could be the murderer. I hoped no one noticed my slight hesitation.

"Like I'd drop so much as a *hint* to a *Tribune* reporter that I suspected a cop? What kind of a dimwit do you think I am?"

I was holding a hand of nothing, seven high. Folding wasn't an option. Bluffing was my only chance.

"You're an idiot," Lennox said. "But I'll grant you, nobody's *that* big an idiot."

Apparently he'd forgotten I was King of the Idiots.

"Sergeant," Lennox said, "you haven't said anything to talk sense into this man."

Seymour looked at the chief, captain, and lieutenant, in that order. He'd been a cop most of his life.

"If he's making a rush to judgment, I'd try to talk him out of it," Sarge said. "Chandler cuts corners, and I've had to pick up the pieces. Still, he's one of the best detectives I've ever seen."

The sweet talk made me blush and grin.

"But I wouldn't underestimate how big a dimwit he could be. He may just be warming up."

I stopped grinning.

"Still," Sarge said, "the evidence suggests we may have an internal problem. I don't see how we can overlook it. Our job is to follow the evidence and solve the crime. How it makes us look doesn't matter."

"You've been a police officer how long, Sergeant?" Lennox asked.

"Thirty-five years, sir."

"And you were last promoted when?"

"Fifteen years ago. I like my job. It's what I—"

"Yes. No doubt. But perhaps you aren't qualified to assess how important our public image is. We work for the people. They pay our salary. What they think of us *does* matter."

"But it's secondary, not primary. And I believe they'll think more highly of us when we catch killers—whoever they are."

I could have kissed Sergeant Seymour. And if you saw his mug, you'd understand what that means.

"No one's saying to look the other way," Swiridoff said. "We're just saying, use discretion."

"It's essential that Abernathy doesn't catch wind of this possibility," Lennox said. "I'm going to tell Raylon Berkley the deal's off. I don't want Abernathy on this case."

"Won't that look suspicious?" Nicks asked.

"I'll give him a good reason and offer alternatives. Meanwhile, I'm counting on you three men to make sure Detective Chandler stays within his limits and does *not* damage our image. When it comes to your future in this department—all of you—there are other fish in the sea. Am I clear on that point?"

The captain and lieutenant nodded. Sarge's neck went rigid.

"Am I clear on that, Sergeant?"

"Very clear."

"As for you, Chandler, if you mishandle this case, it'll be your last. These men are my witnesses. If your career goes down in flames, you won't be alone. I'll hold any or all of your superiors accountable. Do you hear what I'm saying? All of you?"

Everybody nodded. Even me.

I drove home in the darkness. I didn't turn on the radio, or Michael Pritchard reading Nero Wolfe. I even turned off my cell phone. My body was behind the wheel, but my mind was elsewhere. My meeting with the brass was bugging me; so were nagging thoughts about the gum wrapper and rope. My mind landed on the discussions with Jake and Clarence. They'd raised again the two events I can never escape…Sharon's death being one of them.

Maybe it was the looming shadow of Thanksgiving. Holidays can do that to you when you have great memories of a past but no hope for a future. Maybe it's the holiday's name. You know you're far better off than most people who've ever lived, but you're still not happy. And part of you refuses to give thanks because you've lost so much and you feel like you deserve better than what you've gotten.

Then I felt guilty, because I hate entitlement, whining, and ingratitude—three things ruining our country. Yet when I look inside myself, I see the things I hate. Sometimes I think maybe what's wrong with this world is that it's made up of people like me.

During my first years as a detective, I never discussed my work with Sharon. I figured it would depress her. What depressed her was that I shut her out. I kept it inside, but it ate at me.

"Let me in," she'd say.

"You don't want in," I'd say.

"Some wives can live with their husband's silence. I can't. If you don't trust me enough to let me in, it's going to destroy our marriage."

I started doing what my superiors wouldn't approve. I'd fill her in on a case. It made me feel better. We could talk about it for hours. When I said, "You've got to be sick of this," she'd say, "I'd rather have us talk about a murder case than talk about nothing." Then magically, once we talked it out, we could move on to other things. And I was no longer shutting her out.

Sharon was my closest friend and I was hers. Until her last days, that is, when she spent more and more time with Janet Woods, Geneva Abernathy, and Sue Keels. "I love those ladies," she said. "That Geneva—her smile seems lit from the inside, like a big candle flame coming through a carved pumpkin."

My wife said things like that.

"When I'm with them, I feel encouraged," she said. "I feel hope."

"And when you're with me?"

"I feel your love. It seems like the love was late in coming. But now that it's here, I'm so grateful. But…"

"But?"

"But when I'm with you, I don't feel much hope. Long-term hope, I mean. You're always trying to give me hope that I'm going to beat this cancer. But I don't know if I *can* beat it."

"Don't say that."

"You mean well, Ollie. You've become my cheerleader, and I love you for it. But I *am* going to die."

"Stop it!" Hot blood flooded my brain.

"Okay, let's say I *do* beat this cancer. Then what? Does that mean I won't die? Of course not. I'll die at a different time, maybe in a different way. You'll die too. I just want to be ready. Geneva and Janet and Sue are helping me get ready."

"They're helping you give up, that's what they're doing! They're throwing dirt on your grave!"

"No, they're not. They're showing me God loves me and—"

"God loves you? Then why's He doing this to you?"

"I don't know, Ollie. There's a lot I don't know. But I want to spend the time I have left—whether it's weeks or years—learning more about Him."

"Fine. Whatever."

"Following Jesus is like a fresh start. I feel like I've been wasting my life."

"On me? And Kendra and Andrea? We're a waste?"

"What a terrible thing to say. You know I don't think that."

Her tears started flowing, and my stupid heart broke.

"Sorry."

"Even my death is about you, isn't it, Ollie?"

"What's that supposed to mean?"

"You're the detective. Why don't you figure it out?"

My job is figuring out why people died. But I'll never figure out why Sharon died.

When she was near the end, Jake said to me, "God loves you and Sharon."

If God loved us, why didn't He help us? Why isn't Sharon still alive? If He's in control of everything…then He's the one who killed Sharon. So why would I trust my wife's killer?

Thanksgiving? For what?

"They say that genius is an infinite capacity for taking pains. It's a very bad definition, but it does apply to detective work."
SHERLOCK HOLMES, *A STUDY IN SCARLET*

THURSDAY, NOVEMBER 28

THANKSGIVING DAY.

My daughter Kendra hadn't returned my call—she usually doesn't—so I drove toward Jake's house to join his family and the family of Finney Keels, Jake's old buddy who died years ago.

I pulled up across the street from Jake's and tried to find motivation to get out of the car and face another holiday with a group that didn't include Sharon. After ten minutes, I walked to the front door.

The first person to greet me was Little Finn, Finney Keels's Down syndrome boy. He wasn't so little anymore, but his face was still that of a child.

"Hi dere, Unca Ollie!" He put his arms around me.

"Still working at the health club, Finn?"

"Yeah, Mr. Eisenzimmer says I'm his best 'ployee!"

"I'll bet you're one fine 'ployee."

"No, it's 'ployee," he said.

I nodded and smiled.

"Uncle Ollie!"

I turned and looked at the familiar smile of the young woman in the wheelchair. I came close to her, bending down. Carly Woods, brown-haired with a hint of red, reached out and hugged me. She was so thin now it was like being hugged by dried-up branches. She felt brittle, and I was afraid to squeeze lest she crack.

Carly seems to like me. I'm grateful for her naïveté, but I can't stand what she's going through. It isn't right. Her son Finney, named after Little Finn's dad, Finney Keels, shook my hand politely and firmly. I liked that. He looks like his grandfather Jake.

Jake gave me his muscular Vietnam vet handshake. Janet fawned over me, taking my coat and offering me malted milk balls, which she knows I love. When you come to gatherings alone, it helps to have something to do with your hands…and your mouth.

"Ollie!" Sue Keels, still blond and petite, threw her arms around me. "I've really missed you."

Funny how you know when people mean what they say.

I see Sue only a couple of times a year when I pick up Little Finn and take him to a ball game or a movie, usually with Jake. I got to know her while investigating her husband's murder. She's dated a few guys since then, one or two I've met at our Thanksgiving gatherings, but she's never remarried. She's a sweetheart, and she'd be a great catch for any guy with a high tolerance for talk about Jesus. But with her it's more than talk. She gives me hope that her beliefs aren't empty, and that, in the end, maybe Sharon's weren't either.

Sue's daughter Angela and granddaughter Karina were there, with Sue's grandsons Ty, Matthew, and Jake. (People get named after each other in these families). The three boys are an entertaining little trio—binky-sucker, stair-climber, and fridge-raider.

It wasn't long before we'd grabbed hands, Carly on one side and Little Finn on the other. I knew what was coming. Different people pray before meals, but usually Little Finn steals the show.

"God in heaven," Finn said, much louder than necessary, "tank You dat You are dere and here and everywhere else, even under da bed and in da closet and on da roof, and in dat scary corner in da garage by da paint cans. Tank You for takin' care of me and my mom and sister and niece and nephews, and everybody else's nieces and nephews and cousins and children and parents and grandmothers and grandfathers and great-grandmothers, and da people they don't know very well too."

There were amens and nods and smiles. I know because I was looking around the table, not being much of a prayer guy. One time I closed my eyes in a group setting and opened them to see a gun pointed at a hostage. Since then I've made it a habit not to close my eyes in public.

Little Finn was going right on, as if he were talking to a real person.

"Tank You, Jesus, dat my dad's dere with You and he's lookin' forward to seein' me again just like I want to see him. Please make dat happen soon, Lord. Say hi to him for me, and hi to Unca Clarence's daddy, Mr. Abernathy, and his sister and niece and say hi to Unca Ollie's wife, Sharon, who also died. And Carly is going to be joining them soon too, so please tell everybody she's coming, okay?"

I looked at Jake and Janet and saw tears come to their eyes, and when I looked at Carly, right beside me, I saw a huge smile on her face. She nodded and said a soft "Yes, Lord."

"And Jesus," Finn wasn't done, "tank You for this Thanksgiving dinner and for Aunt Janet and my mom, Mrs. Susan Keels, and for everybody who came with food, including da pie somebody bought at Safeway. And God, we also pray for

Unca Ollie dat he repent and come to Jesus and admit that he's a big sinner."

Little Finn squeezed my left hand and Carly squeezed my right, and she looked up at me and laughed hysterically. It was contagious, and others started laughing. I laughed too.

Little Finn went right on, "And God please forgive everybody for laughin' in da midda of my prayer, but we do wanna laugh tonight, just not during da prayer, so help me to finish this prayer so it will be 'kay to laugh. In Jesus' name…"

"Amen!" Five people said at once, and Little Finn was done. Now he was laughing too.

I looked at him and marveled that he could be in his twenties now and still a child. He reminded me of Obadiah Abernathy, a man I'd known in his eighties, who even then was childlike. It made me long for the childhood I'd left behind too soon. One that my father or Nam or job or the realities of life and death had taken from me.

The meal was wonderful—turkey and dressing and gravy and corn and the most wonderful biscuits drenched in butter and strawberry jam. I had three tall glasses of milk, plus sparkling cider that Finn told me I just had to drink.

Afterward we sat around the living room telling stories. Jake and I talked about our tours in Vietnam. They asked me to tell them detective stories. I obliged, and they seemed interested. The children made everybody laugh, and Champ, Jake's old springer spaniel, sat at my side, where I scratched him nonstop. Mulch would demand an explanation.

Dogs know the people who love them, and they know enough not to walk away from a good thing. If only we were that smart.

As it got dark, I looked around for Carly but couldn't find her. The conversation had broken into groups of threes and fours, and I stood and stretched and inched my way toward the hall closet and my trench coat. Jake caught me.

"Carly wants you to say good-bye before you leave. She's in her room."

I knocked on the partly open door.

"Come in."

Carly was lying in her bed, all tucked in, with her right arm outside the covers. Her son Finney's head was on a pillow next to her. Her smile lit up the room. I know that's a cliché worthy of the chief, but I don't care. It did.

"Uncle Ollie, I'm so glad you came."

"Wouldn't leave without saying good-bye," I said.

She whispered to Finney. He jumped off the bed and walked out of the room telling me, "I'm going to have blackberry pie." I smiled my approval.

"How you feeling?" I asked Carly.

"Not great. I get so tired. But I'm grateful. It could be a lot worse."

I stood there and stared, like an idiot.

"It may not be much longer," she said.

"What do you mean?"

"Maybe you missed that part of Little Finn's prayer," she said, grinning. "In case you haven't heard, I'm supposed to die pretty soon."

"No, you're not." I knew it was stupid the moment I said it. Sometimes I need a filter between my brain and my tongue.

"Sounds like you've got inside information. Maybe you could fill me in. And the doctors, too!" She laughed.

How could she laugh?

"Don't feel bad for me. I know where I'm going."

"Good," I said, which seemed better than saying, "How could you *possibly* know that?"

"Jesus promised He was preparing a place for His followers so we could live with Him forever." Her voice was light and airy.

"So I've been told."

"Do you believe it?"

"Sometimes I want to."

"And sometimes you don't?"

I nodded.

"Aunt Sharon believed in Jesus."

"Yeah. She changed her thinking a lot before…" I trailed off.

"She died."

"Before I lost her."

"When you know where someone's gone, you haven't lost them," she said, sticking her thin, shivering arm under the covers.

"I'm just not as sure as you are."

"If you knew Jesus, you'd feel differently."

"I'm not a religious man, Carly."

"Neither am I. I mean I'm obviously not a man, but I'm not religious either."

"You sure sound religious to me."

"Because I believe Jesus and love Him? That's not religion. It's just love and trust. Trust in what I've seen."

"You mean what you *haven't* seen."

"No. First, all those years ago I saw what Jesus did to my dad. How He changed him through and through. You've known my dad a long time. You've seen it, haven't you?"

I nodded.

"Then I saw what He did in my mom's life. And finally I experienced Him myself. He changed me from the inside out. I believe Him. I believe His promises. I believe in the resurrection and the new earth. I believe that He's going to take away all the pain and wipe away all the tears. Those are His promises. I'm taking them to the bank."

"Good for you," I said. I didn't hear conviction in my voice. I suspect she didn't either.

"It's only good for me if God keeps His promises. But I believe He does."

She pulled out that arm again and beckoned me to come close. I could hear her breathing now in little puffs.

"Can I pray for you, Uncle Ollie?"

I nodded numbly. I can't tell you what she said except, like Little Finn, she sounded like she was talking to a real person. I can't explain it. It was really…well, not religious. She said the names Andrea and Kendra. Not hearing what she said about them, even their names stabbed my heart.

An "Amen" yanked me out of my fog.

"I may not see you again here," Carly said. "But I hope I'll see you again there. And if I do, let's make a date to walk the new earth together, okay? Maybe visit the New Grand Canyon or the New Mount Everest or the New Lake Victoria. Maybe even the New Portland. Without any crime or suffering or death."

"What would I do for a living?"

She laughed. "You'd be living all right…and you'd find plenty to do. You'd love every minute of it. I know you would."

I looked at the floor. I couldn't bear to look at her. She was so much more alive than I was.

She stretched her arms out to me, like an angel but better, and I felt her thin fingers on the back of my neck and something light on my cheek. I heard her say, "I love you."

I stumbled out of her room and out the front door. Somebody said something to me. I don't know who or what.

I pushed my way into the cold east wind, weak in my stomach and my legs, feeling something sticking to my face. I barely made it to the car, fumbled with the keys, and dropped them. I swore. I sat in the car a long time before I realized I was shaking. I turned the key and continued to sit. It might have been ten minutes later when I noticed a curtain move and saw Janet looking at me. Afraid Jake would come out, I pulled away.

I went home, thinking of Jake and Janet and Carly and Finney and Sue and Little Finn—and Sharon too. I felt a lingering warmth inside, harpooned by sharp cold.

How could I explain what I'd seen?

How could Carly Woods believe in a God who was letting her just shrivel up and die?

"I'm so happy Carly's coming soon."

"So am I."

"It's going to be hard on Jake and Janet to lose her."

"Did you not hear My daughter's words, Finney?"

"Right. They're not going to lose her because they'll know she's here with You. But they don't know what it's like here. I sure didn't. It's so much better than I imagined."

"I've told them about this place and much more about the new earth, but somehow they don't grasp it."

"Wherever You are, it's heaven."

"So it is, Finney. But the best is yet to come. I will relocate all of this, all of us, to a new realm. There you and your people will at last reign over the earth, exercising dominion as I intended from the beginning when I made your planet and the morning stars shouted for joy."

Finney Keels entered into the Carpenter's joy, He who was the maker and repairer of people and worlds. Finney felt his companion's arm rest on his shoulder, an arm that felt extraordinarily light considering it had created the universe.

FRIDAY, NOVEMBER 29, 9:00 A.M.

"Chandler? Phil Oref, criminalist detail."

"You finally got that fingerprints report?"

"On the gun in the Dumpster? Not my assignment. I'm calling about your gum wrapper."

"You can get me results in two days when you've already taken a week on the gun?"

"I'll say it again. I have nothing to do with the gun. We're understaffed, Detective."

"What you got on the gum wrapper?"

"One thumbprint, 60 percent of a whole, and a partial finger, both yours."

"Mine?"

"Yeah. That's what you were expecting, right?"

"Right. Nothing else though?"

"Just yours. Must have dropped from your pocket. You want me to put this into the evidence room with the rest of the stuff?"

"No," I said a little too emphatically. "I better get it back. I was a dope to touch it with my glove off."

"Yeah, you were."

"At least I didn't contaminate a blood sample."

"It was 3:00 a.m., okay? I'll have it here in an evidence bag, inside a manila envelope with your name on it, for you to pick up. Won't have a case number since it's outside the system. I could get in trouble for this. So could you. You owe me, Detective."

"Actually, we're even now."

I drove ten minutes to the Property Evidence Warehouse at Seventeenth and Jefferson, by Lincoln High School. It's an old cement building with ramps that looks like it was a giant auto repair shop in a previous life. Once you get past sign-in and back to the evidence viewing room, the tables and chairs are bare and uninviting. But rather than go through the hoops of checking out evidence and having to bring it back, I decided to set up camp and tackle four evidence boxes we seized from Palatine's file cabinet the night of the murder. With help, I found the boxes stacked in P-8, on rack shelving like Costco or Home Depot.

It took me two hours to go through three boxes of papers. Talk about panning mud and rocks. I nearly gave up, partly because the evidence viewing room is within smelling range of the two vaults in the back of the warehouse, which contain guns and drugs. I couldn't smell the guns but caught periodic whiffs of marijuana. The primary offender, though, was crank, or meth, which smells like cat urine with a touch of fingernail polish. A couple of hours is all I can take.

In the back of the final box, which had the contents of the lowest file drawer, was a thick folder labeled "Special papers." On top was a student's five-year-old paper with a red grade on it: A+. Under it was a paper two years old, another seven years old, and fifteen more student papers, all marked A or A+, with dates ranging from fifteen years to three months ago.

I started reading these papers one by one. I'm no philosopher, but I've read great writers—including Rex Stout, Mickey Spillane, Dashiell Hammett, and Ross Macdonald. I'm talking the giants. So I know good writing and bad writing when I see it. Most of these papers were not good writing. No one would accuse these students of plagiarism.

Some papers had numbers penciled after the grade. The highest was a ten, the lowest was a one, and most were in between.

It was then I realized that not one of the papers was written by a guy.

I picked one paper I'd read, a treatise on a dude named Hobbes, with a red smiling face next to the A+, and a penciled number 3 next to that. The paper was written by a Cassandra Fields. I barely stayed awake while reading and decided to track her down to find out why the professor gave her an A+ and a smiley face for such mediocre writing.

I drove back to the Justice Center. If you want to find out about somebody quickly, it helps to be a cop. Within fifteen minutes I had a fax of Cassandra's college transcript, knew where she lived and with whom and that she worked in the Multnomah County library, just a few minutes away. After another call, I found she'd be at work for three more hours. She agreed to meet me in a library conference room during her break, as long as I had proper ID.

Cassandra was attractive, though she'd put on weight since college. I knew this because I recognized her flaming red hair. She was one of dozens of young girls in the professor's pictures.

She led me to a conference room with an ancient Greece theme, including a model of the Parthenon.

"As I said, I'm investigating the murder of Professor William Palatine. We're talking to former students. You remember him?"

"Yes."

"You remember what grade you got in his class?"

"I had him for two classes. I think I…got As."

"Did you usually get As in your classes?"

Her face flushed, and she looked down. "Sometimes."

"Well," I said, looking at the top paper in my file, "in four years at the university, you got a total of three As. Two were from Professor Palatine. The other was a PE class."

"You have my transcript?"

"Yes."

"Why?" She was wringing her hands.

"Were you close to the professor?"

"I haven't seen him since I graduated."

"Were you seeing him before you graduated?"

"Yes, of course…I mean, I always saw him in class."

"Only in class?"

"Mainly in class."

"Ever go to his home?"

The best lie detector is experience. I've learned that some people spout lies too quickly, like a counterpunch. Some weigh and measure their lies to get the words right. For others, like Cassandra, the delay comes from a crisis of conscience in which they try to decide whether to lie or tell the truth. Her face and her hands told her story.

"I have a picture of you taken in his home."

Her eyes widened and face whitened. "He took pictures?"

I nodded.

"I was never that kind of girl," she said. "He was the first…" She started crying. "I've always regretted it. It makes me feel cheap. At first I thought I was special. He was never mean, really, but when he was finished with me, I knew it."

"Did he write you poetry?"

She snapped backward as if I'd slapped her. "How did you know that?"

"Still have it?"

"I burned it years ago."

"You remember what it looked like? Was the ink sort of thick?"

She nodded.

"What color was it?"

"Blue."

"Did it look like this?" I handed her a card, the one from Palatine's file drawer, with the three quotes about love.

"How did…? I burned it!"

"This one wasn't to you."

The redness came back to her face, which got wetter. She was using her sleeve. I wished I had Kleenex.

"Can I get you anything? A glass of water?"

She shook her head. "What are you going to do with the photos? Do people have to see them?"

"I only know of one."

I handed it to her. She was standing in the picture with four other girls, two of them between her and the professor.

"That's it?" she asked.

"Yes."

"But I thought you said…"

"I just said I had a photo of you taken in his house."

"Okay. Well…that's good."

"Thank you, Miss Fields. I'll call you if I have more questions."

I stood and moved to the door. She sat motionless.

"Are you coming out?"

She shook her head, no eye contact. "I'll just stay here for now."

"I'm…sorry."

Her face rested on her hands, which were palm down on the table. I saw a box of Kleenex at the front desk, grabbed a handful, and took them back to Cassandra Fields. Still looking down, she sobbed when she clutched them. I put my hand lightly on her shoulder, then left her to her demons.

I grabbed a late lunch at the Pizza Schmizza three blocks south of the library, but it didn't settle, so I left some, which shows how hard Cassandra's story hit me. I returned to the central precinct at the Justice Center and made phone calls. There's no point in telling you details about the other contacts I made, following up on A+ papers in Palatine's file. Five of the nine I was able to reach on the telephone admitted that they'd had a relationship with Palatine. He hadn't kept these papers for their literary value, but as reminders of something else.

But when the afternoon had finished, it was Cassandra Fields who haunted me, because hers was the only face I'd seen. I couldn't shake her vulnerability, hurt, and shame. Had I been her father or brother I might have considered killing Palatine myself.

I'm no Victorian. I don't much care what people do in their private lives. But a professor is in a power position, and if he abuses his power and seduces his students, and especially if he does it repeatedly, I think something should be done to him. Maybe not death, but something permanent.

Short of that, I'd volunteer to beat him within a millimeter of his life, because though I don't use the metric system, I know a millimeter is a lot less than an inch.

I sat down in front of Billy the Bartender at Rosie O'Grady's, munching on pretzels and peanuts. "What time did I leave here a week ago Wednesday night?"

"Like I should remember if *you* don't?" Billy squinted at me. "Haven't seen you since you was here Saturday."

"I'm talking the Wednesday before that. When I came in the door, you were ragging on Mayor Branch's "Beautify Portland" plan and how much it was going to cost Rosie's. Remember when I left?"

"Checking out your own alibi?"

"Just answer my question."

"Little after ten, I reckon. Ten thirty outside. Early for you. I asked if you wanted a cab, but you wasn't in a mood to listen."

"What mood was I in?"

"Ticked off."

"About what?"

"Government. Religion. Education. The mayor. That newspaper guy. The police chief. You name it."

"I mentioned the chief?"

"You called him names. Want I should repeat them?"

"What did I say about education?"

"You was groanin' about liberal communist college professors who act like cops are the criminals."

"I said that?"

"And a hundred other things. You pushed a customer who made a crack about donuts."

"I didn't push anybody."

"Yeah you did. People were backing off. I heard one guy say you're a lot tougher than you look…said he'd seen you knock somebody cold with a head butt. That true?"

"You're sure I was gone by ten thirty?"

"Pretty sure," he said, wiping the bar with a wet towel. "Get a memory, will you? Then you won't have to use mine."

I've had plenty of firsts. My first kiss, Heidi Holstrom, third grade. My first transistor radio—high-tech, costing me a twenty-dollar fortune—on which I listened to Elvis and Buddy Holly. My first date with Sharon at the original Spaghetti Factory in downtown Portland, back when spumoni ice cream had those little candied fruit doohickeys in it. My first NFL game, in Seattle at the old Kingdome, watching Jim Zorn and Steve Largent. My first World Series, in New York, Yankees versus Braves. My first arrest. My first solved homicide.

Most of the firsts, with the exception of my inauguration to the oven of Vietnam, when I melted into a puddle, I remember fondly. But today was another first.

I considered my inability to remember what I'd done after leaving Rosie's. I thought about Wally's Donuts, three lousy blocks from the professor's. I thought about the Black Jack gum wrapper I'd removed from the crime scene. I weighed Billy's testimony that I was mad enough to push people around.

It was another first for me when I wrote a new name on my suspect list.

Mine.

"Nothing clears up a case so much as stating it to another person."
SHERLOCK HOLMES, *SILVER BLAZE*

I HAD MEANS. I had opportunity. I didn't have an alibi, and while it seemed that the alcohol in my system would have prevented me from the crime, it also might have emboldened me. Tangible evidence—both the gum wrapper and the rope—placed me at the scene.

But what could have been my motive? Did it lay in the gaps of my existence, the blackouts that had increased in frequency and duration?

One of the sore points in comics history is that Hal Jordan, Green Lantern, failed to save Coast City, his childhood home, from destruction. That failure turned him mad. Unable to prevent this terrible injustice, he tried to right all wrongs, but resorted to wrongdoing to do it. The great champion of good turned evil.

My meals with Jake and Clarence at Lou's Diner were up to two a week—a bonus for working with Clarence, since it was natural to include Jake, who we trust and who we're both more comfortable around than each other. This time we were meeting on a Saturday, after which Clarence and I would be working on the case. I sat at our booth, getting in a few beers before my buddies arrived, admiring the orange flower Rory called a gerbera daisy.

A dilemma is a problem for which you can see no solution.

When you work with a bunch of guys you'd die for in a heartbeat—even if you don't like them all—and you follow the evidence, which tells you the murder was committed by one of them…and will cause mega-resentment from the other detectives…and make a community that's already suspicious of cops believe they've been proven right…and when you're working every day not just with cops you can't trust, but a journalist…this is a dilemma. It weighed on me enough that it threatened my appetite, though the threat proved hollow.

Jake entered, said hi, then went right to the Rock-Ola, pressing C3. The haunting lyrics of "Bridge over Troubled Water" transported us again, and we were both thinking of Vietnam.

Clarence walked in halfway through, and my companions looked as melancholic as I felt. But eventually Rory came to the rescue, burgers dripping with Tillamook cheese and Lou's special sauce, a doctored Thousand Island dressing. A mouthwatering feast that cures your ailments…or masks them, and I'll settle for that.

"*Buonissimo?*" Rory asked, after we took our first bites.

"Buonissimo," we said in unison, wiping our mouths.

Over lunch, Clarence talked about the hordes of boys interested in his teenage daughter, Keisha. Clarence asked, "What did you guys do when boys paid attention to your daughters?"

Jake deferred to me, which was odd, since he's the good dad and I'm not. Still, it was nice to give an opinion on something besides murder or the problem of evil.

"I remember once we were at Dea's, enjoying a father-daughter time, with extra fry sauce. In the middle of my Long Burger, I notice a guy, maybe seventeen, giving Kendra the eye. While she was looking at him, I unsnapped my SIG-Sauer P226, lifted it halfway out of the holster, and stared him down like he was a stray dog rummaging my flower garden. His eyes turned saucerlike, he left the remnants of his burger, and hit the pavement."

Clarence was smiling, which he should do more often since it makes him look like his father.

"Anyway," I continued, "Kendra was oblivious to what I'd done, which came in handy because these situations started happening a couple times a week. Approximately two dozen teenage boys, seeing me handle my pistol, decided there were other girls to look at besides Kendra. Finally she started noticing. 'It makes me want to totally die when he does that,' she told Sharon. Once upon a time she thought it was cool I was a detective, but eventually it became a great deal lower on the food chain than if I'd been a guitarist or assistant manager at Gap."

"She went off to college, right?" Clarence said, as the Rock-Ola told us our answers were "Blowin' in the Wind."

"When she went to Portland State, she moved downtown, and I saw her a lot less. But I felt just as protective. Even after college, she was dating some loser, and I found out he'd knocked her down and slapped her around. She tried to keep Sharon from telling me, but I found out when I bumped into her girlfriend at Starbucks. Kendra was shuffling around like a bag lady, in a daze, waiting for the jerk to come back and beat her up again. When I saw her at Christmas a month later, she'd heard her ex-boyfriend was limping. Apparently he'd been beaten up in an alley by a guy wearing a ski mask."

"No kidding?" Clarence said.

"Yeah. Her boyfriend bragged that he got in some good punches, even though the guy was 6'5" and used a bat on him. So he wasn't only a woman-beater; he was a liar."

"How do you know he was lying?"

"Because I'm only 6'1", he didn't land a single punch, and I didn't use a bat. It was just Fist One and Fist Two." I held them up.

Clarence started to laugh but looked at Jake and said, "Is he serious?"

Jake nodded.

For once, neither of them knew what to say.

At one thirty, Clarence and I set up camp at the Justice Center, where there's extra elbow room on Saturdays. That's good, because my workstation is too small for the two of us. Anything is. As Clarence sat writing on his notebook computer, I finished the final paperwork on the Lincoln Caldwell case.

Given Chief Lennox's threats, I'd half expected Clarence to be yanked from the case by now. Apparently Raylon Berkley wasn't willing to pull his fox out of the henhouse and was holding Lennox to his commitment.

"Look, Ollie…you found my sister's killer," Clarence said. "I owe you for that. I'm concerned what's going to happen if you pursue this theory that the killer's a detective."

"You want me to back off too?"

"Don't cops make it hard on other cops who…?"

"Who turn them in? Squeal like a pig? Guys believe the golden rule is *cops don't tell on cops*. Since nobody looks after cops—it's not like the *Tribune's* watching our back—it becomes 'we take care of our own.' If you don't, you're a traitor."

"Can't you explore other options first?"

"You think I want this? Nothing's worse than a dirty cop. And since when are you looking out for me?"

"My daddy liked you, Ollie. And he was a good judge of character."

"Still am, son. Still am." The man watching the unfolding events on earth smiled broadly and laughed loudly, reaching up to slap the back of the huge warrior beside him.

It suddenly clicked, seeming to come out of nowhere. I snapped my fingers at Clarence.

"My daughter took a class from Palatine. That's when I visited his classroom. With Kendra!"

"That just came to you?"

"It was one of my sporadic attempts to be involved in my daughter's life. I went to a couple of her classes. She made me promise not to show my gun or arrest anybody for smoking pot. It wasn't a warm and fuzzy day. Maybe that's why I'd pushed it to the back burner. It must have been…maybe ten years ago."

"Call her. Talk to her about the professor."

"There're hundreds of students who took his class recently."

"None of them would be your daughter."

"It's not that easy."

"You've got a reason to meet with your daughter. Take advantage of it."

"No way."

"If you found out where Andrea is, would you call her?"

"Of course."

"Well, you know where Kendra is. Call her."

I shook my head. Clarence grabbed my cell phone from the desk. "I'll call her. What's her number?"

"Forget it."

"You don't know her number, do you?"

"I don't know anybody's number. I speed dial."

"What's her speed dial number?"

When I didn't answer, Clarence pressed 1. "This retrieves messages? Oops. 911." He cancelled.

"If you don't give that back, you'll need 911." I reached for it, but he turned his back, which is roughly the size of Fenway's Green Monster.

"Who's 2? Homicide." Clarence was pressing each number and waiting to see the ID pop up before he stopped the call. "3 is…Lou's Diner. 4 is…Flying Pie Pizza? 5 is…Jake. I'll let him know he got beat by pizza. 6 is…Ollie, I'm touched. I made your top six."

"Only because the video store closed. You got bumped up. I plan to replace you with Krispy Kreme."

"Number 7 is…Kendra! How's that for detective work?"

"Give me my phone or I'll pistol-whip you."

"Is this Kendra?" Clarence asked.

I froze.

"Hi, this is Clarence Abernathy. You know, your dad's friend? From the *Trib*?" Clarence paused. "No, that's Jake Woods. I'm the other columnist. Yes, the big guy. There's something else about me you may have noticed. No? Really? I'm black. Yeah. Most people pick up on that." He laughed. "Anyway, can I ask you a question? Do you remember your philosophy prof from PSU?" He paused. "Dr. Palatine, right. You do? Good."

With a lightning move I snatched the phone out of his ham-bone mitt.

"Hi, sweetie, this is Dad. I apologize for Mr. Abernathy. He can be irritating."

"He sounds nice," she said.

"He's not."

"What do you want?"

"You had Philosophy with Dr. Palatine?"

"I took him for 101, then Ethics and another class. Uh…Logic, I think."

"Do you remember that day, maybe ten years ago, when I went with you to a couple classes?"

"I've tried to forget. Mom was going to come because it was a family visit day, but she got sick. She begged you to take her place. You didn't want to."

"It wasn't that I didn't want to, I just—"

"No, you didn't want to. More important things to do. Like always. You left my other class early."

"Wasn't that the all-women class?"

"Feminist Literature. There were two boys in the class. Anyway, you didn't like it. What's new? So, I hear Professor Palatine died."

"I'm investigating his case."

"Why am I not surprised? What do you want from me?"

"It's been a while since we talked."

"You didn't call me. Your friend Clarence called. About the investigation?"

"Well…sort of." I scowled at Clarence, who gave me a smug look. "Listen, since you had Palatine for three classes, would you mind talking to me about him? Telling me what you remember?"

"I'm busy. My job keeps me going."

"How about tonight?"

"You think I'm not doing something on a Saturday night?"

"Tomorrow?"

"Lots of people knew Dr. Palatine better than me. I was only at his house once."

"You were at his house?"

"He had groups of students over. There were maybe eight of us one night."

"Well…it's been a while since we've gotten together. Could I meet you at Lou's Diner?"

"Do they serve vegetarian meals?"

"Uh, I don't know. I don't think I've seen…Lou's has salads, right Clarence?"

"Their steak salad's great."

"Yeah, right," I said to Kendra. "There's a steak salad with bacon and—"

"Do you know what vegetarian means? I don't eat meat."

"Look, you could order the steak salad without the steak and the bacon, just with…you know, whatever's left. What about tomorrow night at seven?"

"It would have to be Monday night. Eight would be better."

"That's pretty late for dinner, isn't it?"

"No, it's not."

"Okay. Lou's is on Yamhill, near Fourth, halfway between Pizza Schmizza and Chipotle Mexican Grill, you know where—"

"I've seen it. It's near Pioneer Place, Saks Fifth Avenue, Gap, all the great shops."

"Right. There's those too."

"That diner looks…out of it."

"Lou's is cutting-edge retro. Nonsmoking. Has flowers and everything. You'll love it. See you Monday at eight?"

She hung up.

I looked at Clarence and his stupid smile.

"What?" I said. "You've never seen a guy ask his daughter to dinner? No Monday night football for me."

I pressed 3.

"Lou's Diner."

"Rory? Ollie. Listen, do you guys have vegetarian food?"

He chuckled. "This is a funny joke, Mr. Ollie."

"This isn't a joke. My daughter's a vegetarian."

"I am so sorry to hear that."

"Yeah, stuff happens. Anyway I'm meeting her there for dinner Monday night. Could you make her a steak salad without the steak and bacon? And with lots of extra tomatoes and green stuff?"

"Lettuce?"

"Yeah. Lettuce is good. How about cheese? Cheese isn't meat, is it?"

"I do not think so. I am Italian. I never run out of cheese. But some vegetarians don't eat dairy products, no?"

"That's scary. Anyway, be sure you don't run out of lettuce, okay?"

"We have many salads in a part of the menu you perhaps have never seen. All right, Mr. Ollie. I will reserve your booth and have some special flowers, *bellissimo*."

"*Grazie*," I said, hoping I didn't mispronounce it.

I was going to have dinner alone with my vegetarian daughter.

Why did it feel like I was walking the Green Mile?

SUNDAY, DECEMBER 1, 8:15 A.M.

While waiting for Mr. Coffee, I looked across the street at Kyle Hanson's. He'd told me he'd be gone this weekend—he always tells me when he's leaving town, figuring why not have a cop keep his eye on the place. I decided he wouldn't mind me borrowing his Sunday edition of the *Tribune*.

I searched for Abernathy's column. There it was: "Follow the Evidence." Sipping French roast, I read it:

Today December begins. Thanksgiving's behind us, Christmas ahead.

For many people the holidays are lonely. For those whose loved ones have been killed, the loneliness is magnified. I know that firsthand.

Every day I have an unusual opportunity—to observe the investigation of the murder of Professor William Palatine. Detective Ollie Chandler tells me I still can't divulge many specifics since they could compromise the investigation. Some of what's already been uncovered is fascinating. Soon I'll be able to tell you more. It'll be worth your wait.

Meanwhile, let me tell you what I've learned. First, investigative journalists and police detectives have a lot in common. It's their job to suspect people. And to catch those who've done wrong. We are, at our best, seekers of the truth.

Detective Chandler's motto is, "Examine the evidence. Then follow it wherever it leads." He takes nothing for granted. He looks at crumbs on a carpet that seem insignificant. He assumes the opposite. Until proven irrelevant, he treats everything as vital.

Detective Chandler knows that sometimes the evidence takes you where you don't want to go. He told me of a homicide detective who followed evidence that led to the conviction of the detective's little sister, now in her thirties. You can't let your preferences or wishful thinking blind you to the truth, Chandler says.

Since I can't yet release case details, today I want to relate this "follow the evidence" thread to Friday's CBS special, "Investigating the Life and Death of Jesus." Christmas and Easter season are the two times columnists are allowed to raise questions related to the Christian faith. You've read thoughts from *Tribune* writers who are Muslims and Jews. This reflects part of our commitment to multiculturalism and religious tolerance. In light of this, I'm sure readers will be tolerant of this column, even if they disagree with my conclusions.

Here's my thought: Each of us is called to act as a homicide detective to answer the question "Who killed Jesus and why?" There was a murder and a corpse—for three days anyway. Since the apostles died for believing Christ rose from the grave, it raises the question: Would they have died for what they knew to be false when they could save their lives simply by telling the truth? Would that make any sense at all?

Jesus said, "The truth will set you free." He also said, "I am the way, the truth and the life; no man comes to the Father but by me." Not a popular statement. One that helped get Him crucified. But then, Jesus wasn't a popularity-seeker. He was a truth-teller.

The homicide detective has much to teach us. Follow the truth wherever it leads you. Even if you don't like where it leads.

If the evidence suggests that Jesus wasn't who He claimed to be and that He didn't rise from the grave, then we should have the courage to follow the evidence, even if it means walking away from our churches.

On the other hand, it may lead to something even more radical. Perhaps you'll have to abandon your skepticism and accept the claims of Jesus. And—dare I say it—maybe you'll need to give church a chance.

In the wake of Thanksgiving, you may be wondering who you should be thanking and why. Think of Thanksgiving as a signpost pointing to Christmas, and you'll find the answer.

In the four weeks of this Christmas season, as we ponder the person whose birth splits history into BC and AD, let's examine the intriguing evidence concerning Jesus Christ—his birth, life, death, resurrection, and ascension. If we take the time to carefully examine the evidence, then—and only then—we can "follow it wherever it leads."

I put the paper down. My name was mentioned. My motto was the theme. Nothing bad was said about me. Shouldn't I feel flattered?

So why was that knot in my stomach?

Sunday afternoon Jake Woods invited me to go shooting with him in the Mount Hood forest near Zigzag, a fifty-minute drive from Portland. I felt like shooting something—anything that I could pretend was a professor who'd exploited girls.

I sat by Jake in his black Chevy Tahoe, which has approximately enough room for a rugby team.

I figured Jake would ambush me with something spiritual. So far it was just small talk: sports, weather, work, and guns. It was only a matter of time before he'd bring up Clarence's column.

Tired of waiting, I beat him to it. "Clarence thinks we should all take a closer look at Christianity. Okay, if this God of yours is really good and He's really in control, why does all this bad stuff happen? Murders and rapes and starvation and professors taking advantage of girls and child abuse in churches and all that?"

"That's the oldest and most common argument people use for not believing in God."

"You admit it?"

"I don't think it's a valid argument, but it's certainly understandable."

"How do you answer it?"

"Well, first I'd say it's God who gave us a moral compass. It's that sense of justice He put in you that causes you to raise this question in the first place."

"You're giving Him credit for my doubts?"

"In a way, yeah. God isn't afraid of us and our questions any more than a lion's afraid of a gerbil. Read the Bible—it raises the problem of evil again and again. You haven't come up with something new, Ollie. Prophets and psalmists ask why good people suffer and why evil people appear to get away with their crimes. Take Psalm 10. It starts off by asking, 'Why, O LORD, do you stand far off? Why do you hide yourself in times of trouble?' Then it talks about the evil man and how he prospers and imagines he's going to get away with it. But he won't."

Jake pointed to his glove box. "Grab the Bible in there and turn to Psalm 10. I want you to read a few verses."

I took it out. He told me to open to the middle, and sure enough I was in the Psalms. I found Psalm 10, and he told me to jump in and read a particular verse.

"'His mouth is full of curses and lies and threats; trouble and evil are under his tongue.' I've seen plenty of that," I said. "Next it says, 'He lies in wait near the villages; from ambush he murders the innocent, watching in secret for his victims.' Whoa. This guy's a killer."

"You'd be surprised what's in that book," Jake said. "Keep reading."

"'He lies in wait like a lion in cover; he lies in wait to catch the helpless; he catches the helpless and drags them off in his net. His victims are crushed, they collapse; they fall under his strength. He says to himself, "God has forgotten; he covers his face and never sees."'"

"Yeah, exactly," I said. "That's what bugs me. God doesn't seem to be paying attention to what's going on down here."

"Keep reading."

"'Arise, LORD! Lift up your hand, O God. Do not forget the helpless. Why does the wicked man revile God? Why does he say to himself, "He won't call me to account"?'"

I put Jake's Bible down on the floor, still open. It's a little creepy to have a Bible on your lap.

"People appear to get away with evil for a while," Jake said. "But one day it'll be different."

"What day would that be?"

"When they die and face God. And when Christ returns to set up His kingdom. When the final judgment comes."

"If there's a God, why doesn't He just bring that final judgment now?"

"Is that really what you want? God says He holds off judgment because He's merciful to us. He gives us time to repent. Are you ready to face judgment?"

I picked up the Bible and read again. "'But you, O God, do see trouble and grief; you consider it to take it in hand. The victim commits himself to you; you are the helper of the fatherless. Break the arm of the wicked and evil man; call him to account for his wickedness that would not be found out.' Wow, it actually says 'break his arm.' Now we're talking."

We turned left onto the old dirt road headed to our firing range. It was suddenly bumpy.

"There's one last verse, isn't there?" Jake asked. "Read it."

"It's bumpy," I said.

"Don't be a wimp."

"'The LORD is King for ever and ever; the nations will perish from his land. You hear, O LORD, the desire of the afflicted; you encourage them, and you listen to their cry, defending the fatherless and the oppressed, in order that man, who is of the earth, may terrify no more.'"

"Did you catch that?" Jake asked as I closed the Bible and put it back in the glove box, where it couldn't bite me. "God's saying He's going to make it all right one day. I heard Clarence's daddy say once, 'God doesn't settle all His accounts in October.' The judgment is coming—and if you're eager to see it come, you'd better remember that once it comes, it'll be final."

"I'm not going to sit on my hands waiting for God's justice to come."

"Who said anything about sitting on our hands? We're supposed to do what we can to bring justice now. But God's the ultimate judge. Justice doesn't always come here and now, but God promises it'll come there and then."

"There's a cop saying that goes, 'There's no *justice*. There's *just us*.' If we don't make things right, they won't be right. Get it? There's just us."

Jake pulled over by a fallen tree. He turned to me.

"I get it, but you're dead wrong. There's not just us. There's God."

"You really think God's doing His part?"

"Not as fast as you'd like or in the same way maybe, but, yes, I do. Absolutely. Would you be willing to wait an hour or a day or a week for a criminal to come to justice? Well, if God's willing to wait fifty years, your wait to you may be longer than God's wait to Him."

We stepped out of the Tahoe.

"What am I supposed to do, turn and look the other way while people are murdered? Pretend it's all right?"

"Of course it's not all right," Jake said, as we pulled out our guns. "The question is whether it's God's fault or ours."

"That's a lot of blame to lay on people."

"So you blame God instead? Brings us right back to where we started. Where do you get your sense of justice that makes you believe crime and suffering are so wrong?"

"I guess I was born with it."

We took out a dozen pop cans and placed them on stumps and low limbs.

As we loaded, Jake said, "You were born with a sense of justice? Well, then it didn't come from you, did it? It came from the One who made you. You believe evil is wrong because God knows it's wrong and made you to know it too. Ironic, isn't it?"

I lined up the first shot, calling the Mountain Dew can seventy feet away. I squeezed gently. *Boom.* I saw bark fly off a tree ten feet behind. I was two inches high and to the right.

"What's ironic?" I asked.

"You're using standards of justice that could only come from God in order to argue that there is no God."

Jake eyed the same target, then squeezed the trigger gently. The can went flying.

On our way home, after two hours serial-killing pop cans, the CTU headquarters phone rang, and since *24* wasn't on I checked my cell. Incoming call from Criminalist Detail.

"It's Phil Oref. You know Bates was assigned to process prints on the gun ballistics ID'd as the murder weapon? I volunteered to take it off his hands. Went ahead and ran the prints."

"No kidding? What'd you find?"

"Two index fingerprints. From angle and placement on the gun, I'm guessing they're both the left index finger."

"You ran the prints?"

"Naturally."

"Any match?"

"You won't believe it."

"Try me."

"The fingerprints on the gun belong to a Portland cop."

"Which one?" I asked, holding my breath.

"Detective Noel Barrows."

16

MONDAY, DECEMBER 2, 7:00 A.M.

I'D HAD A ROUGH time sleeping Sunday night. As I sat at my homicide desk, floating above the Portland gray, my usually iron stomach felt like I was deep-sea fishing in a typhoon. I was dreading two confrontations: first with Noel Barrows, accusing of him of murder; second, having dinner with Kendra.

Why did Kendra terrify me more than Noel? Part of me desperately wanted to see her. Part of me didn't—the same part that in Nam didn't relish walking through a field of claymore mines.

As for Noel, how would I approach him? And what would I tell his partner, Jack, my old friend, who's like a father to him?

Sometimes when your theory is confirmed, it makes you go back and question your theory. Noel Barrows? I'm not saying Noel's a Boy Scout but…*murder*? Not only Palatine, but Frederick?

When I'm worried, I putter. I pulled open my file drawer and looked at the murder mystery I started writing four years ago, *The Bacon and Cheese Murders*. It isn't Ross Macdonald. It isn't even Ronald McDonald. But at least I wrote it myself, as declared by the header with my name on every one of its 280 pages. Maybe eventually I'd finish it. Meanwhile, I have my real life murder mystery to solve.

I'd asked Manny and Clarence to meet me at 8:00 a.m. in the Justice Center. We claimed a small conference room. Manny and Clarence chose opposite corners of the ring, me in the referee position.

I told them about Noel's prints on the gun.

"You're saying Barrows killed Palatine?" Clarence asked.

"I'm withholding judgment."

"Let me get this straight," Manny said. "First, without any clear evidence, you conclude it's a homicide detective. Now, when you actually have hard evidence, you're backing off? His fingerprints are on a gun I found in a Dumpster two blocks from the murder, which ballistics says was the murder weapon?"

"I'm just keeping an open mind. I'll grant you Noel's not the sharpest knife in the drawer. As Cimma would say, he's no brainiac. But is he stupid enough to dump the gun in a nearby Dumpster?"

"What now?" Clarence asked. "Do you arrest Noel?"

"No. I want to squeeze out anything I can before he hears what we've got and gets his defenses up."

"You're still considering other suspects?" Clarence asked.

"I learned years ago never to decide a case is over until I'm certain of holes in alibis and solid grounds for arrest and conviction. We're not there yet."

"Did you check out those half dozen phone numbers written in the backs of the professor's books?" Clarence asked.

I shook my head. More important things on my mind. "I've got a job for Carp. Think she'd do it?"

"Maybe, if she'd get a photo exclusive if something comes of it."

"You journalists always have an angle."

"Yeah…and you detectives don't?"

An hour later, Noel entered homicide. I poured him coffee and we chatted.

"Heard you had a golf tournament this weekend." You know when you've pushed a man's passion button. He went on for five minutes about what a great tournament it was and how he shaved four strokes off last year and finished in the top ten.

"How's your investigation going?" Noel asked.

I shrugged. "The usual. Panning for gold. You've looked at the reports, haven't you?"

"A little. Pretty busy with our own cases."

"The professor was arrogant, don't you think?"

"Yeah," Noel said, grinning. "A phone message quoting the philosopher of the week? Gimme a break."

I leaned against the wall. "Hey, remember when you came to the professor's house the day after the murder? When you pointed to the pictures on the mantel and noticed something was wrong?"

"Yeah."

"Well, that missing picture idea was really helpful. What exactly was it you kept saying? Was it 'something's funny'?"

"Something's fishy."

"Yeah. Something's fishy." I slapped him on the shoulder. "Thanks again, Noel."

"Okay…you're welcome."

I walked back to my workstation, where I reached in my pocket and turned off the recorder.

↔

"I need you to run a voice analysis," I said to Criminalist Mike Bates, handing him an envelope marked "Voice Needing Identification," 911 recording inside. "But this time I want results pronto."

"You have to give me a voice to compare it to. That's how the sound spectrograph works."

I handed him a second envelope marked "Suspect's Voice."

"Preferably using some of the same words."

"Done," I said.

"Whose voice is the one I'm comparing?"

"I'd rather not say. Just tell me if it's a match."

"I can tell you if it's a positive or probable identification, or if it's a positive or probable elimination. But we're really backed up."

"You're *always* backed up. It's important."

"It's *always* important."

"Look, I waited a week for prints on that Taurus 9 mil before Phil got me results. I can't wait a week for this. I need it tomorrow."

After a drive in pounding rain, Clarence and I ran through the parking lot at Lou's. We hung his overcoat and my trench coat and fedora to drip dry beside our booth, next to the jukebox. I put in a quarter and pressed "I Get Around," "Eve of Destruction," and "A World Without Love." Clarence put in his own quarter and made his selections more carefully.

Jake arrived two minutes after Clarence and I were both seated. "Weren't we just here a few days ago?" he asked. "I love you guys and I love Lou's, but this is going to stretch my waistline."

Rory walked eagerly to our table. "Welcome to my friends. Mr. Ollie, you return tonight? Dinner with your daughter?"

"Yeah. Eight o'clock. You'll have vegetables, right?"

"Many vegetables. Abundant lettuce. And fine pastas, without meat."

My body was at that booth, but my mind was on Noel.

"So, guys, did we do our reading?" Jake referred to *Mere Christianity*, a book by C. S. Lewis that he's been trying to get me to read for years. He'd assigned a portion to read, but I don't take well to assignments.

"Been a little busy," I said. "Solving murders and all that."

"*Mere Christianity*'s opened my eyes."

"So you've said…again and again."

"You could shut me up by reading it."

"If I thought it would work, I'd do it."

"You read detective novels. It's shorter than most of them."

"But there's a big difference," I said. "I *want* to read those novels. I'm a believer in free choice. The right to read what I want."

"Glad to hear you believe in free choice. I hope that means you're no longer blaming God for giving it to us."

"You're becoming a nag, Jake."

"Can't friends try to influence each other when they think it's in their best interests?"

"Say what you want, I'm not reading that book."

"Why? Afraid it might make sense? As a detective, I'd think you'd want to examine the evidence. Didn't you read Clarence's article?"

"Oh, yeah," I said, looking at Abernathy. "Quoting me to encourage people to investigate Jesus? You weren't trying to send me a message, were you?"

"No different than the message I've been trying to send you for years."

"Hey, I've read books. I read *The Da Vinci Code*."

They both laughed.

"I know you didn't like it, but why laugh?"

"Because," Clarence said, "it's full of historical errors and false claims that any junior high kid could refute after spending twenty minutes checking facts on Google."

"Heard of G. K. Chesterton?" Jake asked. "He said that when people stop believing in God, they'll believe in anything."

"Heard of W. C. Fields?" I asked. "He said, 'Everyone must believe in something; I believe I'll have another beer.'"

"Chesterton's point was that when you reject the truth, you become gullible. You lose your common sense. Somebody writes a book like *The Da Vinci Code*, and since people don't know history or the Bible and haven't bothered to investigate the facts, they end up believing stuff that's so ridiculous it's embarrassing."

"You guys think you know it all." I pushed back my empty cup.

"I'm well aware of how little I know," Jake said. "That's why I choose to trust what God has said in the Bible rather than trust myself."

"Does it occur to you how judgmental it is to think you're going to heaven and other people are going to hell?"

"I'm just telling you what Jesus said. He talked about hell more than anyone else, and I think He knew what He was talking about. He doesn't want us to go there. He died and rose so we wouldn't have to go there."

Soon we were munching on cheeseburgers. Clarence's selections were playing, including Chuck Berry wailing, "No Particular Place to Go."

"Okay, guys, this time I've got something for you to read." I pulled it out of my coat pocket. "It's by Bertrand Russell. It's called *Why I Am Not a Christian.*"

"You got that from the professor's," Clarence said, like I'd firebombed a church.

"I'm borrowing it," I said. "The professor won't be needing it."

"I'm afraid by now he realizes the flaws in that book," Jake said.

"It's just one essay by that title," I said, holding it up. "But there's lots of stuff in the other essays you wouldn't like either. So here's my deal. You read this; then I'll read your *Mere Christianity.*"

"Great," Jake said. "I'll pick up copies for me and Clarence; then we can all discuss it." Clarence nodded. Jake reached his right hand across the table and shook mine. "After we're done, you'll read *Mere Christianity* and we'll talk about it. It's a deal."

"You're really going to read this?" My voice cracked, like a fifteen-year-old's.

"I look forward to it."

"But it's not…"

"Not what?"

"Not…Christian."

"No kidding?" Jake said. "A book called *Why I Am Not a Christian* that's not Christian? Man, I feel blindsided. You should have warned me."

"I didn't think you'd want to read it."

"This book doesn't scare me a bit. The Bible always holds up to attacks. Besides, I promised to read it. And if a man's word and his handshake can't be depended on, well…"

"Speaking of the Bible," I said around a mouthful of burger, looking at Clarence, "remember that confession on the professor's computer screen said something about millstones? You said it was from Jesus."

"But you decided Palatine didn't write it," Clarence said.

"He was dying or dead when it was typed. But here's my point: Isn't that the sort of thing *you* guys would say? I mean, you're always quoting Bible verses."

"You think we killed the professor?" Jake asked, smiling.

"No, but it seems obvious the killer wrote it. And if he did, that means the killer was a Bible quoter. What do you think about that?"

I liked the bewildered expressions on their faces. I was grinning when I swallowed a large gulp of my blackberry shake. It gave me a brain freeze, but it was worth it.

When Jack Glissan left homicide at 1:40 p.m., I went to Noel Barrows's workstation and said, "We need to talk—now." I escorted Noel into the conference room, where Manny and Clarence were already waiting in uncomfortable silence.

"Hi, guys," Noel said. "What's up?"

I started on the Seahawks and Rams. He said he was pumped about the big Hurricanes and Gators matchup next Saturday.

I groped for more small talk. "I saw you coming out of the Starbucks by Pioneer Square Saturday morning, didn't I? I was at Lou's Diner. Must have been heading off for your tournament, huh?"

He shrugged. "Are you accusing me of something?"

"Why would I accuse you? It's not a crime to go to Starbucks."

"Why am I here?"

"Okay," I said. "There's no easy way to ask this. Where were you between ten thirty and midnight Wednesday, November 20?"

He studied my face, then Manny's and Clarence's. "Is this a joke? Did Jack put you up to this?"

"It's no joke. Where were you?"

"That was like…two weeks ago."

"Twelve days."

"Night before Thanksgiving?"

"Seven nights before."

He looked down and started mumbling and moving his fingers, apparently trying to sort out what he'd done the last twelve days and what fell on what night.

"That Monday night I was at Jack's for football—same every week. Going over there tonight. Most nights I watch the golf channel pretty late. I guess that Wednesday could have been one of them."

"Anybody see you?"

"I have an apartment. People walk the hallways, but I don't think I came out, so they wouldn't have seen me. No roommate."

"Too bad." I reached into my briefcase and pulled out the gun in its evidence bag. "Ever seen this?"

He looked it over. "Sure, I've seen them. Looks like this one's been around the block."

"It's a Taurus Millennium Pro, 9 mm," I said. "Have you seen this *particular* gun?"

"I don't think so. Why?"

"Because it's got your fingerprints on it."

A long awkward silence. "I've taken guns away from lots of people. I guess they could have my prints on them."

"This gun's special. It was used to kill Professor Palatine."

"And my prints are on it?"

"Yeah."

"How's that possible?"

"We were hoping you could tell us, Noel."

Suddenly the conference room door flew open. I stood, looking at the red face of Jack Glissan.

"What's going on here?"

"I'm having a private interview with Noel."

"Private? With Domast? And Abernathy?"

"You read the memo. I have to include him."

"What's going on, Ollie?" Jack asked. "I heard the murder weapon has prints."

"Word gets around."

"You're not accusing Noel?"

"His fingerprints are on the gun. It was found in a Dump—"

"I don't care if it was found under his pillow. He didn't do it!"

"Were you with him between, say, 10:45 and 11:45 November 20?"

"No, but I saw him at 2:00 a.m. at our murder scene that same night."

"Two and a half hours after Palatine's murder? That doesn't help." I turned to Noel, whose usually tan face was two shades lighter. "Where were you?"

"I told you. Home. Alone. We were on call, right? I must have gone to bed early."

"I'll ask you again: Can anyone confirm your alibi?"

Noel shook his head.

"Hold on," Jack said. "A week ago Wednesday night? I went out that night and dropped your golf DVD by your place. Around 11:15."

Noel stared at him blankly.

"Don't try it, Jack," I said.

"You'd gone to bed early. Remember, Noel?"

Noel's chin dropped. He looked at Jack for his next move.

"I dropped by because you're usually up till midnight. I figured you were gone. So before I got the key from…you know, where you hide it…I rang the bell. And you came to the door. Said I was sorry for waking you up. That's how it happened."

"Stop it," I said. "You're just going to make it worse. Noel said no one saw him home. No alibi."

"Don't you remember, Noel?" Jack pleaded.

Noel raised his hand. "Jack's telling the truth. That's how it happened."

Jack smiled. I looked back and forth between them.

"Except it was on Tuesday night," Noel said. "I'd been at Jack and Linda's. I really did leave Jack the golf DVD. I went to bed early, and he dropped it by and rang the bell, just like he said. Except it wasn't Wednesday night, it was Tuesday."

Jack's and my jaw dropped in unison.

"Jack was telling the truth." Noel turned to Jack, with eyes that said "let it go." "You just got the night wrong."

Jack started to argue. But neither Noel nor I was going to let him win.

I rushed in the door at Lou's Diner, fourteen minutes late. Kendra was in our booth. On the table sat a beautiful arrangement of a dozen red roses, baby's breath and all.

"Sorry I'm late," I told her. "The traffic was—"

She waved her hand, giving me that look that said she'd heard it all before.

"You look nice," I said. She'd put on weight, but so had I. Pointing to her silver chain necklace, I said, "I like that."

"Mom gave it to me for my high school graduation," she said, in a way that sounded like I'd never given her anything. "I wouldn't expect you to remember."

I settled in on my side of the booth. "Been waiting long?"

"Yes," she said. "The man says they have a vegetable plate."

"Good. Vegetable plates are always good."

Silence.

"I'd hoped you'd join me for Thanksgiving," I said, not mentioning that she'd never responded to my messages.

"With all those people? I don't think so."

"We could have eaten at my place. Just you and me and Mulch."

She didn't look up from the menu.

Rory came to take our order. "It is so nice to meet your daughter, Mr. Ollie. She told me she'd like the vegetable plate. Will you have the usual?"

"The usual" means three different things at Lou's, depending on time of day. My breakfast usual is a western omelet and hash browns with a giant buttermilk pancake. My lunch usual is a cheeseburger and fries or onion rings. My dinner usual is New York steak with a baked potato and all the trimmings. I pictured large hunks of medium rare meat in clear view of the vegetable plate. It didn't seem wise.

"I've been having so many vegetable plates, I'm thinking tonight I'll go with a steak *salad*," I said. "With Thousand Island."

Rory looked at me with big sympathetic eyes, but he nodded, took the menus, and left.

The next fifteen minutes were like pulling teeth. I couldn't get more than a sentence at a time from Kendra. She didn't ask me anything. The silence between my questions kept getting longer.

"How about those Seahawks?" I asked.

Nothing.

I pulled out a quarter and asked her if she had any favorite oldies. "Nope." So I chose a few of Sharon's: "I Got You Babe," "Never My Love," and "Cherish." I saw "Honey" by Bobby Goldsboro, but I knew where to draw the line. Still, Kendra didn't appear impressed.

Finally, Rory came with the meal. Kendra looked at her vegetable plate and seemed to reluctantly approve. Then she looked at my steak salad.

"How can you eat that?" she asked.

"What? Thousand Island?"

"Animal flesh."

"I'm having a steak salad because it's the closest I can get to a compromise between what I'd like to eat and what you'd like me to eat. I thought you'd appreciate the lettuce and tomatoes. Look, cucumbers and olives and these little…jobbers. They're vegetables, aren't they? I thought you'd approve."

"It's not just what we eat. It's what we *don't* eat. You wouldn't eat your dog, would you?"

"*Mulch*?" I dropped my fork. I couldn't believe the words had come out of my daughter's mouth.

"Some societies eat dogs," she said. "That doesn't make it right, does it?"

"No."

"Then why do you think it's okay to eat cows?"

"Well, for one thing…they're a lot bigger."

"So it's okay to eat big dogs?"

"Could we stop talking about eating dogs?"

"What's the difference?"

"Dogs are like people. Cows are like…pheasants, except not so gamy. And they don't fly. I mean the aerodynamics…just getting airborne would—"

"I don't think it's right to eat animals."

"Sweetheart, look, you can eat whatever you want. But—and this is just me, okay—I didn't fight my way to the top of the food chain just to become a vegetarian."

She scowled. "You need to get more exercise too."

"I run around all day."

"Don't they have mandatory fitness programs for cops? They should. If you don't watch it, you're going to cut ten or twenty years off your life."

Why would that matter to you?

We ate in silence. She finished her vegetables. I polished off my cow.

Since all attempts at bonding had failed, I took a deep breath and said, "About my investigation—can I ask you a question?"

"You and your investigations."

"If I were Ichiro, would you say, 'You and your baseball'?"

"You're no Ichiro."

"But what I do isn't worthless. It saves lives, you know. I mean human lives. Not cows."

"You didn't talk with me when I was growing up," she said.

"We talked more than you remember."

"There were things I'd ask you about, and you'd never tell me. Personal things, family things. I had to go to Mom to find out. You'd always change the subject. I'd ask you about Grandpa. Nothing. I'd ask you about my br—"

"You were in Professor Palatine's class?"

"Yes."

"Did he ever make a move on you?"

"A *move*?"

"Did he get fresh with you?"

"Dad, you're so out of it."

"Just pretend I'm retro. Retro's cool, right?"

She shook her head at me, but I saw a slight smile.

"So…did Dr. Palatine ever show a romantic interest in you?"

"Well, *this* is certainly awkward."

"You said we never talked about personal things. I'm making up for it."

"Well, it's personal, I'll give you that." Her smile evaporated. "No. He only went after the pretty girls."

"You're a pretty girl."

"I mean the *really* pretty girls."

I would have hated Palatine for coming on to my daughter. Now I hated him for not considering her pretty enough. The truth is, my daughter's history with men is…not so good. Her relationships have been many, and with the shelf life of yogurt.

"I didn't mean to imply you were that kind of girl," I said, then bit my lip.

"I need to be going."

"Okay."

She sat still. Finally I stood. I stepped toward her and put my hand on her shoulder, not close enough for her to bite it.

"Go home," she said, voice strained. "I'll be leaving in a few minutes. I just feel a little dizzy."

"Need help?"

"Just leave, would you?"

"I'll take you to your car. No, I'll drive you home."

"You're so stubborn."

"Your mom used to say we were the two most stubborn people she knew."

Finally, Kendra eased herself out of the booth, standing awkwardly. That's when I realized my daughter was pregnant.

"Of all the facts presented to us, we had to pick just those which we deemed to be essential, and then piece them together in their order, so as to reconstruct this very remarkable chain of events."
SHERLOCK HOLMES, *THE NAVAL TREATY*

TUESDAY, DECEMBER 3, 8:00 A.M.

"DID YOU SEE THIS?" Kim Suda pushed the newspaper in front of my face, at my desk.

I was staring at a photograph of Professor William Palatine, on his back, on the floor, noose around his neck. I checked the paper's date. December 3: today.

"This is a joke, right? Somebody printed one of those dummies. This can't be the real *Tribune*."

"I bought it off a newsstand."

I read the article, written by Mike Button. Among other things, he said, "An anonymous source inside the Portland Police revealed that the leading suspect in the Palatine murder investigation is a street person. He'll likely be arrested within the week."

I punched 6 for Abernathy. No answer. I declined leaving a message lest it be used against me at my murder trial.

I stewed in my juices fifteen minutes, skulking back and forth in homicide, eyes on the glass entrance. Finally, I saw Abernathy. I locked my laser stare on him when he was still twenty feet away.

"You're off this case, Abernathy. It's over!"

A half dozen heads turned our way, secretaries to detectives.

"First I knew of this is when Geneva showed me the paper this morning."

"You expect me to believe that?"

"It's the truth." He raised his right catcher's mitt.

"Your friend Carpenter gave those photos to someone."

"They belong to the *Trib*, not Carp. She's a pro, our best photojournalist. She's turned down offers from the *LA Times* and *Chicago Tribune*. She'd never pull a stunt like this. She says the photos were on file, ready to go in case we got clearance."

"Never happened."

"I know that. Carp's as mad as you and I are. Somebody got hold of them and took it to print."

"Who?"

"Button refuses to identify his source." Clarence's face looked as hot as mine felt. "He's willing to be a first amendment martyr. I think he wants to go to jail. Winston doesn't understand how it got through editorial without coming to him. I told Button he'd be fired. Winston says they're discussing it on the upper levels. Berkley's involved."

"Too late for that, isn't it?"

"I know it's false about the street person, but it's better than spilling the truth, isn't it? Does it really compromise the investigation?"

"Confidential crime scene information in public hands? Of course it compromises the investigation. Until now, if we interview suspects and they make an unguarded comment about the noose around the neck or the skin color or body position, it'd be enough to finger them. Now their only mistake—and I'll grant you it's a big one—is reading the *Tribune*."

"Look, I'm sorry. But I didn't do it. And it wasn't just photos either. It was information, some accurate, some false, like the street person part. It wasn't from you, me, or Carp. Could it have come from Manny?"

Clarence didn't notice Manny had just come up behind him, newspaper in hand.

"From me? I don't work for the *Tribune*, hotshot."

"You didn't leak anything?" I asked Manny.

He gave me his thousand-yard stare, the one that would make Clint Eastwood melt like a salted slug. Manny redirected his stare to Clarence, then threw the newspaper on the floor in front of him. He stepped on it, grinding his heel into it.

My sentiments exactly.

"I heard the scuttlebutt about Noel Barrows," Officer Taylor Burchatz said over the phone at my workstation. "For what it's worth, I saw him the night of the Palatine murder."

"Where?"

"At the Do Drop Inn, 59th and Foster."

"You're sure it was Barrows?"

"Absolutely. It's not like we're friends, but I know him well enough to recognize him."

"What time did you see him?"

"I came at nine thirty. Left late, close to midnight. He was there the whole time."

"You're sure it was Wednesday—week before last?"

"Yeah."

"Nice try. Everybody wants to give Noel an alibi."

"You calling me a liar?"

"Look, Noel says he was home alone that night. What kind of a half-wit would withhold his alibi for murder?"

"All I know is, I saw him."

"Who else was there?"

"Bartender's Barry. He might remember. There were probably a half dozen guys hanging around him. I know a few first names—Stu, Steve, Alan."

"Exactly when did you leave?"

"After sports. I saw highlights of the Blazer game."

"Sports is over about 11:25. You're saying Noel was still there?"

"Yeah."

"This isn't a put-on? If you've talked to Barry and got him to go along with this, we're talking perjury, obstruction of justice, and—"

"I don't know what your deal is, Chandler. I'm calling because I thought maybe you wouldn't want to go after an innocent man. An innocent cop. Figured I should speak up. Maybe you want him to go down? That it? Maybe I should call a lieutenant or captain or somebody who wants to hear the truth?"

"Calm down," I said. "I'll call Barry now and check it out. If it's true, I owe you an apology."

Ninety minutes later, Manny, Clarence, and I sat at the conference table, door closed. Noel and Jack walked in together.

"Why are you here?" I asked Jack.

"Because I'm Noel's partner. And friend."

"But you're not his lawyer. Let him talk, okay? Don't put words in his mouth. Not like last time. Got it?"

Jack's face flushed, but he nodded.

"I've been doing this many years," I said to Noel. "I've told countless suspects that they're lying about their alibi, and that's what I'm going to tell you."

"Hold on, Ollie," Jack said. "You can't just—"

"Shut up and let me finish, Jack." I looked at Noel. "But until now I've never once sat down with a murder suspect and accused him of lying about *not* having an alibi."

"What are you talking about?" Jack said.

I stepped between Jack and Noel to get Noel's full attention. "I got a call from an Officer Burchatz. He saw you that night at the Do Drop Inn."

Noel's face twitched. His hands shook.

"He said you were still there when he left, near midnight."

"Maybe he's got the wrong night," Noel said.

"No. I talked with Barry, the bartender. He says it must have been midnight when you left. You were there with a half dozen guys. He gave me names. I already called Stu, Steve, and Alan. These guys aren't Phi Beta Brilliant, but all three confirm you were there."

Jack looked at Noel. "Is it true?"

Noel looked like a junior high boy who'd been caught red-handed.

"Did I miss something," I said, "or was your bacon just saved? Why in the ever-lovin' world would you deny a murder alibi?"

Noel stood, face flushed, hands darting. "Look, we were the up team, for crying out loud. You know department policy. You're not supposed to be drinking when you're on call!"

"It's not just department policy," Jack said. "It's my policy. No exceptions. Ever."

"I know," Noel said. "But we'd been on call for a week. I figured, what are the chances of somebody getting murdered that night? So I just…went to the Do Drop."

"Let me get this straight," I said. "You have this alibi, with multiple witnesses, proving you couldn't have committed a murder for which there's evidence against you. And you wouldn't tell us this because…Jack would be disappointed you'd had a few drinks?"

"He always tells me to stay off the drinks and go to bed early," Noel said. "I…didn't want to admit it."

"So now you're 'admitting' that you were at the Do Drop Inn between 10:45 and 11:45?"

"No," he said.

"You weren't?"

"It was more like between 9:00 and 12:15. I guess I got home around twelve thirty."

"Actually, Noel, between 9:00 and 12:15 *includes* between 10:45 and 11:45. Jack will explain it to you." I've spent days trying to wring the truth out of people, but this was ridiculous. "Write down the names of guys there that night." I handed him my pad and a pen.

He jotted down five names, two of which were new. Blushing, he handed it back to me.

Jack threw his arms around Noel. "Congratulations, bud. You've got yourself an alibi!"

Noel smiled sheepishly.

"But," Jack said, "if you ever go to a bar again when we're on call, I'll kill you myself!"

I left the conference room, head aching and thinking about that other little item. Noel's fingerprints were still on the murder weapon.

I called Phil, asking how a man with an ironclad alibi could have his fingerprints on the murder weapon, even though he swears he didn't touch it. He couldn't explain it but said he'd get back to me.

For an hour at my desk, I examined with a magnifying glass a hundred of the professor's photos we'd bagged from his house, looking for a particular camera angle. I couldn't find what I was looking for.

I called Manny, who rarely hangs around precinct. "I want you to go over our list of the professor's family and friends and colleagues. Call and ask if they have pictures taken at the professor's house, anytime in the last three years. If they do, I want to borrow them. We'll make copies and return them."

One thing I like about Manny is that he seldom asks why. Within an hour, he called back. He'd already talked with three people who had pictures taken at the professor's. The professor's sister-in-law, easier to get hold of than her doctor husband, said she had a couple dozen.

There were a number of things I needed to do, but I lacked manpower. I needed to recruit some.

I called Paul Anderson, ex-skater and beat cop and now larceny detective. He knows the streets better than anybody. He said he and his partner were on surveillance, but I was welcome to join them. I got his location, grabbed Clarence, and headed for my car.

When Clarence and I approached, Paul was sitting in an unmarked car with his partner, Gerald Griffin. I knocked on their passenger-side back door. After Griffin lowered his hardware, we crawled into the backseat, and I gave them a peace offering…a box of Krispy Kremes.

As Anderson smacked his lips on a warm glazed, I said, "You wouldn't have a half day to spare for an old friend who's an underresourced homicide detective?"

"Wish I did, Ollie. If there were a moratorium on theft, I'd be glad to help."

"Who you watching?'

"Clancy Baines, the guy in the navy blue sweatshirt." He pointed. "Word is he robbed the liquor store on Twelfth and made away with a sackful of bills. Fifteen hundred dollars—way more than they should've had in the till. We're sure the money's in his room. Positive he's behind a dozen other robberies. We take this dude and crime plummets."

"Insufficient grounds for a search warrant?"

"And he knows it," Griffin said.

"He's a drug dealer too," Paul said. "We're hoping to see him sell so we can get a warrant. But he's not going to deal in front of us. He just steps around a corner. He's got his soldiers keeping their eyes out. They know exactly where we are." He nodded toward two teenage boys leaning against the wall ten feet away, pretending not to look at us.

"So," Griffin said, "he's not only robbing the community; he's robbing our time."

"If I get him for you in the next twenty minutes," I said, "would you give me four hours each?"

"You kidding? We'd give you a whole day each. But how—"

"Two entrances to the apartments, front and back?"

"Yeah, but—"

"Okay, after we step out of the car, give us five minutes. Then you get out and stretch. I'll call your cell. Answer, sound excited, say you'll be there right away, and lay rubber when you take off. Then circle the block and wait out of sight. In ten minutes or so, Clancy Baines will be running out the front door, carrying the money."

"What are you talking about?" Griffin asked. "Why would—?"

"When you see the bag or box or whatever, you'll have grounds for believing it's the money and you can look at it. Then you take him in. I'll call you later about your indentured servitude."

"Come on, Ollie, you can't possibly—"

"Just do it," I said.

Clarence and I went to the back of the apartments. He wanted an explanation, but I told him, "Just follow my taillights, okay? I need you right here at the back door. You got a good look at Clancy Baines? He'll be carrying something in his hand. Make a threatening move toward him."

"What do you mean?"

"Just plant your body in front of him, that's all. One look at you will probably be enough. Make it so his only other option is the front door."

"But why—"

"Just do it, okay?"

He sighed and nodded.

I peeked around the corner and saw Anderson outside his car, the two street soldiers within earshot. I punched his number and watched him answer. I said, "There's a bank robbery, kidnapping, assault, rioting, terrorist activity, pipe bombs, and a hijacking at the county courthouse! We need you here now! Pronto! Get going, you lazy no-good cop! Peel rubber! And don't stop for donuts!"

I disconnected and heard his excited voice from the street. He might have over-acted, but when the tires screeched, everybody noticed. He was gone.

I waited, giving Anderson and Griffin time to park and sneak back on foot. I called to make sure they were in position. Anderson said they were lurking in the shadows, with a clear view.

"Ready?" I asked Clarence.

I grabbed handfuls of newspaper that had blown up against the apartment, stepped in the back door, found a metal garbage can in the hallway, then pushed it into a tiled alcove. I put in about half the day's *Tribune*, flicked a BIC lighter I keep in my trench coat, and watched the smoke rise. No one was in the hall, so I let the smoke build. The alarm didn't trigger, so I pulled the alarm on the wall.

This alarm was…well, alarming. Really loud. I yelled, "Fire!" and the manager yelled, "Fire!" and pretty soon a dozen people were yelling, "Fire!" Within ten seconds residents were rushing out their doors. Some took longer, getting kids, pets, pictures, and iPods. Several ran *into* the building, past the manager who was waving everyone out. Clancy Baines rushed in, turned the corner, right through the smoke, and ran up the stairs, three at a time.

Within a minute, Baines was back down the stairs, a bulging Nike gym bag in hand. He ran pell-mell toward the back of the building, where he was met by the hulking frame of Clarence Abernathy. Baines pivoted and ran out the front door, clutching that gym bag like it held ten grand.

I stepped to the front door and watched Baines run into the street, where Anderson and Griffin grabbed him. I watched Anderson zip open the bag and smile broadly. Griffin was talking to Baines while he handcuffed him.

I went to the manager and identified myself as a cop. "The fire's in that garbage can," I said, pointing. Fifteen seconds later he had a fire extinguisher on it, and within a few minutes the smoke was clearing.

I walked out the back to Clarence. "Who says the *Tribune* is worthless? It makes first-class smoke. A man's brought to justice, and we've got a day's work each from two grateful cops."

We walked to my car. Clarence turned back to gaze at the smoky apartment and then at me. We heard the sirens of the approaching fire truck, and when it flashed past, I pulled out and headed to Baja Fresh for lunch. A Steak Burrito Ultimo, with four containers of those chopped tomatoes, was callin' my name.

As I drove, Abernathy looked back at the scene and a couple of times opened his mouth like a goldfish. In a way unusual for journalists, he didn't know what to say.

*"It is fortunate for this community that I am
not a criminal."*
SHERLOCK HOLMES, *THE ADVENTURE OF THE BRUCE-
PARTINGTON PLANS*

TUESDAY, DECEMBER 3, 1:45 P.M.

ON OUR WAY BACK to the Justice Center from the fire and Baja Fresh, Phil Oref
called.

"You're not going to believe this. First, those *are* the fingerprints of Noel
Barrows on the murder weapon."

"So what am I not going to believe?"

"I studied the prints with a close-up lens. I found traces of plastic."

"So?"

"Somebody took the detective's fingerprint, made a plastic mold, then pressed
it down to leave Barrows's prints. In other words, the prints are his, but he never
touched the gun. The prints were planted."

"You're certain?"

"I found definite traces of the kind of moldable plastic you can duplicate a
print from. It's exactly what I'd use if I were framing somebody."

"I've heard that could be done. But it's rare, isn't it?"

"Extremely. I've never seen it. I've played with doing it myself, to see how hard
it would be. But I never would've looked for it if you hadn't told me about the
alibi. You have to look for it to see it. And you'd really need to know what you're
doing to plant it."

"Who would know how to do that kind of thing?"

"People like me. Or you, if you did your homework."

"Can you show me how it's done?"

"Sure. I'll have to pick up a couple of things. Meet me in my office at four."

I set up a five o'clock appointment with Noel Barrows, who wanted to know why.
I told him I might have good news for him, but we'd have to see.

At 2:40 I got a call from the security desk. "Someone from the *Tribune* is asking to see you."

"If his name's Mike Button, have him shot and handcuffed; then dump him on my desk."

"It's a she. Name's Lynn Carpenter."

"I'm on my way." I sucked in my gut and greeted her at the door. "Sit down," I gestured to the empty table by the coffee and donuts, twelve feet from the entrance. Everybody was busy, and it offered more privacy than my workstation.

"What a view," she said, gazing down at the city below.

"Only the best for my special guests," I said, charmer that I am. "To what do I owe the pleasure of your company?" They say stuff like that in the movies.

"I'm really bugged by that photo in the *Trib*." She pulled out an eight-by-ten enlargement of the infamous picture.

"I was slightly bugged by that myself."

"Somebody got hold of a digital photo file and gave it to Button. He won't tell who. To tell you the truth, I figured they knew my password and got into my computer files at the *Trib*. But they didn't."

"How do you know?"

"Because I went through every single picture I took. There's no match. Same subject matter, naturally, but always the angle's slightly off or the flash shadows next to the corpse aren't quite long enough. There's even something on the ground in the picture that wasn't there when I took mine." She pointed to a rectangular object near Palatine's right leg. "Looks like one of those bags the criminalists carry."

"Yeah. An evidence bag."

"But my point is, I didn't take this picture."

"You're certain?" I asked.

"Positive. But you and I and the ME were the only ones taking pictures, right?"

"I wonder who has access to Carlton Hatch's photos?"

"Look," Carp said, "why not get me all your photo files, and the ME's? I'll go through them one by one and make the match. I'll be able to tell you exactly which photo and who took it."

"You'd do that?"

"I can't have the *Trib* pay me for it, but I'll do it on my own time."

"I'll call Hatch and get his photos. I'll give you mine on a thumb drive right now—they're on my laptop. But I took a few hundred. That's tons of work...are you sure?"

"It's really bugging me," she said. "Besides, I figure I'll get a pizza or two out of it."

"Or three," I said. "Double pepperoni, double cheese."

She smiled at me with her eyes.

Man. Things were rollin'.

↔

At four o'clock, an animated Phil Oref welcomed us into an evidence lab. He was happy to see Clarence, who might make him famous once he got cleared to tell the story in the *Trib*. I'd invited Carp to join us, so Phil might see his picture in the paper too.

"Faking a fingerprint 101. Here's how it works." Phil rubbed his hands together. "First you need an original. Latent fingerprints are just body sweat and fat, oil left on items you touch—glasses, doorknobs, ceramic coffee mugs." He pointed to a glass of water. "Hand me that."

Clarence grabbed the glass and passed it to Phil, who wore gloves, and held it up to the overhead light.

"You've just given me your thumbprint, index finger, and a partial of your middle. Let's use the index finger. I sprinkle it with colored powder, which sticks to the oil, and there you see a clear print."

Sure enough, there it was.

"You can spread the powder with a thin brush, but not necessary in this case. You can also use cyanoacrylate, the main ingredient in superglue. It reacts with the fat residue; then it forms this solid white substance. See?

"You can use black tape to grab the substance. You scan it or photograph it with a digital camera."

He demonstrated, then took a few close-ups and downloaded them.

"Once it's digitized, you can do graphic refurbishment to brush up the print's image." He pointed at an enlargement of the fingerprint on the wide-screen monitor. He cleaned up a smeared print line. "The goal is to get an exact image of the fingerprint. Then you can use a standard laser printer to print it out on a transparency slide."

He made the print, pointed, and said, "The printer toner forms a relief." He took us through two more steps involving wood glue, glycerin, and the creation of the dummy print. Then he said, "Now, you pull it off the foil and cut it to finger size. And use this theatrical glue to attach the dummy to your finger."

As Carp took pictures, Phil held up his right hand with the dummy fingerprint on his index finger, rubbed it on his left palm, then picked up a coffee mug from the desk. "And now, with the help of a little body oil, everything I touch leaves the fingerprint of Clarence Abernathy."

"You make it look easy," Clarence said.

"Actually, it's tough. Little mistakes can distort the print. Whoever did this knew what he was doing. Probably practiced."

"But you didn't figure that out when you first saw it?" Clarence asked.

"Nobody would. It was only when I thought to look for trace chemicals that I hit the jackpot. I found traces of glycerin and a little cyanoacrylate."

"You normally don't test for those?" I asked.

"Why would I? This is a one in a million. When you called and told me he had a solid alibi, that's when I checked."

"Eventually Noel would have come forward and admitted where he was, assuming he wasn't willing to endure capital punishment rather than admit to Jack he'd had some drinks. But suppose he'd been home alone that night. The scary thing is, if he didn't have the alibi, Noel could have been prosecuted."

"Any expert would've testified these were his prints on the murder weapon," Phil said. "It could've been enough to put him away."

Clarence, Carp, and I were walking out of Criminalist Detail when Mike Bates poked his head out a door. "Chandler? Just got the results on that voice comparison you gave me. The one where they both use the word *fishy*."

"Yeah?"

"There's a probable elimination. It's not the same voice."

"You're sure?"

"No. Probable means not sure. But I'm 98 percent sure it's not the same guy."

Double elimination for Noel, in the space of twenty minutes.

True, there was a one in fifty chance Noel was the caller. More likely, though, the caller knew Noel and his quirky use of *fishy*. Who would know better than one of the detectives? And if they went to the trouble to plant his fingerprints, why not put another nail in his coffin with the 911 tape?

And if Noel was being framed…why not somebody else?

Clarence went back to homicide, where he'd be joining me for my five o'clock appointment with Noel. Carp lingered at the elevator. She said the magic words "double cheese" as we parted. On the way back, I stopped to scope out the donut situation. As usual, the one with colored sprinkles was the only one left. Why do they even make them?

While contemplating this mystery at 4:45, I noticed my workstation fifteen feet away. I happened to be in a position to see something under it. Specifically, a pair of legs. And whoever they belonged to was wearing panty hose. Tentatively, I eliminated Cimma, Manny, and Clarence.

The top of the divider panel above my desk has thin cracks. I sometimes look through them from the desk side to see who's stalking the donuts, but I'd never looked through from this side.

The head was definitely female, bent over, searching my file drawers. My instinct was to say "Gotcha," but I decided to watch. If you stop people then ask them what they were doing, they lie to you. The best way to find out what they're doing is to watch them do it.

Apparently she wasn't finding what she was looking for. She stood up and went through the papers on my desk—notes and messages, business cards and mail. I had the feeling she'd done this already, and this was a retry.

She looked up at the crack and seemed to stare right at me. I froze. She glanced back down and quickly shuffled papers again.

Was she looking for my case notes? I had them. This was a wake-up call never to leave them at my desk, not even for a bathroom break. She walked to the aisle, turned and looked toward the security entrance, and returned to her desk, which fortunately is on the far side of where I was hunched over.

Now I had another question to deal with.

Why was Kim Suda snooping in my files?

At 5:00 p.m., Noel, Jack, Clarence, and I met in the conference room. I'd baked the crow, now I had to eat it. I explained Phil's demonstration of how Noel's fingerprints had been faked. I said that since Clarence had been there when I accused Noel, it was only right that he witness my apology. So…I apologized.

Noel took it pretty well. Jack? Not so well.

"They said it was one in a million," I told Jack, my oldest friend on the force. "The fingerprints seemed definitive. I was just following the evidence. What would you have done?"

"I'd try knowing the people I work with," he said. "And maybe trusting them."

I extended my hand to Noel, and he shook it.

"No hard feelings?" I asked.

"No." He blushed.

"Jack?"

I stuck out my hand. He shook it unenthusiastically. I saw the hard feelings in his eyes. He walked out the door behind Noel.

"I may have just lost a friend," I said to Clarence.

"You were doing your job."

"Things are not as they appear. Another of my mottoes, but I was blindsided. What bugs me is I didn't think to ask the forensic guys to look for a fake print. I'd read it could be done, but it never occurred to me."

"You can't think of everything," Clarence said.

"When it's this important, I have to. Whoever did this isn't dumb enough to leave their prints on a gun. And if they do, they're not going to dump it two blocks from the scene. Why not dump it in the river three miles away? They knew we'd check Dumpsters. That's standard procedure."

I flipped to my list of five observations that pointed to a detective. I wrote down two more beneath.

6. The killer knew how to fake fingerprints and place them on the gun.
7. The killer knew it would be SOP to search all Dumpsters within four blocks of the scene. He knew where to put the murder weapon so it would be found, while appearing that he didn't want it to be found.

So far the killer had planted evidence against at least two of us, Noel and me. Was this his joke, trying to send the department into confusion, give us bad PR? Or was he really trying to put me or Noel away?

Why Noel? And why me? What did we have in common? Were we arbitrary choices? Or did the killer have an ax to grind? And if so, was he planning to grind it again?

"Circumstantial evidence is a very tricky thing. It may seem to point very straight to one thing, but if you shift your own point of view a little, you may find it pointing in an equally uncompromising manner to something entirely different."
SHERLOCK HOLMES, *THE BOSCOMBE VALLEY MYSTERY*

THE FOLLOWING HAPPENED between 1:00 a.m. and 2:00 a.m.: no sleep.

I was watching *24* on a portable DVD player in my car. I know I really shouldn't do that, but it keeps me awake in the wee hours of noncritical surveillance.

Critical surveillance requires unswerving attention. This didn't. I was scoping out a house one hundred feet away. I looked up every three seconds, and a second later I looked down. A world-class sprinter couldn't move to or from the house out of my line of sight.

Jack Bauer and I are alike. We take down the bad guys. We're tough as nails, yet tenderhearted. We're misunderstood, Jack and I, tragic and heroic. We're both always in trouble with our superiors. We've both lost our wives and have complicated relationships with our daughters. We're both handsome. The ladies love us. But the biggest similarity is this: Neither of us gets any sleep.

I sat there nursing my Big Gulp, neck aching from turning to the right. If I didn't reposition the car soon to equalize my neck twists, I'd have a chiropractor on my back.

I turned my flashlight to my shirt, recognizing a spot from yesterday morning's Egg McMuffin. The second stain was coffee, probably last night's venti latte.

It was the third spot that intrigued me. Using my detective skills, I pulled the fabric up close and put my tongue on the reddish-brown spot. Of course. The steak Burrito Ultimo, Baja Fresh.

I wondered if the department would cover charges for a cleaner's bill for food stains. I pictured Sarah Ballenger in accounting rolling her eyes.

In novels, detectives on surveillance see and hear all kinds of things. Suspects raise their voices and say, "Okay, now that we stole his diamonds, let's go dump Harvey's body in the lake." They may even say "in the lake, eh?" so you know the killer's a Canadian.

Unfortunately, in real life people don't say things they already know for the benefit of the eavesdropper. And if you're sitting outside someone's house for the night, chances are they'll do nothing more exciting than go to bed. They sleep soundly; you don't.

But Kim Suda was a light sleeper, I'd heard her say, and seeing her rifle through my papers got under my skin. It would probably be a wasted night, but I was willing to chance it.

I have nothing against time. Time is what keeps everything from happening at once. But on a stakeout, time can get on your nerves.

Good thing I had a companion.

"Want another Cheeto?" I stuck back my hand, and Mulch gratefully closed his lips, taking care not to bite me.

Clarence called. "Still on your stakeout?" he asked. "Geneva's asleep."

"I'd hope so. It's 2:10 a.m.!"

"Thought I'd come join you."

"Suda's light's still on, but she's probably reading and won't emerge from the cave until daylight. This cul-de-sac's dead."

"I want to write up a stakeout."

"Imagine sitting in a car doing nothing for eight hours. That's pretty much it. Just go out in your garage right now and sit there all night. You'll get the idea. Besides, I don't want somebody seeing Goliath get in my car."

"You said nobody's around."

"Okay. Park around the corner. No lights. Then walk to my car nonchalantly. Knock twice on the passenger window, or I might have to shoot you."

Fifteen minutes later the double knock came. I unlocked the door, and the offensive line of the New England Patriots sat beside me.

Mulch growled as Clarence got in, but I gave him another Cheeto, and soon he was licking Clarence's face.

"You bring a dog on a stakeout?"

"Only when I can pull him away from his poker game."

No response.

"You ever seen that art with the dogs playing poker? I got mine with my velvet Elvis."

No response.

There's nothing like stakeout conversation. Sports, politics, how to reach out to your pregnant thirty-year-old unmarried daughter, guns, movies—you bounce in and out of stuff. The next hour was a panoply of randomness. (Sharon used *panoply* once in Scrabble, and I liked it.)

"Your eyes'll get used to the dark."

He picked up a corn dog wrapper and mustard packet at his feet. "I'm not sure I want them to."

Clarence stared behind the driver's seat at the archaeological dig. He excavated a berry pie wrapper from the Neolithic era.

"You are what you eat," he said.

"That makes me an Izzy's pizza," I replied. "There's one piece left." I opened the glove box and pulled it out. "Want it?"

Clarence refused. I put it back, and pretty soon we were talking about family.

"I stopped going to my family reunions after my sister's second marriage," I said. "She showed up with this guy at a family gathering, called him Bob, but never introduced him. No explanation. It was like *Bewitched*, with the two Darrins—like if they don't say anything, we won't notice *this isn't the same guy*! You know what I'm saying?"

"Who's Darrin?"

"*Bewitched*."

"I never saw *Bewitched*."

"It's on cable. Wouldn't take you long to catch up." This was another reminder that Clarence and I grew up on different planets.

"Daddy wasn't much for TV. He wanted us to read."

"Wish your daddy were here right now. With him, a stakeout would be a pleasure. I could listen to his stories forever."

"I'm sure he'll be telling them forever," Clarence said. "And there'll be lots of fresh stories to tell on the new earth. He always said it would be the great adventure. If you're with us, you'll get to listen to his stories…and they'll be better than ever."

"You managed to work it in, didn't you?"

"What?"

"The Christian stuff. Heaven. The whole nine yards."

"Hey, you pitched the ball to me. I just took a swing." He tried to stretch, unsuccessfully.

"For future reference, on stakeouts you need to be shorter than six five," I said, "or bring your own car. It also helps to have the bladder capacity of five people."

After five minutes of silence I said, "Ever notice that stakeout rhymes with takeout? If you get a Bonzer Steak from Outback, like I do sometimes, then it's a STEAK-out. Get it? I mean, spelled S–T–E–A–K–O—"

"I get it!"

"I've got a surprise for you." I pushed the seat back, reached past my coat, and pulled a box from the sealed plastic container I use to keep Mulch out of the food.

Clarence looked at the box. "Krispy Kreme donuts?"

He said it like they were bad. "You Christians got something against donuts?"

"Per capita, Christians eat more donuts than anybody. You should come to our men's meetings."

"How much are the donuts?"

"Voluntary donations. For you, free."

"Do you have to stay for the Bible study, or can you just pick up the donuts and leave?"

"You have to stay ten minutes for each donut you eat. That'll keep you there for the whole hour."

I opened the box and handed it to him. "I have a buddy who writes murder mysteries, and he's always calling me for advice. This guy mentions Krispy Kreme in his books, like three times on a single page, hoping somebody who works with the company will give him a gift certificate or a year's supply or something."

"That doesn't sound professional."

"Yeah, people can be so pathetic. Pass me a Krispy Kreme, will you?"

Clarence reached for the glazed raspberry.

"No, give me the New York cheesecake. No, that's a chocolate iced glazed cruller, Mulch's favorite. Pass it over to him, would you? Sorry, that's key lime pie." He closed the box and dropped it on my lap.

I pointed at the house. "Look, Suda's moving. Light went on in the front room."

I saw blinds open slightly and a face peeking out the bay window, looking the other direction, straight out, then at us.

"Don't move," I said. "Stay exactly where you are."

Ten minutes later it was boredom as usual. Hopes rise and fall on stakeouts.

"So, tell me about your world," I said. "Berkley's concerned about subscribers?"

"Revenues are down. Too many competing news sources—TV, radio, the Internet."

"Plus people finally realizing the *Tribune*'s garbage."

"You say you don't read the paper, so you don't know what you're criticizing, do you?"

"You walk the beat with our street cops? Didn't think so. You don't know who you're criticizing."

"Where I come from 'beat cop' has another meaning. When you've been beaten just for being black, you don't overflow with trust."

"Don't judge us all by the bad ones."

"My point exactly," Clarence said. "And if you think you could write better than what you read in the *Trib*, submit me a column. If it's good enough, I'll see that it's printed."

"No kidding?"

"No kidding. Tell your own story. First person, detective talking to the people about investigating murders. Go for it. Turn it in when you're ready."

"I will."

"Pardon me if I don't hold my breath. Anyway, tell me about this police morale problem."

"You think I'm going to say something you can use against us?"

"Off the record."

"Morale? Well, there's the budget cuts, not to mention all the bad publicity the *Trib's* given us."

"The *Trib* didn't shoot an unarmed law-abiding citizen."

"That was one in a million, okay? People don't appreciate cops. Truth is, we risk our lives every day for whiners and gripers. And cops are getting laid off. Guys come to work, check for blood on their office doorposts, and hope the angel of death passes them over."

"Sounds like you've been reading the Bible."

"Just a figure of speech." I hesitated, not knowing how to say it. "Listen, I know there are racist cops. And I know what they did to your daddy. I want you to know I'd have been proud to have him as my father."

"You would've gotten funny looks if he were your father. Still, I appreciate what you're saying. Daddy really enjoyed the time he spent with you. He liked you. I never thought I'd tell you this, but Geneva says I should…"

"What?"

"Before he died, Daddy asked me to keep an eye on you."

"Why?"

"Well, since you asked…he wanted you to know Jesus."

"He said that?"

Kim Suda's front door opened. She walked briskly to her car, got in, and pulled out of the driveway. We ducked low, though she probably wouldn't have seen us anyway since I'd parked past her place behind another car.

I waited until she turned right off Patty Court onto Woodard, then started the car and followed her to the next turn, right again on 78th, then left on Jackson. Eventually we were on Stark. I had to stay way behind her because of the light traffic. She drove Stark to 162nd, turned right, and took a quick left into the parking lot of a 7-Eleven. I pulled into a real estate building lot across the street. I turned off my lights and backed around so I had a clear view of the store Suda entered. I grabbed my binoculars from under the front seat.

"There's a small pair in the glove box," I said to Clarence. "Just toss the pizza to Mulch."

He handed the pizza back, where an invisible entity dismembered it. Clarence held up his binoculars. "We're going to watch what she buys? Seems a little…intrusive."

"That's surveillance," I said.

She'd veered left and gone to the far end of the store by a glass cooler filled with milk. She slowed down near a man whose back was to us. He was flipping through a magazine. I got out of the car and found the best place in the shadows, which put me right next to a rhododendron bush. I had to keep moving to keep her in view, but fortunately the front of the store was glass.

Suda turned up an aisle where she appeared to be looking at medications. Sominex? I could see her face once in a while, but a slight move one way or the other obscured her. I saw her face and realized her lips were moving.

"She's talking," I said to Clarence, who'd exited the car and was now mostly behind the rhody, eclipsing the moon and looking over my shoulder.

"Talking to herself?"

"No, to that guy in the black coat standing a couple of feet from her on the other side of the aisle. See him?"

"Why don't they stand closer if they're talking?"

"Because they don't want to *look* like they're talking. Suda and this guy didn't come together, and they won't leave together."

They talked for five minutes. I could see only the guy's back. He was wearing a navy blue stocking cap. I looked away only to take an occasional glance at Mulch, who was exploring the inside of the car without supervision. I could see Suda's lips moving periodically. I wished I'd studied lipreading. The man handed her something.

"What's that?" I asked.

"A brown envelope."

"Evidence? A payoff? Bet it's not a birthday card."

Suda stepped to the cooler, opened the door, and grabbed a bottled water. Walking up a different aisle, away from the guy she'd been talking to, she made her purchase, got in her car, and headed back onto Stark.

"Why aren't we following her?" Clarence asked.

"Because we know who she is and where she lives."

The man continued to gaze at his magazine. A minute after Suda pulled away, he took it to the front desk. Paid cash. With his stocking cap pulled down and various things blocking my view, it was hard to get a good look at his face. But just as he pointed his remote to unlock his car, he looked up. The streetlight caught his face.

"I don't believe it," I said.

"It looks like…"

We both slunk back to the car. I turned the key, but kept the lights off. "Stay low."

After he was a hundred feet down the road, I followed. No traffic, either to fight or cover me. He went all the way down to Foster, turned left, then turned right exactly where I knew he would. Still a hundred feet back, I saw him slow down, turn into a driveway, and stop. I couldn't see it, but I knew he was punching a code and a gate was swinging open.

We sat there, car idling.

"Was it really him?" Clarence asked.

"Yeah. If I had the slightest doubt, I don't now because that's his driveway he just went up, security entrance and all. I don't know what it means, but we just found a gold nugget in the rocks and mud. Kim Suda had a clandestine meeting and a handoff at 3:15 a.m....with Edward Lennox, chief of police!"

20

WEDNESDAY, DECEMBER 4, 10:00 A.M.

I DIED IN 2003, when Sharon died. I went on breathing, but it was a technicality.

Since then I've felt alive only at key points in an investigation when the adrenaline flows, or in isolated moments with close friends, like Mulch or Jake.

These thoughts came over me at 10:00 a.m., which is late to sleep in, unless you've gone to bed at 5:00 a.m. I sat up in my bed, sipping French roast and feeling Mulch's hot breath on my toes. He seemed to have a stomachache; he'd been emitting fumes reminiscent of a paper mill.

My old brownstone is a sanctuary from human beings, which is why I usually don't answer the door and seldom answer the phone. When Sharon was around, I enjoyed people more.

She was kind, but honest. Once she told me, "You dance like a guy tilting a pinball machine. Relax." So I learned to relax, becoming suave and debonair. At least I stopped tilting her.

We danced the jitterbug. The slow jitterbug, not the fast one. Neither of us ever wanted it to end.

But it did.

The coffee was cold now. Not much reason to get out of bed. But even less to stay there.

As I drove to downtown Portland, I phoned Officer Paul Anderson, calling in the hours he and Griffin owed me for flushing their holdup man out of his apartment. Tomorrow was Kim Suda's day off. Could one of them follow her to lunch, to her martial arts class, to anywhere and everywhere? Maybe take pictures?

I walked into Grayson's Fine Pens, a store for fountain pen connoisseurs. I'd never been in such a store and didn't know they existed until seeing it on a website. The fountain pen specialist had a contemplative look on an expansive face, with cheeks so fleshy they could use support. There were two sets of shoulders, his and the suit's. His tie had been loosened, and his white dress shirt was a mass of wrinkles.

"Rupert Bolin at your service," he said.

When he leaned over, a ridge of white flesh emerged above his low-slung belt. I thought of taking his picture and posting it on my refrigerator as a warning. Relatively speaking, I'm still a fine specimen. Rupert was about nine hundred Krispy Kremes ahead of me.

I showed him a half dozen of the professor's fountain pens. He looked them over, called them by name, nodded appreciatively at two of them, and dismissed the other four as pens for lowlifes. He spoke rapturously of the joy of fountain pens. Here I'd wasted my life bringing killers to justice when I could have been a pen collector.

"What do people do with fountain pens?" I asked.

He looked at me as if I'd asked, "What do people do with a porterhouse steak?"

"Humor me," I said. "Pretend I know nothing about fountain pens."

He sighed, looking upward. I followed his gaze. Ceiling tiles.

"Where do I begin? A fountain pen is a fine instrument in the hands of a master artist. Artisans use fountain pens for special occasions. For important documents. For poetry and love letters. And sketch art, the type you might frame."

I nodded earnestly.

"It's a hobby you should consider. We had our first Portland fountain pen show in 2004, at the Embassy Suites. It was a big success. You must have heard about it."

"I'm sure I must have. Was it on ESPN?"

"It was thrilling."

"I can only imagine. Who wants to watch the Packers play the Bears when you can go to a fountain pen show?"

"My sentiments exactly. We have a strong presence on the Internet, you know."

"Do we?"

"There are over fifty websites of fountain pen dealers, hobbyists, and enthusiasts."

"Fifty? I wouldn't have thought there'd be more than thirty-five."

"You've no doubt visited the sites."

"No doubt." I'd visited one. "I found you on Bill's Fountain Pen website."

He beamed.

"Look," I said, "I adore fountain pens, but I'm having a hard time explaining my devotion to…the uninitiated. Novices. You know what I'm saying?"

He nodded sympathetically. "In an age of e-mails and BICs—" he nearly spat the word—"and cookie-cutter mass production, fountain pens are elegant. They tie us to the past. They are handheld history. In an age of encroaching illiteracy, they make us more cultured, more refined, more literary."

"More literary?"

"They make us better wordsmiths. They stimulate thought and reflection. They are tools of articulation and civility."

"Okeydokey," I said. "And…how does that all work?"

"When you put the nib of the pen in the ink, you can write perhaps eight words. Maybe a short sentence. Then you have to dip the pen again."

"Seems inconvenient."

He looked like I'd called his mother a name. "The best things in life take time. A love letter takes time. People are so used to keyboards and e-mails that they've lost the love of thoughtful language. They don't stop to think. They just spew out words. No wonder the writing is so thoughtless, so careless, so urbane, so…"

"Quick?"

"Quick is not always good."

I thought of a few instances when it isn't and nodded.

He insisted that I drop my business card in the drawing for a set of three fancy fountain pens on display. The sign said the set was worth two hundred dollars, which was about $198 more than I would have paid for it. He also insisted that I sign up for his monthly fountain pen newsletter. I pulled out my BIC pen, saw his shocked stare, assured him I'd found it on the sidewalk, then took the green Paradise fountain pen he handed me and started to write the address of Clarence Abernathy. But I wasn't sure on the house number, so I wrote my address instead.

For a change of pace, I met my cronies at Powell's City of Books. Occupying a whole city block, with over a million new and used books, it's a book lover's paradise. They display a framed article from the *Washington Post* calling it "the best bookstore in the world." Powell's probably thinks the *Washington Post* is the best newspaper in the world, but that's another issue. I don't go to Powell's for the politics.

I came an hour early to find a space at the world's largest bookstore, with the world's smallest parking garage. Six thousand in-store customers a day, and they have forty lousy spaces. I wedged into an imaginary space, and when an attendant scowled, I showed him my badge and he backed away so I wouldn't smell the marijuana.

No matter what you believe, you can find a section in Powell's to make you feel better about it and another section to make you question it or get mad at somebody. I go there when I want to feel literary and absorb wisdom. Looking at the bestseller tables near the entrance, I wonder about the wisdom part. But I love that old-book smell, and they've got the great detective novels buried amidst the not-so-great.

I entered at Tenth and Burnside determined to book my way to World Cup Coffee and Tea, passing by new arrivals, literature, classics, and reference works to get to sci-fi, thrillers, and mysteries. With seven thousand mysteries to sort through, there's lots of rocks and mud but plenty of gold awaiting discovery. Everybody's a detective at Powell's. Right when I got to the section I wanted, I had to stop. One minute of Powell's time is one hour of real time.

I put on imaginary blinders to beeline to Clarence and Jake at the World Cup, by the humor and audio books, where some come for free Wi-Fi and I come for the walnut sticky buns and chocolate croissants. They trust you with five books, so I've spent lots of time here with Ross Macdonald and Raymond Chandler—no relation—occasionally getting goo on their pages. That's part of the character of used books.

Joining Clarence and Jake in the cafe, I chose a grilled chicken and Gouda cheese sandwich, while Clarence took the egg salad and Jake a corn and black bean salad with chicken tortilla soup.

Two minutes after ordering we were talking about issues raised in Russell's *Why I Am Not a Christian* and Lewis's *Mere Christianity*. Though I didn't bring the books, it took Jake and Clarence only five minutes to find both on the shelves while I worked over my sandwich.

"God's existence is wishful thinking," I said after ten minutes of discussion. "It makes people feel better to think there's a supreme being."

"For me it was the opposite," Jake said. "The last thing I wanted was to believe in God. It required changes I didn't want to make. God has a way of interfering with your life. Big time. It was only later that I realized the changes were in my best interest."

"So," Clarence said, "your wishful thinking wasn't that God existed, but that He didn't?"

"Exactly. That's what C. S. Lewis experienced. Ultimately, he bowed to the God he desperately didn't want to believe in. When he became a theist, before he became a Christian, he called himself the most reluctant convert in all of England. Lewis went from atheism to agnosticism to belief in God. Later he came to believe in Christ. And that's when he really found joy."

I'd left room for a walnut sticky bun with extra butter. (I may die a few years sooner, but I'll die happy.)

"But what if I don't *want* to become a Christian?"

"Isn't that where the wishful thinking comes in?" Jake asked. "Shouldn't you just want to believe whatever's true? I mean, if Jesus isn't who He claimed to be, then *don't* believe in Him. If He is, then do. It's not about what you want to believe, but what's really true."

"You don't want to believe the murderer's a detective," Clarence said. "But you do believe it, right?"

"I go where the evidence leads."

"So ask yourself where the evidence leads when it comes to Jesus," Jake said. "It's not about your preference, like choosing between a walnut sticky bun and a chocolate croissant."

"Don't mock me. It was a tough call."

"My point is, faith shouldn't be about what suits our tastes, but about the truth the evidence points to."

"So if you disagree with what we believe," Clarence said, "then try to talk us out of it—take your best shot. We don't want to believe what's false."

"You guys will get talked out of your faith when hell freezes over."

"What is it that holds you back?" Jake said. "Not only from Christ, but from the idea that there's a God?"

"The Holocaust. Stalin. The Killing Fields. Idi Amin. Rwanda. Jeffrey Dahmer. What I saw in Vietnam. A couple hundred murder cases. How's that for starters? People get away with murder. Where's the justice?"

"Daddy used to say, 'Nobody gets away wid nothin',' " Clarence said.

"How could he say that? After what those dirty cops did to him?"

"It used to bother me how Daddy would forgive people. It made me think he was weak." Somebody with green hair, waiting for coffee, heard Clarence's voice and stared. If I had green hair, I wouldn't stare at anybody.

"I couldn't have been more wrong," Clarence continued. "He knew God would bring justice, but he was willing to wait. He said to me, 'They still has time to repent. If they doesn't, yo' daddy would sooner be the mule they whip than stand in their shoes before almighty God and be burnt to ashes by the fire of His holiness.' "

"He really said that?"

"I've never forgotten it. My point is, what makes you think God will let people get away with all this stuff? The Bible teaches that He won't. There's going to be a judgment for everything that's been done, good and bad. God promises that repeatedly."

"But why wait? I've seen parents kill their children, children kill their parents, a teenage boy torture his little brother. Why didn't God just throw lightning bolts and fry these lowlifes?"

"I've seen evil too, you know," Jake said. "I was in Nam. I saw Finney and Doc die. They were my best friends. My Carly's dying as we speak."

"My sister and niece were murdered," Clarence said. "Daddy saw a lot more evil than I ever have, probably more than you. He believed God has reasons for allowing these things that we can't understand."

"I don't buy it. Sometimes I just want to go out there and save hundreds of people by performing a few executions. You know how many people die because of drug dealers?"

"So if you were in charge," Clarence said, "there'd be no mercy, no opportunity to repent? Bad people would all die. But…maybe you deserve to die too. Maybe we're all worse than you think. That's what the Bible says."

"Don't try to put me in the same box with murderers and rapists. That's one of the things that frosts me about you Christians," I said, standing up. "One of the many things."

When I returned to detective division, two attractive women were standing near my workstation. One was dressed in fashion magazine clothes. Her outfit screamed money. The other was Linda Glissan, Jack's wife. Linda always looks nice, but she and Sharon used to shop for bargains at Nordstrom Rack. Even that can strain a detective's salary.

"Hi, Ollie." Linda hugged me. I don't get hugged often. "You've met Sheila Phillips, Brandon's wife, haven't you?"

"I don't believe I've had the pleasure," she said, stretching out her hand, which momentarily unnerved me, since her fingernails looked like red-polished Ginsu knives. So this was Phillips's wife. He'd married her a year ago, eighteen months after his divorce. I'd heard about Sheila. She lived up to it.

"I brought you some of those chocolate pecan muffins you like," Linda said, handing me a bag.

"Thanks."

"Jack and I miss you."

"Look, Linda, I'm sorry. I…"

"It's okay. I miss Sharon too. She was one of my best friends."

I nodded, aware of Sheila, who seemed to be studying us.

"We've stopped asking you over because we don't want to bug you. But when you're ready, let us know. Or just drop by, okay? You're always welcome at our house."

Her invitation reminded me that it was approaching twenty-four hours before my second dinner with Kendra, this time at her home. I was shocked when she'd asked. I wanted to see her again, but if they made body armor for the heart, I'd be bidding for it on eBay.

I said good-bye to Linda, pretending I had to make a phone call. As I called to check my messages I watched Sheila Phillips out the corner of my eye.

Why was she staring at me?

↔

Clarence and I planted ourselves in an empty conference room, where the boxy wooden chairs weren't comfortable but we could talk more freely than at my workstation.

"When you have a limited number of suspects," I said, "you start by eliminating people, one by one. Suppose it's one of the detectives. Who do we eliminate?"

"You?" Clarence asked.

"I hope so," I said, followed by a laugh I hoped didn't sound forced. This wasn't the time to bring up that I couldn't remember anything between my first half hour at Rosie O'Grady's and getting the phone call at 3:07 a.m.

"Manny?"

"I can't see a motive. His alibi's as good as you could expect—home with wife and kids. But I'll call Maria and worm it out of her, just to make sure."

"You're going to check up on your own partner?"

"He'd understand. Well, maybe he wouldn't. But he'd check up on me."

"Who else is off the list? Jack?"

"Why?"

"For one thing, when you called him to the crime scene, he didn't seem nervous."

"Jack's an old friend. But for now he stays on the list. But do I think he'd do it? No way."

Clarence looked at his list. "Tell me about Brandon Phillips."

"Efficient, smart, observant. Heck of a poker player. Cleans out guys in the Friday night games. I was losing too much money, so I don't go anymore. Brandon's a good detective."

"He's nervous," Clarence said.

"Why do you say that?"

"Remember at the professor's house? Said he had allergies, but it seemed like an excuse. He was twitching and seemed anxious to leave. He wasn't responsive to your questions. "

"He knew that Dell computer was a mail-order only model. Like I said, he's observant."

"You and Noel both noticed the missing picture on the mantel. Phillips didn't."

"Did you?"

"No, but I'm not a detective." Clarence looked at his list. "How tall is Suda?"

"Five one?"

"You've thought about—"

"The desk chair adjusted for a short person? Suda can be a pain, and she's up to her eyeballs in something. But…a killer?"

"How about Tommi?"

"She's a mom—five kids, ranging three years old to high school."

"Moms never kill people?"

"If the professor told her kids not to wear seat belts or breathed on them when he had the flu, maybe."

We talked until Clarence had gone through the whole list. "Congratulations, detective," he said. "You've eliminated everybody. Since none of your suspects killed the professor, he must still be alive. Somebody better dig him up."

Smart guy.

I headed home to the old brownstone in the dark. I turned onto 150th, eighty feet from my house, then threw on the brakes. A shadow moved, then disappeared behind my garage. I pulled my car over the curb onto my lawn, headlights pointed where I saw the shadow. I jammed it into park, grabbed a flashlight out of the glove box, and popped out, gun pulled.

"Police officer! Don't move!"

Somebody pulled himself over the wood fence on my side yard. I ran through my neighbor's side yard, flashlight in one hand, Glock in the other.

"Stop or I'll shoot!"

As I passed the window on my right, I saw Donna, the neighbor lady, horrified. When I got past the back edge of their house, I heard a crack and felt an explosion on the right side of my skull. I felt warm blood before I hit the ground.

Someone wearing a ski mask was on top of me. He had both his hands on my gun. I hit the left side of his face with my flashlight. He stood, staggering, and threw my gun over the fence.

I tried to stand, then fell back to the ground. I saw him disappear into the hedge at the back of my neighbors' yard. That's the last thing I remember until hearing somebody yell, "Donna, call 911!"

"Did you see him?" I asked.

"The guy in the magazine?" someone said. "I saw his grump. He was over the fence in a frimbo. I came out when I heard the yardarm. He threw something over the brumbello."

"What?" I tried to say.

"You're the car, right? My mother the car."

That's what it sounded like. In retrospect, I think he must have said, "My neighbor the cop."

Patrol arrived, then the EMTs in an ambulance. Despite the objections of the good-hearted Obrists, who'd brought me into their house, I staggered out the back door to point out things for the officers to look for. I told them they needed to find footprints and fetch my gun and make sure nobody contaminated the crime scene. They seemed to think they didn't need my advice.

Next thing I knew, the uniforms were escorting me back into the house and telling the Obrists not to let me move. Donna had just fixed me tea, Earl Grey, which is what Jean-Luc Picard, my favorite captain, drinks on *Star Trek: The Next Generation*. I'd never tried it. It was awful. But she was so attentive that I kept thanking her for it.

The EMTs thought I had a concussion and insisted on taking me in. I insisted otherwise, telling them I didn't need a doctor—it was only a little crack in the skull and I get a couple a week. No brain fluid leaking out my ears, so no big deal.

Manny showed up and seemed almost concerned. I should get cracked in the head more often. I told him I wanted to check out signs of entry at the old brownstone. We went to my back porch. I was more light-headed than I let on, grabbing on to a tree limb and a fence post to keep me up. Mulch looked out the sliding glass door at Manny, showed his teeth, and barked like crazy until he saw me and began his doggy dance of joy.

I unlocked the back door, and next thing I knew Mulch was licking my head wounds.

"Give me a minute," I said to Manny, going into the bathroom. Mrs. Obrist had wiped off most of the blood before the EMTs got there, which made it easier to call them off. But there was still wet blood in my hair. Red puffiness was working its way over the right side of my face.

I put my head in the sink. After the water drained, the sink had a reddish stain. I dried my hair with a bath towel, then walked out when I heard Mulch's growling and a string of Hispanic swear words. Between Manny and Mulch I wasn't sure who was doing more growling, but when I thought I heard Mulch swear at Manny in Spanish, I decided it was time to sit down, take it easy, and avoid Earl Grey.

When you're a detective and also the victim, you want to question yourself, put the pieces together, and solve the crime. But I wasn't thinking clearly. Manny, apparently, was doing the thinking for me. He had me sitting on my recliner and even took off my shoes and brought me my slippers.

An hour later, my face was experimenting with new and different colors. Having abandoned a pinkish brown, it had settled on a puffy purple.

I heard Mulch barking again. Next thing I know, Jake and Clarence are in my living room. Sue Keels showed up and tried to talk me into going to the emergency room. She said a concussion was possible, that my eyes didn't look right. I was a

Klingon warrior who'd been assimilated by the Borg, and she was worried about me going to sleep. Being a man and a cop, naturally I refused. Bart Starr, who was feeding pineapples to my kangaroo, agreed with me. Since Sue's an emergency room nurse, I figured she could take care of me even without all those machines. She messed with my head and did stuff that made it feel worse at first and better later.

Finally Sue said, "Looks like you guys are ready for a men's night," and took off. Jake and Clarence and I hung out for a couple more hours. They made popcorn and dug out the cookie dough ice cream I'd bought the day before at WinCo. I try to eat ice cream within two days; no point risking freezer burn.

Sergeant Seymour called and ordered me to stay home the next day. He said that if he found out I'd conducted interviews or done surveillance, he'd suspend me. He also said something about the Nebraska Cornhuskers taking the Space Shuttle into Lake Michigan to find the lost city of Atlantis, but after that he stopped making sense.

Jake and Clarence and I talked and laughed. There were lots of stories, the best ones about Clarence's daddy. It reminded me of Vietnam, how hard you laugh when you've lived through an attack.

Occasionally I nearly forgot my head was about to explode.

21

"There is nothing more stimulating than a case where everything goes against you."
SHERLOCK HOLMES, *THE HOUND OF THE BASKERVILLES*

I WOKE UP with a jackhammer beating on the little gray cells.

Sometimes you're the dog; sometimes you're the fire hydrant. I wasn't fond of being the hydrant. I couldn't have managed three eggs, five strips of bacon, and two English muffins without Mulch's help.

Later Manny dropped by my house and left me forty-one pictures of the professor's living room, which he'd collected from Palatine's family and friends. I quickly eliminated thirty-eight of them, then looked under the magnifying glass at the other three, examining the professor's mantel. One photo showed nine pictures on the mantel, with one dead center, four on each side, evenly spaced. I focused in on the second picture from the right. I could tell only that there were a few people in it, like most of the other pictures. I assumed one was the professor.

I picked up the phone and called Lynn Carpenter at the *Tribune*.

"Lynn?" I asked. "Can I call you Lynn?"

"Give it a try and see what happens. I'm calling you Ollie. Clarence said you had an eventful evening. I've been worried about you. You okay?"

"No permanent damage. Can I ask you a favor?"

"Name it."

An hour later a courier picked up a pile of photos. I'd taken photos of the photos with my Olympus, for fear they could be sucked into the *Tribune*'s black hole, never to see the light of day unless it was on the front page. Carp assured me no one else would even see them. But I've heard too many assurances from journalists to believe it. Even if they like double cheese and they're worried about me.

Jake and Clarence had promised to help me get through an entire day away from investigating. A little late for that, but they said they'd bring over lunch from Lou's, and who was I to argue?

By the time they arrived at the old brownstone at twelve thirty, the jackhammer had mellowed to a bass drum, and I had an appetite.

"Rory insisted lunch was on him," Jake said. "He threw in onion rings, extra fries, extra sauce, and—you're not going to believe this—an orange malt." He pulled it out and held it up for me.

"But Lou's doesn't make orange malts."

"They do now. Rory went out and got the mix. When he found out you'd been two-timing him at Dea's, it lit a fire under him. He said, 'Only the best for Mr. Ollie.'"

I grabbed the metal container—Rory had gone all out—and pressed the cold against the right side of my face.

"Food from Lou's again…almost makes the assault worthwhile."

What followed was a feast that food critics—who prefer French meals consisting of small, wet animals you try to exterminate in your garden—would raise their noses at, but that real people love.

"Did you know I'm having dinner with my daughter tonight?"

"Terrific," Jake said. "At Lou's again?"

"No. Her place. She invited me. Probably regretted it the second she did it, but I said yes. I think we're both bracing ourselves. The gloves always seem to come off when we talk privately."

"Just getting together is progress," Clarence said.

"Between the two of us, we'll find a way to ruin it."

My cell rang just as I was polishing off the onion rings, dipping them into the last bit of horseradish. It was the professor's brother, returning my calls. Finally.

"I'm scheduled for surgery, so let's make it quick."

"I haven't been doing squat myself. Just eating burgers with my homeys. You know how it is—the cop's life. Okay, here's my question. Did you ever drink with your brother?"

"What makes that your business?"

"Was he a wine drinker?"

"Wine was all he drank."

"What kind?"

"Mostly merlot and cabernet sauvignon. The merlot was Beringer Brothers. Not sure about the cabernet."

"Are those…red wines or white?"

He laughed. "Red."

"I'm a beer drinker."

"Obviously."

"Okay," I said. "Name three beers made by Anheuser-Busch, besides Budweiser."

"Uh…I'm not sure."

"Obviously." Wine snob. "Okay, what white wine did your brother drink?"

"None. He didn't like white wine."

"But…there was residue of white wine in two glasses in his house. The lab hasn't confirmed it officially, but one tech said it smelled like a Riesling."

"I can guarantee you Bill wasn't drinking it. Unless he was out of reds."

"There were two bottles in the rack and more in the garage. All red."

"They're waiting for me in surgery."

"Knock 'em dead." I sucker punched the red key to hang up before he could.

"You already knew somebody took the bottle of white wine," Clarence said.

"But now it looks like they brought it too. Why would the killer bring wine to the murder scene? Did he offer it to the professor? Did the professor drink it or turn it down? And if he turned it down, maybe the killer drank from both glasses. That's why he wiped them both."

"Your sergeant told you not to work on the case," Jake said. He and Clarence cleaned up after the meal like a couple of housemaids.

"I should have you ladies come more often."

Clarence looked around. "Yeah, you really should."

Jake picked up *Why I Am Not a Christian* from the coffee table, where it sat on top of *Mere Christianity*.

"Been doing your reading?" I asked him before he could ask me.

Jake smiled and pulled his own copy of *Why I Am Not a Christian* out of his briefcase. He turned pages, then read aloud.

"Russell says, 'I think that you must have a certain amount of definite belief before you have a right to call yourself a Christian. The word does not have quite such a full-blooded meaning now as it had in the times of Saint Augustine and Saint Thomas Aquinas. In those days, if a man said that he was a Christian it was known what he meant.' He's right on target," Jake said.

"I didn't think you'd agree with *anything* this guy says."

"Why not?"

"Well, he's no friend of Christians."

"No, but that doesn't mean he's always wrong. I'm not afraid of the truth. I read lots of people I disagree with. How about you?"

I shrugged, which is what I do instead of answering when I don't like my answer.

"Obviously," Jake said, "I disagree with Russell's view of Jesus as being just a good man and a decent teacher."

"You fault him for saying Jesus was a good man?"

"No. For saying Jesus was *just* a good man. That He wasn't God. When I first read *Mere Christianity*, Lewis got through to me when he argued that people can't logically say that."

"Why not?"

"Because Jesus claimed to be God and to forgive sins. So He was either deceived or lying. The only other possibility is that He was telling the truth. When I considered the possibilities and weighed His words, I decided He wasn't a liar and He wasn't deceived. He was really who He claimed to be."

"At least look at the evidence," Clarence said.

"Look guys, I'm tired, and I'm expected at Kendra's tonight. I'll need my strength. I'd better take a nap."

Jake stood and put his hand on my shoulder. "Give our love to Kendra. Tell her we miss seeing her. Anything we can get you before we leave?"

"Warm milk, maybe, and you can read me a bedtime story, from C. S. Lewis no doubt. Then you can warm up my jammies in the microwave and tuck me in for my nap."

Right then the doorbell rang. Clarence opened the door, and Mrs. Obrist marched in holding a tray with delicate china on it.

"Feeling better?" she said to me. "Since you liked it so much, I brewed you another pot of Earl Grey."

The phone jarred me awake, and I saw 3:00 on the clock. Why was I not surprised? But the room wasn't dark enough. That's when I realized it was p.m., not a.m.

"Sarge here. Chief Lennox wants to see you right away. I told him I'd ordered you to stay home after last night's incident, but he was adamant."

"I'm right here if he wants to drop by."

"I'm afraid he meets everybody at his office."

Everybody but Kim Suda, whom he meets in the middle of the night at a convenience store.

"He says he needs you here by four. Sorry."

It was 4:48, and I'd been waiting outside the chief's office fifty-one minutes. This time his door was closed. I'd just squished chewed-up Black Jack gum between two pages of *Architectural Digest* when he appeared, shaking the hand of someone in an expensive suit.

In public the chief kisses not only babies but a particular part of the human anatomy, mentioned by cops two hundred times a day, which I will not name in case my grandchildren—if I could be so lucky—one day read this.

In private, when dealing with those under him—which is everyone wearing a badge—the chief acts like the animal with the same anatomical name.

The chief walked the suit down the hall, then reappeared, all smiled out. Eyeing my trench coat, he beckoned me inside like snobs summon a waiter.

"Don't bother sitting—you won't be here long."

I sat. "I'm feeling dizzy after being attacked last night. Thanks for sending the flowers."

He did a double take. I saw him make a mental note to tell his assistant not to send me flowers next time. That's when he'd find out she hadn't.

"I've been looking over your paperwork," Lennox said. "Despite our warning, you're insisting that one of our own is guilty."

"I'm not insisting. I'm just concluding it, based on the evidence."

"And now you have a supposed assault?"

"*Supposed* assault?" I said, pointing at my face, sporting all the colors of the rainbow and—I might add—not covered by makeup.

"Are you going to say next that one of your fellow detectives was skulking around the back of your house, lying in wait for you?"

"I don't know who it was. But detectives can skulk. We're professional skulkers. Cimmatoni skulks. Why couldn't he do his skulking in my backyard? And furthermore—"

"If you don't resolve this case in a satisfactory manner, it'll cost you your job. If you do it right, I'll offer you a transfer anywhere, a promotion, a pay raise—you name it."

"You're offering to pay me to ignore evidence pointing to a cop? If that's what you're saying, tell me directly."

The chief sat there uncomfortably, as one does when his head is in that location. He knew enough not to answer my question with a yes. But neither did he say no. He waved the back of his hand at me.

"I think we know where we stand, Detective. Close the door behind you."

As I walked out of the chief's office and shut the door, my eyes fell on that photo of him, his wife, and his daughter. The moment I saw it, lightning struck. I pulled my Olympus from my trench coat pocket and took a picture of the picture.

I fought traffic and returned home at 5:50. Hours of time to experience eight minutes of being threatened and bribed.

I opened my laptop to the crime scene pictures, then to the photos of the photos on the mantel. I scrolled through them until I landed on one in particular. There, in the third frame on the left side, was a picture with the professor's arm around a girl on his left and another on his right, with two boys to the outside. I didn't need to look at the picture I'd taken an hour ago to recognize that one of the girls was Chief Lennox's daughter.

❧❧

I fell asleep, this time in the recliner, and woke up at seven. I showered and found a clean shirt and was heading toward Kendra's house when I got stuck behind a fender bender. I considered calling her, but I knew whatever I said would sound like an excuse. I had such a track record of excuses that legitimate reasons don't count. I'm the dad who cried wolf.

I rolled down the window. The smell of brakes and wet asphalt didn't help my head. I thought about flipping on the siren, but I didn't want to get another reprimand, like the time I used sirens to get home in time to watch the season finale of *24*.

I pulled up to Kendra's apartment; she'd been here eighteen months. It was only my second visit, though I'd driven by a dozen times hoping to catch a glimpse of her. As I walked to her door, I noticed the bushes, the bad lighting, and figured out six hiding places and three escape routes for an assailant. I'd talked to the manager about it when I was here the first time. I'd do it again, but this time I wouldn't make the mistake of mentioning it to Kendra.

The number on her door was hanging loose, so I reached for my Swiss Army knife that hangs from a thin metal wire on the inside of my belt. It was the only gift my father ever gave me. He'd thought it clever that it wasn't kept in the pocket but hidden under the belt. As far as I knew this was the full extent of my heritage from my father. I wondered what my daughters would say I'd passed on to them.

I straightened the number, then tightened the screw. I breathed deeply and knocked. I heard her on the other side, looking through the fish-eye lens.

"What were you doing?" she asked, before the door completely opened. She stepped out and looked at the door. "I should've known. Like I'm not capable of fixing a crooked number."

"I know you're capable. I just—"

"I didn't open the door before looking through the peephole."

"Good. Did you have the Mace in your hand just in case?"

"No. But when I saw it was you, I wished I did."

I laughed. It would have been one of those perfect father-daughter moments…if she'd laughed too.

Not that it was a full-fledged scowl. It was more a look of moderate disapproval. But I learned many years ago that the mildest disapproval from a daughter is a twisted knife in her father's heart. In my visits to Kendra over the years, I'd walked away with bloodstained shirts. Andrea was a long-term hemorrhage. Kendra was a recurrent stabbing.

In all fairness, I've fired off my share of rounds at her too. I always found myself looking back and rewording things. But it was too late. It's always too late.

She'd invited me to dinner, yet I was sure an hour later she'd regret it. I looked at her knowing that whatever I said or didn't say would be wrong. Just then I remembered I had something in my hand. I held them out to her.

"What are those?"

"Gerbera daisies," I said.

She didn't take them. I set them on a magazine on the coffee table. Apparently this wasn't right, since she quickly scooped them up, rescuing the magazine.

"Kendra, is there any chance we could…you know…have a good relationship?"

"It's a little late for that."

"Could you just…give it a try?"

"Am I supposed to feel guilty? Like it was my fault?"

"I didn't mean that. It was my fault, not yours. Really. But I was hoping maybe the judgment would expire."

"*I'm* being judgmental?"

"No. A judgment's a legal decision against somebody. It expires after ten years. I just meant—"

"You think I don't know what a judgment is? You've always thought I'm stupid."

I'd never thought that. But I was beginning to wonder.

"Remember Stephen, the guy I was in love with?"

"Short guy with the goatee?"

"That was Sedgwick. He loved me too. Stephen was the guy you harassed."

"Remind me."

"We see you at a restaurant, and I make the mistake of going to the restroom. You tell him if he ever hurts me, you'll kill him and make it look like an accident."

"Okay, the guy with all the piercings. I said it good-naturedly."

"Right, which is why you gave him three examples of how you might kill him."

"It was two examples. I'd just started the third when you got back. I never even finished."

"It's funny to you, but he was terrified. And it's my life you messed up."

"You think Stephen was the right guy for you? Because if you do, I'll get a metal detector and go find him tomorrow and apologize. I mean it."

"You'd do that?"

"In a heartbeat. Just say the word."

"No. He wasn't the right guy for me."

"Is he the…" I paused as if I'd stepped on a land mine, and any attempt to lift the foot would blow off a leg.

"Father of my child? No." Long pause. "You wouldn't like him."

"Do you?"

"I thought I did, but he's gone. Didn't want the responsibility. Anybody who'd leave me because I'm having his baby would leave me for a dozen other reasons."

"Or a hundred. I meant what I said, sweetheart. I'll help you financially. Or any other way."

"Abortion? That was the father's solution."

"I'd never want you to hurt yourself like that."

"Thank you."

"I'll do anything, and on your terms. I love you. I want to help you."

She stared at me, as if trying to figure out a Rubik's Cube.

"The side of your face is bruised," she said. "What happened?"

I told her the story. As I did, her face softened. She got me a cold pack and medications, natural ones, the kind that didn't require the killing of ducks or armadillos. She asked me to put on some orange ointment made out of kumquats or something. It smelled funny but felt good. Mulch could lick it off when I got home.

Over dinner we talked civilly. I asked her about her work as a real estate agent. We stayed away from the hundred subjects that would divide us and talked about the dozen we had in common. Especially Sharon. This was the first time since her mother died that Kendra and I had gone thirty minutes without fighting.

It was the best meal of vegetables, fruits, nuts, and carrot juice I've ever had. To be there with my little girl, no darts flying for the last two hours, was…a taste of heaven.

As I left, she thanked me for the flowers. I wouldn't have traded that moment for all the cheeseburgers and orange malts in the world.

22

FRIDAY, DECEMBER 6, 10:30 A.M.

MY REGRET IN NOT REPORTING to work the day before was that I hadn't seen the other homicide detectives and couldn't study their faces. Whoever had attacked me Wednesday night would likely have a bruise, where I struck him with the flashlight. But only four others were in Friday, and by then a bruise could have been covered. Cimmatoni was gimpy, probably his rheumatism. No bruises were obvious. Everyone kept their distance but Tommi. And she hadn't been my assailant. He'd been too strong. It must have been a man.

I left headquarters to meet Carp in her home office in Northwest Portland, near Wallace Park, twelve minutes from downtown. Her furniture was modern. No clutter, yet the house seemed comfortable and fit her. I admired her wall hangings—award-winning photos she'd taken of bridges, buildings, forests, mountains, lakes, animals, and people. I've done enough crime scene photography to appreciate good stuff. I vaguely sensed that something was missing. Then it came to me—no photos of dead bodies.

She took me into her photo lab and sat me down next to her in front of a twenty-one-inch monitor displaying a wallpaper of multicolored flowers in a meadow with breathtaking clarity.

"That's beautiful," I said.

"Thanks." I was slow to figure out she'd taken the picture.

"I've superenlarged the mantel and the photos on it in five of the pictures taken in the last year before the murder." Then she took my own photos of Palatine's mantel, and my close-ups of each picture. "Each of these pictures shows nine photos, but there were eight after the murder. The ninth is missing. Just like you figured."

I nodded.

She called up another image on the monitor. "Here's my best resolution of that missing photo, using a computer enhanced sharpening feature. It shows the professor and two females, a blonde and a brunette. Based on his height you can judge theirs. Obviously their faces are blurred. Even eye color's questionable with this degree of enlargement and enhancement. Sorry."

"Considering they were just tiny spots in the background on the originals, I'm amazed you got this much." I pointed to something shiny. "Jewelry?"

"Earrings on this girl and part of a chain necklace on this one. If not for reflection from the original flash, we wouldn't see them. You're positive you don't have anything taken with a digital camera?"

"These were from Palatine's camera, a Canon SLR," I said.

"Good camera, but it's all film, not digital. For magnification this extreme, I need a digital file."

She pushed her chair back from the computer. "So who swiped the photo from the mantel?"

"My money's on the murderer. The question is why."

"Because of the identity of the girls in the picture, right?"

"One of them anyway."

"You think the professor had a compromising relationship?"

"He seemed to have a pattern of compromising relationships. But the killer must have thought the girls would point a finger at him."

"Or maybe the girls' jewelry?" Carp said.

"I never thought of that."

She smiled. "Find me another picture, taken with a digital camera, even if it's just the mantel in the background again. Maybe I'll get you faces you can recognize."

"Thanks."

"Don't mention it. I'm one of those helpful journalists."

"Lunchtime," I said. "Thinking what I'm thinking?"

She raised her eyebrows. "Double cheese, double pepperoni? I know just the place. I'll drive."

She took my arm, pulling me to her front door. Once you know their love language, everything falls into place.

Two hours later I took Abernathy with me to meet Jenn Lennox, who insisted we meet at a Starbucks in Gresham, on Division, next to Red Robin.

"Interviewing the chief's daughter is strictly under the lid," I said.

"Won't she tell her father?"

"Let's hope they don't have that kind of relationship."

"What kind?"

"The talking kind."

"Why are we at Starbucks?"

"She didn't think a donut shop was cool. I had to guarantee she could have a venti Frappaccino. Told her the sky was the limit."

We sat in the most private corner, not wanting to bump elbows with the Wi-Fiers or buoyant caffeine-happy greeters or be seen by passersby. Truth is, I used to spend lots of time at Starbucks. I was named employee of the month twice without ever working there. But one-third the price plus unlimited refills at Lou's lured me away.

The girl appeared, dressed like she'd raided the giveaway table at Salvation Army. If she didn't live up to *my* apparel standards, you can imagine what a sight she was.

She had a face that could have set off a thousand metal detectors. Rings everywhere—lips, cheek, eyebrows, half a dozen on the ears. She was a walking jewelry store. It was the same unhappy face from the family portrait, but it weighed a few pounds more, both in flesh and metal. Her hair was purple and orange.

"Jenn Lennox?"

"Mr. Detective?" she asked through her chewing gum. Her voice was baby talk, and her eyelashes batted like a butterfly. I don't know if her flirtatiousness was conscious. Maybe it was her way of fishing for Frappaccinos.

I ordered the drinks from a friendly young guy named Matt, plus the double chocolate brownie she informed me she couldn't live without. She marched over to a stack of coffee mugs near a CD rack displaying a young male musician. She took out her cell phone and held it up to take a picture. She squealed, thrilled she'd gotten this photo. While we waited, she popped her gum, then picked it off her lip rings. Her hair was making its way to her left eye. She pulled it back, but it kept obeying the law of gravity. She kept pulling down her skirt. It obeyed a different law.

She was a little girl trying to look grown-up. It wasn't working. No coffee or chocolate yet, and she was already so jittery she could jump-start a car. She kept chewing her fingernails, but there was nothing left. I was afraid she was going to start on mine.

After sitting with her five minutes, we learned that she knew everything and hated everyone. Kids have always been know-it-alls. I was, I guess. But I don't recall the cynicism going so deep. The chief's daughter reminded me of my Andrea at that age.

"How did you know Professor Palatine?"

"That's what this is about? You said you wanted information." Her voice was no longer baby talk, but nasal and whiny. Made me miss the baby talk.

"You said you wanted a Frappaccino. You got what you came for, and a brownie too. How about the information? If it's good, I'll give you a Frap to go. Tell me about the professor."

She leaned forward. "I'm a senior, and they said we could take a course at Portland State. Figured I'd do it to meet guys. Philosophy was one option. It sounded cool."

"Why were you at the professor's house?"

"He invited new students over."

"Do you remember who took this picture?" I handed it to her.

"Gross," she said. "I don't know who took it."

"Who else was there?"

"The four of us in the picture and the professor."

"Plus whoever took the picture."

"The professor mainly talked with the other two girls. Cheerleader types."

She said it with a secretive voice—the type that makes you want to ask questions to find out what she's hiding. So I asked for a while before I figured out she had nothing to hide. Any secrets were an inch below the surface, eager to get out…and absolutely useless.

"I have to pee," she said. In a moment she was gone.

I saw the look on Clarence's face. He appeared unsympathetic both to her and her bladder. I had the feeling she'd used a word his children don't.

She returned, talkative, caffeine sinking in, along with the promise of imminent sugar from the Starbucks chocolate-hazelnut biscotti and the package of chocolate-covered coffee beans she'd wrangled from me in exchange for renewed interest in our conversation. I looked at the drinks and minidesserts and considered that I'd already paid for three full lunches at Burgerville. *This better be worth it.*

High on the list of things cops don't like are: wandering, and inability to answer a question without interjecting irrelevant self-disclosure. (Relevant self-disclosure: I killed the guy; I saw the guy who killed the guy. Irrelevant self-disclosure: I was finishing up my skinny vanilla latte when I saw this dress at the Gap, and I thought Brandy would be so jealous if she saw me in it, and I…")

"How'd you like the philosophy class?"

"I hated it."

"What'd you think of the professor?"'

"I hated him."

"The boy with you in the picture?"

"I hated him."

"What'd you think of the cheerleader girls?"

"I despised them."

Good. There *was* a thesaurus in her brain.

She looked at Clarence, then me, then said, "Boring."

Two boys walked in the door, and in an instant she was up greeting them. She took out her cell phone and took pictures of them. Then she posed with one of the boys and coerced the other into taking a picture of the two of them, Starbucks counter behind them. She said her friend Tasha "just won't *believe* I saw you here." She punched buttons on her phone and sent the photo to Tasha apparently and said she'd have to download it when she got home and post it on MySpace.

I took note that caffeine helps people say and do stupid things with more energy and enthusiasm. I beckoned her over and asked if we could wrap it up.

"Do you think I'm silly, Detective?" It was one of the first nonsilly things she'd said.

"The thought occurred to me," I said. "But if you have evidence to the contrary, now would be a good time to present it."

"My parents think I'm no good."

"Are they right?"

"What?"

"*Are* you no good?"

She thought about it. "My father thinks he knows everything. He's always telling me what to do. And he's never happy with my choices."

It struck me—that's how I felt about God. A killjoy who never liked what I did, so why try? And if He didn't like me, okay, I didn't like Him either.

"It's not easy being a dad," I said.

"Sometimes he's just mean."

"My guess is—" I couldn't resist—"his bark is worse than his bite."

"You sound like him."

"Listen, if you remember something about the professor, or about someone who hated him, I mean way more than you did, call me, would you?"

I handed her my card.

"Will my dad find out?"

"Not if you call this number. Your dad doesn't answer the phone in detective division."

An hour later, weather cooperating, I decided not to take on city traffic and instead walk the half mile to Portland State University. I passed Seattle's Best, a caffeine oasis located in the middle of a three-hundred-foot desert between two Starbucks. Had I not just been at a Starbucks with Jenn Lennox, I would have stopped. Suddenly, realizing I could justify it on the basis that I needed to warm my hands, I turned around and ordered a large coffee.

I walked to Broadway, then headed south to the Park Blocks and Portland State

University. The artsy attractions along the way made it more interesting than two laps around a track. I've never actually entered the Portland Art Museum, but I feel cultured walking by it. Besides, there's a Polish sausage vendor on that sidewalk who's made meat into an art form.

At the University Station Post Office, I asked a vacant-looking underclassman where I'd find the academic dean. He scrunched his face, mumbled about a provost, then pointed, as far as I could tell, to the second building, Cramer Hall. The directory led me to the third floor.

A secretary assured me they didn't call them deans, but provosts. The academic provost was Dr. Hedstrom. He'd been a highly reputed sociology professor before that, she explained. I nodded, like I cared. She told me to wait in an undersized chair while she fetched him. I paced. The hallowed halls of academia are not my home.

Two minutes later, the secretary returned to the reception area, followed by a provost-looking individual. He was a thick-throated, chinless man who could have shaved from cheek to Adam's apple without angling the blade. There's a lot of gravity in this world, and Hedstrom was carrying more than his share. I'm no lightweight, but if I'm a moon, he's Jupiter. Shoulders stooped, head tipped forward like it needed something to prop it, he made eye contact with the floor tiles. He beckoned with his fingers. I followed, shifting to my lowest gear not to rear-end him.

We entered his office, which smelled of polished wood. His redwood bookcases were masterpieces. A picture on the wall showed him standing straight and slim forty years ago with a college basketball team. He'd probably shrunk three inches since then. It's a tough world that makes a man shrink. One day, like all of us I thought, he's going to just disappear. And then what? What's on the other side? Nothing? Something? What?

Hey, he'd been a highly reputed professor. Maybe I should ask him.

Nah.

"I am Dr. Elwin Hedstrom," he said, as if I should be impressed.

"Nice to meet you," I said, lying.

He laced his fingers at the Greenwich median of his equator and plunged into what I'd told him I wanted to discuss.

"I had my issues with Dr. Palatine."

"Did you?"

"He assumed that humans are social beings by their nature and subscribed to the position of Francisco de Vitoria that statally organized peoples were in need of a legal order to govern their mutual relations."

It's hard to know what to say to such a statement.

"A rather Thomistic assumption, don't you think?" Hedstrom said. "He was too eclectic and in many respects Hegelian."

"I know that name. Pro bowler or NASCAR driver?"

He produced an unfriendly chuckle. "How quickly we make light of what we don't understand."

"That was a Wolfian assumption," I said.

"Thomas Wolf?"

"Nero Wolfe."

The professor grinned, but the grin started at his teeth. My inner child, wishing to correct this, considered whether to raise his lower teeth or drop his lower lip. I chose to resist the instinct to give him, as the old philosophers might have put it, a knuckle sandwich.

The verbal sparring continued: He tested me by using bigger words and more abstract concepts, citing names of sociologists and philosophers. I tested him by dropping the names Sam Spade, Philip Marlowe, Lew Archer, and Jack Bauer. Before long we each knew the other was a moron.

"Anything unusual you can tell me about Professor Palatine?"

"Unusual?"

"I didn't make the word up. It means different or remarkable."

His head shook slowly, as if someone else were doing it for him. It was then that I noticed a little wooden mount on his desk, which contained a small ink bottle and a dark blue fountain pen.

"As the academic dean, sorry provost, you've probably heard your share of gripes about teachers, right? I'm looking for people who disliked Dr. Palatine. Any complaints lodged against him?"

I learned years ago never to take my eyes off someone's face when I ask a question or when they're answering. At the sound of one particular word, maybe a name or place, there's a facial twitch, smile, frown, smirk, a flash of anger in the eyes, a look of fear or discomfort. That look may disappear in a heartbeat. Miss it, you miss everything. I'd just seen something in Hedstrom.

It took him time to find his tongue. Soon after he did, I wished he hadn't. He jabbered ten minutes without saying anything. He spoke Sominex, wrapping it up with: "One would, indeed, have to have had a long history in academics to appreciate the high standards we have rigorously met over the decades. We are absolutely aware, if I may put it that way, of our responsibility to maintain the highest standards of academic achievement and with that to provide an example of personal and contextual fidelity to certain established ethical norms, as recognized by and indeed fostered by the larger university. We must operate consistently within our own consensus of mutually acceptable norms. Inevitably certain concerns are raised, but we cannot assume these to be authentic. We have a responsibility to our faculty, our students, and, yes, to our constituency. We make no pretense of perfection, but we maintain the highest standards of humanistic ideals, as it were. Do you follow my meaning?"

"Indeed," I said. "Actually, I may possibly, to put it that way, have missed your meaning, so to speak. If there was one, as it were."

He stared impassively, but I saw fire in his eyes, and I was glad to have lit it.

"This university," Hedstrom continued, "must operate by our own consistent standards which may be beyond your grasp. I am not certain you comprehend either the intricacies or, shall we say, the delicacies incumbent upon one entrusted with the position that the stewards of this academic community have seen fit to bestow upon myself."

"That sounds like a Plutonian approach."

"Do you mean Platonic?"

"No. Plato was a philosopher. Pluto was a dog in the Disney cartoons. Smaller than Mickey Mouse, but he's a dog…go figure. You may be more familiar with Goofy, who reminds me of some of your statements."

He looked at me through half-closed eyes, trying to appear above it all. He wasn't. The fire in his eyes was raging now. All the better, as I hoped it would cause him to say whatever he was holding back.

"Where were you the night of November 20, between the hours of 10:00 p.m. and midnight?"

"See here. I have been academic provost of this university for fifteen years, am a graduate of Dartmouth, and have been honored by the American Society of College Professors."

"You must be proud of yourself. Where were you the night of November 20?"

"I wouldn't know. That was last month."

"Sixteen days ago. Care to guess?"

His head shook again, the same way, as if pulled by strings.

"In the Ivy League you had to use the little gray cells occasionally, didn't you? Summon up that genius that got you through Dartmouth. Check a calendar; then tell me what you were doing two weeks ago Wednesday night."

For the next fifteen minutes I tried to shake him empty, like a bag of peanuts. But he was a lot to shake, and I had little to show for it. He wasn't telling me what I needed to hear. Feeling I'd lost a battle, I decided to leave him with something to ponder.

"Our discussion raises a question, something you can ask your students. If Goofy and Pluto are both dogs, and the world of Disney should operate by its own consistent standards, then how come Goofy stands on two legs and Pluto on all

four? And why is Pluto's nose on the ground, w

to his doctoral certificate in its golden frame. "

been written on the Pluto/Goofy conundr

"What did you say your name was, De

tain pen, dipped it, then rested its point on fan

"Cimmatoni, two *m*'s. Bryce Cimmatoni."

He wrote it down.

It was getting dark, so I boarded a TriMet bus to get me back to the par

As I drove home, I kept rolling Hedstrom over my investigative tongue.

like the aftertaste.

I considered changing my policy and conducting interviews unarmed. One of these times I was going to lose it. Pistol-whipping a professor does not look good on one's résumé when you're trying to get your next job as security cop at Toys "R" Us.

Maybe you wonder if I regret not having punched the academic provost in his piehole. The truth is, I *do* regret it. I wish now I would have.

Because if I had, he might not have stayed late at his office. And if he'd gone home early and his wife had nursed his aching jaw, fixed him chicken soup, and fed him Rocky Road ice cream, maybe he wouldn't have taken Polo, his Yorkshire terrier, out for a 9:30 p.m. walk in Montavilla Park.

And if he hadn't done that, maybe at 9:46 p.m. he wouldn't have been shot to death.

"She is the daintiest thing under a bonnet on this planet."
SHERLOCK HOLMES, *A SCANDAL IN BOHEMIA*

SATURDAY, DECEMBER 7, 9:15 A.M.

"WHY WOULD SOMEONE KILL Dr. Hedstrom?" Clarence asked.

"His wallet was stolen. Looks like a mugging."

"You believe that?"

"Not for a second," I said. "The killer thought Hedstrom knew something. You attended university. What would an academic dean know about professors?"

"He'd know the complaints filed against them."

"I need to see those complaints."

Hedstrom's murder investigation fell to Chris Doyle and Kim Suda. Obviously, they'd be consulting me since I was one of the last to see him alive. I left them a message that I'd be spending most of my Saturday at the precinct. They dropped in around 11:00 a.m. Doyle's lazy eyelids reminded me of a frog.

"Okay, that's it," he said, after five minutes.

"That's what? You asked me three questions."

"Lots of people to talk with."

"You'll be getting back to me?"

"We know where you work."

"I'll give you my notes from the Hedstrom interview."

"If we want them, we'll ask." Doyle smirked at Suda. They seemed to be enjoying an inside joke.

"I need to search Hedstrom's files to see what he had on Palatine."

"Don't think you can do that," Doyle said, setting his meaty chin.

"Why not?"

"His records are part of our case. You handle yours, we'll handle ours."

"The cases are related."

"You don't know that. You're the one who's been saying the killer's a detective. People are wondering if it's you."

"Who's wondering that?"

"It's our case. We don't want any tampering."

"And nothing picked up and removed from the crime scene," Suda said. "Like gum wrappers, for instance." She eyeballed me.

Pretending to ignore her comment and wondering who'd talked to her, I said, "Find out what complaints are on file against William Palatine. It's vital to my case."

"You're on a fishing expedition," Doyle said. "Outrageous speculations are your style."

"Is it just me, Chris, or did you have a second bowl of stupid for breakfast?"

He glared.

"Really, what's your theory?" I asked. "Why'd Hedstrom get killed?"

"Robbery that went south. Doubt they meant to kill him."

"A shot to the head wasn't meant to kill? Somebody could've watched and studied, then laid in wait. Is taking his dog out for a late walk a habit? After a nine o'clock program's over?"

"Oh, is that how detectives do it? We talked with Hedstrom's secretary. She said you picked a fight with him. The guy who picks a fight shortly before someone's murdered is a suspect."

"Hedstrom was arrogant and irritating, but I can handle that. I haven't killed you yet, have I?"

"One other question, Chandler," Doyle said. "Where were you between 9:30 and 10:00 last night?"

"You're wearin' cheese underwear, Doyle."

"What's that supposed to mean, goofball?"

I turned my back on him. I needed to create distance between my fists and his face.

I came home early and found the television on. I pulled my gun, but I wasn't that concerned since when I leave the remote on the couch Mulch sometimes sits on the power button. Sure enough, he was watching the Fighting Irish at Nebraska.

Mulch had raided the garbage can under the kitchen sink. I'd forgotten to stretch the little bungee cord across the knobs. I gave him a stern look and threatened to reduce his bacon ration, but when I saw his face pucker up, I took it back.

I hadn't fixed Mulch a home-cooked meal for a while, so I took out the George Foreman grill and treated us to Hillshire Farm sausages. I had Koch's horseradish and Sweet Baby Ray's barbecue sauce and a pan of Brussels sprouts for Mulch. He loves those puppies when the butter's meltin' all over them. It's one of the few health foods Sharon introduced us to that stuck.

The kitchen phone rang. While I was looking at the phone waiting for the message, Mulch, seeing I was distracted, went for the plate. Sausages fell to the ground. I quickly crouched to put my body between Mulch and the sausages. Just then the room exploded.

Glass flew everywhere, and I didn't know what hit my left shoulder, buckshot or window pieces. It sounded like a shotgun at close range. I wasn't aware of feeling anything until I looked at my gray Mariners sweatshirt, with three holes in it, inches apart. My right hand reached above me to the King Cobra revolver, duct-taped beneath the kitchen table. I yanked it off, slowly opened the back door, and peeked out. Mulch rushed out, growled ferociously, and raced the intruder to the swinging gate. I heard him yelp when it slammed into his face.

Our neighbor, Mr. Obrist, looked over his fence.

"What's going on now? A bomb?"

"Uh, no, it was just an…incident. Somebody paid me a visit."

"Who?"

"My wife's sister, maybe? Not much damage. Some glass to sweep up."

"You're bleeding."

"No big deal…I just…" I looked at my sweatshirt. I could swear it had been gray. I didn't remember having a red sweatshirt. It's the last thing I recall, except my gun slipping from my fingers.

This time no wrangling with the EMTs about whether to go to the hospital. Unconscious men who've lost a quart of blood aren't in a position to wrangle.

Next thing I knew I was hearing electronic noises and looking up at Jake and Clarence. Jake handed me a cup of ice.

"You guys keep showing up when I have an incident."

"Incident?" Clarence said. "You were nearly killed."

"Mulch okay?"

"He wasn't hit," Jake said, "but he's concerned about you. Janet's with him."

"Mulch saved my life."

"How's that?"

"My left shoulder was where my chest had been a quarter of a second earlier. If Mulch hadn't gone for the sausage right then, I wouldn't have ducked."

"Sounds like the providence of God," Clarence said.

"I'm thinking it was Mulch liking sausage."

"They're not mutually exclusive," Jake said. "You think God couldn't use the instincts He put in Mulch to save you?"

"That phone call? I wonder if I wasn't supposed to stand and answer it to give the shooter a clearer look."

"This is getting way too dangerous," Clarence said.

I nodded. "Good thing I've usually got a bodyguard the size of a buffalo to take a bullet for me."

SUNDAY, DECEMBER 8

I escaped the hospital the next day, leaving the other inmates behind. After being face-licked by my bullie, I entered the old brownstone and found my big Glock still on the coffee table in the living room, where I'd left him before heading to the kitchen and almost getting my head blown off while eating sausage. I held Daddy Glock close because it'd been years since we'd spent a night apart. He seemed okay.

Thanks to Jake, my kitchen now featured a four-by-five-foot piece of plywood where a window had been. I walked the house, checking my other guns. At the back of the closet was my original pellet gun, the one I shot out streetlights with forty-five years ago. Mom had threatened to confiscate it, even though I warned her that if she wanted to take my gun, she'd have to pry it from my cold dead fingers. She said she was glad to oblige and cracked me over the head with a broom handle, then hid my gun for thirty days. That was the last time I messed with Mom.

I like my guns spread around the house, like drink coasters. But I'd rather have to put all of them away someplace safe because grandchildren are visiting. Would Kendra let her kid come over? Did I dare hope? She'd visited me in the hospital, and though she'd scolded me for not being more careful, it was a Sharon sort of scolding.

Mr. Obrist had retrieved the King Cobra from the deck after I fell. I duct taped it back under the kitchen table, a three-foot portion of which was battle-scarred by buckshot. I considered replacing it, but now it was wartime memorabilia. Better than anything I could buy on eBay. Maybe someday my grandchild could point to it and say, "Tell me that story, Gramps!"

You can't blame a guy for hoping.

The table would also remind me that life is short…and I'd once more teetered on its edge.

I thought about all those close calls, the times in Vietnam and on the streets as a patrol cop and a couple of car accidents and the situations I'd faced hunting down killers. The more I thought about it, the more I came to a realization.

I was one lucky guy.

"How blind we were to Your presence there," Finney said to the Carpenter, shaking his head. "Looking back, with my memory so clear now, I've begun to see how You were with us, guiding, protecting, providing, hundreds of times each day."

"Ten thousand times a day," Obadiah Abernathy said. "We couldna got single breath widout You, my sweet Lord. Every heartbeat was a gift. Yet we was fools enough to wonder if You cared. We was so impatient. And ungrateful."

"But you know better now, My friends," the Carpenter said, smiling. "And even there, you'd begun to realize and to say thanks. For that I commend you both. Well done."

"It was so cloudy then," Finney said. "Now it's so clear."

"It will become clearer still," the Carpenter said, stretching out His right arm. "You have much more to learn. When you look back at your lives on earth, you'll see much I was doing that you never guessed. What you called luck was My providence. I was there even in what you considered disaster. In the new world you'll experience new joys daily. But you'll also discover, as I peel back the layers, what I did for you in the old world. This is what My Father promised you: that in the coming ages He might show you the incomparable riches of His grace, expressed in His kindness to you…the kindness He demonstrated in Me."

Sunday evening, December 8

That night my tender shoulder, which was in far better shape than it could have been, was talking to me. Other aches and pains joined in. I sat back in the recliner and sipped a cream soda while Mulch chewed a soup bone.

When you make a living related to dying, it puts a curious spin on your life. I suppose morticians feel it and medical examiners and oncologists. I know homicide detectives do. On the one hand you feel sorry for the victim and his family. On the other hand, you're excited, because there's a problem to be solved. Mathematicians and scientists and accountants enjoy solving problems. I doubt they feel any guilt about it.

You'd think anyone who deals constantly with death would be forced to come to grips with his own mortality. But it's possible to see your death as inevitable, as I do, yet never as imminent. Sure, I'll die, but not this minute or hour or day or week or month or year. Always death seems decades away, years at least.

But when you take metal and glass in your flesh and realize how close it came to your head, it makes you stop and think. And yet, I found myself denying it even then. I've cheated death before, and I'll do it again. Will I tell myself that until the moment I die?

I looked at my left hand and imagined it was the hand of a corpse, then a skeleton. The destruction of the flesh, accelerated in the *Indiana Jones* movies, seems fiction. Yet what is more certain than death?

When Sharon was dying, I wished her doctors were as good at finding out reasons for death as I am. I wished the problem could be solved with one more night's work. And I wished that her Christian friends would just shut up. When I heard several of them say, "I know God's going to heal her," I almost believed it. When He didn't, I wanted to hunt them down and smack 'em.

I'm not sure how I went from pondering my mortality to being ticked off at Christians, but it happened. See, in my thinking, Christians tend to be either idiots or hypocrites. I'm not fond of either. I'm not saying there aren't good Christians—Jake and Clarence are, and Obadiah Abernathy certainly was. What I'm saying is that, to me, looking for honest Christians is like searching to find clams in a bowl of cheap chowder.

These people who think they can beat the devil with a big toothy smile ought to work homicide or vice or sex crimes for a week. Reality will put a sag on the corners of your mouth.

I hear this stuff about Jesus taking away people's sickness and financial woes. Yet Christians are poor and get sick and die like everybody else, don't they? I mean, do you know any two-hundred-year-old Christians? Sharon prayed to be healed. Her Christian friends prayed for her healing. Didn't happen.

All that health-and-wealth mumbo jumbo on the Big-Hair Channel? It's just pretense, isn't it? And all those "Jesus wants you well" televangelists that collect offerings from people trying to buy their way out of suffering and death—don't those preachers just quietly grow old and die of cancer and strokes like everybody else?

I can't stand these holier-than-thous, with their swaggering self-righteousness, their spiritual one-upmanship.

Buddy Darson was my partner for two years when I wore a uniform. Buddy's a deacon or a trustee or a grand pooh-bah in some church. But he lied on his reports, cheated the clock, stole supplies from the department, and looked down the barmaids' blouses.

Some of the most racist cops I've ever known say they're Christians. If that's what it means to be a Christian, I'm better off a pagan. At least I'm not a hypocrite. That counts for something.

I hope.

I don't live in the sweet by-and-by. I live in the nasty here and now. And if I can take down perps and save kids' lives and keep women from being raped, it may not make me Saint Francis of Assisi, but hey, it's better than turning my cheek while scumbags rule the city.

These are thoughts that go through my mind when it dawns on me that at any moment someone in the shadows could put a bullet through my head.

MONDAY, DECEMBER 9

Jake told me it doesn't make sense to be at work two days after you're shot through your back window, but I wanted to make a statement to someone who likely would see me at work: "You missed me, bozo." Well, not missed, but the damage wasn't that serious. I practiced not wincing in front of the mirror, but sometimes, after a quick movement, I felt the tears in my eyes. Since my doctor wasn't watching, I doubled my pain meds.

When Manny came to my desk and asked me if I was okay, I assured him it was nothing. I no longer point to my extra chair because neither of us wants him there. Apparently I convinced him not to feel sorry for me, since within five minutes he was waving a handful of papers in my face.

"I got to the professor's house late, remember?" Manny said. "So this morning I asked for their report."

"Whose report?"

"Patrol's. Dorsey and Guerino. Obviously you didn't read it."

"Why should I? They filled me in when I got there."

"They tell you they left the scene?"

"They what?"

"It's right there." He tossed the report on my desk. "A guy across the street grabs another guy, takes something and runs. So they run after him."

"Dorsey and Guerino? Both of them?"

I looked over the report. I felt the heat rising off my forehead.

I called patrol. "Sergeant Parfitt? Did you know Dorsey and Guerino abandoned the Palatine crime scene?"

"I knew. There was good reason. Didn't you read the report?"

"Just did. But there's no such thing as a good reason. I need to meet with those guys pronto. The scene may have been compromised."

"Day off for both. You really need me to call them in?"

"Absolutely."

Time passes slowly when I'm mad. An hour later Dorsey and Guerino, in plainclothes, walked in. I know the look of two guys trying to get their stories straight.

"What's he doing here?" Guerino asked, pointing at Clarence.

"He's my bodyguard. And he's been assigned to this case."

"I'm not talking in front of him."

"Chief says he stays. This meeting's off the record, right Clarence?"

He nodded.

I held up their report. "You left the crime scene."

"We were only gone three minutes," Dorsey said. "Five at most."

"Your job was to protect the scene."

"The professor was dead," Dorsey said. "Somebody pulled a knife on a living person."

"One of you should have stayed."

"Pursue a criminal without backup? The same manual that says we stay at the crime scene also says we can't ignore a crime against a person. And we shouldn't pursue without backup if a partner's available."

"He wasn't available. He was confined to the scene." I sighed. "Tell me exactly what happened."

"The guy with the knife yelled at the other guy to give him his wallet," Dorsey said.

I turned to Guerino. "Describe the men," I said, holding up my hand to silence Dorsey.

"I can't."

"Why not?"

"They were wearing ski masks."

"You mean the assailant was wearing a ski mask?"

"Both were."

Words escaped me.

"Look, one of them pulled a knife on the other one," Dorsey said, through my hand.

"You're saying the victim was wearing a ski mask?"

"It was cold," Guerino said.

"Yeah, all kinds of innocent citizens wear ski masks in Portland."

"We didn't dress him," Dorsey said.

"Victims don't wear ski masks. People who don't want to be identified wear ski masks. Criminals wear ski masks. Who else wears a ski mask?"

"Skiers?" Guerino said.

"Was there snow on the ground?" I asked. "Did they have skis and poles and goggles and an SUV and mugs of hot chocolate? Was there a Saint Bernard?"

"You're a jerk," Dorsey said.

"Why didn't you tell me you'd left the scene?"

"We knew you'd be mad, and—" Guerino stopped when he saw Dorsey's eyes.

"You and Abernathy here were having a tizzy fit," Dorsey said. "You never asked us for a report, and we had no chance to tell you. You wanted us to stay out of your precious crime scene. We put it all in our report. Not our fault if you didn't read it. Speaking of which, if we hadn't gone after a guy running around threatening people with a knife, you realize the liability?"

"But two guys in ski masks?"

"Okay, looking back at it…but at the time we saw a knife pulled and some-body accosted. We can't ignore that. Maybe it looks different from behind a desk, but that's how it works on the streets."

"Don't tell me how it works on the streets. I wore a uniform for ten years."

"Bet you couldn't fit into it now," Guerino said.

"Bet your brain could fit in a walnut shell." I started pacing. "Once you chased them, did you keep them in sight?"

"The guy on the ground said, 'I'm okay—get him.'"

"So you took orders from a man wearing a ski mask?"

"Stop with the ski mask, would you? We chased the guy. He went over a fence, into a backyard. Guerino went over after him, and I ran on the sidewalk hoping to head him off."

"And?"

"He disappeared."

"Like you disappeared from the crime scene?"

Dorsey stood, leaning forward on the table. "Look, as soon as we lost the guy, we ran back to the scene."

"Let me guess. The victim was gone."

"Yeah."

"No way anybody bothered the scene," Guerino said. "It was just a few minutes."

"You think they would have left you a note saying they'd been there? You know what can be taken from or left at a crime scene in three to five minutes? They say intelligence skips a generation. The good news is, your kids will be brilliant."

"Word is," Dorsey said, "you're blaming detectives for the murder. So—now you can blame patrol for something else. That seems to be your way. Blame cops. Me, I blame criminals."

"My way is to do my job. I expect you to do yours."

Guerino started to talk. Dorsey tugged him out the door.

"You were hard on them," Clarence said.

I'd forgotten he was in the room. "Now you're defending cops? Make up your mind."

"They were trying to protect someone."

"Someone wearing a ski mask." I felt my fist hit the table. "Compromised crime scenes drive me crazy. Gawkers come through, neighbors, passersby. Footprints and fingerprints and dirt falling off pant legs and fibers from uni-forms…you know what that does?"

"It irritates you."

"You still don't get it. Why would two men in a fight, right in front of police officers, both be wearing ski masks? Nobody pulls a knife when cops are standing across the street. The ski mask guys were putting on an act."

He pondered it a moment before the light turned on. "To distract the cops and pull them from the crime scene?"

"Exactly. And then what happened?"

"The cops chased one guy."

"And what did the so-called victim do?"

Clarence whistled softly. "Walk across the street and enter Palatine's house?" He opened his notebook computer and started typing.

"So," I said, "do we have *two* killers or one? Was the second guy his accomplice for the murder, too? Had the killer left something at the crime scene? Or did he go back to plant something? Either way the scene was contaminated. He had to evacuate when patrol arrived, but he got back in long enough to do what he wanted. Whatever that was."

I threw down my pen and stretched back in the chair, moaning when a sharp pain went through my shoulder. While Clarence eyed me, I checked the bandage. The blood stain wasn't too bad, and I didn't feel like changing it again.

"I need more manpower. Too much to check out."

"You could set another fire in an apartment," Clarence said.

"Don't think it hasn't occurred to me."

"What would you think about using Ray Eagle?"

"Ray's great," I said. "Best private detective I've worked with. But the department's not going to pay him."

"He'll do it for free."

"Why would he do that?"

"I called this morning. He said business has been light. I told him if he volunteered, his name would make it into my articles, several times. It's an opportunity to make a name for himself."

"Free advertising?"

"Not exactly free. Like you said, he won't get paid for his work. But it'll buy him advertising."

I found Ray's number in my Rolodex.

"Ray? Ollie Chandler. How soon can you start?"

He said he was ready to go.

"How will the chief feel," Clarence asked, "when he hears you've brought in a private investigator to do police work?"

I shrugged. "I'll jump off that bridge when I come to it."

"Elementary. It is one of those instances where the reasoner can produce an effect which seems remarkable to his neighbor, because the latter has missed the one little point which is the basis of the deduction."
SHERLOCK HOLMES, *THE CROOKED MAN*

TUESDAY, DECEMBER 10

BEFORE OUR MORNING WALK, Mulch emptied his half-gallon water bowl. Fully loaded, he was ready to reclaim the city. Mulch's life consists of eating, playing, and sleeping. And while sleeping, he dreams of eating and playing.

Not a bad life. I've considered trading straight across. Right now, with my aching shoulder, it seemed particularly appealing, though I'd never do that to Mike Hammer.

Ever walked into a room and forgot what you came for? This is how dogs operate, except they aren't frustrated by it. They just find something interesting in the room they've entered for reasons now forgotten. Considering all that's happened in my life, a case could be made for a dog's memory.

Speaking of dogs, I spent most of the day like a dog chasing a parked car. I had nothing to show for it but a flat nose.

"I wish we had the DNA results," I told Abernathy as we sat in the Paradise Bakery in Pioneer Place, at Fifth and Morrison. "Palatine's blood could be mixed with the murderer's for all we know. The killer's saliva could be on the beer bottles. We might have collected all the proof that first night."

"What's the holdup on those tests?" Clarence asked. "It's been three weeks."

"Three weeks? That would be a record for DNA evidence. We could only wish."

"I've got another article due tomorrow. You won't let me say much more about the case—talk to me about DNA evidence."

"If we get a DNA match, it's definitive," I said, sounding brilliant. "There's a one in ten billion chance of one person's DNA matching another's. Chances of winning a fifty-million-dollar lottery are way better. Takes a lot more than chemicals and plastic impressions to fake DNA."

"So the rate of solved cases has gone way up, right?"

"That should be happening, but we didn't even start our DNA database until 1992. There's a bunch of criminals we have no DNA for. They can't get flagged because they're not in the database. Then there's this ridiculous wait for results."

"How long?"

"Guess."

"More than three weeks, obviously. A month?"

"Try three to four months."

"You can't be serious."

"While waiting, we're supposed to keep building our case. Fine, unless we're building it against the wrong guy! I spent three months building my case against a woman. Then the DNA samples we'd collected two hours after the murder ended up proving it was a guy who wasn't even on our radar screen. The temptation is to wait and see so you're not wasting your time. But if there's no match, it's a cold case. Lieutenant says 20 percent of the findings absolve the primary suspects, whether it's homicides or burglaries or gas station holdups. You wait three months to discover you've focused on the wrong people."

"And if not for the DNA you might have put them away?"

"If a jury thought the evidence was persuasive."

"So you're telling me those blood samples from Palatine's house are just sitting at the crime lab?"

"Blood, saliva, you name it, sitting there waiting. And that's not the only backlog. Since 2001 they've required DNA samples of all convicted felons to be entered into the database. Over seventy thousand have been entered, but last I heard we had more than twenty thousand DNA sample cards waiting to be processed."

"What's stopping it?"

"Funny you should ask. The *Oregon Tribune*."

"What are you talking about?"

"Remember how the *Trib* advocated police budget cuts? Back in 2003 we cut the state's forensic staff from 135 to 50 people. Far more samples, far more work to do, and fewer and fewer workers to do it."

"I didn't know that."

"It's your job to know. Why haven't you investigated it? Every time cops do something wrong, you tell everybody the juicy details, including false ones."

"The concern is citizen safety. The police department has had its problems."

"Wouldn't citizens be safer if we didn't have to wait three months to get violent criminals off the streets?"

"Can I quote you on that?"

"You can quote me as saying that, by defending police budget cuts, the *Tribune* is responsible for deaths, rapes, and robberies that wouldn't have happened if we'd had data entered sooner."

"I don't agree."

"You don't have to agree. Just quote me."

"It's…unnecessarily accusatory."

"In other words, the *Trib* can dish it out, but you can't take it."

"Look, I'm just trying to inform people. People love this investigation stuff. We can capitalize on the popularity of *CSI*."

"*CSI* is television magic," I said, downing my milk, which I'd rationed perfectly to cover my last bite of an apple fritter. (If you don't gauge it right, you have to get more milk or another fritter.) "They take in a sample and ten minutes later, or an hour, or a day, they have results. In the real world, we wait a hundred days. With enough people, everything could be processed in two days. Go over to Clackamas crime lab headquarters and check out the high-tech gear. They can turn molecular evidence into digital data, then put it into a database. But staff's so limited, it takes forever."

"You're saying it could get done in two days instead of a hundred?"

"And you know what burns me? If the killer's a detective, he knows how long this takes. He probably didn't leave DNA evidence at the scene, but even if he did, it drives me bonkers that he knows he's safe for another two months!"

At three thirty Clarence and I needed to surface for air, so we met Jake in Terry Schrunk Plaza, a block from the Justice Center and three from the *Tribune*. It was sunny but chilly, so we talked as we walked.

A man had been beaten up yesterday and was in critical condition. I pointed to chalk marks on the pavement and blood residue. "I still say there's no way a good God allows this kind of evil and suffering." I wasn't going to let them worm out of it.

"What are your favorite movies?" Jake said.

"What's that got to do with anything?"

"Humor me."

"*Braveheart. Gladiator. Saving Private Ryan. Schindler's List. Amistad. Air Force One.* Stallone and Norris movies in Vietnam. *Twelve O'Clock High. The Shootist* and everything else with John Wayne. *Star Wars. Lord of the Rings.*"

"Okay, good. Now think about the qualities of the characters you admire in each of those movies. What are they?"

Cold wind made me catch my breath. "Courage. Heroism. Sacrifice. Justice."

"And compassion, mercy, love?"

"Those are good too."

"These are the same things you admire in people in real life, right?"

"So?"

"So think about it. Would you ever have been able to see courage without danger? Or heroism without desperate situations? Compassion without suffering? Justice without injustice? Sacrifice without a need?"

I shrugged.

"The virtues of good people inspire us. And in the movies you named, just like in real life, we wouldn't see those virtues if not for evil or suffering."

"I guess that's one way to look at it, but it's a terrible price to pay, isn't it?" I pointed back to the crime scene.

"So, if you could snap your fingers and remove all evil and suffering that's ever existed, would you?"

"Wouldn't you?"

"Well, if we did, there'd be no Helen Keller, Frederick Douglass, Sojourner Truth, Abraham Lincoln, Harriet Tubman, Corrie ten Boom, Dietrich Bonhoeffer, Martin Luther King, or William Wilberforce."

"Who's Sojourner Truth? Or Harriet Tubman?"

Clarence turned and gave me a look. Suddenly I had a good idea.

"And think about Jesus," Jake said. "How would we know the extent of His love and grace if there'd never been evil and suffering?" He put his hand on my shoulder as we walked. "Don't you think it's inconsistent to say on the one hand that all these virtues that surface in the face of evil and suffering are good, then claim there's no way a good God could allow evil and suffering?"

I shook my head. "When people maim and kill each other, it throws a switch inside me. I do what I can to bring justice now. God seems to wait around a lot."

"He says He waits and withholds judgment to give us time to repent and get our lives right with Him," Jake said. "Justice has been restrained. What you're mad at God about—that He's been withholding judgment—is what's kept us all alive, giving us opportunity to repent and accept His grace."

"Isaiah says," Clarence added, "that God will bring justice 'like a pent-up flood.' He's not going to wait forever."

"That time should have come by now," I said.

Jake stopped in the middle of the plaza, so I stopped too. He looked at me and said, "And if it would have, where would you be?"

I sat at my desk, reading the *Tribune* again. It was getting to be a habit. Pretty soon I'd need a support group.

I have to give Clarence credit for his article. Not only did he write about the backup at the crime lab; he called on citizens to raise funds to help us catch up. He proposed fund-raising dinners and car washes. He even suggested a bumper sticker: "Support your police crime lab," and he said he'd put one on his own car.

I called a novelty shop to get one made for him.

My neck tensed when I saw Karl Baylor coming my way.

"Hi, Ollie. How are you?" His thick fingers looked like pork sausages, pressed together. When I shook his protruding hand it was a pliable lump.

"I need to talk to you about the moider."

Detective Baylor grew up in New York before moving to Oregon when he was in high school. I don't know the difference between Brooklyn, Queens, and the Bronx. All I know is that Baylor never says "murder"; he says "moider." This wouldn't be annoying if he were an accountant. But when you're a homicide detective, you use the word, what, three times a minute? Hearing "moider" 180 times an hour can drive you bonkers. Which I believe is also near Brooklyn.

"I've heard you think it's one of us," he said.

"That committed the moider?"

He nodded. Baylor has a reddish face that's big and broad, with insufficient features to fill it. I keep thinking something's missing, but when I count eyes, ears, nose, and mouth, they're all there.

He smiled broadly. It irritated me. Baylor lives under the curse of self-imposed merriment. Unfortunately, the rest of us have to put up with it.

"Isn't it a beautiful day?" he said in an auctioneer's voice, pointing out through the windows to the blue sky overlooking Portland. "Doesn't it just make you want to thank God for His goodness?"

"No."

Someone needs to tell Baylor it's not smart to talk like this to people who are strung tight at three hours of sleep, drink eight cups of coffee a day, and carry loaded weapons.

"You don't like me, do you?" Baylor asked.

The truth is, I disliked him from the first time I saw him, with that toothy tel-evangelist smile and Christian paraphernalia in his cubicle. I feel guilty enough. I don't need large-print Bible verses screaming at me every time I walk by his work-station.

"Look, Detective, I'm all for jolliness. I manage a respectable amount myself. But when someone acts jolly because they think they're supposed to, it bugs me. I know you want to spread your happiness. But it would make some of us happier if you'd keep it to yourself."

He stepped toward me, leaning forward. Baylor's a personal space invader and has the kind of breath no mint can cure. He carries a tin of jiggling Altoids; thousands have perished in vain.

"I'm sorry I bother you," Baylor said.

"Look, nobody from New York is supposed to be happy. LA, okay. It may be drug-induced happy. It may be fake happy, but at least it's…conceivable. But New Yorkers are supposed to be rude and sullen." I paused. "Is Cimmatoni from New York?"

"Pittsburgh. You want me to act like Cimmatoni?"

"It's a start."

He smiled ear to ear. I wanted to deck him.

"What are you after, Detective?" I asked.

"I just wanted to let you know that people are getting concerned. They're…wondering if it's true you think one of *us* was involved in the Palatine moider."

"Tell them to come talk to me, would you?"

"Good idea," Baylor said. "God bless you."

"And you too, Tiny Tim. God bless us, every one."

WEDNESDAY, DECEMBER 11, 9:00 A.M.

Homicide was decorated for Christmas, tree and all. An elf had been busy last night. But thanks to the killer and me, the prevalent spirit wasn't the spirit of Christmas.

I arrived ten minutes early for the detective meeting and sat at a far corner of the conference room thinking of Kendra's visit the night before. I was sure I'd done everything right. I'd hidden the meat at the back of the freezer behind extra-large Costco-size bags of carrots, peas, and string beans, enough to feed a vegetarian army.

For an hour straight we'd been getting along without noticing it. But the moment I did notice, it all fell apart. In my relationship with my daughter, I am Wile E. Coyote, who can blissfully run ten feet beyond the cliff's edge…but only until he notices.

It was 10:15 when, out of the blue, Kendra declared that condoms should be distributed in schools to prevent diseases and pregnancies. So I said yeah, and how about we use the same strategy to solve the problem of battered women by handing out boxing gloves to abusive men.

At 10:23 Kendra marched out the door, slamming it. Mulch hid under Sharon's old hutch. My Wile E. Coyote face, succumbing to gravity, was plastered at the bottom of Father-Daughter Canyon. Somewhere in the distance I heard Road Runner's *beep-beep* mocking me. Every fatherly device I've ever tried was made by Acme.

↔

"Settle in," Sergeant Seymour said. I looked up to see a full room. The closest person was six feet from me.

"First, we're glad Ollie's still with us." Light applause followed—very light. Tommi and Karl. "We're hoping it was a freak incident and it won't happen again, but we're encouraging him to be cautious. Meanwhile, everybody's overworked and we've got to prioritize. I've asked Jack and Noel to help Karl and Tommi on the Frederick case. We've got more to work on there than with Dr. Hedstrom, which seems to have quickly dead-ended. I've got to keep Ollie and Manny on Palatine, so they're out of the rotation for now. This is triage. It's not ideal, but we've got to pull together and make it work."

"So why were we told to block off ninety minutes for a meeting?" Cimmatoni asked.

"It relates to the Palatine case. Detective Chandler's going to carry the ball."

"Great," Suda said.

Tommi gave her a disapproving look. I noticed dark swollen bags under Tommi's eyes.

Sarge didn't know I'd come at 5:00 a.m. to place Ray Eagle's miniature camcorder, looking like a nondescript plastic container, sitting on a front shelf surrounded by manuals. It was pointing at the detectives.

It's easier to get forgiveness than permission, and if no one finds out, you don't have to get forgiveness either. I pressed the record button on the remote in my coat pocket.

"Sarge asked me to read my conclusions about the Palatine case." One look at Sarge's face caused a revision. "He didn't ask me. He gave me permission." Here's what Manny and I are thinking." I saw Manny's expression. "All right, Manny's not so sure. Here's what *I'm* thinking."

"Can we move this along?" Doyle asked.

"Tonight it'll be three weeks since Palatine was murdered. Since then two others have been murdered because of what they knew or saw."

"Speculation," Doyle said. "And those aren't your cases."

"I'm going to read this," I said, holding up a paper. "Please withhold comments till I finish."

"First, the killer planned this meticulously, including the bizarre elements with the noose and ink injections.

"Second, the killer stayed dangerously long at the site. Apparently he knew nobody heard anything, even the broken window, and nobody called 911. Why would he stay unless he knew cops wouldn't come sooner, and he wouldn't be caught? Maybe he had access to a police monitor or experience with police procedure.

"Third, the killer took unnecessary measures that could make him vulnerable, as if he were daring detectives to catch him. He knew enough to avoid being caught, yet he took the time to inject the ink and remove items from the scene."

"What items?" Phillips asked.

"At least one framed photograph and a wine bottle."

"How do you know that?" Doyle asked.

"It's in his report," Tommi said.

"Fourth," I said, "the killer probably came back to the scene after patrol got there and before the detectives arrived. That's in my notes too."

"Fifth, the killer knew how to fake fingerprints and where to place them on the gun."

"We're sure those were fake?" Cimmatoni said, looking at Noel.

"Positive," Sarge said. "Internal Affairs had three lab experts examine it to make sure. They all agreed. Noel's in the clear."

"Leave it to IA," Suda said. "Bet they were disappointed not to hammer one of us."

"Sixth, the killer—I think—knew it was department SOP to search Dumpsters within four blocks of the scene. So he knew where to put the murder weapon—the one with the planted fingerprints."

I got several nods on this one.

"Seventh, the killer—most likely—knew the private phone number of a homicide detective, my number, and called me from the scene."

"Anybody can get a phone number," Cimmatoni said.

"I thought the professor made the call," Kim said.

"We think it was the killer," I said. "Anyway, the killer seemed to know homicide investigative procedures well enough to get around them. And because he took chances and left unnecessary evidence, this may be a game for him."

"That about it?" Sarge asked.

"Any…tentative conclusions based on what I've said?" I asked the group.

I saw the dissatisfied faces.

"Are you thinking…" Karl Baylor stopped and thought how to rephrase it. "The killer's a cop?"

Brandon Phillips looked around the room. "He's thinking more than that. He's thinking the killer was a homicide detective. He's thinking the guy's right in this room."

"Guy or gal," I said, nodding at Tommi and Kim.

"Nice to be included," Tommi said, laughing unnaturally. Suda wasn't smiling.

There's an old theory about announcing something shocking to a group and watching each person's expression to see who's least shocked. Old theories don't always work. And when your pool of suspects is homicide detectives, they're even less viable. We're used to studying people's faces. We know what we'd be looking for—and therefore how to avoid looking ourselves.

But I also knew that gradually faces would become less guarded. That's why I had the video running. It would be my game film.

"Since Noel was framed, does that eliminate him?" Tommi asked.

"Not necessarily," I said, trying to be inclusive. "He has access to his own fingerprints. He could have done it."

"Yeah," Noel said. "I've always wanted to frame myself for murder."

"What about you, Chandler?" Doyle asked. "Eliminated yourself as a suspect?"

"I didn't do it, if that's what you're asking."

"Right," Cimmatoni said. "Why don't we just take a poll and find out which of us *did* do it. That would save time."

"I know this is awkward," I said.

"It's not just awkward," Suda said. "It's ridiculous. I can't believe you're doing this, Chandler. Did Internal Affairs put you up to this?"

"The evidence put me up to it."

I pulled out of my coat pocket a handful of scrap papers. "Everybody gets a paper. Write your name on it, fold it, and pass it in." One minute of corporate whining later, Tommi picked them up.

I held up the scrap papers. "The person whose name is drawn will be the first to say where they were between 10:45 and 11:45 November 20."

"I don't believe this," Phillips said.

"Chandler's a horse's rear end," Cimmatoni said, or something to that effect.

"Okay," I said, pulling scraps out of my pocket and setting them on the table in front of Tommi. "Draw."

Tommi picked out of the middle, unfolded it, and read, "Kim Suda."

So began an hour of alibis.

"Professor Moriarty is not a man who lets the grass grow under his feet. You will not wonder that my first act on entering your rooms was to close your shutters, and that I have been compelled to ask your permission to leave the house by some less conspicuous exit than the front door."
SHERLOCK HOLMES, *THE FINAL PROBLEM*

WEDNESDAY, DECEMBER 11, 1:00 P.M.

THREE HOURS LATER, Clarence and I sat in Ray Eagle's living room, in Vancouver, Washington, across the I-205 bridge from Portland. His furniture was brown, red, and gray, with American Indian paintings on the wall. The chair I was sitting in disproved my theory that attractive furniture is uncomfortable. I rested my feet on a soft bulgy thing Clarence called an ottoman.

Ray connected his camcorder to his TV. He said to me, "So, you see Suda rifling your files, tail her, see her secret meeting with the chief, and her name gets drawn first? A one out of ten chance."

I reached in my right coat pocket and pulled out a bunch of folded paper scraps. I handed them to Clarence.

He looked through them.

"But…they all say Kim Suda."

Ray laughed.

"The trench coat has a pocket divider," I said. "I took the papers they wrote on and stuck them in back. The ones I wrote on were in front."

"You did this in front of a group of professional detectives?" Ray laughed again.

"I didn't want to give Suda more time to think. I wasn't going to take Clarence's approach and leave it up to providence."

"But…Tommi drew other names, right?" Clarence said.

"I replaced my scraps with theirs while everyone watched Suda."

Ray turned on the video and handed me the remote control, making me king.

"Wait," Clarence said. "Did they know they were being videotaped?"

I tried not to laugh.

"Isn't that illegal? Or unethical?"

"Go check with a lawyer or a priest, and get back to us," I said. "Me, I'm just looking to solve a murder. If it helps, pretend I have a photographic memory and we've hired professional actors to re-create the scene as I recall it. That would be just as unfair as this is. We're here to evaluate their body language, responses, anything that could indicate innocence or guilt."

I passed out that photo of the detectives and spouses, taken before Sharon died. Carp had made a dozen copies for me since I needed to flash detective faces around.

"Before Suda answers, let me fill you in. She's short, maybe five one. Fit. Strong but feminine. Great conditioning. She chased a twenty-year-old gangbanger ten blocks before taking him in. Her partner, Chris Doyle, was her backup, four blocks behind. They say he was lying in a heap hyperventilating while Kim handcuffed the perp. Suda moves to her own beat, music playing in her head."

"What about Doyle?" Ray asked.

"A Hercule Poirot when it comes to his soft mannerisms, but the similarity ends there. Reminds me of Jessica Fletcher because people around him have a way of dying. Smokes himself to death, and nobody's eager for him to stop. Anyway, here we go."

I pressed play and was back in the room where all this had happened four hours ago. Except this time I had two more sets of eyes, could see faces at will, and had the freedom to pause and rewind.

"I was at a friend's house pretty late," Suda said.

"What friend?" I heard myself ask.

"Someone who doesn't want to be identified."

Long pause, then Chris Doyle said, "She dropped by my house."

The room was one collective smirk.

"It wasn't what you think," Chris said.

"What would be wrong with what they think?" Suda asked him, ignoring the tittering.

"We were together until you got that text message from your mother about 11:20."

"Your mother sends text messages?" Cimmatoni asked.

"She's high-tech. Was spending the weekend with me and wasn't feeling well. I needed to get home."

"We were together until 11:20," Doyle said. "That's close to time of death, right? And wasn't the killer supposedly there forty minutes earlier? Then you called me when you got home, say 11:40."

"Proves nothin'," Cimma said.

"Yeah," Suda said. "I always make calls while I'm murdering someone. It calms my nerves."

"Clears me though, right?" Doyle said. "I mean, I was home at 11:15 and 11:45 when you called, right, Kimmy? I mean Suda." His chubby face glowed like a Christmas light.

"Kimmy?" Noel said.

"*Kimmy*," Tommi said, putting her hand over her smile.

Suda glared.

"Why didn't you stay home with your mother?" I asked. "What brought you back out at four in the morning when you dropped by our murder scene?"

"None of your business."

"Hiding something?"

"I'm a light sleeper. Occasionally I get up and drive. I had the monitor on and heard about the murder. It was close to my place, so I stopped in."

"Anyway," Chris said. "Back to Kim's phone call at 11:45. That covers me, right?"

"It would," Suda said, "if I'd called your home phone. But I called your cell."

"Way to take him, Kimmy," Cimma said. "You could've been anywhere, Doyle. You're what, ten minutes from the dead guy's? You could have been standing over his body when she called…if she called."

Doyle froze, dragging me back to the present, where we were sitting in Ray's living room. Ray had grabbed the remote and paused.

"Look at his face," Ray said.

Chris's face had gone from red to stark white. It's as if a plug had been pulled, and all the blood drained out. His Adam's apple was moving, but he was swallowing nothing. I didn't need a polygraph to measure his nerves, not when I'd heard him live, and not now that I watched him again.

Clarence typed furiously on his notebook computer.

"You're going to keep that to yourself, right?" I asked him.

"For now."

"Maybe forever. You can't tell anybody I taped this."

He pretended to ignore me.

"He looks guilty," Ray said.

"Doyle or Abernathy?"

"Tell us more about Chris Doyle," Ray said.

"He worked a couple of cases with me when Manny was out and Suda had a family emergency. Doyle's…like a duck on the lake. He's calm on the surface, looks like he's doing nothing, but underneath those legs are paddling. If the perps leave their fingerprints on everything, or they look into surveillance cameras and hand notes written on the back of their phone bills to bank tellers, saying 'Give me all the money,' Doyle will nab them. But he's no creative genius. This crime seems too intricate for him."

"Somebody told me, 'Things aren't always as they seem,'" Clarence said.

Ray walked behind me. "He just looks like your average red-faced guy drinking beer and watching his Buffalo Bills play in December."

"Except Doyle would be more likely to watch ballet," I said. "I think he has sugarplums dancing in his head.

"Okay." I pointed to the screen. "This next guy's Noel."

"The guy who was framed? Plus he's got a solid alibi? Six guys in a bar plus the bartender?" Ray asked. "Are they all close to him…and each other?"

"Just bar buddies. Acquaintances."

"Hard to believe six guys and a bartender would be in on a conspiracy to protect him," Ray said. "What's Noel like?"

"He's a good old boy, nice golfing tan. Smart enough to be an average detective. Doesn't have to be brilliant. He works with Jack."

I stepped toward the screen and pointed out Jack Glissan. "Jack can tell you the names and dates of crimes committed twenty years ago. He's the brains."

We heard Noel's alibi then listened to Manny's. Home with Maria until she left at 10:45 to work night shift at the hospital. Manny was at the house with three kids, who were sleeping until the 3:00 a.m. murder call. He dropped the kids at his sister's. He seemed agitated just talking about it, saying "We weren't the up team" and complaining about journalists coming to a murder scene.

"Okay, Brandon Phillips is next," I said. "His name's about to be drawn."

Ray zoomed in.

"He's looking at his BlackBerry," Clarence said, getting up to point at the object in his hand. "Checking e-mail?"

"Or rehearsing his alibi?" Ray asked.

"Phillips is a detail man," I said. "Precise. Methodical. We did a couple of cases together. Nice guy, but he drove me nuts. He was like a fussy little maid looking for dust in every corner."

"The scars on his face," Ray said. "Acne?"

"Golden Gloves boxer. He reminded us, maybe to make excuses for his face. He's okay, but when you press him, he can get a steel rod up his back. Last year I happened to be driving down his street to avoid traffic. He was shoveling snow in his driveway, and it was like a Wayne Gretzky slap shot."

I pointed to the screen. "The next part's interesting."

After I asked his alibi, Phillips seemed to be thinking for five seconds, then finally looked at Jack and said, "Was that the night we were at your place talking about that cold case at Lloyd Center?"

Jack nodded.

"It was a couple of hours," Brandon said. "Maybe I got there at ten? I had a couple beers, but you were on call, so you couldn't drink. So I left when? Midnight?"

"Closer to twelve thirty," Jack said, a little red-faced when he caught my eye. After all, he'd claimed to drop by Noel's at eleven thirty that night—back when Noel needed an alibi. "Linda came downstairs and reminded me I needed sleep."

"She'll confirm that?" I asked Jack, instantly regretting it when I saw his face.

I paused the tape, then rewound. "So when I ask Phillips for his alibi, what do you see?"

"He's…trying to remember," Clarence said. "Then suddenly he does."

"Which makes you think what?" I asked.

"He hadn't given it much thought?"

"Hold it," Ray said. "The guy's been sitting there twenty minutes. He *had* to be thinking about how he'd answer the question."

"Exactly," I said. "This isn't a man trying to remember. This is a man pretending to try to remember."

"What's the difference?" Clarence said.

"The difference between innocence and guilt?" Ray asked.

"Would Jack and his wife lie for him?" Clarence added.

I've tried not to like Phillips—maybe because he's strong and good-looking and fifteen years younger and the consummate detective. But he isn't an easy guy to dislike. There're those little things. Like him calling me after he'd seen me at Rosie's, wondering if I was okay.

Besides, Cimmatoni was his partner. If he was going to murder somebody, wouldn't he have taken out Cimma years ago?

I froze the frame, and we studied Bryce Cimmatoni. He's a specimen—looks like he was born to conduct mysterious business in nightclub back rooms with guys named Giuseppe and Bruno. You could see him breaking a piano player's fingers for being delinquent on his loan or putting a horse head in somebody's bed. Cimma doesn't give an inch, a cent, or a rip.

But I'd still take a bullet for him. That's how it works.

As I looked at Cimma on film, he was pale with four or five splotches of red. His face had no insulation between lumber and Sheetrock. His hair was gray and receding. His jaw—pit-bull solid—looked like it had been clamping down on people for decades.

His face seemed incurably unhappy and therefore unreadable since it always looked the same—disgusted.

"Is he as tough as he looks?" Ray asked.

"Tougher. He gets no points for personality, but he's a decent detective. His wife Martha was drop-dead gorgeous in her day and at sixty is still striking. She's an oncology nurse. Sweetest person you'll ever meet. She rivals Tommi. How she ended up with Cimma, I don't have a clue."

Come to think of it, I don't know how Sharon ended up with me. When Tommi drew Cimmatoni's name, he set his jaw and said, "I'm not answering."

"Why not?" Sarge asked.

"I have my reasons."

"If you have an answer that clears you," I asked, "how will it be helped by aging?"

"I need to think about it."

"When people need to think about it, it's to get their lies straight."

Cimmatoni might not have killed Palatine, but if looks could kill, I'd have keeled over on the spot.

"He doesn't look happy," Ray said, which was like saying water looks wet. "He never answered?"

"Nope. If he has an alibi, he's not talking."

"What do you think?" Ray asked. "Could Cimmatoni kill Palatine? And Frederick? And the academic dean?"

"He could kill a man in a heartbeat," I said, "if he thought he had good reason to and could get away with it. He worked vice and sex crimes for years. Transferred to homicide four years ago."

"Do you know why?"

"Because he likes to see dead people?"

"What exactly are we looking for?" Clarence asked.

"It's like studying game film," I said. "There's a lot to see. Isolate it. What do you notice about their sitting positions and eye contact and body language? A murderer's always interested in discussions of a murder, just like a home run hitter's interested in discussions of his home run. Even more, since his life could be on the line."

Ray pointed at the screen. "Tommi and Noel look casual. Jack and Cimmatoni interested. But I'd say there's extreme interest by Kim Suda, Chris Doyle, and Brandon Phillips. Look where Phillips is seated. Freeze that frame."

"He's on the front of his chair," I said. "The front eight inches. Why? Nervousness, uncertainty, fear? He's extremely absorbed."

We did this for two hours, starting and stopping, rewinding and commenting, each of us, especially Clarence, jotting down notes. We were only halfway through and it was three o'clock.

"Snack break," Ray said, reading my mind. He threw stuff in the oven while Clarence and I made phone calls. Minutes later we were at Ray's kitchen table, eating Hot Pockets sausage and pepperoni pizza snacks.

"We've got a ways to go," I said. "Let's watch while we eat."

Thirty seconds later I pushed pause again.

"You can enlarge this?" I asked Ray.

"Who you interested in?"

"Noel. He keeps looking down. Why?"

Ray fast-forwarded until Cimmatoni got up for a drink. Suddenly there was a clear view of Noel. Ray zoomed in.

"He's reading something. A magazine I think," Clarence said.

Ray enlarged it as far as he could. "The picture has lots of green and blue above it. Something yellow there and a little white object and a—"

"It's a golf green," I said. "He's reading a golf magazine. Figures. In Noel's mind, work's for people who don't know how to golf."

"What about that guy?" Clarence asked, grabbing the remote and freezing the frame on one man.

"Brilliant, athletic, witty, uncommonly handsome," I said. "Oliver Justice Chandler. Look at that kisser. What does it say?"

"That you need more sleep," Clarence said.

"Question," Ray said. "Has Tommi ever had a romantic relationship with any of these guys?"

"Ten years ago she had something with Phillips," I said. "He's on his second marriage since then. Anyway, Tommi's no whiner, but she got hurt. Felt like Phillips used her, I think."

"She reliable?"

"Tommi? Cal Ripken reliable."

"Married?"

"Yeah. Her husband Peter's a veterinarian."

Tommi offered her alibi in the video. "Peter and I were home alone. Went to bed probably by 10:30. We talked and read."

"Talked and read?" Cimmatoni grunted.

"We love to talk—we're soul mates."

She took ribbing for this.

"Well, we are," she said. "On our five-year anniversary, I put on my wedding dress and Peter rented a tux, and we stood in the same spot we were married."

In the secretarial pool they would have said, "How sweet." Homicide is not the secretarial pool.

Tommi's alibi was simple, straightforward, and the next worst alibi to "I was home alone." It meant that only one other person needed to lie besides her. And that person happened to be her soul mate.

When I asked his alibi, Karl Baylor said, "Tiffany and I were on a marriage retreat. At the Gresham Holiday Inn."

"Just that night?"

"Tuesday and Wednesday nights. Wednesday we visited friends from church, in their room."

"Write down their names, would you?" I felt the ice, not as much from Karl as from Tommi.

"What time did you go back to your room?"

"10:30? 10:45?"

"And you just…went to bed?"

"Lights out at eleven or so, I guess."

"That was it?"

"One final session after breakfast the next morning. I didn't see the paper. When we were driving home Thursday, we heard about the moider on the radio."

Tommi drew Jack Glissan's name.

"Jack's like the coach every guy loves, the one who brings out the best in them. Mind like a steel trap. Last month he took me out to dinner for the twentieth anniversary of the first day we worked together as partners. Not perfect, but I'd trust my life to him. I have. Heck, we were in a bowling league together."

"That settles it," Clarence said. "Killers don't bowl."

"Could Jack be a killer?" I asked. "Anybody could be. Ray could be the killer. His phone number was in the professor's desk. I could be the killer."

"Could you?" Clarence said.

"I don't mean in this case." I hoped my face didn't look like my gut felt. "But with a strong motive, like if somebody pilfered my Fritos…" I eyed my plate, then Ray.

"I only took two."

"It starts with two, then it's a bag, then it's my car, and next my retirement funds."

"I bought that bag of Fritos," Ray said.

"Once they landed on my plate they became mine. That's the law."

"Can we get back to Jack Glissan?" Clarence asked.

"Jack's retiring in the next year or two. Loves to golf, travel with Linda. I don't think he'd do that to her—run the risk of leaving her alone if he was caught."

On the video, Jack told the same story Phillips had, sitting in his living room and Linda coming downstairs and seeing them after eleven.

All in all, some detectives had convincing alibis and some weak ones. But what alibi can you expect for ten thirty until midnight? Playing poker with a half dozen federal judges?

Sitting on Ray's couch I was lost in this thought, then realized one last question remained on the video. I groped for the remote, which had slipped behind a cushion.

"What's your alibi, Chandler?" Doyle spouted off.

I almost pressed fast-forward but knew how it would look.

"At Rosie O'Grady's pub."

"Figures," Cimmatoni said. "How late?"

"Got there at nine, then drove straight home." As I said it, Wally's Donuts, one of them in particular, filled my brain. For all I knew, I'd been abducted by aliens. The hours were missing.

"Then what?"

"Went to bed, slept until I got the call about the moider." I eyed Baylor and pulled a chuckle from Jack.

"So you don't have an alibi?"

"Just my dog, Mulch."

"I called you from Jack's just after eleven," Phillips said. "You didn't answer your cell or your home phone. I'd seen you leaving Rosie's before I went to Jack's, and you didn't look—"

"I didn't feel like answering," I said. Never mind that I didn't remember the phone ringing…or being home to hear it ring.

Clarence and Ray both looked at me silently. The tape finished five minutes later. I turned it off when Sarge dismissed the group. Ray restarted it to watch people's reactions after the meeting. I could feel the same chill in the air as I had that morning. Not one person talked to me—except Tommi, who doesn't count since she would tell Charles Manson to have a nice day.

"Wish we had tapes of their private conversations afterward," Ray said.

"This hasn't made you popular," Clarence said.

I shook my head. "Law enforcement's most sacred credo, on a par with don't shoot innocent bystanders, is *don't tell on another cop*. Nobody seems willing to take care of cops. People take cheap shots at us. The *Tribune* comes to mind. So, as they say, 'we take care of our own.' You're not supposed to violate that. I've crossed the line. And there's no going back."

"One way or the other," Ray said, "somebody's going to make you pay."

"It is one of the curses of a mind with a turn like mine that I must look at everything with reference to my own special subject. You look at these scattered houses, and you are impressed by their beauty. I look at them, and the only thought which comes to me is a feeling of their isolation and of the impunity with which crime may be committed there."
SHERLOCK HOLMES, *THE ADVENTURE OF THE COPPER BEECHES*

THURSDAY, DECEMBER 12

WHEN IT COMES TO RELATIONSHIPS, I'm like a battery-operated screwdriver that has to be recharged for twenty-four hours to be useful for ten minutes.

For twenty years, whole weeks of my family life went by without my family. All things considered, it's amazing our marriage lasted. Sharon gets the credit. I didn't deserve my wife. And she didn't deserve me. She deserved a lot better. I'm ashamed to say I love her more now than I did when she was alive. I'd like to tell her I'm sorry.

Part of me says there's no way I'll ever see my wife again. One, there may be no heaven. Two, if there is a heaven, I won't be there.

As for Kendra, there's a hint of progress. I keep calling her. She doesn't seem to resent me as much. I'm holding my breath because one wrong move and I may not see her for another two years. I told her again I'd do what I could to help with the baby. Kendra may be there to choose my nursing home. But I wonder how much I'll see her between now and then.

We met at the parking garage. Jake would drive us out in the country, past Sandy to Calamity Jane's, a great burger place. We figured we'd take a break from Lou's and use the extra drive time to discuss the case.

Before Jake got us across the Morrison Bridge, I decided to stir things up.

"Why would anyone want to go to heaven? When my grandmother spoke about heaven, it was the last place I wanted to go. Who wants to be a ghost anyway? My idea of utopia was a place like earth, where you could have fun and ride bikes and play baseball and go deep into the forest and dive into lakes and eat good food."

"Sounds to me like the new earth," Clarence chimed in from the backseat.

"Exactly," Jake said. "The Bible says the heaven we'll live in forever will be a new earth, this same earth without the bad stuff. God doesn't give up on His original creation. He redeems it. And we'll have these same bodies made better. The Bible teaches the exact opposite of what you're saying—we won't be ghosts. We'll eat and drink and be active on a redeemed earth."

"So you'll still be Jake Woods?" I asked.

"Yeah—without the bad parts. We'll be able to enjoy creation's beauty and rule the world the way God intended us to. Baseball and riding bikes? Why not?"

Clarence leaned forward. "The thing you want is exactly what God promises. Earth with all the good and none of the bad. Heaven on earth."

"Wish I could believe that."

"What's stopping you?" Jake asked.

"Same song, different verse. A world of injustice and suffering is part of it. Another part is hypocrite Christians."

"Okay," Jake said, "suppose there is a God and Jesus really died on the cross for people's sins. Suppose He rose from the grave and offers eternal life to everybody who trusts Him."

"That's a lot to suppose."

"And suppose there really is a devil. Now, if you were the devil, what would you do to keep people from believing in Christ?"

"Never thought about it."

"I know what I'd do. I'd get people to claim they're Christians when they aren't. I'd get them to do terrible things in Christ's name. Then I'd try to persuade unbelievers to focus on those terrible things done by so-called Christians, instead of on the wonderful things done by Jesus. Then I'd try to get Christians to be self-righteous hypocrites who don't care about the needy, but only themselves."

"You're blaming the devil for what Christians do? Like the Crusades?"

"I'm saying the devil's behind lots of evil, yeah, but so are people. And I'm saying people can claim to be Christians even though they aren't. And sure, people can be real Christians and mess up, big time. But true, humble followers of Jesus are everywhere, and if you knew them, Ollie, you'd be drawn to Christ. If not for Clarence's sister being murdered, you'd never have met Obadiah Abernathy. You wouldn't have been touched by him because you wouldn't even know he existed."

"He was one of a kind," I said.

"Actually," Clarence said, "there are plenty of good-hearted, humble, and lovable Christians like my daddy. All the attention falls on false Christians or loudmouths or hypocrites. But the gospel's about Jesus."

"The fact remains: Some Christians are mean and hateful. I've met them."

"So have I," Clarence said. "Read some of those Christian blogs, and look at how they love to gang up on people, kicking them with their words when half the time they don't know what they're talking about."

"Christians can be jerks," Jake said. "We're unanimous on that one. Sometimes they're just nominal Christians. Other times they may be real Christians full of flaws. I have plenty myself."

"At least you admit it," I said.

"But it makes no sense," Jake said, "to reject Jesus because some of His followers are hypocrites. The Bible never says that to be saved you have to believe in Christians. It says you have to believe in Jesus."

"I still don't want to be associated with judgmental hypocrites."

"It's pretty judgmental to call all of us Christians hypocrites, isn't it?" Clarence asked. "Speaking of which, if you discovered other detectives were withholding evidence because they thought it had been planted against them, wouldn't you say they were wrong for covering it up?"

"Yes, but—"

"By your own standards you—Oliver Justice Chandler—have been unjust. That's hypocrisy, isn't it?"

"Well, I don't claim to be godly."

"You claim to love justice, don't you? Yet you violate standards of justice. Lots of people, including you, don't live consistently with what they profess to believe. Christians don't have a monopoly on hypocrisy. The justice you believe in is good, even when you violate it, right? Well, the Jesus that Christians believe in is good, even when we violate His teachings. Even when we're hypocrites."

It's scary when Jake and Clarence make sense.

"Mind if I change the subject?" I said. "I've been thinking about our murderer. This guy doesn't kill as a last resort. It's become a habit."

"Which puts you in danger," Clarence said. "You could have been killed."

I shrugged it off. "I'm still kicking, aren't I?" We pulled into the Calamity Jane's parking lot. I could taste the County Fair Burger, smothered in grilled onions. I jumped out of the car, eager to get moving. As we walked to Jane's door, I said, "To catch a killer, you have to think like a killer. If the killer's a bricklayer, you have to think like a bricklayer, know how he'd kill someone. In this case, you have to think like a homicide detective. The bad news is, any homicide detective is going to be tough to catch because he knows the ropes. The good news is, I'm a homicide detective, so I know how they think. But we've had three deaths and a shotgun blast through my window. I've got to do something to get ahead of this guy."

THURSDAY, DECEMBER 12, 6:00 P.M.

Clad in an extra-large A&E Nero Wolfe T-shirt and my blue plaid boxers, I sprawled back on my faded brown recliner. With a plate of Ritz crackers on my lap, a jar of Skippy peanut butter between my saggy white knees, and a tall glass of milk in my right hand, I was unlikely to make the cover of *Gentleman's Quarterly*.

I plunged into my Wolfe book, *Over My Dead Body*, enjoying the artistry of

Rex Stout, who as far as I'm concerned is twice the writer Faulkner ever was (not that I've ever read Faulkner).

After finishing a chapter, I rewarded myself by spreading Skippy on Ritz. I wasn't sure there was a heaven, or the heaven on earth Jake and Clarence said was coming, but this might be a foretaste.

Mulch was working peanut butter off the roof of his mouth. Suddenly he froze, his tail rigid. He stared out the dining room window looking out on my backyard. I heard a slight growl, then the first of dozens of loud barks. He ran to the back door and scratched. I looked outside the window. Nothing.

Mulch has conned me into checking the backyard for intruders countless times, and I wasn't about to fall for it again. I finally managed to calm him down.

Sitting back in my recliner, I thought I heard a creak on the back porch, the sort of creak that bothers women, like Sharon, who thought that every noise required an explanation. Being a man, I ignored it.

I leaned the Nero Wolfe book against my chest, dabbed my knife into the peanut butter, lifted the cracker to my lips, then bit slowly. Oh, yeah.

Thump. No denying the noise, but it sounded more distant and higher. Mouth full, I set down the jar and moved the recliner forward as Mulch attacked the back door.

I reached underneath the recliner on the left side and pulled out my SIG-Sauer, removing the duct tape. With my right hand I grabbed my Glock out of its shoulder holster, lying on the coffee table. People occasionally have good reasons to be on my front porch. Never the back. Like young Kevin Costner in *Silverado*, I was going out a two-fisted gunman, covering both sides. And for good measure, I put on my Baby Glock ankle holster, which may have looked a little funny considering I was in my boxers.

I walked to the kitchen, mouth dry with peanut butter. I moved past Mulch, peering out the new, clean window. Nothing. Same thing I'd seen before a shotgun blast nearly answered my questions about the afterlife.

I opened the door slowly and stepped out, nudging it shut with the Glock's barrel. I heard a shuffling noise in the garage, six feet to my right. If these were mice, they must be fifty-pounders.

I pivoted, pointing both guns at the roof. I stepped backward to the edge of the porch. Nothing above. Nothing in the yard. I turned toward the garage. Due to a gap at the bottom of the garage door, I'd had a cat in the garage, an occasional bird, even a possum. But when a shotgun has been recently fired at you from your back porch, you have no assurances concerning noises in your garage.

I turned the handle to the garage door and pushed it open, hugging the side of the frame. I pointed inward, SIG in my left hand, waiting to see if it would draw fire. Nothing.

I stepped into the garage, flipped on that wimpy overhead light, and treaded

slowly by boxes, looking backward and forward. I hadn't been out here since finding the nautical rope.

The garage was still. I heard nothing. Elvis, framed in the corner shadows,
looked like he wanted to warn me. Just then I realized I'd looked forward, backward, and down. I looked up just as something dropped around my neck.

I was choking, unable to breathe, spitting out chunks of Ritz crackers and
peanut butter. My legs were flailing wildly, as if detached from my body. I was dangling a foot above the concrete floor. I heard my gun bounce beneath me.
Something was pulling me up. A noose. I was suffocating.

I heard a noise above me, quick movement, and the sense of someone coming
down a ladder ten feet away in the shadows, then rushing by under me. I thought
I saw a ski mask, but wasn't sure. Whoever it was exited out the door I'd entered.

Hanging there in my boxer shorts, time seemed to slow as I contemplated what
a humiliating way to die this would be. I pictured my detective colleagues taking
my photograph, Kim Suda laughing at my underwear and Cimmatoni shaking his
head in disgust. I even saw Carlton Hatch looking at my body—a still, blue
corpse—then in a moment of drama declaring my death. I hoped Carp wouldn't
see me this way and, above all, Kendra.

I tried to scream as I dangled. What came upon me next was a profound fear:
that Jake and Clarence were right. And I was too late to do anything about it. Sharon
had sensed light and comfort shortly before she died. I felt only darkness and dread.

The more I fought the rope, the quicker my life eked away. The garage light
dimmed completely. I lost all hope. Suddenly, a voice spoke inside my head.

Your gun.

I sensed something in my right hand. It seemed impossible I hadn't dropped it.
The SIG had fallen from my left hand, but my grip on the Glock had tightened.
It felt like part of my hand. Somehow I managed to pull it upward. I put the barrel an inch from the rope above my head. Despite the dimness, I saw an old wasp's
nest and a spiderweb.

I tried to find my trigger finger and move it, then heard an explosion. The
recoil nearly knocked the gun from my weakened hand. I pointed it at the rope
again and fired, hanging on. Nothing. My feet were still a foot above the garage
floor. Finally, darkness enveloping me, in what I knew was my last chance I lifted
the gun again, put the barrel near the rope, and pulled the trigger.

Still hearing the explosion, I felt my feet touch ground and my dead weight
crumble onto concrete. Simultaneously, I felt relief on my throat and severe pain
in my lower body. I felt and heard, in the same awful moment, my head hit the
concrete. In the split second before unconsciousness, I knew I was slipping into a
pool of darkness, either sleep or death.

"It is cocaine, a seven-per-cent solution.
Would you care to try it?"
SHERLOCK HOLMES, *THE SIGN OF FOUR*

FRIDAY, DECEMBER 13, 9:00 A.M.

SOMETIMES IN THE NIGHT wind I hear the world groaning like it knows it was made for something better. I see it in Mulch's eyes. He knows something's wrong. When I flip past those lame reality shows with pathetic people unveiling their emptiness for everyone to see, it's like they're crying out, "Something's wrong, and I don't know how to make it better; will somebody help me?"

These vague notions swirling in my brain suddenly gave way to the blurred image of Jake Woods.

"What happened?"

I was talking, but what I heard wasn't me. I sounded like one of those cowboys in the movies that survived a hanging and never got his voice back. My normal voice wasn't much different, come to think of it.

Seeing Jake above me, I wondered if he'd died too.

"You're going to be okay," Jake said. "It was a close one."

"How…?"

"Your neighbor, Mr. Obrist, heard the shots. He found you in your garage. He loosened the rope around your neck and called 911."

"Where?"

"Emmanuel Hospital. They just moved you from Emergency."

"Throat…sore."

"Yeah," Clarence said, obscuring the ceiling light. "That comes with being hung."

"Making fun of me?"

"No," Clarence said. "If we were making fun of you, we'd be mentioning your boxer shorts."

"We've been praying for you," Jake said. "We didn't want to lose you."

It was a tender moment of male bonding, so I said, "Get me a beer?"

"Can't do that," Jake said. "But I think I can manage water."

"Ice chips," a kind voice said.

I looked up and it was a young brown-haired nurse whose name tag said

"Emily Arnold." She tipped the ice chips to my mouth. I took them in and they felt good, until water made its way down to my throat. I flinched.

"I'll get the doctor," she said.

The doctor was apparently playing the back nine, so it was just me and Clarence and Jake. I told them the part of the story they didn't know; they told me the rest. Nurse Emily came back and checked on me a few more times. She seemed smarter and more helpful than a doctor anyway. When I asked when I could eat onion rings again, she thought it would be within a few days. That's my kind of nurse.

When she left, Jake said, "I'm so thankful."

"That somebody lynched me in my own garage?"

"That you weren't killed."

"And here I was wondering why God thought He needed to hang me."

"So instead of thanking God, you're blaming Him?" Clarence said.

"It was a miracle," Jake said. "God saved your life."

"Didn't I save my own life by shooting the rope?"

"That's one way of looking at it," Jake said.

"Yeah. The wrong way," Clarence said. "The doctor told us it's nearly impossible for you to have held on to the gun in the first place—and then to have fired it right through the rope?"

"I'm a man who does the impossible," I whispered. "What can I say?"

"You can say, 'Thank You, God,'" Jake said. "Because if He hadn't kept that gun in your hand and steadied it in front of that rope and given you strength to pull the trigger, you'd be dead."

"God's given you another chance," Clarence said.

"Another chance to get this killer."

"Another chance," Jake said, "to prepare for the death you narrowly escaped."

Two hours later Manny and Sergeant Seymour came to my room. Despite getting the evil eye from the new nurse on shift, they explained how someone had screwed my own block and tackle unit into the upper storage platform of my garage. This jury-rigged gallows had taken a half hour's work anyway, so when I heard the noise, it was exactly when he wanted me to hear it, to lure me out to the garage. He had every intention of hanging me. That I was in my underwear was an unanticipated bonus.

"Let me get this straight," Manny said. "You had a gun in your hand, and you saw the person who hung you running out the door—and you didn't fire at him?"

I explained that I didn't know I had the gun, but it sounded lame. Finally I said,

"Wait until you get hung, then you'll understand."

Manny had talked with all my neighbors, including the Obrists, and no one had seen the guy. Naturally.

"We're considering posting a guard at your house," Sarge said.

"What? I can take care of myself."

"You got assaulted by a guy in your backyard, someone unloaded a shotgun at you, and now you were hung in your garage? I'm thinking maybe you can't take care of yourself."

I pleaded with him not to do it. I'm the type of guy who protects people, not who's protected by them. I mean, did Green Lantern have a bodyguard?

"You're just lucky you're alive," Sarge said.

After they left, I lay there in that empty room, wondering if it was more than luck. I thought about what Jake and Clarence had said. And in case anyone was listening, as I slipped into a semidrugged sleep, I whispered, "Thank You."

SATURDAY, DECEMBER 14

When the Friday afternoon examination showed no damage beyond a raw neck and a bruised trachea, a six-inch melon bruise on the right side of my head, a gash in my knee, and a general sense that I'd been pushed through a cheese shredder, the doctor reluctantly gave in to my pleas to go home to Mulch, provided I wear the protective collar around my neck and stay home for three days.

I solemnly agreed.

I kept my promise for one evening, but Saturday morning I couldn't sleep, so I was first on the detective floor at five thirty. Not many show up on Saturdays, so it's a good day to work. I'll grant that I was making another statement. Even if few people saw me working Saturday, word would spread. "Missed me again." I sat down at the snack table, looking out the window at Portland drizzle.

A hungry dog hunts best. Being the target of a second assassination attempt increased my hunger to capture this guy; third strike and I felt sure I'd be out.

At six thirty a voice behind me said, "Hey, man. You don't look so great." It was Jack Glissan. He sat across from me, drinking something that smelled suspiciously like Earl Grey. He said, "It's a ghost town this time of day."

I nodded.

"I heard you had to wear one of those collars," he said.

"I gave it to Mulch. He loves foam rubber. I'll clean up the shreds tonight."

"You haven't changed," Jack said, smiling but showing his age.

This episode had strained our relationship, I knew. It had strained my relationship with everybody.

"Sorry about what happened," Jack said. "And sorry I didn't visit. So somebody really wants to take you down?"

Suddenly I was saying, "You know when Linda and Sharon used to go to AA?"

"Yeah. Every Tuesday night."

"Linda still go?"

"Sometimes. Not often. Drinking's not as big for her anymore. I've learned to keep the stuff out of the house. Except small quantities of beer, which she doesn't like, so it's no threat. Have to keep her away from wine."

"Any problem with it yourself?"

"A drinking problem? No. But no reason for me to bring it home when it could trip her up. We have to look out for each other, you know?"

"Yeah." I poured more coffee and stirred in French vanilla Coffee-Mate. "Has Linda ever...blacked out?"

"Couple of times, when it was really bad. Why?"

"Because...I've blacked out. More than a couple of times. And I can't remember what happened. I drink because I don't want to remember. You know, Sharon and...all that."

"I know. I'm sorry. She was a good woman."

"The best. I've had times when I've been out places, and I can't remember what I was doing. Especially between when I leave the bar and get home. It's like a big gap. Sometimes not just the fifteen-minute drive. An hour or two. Then I wonder, what was I doing all that time?"

"Still going to AA?"

I shook my head, pouring in more creamer.

"You should."

"It's not my thing."

"That's what everybody says till they realize how much of their lives they've been missing."

"Yeah," I said. "But sometimes missing part of your life is the whole point, isn't it?"

"Ain't it strange what these folks think?" Obadiah Abernathy asked.

"And what they don't think," said Ruby Abernathy.

The Carpenter nodded. "They cling to youth and health with a white-knuckled grip. But they don't take time to prepare themselves for what awaits them on the other side."

"Looking back," Ruby said, "I wonder why I was so afraid to grow old. Every day brought me one day closer to being here with You."

"So many of them store their treasures there," He said. "So every day they move toward their deaths, they're moving away from their treasures. But if they store their treasures here, every day they're moving toward their treasures."

Obadiah nodded. "The one who spends his life movin' away from his treasures is goin' to despair. But the one who spends his life movin' toward his treasures is goin' to rejoice!"

The Carpenter smiled and nodded.

"Ollie Chandler's lost hope, hasn't he?" Obadiah asked.

"He once looked forward to the future," the Carpenter said, "yet it didn't materialize as he'd hoped. Even when it did, it failed to satisfy. Now he no longer dares to hope. It saves him disappointment. He doesn't yet realize that I am the One he longs for."

"And You never disappoints," Obadiah said. "I can testifies to that. Elyon's Word tells us to look forward to a new heaven and a new earth, the home of righteousness. Yet how often they seems content only to look forward to a new car. Or business deal. Or the next round of golf." He shook his head in wonder. "Rarely do they look forward to that glorious world You promised."

"As they age, they imagine they pass their peaks," the Carpenter said. "But Elyon's children never pass their peaks. The best is never behind God's children. The best is always ahead."

"I wish sometimes we could talk to our Clarence," Obadiah said. "And Harley. And our grandchillens. And Ollie Chandler. I could tell 'em that the last of their lives before they dies is *not* the last of their lives. When they dies they go on a-livin'. They just moves to another place. Clarence believes it in his head, but maybe not his heart. Ollie doesn't believe it at all."

"Our lives here are so rich, better by far than our lives ever were there," Ruby said.

"Yet even here we awaits resurrection mornin'," Obadiah said, smiling broadly. "And the meantime's as sweet as lickin' the spoon of Mama's beef stew on the stove. We long for Elyon to bring His kingdom to earth, where we gonna live again on that world *You* made for us," he said to the Carpenter. Obadiah bowed his knee before Him, Ruby bowing by his side.

"What I have planned is far beyond what even you imagine," He said to Obadiah, placing His hands on their heads. "Together, as My kings and queens, you will reign with Me over a new universe. And billions of years from now, you will still be young."

Though I told myself I didn't want attention, I was disappointed at how few people came by my desk to give me their sympathy so I could brush them off and be the tough guy, saying something like, "Hanging, what hanging?" But after Jack left, only Cimma had come in, and he only said, "You okay?" without breaking his gimpy stride. Paul Anderson and a couple of larceny detectives came by and asked for my story, but that was it.

So I sat and read the *Tribune*. Then I decided to read one last time an article not yet printed in the *Trib*, but which was about to be submitted. It was a guest column written by a cop:

Call me Ollie.

The full name's Oliver Justice Chandler.

I am a detective.

The detective must set aside assumptions that blind him to the truth. He must follow the evidence wherever it leads.

Beneath every mystery, every unsolved crime, is an unseen world of habits, attitudes and motives. It's a world detectives must explore. That's why I walk our city's asphalt jungle.

Detectives must familiarize ourselves with what lies in the shadows. We must learn to see the unseen. Optimists believe the human heart is good. They're surprised by evil and quick to deny it, in themselves and others. Many murderers show regret at being caught. But they believe their crime was justified.

There's good in the unseen realm, but there's also evil. There's a malice that drives men's hearts toward unspeakable crimes. The detective is a truth hunter. He must pursue truth relentlessly.

I've known model sons who've given their frail mothers love and care. "He's a wonderful boy," everyone says. But probing deep, I have broken the skin and exposed the pus underneath. A homicidal pus. It surfaces in an over-heard conversation, a scrawled note, subtle signs of resentment and blame.

After discovering these threads of evidence, I sew them together to prove that a model son was his mother's murderer.

Right now at least one murderer is reading this column. He thinks he'll get away with three murders and attempts on my own life. He's wrong. I'm going to catch him.

Like Green Lantern of old, I am a relentless seeker of truth and upholder of justice. I make my pledge to this city as Green Lantern did: "In brightest day, in darkest night, no evil shall escape my sight. Let those who worship evil's might, beware my power…Green Lantern's light!"

Crime must be punished. Justice must be done. The boil must be lanced, the pus removed.

The name's Chandler. Ollie Chandler. I am a detective.

Justice is my middle name.

↔

Crossing the Morrison Bridge heading east, I decided to drop off my masterpiece at Clarence's house in North Portland.

Clarence's house is immaculate, lawn edged and alive even in winter, and picket fence a perfect glossy white. It doesn't remind me of my place. Geneva hugged me, and a couple of teenagers—Clarence's daughter Keisha and her cousin Celeste—extended their hands, made eye contact, and distinctly said "Hello." No mumbling. Respect is big in the Abernathy family. Clarence's daddy would be proud.

"Here's my guest article," I announced to Clarence, handing it to him, neatly printed out in a cool font called Franklin Gothic Medium, which I picked out after trying a couple dozen.

"I'll read it and let you know."

"Why not read it now?"

He sat down at the kitchen table while Geneva offered coffee. Earl Grey was mercifully absent. She took me in the family room and showed me another Negro League team picture they'd located, the 1949 Birmingham Black Barons. There was Obadiah Abernathy, smile bigger than life.

After fifteen minutes lost in memorabilia and telling Geneva how much I missed her father-in-law, I came back to Clarence, now sitting in the living room. My eye caught a furry little creature in a cage, spinning on a wheel.

"Didn't know you had a hamster," I said.

"Clarence brought him home last week," Geneva said. "He's adorable. The kids love him."

"What's his name?"

"Brent," she said.

Clarence pretended to read, ignoring my grin.

"What do you think of my article?" I asked.

"Well," Clarence said, "I hardly know what to say."

"That good?"

"It needs…a little editing."

"What do you mean *editing*?"

Clarence pointed toward an *American Heritage* dictionary on the shelf. "Look it up."

"What's wrong with it?"

"It's a bit…melodramatic. 'Call me Ollie'? 'The name's Chandler. Ollie Chandler. I am a detective'?"

"You make it sound silly."

"It sounds silly on its own. Reminds me of *Dragnet*."

"I like Joe Friday."

"It shows."

"What else?"

"'Justice is my middle name'?"

"Justice *is* my middle name."

"I know, but… Anyway, who's Green Lantern?"

I looked at him. "Charter member, Justice League of America. Dell Comics. Hal Jordan, test pilot. What college did you go to?"

"Oregon State University."

"What'd they teach you anyway?"

He pointed at my article. "Asphalt jungle? And the pus thing's got to go."

"Why?"

"People read the paper over breakfast. We don't want them puking on the *Trib*."

"Isn't that redundant?"

"And yet you want to write for it, don't you?"

"You said I could."

"No pus. I'll ratchet down the melodrama so nobody laughs at you."

"I want to see your edit before it goes to press."

"I've got to get Celeste to volleyball."

"Go ahead. But you and your loved ones sleep peacefully tonight because of the work I do. You and Geneva and the kids and Brent."

He straightened his back and saluted me. "Go, walk our city's asphalt jungle, Green Lantern. For your middle name is Justice. And you are Ollie Chandler, detective…lancer of boils and relentless foe of pus."

I suspect he wasn't entirely sincere.

*"When Gregson, or Lestrade, or Athelney Jones are
out of their depths—which, by the way, is their
normal state—the matter is laid before me."*
SHERLOCK HOLMES, *THE SIGN OF FOUR*

IT WAS A COLD DAY but sunny; time for lunch at Lou's again. On our table was one big light blue bloom. Rory called it a hydrangea. I took his word for it.

"You used to come only on Thursdays," Rory said. "I am happy to see you more often."

"We've got more to talk about right now," I said.

"It is always a pleasure to serve the three of you." I found myself wishing more people were like Rory Santelli. It would be a better world.

I asked the guys if this time we could put a hold on the Christian stuff. I wasn't in the mood.

They asked me what was next on the Palatine case. I said hang on and pulled out the only quarter I had. I looked for "MacArthur Park," history's longest song, with the quality of lyrics—sung by an actor, not a singer—that makes it seem even longer. I pressed C5 three times. If we needed it, that should cover us a couple of days.

"I'm going to check out a few alibis myself," I said as I sat down. "Karl Baylor first."

"Why Karl?" Clarence asked.

"I don't like the way he struts around showing off his gun."

"You're criticizing a man for being attached to his gun?" Jake asked.

"He's a Jesus freak. Isn't he supposed to be a pacifist?"

"If he were a pacifist, you'd berate him for that too," Jake said. "You're not judging him because he's a Christian, are you?"

"He can kiss the Blarney stone or worship the dung beetle for all I care."

"Listen to yourself."

"You try listening to me first, and let me know how it is."

"I *have* been listening—and trust me, you're not missing much. Seriously, Ollie, what have you got against Baylor?"

"I just don't like him."

"I detect a history, Detective. You going to deny that?"

"Okay." I gestured too dramatically, then put my hands around the coffee cup to keep them down. "After Sharon died, I came back to the office. It was…weird."

"Like people didn't know what to say."

"Yeah. Exactly."

"Same thing happened when Finney and Doc were killed."

"Same with Dani and Felicia," Clarence said. "People say nothing, or sometimes they say the wrong thing."

"Anyway," I said, "most guys looked the other way or said 'Sorry' when they passed by. Jack and Noel took me out for a beer. We talked about sports. Tommi was the only one who hugged me, which was fine. I don't want to be hugged by Cimmatoni. Kim Suda got me a Hallmark card. Point is, I didn't have to say anything back."

"What did Baylor do?"

My hands started moving, and I restrained them again. "He comes up to me by the snack table and says, 'I'm sorry.' Okay. Thought he was done. But no, he's a *Christian*. He has to say something more. So he says, 'She's with Jesus; she's better off.' She's better off? She's dead, for crying out loud. And if there's a Jesus, He's got plenty of other people with Him. Why did He need my wife? But Baylor still wouldn't stop. He says, 'Somehow it'll all work out for the best.'"

"He really said that?" Clarence asked.

"I'll never forget it. Then he quoted from the Bible, saying her death was really a good thing."

"I'll bet it was Romans 8:28," Clarence said. "'All things work together for good to those who love God.'"

"That was it. He was saying my wife's better off without me."

"That's not what he meant," Jake said.

"You're as big a know-it-all as he is, aren't you?"

"I'm just saying that—"

"Jesus has Sharon, but I don't. I'm supposed to be happy about that?"

"MacArthur Park" started over. They both looked at the Rock-Ola, then at me.

"Not again," Clarence mumbled.

"Hey, I only had a quarter. You wanna limbo with Chubby Checker, cough up your own two bits!"

"Okay," Jake said, "Baylor shouldn't have said it that way. I think he was trying to comfort, but he used the wrong words. The passage he quoted is true, but there's a right place and time and way to say it. That was the wrong one. I've done the same thing…we Christians can be dopes, just like everybody else."

"*More* than everybody else. Give me an atheist any day. Give me Bertrand Russell. He'd never say something stupid like that."

"Don't set up atheists as your role models. Professor Palatine was a Bertrand Russell fan. You don't idolize him, do you?"

"I don't even think God exists," I said.

"If He doesn't," Jake said, "then why are you so mad at Him?"

I stared at him, but he didn't melt. "At least an atheist wouldn't tell me God had a reason for killing Sharon. What it comes down to is if there's a God and He's all-powerful, then He chose for her to die. Am I right or am I wrong?"

"There's truth in it, but I wouldn't put it that way exactly," Jake said.

"Right. Because your job is to be God's PR guy, to run interference, bolster His public image."

"He doesn't need me for PR."

"Yeah? Well, He's not doing so well on His own."

"He doesn't look at His approval ratings. And we don't get a vote." Jake cocked his head. "Did you tell Baylor how you felt when he said that?"

"No, Dr. Phil. I didn't."

As I walked out the door Richard Harris was singing "Someone left a cake out in the rain."

Right, I thought. *Exactly.*

MONDAY, DECEMBER 16, 3:30 P.M.

Two hours later I sat in the Gresham WinCo parking lot, wearing a Mariners baseball cap and an old camo jacket, faded green and brown. No trench coat, no fedora. I don't wear glasses except for reading, but I have a pair of thick ones with uncorrected lenses for special occasions. I'd never met Karl Baylor's wife, but if I ever saw her again, I didn't want to be recognized.

I'd followed her from her house. I watched her get out of her navy blue Toyota. She was short and energetic, walking briskly, two kids in tow.

After studying her movements in WinCo, I positioned myself at the end of the next aisle. As she was slowly moving her cart, looking at a display of Nalley bread and butter pickles, I backed into her, assuming the posture of someone who'd established position. It's an art form, like Allen Iverson drawing the charge.

Her cart hit me.

"I'm so sorry," she said. "I should have been watching."

"No problem." I looked at her, like she was familiar. "Didn't I see you at that church... Um, Good Shepherd, was that it?"

"Yes. Good Shepherd Community Church. You go there?"

"Not often." As in, not ever.

"I'm Tiffany Baylor," she said, reaching out her little hand. "My husband's Karl.

These are our children, Matthew and Kivren."

I smiled at the cute kids. "When I was at your church, seems like they were talking about a couples conference. In Gresham, right?"

"The Holiday Inn on Hogan. Karl and I went. It was great."

"Nice you could get the time off."

"Usually they're on weekends but this was a Tuesday and Wednesday night. Karl's schedule's weird. He's a police officer."

I raised my hands. "I didn't do it."

She laughed. "People always say stuff like that. He's a detective. Anyway, he works weird hours. Sometimes in the middle of the night."

"You were lucky to make it through the conference without him getting called out."

"Actually he did get called out on police business after we'd gone to bed. But by the time I woke up, he was back. He was tired, but he can get by on a few hours' sleep."

"Too bad he got called away your first night."

"Second night. Tuesday we were together every minute. It was glorious."

"I have a buddy who's a police detective in LA. He and his wife go to bed at ten, but she says he gets 3:00 a.m. calls."

She nodded. "Same with Karl. That night he got called after 10:30, but I was asleep, barely heard the phone. He gets up, kisses me good night. Next thing I know it's morning, and he's there beside me. Said he was gone just a few hours. I sleep like a log when we're away from the kids." She giggled like a schoolgirl, taking a jar of red hot salsa from Matthew and putting it back on the shelf.

"What do you do?" she asked.

"Self-employed," I said. "Management consulting. Pays the bills while I write a novel."

"I lead a women's Bible study at church on Wednesday mornings. Your wife might enjoy it."

"Oh. My wife isn't...she died."

"Oh, I'm sorry." At least she didn't quote the Bible to tell me it was okay. "I shouldn't have assumed you... Sometimes I talk before I think. I'm really sorry. I hope we see you in church again. I'd love for you to meet Karl. I know you'd like him. What did you say your name is?"

"Uh, Joe. Joe Greenley. Pleasure to meet you, Tiffany."

"What'd you learn about Karl Baylor?" Clarence asked as we sat at my workstation.

"I like his wife better than I like him. Also, he's a liar. His alibi doesn't hold."

"No kidding?"

"That Wednesday night he left around 10:30. Supposedly he was called away on police business. His wife didn't see him until morning. He could've been gone five hours, and she wouldn't have known."

"He wouldn't have needed five hours," Clarence said.

"Two would have been plenty. Hotel's maybe twenty minutes from Palatine's."

"Who called him?"

"Couldn't have been homicide. There were just two cases that night, ours and Jack and Noel's. But he told his wife it was police work. He lied to her. And to us."

"You got all that out of her?"

I nodded.

"Think Baylor will be mad at you for interviewing his wife?"

"She didn't know she was being interviewed."

"How could she not know?"

"You'd be surprised what people don't know. Things aren't always as they appear, remember? That can work in the detective's favor too. It's a game, really. We have to outplay other people in order to outplay the killer."

"You make it sound like chess."

"I play chess. Most criminals play checkers. Take my murder before last. Lincoln Caldwell blows away Jimmy Ross. He lets himself be seen in the hallway, in his red sweatpants, of all things. Then he leaves fingerprints at the scene. And manages to cut himself and leave blood! Stupid is as stupid does. Caldwell holds a patent on stupid."

"Stupid." Clarence said, pointing pen at pad. "Got it."

"The smart ones have a plan. They wear gloves. Disguises. Even a ski mask works. If they know police procedure, they know if they're not holding a gun they won't be shot, even if they're running away, not without multiple warnings. Even then it's a last resort."

"And he'd know they'd have to get back to the crime scene quick," Clarence said.

"Right. He knows they'd have to break off pursuit and hightail it back to Palatine's."

Clarence scratched more notes. "A homicide detective would make a smart killer."

"Sure. Take your friend Karl Baylor, who told one lie to his wife and another to us to give him an alibi."

"He's not my friend. I met him two weeks ago."

"Suppose the killer's disguise isn't a ski mask. Suppose it's being a church-attending guy. Going to church places him above suspicion."

"Sounds to me like that's what makes you suspect him."

"I've tagged killers who go to church every Sunday."

"You've probably tagged killers who help the poor. That doesn't mean people who help the poor should be your primary suspects."

"A homicide detective would think it through, do his homework, draw up a plan. Wouldn't use a credit card to buy fertilizer for an explosive. Doesn't ask, 'Anybody know how much cyanide it takes to kill someone?' People remember those questions. He doesn't Google 'how to kill your boss' so his hard drive has a history of murder tips. If he does, he uses someone else's computer or knows how to erase his seven times so computer forensics can't recover it. If he prints hard copy, he burns it, doesn't put it out in his trash. Doesn't stand in front of surveillance cameras at the department store where he buys a pickax."

"He knows how you think as well as you know how he'd think, right?"

"Detectives peel away layers of lies to find the truth buried beneath. A smart killer creates the illusion he didn't do it. He makes sure no evidence points to him and some evidence points elsewhere."

"Like the fingerprints?"

"Nearly worked. But he also raises suspicions. This investigation's like walking through a circus fun house. You see a lot, but it's distorted. We have to get past the deception to see things as they really are."

"You're a truth seeker," Clarence said. "And truth seekers have open minds?"

"Sure. It's not enough to know somebody's lying. Many people lie. We need to know why they're lying. Sherlock Holmes said people lie for three reasons: to gain, to cover, or to protect. So what's your friend Karl Baylor hoping to gain by his lies? Who's he covering? Who's he protecting? My guess? Just himself."

WEDNESDAY, DECEMBER 18, 7:00 P.M.

The homicide detail gathered for a reception at the Heathman Hotel in downtown Portland. Sergeant Seymour kicked it off by saying, "Things have been tense lately. We got permission from the captain to use some budgeted funds for this party. No offense intended in not inviting spouses, but we thought we needed some positive time just for the team. We've got crab cakes, deli cheeses, baked breads, Greek salad, cheesecakes, and blackberry pie. You're off duty, and we've got your favorite drinks. Karl and Tommi are the up team, so there's water and coffee and pop for them. Everybody else, drink up!"

While Bing Crosby sang "White Christmas" in the background, Chris and Kim huddled, giving me dirty looks.

I'd suggested to Sarge that we have this party. I'd done my homework and made sure everybody's favorite alcohol was present, from Chris's Coors Light, to Cimmatoni's Scotch, to Phillips's wine coolers, to Tommi's Chablis, to the Budweisers that covered the rest of us.

It was then that Phillips dragged out of his pocket a compact surveillance device detector and started sweeping the room with it.

Jack teased him as he walked around the edges of the room, moving it up and down the walls, sweeping it under the tables, and even into the Christmas tree.

"Who'd be bugging us?" Tommi asked when he was half done.

Phillips said nothing but looked straight at me. It had come to that.

Ten minutes later, after the room passed the test, I said with all the indignation I could muster, "You actually think I'd rig something up at a Christmas party and treat you like you're a bunch of lowlifes?"

"Sorry," Phillips said. "I had to check."

I walked away, shaking my head in disgust. I leaned against the wall by myself, next to a tall decorative plant. Tommi came over and put her hand on my arm. "Everybody's under pressure, and things have been tense. Brandon didn't mean anything by it."

"I may not seem like a sensitive guy," I said. "But I gotta tell you, that really hurt."

Tommi talked to me another five minutes, trying to cheer me up. When she walked back toward her table, I turned away, looked into the camera I'd rigged up inside the thick plant, and grinned.

An audience of three was watching me in the small room next door, requested from the Heathman for "police business." Officer Paul Anderson still owed me three hours, and I promised to bring him some refreshments. Ray Eagle was taping through the surveillance device that he told me had an 80 percent chance of not being seen even if someone brought a bug sweeper. I told him nobody'd do that. I don't know what made Phillips suspicious, but I could've kissed Ray.

I couldn't see the camera lens peeking out of its green and brown casing, but I knew it was there. I looked that direction and mouthed, "Ray, I owe you a donut." Then I said in a hoarse whisper, "Hi, Paul. Hey, Clarence…how's Brent? Can you dunk it?"

It was Clarence's job to record everybody's drink intake. I'd explained my theory: "The murderer has to stay alert. That means if he's smart—and this guy's smart—he'll drink less. He knows he needs his wits. He knows it's important not to let something slip. If you're innocent, you're not worried. You can drink all you want."

Clarence had been there an hour early to see exactly where each drink was. The camera had a wide-angle lens, but he wouldn't be able to read labels. Cimmatoni was drinking Scotch like a fish. Jack and Noel downed beers at a fair pace. Tommi had Diet Coke but worked in half a Chablis before someone reminded her she was on the up team. Karl Baylor had Dr. Pepper. Kim Suda, V8. Manny seemed under par with the drinking. I felt guilty keeping him out of the loop on the surveillance but had to treat him as a suspect.

Chris Doyle opened a beer, but I never saw him drink it. That's way under par—not just a birdie, but an eagle, maybe a hole in one. Though the Coors Light was right beside him, he resorted to water. I had water in a dark cup so it wasn't obvious I wasn't drinking booze.

People ate at one of three tables. Lots of hushed tones and private conversations. By 8:30 desserts had been eaten. The room grew quiet.

"Still chasing one of us, Chandler?" Chris Doyle boomed.

After an uncomfortable silence I said, "There've been three murders, and they're all linked to Palatine. Anybody can see the evidence suggests it could be one of us. They're threatening to turn it over to Internal Affairs or bring in an outside agency. Then we'll all be guilty until proven innocent. That what you want?"

"So instead you're going to be our judge?" Suda asked. "I'd take my chances with the outside agency."

"State police?" I asked.

"Or Department of Justice?" Sarge said. "Attorney General's office?"

A hotel staffer walked in, but when eleven known cops turned and stared at her, she said, "Let me know if you need anything," then pivoted on her heel and disappeared.

"Ninety percent of us are innocent," I said. "But the only way to establish our innocence is to establish someone else's guilt. If the killer isn't in this room, I'll be relieved. But if he is…then don't all the rest of us want him caught?"

"Easy for you to say," Chris Doyle said.

"Easy for me?" I opened my shirt collar, showing the rope burns.

"Not to mention the shotgun blast through his kitchen window," Tommi said.

I was hoping Ray could zoom in and get a reading on faces.

I pride myself on my ability to expect the unexpected. But what happened next confirmed that truth really is stranger than fiction.

Bryce Cimmatoni, who'd been downing Scotch for an hour and a half without saying a word, cleared his throat. "I have something to say."

Everyone was riveted, because Cimmatoni has a history of making his normally rude remarks without asking for the floor.

"I planned the murder," he said. "I scoped out his house. I knew what I had to do. I knew I could get away. I hated the man. He didn't deserve to live. I thought through every step, every detail. I remember the night I decided to kill him."

29

WEDNESDAY, DECEMBER 18, 9:30 P.M.

I'VE NEVER SEEN a group of cops more stunned. The room was completely silent. Everyone froze, including me.

When Cimmatoni talked, he kept his chin low, against the crown of his chest, then looked through the tops of his eyes like a boxer in a crouch. His head tilted forward, and he gazed up from under his brows. Even in a confession, I felt like an uppercut was coming.

"What'd you do?" I asked.

"Went to his house. I'd picked the murder weapon. Untraceable."

"Did he come to the door?"

"Yeah."

"Let you in?"

"Yeah."

"Then what?"

"I pulled my gun."

Tommi did something no one else would have considered. She went and sat down next to Cimmatoni. "Why, Bryce? What did he do to you?"

"Sold drugs to my nephew, my sister's only kid. Kenny overdosed, went into a coma. Year later they pulled the plug."

"The professor sold drugs to your nephew?" I asked.

He looked up, dazed, trying to think his way through the Scotch. He scrunched his forehead.

"Professor?…No. He was a drug dealer, on Fourth and Alameda."

"You killed him?"

He gazed long and hard. "Threatened him. Waved my gun in his face, stuck the barrel up his mouth till I couldn't push it any farther. Sometimes I wish I'd pulled the trigger. They let him out of prison six months ago. He's selling drugs again. I drive by and look at him once a week. Sometimes I pull my gun and just sit there, thinking about it."

"What's stopped you from killing him?" I asked.

"I knew I could do it. I knew I could get away with it. I knew he deserved it. But…I'm a cop."

"So, Bryce, you didn't really kill anybody?" Phillips asked.

"Came so close I could taste it. Felt the pressure on my trigger finger. Close enough to see it in my mind, to see the blood splatter."

"But you didn't really do it," Tommi said. "Right?"

Cimmatoni nodded.

Never was a party as over as that one.

While everyone collected their things and headed for the door, I stood and stared at Bryce Cimmatoni. I wondered how many skeletons were in his closet, and how many things didn't come out of his lips that could've. I've seen a lot of drunks, including the one who looks back at me from the mirror. But never have I seen a better argument for not getting drunk around people you know.

I knocked on the room next door, one light, one heavy, one light. Paul Anderson peeked out and let me in. Clarence handed me his list:

Cimmatoni—Six Scotch and waters

Phillips—one wine cooler

Jack—two Budweisers

Noel—three Budweisers

Manny—one Irish Cream, one beer

Tommi—one glass of wine, half-finished, one Diet Coke

Karl Baylor—two Dr. Peppers, one decaf coffee, no alcohol

Kim Suda—one V8, one diet Sprite, no alcohol

Chris—one Coors Light (unfinished), two waters, two cups decaf

Ollie—water

"We'll talk about it tomorrow," I said. "We're done for the day."

They nodded. I drove home, but stopped for two hours at Rosie O'Grady's, where I didn't drink water.

I don't have many dreams I can remember. And I've found that the wonder and terror of a dream dissipates in telling it.

My dream that Wednesday night doesn't remember like a dream. It remembers like reality, which is why I'm still shaking from it.

It began in a fantastically beautiful place, with trees, flowers, gardens, rivers, lakes, and animals, including dogs of every breed. It was a huge city with stunning architecture, massive gates, and colorfully dressed people coming in and out. The people smiled and laughed—not the forced smiles and guarded laughter of someone trying to be happy. It was the irreplaceable joy of a person who *is* happy, with no thought of trying. The people there reminded me of Little Finn and Obadiah Abernathy.

I saw a writer and two artists contemplating boats going down the great river. People on the boats waved and occasionally jumped into the water, laughing. Those beside the river picked fruit off trees, smiling broadly at unprecedented tastes. They offered fruit to each other, freely taking bites and comparing. And the fragrances—I can still smell them, like the gardenias at Lou's but far more fresh and potent. A hundred different fragrances, each distinct. And a spectrum of colors, thousands of colors, including ones I remember but can't describe.

Some people ran, some played basketball and tennis, some chased and wrestled on the ground with animals—including lions, cheetahs, and panthers. Others rested. Everyone did what they wanted. I saw no scars, limps, disabilities, no one dragged down by age or disease or bad memories or emotional baggage. No one appeared cynical, suspicious, or threatening. No one taped guns under tables. A city with all the beauty of the country and with no hint of fear.

People's nods to each other seemed to say, "We're passing each other now, but one day we'll be introduced, and we'll eat or walk or play together and enjoy each others' stories."

It dawned on me that while there was much to do and the place called out for me to explore it, I was out of a job. The last thing this place needed was a homicide detective. It was like a brand-new earth, a planet that couldn't be bad any more than water can be dry. I knew that everything in me, every skill and gift and passion, every thirst for knowledge, could be invested forever in the endless pursuits of this fascinating world.

I was immersed in sweetness, in joy itself. I saw two great warriors standing at the gate of the city, admitting some while turning away others, according to whether their names were written in a huge open book on a great wooden stand just inside the gate.

A realization suddenly hit me like a spear thrown hard at my chest. I wasn't really inside this world. I'd been outside looking in.

Right then there appeared an old-fashioned train, vintage 1920, bound for the city gates only a hundred feet away. It pulled up next to me. From inside the train an arm reached down to me. A hand rested on my shoulder, a strong, coal-black hand, white under the fingernails.

I looked up through the train window into those big moist eyes. He said something to me. Though the dream itself began to fade after I wrote it down, that voice and these words are as clear now as when they'd just been spoken: "Son, it's gettin' late now. Soon be time to go home. Can't get on board widout yo' ticket. You has yo' ticket yet?"

Suddenly the train pulled away. Obadiah Abernathy never took his eyes off me until he was at the gate. Then he turned to enter that glorious world. In a moment the train had entered the city and disappeared into its wonders. I'd been left on the outside, standing under the forbidding glare of the guardians at the gate.

I awoke shivering, T-shirt soaking wet. I had no instinct to reach for my gun. I knew this was a danger no gun could save me from.

THURSDAY, DECEMBER 19

"It's all about perspective," I said to Ray and Clarence at Lou's, admiring the yellow flower I didn't recognize but that smelled like honey. Ray had pressed "Hey, Jude" and was timing it, betting me a milkshake it was longer than "MacArthur Park."

"You have to see things not as you assume they'd be, but as they truly are. In the face of the truth, your assumptions are often proved wrong."

"So sometimes you have to let go of your assumptions to see the truth?" Clarence asked.

"Exactly."

"And some people are too stubborn to let go and take a fresh look at the situation?"

"Yeah. But you'll never be a great detective if you can't reexamine your assumptions."

"Assumptions," Clarence said, "like…a good God can't allow suffering? And because some Christians are jerks, Jesus isn't worth believing in?"

"Those are more like conclusions than assumptions," I said. "But that's not our topic, is it? Any thoughts on last night's drama at the Heathman?"

"Quite a performance by Cimmatoni," Ray said.

"Crazy as it was, I sympathize with Cimma," I said. "I've committed hundreds of murders."

"This a confession?" Ray asked.

"I've committed murders in my mind. In detail. It's my job. If I hadn't, I wouldn't be such a great detective."

"And the other detectives, they do the same, right?" Ray said. "Play out murders in their minds?"

"Like a manager plays out a baseball game. To catch a thief, you have to think like one."

"Hey, Jude" ended. "Seven minutes four seconds," I said. "'MacArthur Park' beats it by seventeen seconds." Ray coughed up for an orange malt. "'American Pie' is eight minutes, but it came on two sides of a 45, so it doesn't count," I said. Ray took off, knowing he'd been schooled. After my malt, Clarence and I stood by my car discussing the case.

"Chandler!" It was Manny, face strung tight, eyes on fire. He came uncomfortably close to me and Clarence. "You homeboys cookin' it up?"

"Settle down, Manny," I said. "What's up?"

"What's up is that you called Maria to check my alibi."

"Well, you said you were with the kids. Who else was I supposed to call? Your kids?"

"Ever do that and I'll take you down myself," he said, index finger thumping my chest. "Hear me?"

"Threatening murder isn't the best way to get your name off a suspect list."

"Why am I even on the suspect list?"

"Because *everybody's* on it."

"You suspect me of something, you come to me first. Got it?"

"Well, that's a great relational principle there, and I'm sure Oprah would approve, but when it comes to suspect lists, you don't check out alibis by asking people if they're telling the truth. It's too easy for the killer to say yes, don't you think?"

"And what's *your* alibi?" Manny spat.

"Rosie O'Grady's pub."

"So if I was to talk to the bartender, he'd say you were there?"

"Yeah."

"What if he says you left before 10:00?"

"I'd say you checked up on me."

"Yeah. How does it feel?"

"I thought you were there until midnight," Clarence said.

"That what he told you?" Manny asked. "Then he's a liar. Maybe there's a job for him at the *Tribune*! You could always use another liar."

"The truth is…I don't know when I left Rosie's."

"You do know because the bartender told you, like he did me."

"My partner, who was checking my alibi."

"After I found out you were checking mine."

"So we're even."

"We're not even. You threw the first punch."

"And you punched him back," Clarence said. "Sounds even to me."

"You don't know nothin' about street fighting, do you, Mr. Suit and Tie suburb boy?"

"Don't call me boy."

"I'll call you boy if I want to, boy." He pivoted, standing ten inches from my face. "And what about the Black Jack you stole from the crime scene, Detective?"

"A blackjack at the crime scene?" Clarence asked.

"Not the weapon, the gum, goofball," Manny said.

"The weapon's a lot more dangerous than the gum," I said. "You could slap a guy with the gum, and it wouldn't even draw blood."

"This wise guy here found a Black Jack wrapper at the crime scene and picked it up, hid the evidence."

"Is that true?" Clarence asked.

I nodded.

"Why didn't you tell me?"

"It had his fingerprints on it," Manny said. "He knew it would. Didn't you, Chandler?"

Somebody'd been spilling my secrets.

"Your fingerprints were on something found at the crime scene?" Clarence asked.

"Finally sinking in, boy?" Manny turned back toward me. "You don't know where you were at the time of the murder, do you?"

"No."

"Instead of withholding evidence and treating us like we're killers, you should be turning yourself in." Manny thumped me on the chest again with the knuckles of his closed fist. Hard.

"You need to calm down." Clarence stepped between us.

"Stay out of this, *boy*," Manny said.

Before I knew what was happening, Clarence bear-hugged Manny and squeezed him like a bagpipe. Manny's wiry, athletic, and quick. But Abernathy had him in a death grip. Manny kicked and grunted, but his feet were eighteen inches off the ground, and all he was getting was Clarence's shins. He was a Jack Russell wrestling a Rottweiler.

"Let him go," I said.

Then I saw something in Clarence's eyes that scared me. I heard a sickening crunch. I pulled my Glock and pointed it at Clarence's forehead.

"I mean it, Abernathy. Let him go."

Clarence's eyes were wild one moment and tame the next. He dropped Manny to the parking lot like a rag doll.

Gun still in my right hand, I knelt by Manny. He was catching his breath and drenched with sweat. "You okay?"

"Rib's…broken."

"I'm…sorry," Clarence said to me, from above.

"You might want to tell Manny," I said. "My ribs are still attached."

"Sorry," Clarence said.

Manny stood up, more quickly than he should have. I was trying to support him when he threw a hard punch that landed short of Abernathy's chin, right on his left pectoral. Apparently the rib wouldn't let him extend the punch, because it's the first time I've ever seen Manny miss a punch.

Clarence made no effort to retaliate. His usually straight neck was bent.

"We're not even yet," Manny said. "But we're gonna be, *boy*."

"I'm sorry," Clarence said, dazed. "I shouldn't have…"

"Let's get you to the hospital," I said.

"I'm fine," Manny said, wheezing.

"Either I drive you or I'm calling 911."

I tried to support Manny on one side with Clarence on the other, but it wasn't working. His eyes were drooping now. I was trying to ease him to the ground when Clarence picked him up in his arms. Manny offered no resistance.

I put my gun away and held my 1 button for 911.

THURSDAY, DECEMBER 19, 3:00 P.M.

On the bright side, the fight between Clarence and Manny took the focus off my belonging on the suspect list. And lying about my alibi. And blacking out. And withholding self-incriminating evidence from the crime scene.

If I wasn't sure I was innocent, why should anyone else believe I was?

Clarence and I sat in another emergency room, this one at Adventist Medical Center. It was my third trip to emergency in two weeks. Nice not being the patient for once.

"I'm sorry," Clarence said.

"You've mentioned that," I said. "Repeatedly. Manny had it coming. He always has it coming. But if we were to give everybody what they had coming, we'd all be in jail, wouldn't we?"

"I won't blame him if he presses charges."

"Manny? An old street fighter like him? He won't press charges. He handles things himself. How's your insurance?"

"Insurance?"

"Health? Disability? Life? You might want to check it out. But the good news is, Manny hated your guts already. I doubt this is going to make it much worse."

"I'm a Christian. I shouldn't have done that."

"Yeah, well, I've seen lots of Christians do what they shouldn't." I looked at him. "On the other hand, I've rarely heard them admit they were wrong. It's refreshing."

"Daddy'd be ashamed of me."

"I got to know your daddy pretty well. He's the main reason I'm willing to put up with you. But he was awfully proud of you. I think he'd be proud of you for admitting you're wrong."

Something inside me, like a voice, suggested I should admit I'd been wrong about some things too. Fortunately, I could ignore it.

A nurse came out. Her name tag said Angela Stiz. "You're police officers, right? Manuel's your friend?"

I nodded, letting Clarence become an honorary police officer and honorary friend of Manny.

"Dr. Nakamura sent me. He's with another patient, but he'll be out when he can. Your friend, Manuel…he's got a broken rib with a contusion. Bruised lung but not punctured. He's lucky. He says some wild man squeezed him. Probably a meth addict. When people are on meth, they do crazy things."

"We deal with lots of crazies," I said.

"We get our share in here too," Angela confirmed.

"Somebody's got to protect the decent folk from the crazies," I said. "Right, Officer Abernathy?"

Clarence didn't give me the satisfaction of looking my way.

"The guy's in jail, right?" Angela asked. "Off the streets?"

"Well, he's not on the streets," I said. "Probably having a pleasant conversation with someone who doesn't have a clue that he broke a cop's rib while suffocating him. But he'll be out on the streets again. I pity the people who'll have to deal with him."

"Me too," Angela said. "I wish there weren't so many nutcases out there."

"He's really going to be okay?" Clarence asked.

"I think so. He's a little cranky, but anybody would be after what he went through."

"Yeah," I said. "Usually Manny's a sweetheart, but when you're attacked so viciously, it can change you."

"Listen," Nurse Angela said, "why don't you go visit him, one at a time? Seeing his friends will cheer him up. You want to go first, Officer?" she said to Abernathy.

"Yeah, you go first, Clarence," I said. "That'll make him feel better. You've always had a calming effect on Manny."

"Follow me," she said.

"Come on, Clarence. It'll do him good. Do you have your Bible with you?" I looked at Nurse Angela. "He's sort of a police chaplain. He can quote Scriptures about turning the other cheek and things like that. He's like a big brother to Manny. Extremely big."

"If you don't have your Bible, I can get you one," she said, cheerfully.

"No. Thanks."

"Tell you what," I said. "We'll give Manny a little more time before we see him. We'll just be out here…praying for him."

"That's nice," she said. "He's fortunate to have friends like you."

I sat there, feeling a warm smugness. After a minute of silence it still felt good.

"What about you?" Clarence said.

"What about me?"

"You said it was refreshing to hear me admit I was wrong. What about you? You lied about your alibi? And the Black Jack wrapper had your prints on it? And you removed incriminating evidence from a crime scene?"

"Okay, I lied, but it wasn't a big lie. In Washington DC it would pass for the unvarnished truth. Senators would swear by it on their mothers' graves."

"The great defender of justice rationalizes his injustice," Clarence said. "Guess I'm not the only hypocrite, am I? You were really so drunk you don't remember where you were?"

"I don't."

"That's a serious problem," Clarence said.

"Yeah."

"So you're not only a hypocrite, but you're on the suspect list, aren't you?"

I no longer felt smug.

"While the individual man is an insoluble puzzle, in the aggregate he becomes a mathematical certainty. You can, for example, never foretell what any one man will do, but you can say with precision what an average number will be up to. Individuals vary, but percentages remain constant."
SHERLOCK HOLMES, *THE SIGN OF FOUR*

FRIDAY, DECEMBER 20

CLARENCE AND I walked the streets on a beautiful Portland morning, sunny, crisp, and chilly. Christmas was on the signs, in the shops, on the trees, and in the air. A blue-jeaned, red-jacketed guitarist played "Silent Night." I dropped a buck in his open guitar case. Call me a philanthropist. Me and Bill Gates. I don't tire of Christmas.

What I do tire of are the things that keep me from enjoying Christmas. Unsolved murders are among them. We were walking toward the parking garage to Clarence's SUV, which had two bicycles in the back since I'd given in to Clarence's badgering and agreed to go for a ride.

Clarence drove across the Hawthorne Bridge and southeast to Johnson Creek, where we parked and got on the Springwater Corridor Trail.

"Motive is everything," I told Clarence between huffs and puffs as we rode our bikes toward Gresham. "If we find the motive, we have him…or her. And to find the motive, we have to learn what we can, not just about the professor but about each detective. That's how we find out where they crossed paths, how the circles of their lives overlapped—where they came from, where they've traveled, common interests. And why a homicide detective would murder this guy."

I raised my hand, signaling him to slow down. My face was freezing even though I was dressed like the Stay Puft Marshmallow Man. Sharon wouldn't have let me out of the house.

"You work with these detectives," Clarence said. "Don't you know them well enough?"

"Everybody has things they don't want other people to know. But I have a theory that's proven pretty reliable. My theory is that most murderers can be understood by the kind of person they were in high school. Stop pedaling faster when I'm talking! Why are we doing this anyway?"

"To get you in shape," Clarence said, looking obnoxiously snazzy in his black Adidas sweat suit. "So far we've worked off maybe half a donut. Keep talking. I'm slowing down."

"Anyway," I said, "when you look at a murderer and his type of murder, 90 percent of the time you see the seeds scattered back in high school. If somebody was killed with a cello, and you find out one of the suspects was a high school cellist…well, there you go."

"A cello?"

"Just an example. Not a great one. Anyway, I'm going to be asking the detectives some questions, and I'll ask Ray to compare their answers with what he digs up. If something doesn't jibe, or they leave out something important, we'll ask why."

"Sounds like you're fishing."

"Yeah," I said, turning off the trail at 181st when I saw a McDonalds. "And a good fisherman knows where to cast his line."

The detective floor conference room was chilly in more ways than one.

"You're going to interrogate us as a group…again?" Chris Doyle asked.

"It's not an interrogation," I said.

"Who you think you're kidding?" Brandon Phillips said. "We do this for a living."

"I'm going to ask you questions about growing up, family, and school."

"I'm not going to waste my time with this," Bryce Cimmatoni said, standing.

"Cimma, sit," Sergeant Seymour said as he would to a Doberman. "I don't like this any more than you, but we're on the verge of losing control. If Internal Affairs takes over, it'll get ugly. If an outside agency comes in…it'll be a nightmare. We're going to do this with everyone present, because we're accountable to each other. If someone's lying, someone else may know. If you do, challenge them on it, here and now. Or come to me or Chandler afterward. Time's running out."

"You don't have to confess this time, Cimma," Kim Suda said, followed by a ripple of laughter and whispers. Cimmatoni didn't smile.

"This time I'm starting," I said. "I grew up in Milwaukee, Wisconsin. Moved to Portland when I was fifteen. Went to Franklin High. Have one brother, one sister. My dad was a tavern owner. He also had an amusement machine business: pinballs, jukeboxes, pool tables, shuffleboards. My house was full of the stuff. Everybody came over for parties."

I looked out at the blank faces, all except Tommi Elam's. She seemed fascinated.

"I bet most of you didn't know that," I said. "See what a bonding thing this can be?"

"It would help if we even slightly cared," Doyle said.

"In high school I played football and did track and field, shot put and discus."

"Don't care," Doyle muttered.

"Tommi? Tell us about family and high school."

"Born and raised in Portland. Dad owned a marina. We were always boating. I was into waterskiing. Went to Grant High School. Go Generals! Two sisters and a brother. In high school I was shy. Enlisted in the army after graduating. At my reunions, no one can believe I became a cop."

"What kind of school activities?"

"Volleyball. National Honor Society. That was about it."

"What about you, Cimma? What'd your dad do?"

"Steel mill."

"You must have been into sports, big strapping guy like you. Football?"

"Linebacker. Three years varsity."

"Clubs or social groups?"

"No."

"School dances?"

"No."

"Anything you liked to do? Hobbies?"

"No."

"Macramé? Decoupage? Scrapbooking?"

He glared.

"Well, that was helpful. How about you, Kim?"

"Born in Santa Clarita, California. Just a regular high school kid. But I did go to dances." She smiled at Bryce, not warmly. "My friends and I hung around Magic Mountain. Had annual passes."

"Cheerleader?"

"No way. I played basketball and softball. First base. Batted third. Won the state championship my senior year. We were up by one, and their best hitter tried to stretch a right field triple into a homer. I was the cut off. Threw her out at home." She acted it out, winding up her left arm and emulating the throw.

"How's this going to help catch a killer?" Doyle asked in a whining nasal tone that made me want to Glock-whip him on the spot.

"Just go with it, okay?"

"None of this is okay," Phillips said. "It's irrelevant. A total waste!"

"Manny?" I asked.

He winced from his rib injury, which defanged his glare. "I dropped out of high school."

"Family?"

"Three brothers and a sister."

"Activities?"

"Gangs and drugs. Reformed, then became a cop." Manny's concise. "This is stupid," he added.

When you're doing something awkward, such as accusing coworkers of murder and trying to accumulate incriminating information, it's always nice to have your partner behind you.

"Karl?" Baylor's face wasn't as sour as the others. It was worth a try.

"One brother. Raised in Brooklyn, then moved sixteen miles from here. Went to Barlow High School. Graduated 1996. I was the starting point guard on the basketball team. Tennis, second doubles."

"Favorite teachers?"

"Tom Johnson, Gene Saling, Linda Saling, Tom Starr, Andrew Pate."

Wow. He knew his favorites. I looked at Jack Glissan. "I know all about you, Jack."

"So since you're old friends," Doyle said, "he's not a suspect, but we are?"

"Didn't mean it that way."

"Look, who cares?" Jack said. "Raised in Bellingham. Played football, basketball, and baseball. Came down here to Linfield in McMinnville, then moved to Portland. Never left."

"Noel?"

"Grew up in Liberty Lake, a suburb of Spokane. Only child. Dad was a mail carrier. Took up golf after high school. I was visiting Portland, checking into law enforcement, and somebody introduced me to Jack. He talked me into police academy."

"Anything else?"

"Well, high school four years. Anything in particular you're looking for?"

Three people checked their watches at once. One of them was Sarge.

"Chris?"

Doyle looked up from his watch. "Grew up in Indianapolis. My father was a teacher."

"High school?"

"College."

"What subject?"

"History mainly."

"Mother?"

"She was born and raised in Stratford, England. Graduated from Oxford, King's College. Taught literature there before marrying my father. She tutored my sister and me in the queen's English."

"I never knew that, Chris," Tommi said.

"Sports?" I asked.

"Wasn't into sports then."

"Not a stud like you are now?" Cimmatoni asked.

"Other activities?"

"Not really."

"Chris," Suda said, "didn't you tell me you were on the chess team?"

In a room starved for laughs, the effect was immediate.

"He went out with an injury his senior year," Noel said, "or he would've nabbed a scholarship."

More laughter. Chris steamed. I play chess and respect it. Chess is difficult and challenging and a lot saner than rugby. But cops generally don't wear their chess club sweaters to work.

"Five more minutes, Chandler," Sarge said, pointing at his watch.

"We're down to you, Phillips," I said, realizing that without an outright confession of guilt, this session had been an unqualified disaster.

"Where'd you grow up, Brandon?"

"Texas."

"Where in Texas?"

"Dallas area."

"Remember the name of the town?"

He glared. "Irving."

"Sports?"

"Cross-country. Baseball."

"What school?"

He shook his head like it didn't matter.

"That's it." Sarge dismissed us.

"Well, that was productive," Doyle said, looking at me like I was as dumb as I felt.

"Genius, Chandler," Cimmatoni said, his shoulder bumping me hard as he pushed past me.

"Wasn't a total loss," Noel said. "We found out Chris was on the chess team."

After I'd spent an hour being ragged on one at a time by a half dozen of the detectives about my stupid little meeting about family and schools, Lieutenant Taylor Nicks called me in. My favorite part of his office is the sign saying, "Complaints? Take a number." The number's attached to the pin of a hand grenade.

"I'll get right to it," Nicks said. "You need to back off from your—" he looked down at a piece of paper—"wild accusations."

"Are you saying this on your own?"

"You've…" he looked at the paper again, "gotten completely out of hand. You're a bull in a China shop. You're not a team player. You need to toe the line or you'll…" he looked down again, "be sent packing."

"That doesn't sound like you, Lieutenant. But it does sound familiar."

"It's my job to tell you this. I'm following orders."

"Like I'm following the evidence."

"I understand," he said. "But if you keep it up, you may be asked to resign. If you don't resign, you may be dismissed."

"Fired? You'd do that?"

"I wouldn't. But I don't know how I could stop it. Anything you want me to tell someone who thinks the department would be better off without you?"

"Only that I think the killer would agree."

"Anything else?"

"Remember when you came by my house when Sharon was sick? You met my bullmastiff, Mike Hammer."

"Sure. Nice dog."

"Mike Hammer likes to sink his teeth into tennis balls, sticks, stuffed animals, you name it. Now when he's ready to, he'll drop those things at your feet. But try to take them away, and he'll latch on to them with the teeth-clamp of death."

Long pause.

"You're like your dog. That what you're saying?"

"We both like red meat—and we don't like it when somebody tries to take it away."

"That all?"

"No. If I were fired, I think Clarence Abernathy would just tell the world why, without regard for our precinct's image. You know how journalists can be. Everybody'd know I was fired because I was going after a guilty cop."

"I can say that to…whoever might be interested?" Nicks asked. He jotted a note.

"And you can say I won't go down easily. You can tell him he's bit off more than he can chew. And I smell a rat. And no snake in the grass is going to keep me from doing my job."

"Good. You're dismissed."

I stood. "And something's rotten in Denmark. You can say that too."

He nodded.

"And all's fair in love and war."

"Get out of here." He seemed to be biting his lip. "And shut the door."

I did.

Parting is such sweet sorrow.

↔

The Chief, even when he has somebody else do his dirty work, makes you feel like a rat being shaken by a Rottweiler.

Truth is, I don't want to lose my job. It's a little late to start over as a professional hockey player or home decorating consultant or Cinnabon employee, though the fringe benefits are tempting. Nobody hires guys to wear capes and come to their parties as Green Lantern.

I retreated to my cave, the old brownstone, guarded by my trusty sentinel. I sat on the couch because I still smell Sharon there. She didn't wear much perfume. It's actually her I smell.

I went to the closet and pulled out a Seahawks blanket I got her for our anniversary, on April 3. You may think it was a lousy gift, but she loved it. She was that kind of woman—a football-loving woman, a pizza-loving woman. A Hall of Fame woman. She bundled up in that Seahawks blanket all the time and still thanked me for it five years later. I'll never wash it because her scent's stronger there than anywhere else.

I can't smell Sharon as much as I used to. I'm afraid one of these days I won't smell her at all. And then the last living trace of her will be gone forever.

I have thousands of pictures of dead bodies and less than a dozen of my own wife. If I were a contortionist, I'd kick my rear end for this.

Will she just disappear as my memories fade? When I'm gone, will Saint Sharon be no longer?

"Open his eyes, Lord," she said. "Help him see the unseen—to behold Your kindnesses to him."

"I grant him hundreds of graces each day, from the air he breathes to the food he eats to the roof over his head. He sees none of them, so it's no surprise that he doesn't see the greatest gift I offer him. I've been patient, not wishing him to perish."

"But the clock's ticking."

"Yes, Saint Sharon," He said with a smile, placing His arm around her. "But I am bigger than the clock."

I left home for Rosie O'Grady's, returning three hours later. I'd managed to sip a few beers slowly and was proud of not being drunk. I turned the corner and saw a flashlight on in my dark house.

Not again. My head instinctively ached.

I drove past the house and pulled to the curb sixty feet away. I waited two minutes before the flashlight came on again.

I called Jake's cell. "Where are you?"

"Home," he said.

"Can you drive to the old brownstone right now? Just pull in the driveway and sit there. That's all I'm asking."

"Do I bring my service revolver, Sherlock?"

"Good idea."

"You're serious?"

I hung up and worked my way into the backyard behind the elm tree, next to the moldy pile of bark dust.

Five minutes later I saw the front of the house light up and knew Jake had arrived. The inside flashlight went off. Within five seconds the back door opened.

Fear kicked in when I realized Mulch wasn't barking.

I followed the guy over the fence, through the Atkins' backyard. I was grateful for that much, since as far as I know the Atkins don't drink Earl Grey tea. He ran to a parked car, opened the door, and as he did, I saw he wasn't a he.

He was a she.

He was Kim Suda.

I couldn't follow her. I decided it was in my best interest to know it was her without her knowing I knew. I was also worried about Mulch. As Suda drove away, I ran back to the house, legs sore from my bike ride.

I ran to the front yard and raised my hands until Jake lowered his Walther from its bead on the center of my chest.

"What's going on?" he asked.

"Intruder. I followed him. Her."

"Her?"

"Tell you later. I think Mulch's down."

My keys rattled, but still I heard nothing. Truth is, I prayed Mulch was okay. There are no atheists when your dog's in a foxhole. Or something like that.

I opened the door, where Mulch is positioned 100 percent of the time when I enter. Nothing.

"Mulch! Mike Hammer?"

I tripped over something big and baggy on the floor. Mulch. No movement.

"No. No."

The light flipped on and I was looking at Jake six feet behind me.

"He isn't moving," I said. I smelled something, then saw it. A half pound of raw hamburger six inches from his mouth.

"It's like he's asleep," Jake said.

"Is there a 911 for dogs?" I asked.

"There's a vet named Megan at our church. I'll call her."

I lifted Mulch onto the couch. I shook him. One eye opened just enough to show his inner eyelid.

Five minutes later Dr. Megan Wood showed up. She put her hands on Mulch's chest and by his snout. I pointed out the hamburger.

"We hide pills in hamburger. I think someone gave him a sedative."

"They slipped Mulch a mickey?"

"Hamburger's the best way."

"It'd work for me," I said. "What should I do? Make him coffee? Coke? There's a hangover recipe with Tabasco sauce and black pepper."

"Sounds like you've had some experience. His breathing's normal. I don't think it's an overdose, just a deep sleep that he'll come out of eventually. No sense taking him to my office. He'll be more comfortable here."

She wrote down her cell number and handed it to me. I told her I'd never forget her, and if she needed a homicide detective, I was her man.

Jake was checking out the whole house, pointing his father's Walther P38, taken from a Nazi soldier, into every nook and cranny. I put Sharon's Seahawks blanket over Mulch and sat beside him. Jake's one of the few people I trust with a gun as much as I'd trust myself. He was a Green Beret in Nam.

Half an hour later I talked Jake into leaving. For the rest of the evening I thought about Kim Suda, trying to connect the dots. I never left Mulch for more than a few minutes, but I noticed a few things in my office that seemed out of place. The phone on my desk was positioned perfectly, at a right angle to the front edge of the desk. Too perfect.

I disconnected it from the wall. Then I opened the mouthpiece quietly. In it I found a tiny device.

Kim Suda had bugged my phone.

I heard a gurgle eight feet away. I rushed back to see two tired eyes peering at me. I stretched out my hand, and he licked it. I hugged him and fried him some bacon, unleashing its magical healing properties. He ate it slowly but gratefully.

Mike Hammer was back.

And I vowed to make the dog drugger pay.

*"Come, Watson, come! The game is afoot.
Not a word! Into your clothes and come!"*
SHERLOCK HOLMES, *THE ADVENTURE OF THE ABBEY
GRANGE*

SATURDAY, DECEMBER 21, 9:00 A.M.

MULCH SLEPT NEXT TO ME. For breakfast, I made him waffles and threw an extra egg into the mix. He likes them fluffy. I usually toss him waffle portions, and he jumps to catch them. Never misses. But this time I hand-fed him, in bed. He seemed to appreciate the extra butter.

When Ray arrived two hours later, we stood on my front lawn, Mulch on his leash, breathing deeply. Some places you want to close your mouth and keep the air out. Not Oregon. The air's so incredibly good, you want to keep breathing just to remind yourself.

"Suda's toast," I said. "She invaded my home, planted a bug, and drugged my dog. That's as low as it gets. *Kim Suda.* Even her name sounds dark and slippery. Just try it on your tongue—*Kim Suda.* Close your eyes. Whisper it in the dark a few times. It'll give you the willies."

Ray closed his eyes and whispered, which is more than I could've gotten Abernathy to do.

Then he pulled out his bug detector, a TD-53, to sweep my house. He told me he'd test it on the phone I already knew was bugged. He said I should just do what I usually did, talk to Mulch but not to him. He suggested I turn on music too. Johnny Cash, the only country singer I ever liked, sang in the background to cover for us.

When we got two feet into my office, three feet from the phone, the audible tone on the TD-53 clicked faster and faster, like a Geiger counter. Ray turned it low enough not to be heard by whoever was listening in. The signal was strong.

Ray found two other bugging devices, one by the kitchen phone, perfectly hidden in the seam of a pen holder. The other was inside the lamp shade by my recliner.

We stepped outside to discuss it. I wanted the two we'd just found deactivated, but we'd leave active the one in my office phone.

We went to the front of the house, and he turned on the bug sweeper to check my car. Nothing. Still, he beckoned to his car and we got in to talk.

"A phone bug and two others?" Ray said. "Wow. I'm pretty sure I found everything, but some bugs can be turned on and off remotely, and when they're off they can be missed."

"They're department issue, aren't they?" I asked.

"Technically a private party can get them, but given these brands and considering the cheaper equipment you can buy publicly, I'm sure it's police department hardware. Which means she's in big trouble."

"Can you access e-mail without someone knowing?" I asked.

"Private? On a secure system?"

"Her computer's thirty feet from my desk, but she's usually carting around her laptop."

"Wireless?"

"I guess. Is that good?"

"I'll let you know."

Ray called me at 11:00 a.m.

"Suda's home and her computer's running, but she's not on it. I'm parked curbside at her neighbor's, inside her wireless range. She's got a good firewall. Can't get in without an alphanumeric password. You're going to have to check her desktop. Computer stays on at the precinct, right?"

"Unless there's a power outage."

"That means some people will leave their e-mail open," he said. "It's Saturday, so she probably won't be in, right? If Outlook's open, just watch the screen and make sure there's no movement. Otherwise if she's accessing remotely you'll bump her off."

I went to detective detail and moseyed over to Kim Suda's desk. Outlook was open. I did an MSN desktop search for "Ollie" and "Chandler." It turned up some old e-mails to and from me, as well as a few recent derogatory comments about me exchanged by my fellow detectives, referring to me by a variety of anatomical terms. I opened her sent file and looked at the last ten e-mails.

Found an e-mail sent at 11:45 last night. It was the shortest I'd come across. All it said was, "Job done. Everything set."

She'd done a job on me and Mulch, and I wondered if that's what she meant. The e-mail went to an address without a name: wearp@verizon.net.

I Googled "wearp" at my desk and tried searching for listed e-mail addresses. I found only forty-six people in America with the last name Wearp. Glad it wasn't Jones. Finally I called Ray Eagle and briefed him.

I sat there thinking about dinner for me and Mulch. It was Saturday night, so my thoughts went to one place. One of the greatest natural resources of the Pacific Northwest—found nowhere else—is Burgerville USA, where hot beef under Tillamook cheddar cheese with the works can be bought alongside an unforgettable blackberry shake.

Sharon worked in a Burgerville on Eighty-second and Glisan, before we had kids. She'd give me extra fries and sometimes another slice of cheddar. In our last ten years together, besides Lou's and Dea's, it was my next favorite place to take her for special occasions. We used to kick up our heels and go there on Saturday nights. Sharon would call me a romantic fool.

Hugh Mulhaney, a cynical cop who's been divorced three times, told me, "Being single's really great. You make up the rules. You don't call anyone to say you'll be late. Don't have to justify yourself to anyone. No one pokes you when you snore. No one suggests you clean out the rain gutters when the Cowboys are playing the Giants."

Sharon would never make me miss a game over gutters, but if she were here, I'd do it for her in a heartbeat.

Ray called. "Name's not Wearp. It's W. Earp, as in Wyatt Earp."

"Shootout at the OK Corral?"

"Got a billing address for the account."

"So who's Wyatt Earp?"

"Would you believe…Edward Lennox?"

Two things I've learned. First, never stand between Mulch and a bush he's sniffing. Second, never trust Chief Lennox.

Ray, Clarence, Manny, and I sat in Ray's living room. Manny, moving stiffly due to his broken rib, eyed Abernathy repeatedly, despite the big guy's continual apologies and offers to help. Manny didn't want to be there with us, but then Manny doesn't want to be anywhere. He went on and on about the miserable failure it had been when I quizzed the detectives about their backgrounds.

Finally I stopped him. "We've got to know motives, and to do it we've got to find out people's backgrounds, families, interests, habits. Their secrets. Since it didn't work in our group setting—"

"Disaster," Manny muttered.

"I asked Ray to do his own checking." I looked at him. "You're on."

He glanced at an old brown clipboard, like a coach would use. "Truth is, I started on this a week ago. It represents lots of phone calls, Internet research, and beating the bushes."

"We supposed to be impressed?" Manny asked, bringing Christmas cheer. "You haven't told us anything."

"Tommi Elam first," Ray said. "Her father was a writer. He grew up in England—like Chris Doyle's mother. Her dad met her mom while she was vacationing in England. He moved here to marry her. He's successful enough to pay the bills. And he was involved in the kids' education. Taught them to read and write."

"No kidding?" I asked. "Never heard her say that."

"He was a collector. Music, coins, stamps, baseball cards, pens, rare books, even a dozen typewriters from various eras."

"How'd you find this out?"

"Somebody who admired his work made a website about him. Tommi's divorced. Her first husband was a radical activist. Environmental stuff—chained himself to a tree. And animal rights. She got a restraining order against him. Said he was abusive and that he cheated on her."

"She ever get violent with him?"

"No record of it. There were custody disputes. Two kids by that marriage. Now they're in high school."

"Where's the ex-husband?"

"Passed away at age forty-four, two years ago, five years after their divorce. Surprise heart attack while jogging. No prior condition. Here's something. Tommi went to Grant, same high school as Palatine. But he was older so they weren't there at the same time."

"She have brothers or sisters?" I asked. "One of them might have known him."

Ray jotted a note, then continued. "Bryce Cimmatoni grew up in Pittsburgh. He's a congenital Steelers fan, but we can't blame him for that. His father worked in a steel mill. Most people of that profile resent those above and below them on the social ladder."

"You're a psychologist, too?" I asked.

"Does it describe Cimmatoni?"

"Yeah, except he also resents those who are level with him on the social ladder. I don't think he's ever met anyone, on or off a ladder, he doesn't resent. Except his wife."

"About his upbringing—his records are sketchy. Doesn't look like he was popular."

"Surprise," Manny said.

I looked at him. "Not everybody can be Mr. Sunshine like you."

"Not many social activities," Ray said. "Won a chemistry award. First two years in college he was premed."

"Cimmatoni?" I said.

"Yeah. He was accepted into med school. His sister was murdered, and next thing you know he became a cop."

"No kidding?"

"Shot in the head."

"He's never mentioned his sister's murder," I said.

"You hang out with him?"

"No. But cops are like old ladies. There's always gossip. How come I've never heard that story? You heard it?" Manny shook his head.

"Some people don't like to talk about stuff like that," Clarence said. "I don't talk about my sister's murder."

"How'd you find this out about his sister?"

"Cimmatoni's other sister has a blog. I did a search on Bryce Cimmatoni, and three minutes later I'm reading the inside story of the family, including the sister's murder. She's the one who said her brother decided to be a cop instead of a doctor."

"A blog?"

"Yeah, I forgot—you don't know how to use your answering machine either. I was able to access Cimmatoni's Internet history—don't ask me how."

"Let's leave it there unless it's relevant," I said.

Ray flipped a couple of pages. It's odd to be a detective for a living and find yourself scared to hear what a detective can find out about you.

"Kim Suda," Ray said. "There's some interesting things she didn't mention. In high school she got in big trouble for fighting three times. Twice with girls."

"Catfights?"

"She was the Queen Cat. In one case she broke two teeth of the cheerleader who was homecoming queen."

"Ouch."

"Suda was suspended and the other girl wasn't."

"What about the third time?"

"She decked a male teacher."

"You're kidding."

"She claimed he made a lewd comment to her. He went to the hospital. There were rumblings of a lawsuit, but he didn't pursue it. I checked court records."

"Sue a teenage girl for decking you? No thanks."

"Suda has an old boyfriend, Skeets, some brainiac at Microsoft. He supplies her software. Still has a crush on her, I think."

"Where do you come up with this stuff?" Clarence asked.

"Karl Baylor." Ray flipped another page and smiled as he ignored Clarence's question. "Single-parent home. Dad wasn't around. Close to his mom. No great student, but he didn't get in trouble."

"Figures," I said.

"Transcript said he was a journalism student. In Barlow High School's library I got a copy of a school newspaper editorial he wrote. Baylor was a Christian."

"Still is," I said, restraining myself.

"Good article. You should read it."

"This stealth evangelism, Ray?"

"No. If it were stealth, you wouldn't have seen it coming. Baylor has a petite wife, two kids, and two hamsters."

"Hamsters? Don't let Clarence near them. He'd dunk 'em in a heartbeat."

Abernathy's eyes threw darts at me.

"How's Brent doing, anyway? Remember that Boys Town emblem? You and Brent could do one, with Brent on your shoulder: 'He ain't heavy, he's my hamster.'"

All three of them stared. I can't help myself.

"Jack's records are harder to get to," Ray said to me. "He's even older than you."

"Funny."

"Everything checks out. Wrestling. Student body president. Model citizen. Did you know his daughter died when she was at Linfield College?"

"Yeah," I said. "She was friends with my daughter. Kendra was at Portland State while Melissa was at Linfield."

"How'd she die?" Clarence said.

"Suicide. She got on drugs. Coke and meth. Grades dropped. Became despondent."

"Jack's wife's an alcoholic," Ray said.

I felt my neck tighten. "What's that got to do with anything?"

"You're looking for information. Secrets. Problems, you said. Doesn't that qualify?"

"She's been sober for years."

"Glad to hear it," Ray said.

"It's private information."

"So's everything else I'm giving you. I didn't know some of the detectives had immunity."

"They don't."

Everybody was looking at me. Ray went on.

"Noel Barrows grew up in Liberty Lake, Washington. Dad was a postal worker."

"So he said."

"Found a couple of job references from back in the day. They were good. No rocket scientist, but competent, dependable. In high school, average grades. Got into trouble once. Caught smoking dope. Played baseball two years."

"Not golf?"

"He took up golf after high school," Clarence reminded me.

"He's good," Ray said. "Two years ago, he placed fifth in a big club tournament."

"Dirt on Noel?" I asked.

"No, but something sad. His senior year, two weeks before graduation, his parents went to Idaho for the weekend. When they were coming back, fifty miles from home, a drunk driver hit them head-on. Killed both parents."

"Amazing what you don't know about people you work with," I said.

"Clarence's report says Chris Doyle was on the chess team," Ray said. "Turns out he was also into drama big time. Four years. Six plays. Three starring roles."

"Doyle?" I said. "You gotta be kidding."

"But get this. His dad taught at the University of Pennsylvania. According to Clarence's notes, Doyle said his dad taught history."

"Yeah?"

"He did. Two years. But his main subject, for twenty years, wasn't history. It was philosophy."

"Doyle's father was a college philosophy prof?"

"Yep. Like he said, his mother was from England and was hands-on with the kids' education."

"A cop with a white collar background," I said.

"Something else. He declared bankruptcy five years ago. Had a gambling problem. Impulsive buyer. Turns out he's a rich kid who squandered his inheritance, mostly from his mother's side. This was interesting: When he was twenty, he lied on his résumé to get a job at a retail stationery store. Didn't get fired, but his employer put it on record. Also, he's been in therapy."

"You mean counseling?"

"It's in department records, but it's confidential."

"How does a private eye get into police records?"

"I've done some favors for cops. Including one in records."

"They must've been big favors."

Manny's phone rang. He nodded a couple of times and said, "Okay, be there in fifteen." He hung up. "Gotta go," he said and was gone. No tears at his parting.

"What about Brandon Phillips?" I asked Ray.

"Got some police personnel stuff. You know the competency tests?"

"Yeah?"

"He scored second highest in the department. Near genius."

"I was highest?"

He laughed. "Not quite. But among the detectives, you were third out of ten. Phillips scored one of the highest in the physical fitness tests too, the ones with aerobics, weight lifting, and flexibility."

"He outscored me there, too?"

"Slightly."

"Years ago Phillips and I played together on the precinct fast-pitch softball team. He could knock a home run from either side of the plate."

"Something else," Ray said, putting a check mark in his notes. "Phillips has lots of money…and unlike Doyle, he hasn't run out of it."

"I've seen his Audi," I said.

"And his wife drives a six-month-old Porsche. But here's something odd. She doesn't work outside the home. And have you seen their house?"

"No. Heard it's nice."

"Ninety-eighth percentile nice. CEO type nice. I drove to it. So where does the money come from? Not a detective's salary. Not an inheritance—parents alive on both sides. He's a heck of a card player, I hear, but that's a lot of lifestyle to buy with poker winnings."

"Check it out, will you?"

"I've got his date of birth, but I can't find a Brandon Phillips who was in high school near Irving, Texas, during those years. Okay, the other person with a history of violence was your partner, who just left us."

"Fortunate for you," I said. "Manny was a gangbanger. Took down some rival gang members."

"Always a fighter. Expelled his sophomore year."

"Then went back and got his GED. I know."

"Did you know he was convicted of assault and battery twice, and assault with a deadly weapon as a sixteen-year-old?"

"I knew it was serious and he did time as a juvie. Don't know details. Manny's not the type to open up over a latte."

"He might get mad enough for his violent instincts to be triggered," Ray said.

"Manny has a go-nuts button. I try not to push it. I'm not one to pick a fight." I looked at Clarence, who didn't look back.

"Four years ago," Ray said, "Manny's wife went down in a hit-and-run."

"She nearly died," I said. "Still limps. Lots of rehab."

"Never found who did it, right?" Ray asked.

"Two witnesses, but neither got the license. Drove him crazy that it was a hit-and-run."

I stood and extended my hand to Ray Eagle. "That's the whole gang. I gotta say, you're good, Ray. Not the kind of incompetence I expected from a private eye. You ever want to be a real detective again, I'll give you a reference for Portland Police."

"No thanks. Left that behind me in Detroit. I like my freedom. Call my own shots. I figure out the best way to do it, then I just do it. No bureaucracy. Don't have to raise my hand and ask to go to the bathroom. Don't get called into the chief's office. Plus, I can go to my kids' games. And usually my wife isn't wondering whether I'll be shot today."

"On second thought, keep me in mind if you ever want to hire somebody."

He laughed. "I'll do that. Listen, I wasn't sure if I should mention it, but I did check out somebody else."

"Who?"

"Detective Ollie Chandler."

"You checked on me?"

"Are you a Portland homicide detective?"

"I didn't ask you to check on me."

"So...you're off limits? You don't want to hear it?"

"I'm guessing I already know it."

"In your case I didn't go back to high school. They didn't keep records in those days, or they were all on papyrus and it's crumbled."

"You should be on TV."

"I did get access to some department records. You've got a history of insubordination. And anger management issues."

"That's your best shot?"

"According to a couple of records you've got a serious drinking problem. In at least one case, you blacked out."

"I...where did you get that information?"

"That same somebody who owed me a favor."

"That somebody could lose their job."

"They could but they won't. Since your file says you're known for taking short-cuts, I figured you'd understand. Then there was the investigation into the police brutality charge."

"I was cleared of all charges. The guy was on drugs and was threatening innocent people. I was doing my job."

"I figured you were, but—"

"You don't have to figure anything."

"The last thing was about some difficult things in your own family history. Especially your wife and your—"

"Stop right now! That's enough!" I was standing, my finger pointing at him.

"Oookay then," Ray said. "Sorry. I thought..." He looked at Clarence.

"Anything else you want me to do?" Ray asked.

"No."

"I could check everybody's alibis."

"I've got that covered."

"I could double-check, and we could compare notes."

"It's covered. Your job's done."

I was out the door in ten seconds, stalking game in the asphalt jungle, looking for a jaywalker I could take down and handcuff.

After my forehead sweat was cooled by the wind, I started to wonder what Ray and Clarence were discussing right now. I suspected there might be mention of drinking and anger management.

And I resented it.

"You see, but you do not observe. The distinction is clear."
Sherlock Holmes, *A Scandal in Bohemia*

Sunday, December 22

ALL YOUR LIFE you're a wannabe, until you wake up one morning, and you're a has-been.

And you think, where was that part in the middle when you arrived, when you were living the dream?

Did I miss it?

This is why days off aren't the draw they once were. With time on my hands I find myself asking these kinds of questions. In lieu of answers I consult the bottle, which disappoints, but I know that, so my expectations are low. Anesthetics don't have to offer anything great—pain relief, though temporary, is often the best offer on the table.

I told myself I wouldn't start drinking until after lunch. Since I hate violating my commitments, I adjusted that to not taking my third drink until after lunch.

I opened up the Palatine file, now three folders. Unlike 90 percent of us Oregonians, Clarence and Ray go to church Sunday mornings, like Jake does. They look to the Bible for inspiration. Others look to the newspaper. I look to my case notes.

Seven thirty that evening, Ray Eagle called, waking me from a postpizza nap.

"Turns out Tommi's brother and the professor were the same year. On the same water polo team. Looks like he's a dentist in Portland—names and ages match anyway. Don't know if they hung out besides that. I'd have to call people in their class. I've got some names. Worth my time?"

"Low priority."

"Also, did you know Tommi has a medical condition?"

"No."

"Severe migraines. She takes Imitrex. Comes in pills and injections—she uses the injections."

"Never seen her do it. Or heard her mention it."

"She's had it for years."

"Can you really afford to contribute all this work, Ray?" I was being extra nice after walking out on him the day before.

"Even though Clarence can't put into print all I'm doing, he gave me a favorable mention in his last article."

"I noticed."

"I've already gotten four phone calls. Two of them are new jobs. It's paying off. And even if it wasn't, I'm glad to help."

Every police detective should have a Ray Eagle.

MONDAY, DECEMBER 23, 10:15 A.M.

The chief left a message that he wanted me at his office by 9:30. I took files and phone and set up for business in his waiting area. I brought in a Coke, an apple, dry-roasted peanuts, a Swiss Miss Pudding cup, and a plastic spoon.

Okay, maybe I was making a point. It wasn't lost on Mona, who repeatedly insisted I clean up. I cheerfully ignored her. I overheard her explain to someone around the corner that her duties now included working with the chief periodically at his home office, and, yes, it was perfectly fine with the chief's wife, who was always home anyway.

I file information, never knowing when it'll come in handy.

Lennox finally emerged and stared at everything I'd spread out on the table. "Pick up your mess."

"Yes, sir. Didn't know the wait would only be forty-five minutes this time."

He talked at me, not to me, for ten minutes. "You've been living off the fat of the land around here. You better wake up and smell the coffee. Keep your fingers crossed, mister, because I have the power to take you down. And don't think I won't."

"Yes, sir. You are a mover and shaker. A force to be reckoned with."

"You'd better believe it!"

"It's always darkest before the dawn," I said. "When the going gets tough, the tough get going."

"Are you mocking me?"

"When in Rome, do as the Romans do."

"Who do you think you are?"

My plan to anger him was working. We were at war.

"To be or not to be."

"Get out!"

I turned, and as I did something fell out of my hand.

"Pick up that garbage."

I pretended not to hear him. As I looked back I saw him pick up the wrapper and put it in his wastebasket.

I joined Clarence and Manny in a small conference room. Clarence had stopped returning Manny's glares since breaking his ribs, but Manny was his typical cheery self, with all the charm of a DMV employee.

"Been checking on family members," Manny said. "Brandon Phillips's wife and Linda Glissan took a class with the professor last year."

"How could so many people have been in that guy's classes?" Clarence asked.

"The department has an arrangement with Portland State," I said. "Spouses of officers can take classes at reduced rates, something like fifty bucks a class. Dozens of PPD wives have done it. Some are working on degrees. Sharon took a couple of classes with Linda. Palatine's taught twenty-five years. He was popular. Maybe it's not as odd as it seems."

"Brandon's wife's a looker," Manny said.

"I noticed. The professor would've definitely noticed. Phillips never mentioned his wife was in Palatine's class. You worked with Phillips while Cimmatoni and I were away, right? I think Cimma's knee went out, and I was…"

"Sharon had just died."

"Anyway, what were his habits?"

Manny turned up his palms. "We were on two stakeouts."

"You must have missed my stakeout wit and charm."

"Phillips keeps his mouth shut. I like that."

Manny and Clarence looked at each other, Clarence nodding. Glad to give them this bonding moment.

"He must have drunk a gallon of coffee," Manny said. "And he ate a half dozen granola bars."

"Granola bars? Soft or crunchy?"

"Who cares?"

"I'll bet they're crunchy."

I walked out the door to Phillips's desk. He was out. I looked at his keyboard closely, with the light on my keychain. Down between the keys I saw yellowish-brown particles. I looked both ways, then opened two of his desk drawers. At the back of the second, I found his stash—six Nature Valley pecan crunch granola bars. I took one and shut the drawer.

I showed Manny and Clarence my discovery. They weren't impressed. I decided not to explain. Nero Wolfe holds things back from Archie, like Sherlock Holmes did from Watson, so at the unveiling of a crime's solution, his deductions seem more brilliant.

Manny took off, and Clarence and I settled down at my workstation. I pulled open a file drawer between us. Clarence spotted a file in the front. He pulled it out.

"*The Bacon and Cheese Murders*?" he asked. "Wait…it says Ollie Chandler. You wrote this?"

"It's my first fiction."

"You've written nonfiction?"

"Just that article I gave you the other day."

He flipped through it, then read aloud: "Frankie the Knife tried to shake me, but I stuck to him like a mustard plaster. Frankie was hog ugly, face like a bucket of mud. Walking down Broadway, he was as inconspicuous as a tarantula on a slice of angel food cake. When I jumped him on Alder, the streetlight showed the vein in his forehead beating like a ragtime drummer on bathtub gin. Next thing he knew I was slapping him around like a pinball machine with body English."

"What do you think?" I asked.

"I'm speechless," Clarence said. "A pinball machine with body English?"

"Pretty cool, huh? Raymond Chandler was the greatest writer of hard-boiled detective stories. Lots of people ask if we're related, but I've never found a link between my Chandlers and his."

"You think about crime, you read about crime, apparently you even write about crime." Clarence stopped, appearing to weigh his words. "Off the record, could you have killed the professor?"

"I'm capable of it, if that's what you mean."

"Really?"

"So are you. Suppose somebody murdered Geneva and got away with it. He was cleared, but you know for a fact he did it. And suppose you know he'll kill someone else, even your own kids. He's threatened to do it. So tell me, would you just turn the other cheek? I'm not saying I'd kill him. But if no justice was coming and more people were in danger? I'd consider it."

"I'd take him out in a heartbeat." It was Manny, who'd suddenly reappeared at his desk. Manny has no future in politics.

"I'd like to believe I'd leave justice to God," Clarence said, "not take it into my own hands."

Manny groaned, putting his hand on his rib.

"With your family's lives on the line?" I said. "The first question about these homicide detectives is, are they smart enough to kill and have a good chance of getting away with it? In each case, given their experience and knowledge of murder investigations, the answer's yes. Second, are they bold enough to do it? And third, are they motivated enough? You can't answer the last question until you figure out what that motivation could be. If it's revenge for something horrific or prevention of future crimes, that might be enough."

"What if two detectives were in on it together?" Clarence asked.

"What are the chances of two homicide detectives working together who are both cold-blooded murderers? Okay, they might rough somebody up. But plan a murder?"

"Have you talked about how to kill someone?" Clarence asked.

"Sure." I looked at Manny. He nodded. "But pharmacists probably discuss what drug they'd use to kill someone. And mechanics probably say if they were going to sabotage a car, that's how they'd do it. But few of them actually do it. Especially not together. If I were going to murder someone, I wouldn't let anybody in on it. Nobody would see me do it."

"Nobody but God."

Clarence has this way of ending conversations.

MONDAY, DECEMBER 23, 6:20 P.M.

I talked with McKay Kunz, the night shift's head custodian at the Justice Center, about timetables and procedures for dumping garbage. Then I headed for the parking garage to bail out my car.

"I finally got around to checking out the six phone numbers from the backs of the professor's books," Ray Eagle said as I crossed the bridge and negotiated the ramp onto I-84 in a rainy rush hour. "Two are nonworking numbers, two belong to someone else now, and two to the original owners. But I linked up the old ones to past owners. In four cases I confirmed numbers belonging to women who at one time knew the professor. Two had been in his class; two others had dated him. One remembered him fondly; two sounded pretty cold. One ice-cold."

"Why didn't he put names next to the numbers?" I asked.

"For fear someone would see it? Maybe he didn't want to have to explain why he had their numbers. But how could he remember who the numbers belonged to?"

"Probably thinking one at a time," I said. "The girl was on his mind, and he figured he wouldn't forget. Years later he wouldn't care. He always had a book with him, so books were his scratch pads. Fountain pens and love letters aside, to the professor women weren't much more than numbers anyway."

By 7:30 Mulch was walking me through his day. I usually don't grasp the details, but his general points come through. He'd had a good day, barked at a number of joggers, but missed me. And was thinking about bacon.

I did this interacting with Mulch in my office so whoever was listening to the recording on the chief's behalf would know their bug was still working. When Mulch had gotten everything off his chest, including his guilt in the confiscation and mangling of a Zero candy bar I'd left on my desk, I opened my Picasa photo program, called up the Palatine murder scene pictures, and turned on the slide program. As hundreds of slides appeared for three seconds each, I looked, hoping to see something new.

I'd taken six pictures of the hallway, and the last of those showed Kim Suda, at the far end, coming out of the professor's bedroom, talking with a criminalist. I hit the space bar, pausing it, studying the picture. Something seemed peculiar, but I wasn't sure what.

I hit the escape key, called up the picture for editing, and enlarged Suda's face about six times. She looked different. In particular, her hair was mussed. Usually it's perfect. Yeah, she'd come in from the cold, but Suda's the type to find a mirror. But there was more. Suda seemed…something about her face. She looked…nervous.

In the darkness of December 23, I gave in to Mulch's begging, forgave him for the Zero bar, and took him for a walk. A light snow fell, swirling in the streetlights. I opened my mouth and caught snowflakes on my tongue. Mulch barked and jumped up, mouth open, and caught some flakes himself. I laughed and Mulch strutted happily beside me. He's fascinated by the outdoors each time, like he's never seen it before. I was that way as a kid. Snow was magic back then. Usually magic has no hold on me anymore. But the snow drew me out of myself and into something beyond me, an enchanting greatness.

There's something about fresh Oregon air. It gives me an electric charge to the little gray cells. That's what happened at 8:23 as we walked by the yellow house with the yappy dog who's always on his fourth espresso. When lightning struck inside my head, I stood still ten seconds, then turned and ran toward the old brownstone, dragging Mulch on his leash. He thought it was a grand romp.

I charged in the front door, went to my office, and pulled out one of the three thick files from my briefcase. I flipped through papers.

Finally I found what I was looking for: my copy of the crime scene log sheet, signed off by officers Dorsey and Guerino. I examined it to see exactly who had been granted entry to Palatine's house that night.

Nowhere in the log was the name Kim Suda.

"You will remember, Watson, how the dreadful business of the Abernetty family was first brought to my notice by the depth which the parsley had sunk into the butter upon a hot day."
SHERLOCK HOLMES, *THE ADVENTURE OF THE SIX NAPOLEONS*

TUESDAY, DECEMBER 24, 8:00 A.M.

YESTERDAY HAD BEEN A LONG ONE. After my discovery that Kim Suda wasn't in the crime scene log, Mulch and I had driven back to the Justice Center to meet with McKay Kunz, head custodian. I told him I needed something a suspicious character had tossed in the fifteenth-floor lobby garbage can.

Unfortunately, Kunz said, and he thought he'd made this clear to me when I called earlier, all the trash from the floor had been dumped into two giant bags at 8:00, so now I'd have to sort through everything from that floor to find what was in the lobby trash.

Wearing plastic gloves, I found what I was looking for after thirty minutes, put it in a plastic bag, joined Mulch in the car, and headed home.

This morning I called the patrol sergeant at 8:00 a.m., hoping to meet again with Dorsey and Guerino. He said they couldn't be accessed until 1:00 p.m., and then only if it was absolutely necessary since this was Christmas Eve day, for criminy's sake. I assured him it was absolutely necessary.

I was going to have to wait five hours to hear their story about Suda. I called Jake and Clarence and told them I'd have to leave by 12:30, so we met for lunch at 11:30. In honor of Christmas, Rory had six long-stemmed red roses and six white lilies at our table. Only one problem with this festive setting: Rory was wearing an elf hat. I'm all for civil liberties, but I draw the line at grown men wearing elf hats. He offered us complimentary hats, but we declined, though Jake and I tried to get Clarence to try one on.

We were deep in discussion when I heard a familiar voice behind me.

"Ollie! Merry Christmas!"

I cringed. What was Karl Baylor doing at my restaurant? I looked up at him. He was wearing an elf hat.

"I've heard you talk about this place," he said. "Thought we'd try it today since we start fixing Christmas breakfast tonight."

"Noting the 'we,' I turned further to see a smiling young woman.

"Ever met my wife, Tiffany?"

I paused a moment too long. "No."

"Sweetheart, this is Ollie Chandler. I've mentioned him."

I saw the glimmer of recognition. "I think we've met."

"Maybe at the detective dinner last spring," I said, knowing I'd skipped those dinners since Sharon died.

"Seems like recently."

"I was working undercover as your mailman."

She laughed. "That was it. Nice to meet you."

Karl removed his elf hat and held it in his hands while he talked with Clarence and called him "brother" and introduced him to Tiffany. She seemed impressed to meet Jake, another columnist she enjoyed. I was glad to have her occupied with anyone besides me.

Rory pointed the Baylors to a booth fifteen feet away. They sat down across from each other. Fortunately, Tiffany faced the other direction.

"The Baylors seem nice," Jake said. "I was expecting a couple of terrorists."

"I'll take a rain check on laughing."

After a few minutes, the Baylors stood and switched sides. Tiffany stared at me. She looked away only when I glanced at her. Every time this happened, I scooted a few more inches into the booth. Soon I was out of her line of sight.

I needed to get back for Dorsey and Guerino, and Jake was taking off early for Christmas Eve, so we parted, wishing each other Merry Christmas. They invited me to join their families, and I said no. Kendra and I were going it alone.

"See you at the *Tribune* at 3:00?" I asked Clarence.

"Need to be home by 4:00. Sure it can't wait?"

"Positive. Doesn't anybody put in full days anymore? Carp's expecting me. You can leave by 3:30."

Afterward I sat in the parking lot, finding in my briefcase the typed notes of my interview with Rupert Bolin, fountain pen aficionado. I glanced at his business card and called him as I drove back to the Justice Center.

"Remember telling me about the different reasons people use fountain pens? You mentioned love letters."

"Oh, yes, it's so romantic. Women love the old-fashioned ways. It's not like scratching out something with an ordinary pen. Or, heaven forbid, sending an e-mail. Every letter written with a fountain pen is an original. Sometimes I write a saucy one to my wife, with the finest pen and ink money can buy."

"I'm sure she's overcome with excitement," I said.

"Yes, indeed," he replied. "We have several special pens and superior stationery that I highly recommend for you to write exquisite letters to that special woman who has captured your heart."

"I don't have…"

I stopped. I wondered how the phrase "double cheese, double pepperoni" written in fine fountain pen ink on a superior stationery, might move the heart of Lynn Carpenter.

I opened the official crime scene log from Records, so it'd be ready for Dorsey and Guerino. They arrived at 1:05 p.m.

"What'd we do this time?" Guerino asked.

"You guys know Kim Suda, right? She's standing by the watercooler, but don't stare, okay?"

They both stared, then nodded.

"Do either of you remember her coming into the professor's house that night?"

"She was there," Guerino said.

"I know she was there. I'm asking if you remember her arrival."

Dorsey shrugged. "Must have been when I was talking to the gawkers." He looked at Guerino. "You signed her in, right?"

"I don't remember her coming to the door. But I went inside a couple of times to point stuff out to the criminalists. You must've been there when she came."

"Nope."

"Here's the logbook," I said. "Check it out. Neither of you signed her in. Her name's not there."

"But…one of us was at the door at all times," Dorsey said. "That's SOP."

"Not leaving the scene's SOP too."

"You say the words *ski mask* once," Dorsey said, "and we're going to duke it out right here."

"Forget that. Now think, guys." I looked at the log and pointed name by name. "Remember the ambulance, the two paramedics coming in? Two criminalists? Then me and Clarence? Hatch, the medical examiner? Lynn Carpenter, *Trib* photographer? Then Manny, the grouch. And three uniforms named Nick Goin, Chris Warren, and Alex Helm, who you let in for reasons I don't understand."

"It was because—"

"I don't care. I only care whether you remember them."

"Sure," Dorsey said. "I told Guerino you'd have a cow if we let them in."

"It was a pretty big cow," I said. "Okay, then there were two more criminalists they called for, after I left the scene. They were the last two you signed in. Remember them?"

"A wiry guy." Dorsey looked at the log. "Carlo Failla. And a young gal, red hair…Kristin Wennerlind."

"Okay," I said. "So you're telling me you remember every single one of these people who logged in? Now, I'll ask you again. Do you remember Kim Suda arriving?"

They both shook their heads.

"But we know she was there," Guerino said.

Their faces showed they didn't understand what it meant.

I did.

34

*"My body has remained in this armchair and has,
I regret to observe, consumed in my absence two
large pots of coffee and an incredible amount of tobacco."*
SHERLOCK HOLMES, *THE HOUND OF THE BASKERVILLES*

TUESDAY, DECEMBER 24, 1:50 P.M.

I HAVE FOND MEMORIES of Christmas Eve day as a kid. My brother and my buddies Gary Swan and Wayne and Lynn Kim and I, and my black lab Ranger, would gather at the Kims' house, sleds and saucers in tow. I had a hot pink saucer that, on the snow, could be seen from Mars.

We'd spend the day sliding down any slope within walking distance and make it back, fingers frozen, to Mom. She thawed us out with Ovaltine while Bing Crosby sang "White Christmas" on the big old 33 album platter, back when our RCA record player let us choose between speeds—33 or 45 or 78. We loved to switch them to the wrong speed so Bing sounded like Alvin and the Chipmunks.

I could still taste the chocolate malt of the Ovaltine and remember looking longingly at all the presents under the Christmas tree, a bunch with my name on them. Before the night was over, I'd unwrap those treasures.

Now, forty-five years later, this was Christmas Eve day too. But my life was no longer spent dreaming dreams. My job was unraveling nightmares. Still, truth is, since my childhood dreams of being an astronaut or a pro-wrestler or Green Lantern hadn't materialized, I couldn't think of any way I'd rather spend the day than solving a murder.

I phoned the chief's daughter. "Jenn Lennox?"

"Yeah?"

"Detective Chandler."

"What do *you* want?"

"When you were at the professor's house…that was just two and a half months ago?"

"I don't know. Couple of weeks after the first class."

"According to records, your class started in late September. That would put the get-together mid-October?"

"I guess."

"When you were at Palatine's that night, did you have your cell phone?"

"Always."

"You didn't take any pictures with your phone did you?"

"Probably. Wait, yeah, I did. Pictures of the professor and other students."

"In front of the fireplace?"

"I think so."

"Still have them?"

"Probably not."

"Don't you save any pictures?"

"Only ones I want. I don't keep pictures of people I hate. Not like Tasha. She keeps everything on her computer. She's a geek."

"You're sure you don't have those pictures? Can you check?"

"Why?"

"If you find them I'll give you a Starbucks card."

"How much?"

"Ten dollars."

She laughed. "Not worth it."

"Twenty-five dollars?"

"Thirty."

"Okay. You find me some pictures taken in the professor's living room that night—but they have to be where the fireplace mantel is visible—then I'll give you a thirty-dollar Starbucks card."

And they say we don't negotiate with terrorists.

At 2:00 p.m. Suda entered the conference room. To soften her, I'd brought in a cup of coffee and a white frosted donut with those colored sprinkles that irritate me.

"Coffee and donut?" I asked.

She shook her head and sat down. "I have twenty minutes, that's it."

"What time did you come to the professor's house November 20?"

"Near four, I think."

"I guess if I needed to know, I could just check the log."

"I guess." No twitch.

"You did sign the log, didn't you?"

"Probably."

"Could you point out your signature?" I handed her the log. "We've got para-medics, criminalists, Clarence and me, Hatch, Lynn Carpenter, Manny, and the uniforms you ushered out. You must have come in somewhere between me and the uniforms. So...why didn't you sign in?"

"They know me."

"They know me. And Hatch. And Manny. They signed us in."

"It was a zoo when I got there."

"Guerino and Dorsey remember talking with you inside and when you left. They don't remember you arriving."

"What's your point?"

"Where'd you park?"

"Around the corner."

"What corner?"

"The street next to the professor's. 22nd?"

"I left before you did, to check my messages at home. I took 22nd down to Stark. I didn't see your car. And it wasn't on Oak either."

"There were lots of cars."

"I notice cars. Was it your red Toyota Camry?"

"I guess."

"Why would you have to guess?"

"Yeah, it was my car. It's a Camry. It's red."

"How many feet from Oak were you parked?"

"Forty?"

"East side of 22nd?"

"West. Look," she said, "you showed up at one of my investigations, remember? Did I harass you about it?"

"I'm not harassing you."

She got up, teeth clenched, and stormed out of the room in a cold front. If she'd had a broom, she could have flown.

Have I mentioned I have a way with women?

I removed a few of the sprinkles and ate her donut.

I was going to meet Clarence at the *Trib*, but I had an extra fifteen minutes, so I stopped by to see Phil in crime lab. He wished me Merry Christmas. At least he wasn't wearing an elf hat. I handed him a clear evidence bag.

"Look," I said, "here's that gum wrapper, still sealed in your bag. I realize it was careless of me to drop it at the crime scene, but I shouldn't have picked it up. And I shouldn't have asked you to give it back to me. It puts us both at risk. I don't feel right holding on to it."

"Conscience?"

"You don't need to mention this. You'd be in as much trouble as I would."

"Okay. I'll just put it with the other evidence. I'll just change the date and leave it unmarked. Doubt if anyone'll notice. Nobody needs to know. As long as nobody needs to know about that contaminated blood sample."

"Merry Christmas," I said.

Clarence had been routinely invading my workspace. I returned the favor that afternoon. It was dry, so I decided to cut through Terry Schrunk Plaza south to Jefferson and head four blocks west to Broadway, where I turned left and entered the front door of the *Oregon Tribune*.

When the two gals at the front desk of the *Trib* asked for my ID, I showed them. When that didn't appear good enough, I showed them my Glock in my shoulder holster. I showed it to the security guard, along with my ID. He told me I might have to surrender my weapon. I told him that my Glock and I are conjoined twins and it would require a delicate surgery. I wondered if he felt up to it. He got on the phone. They let me through, then said, "Mr. Abernathy will come down."

"No thanks," I said. "I'm going up." Not that I knew exactly where I was going. I'd visited the *Tribune* about as often as I'd visited the Kremlin. No offense to the Kremlin.

Journalists are nervous about people with guns. This is understandable since they do so much to aggravate gun-owners. They write columns about how regular people shouldn't be allowed to have guns. Of course, I don't think journalists should be allowed to write words, which have destroyed more lives than guns. These thoughts contributed to my self-righteous swagger as I walked through the state capitol of self-righteousness.

I bumped into Clarence as I was about to get in the elevator. Clarence is a lot to bump into.

"I told them I'd come down to meet you," he said.

"What a coincidence. I told them I'd come up to meet you. Apparently we were both right. I'm tired of you occupying my world. I feel like occupying yours for a change."

"It's my job to be part of your world. It's not your job to be here."

"Here I am. Loaded firearm and all." I said the words loud, drunk loud, though I hadn't had a drink since yesterday. I patted my jacket and watched people look at us nervously.

"Homicide," I said loudly.

One woman in dress and high heels and fancy scarf, who I recognized as a columnist, turned pale.

"Don't worry," I told her. "I don't commit them. I investigate them. There've been threats about vigilantes going after journalists because of slander. I'm here to guard your life."

"He's joking," Clarence said.

It was fun, a Christmas present to myself, turning the tables and making people nervous who make their living making others nervous.

Clarence's editor Winston blew in like a hurricane. "Who do you think you are, barging in here?" he bellowed, Louis Armstrong-like, with cheeks to match.

"I think I am Police Detective Ollie Chandler. Wait, hold on." I pulled out my ID card, read it, and said, "I *am* Detective Ollie Chandler, and I'm paid to barge into places. Excuse me if my presence is inconvenient and uncomfortable. You journalists have always been sensitive to my convenience and comfort, and I certainly want to reciprocate."

Winston, his mammoth cheeks red, scowled. I scowled back. His natural face gave him a big advantage. He was the Grinch who stole Christmas. If an elf hat had been nearby, I would have crammed it over his head.

"Okay, enough holiday cheer," I said to Clarence. "Where's Carp?"

Clarence led me through the giant maze, explaining that most photojournalists just had workstations but Carp had her own office.

She greeted us warmly. I presented her with three Papa Murphy's coupons. "Clipped them myself." She gave me an endearing look.

I sat down and showed Carp the crime scene log. "You signed in at 3:51, but they didn't sign you out when you left to take the pictures on the street. When was that?"

"That'll be easy," she said. "The pictures all have a date and time stamp." She maximized her photo program and looked at the slides on her screen, then checked Properties. "Looks like I took all those pictures in eight minutes, between 4:46 and 4:54."

"That was quick."

"It was spooky out there. I don't hang around murders like you do."

I flipped through the neighborhood pictures on her computer screen three times. "No red Camry. Suda's car wasn't where she said it was."

"Why would she lie?" Clarence said.

"And why would she park away from the scene? Above all, why didn't she sign in? And why don't Dorsey and Guerino remember her arriving?"

"Is it really that important that she didn't sign in?" Clarence asked. "I mean, obviously she was there. We all saw her."

"Suppose the officers were right and she didn't slip by them," I said.

"But she had to slip by," Clarence said. "What other explanation is there?"

I looked at them both, preparing to say what I'd been thinking: "When Dorsey and Guerino arrived at Palatine's, Kim Suda was already in the house."

35

"That hurts my pride, Watson. It is a petty feeling, no doubt, but it hurts my pride."
SHERLOCK HOLMES, *THE FIVE ORANGE PIPS*

TUESDAY, DECEMBER 24, 7:30 P.M.

KENDRA ARRIVED at the old brownstone for Christmas Eve dinner, bringing a vegetable stew, a fruit salad with watermelon and grapes and pineapple, and a festive display of raw vegetables, including minicarrots and those little jobbers that look like corn on the cob. I pulled out some Thousand Island dressing for dip, so it wasn't a total loss.

Bing Crosby was dreaming of a White Christmas, and Nat King Cole sang about chestnuts roasting on an open fire. Kendra pretended that wasn't cool, but eventually sang along. And when the snow started falling, we stood on my deck and enjoyed it together. Kendra insisted we hear from Bing again. It was just my little girl and me and Mulch and the snow and the music. It was Christmas, and I didn't want it to end and tried to stop reminding myself it would.

We sat on the couch, her under her mom's blue Seahawks blanket, me covered with Mulch. We reminisced about Christmases past and how her mom always loved watching *It's a Wonderful Life* with Jimmy Stewart. Kendra opened a Target gift card from me and a scarf she'd never wear. I opened up a Best Buy gift card from her and a tie I'll never wear. Our hearts overflowed with yuletide thanks.

Kendra also gave me *It's a Wonderful Life* on DVD, beaming in light of our remembrances, and one other gift. At first I thought it was a big red handkerchief. Then I saw it had a point and "Merry Christmas" embroidered on it in green letters.

"Put it on, Dad."

"Yes, ma'am."

We watched Jimmy Stewart and laughed and cried and ate popcorn and talked about the movie and her job and her pregnancy and how she missed her mother and sister, all with a tray of rabbit food in front of us, Mulch wondering when the baby back ribs were coming, and me wearing an elf hat.

WEDNESDAY, DECEMBER 25, 7:30 A.M.

I sat in my UCLA Bruins sweatshirt in Carly Woods's room at Adventist Medical Center. Her face was pale, eyes red. After their Christmas Eve celebration, at 3:00 a.m., when most bad things happen, she'd had a seizure.

Janet and Jake insisted on stepping out of the room to grab something to eat. They took Carly's boy, Finney. An empty Christmas stocking hung from the tray, which had a cup of ice water on it, surrounded by some wrapping paper and candy.

"Want a Whitman's Sampler?" Carly asked. I declined. "Milk Duds?" Shook my head. "You're looking at my Whoppers, aren't you?"

"Okay," I said, holding out my hand. She filled it.

"What'd you get for Christmas?" I asked.

"Some CDs and clothes, but best of all, books." She pointed at the stack. They included a slipcased set of the Chronicles of Narnia and *Perelandra*, *The Problem of Pain*, and *Mere Christianity*.

"A C. S. Lewis theme," I said. I noticed there were no books by Bertrand Russell and decided he wasn't a popular writer for people in hospitals.

"Two were presents. I asked Dad to bring the rest. I wanted to reread them. *The Problem of Pain* is pretty relevant right now." She smiled like she had no reason not to. "Have you read the Narnia stories?"

"I saw the first movie."

"What'd you think of Aslan?"

"What about him?"

"Wouldn't you like to meet him?"

"Yeah, I guess so."

"He's Jesus, you know."

"I was thinking of him as a lion. King, protector, defender of justice."

"He's all that and more. Have you thought about the self-restraint and love it took for Aslan to let the witch and the evil creatures beat him up and shave him and kill him so he could take the punishment Edmund deserved?"

I nodded.

"The real King didn't just die for Edmund. He died for me. And you."

"I never argue with young women in hospitals."

"I can take it. Argue with me."

"I'm glad you find comfort in it. But to me, it's just a story."

"Some stories aren't true. Some are. This one is."

I looked at her, wanting both to agree and to argue.

"Let me read you something." She picked up her copy of *The Lion, the Witch, and the Wardrobe* and flipped back a few pages from the dog-ear.

"When the Beavers first tell the children about Aslan, Susan asks this question:

"Is he—quite safe? I shall feel rather nervous about meeting a lion."

"That you will, dearie, and no mistake," said Mrs. Beaver; "if there's anyone who can appear before Aslan without their knees knocking, they're either braver than most or else just silly."

"Then he isn't safe?" said Lucy.

"Safe?" said Mr. Beaver; "don't you hear what Mrs. Beaver tells you? Who said anything about safe? 'Course he isn't safe. But he's good. He's the King, I tell you."

"What does it mean that he's not safe?" I asked.

"For one thing," Carly said, "I love Him, and I'm dying." She laughed without a hint of cynicism. "He's faithful, but not predictable. I know He loves me; I know I'll go to heaven. I know the best is yet to come. But I also know that meanwhile, life here under the curse isn't real easy."

"I've noticed."

"We can ask Him to take away pain and suffering and death, but for now it's part of our lives. But He's going to get rid of it, once and for all. I was reading this morning in Isaiah 25…pass me my Bible, would you?"

She took it with both hands, so frail I cringed. "I'll read you three verses, where He's talking about the new earth:

On this mountain the LORD Almighty will prepare a feast of rich food for all peoples, a banquet of aged wine—the best of meats and the finest of wines. On this mountain he will destroy the shroud that enfolds all peoples, the sheet that covers all nations; he will swallow up death forever. The Sovereign LORD will wipe away the tears from all faces; he will remove the disgrace of his people from all the earth. The LORD has spoken. In that day they will say, "Surely this is our God; we trusted in him, and he saved us. This is the LORD, we trusted in him; let us rejoice and be glad in his salvation."

"A banquet?" I asked. "Best meats? Finest wines?"

"I thought that might get your attention."

"My grandmother, who was a church warden or something, never talked about feasts and wine. She just warned against gluttony and drunkenness."

"Right now I don't have an appetite," Carly said, "so I'm thinking about God swallowing up death forever and wiping away the tears. I can't tell you what that means to me."

She reached her hand out. I held it, so delicate and fragile.

She said, "I asked Mom and Dad to leave when you got here because I wanted to make you an offer."

"An offer?"

"You probably don't think I have much to offer right now, but really I do."

"I'm listening."

"If you want me to…I could say hi to Aunt Sharon for you."

"Carly, stop it."

"I could give her a hug for you."

"But…I mean…" I put my face in my right hand, still holding hers with my left. "Yeah. Hug Sharon for me."

"You know, you can go to heaven some day, Uncle Ollie. Then you can hug her yourself."

I couldn't think of anything to say.

"The clock's not ticking just for me," she said. "You spend your life around dying people. You should know."

"You never give up on me, do you, Carly?"

"Nope. Neither does Little Finn. Or Dad. I know I'm going to see Mom and Dad and Finney and Uncle Clarence there some day. I'm going to see Uncle Finney real soon, I think. And I really want to see you again too." A little tear fell from one of her Bambi eyes. "I want to see you in heaven."

She squeezed my hand. There was no strength in me. But in that weak little hand I felt a superhuman strength.

"You know what you need to do, don't you?" she asked.

"Trust. Believe. Accept. Confess. Repent." I recited the checklist.

"Wow." She grinned. "Not bad."

"I can repeat what your dad's been telling me for years. Doing it's the problem."

"Why?"

"Okay, if there's a God and He loves you, then why are you…like this?"

"Dying? It's okay, you can say it."

"I don't want to say it."

"I'll say it. I'm dying. Can't say it's fun. I mean, I'd rather be playing tennis or at the mall. But then if I was, I wouldn't be talking with you like this, would I? And I wouldn't be spending hours with my parents every day. And I wouldn't be seeing Mom and Dad care for Finney. Sad as I am about leaving my son behind, I know that soon I'll be happier than I've ever been in my life."

"You really believe that."

"I really do."

"Wish I could."

"You can."

"It's not that easy."

"I didn't say it was easy. It's your choice. Make it while you still can." She smiled. "You like being the rogue, the unbeliever, the black sheep. Kind of your identity, isn't it? I know you get tired of people saying they're praying for you. So I won't say it."

"Thanks for restraining yourself."

She laughed. "You're funny. You're just a teddy bear. You're this big skeptic with all your tough questions and smart remarks. I love you."

In a flash I saw Kendra as a four-year-old saying she loved me. When I heard Carly say it, I felt like she was my daughter. I didn't want to lose her. I could barely see her now. Something was in my eyes. Carly leaned forward. I felt her arms around me. She couldn't squeeze me, but I squeezed her, gently.

"It's okay," she said. "Don't worry. I'm going to be fine. I really am. And I'm going to give Sharon a really big hug for you."

I stumbled out the door. Carly was on the inside of something, and I was on the outside. And I knew, without doubt, she was in a far better place. Part of me wanted to join her there, and part of me just wanted to run to the elevator. Instead I walked briskly. When I got to the parking lot, snow pelting me, washing my face, I ran to the car.

I sat there, head against the steering wheel, smelling wet upholstery, and wondering why that dying girl was so much happier than I was…so much happier than I've ever been.

36

"Stand at the window here. Was there ever such a dreary, dismal, unprofitable world? See how the yellow fog swirls down the street and drifts across the duncoloured houses. What could be more hopelessly prosaic and material?...Crime is commonplace, existence is commonplace, and no qualities save those which are commonplace have any function upon earth."
SHERLOCK HOLMES, *THE SIGN OF FOUR*

THURSDAY, DECEMBER 26, 9:30 A.M.

CHRISTMAS DAY had been a disappointment. Kendra, long ago, had planned to be with a friend's family. I was grateful we'd had Christmas Eve together, but Christmas was an anticlimax. Mulch and I lounged around the brownstone after my visit to Carly. Bing and Nat weren't enough to pick us up. Not even Alvin and the Chipmunks singing "Christmas, Don't Be Late." Mulch loves those Chipmunks, but the merriment was fleeting. The snow stopped falling. As the day spent itself, the gray morphed into darkness.

In those hours of melancholy I decided that Sharon was Christmas, and Christmas died with her. Mulch's eyes were pitiful, like he was remembering bygone days as a Russian refugee. Dogs can't be happy when their people are sad.

I turned on the radio to the all-Christmas-all-the-time station and heard Andy Williams croon, "It's the most wonderful time of the year." I turned it off. I agree with the sentiment, when Christmas is still ahead. But when it actually comes, I ask myself, *Is this all?* Why is it so much better in the anticipating than in the reality? Or is there a reality that's supposed to last beyond the day itself?

I understand why the suicide rate's higher on holidays. Ironically, so's the murder rate. People alone kill themselves. People together kill each other. What a messed up world. We could use a new one.

I read Sherlock Holmes's *The Red-Headed League* for the sixth time. (I put a checkmark on the stories every time I read them.) Sometimes they pull me up. But not on a lonely Christmas. If Christmas can be lonely, what hope is there for other days?

The more I drank the darker it felt, until I stopped feeling. The bottle never brings happiness, but it can cover misery for a while.

Thursday morning I dragged myself to the office, bleary-eyed. Forty ounces of coffee hadn't facilitated a resurrection. I drank the last twelve ounces without looking at the mug any more than I'd look at a needle when the nurse gives me a shot. If there were a caffeine IV, I'd have plugged in.

I sat there alone, I don't know how long, the Christmas blues and the hangover keeping me from focusing on the case.

I remembered my grandmother talking to me about heaven once. We'd no longer have these corrupt bodies, she said. We'd no longer be doing earthly things like eating or drinking or going to carnivals or pizza joints.

I asked her if we'd be able to swim, run, and play baseball. She said we'd no longer want to do worldly things like that. All we'd want to do is sing and play zithers and go to church. That sealed it for me. I didn't want to go to heaven.

Strange how Grandma talked about heaven but made me not want to go there. Obadiah Abernathy, on the other hand, was one of the few who made me want to go there. Most people I'd never want to spend a day with. It takes a rare person to make me think I'd enjoy spending forever with them.

When Clarence showed up, it was obvious his Christmas had been better than mine. He nearly bordered on being cheerful. Trying to cure that, I said, "Mark Twain claimed it was heaven for atmosphere but hell for company."

"Meaning what?" Clarence asked, in a voice that makes Darth Vader sound like he's in the Vienna Boys Choir.

"Meaning that heaven might keep your feet from the fire, but you'll have more fun with your buddies in hell."

"You think anyone will have fun in hell? It's God who made fun. He invented laughter. God has a sense of humor. The devil doesn't."

I kept thinking about that dream. And hearing the voice of Obadiah Abernathy: "Can't get on board widout yo' ticket."

I didn't tell Clarence about the dream, for the same reason I wouldn't hand ammo to someone pointing his gun at me.

Obadiah Abernathy shook his head. "I loves that man, but he gots it all wrong. It's You he should be thinkin' 'bout. With You, any place is heaven. Widout You, any place is hell. And hell's got nothin' to offer nobody, that's fo' sure."

"You're a loyal servant, Obadiah." The Carpenter laughed and put His arm around him. "Ollie Chandler's mostly wrong, yet…he's closer to being right than you think."

"What do you mean?"

"He saw something in you. He saw *Me* in you."

"He did?"

The Carpenter smiled. "Those most like Me never seem to realize it. They're more aware of their failings."

"That's somethin' I knowed plenty 'bout."

"Yes. And I love you for it. Ollie Chandler's far from Me, yet not so far. For in

Me he moves and breathes and has his being. He loves what he does because I'm in it. He loves logic and deductions and the exhilaration of search and discovery, all from Me. What he hates about life is the part that's not from Me. Even what he loves in food and football is a reflection of the way I made him and the earth itself."

"I saw You in baseball, Lord, all those years. I played it for You, You know I did. It drew me closer to You, my sweet Jesus. Some of us ball players been talkin', You know."

"Yes, I know." His smile broke out again.

"We're thinkin' on the new earth there'll maybe be baseball again."

"Can you think of a single reason why there wouldn't be?"

"Before I got here, I could have thought of some. Now I can't."

"Ollie's love for sports is a love for being connected, being part of a team with a common goal. I made your bodies and minds to reach upward, to improve, excel, have dominion, find joy and pleasure in the small and large. To see and draw close to Me."

"I don' think I really knowed that."

"You sensed it. And you lived it. Ollie saw Me in you. So you see, it's not only you he wants to be with. It's Me."

"But he doesn't know that."

"No. Clarence and Jake and Carly and the others must help him understand. I've put them there for him. It's their job to point him to Me, just as you did."

"What a wondrous job that is," Obadiah said, smiling remarkably like the One he spoke to. "What a truly wondrous job."

An e-mail appeared from Carp. It said "Photos attached." Manny had collected the originals, all taken in Palatine's living room, from various people, including Palatine's sister-in-law. I'd asked Carp to enlarge them, hoping to find what was in the "missing picture." I clicked open Photoshop.

Doyle stood with a cup in his hand and pretended he wasn't staring at my screen. I turned the screen away from him.

The first three pictures were terrible, but Carp had ordered them worst to best. The fifth picture was clear enough to make out a blonde and a brunette by the professor, but the facial features were indiscernible.

I felt a presence behind me and turned to see Tommi.

"Pictures?" she asked. "Family?"

"This is private, Tommi. Sorry." She walked away, pretending her feelings weren't hurt.

I called up the last picture, which was slightly better overall. The jewelry was a little clearer, including the chain necklace. Still, these could be any of a million girls. Whoever they were, the killer had wanted this picture—and not wanted the homicide detectives to see it.

What I'd give for clarity. I was so close I could taste it.

I decided to print it anyway, on the color printer by the copy machine. When I went to get it, Chris Doyle bumped shoulders with me.

"Sorry," I said.

"Watch where you're going." That's when I realized he'd done it deliberately.

"Got a problem with me, Chris?"

"Everybody's got a problem with you."

"Just doing my job."

"You're doing a lousy job. And we're sick and tired of you."

I thought of eight different ways I could take him. But I had other things on my mind.

Chris Doyle, the Pillsbury Doughboy, was wearin' cheese underwear and walkin' down rat alley.

He was beggin' for a whuppin'.

"It was a straight left against a slogging ruffian. I emerged as you see me. Mr. Woodley went home in a cart."
SHERLOCK HOLMES, *THE ADVENTURE OF THE SOLITARY CYCLIST*

THURSDAY, DECEMBER 26, 11:00 A.M.

I STEPPED OUT for a brisk walk in the asphalt jungle.

Walking to the west side of the Justice Center, I looked across Third Street to Chapman Square, with its shade trees now skeletal and even its resilient evergreens flinching in the cold wind. I considered crossing to Terry Schrunk Plaza but instead turned around and headed east down Madison, toward the Hawthorne Bridge.

Despite the teaser on Christmas eve, the dream of a white Christmas hadn't materialized. It seldom does in Portland. Now the day after Christmas, a heavy twenty-five-degree air pressed on my eyes, which watered, threatening to freeze. Tough as it can feel, winter has its own mystique, one of the reasons I like living in Oregon, where the seasons are well defined. Going out in the cold is an escape for me.

And perhaps a metaphor of my life.

I crossed Madison, then walked by two homeless guys, hands out. I ignored them. Then, on the corner of First Street, I came to a woman in bulky layers of old clothes under what looked like a Russian soldier's survival coat. She stood, leaning on a rusted shopping cart, exposed to cold and wind, unprotected by buildings.

She didn't look at me, didn't ask me for anything. Turning to make sure no one saw me, I removed my wallet and gave her a five. "Get some hot coffee," I said, pointing to Kaffee Bistro. She said a quiet "thank you," but didn't go for coffee. Maybe it was free somewhere in her world, at a rescue mission or something. I don't usually give cash to street people, but on a cold day after Christmas, I couldn't stand that she was out on the streets, with all she had to show for fifty years stuffed in a lousy Safeway cart.

I walked toward the southwest edge of the Hawthorne Bridge, knowing it would offer an arctic wake-up, especially with the twenty-mile-an-hour wind. In my four-block walk thus far, in one moment I'd inhaled absolute freshness, with all its promise, then the next exhaust fumes, then garbage, then urine, then a poor woman who hadn't bathed in months.

It reminded me that this world has survived two thousand Christmases, but somehow the promise of Christmas hasn't yet been kept.

I walked on to the bridge's pedestrian path, where the wet air over the Willamette River, splitting Portland in half, assaulted my face. I looked east hoping to catch a glimpse of Mount Hood. Nothing. I looked north at Tom McCall Waterfront Park, so alive in summer, so dead now. I looked west at the Justice Center and KOIN Tower, then southeast, across the river, toward the Oregon Museum of Science and Industry. I contemplated all the creativity, the ingenious design and countless man-hours invested in this great city.

I considered the paradox of its stunning outward beauty coupled with its stinking underbelly, two worlds impossibly coexistent. I thought about how great Portland could be if only things were different. If *we* were different. I thought it's the same with every city, every town. And I thought about how every day our leaders, local and national, keep spouting off promises that never come true.

I still vote because I couldn't sleep if I didn't. But I don't read the literature anymore, the latest blueprints for utopia. I refuse to listen to the campaign commercials that no longer stop in November. I can't change the channel fast enough.

There must be sincere leaders concerned about justice and helping people who need help and stopping crime. There must be leaders who know what to do besides point fingers and make promises. But I can't find them.

The political parties and talking heads serve up words that are shelled husks. I'm sick of them. I wished the cold east wind on my face would blow away empty words forever, or bury them beneath the icy river I peered down upon.

I wondered how many people had jumped off this bridge, how many finally gave up on a life that offers dreams only to kill them. I wondered how many jumpers had once believed that this world offers solutions to the problems of evil, suffering, and death.

I used to try sifting through the political rocks and mud, but I never found the gold. I can't stand the wonks and opinion polls and PR automatons who conduct their stupid studies and put their finger in the wind to find out what they should say next. The world will never be rescued by opinion polls. And from where I stand, rescue is what we need.

For ten years I listened to Rush Limbaugh and Bill Maher and others on every side. I'd agree with one, then the other, but I couldn't stomach the arrogance and word-wrangling and oversimplification and disdain. I didn't need help getting angry. I couldn't see conservative rage or liberal rage doing anything more than propagating themselves into sanctified smugness, which smells no better on one side of the political aisle than the other.

So now I just say no to news. I try to catch killers by day, then retreat by night to Nero Wolfe and *24* and *Star Trek* reruns, leaving the universe to self-destruction or Borg invasion or spontaneous utopia, not putting my money on the latter.

I would never jump off a bridge, I thought as I stood there. I recalled two occasions in the last year when I'd sat on my bed, Glock loaded, once having felt its muzzle on my right temple. That's how I'd do it if I ever did.

I gazed east one last time, still hoping to catch a glimpse of Mount Hood, outrageously beautiful, a giant snow cone this time of year. But what is to me the world's most beautiful mountain remained hopelessly hidden in the clouds.

A hundred feet onto the Hawthorne Bridge, I leaned over the south side, raised my arms, and clenched my fists. I screamed into the cold wind, knowing nobody could hear me.

My scream lasted five seconds. When it was done, I put my hand to my raw throat, then walked back past other cold people, homeless and hopeless, to the Justice Center.

When I returned to detective division, I wasn't the only one with a red face. Chris Doyle was on the prowl, face sweaty, a pale crimson, looking for someone to bump into.

Not just anyone. Me.

"You're pathetic, Chandler," Doyle shouted, posturing like a peacock without the goods.

Eight pairs of eyes locked on us. Apparently he'd let it be known that he was going to teach me a lesson. He could have let me thaw first.

"We don't want you here anymore," Doyle said.

"Does this mean you're going to stop paying my salary, Chris?"

"We don't deserve to be treated like criminals."

"Suspects. Criminals are the ones we arrest. Nearly everybody here is innocent. Are you?"

"You think I did it?"

"I don't know. Did you?"

His fists were clenched so tight his knuckles were white.

"I think you're a disgrace," he said.

"I don't give a rat's patootie what you think, chess boy."

He took a step forward. I held my ground.

"That's your opening move?" I said. "If the professor had been bored to death, you'd be my prime suspect."

His fist connected with my jaw half a second later. I staggered backward.

"Over here," Phillips yelled. "Chris and Ollie. Hog fight!"

It was like high school, everybody running to the end of the courtyard to see the fight.

I stood there fingering my lip and opening and closing my jaw, testing the hinges. I sized up the Pillsbury Doughboy.

"It's smackdown!" Noel said, grinning like a moron.

"Take him, Doyle!" Cimmatoni called.

"Twenty bucks on Ollie," Jack said. He pulled a Jackson out of his wallet and waved it. Jack had seen me head butt guys into tomorrow, so he figured it was easy money.

Doyle was waiting for me to make the next move while he caught his breath. I was waiting for the crowd to settle in at ringside.

"Chandler couldn't take my grandmother," Suda said.

"He's not fighting your grandmother," Jack said. "He's fighting Doyle."

"They should sumo wrestle," Cimmatoni said.

"That's not a pretty picture," Phillips said.

"Nobody tell Tommi or she'll call Sarge," Suda said.

"Sarge is over there," Barrows said, pointing, "pretending he's not watching."

I wiped blood with the Taco Bell napkin from my trench coat pocket. "Just a flesh wound," I said, ditching the coat.

"He's taking off the Sam Spade coat," Phillips said. "He means business."

Doyle ran four steps to me and took another swing. I smelled tobacco as it whiffed by. I ducked then punched him twice, first with a left, then with a right, both in his doughy center. With another right, I plastered the pack of Marlboros in his shirt pocket, sitting him on the back of his lap. But the Doughboy rose again, asking to be popped back in the oven. Doyle surprised me with one more solid crack on my chin. I saw fog and stepped backward. Then I came back with two more stomach punches. I've learned from Jack Bauer not to leave a mark.

"Chess players are slow movers, aren't they?"

He lunged forward, and I swung a haymaker with my right and dropped him like a manhole cover.

I was ready to finish him with my killer head butt, but your opponent needs to be standing to head butt him right. Doyle was rolling on the floor holding his jaw, then stomach, then jaw, then stomach. I wished I'd got him somewhere lower to give him a third choice.

I stood over him and leaned down. "Checkmate, bozo."

Suda tended to Doyle and glared up at me like I'd jumped him with a two-by-four and stolen his lunch money.

I pointed both index fingers at her and bounced on my toes: "Your grand-mother's next, Suda."

"My grandmother has a fourth degree black belt in Tae Kwon Do."

"Dog drugger," I said without thinking. She looked surprised.

Chris Doyle's what Nero Wolfe calls a nincompoop. But I gained some respect for him that day. He wasn't the pushover I expected. The Pillsbury Doyleboy showed some game.

Things aren't always what they appear.

THURSDAY, DECEMBER 26, 12:30 P.M.

Jake and Clarence and I planned to meet again at Powell's City of Books, where an hour's browsing gets me through about one percent of one of the nine color coded rooms with something like seventy thousand square feet. They boast 122 major subject areas and thirty-five hundred different subsections, about a hundred of which interest me. But that hundred contain tens of thousands of books. Powell's buys three thousand used books a day over the counter, so if you can't find it today, you'll have twenty thousand new titles to choose from next week.

I spent my "hour early" in the Gold Room, where aisles 313–319 are myster-ies, maybe ten thousand of them. On the other side of the Gold Room I spied a man reading *Green Eggs and Ham* to a five-year-old Sam-I-am sitting in a tiny wooden chair beside him. I froze, wondering if I would ever have the chance to read books to grandchildren and wondering why I hadn't taken time to read to my own kids. Was reading to my grandchildren another dream that wouldn't come true?

Next thing I knew, the hour had flown by and I'd moved through maybe five feet of books, which at Powell's is like a quarter lap in the Indianapolis 500.

There were too many ears in World Cup Coffee and Tea, so after some chitchat over sandwiches and fabulous Sumatra Mandheling coffee (according to the sign) and a walnut sticky bun to go, Clarence and Jake and I searched the endless nooks and crannies for the right place to talk. We settled, appropriately, near religion in the Red Room, in view of philosophy and journalism in the Purple Room.

I'd caught him staring, but when we finally settled down in our place, Jake asked for a full explanation of the bruises on my face. I walked them through the brawl with Doyle, blow by blow, like it was Frazier versus Ali.

There in the City of Books, Jake handed me one he'd brought with him: Bertrand Russell's *Why I am Not a Christian.*

I pointed to the philosophy stacks. "There's twenty more of those over there. You didn't have to bring your own."

"It's not mine," Jake said. "Last time we talked about this, I accidentally took your book. I finished the final essay last night, and guess what I found on the back page."

He opened it up to show a phone number: 555-570-6089.

"That's the seventh number," I said, halt in my voice.

"Something wrong?"

"It seems…vaguely familiar. Ray'll check it out."

"I had an interesting conversation with Raylon Berkley," Clarence said. "He told me Lennox wants to pull you from the Palatine case."

I wasn't surprised to hear this secondhand, considering the source. "Why'd Berkley tell you?" I asked Clarence.

"He wanted to see how I'd take it."

"I'm working on how I'm taking it. How did you take it?"

"I said you were smart-mouthed, opinionated, stubborn, outrageous, difficult to deal with. That you're always stepping over the line. I didn't mention that you confiscated from a crime scene self-incriminating evidence, lied about your alibi, and set a fire in an apartment complex."

"Nobody's perfect," I said. "I also threatened a hamster, but when you tuck Brent in tonight, tell him I didn't mean it."

"I informed Berkley that if Lennox pulled you from the case I'd tell the public why."

"He try to talk you out of it?"

"He told me he wouldn't let the *Trib* print those kinds of accusations against Lennox. I said I thought the *Trib* was committed to print the truth."

"What planet you been living on?"

"That's the smart-mouthed part of you I mentioned. Anyway, we went toe-to-toe. I told him if the *Trib* wouldn't let me write the truth, there's an alternative paper that would. An alternative paper that's already offered me a job twice. I told him my first article for my new employer would be about the chief's sabotage of the Palatine investigation and Berkley and the *Trib*'s complicity in it."

"You really said that?"

"I told him I wondered what that would do for the spiraling sales of the *Trib*." Clarence looked me straight in the eyes. "You're not the only one who cares about justice."

"Them boys is gettin' themselves in trouble, ain't they?" Obadiah said. "But I has to say, I'm proud of 'em for it."

"So am I." He nodded thoughtfully. "So am I."

❖

Lack of sleep and frustration at not having my hands around the killer's throat were bringing me to a boil. What began as a discussion among friends had degenerated into something else. Still sitting in our nook at Powell's, I raised my hands, knocking three paperbacks out of alignment. "You want me to just blindly believe without asking questions?"

"No," Jake said. "Ask your questions. I just think you need to listen to God's answers. He's in charge of the universe. His fingerprints are on everything."

"That's a bad analogy to use with a homicide detective, bucko. If God's fingerprints are on everything, doesn't that mean they're on every weapon used to kill the innocent? Is He behind my daughter's disappearance too? If good people aren't rewarded and bad people aren't punished, the universe isn't fair. Injustice drives me nuts. If I could take it all away, I would. If He can, why doesn't He?"

"What makes you think He doesn't…or won't?" Jake said. "Is justice ever done in this life? Sometimes. But those times it's not done here and now, it will be done on the other side of death."

"How can you know that?"

"Because God promises it in the Bible." Clarence pointed to a long line of them forty feet away. "It says, 'Man is destined to die once, and after that to face judgment.'"

"I get tired of you quoting these verses when the fact remains that people who don't deserve to die do. All the time. Every day. And where's God when they die?"

"He's right there offering love and forgiveness," Jake said.

"Stop kidding yourself. God doesn't give a rip."

"You're drawing conclusions about God without knowing Him," Jake said.

"I know He killed my wife!" I'd raised my voice. "And that isn't all He did."

"What else?" Jake asked.

"None of your business."

"You need to give God a chance."

"Why give him a chance? He killed Sharon." I shouted it, jumping to my feet. "And He killed our son!"

38

"It is quite a three-pipe problem."
SHERLOCK HOLMES, *THE RED-HEADED LEAGUE*

I'D YELLED "He killed our son" before I knew what I was saying. Dozens of people at Powell's turned like I'd dumped kerosene on the New Age section and torched it. The place fell stony silent.

"Your *son*?" Clarence whispered, standing next to me. "But…you don't have a son."

"Not since your God killed him."

Jake said, "Ollie, I'm so sorry about Chad."

"You know about Chad?"

"Sharon told Janet."

"Why didn't you say something?"

"Sharon said you didn't want us to know. I was hoping eventually you'd bring him up."

"You had a son?" Clarence asked.

I blew out air and sat down, trying to ignore the stares.

"Chad was born three years after Kendra. When he was two years old, some bozo rear-ended us. Chad was strapped in, but it jarred him. Apparently he had some…condition. I've forgotten the name. They say if it wouldn't have been the car, it would have been something else."

Clarence's eyes watered.

"I don't want your pity," I said. "But I'm never going to forgive God for taking away my son. What does He know about how we suffer? I wouldn't take wives from their husbands and sons from their fathers. I'll never see my son again. Trust a God who looked the other way? No, I won't do it."

I was down the stairs and headed to the garage before either of them could answer. I didn't want to hear answers when there were none. In the face of what happened to Chad and Sharon, words were an insult.

I drove west on Burnside, not knowing where I was going, under the gloom of dark clouds that buried the sun. Appropriate, because when Chad died, thick clouds surrounded me, and I couldn't see or hear or breathe. I didn't console myself with Sharon; I consoled myself with booze. Like someone said at an AA meeting, first I took a drink, then the drink took a drink, then the drink took me. It was ten years before I sobered up and saw the sun again. Then, when Sharon died, the stars dropped out of the sky. Since then I haven't found much reason to stay sober.

Randomly, now deep on the west side, toward Beaverton, I drove by an abandoned graveyard, where the headstones seemed arbitrarily placed, many of them bleached, crooked, and sinking. Part of me welcomed the day when my name would be on such a stone. Part of me dreaded it, with a fear that tore up my insides so much my hands shook on the steering wheel.

"He doesn't understand."

"No."

"He doesn't realize that though he's tortured by his memories of me, my life's gone right on in a better place. And he doesn't have a clue that sometimes I'm allowed to see and hear him."

"They don't believe the Scriptures," Sharon said, "that there's rejoicing here in the presence of the angels over the work God's doing in their lives on earth. They think of this place as disinterested in what's happening there. They don't realize their planet is center stage in His unfolding drama of redemption. They're on the playing field. Those in the grandstands are watching."

"Here with my Father, I've gotten to know my earthly father too."

"You know him far better than he ever knew you," Sharon said.

"Will I be with him again?" Chad asked. "Will Elyon answer that prayer?"

"He says we must wait and see. But we don't need to wait to know that He's always good. Your father doesn't understand Elyon's purposes. What's now clear to us makes no sense to him. Yet even we don't understand it all, do we?"

"His ways are above our ways, and His thoughts above our thoughts," Chad said smiling. "But to me, that's beautiful. Whatever we don't yet grasp leaves us more to learn about Him."

Chad grasped his mother's hand. "I hope to walk beside my earthly father again—this time on an earth no longer cursed."

"His relationships with us, though interrupted, need never end. But he must come to trust the One he blames—and that will not be easy."

"Let's pray for him again, Mother."

Arms around each other, mother and son talked to Elyon about a man driving aimlessly on back roads, a man so far away he had no idea they were there, yet so close they could almost reach out and touch him.

A night-after-Christmas party had been scheduled at Chief Lennox's house. I'd never been in the chief's house, only by it. Most recently in the middle of the night, when we'd followed him from the 7-Eleven where he met Kim Suda.

This time the gate was open, and an officer was letting people pass because he recognized them or they showed ID. Turned out the mailbox was in a different zip code than the house.

I'd heard a lot about that house. What I'd heard didn't do it justice.

I'll probably never marry again, because if I did, my wife would want to buy this house, and if I took my retirement savings and held up a couple of banks, I still wouldn't be able to afford the down payment, and then she'd dream about it and show me pictures of it, and then she'd cry and I'd feel like a loser for letting her down, and my daughter would end up siding with her, and pretty soon our formerly romantic evenings of blackberry shakes at Burgerville and bowling at Mt. Hood Lanes would have a cloud cast over them. So it's better all around for me never to marry again.

About forty people showed up, but only three other homicide detectives—Suda, Chris Doyle, and Brandon Phillips, without his wife. There were fancy hors d'oeuvres. I searched for Cheez Whiz and cocktail wienies on a toothpick but finally settled for what was there, though I couldn't tell what it was. I wrapped up items in a napkin and stuffed them in my trench coat pocket for Mulch. When he smells it on me and I don't come through with the goods, he sulks.

The chief's wife was the perfect hostess. Thirty minutes into the party I told her, red-faced, that I was having some…personal problems and I needed to be in the bathroom for a while, but I didn't want to keep anybody out of the main bathroom.

She looked at me sympathetically. "Go all the way to the end of the hall and turn left. There's a bathroom on your right just past Ed's office."

"I'm embarrassed," I said.

"Happens to all of us. I won't say anything."

I thanked her profusely, then followed her directions. I came to the chief's office, looked both ways, and disappeared inside.

Twelve minutes later, I reappeared, looking for something to drink to calm my shakes and hoping the wienies and Cheez Whiz appetizers had shown up.

No such luck.

39

"The pressure of public opinion can do in the town what the law cannot accomplish."
SHERLOCK HOLMES, *THE ADVENTURE OF THE COPPER BEECHES*

FRIDAY, DECEMBER 27, 2:15 P.M.

"THE OPEN HOUSE was a big hit," Mona said.

"I expected more men would attend," Chief Lennox said.

He sounded like he was sulking. I couldn't see him, since he and his secretary were in his home office and I was in mine, sipping A&W root beer. The remote unit was picking up a clear signal, thanks to Ray's high-tech booster.

"I was surprised to see Chandler here," she said.

"Maybe he's seen the light and realizes he needs to get on my good side."

I'd just swallowed some root beer, and suddenly it was spurting out my nose.

"Did you hear something?" the chief asked.

I grabbed a paper towel to clean up. Though I was in the far corner of my office, I'd been heard. I'd turned my monitor low so their voices wouldn't be picked up by their own bug. But I'd assumed my office audio was being recorded and monitored at the precinct, not in the chief's home office. With bugs going both directions, I'd need to be careful.

Great thing about that bug on the chief's phone, one of the two spares Suda planted at my house, was that it not only picked up calls but also any voice within five feet.

"Chandler's at home today?"

"Our friend in detective detail says he's working at home today. I've heard him off and on," Mona said. "It's all recorded, but most of it's wasted. Thirty minutes ago I checked, and he was singing to his dog. Something about bacon and eggs and cats."

"Pathetic," the chief said.

"You'd think we'd hear something interesting. Occasionally he's on the phone, but he never says anything significant. He calls out on his cell phone from another room, for better reception I think, but then I can't hear him. We've had a week of voice-activated recording, but it hasn't amounted to much. And the bugs in the other parts of the house still aren't working."

"Maybe I should send Suda back. If he'd just talk with Abernathy or that PI in his office, we'd know what's going on. And maybe be able to head him off."

"You could get in trouble for this, Ed." I heard Mona's voice tremble. "Is it worth it?"

"If we're caught, I'll say it's because I had substantial reason to suspect him of murder. Including that gum wrapper he stole from the scene."

How'd he know about that?

"We need to find out what he's up to. Maybe we should bug that Ray Eagle character too."

"Could you justify that?"

"You know how I feel about this, Mona. That's one reason we need to have these conversations away from the precinct. As chief I have to make difficult judgment calls. I feel more freedom here in my home office."

"Has that *Tribune* reporter come through?"

"Button promised me he'd deliver Abernathy's notes on the investigation, but nothing so far. I told him no more leads if he doesn't."

I double-checked my recording device. Lights on.

Mona said, "The last inside tip the public got related to the vagrant."

"Right. Let's get the names of all the bums in that area then run background checks. Find the toughest record. We can provide some evidence, get a positive ID, and at least bring him in as a suspect."

"But..."

"What?"

"If he's innocent..."

"You aren't listening. I don't want you to find someone innocent, I want you to find someone guilty. That's the point of the background check."

A cynical laugh came out of my mouth. Covered it too late.

"What was that?" Lennox asked.

"Sounds like Chandler laughed. Wonder what he's laughing at?"

"He doesn't need a reason. The man's a clown. An idiot."

King of the Idiots. But Lennox was in danger of dethroning me.

Obadiah Abernathy. Why do I keep thinking about that old man? Was it because I wished I'd had a real father? Mr. Abernathy's gone. I attended his funeral. And yet...his faith was so real, his life so...right. I just can't believe it ended when he died.

Clarence told me what his daddy said on his deathbed, about the people he was supposedly greeting in heaven. Was he delusional? Or was he seeing things I'll never see?

That old man haunts me, comforts me, gives me hope. But he also unnerves me. Because if he was right about heaven, maybe he was right about hell. And that scares the bejeebers out of me.

Especially when I think about him asking me if I have my ticket because the train's about to leave.

"Lord, put Yo' gracious hand on Mr. Chandler." Obadiah's eyes shone bright.

The great guardians standing around the small but powerful man bowed their heads in respect for the One he addressed.

"Do what it takes to make him not so full of himself. Show him who he really is. And who You really are. Would You do that? For me? And for him? And for Your glory? Would You do that, my sweet Jesus?"

I sat at my detective division workstation making phone calls, looking around and turning my head, my voice low. I alerted Clarence to keep his notes under lock and key because the chief wanted them. And to keep his eyes on Mike Button. I warned Ray to look out for somebody bugging him, even though it was hard to believe the chief would go that far. Ray told me the number Jake found in the back of the professor's *Why I Am Not a Christian* was a convenience store's. Dead end.

I sat down, trying to clear my mind, attempting again to think like the killer. It isn't easy for me to think like a drug dealer, a lawyer, a con artist, or a Pistons fan. But thinking like a homicide detective? That should come naturally. What would I do if I were…what I am?

Frame somebody for my murder? Only if they were guilty of a crime just as bad or worse. I hated to admit it, but I understood the chief's logic about framing someone if I knew that person was guilty of something else.

Would I leave conflicting evidence to confuse investigators and delay resolution with rabbit trails? This could force the detectives to move on to the next case, making it likely they'd never solve this one.

Like the first glimpse of sunrise, another possibility hit me. If I were a Portland homicide detective planning a murder and wanted to be sure I wouldn't be found out, what would I do?

Of course. There it was. So simple. So obvious.

Why hadn't I thought of it before?

40

FRIDAY, DECEMBER 27, 3:40 P.M.

I SAT AT MY WORKSTATION, but my mind kept going back to Chad. Saying his name aloud to Jake and Clarence had unlocked the closet I'd hidden him in.

I was thinking if Chad hadn't died, maybe I'd have been a better father to Kendra and Andrea. Maybe everything would have been different. When the girls brought him up, I'd refused to talk about him. We'd all paid a price for that.

"How's the investigation going?" Karl Baylor asked.

Startled, I looked up at him. My instinct was to go on offense. "What if I told you that one of the detectives who says they were alone with their spouse at the time of the murder was lying?"

"That's a serious charge."

"As a Christian, you have convictions against lying, don't you?"

He hesitated too long. "Of course."

"Lying to a police investigator, and to your wife, is pretty serious, isn't it?"

I packed up my stuff from the table and headed off the floor, leaving him squirming.

SATURDAY, DECEMBER 28

By bringing up Chad, I'd opened Pandora's box. When I got the Saturday lunch invitation from Jake and Clarence, I knew what we'd be talking about.

I walked in and they were both sitting there, with "MacArthur Park" playing. "It's still going from the last time," Jake said, grinning.

"No better way to stretch a quarter," I said. But after it finally ended I was relieved to hear subsequent songs with more sophisticated lyrics, such as "Go granny, go granny, go granny, go."

We'd been seated at Lou's Diner only five minutes when Jake brought up Chad, like I knew he would. Before he could rationalize or minimize, I jumped on it.

"You can't understand what it was like to lose my only son," I said. "Or Sharon."

"No," Jake said, "but I understand what it's like to have my two best friends killed and to have my only child dying."

"And I understand," Clarence said, "what it was like to have my sister murdered. And my niece. And to lose my mama and daddy. And I know something about injustice too. I have a forty-year-old memory of his screams when those cops tortured him in that Mississippi jail. Just a month ago I woke up hearing his screams."

"So maybe," Jake said, "we understand more than you think."

"You believe God has hidden purposes," I said. "Well, I'm not one for hidden purposes. I say, lay them out on the table. I don't like being kept in the dark."

"But you're not God," Jake said. "If we were running the universe, everything would be a mess. Our minds just aren't big enough to wrap around God's purposes. That's where trust comes in."

"Right," I said. "You trust Him. I don't."

"You said you don't believe in hidden purposes?" Clarence asked. "And you don't want to be kept in the dark. Aren't you being hypocritical?"

"How?"

"In the Palatine case you've withheld self-incriminating evidence, placed hidden cameras, and now you've bugged the chief of police. I'll bet you had good reasons for all those, didn't you?"

"Yeah," I said. "Just like I had a good reason for setting the fire at the apartments."

"So you've done outrageous things and kept people in the dark, but you had hidden purposes. And you thought you were accomplishing something good. But do you think other people would understand and appreciate you for it?"

"No, probably not."

"Well, then, don't you think God might have some hidden reasons for doing what He does and allowing what He allows and even for keeping you in the dark? Some of your reasons probably aren't as good as you think, but is it possible God's hidden reasons might all be good, even though we can't understand them?"

I squirmed. "My son, my wife, your friends, your sister. Your God sits off in a corner of the universe, nice and safe. And we get stuck with the injustice and heartache."

"You couldn't be more wrong," Jake said. "God never sat off in a corner of the universe, nice and safe. He did the opposite. To save us, He became one of us. He faced all the hardships. Nobody ever suffered like Jesus did. He took on all our sins and sufferings. He endured the Holocaust and the Killing Fields and the sufferings of the slaves and everything else—including Chad's and Sharon's deaths—on that cross."

"You really believe that?"

"With all my heart. The Bible says that God's Spirit groans for us, awaiting our redemption. You think God doesn't care? His Son was innocent. After they beat Him mercilessly, they sent Him to a shameful and excruciating death."

"You'd think if He was God, He could've stopped them," I said.

"He could have. But He restrained Himself because it was the only way to rescue us. God had to forsake His only Son on that cross, causing Jesus to cry out in agony, asking God why. You feel like you're in the dark? He was in the dark, literally, as He hung on that cross. The Father buried His only Son in a foreign land. Talk about heartbreak. That was the biggest heartbreak the universe has ever known. Or ever will."

After a long silence, Clarence said, "Daddy used to say to me, 'Son, never waste your suffering—God has a purpose for it.' He doesn't want us to suffer alone, Ollie. He's there for us. And we're here for you."

"We'd do anything for you, old buddy." Jake put his hand on my shoulder. "But don't ever forget: God's no stranger to suffering. He knows exactly what it's like to lose His only Son."

41

*"However, wretch as he was, he was still living under the
shield of British law, and I have no doubt, Inspector, that you
will see that, though that shield may fail to guard, the sword
of justice is still there to avenge."*
SHERLOCK HOLMES, *THE RESIDENT PATIENT*

MONDAY, DECEMBER 30

UNDER THREAT of being prosecuted for aiding and abetting a murderer, Mike
Button, esteemed *Tribune* reporter, kissed good-bye journalism's bill of rights,
singing like a bird. Unfortunately, what he sang wasn't helpful. He claimed an
anonymous source mailed the crime scene photo that the *Trib* had published. An
anonymous source would have lacked credibility. An "unnamed source" sounded
better. He'd withheld the name not on principle, but because he knew no name.

Button produced the mailing envelope. The lab was examining it for possible
prints and saliva on envelope and stamp. I figured each would prove a dead end.
I knew Chief Lennox had fed a false lead to Button, but I still didn't believe he'd
supplied the photograph.

Carp and I discussed these developments in her office, perfectly neat except
for two rows of empty Diet Coke cans on her windowsill.

"Remember that evidence kit by the professor's leg in that photo in the
paper?" she asked. "Take a look at this enlargement." She pointed to the screen
and lightened the picture. "Watch what happens when I sharpen it."

She sharpened it twice. The second time it came to life. I saw perforation
marks, six clamps evenly spaced near the edges, and what appeared to be a flap,
raised from the object and pointing to the five o'clock position.

"That's no evidence kit," I said.

"If I superimpose this ruler, it shows you true size. Look at its depth."

"Less than an inch! It must be six inches across and eight inches tall."

"Pretty close. It's the back side of a five-by-seven photo frame."

TUESDAY, DECEMBER 31, NOON

I'd asked Jake to meet me alone at Lou's. I'd had a few beers when some misguided
stranger selected a song Rory had apparently just added: "Achy Breaky Heart." I
had to call Rory over and explain to him why this song didn't belong at Lou's
Diner and why, if it wasn't removed within ten minutes, I would have to empty

my Glock into the Rock-Ola, which I didn't want to do because I always liked that robot in *Lost in Space*.

Rory was extracting "Achy Breaky Heart," looking at me nervously, and Jake arrived, while the beer bottles were still on the table.

I asked him about Carly. She wasn't doing well.

"Sorry to bug you today," I said. "You must be exhausted."

"You're not bugging me. Carly's sleeping, and Geneva's at the hospital with Janet. What's up?"

"I need to…tell you something," I said. "I don't know why, but I do. Clarence knows some of this but not all. Promise not to tell him?"

"I guess."

I cleared my throat to shift the gravel.

"I don't know where I was when Palatine was killed."

"What do you mean?"

"I came home from Rosie's bar, but I lost at least two hours."

"You…lost it?"

"It's a blank. And it's not the first time."

"Blackouts?"

I nodded. "I'm on my own suspect list."

"You think you might have killed him?"

"Not really, but…I'm sure that Black Jack wrapper was already there. And when I drove to the murder scene there was a box in my car from Wally's Donuts, which is just three blocks from the professor's house. I don't remember going there. But…I've done other things I don't remember. I don't know why I'd kill the professor, but…something doesn't feel right."

Rory came to our table with another beer. When I lifted it, Jake grabbed my wrist.

"You've had four," Jake said.

I shook his hand off. Rory retreated.

"Now you're counting my beers? Counting my calories too?"

"I can't count that high. But I can count to four. Or five."

"What's your point?"

"You've been drinking more. It shows."

"Who made you my judge?"

"I'm not judging you. I want to help you."

"I don't need your help. It's New Year's Eve." I lifted the bottle. "Beauty's in the eye of the beer holder."

He yanked it out of my hand, and it spilled over my right arm and onto the table.

"It's not funny, Ollie."

"I'm not laughing." I stared him down while wiping my sleeve on my pants.

"I needed your help once, remember?" Jake asked. "I came to you about Doc and Finney after…what happened. I asked you to stand with me when Janet and I remarried. And I hope I've been there for you a few times."

I nodded. "When the *Trib* smeared me, you stood up for me. And when Sharon was dying…"

"Ollie, I'm going to say something you won't like."

"You already have."

"Think you know what it is?"

"You're going to tell me I need help."

"Yeah, but maybe not the help you're thinking."

"You're going to go Christian on me."

"I'm not *going* Christian; I am a Christian. Beneath your drinking problem there's a thirst for something more. Someone more."

"Yeah, yeah, I know this script."

"Just listen. One time Jesus stood before a crowd and said, 'If anyone is thirsty, let him come to me and drink.' He's the only one who can quench your thirst."

"I'll stick with beer, thanks."

"Beer isn't what you're thirsty for. Jesus went on to say, 'Whoever believes in me…streams of living water will flow from within him.' If you ask Him, God will give you peace and a perspective you've never had."

"I'm not looking for peace and perspective."

"Yes, you are. You've just been looking in the wrong places. Maybe you haven't been looking that hard, but don't kid yourself. You're looking. Everybody is."

"You seem pretty sure of yourself."

"I've been where you are, without Christ. Even when I didn't know it, I was searching for Him. He invites you to believe in Him and accept the gift He bought for you when He died."

"You sound like an evangelist."

"I'm just quoting Jesus, okay? I'm telling you how He changed my life."

"You want me as a notch on your Christian gun."

"You know me better than that. I'll love you and be your friend if you never come to Christ. Sure, it'll break my heart because I love Him and I love you. And I know how much you need Him."

"What's this got to do with me having a beer?"

"When you're reaching for your fifth beer, you're looking for something the beer can't give you."

"You know how many times I've said good-bye to the bottle?" I said. "It's like 'just say no to drugs.' Nice thought. Well, some people just say no to drugs, but the drugs don't listen. I was sober for years. But after Chad and then Sharon, and Andrea dropping off the face of the planet, and my problems with Kendra, and some of the cases I've worked…"

"It's been tough for you."

"You going to tell Clarence about this conversation?"

"Not if you don't want me to."

"I don't."

"Fine. But Clarence is in your corner too. He's rooting for you. So's Carly." When he said her name, he choked and his eyes misted. "She loves you, Ollie. Janet does too. Anyway, I wanted to tell you that at my church we have recovery groups."

"For alcoholics?"

"Yeah, for alcoholics and for other issues too. One group is called grief recovery."

"No thanks. I can take care of myself."

He looked at me long and hard. "Actually, Ollie, you can't."

The chief was working at home again. After fifteen minutes I fell asleep listening to the chief's fatally boring conversation with a city councilman. Mulch licked my face awake.

"Paul Hines, crime lab. Calling back about that Black Jack gum wrapper in the evidence bag, from the Palatine case."

"Yes, it took you long enough to get back to me," Lennox said. "I'd have thought the chief of police wouldn't have to wait for a return call. Were you able to confirm that it has the detective's prints?"

"Detective?"

"Yes, Detective Ollie Chandler. That's whose prints are on the wrapper, right?"

"No."

"You're sure? No prints?"

"No. I mean, prints, yeah, but…"

"Speak up, man. Whose prints did you find?"

"Well, sir, they're…*yours.*"

The pause was so long I thought he'd detected the bug. Finally he said, "Hines, this is a setup. Don't breathe a word to anyone. Understand? I need you to take home those results and keep them until we meet… Tomorrow's New Year's…all right, you come in Thursday, day after tomorrow, 9:00 a.m. No. Forget that. Bring it to me right now. Come straight to my home office. You know how to get there?"

"Yes, but, sir…"

"Listen to me. Bring the evidence bag with the wrapper inside. Understand?"

"But sir, I can't remove an evidence bag—"

"Yes. Yes, you can. I'm the chief of police. You answer to me. Put it in something inconspicuous, and leave as soon as you can. Press the button at my gate, identify yourself, and I'll let you in. I'll expect you within the hour. Cross me on this, and you'll be sorry. Cooperate and you've got a bright future. Follow me?"

"Yes, sir."

I looked at the recording device, saw the numbers moving, and grinned. I fixed Mulch and me some Ovaltine, mine hot, his lukewarm. We might not have much of a New Year's Eve party, but this was cause to celebrate.

Mulch listened attentively as I nuzzled him and whispered in his ear, "Getting the chief's print on that gum wrapper, sorting through the trash, and making the switch in the evidence bag paid off, fella. You were the first to wet on the chief's pant leg. But you won't be the last."

42

"You have been in Afghanistan, I perceive."
SHERLOCK HOLMES, *A STUDY IN SCARLET*

WEDNESDAY, JANUARY 1, 8:15 A.M.

IT HAD BEEN A TAME New Year's Eve. After Mulch and I celebrated with the Ovaltine, I met Kendra at Starbucks. She had a triple-shot macchiato because she wanted to stay up past midnight at a party with her friends. It felt wrong that I didn't know her friends anymore. And I forced myself not to ask how her baby would feel about three shots of coffee. It was part of my new strategy of avoiding fights with my daughter.

Jake's New Year's party, my original plan, had been cancelled because Carly was still in the hospital. I'm not a Times Square fan. Watching the events prior to the ball drop is as entertaining as C-SPAN. Mulch and I welcomed the new year reading Nero Wolfe by firelight.

Groucho Marx said, "Outside a dog, a book is man's best friend. Inside a dog, it's too dark to read." At midnight I gave Mulch a second Budweiser.

As the fireworks went off, I contemplated another year of my existence, wondering if this would be my last and trying to figure out how much it would matter.

Now, the day after, sleeping fitfully and getting up at eight, I'd gone to Mr. Coffee to plug myself into French roast.

Last night images and voices had haunted my dreams. Obadiah Abernathy and Sharon and a young man I didn't recognize were talking. Then something happened. I wasn't sure what. I woke up, heart racing, at 3:14. But I fell back asleep ten minutes later and resumed my dream, where a girl had joined Obadiah, Sharon, and the young man. I thought at first she was Kendra. Then I realized it was Carly Woods. The four of them and some other people hugged and laughed. They all seemed so alive, so happy.

And, once more, I stood outside the circle of their happiness.

Jake called at 9:45.

"I have bad news," he said. "It's Carly."

I froze.

"She's gone."

My tongue stuck.

"You don't have to say anything, Ollie. But…pray for us, would you?"

"Pray?"

"I'm sorry. I forgot."

"It's okay," I said. "Is there…anything I can do?"

"No. Thanks."

"When…did she die?" I asked.

"A little after three."

"Is Janet…okay?"

"No. But we gave Carly to God years ago. Really, she was just on loan to us. She belongs to God, and now He's taken her back. Not easy to let go. God's been preparing us for this…except I guess you're never really prepared. You know how it was with Sharon."

"Need anybody there?"

"Clarence and Geneva are here. Friends from church are coming, already bringing meals. We'd love to see you if you want to come sometime."

"I don't have much to offer."

"You're our friend. That's enough."

"Okay…hang in there."

That was stupid. I've been around death more than my share. But I've never known what to say beyond "I'm sorry" or "I'll fry the guy who did it."

It's harder when you can't go after the killer.

I didn't want to go to Jake and Janet's and hang around with Christians. It bugs me that they think they know something about death the rest of us don't. On the other hand, who had more to offer Jake and Janet now—them or me? Not me. They'd be reading the Bible. What would I read? Nero Wolfe? Bertrand Russell? *The Wizard of Id*?

I shut my blinds, made sure the door was locked, and got on my knees. Mulch climbed on the couch and put his nose up to mine. His eyes looked sad. Dogs know.

"God, I guess You heard Jake ask me to do this. I've only done it once before, when I asked You to spare Sharon. You didn't. I don't know if You're there. Probably not. But if You are, please help my friend Jake. And Janet. And if Carly…I mean if people still live after they die…well, I hope she's okay."

I was embarrassed. I told myself, if there's no God, there's no one to be embarrassed in front of. Somehow it didn't make me feel better.

Once again, somebody wonderful had died. Somebody who didn't deserve to die. Meanwhile a million people who deserved to die went right on living.

Why?

I had no words of wisdom or comfort. I had nothing to offer my friends.

Maybe that's what really bothered me. Others could offer them the one thing I don't have—hope.

Funny though. Now I had a third reason to want to go to heaven. Sharon Chandler, Obadiah Abernathy, and Carly Woods. The Christians would tell me I should only want to be with Jesus. But I don't know Jesus. I did know them.

For a moment I wondered, did what I loved about Sharon, Obadiah, and Carly come from Jesus? Then my thoughts went to someone else, someone I'd tried to put out of my mind for twenty-five years. Chad.

I felt wetness on my face. Mulch, sad-eyed, licked the tears. I hugged him.

Mulch kept me from feeling alone in the universe.

One moment Carly Woods was awake in a world of pain. The next moment she felt herself falling to sleep. A rush of sound and light awakened her.

At first she thought she was walking through a glowing passageway. Then she realized she was being carried, effortlessly, in mighty arms.

Behind her was a ruined paradise, a wasteland waiting to be reclaimed. Ahead of her was a world of substance and light, overflowing with color. The place beckoned her to come dive into it, to lose herself and find herself in something greater than she'd ever known. In one moment, Carly Woods had moved from midnight to sunrise.

"Awesome!" she said.

"Yes," said a deep, resonant voice above her. She turned and looked up at the rock-chiseled face of a great creature, a shining warrior, looking like a man, yet different. She'd never seen anything like him. Yet somehow she thought she'd known him for years. She sensed he was rescuing her, that his job was to carry the wounded to where they'd be made well.

"I am Tor-el, servant of Elyon, God Most High. I have served Him by watching over you each day of your life in the Shadowlands."

"I never knew."

"Elyon knew," he said, the edges of his lips turning barely upward. "That is all that matters."

She turned to look where she was going. With every step the warrior took, she saw more color, detail, and activity. She could taste and smell life. The place reached out to her, pulling her in, as a magnet pulls iron filings.

"I'm getting stronger," Carly said, recognizing her voice, but realizing it was much fuller. She'd never liked the sound of her voice. Now she did.

"I thought my life was over. It feels like it's just begun."

The voice above her spoke again. "The end is behind you, little one. This is the beginning that has no end."

People crowded against a beautiful white fence, reaching their arms toward her. She heard their applause and an enchanting laughter. The warrior put her down.

She turned and said, "Thank you, Tor-el. For everything. I...I'd like to talk more."

"We will. There is much for you to discover in the new world and much to learn about what happened in that world. It will be my honor to guide you. But now is the time for celebration and greeting. Your welcoming committee awaits you."

She ran toward the joy and leapt carelessly into it. The years of sickness had been but labor pains. Now she was being born into heaven.

Uncle Clarence's father, smiling broadly, waved to her, beckoning her to come in. Standing next to him was a woman she'd seen only in pictures...Ruby Abernathy, Clarence's mother.

"Carly!"

It was Uncle Finney, a voice she hadn't heard in many years. She ran toward him and threw herself into his arms. They laughed. He whispered to her. Then they danced. And as they danced, Carly caught a glimpse of a young man she didn't know but thought she should and next to him a woman so beautiful and vibrant that she felt unworthy to speak her name.

"Aunt Sharon?"

"We've been waiting for you, Carly," she said. They hugged hard. And then Carly hugged her a second time, even tighter.

"That was from—"

"Ollie," Sharon said. "I know, sweetheart. Thank you. But there's someone else waiting to greet you."

Sharon bowed her knees to the ground, and bright light shone on her face. All who were around her bowed too, eyes fixed behind Carly, who turned to behold the most beautiful sight she'd ever seen.

She saw the brightness of a billion galaxies, contained in one person. She beheld a man who was God, Creator of the Universe. His face was as young as a child's, yet His eyes had seen all that had ever been and all that ever would be. This was God Himself. He put His hands upon her shoulders. She thrilled at His touch.

"Welcome, Carly, daughter of God!" He smiled broadly, the smile of a Galilean carpenter. "Well done, my good and faithful servant. Enter into your Master's joy!"

He hugged her and she hugged Him back, realizing she'd felt this embrace before. She'd been sad not to marry a man on earth. But she knew now that this was her Bridegroom, the object of all her longing, the fulfillment of all her dreams.

"My Jesus," she whispered.

"My Carly," He whispered back.

When the embrace ended, it continued, even as they stepped back to gaze upon each other.

He put out His hand to her face, and she saw on it a terrible scar. She stared at His other hand and at His feet. She fell to her knees, overcome.

He knelt beside her and looked into her eyes. She saw in Him an ancient pain that was the doorway to eternal pleasures.

"It was worth it, Carly," He said. "For you, I would do it all again."

"On the contrary, Watson, you can see everything. You fail, however, to reason from what you see. You are too timid in drawing your inferences."
SHERLOCK HOLMES, *THE ADVENTURE OF THE BLUE CARBUNCLE*

THURSDAY, JANUARY 2

I'D ASKED CARP to provide me a copy of the photo mysteriously given to Mike Button at the *Trib*. She'd made the comparison to all the photos taken; no match. Nothing with the photo frame we'd mistaken for an evidence kit.

"So…" I said, "you didn't take the picture. I didn't. Carlton Hatch didn't."

"Who's left?" Carp asked.

"The criminalists. The paramedics. The patrol cops on guard, Dorsey and Guerino. It's SOP to have a camera accessible."

"What about that other detective who showed up?"

"Kim Suda—of course! Detectives always have a camera."

"And she sent it to Button?"

"Why not? She was working with the chief when she bugged my place. Maybe she was working for him when she gave the photo to the *Trib*."

I must have scowled when I said *Trib*, because Carp asked, "To one of those dirty rotten journalists, huh?"

"Yeah," I said. "I mean…*Trib* photographers are great. It's the writers I don't trust." I searched her face to see if I'd closed the door on future pizzas.

"That's okay," she said. "I don't trust half of 'em myself. From what you've told me about police detectives, I trust them even less."

Our booth at Lou's is secluded, in the far right-hand corner, at the back. It allows us to see every direction. We know when we're being approached. The speakers connected to the jukebox that keep it relatively quiet in our corner but send out a layer of filtering sound. You don't discuss a murder investigation where someone can eavesdrop.

I'd invited Ray Eagle, but Clarence and I arrived fifteen minutes early. Jake was out of the loop until after tomorrow's funeral. Clarence pulled out four quarters, apparently motivated by fear of "MacArthur Park." We listened to Ray Charles, "The Night Time (Is the Right Time)," and the Drifters, "Under the Boardwalk," then Mahalia Jackson, "He's Got the Whole World in His Hands," singing like she believed it. Okay, the lyrics weren't as notable as "someone left a cake out in the rain," but it was mood music, one of the reasons I go to Lou's Diner.

"I'm going to tell you something I never thought I would," Clarence said, seeming nervous. "You know how I said my daddy liked you and asked me to look out for you?"

"Yeah. Made me feel pretty good."

"Well, he said something else. He said, 'Son, won't be easy for you, but you need to be full of grace and truth so Mr. Chandler can see Jesus in you.' He said, 'Truth comes hard for some, Antsy, but for you truth comes easy. It's grace that comes hard.'"

I laughed, partly at how Clarence's voice was a bigger version of his father's and partly at how perfectly he captured his daddy's inflections.

He went on: "'Ollie Chandler needs to sees grace in you. You hear me, boy? And when he does, he'll know he's seein' a miracle.'"

We both laughed.

"Daddy's eyes sparkled when he said it. You know, he could rebuke me, and somehow I still felt loved. Anyway, Ollie, I've done better praying for you than looking out for you. And I'm not sure you've seen much grace in me."

"More than you realize," I said. "Now Manny maybe hasn't been overwhelmed by your grace, but..."

"Don't remind me," Clarence said, shaking his head.

"One of the biggest regrets of my sorry life is that I knew your daddy for such a short time."

"You know what I'd say to that, don't you?"

"Yeah. That if I want to know your daddy longer, I could choose to live where he's going to live forever."

"See, I didn't even have to say it, did I?"

By the time Ray arrived, I'd moved the gardenias to make room for an album Carp had put together for me, with photos of each homicide detective.

"Helps to visualize suspects," I explained. "But it's weird that I've known all the suspects for years."

After Rory took our orders, we ran out of water. I brought the pitcher over to the counter for a refill.

"*Scusi*, Mr. Ollie. I noticed your pictures on the table," Rory said. "I know you talk about important things, so I stay away. And if I see or hear something, I never tell anyone."

"I trust you, Rory. You know that."

"It is probably not important, but I have a good memory for faces. I recognized two of the people in these pictures. They have come here before."

I took the water pitcher to the table and exchanged it for the pictures. I brought them back to Rory.

He pointed first to the picture of Karl Baylor. "This man was in last week, Christmas Eve day. You were here and greeted him."

"Sure. I know him."

"He and his wife seemed nice. They left a generous tip. But a woman in one of your pictures came at 6:00, when I opened."

I showed him Tommi Elam.

"Not her."

I turned two pages. The moment he saw Kim Suda's picture he said, "That is the woman."

"You're positive?"

"She was by herself. Acting strangely. I would look over, and she seemed busy doing something; then she would see me looking and would talk into her cell phone. She would turn and twist in the booth as if she was trying to get better reception. She even moved to the other side."

"Interesting."

"But something else very odd. Because she was alone, I offered her to sit at a table or small booth. But she wanted the big booth." He pointed.

"*Our* booth?"

"Yes. I told her up to six people can sit there. Naturally, if it is you and Mr. Clarence, then not so many—"

"Yeah, I know."

"She is a small person, and it seemed strange for her to sit in that big booth by herself."

"When was this?"

"A Wednesday morning—she had the special, my vegetable omelet, with the sautéed red peppers. A week ago yesterday. I am certain."

"Thanks, Rory. You have a sharp eye. Don't mention this at our booth, all right?"

He put his finger in front of his lips.

I went to the booth and promptly knocked the water pitcher onto the table, requiring a mass exodus. I apologized for being a clumsy fool. Rory came to clean up, but I said we should move. When we'd relocated to another booth at the opposite side of the diner, I asked Ray Eagle if he had the bug sweeper in his van.

While Clarence watched from twenty feet away, Ray ran the TD-53 over our booth. It activated. I turned on my miniflashlight, opened my pocketknife, and pointed with the blade at a bug, skillfully planted in the woodwork. I went to the other side, guided by his detector, and pointed to a matching bug. They were barely noticeable even under the light.

Ray went to our new booth and ran the sweeper. Nothing. He walked around to all the other booths. Nothing. Only one booth made the TD-53 excited—the one I'd been spending three hours a week in, discussing a murder case.

"Killing people's bad," I said, as my fingers became fists. "Shooting at me's irritating. Hanging in my garage? Unpleasant. Placing a bug in my house? Annoying. Drugging my dog? Let's not even go there. But now…planting bugs in our booth at *Lou's Diner*? This time they've gone too far."

44

"You must play your cards as best you can when such a stake is on the table."
SHERLOCK HOLMES, "THE ADVENTURE OF CHARLES AUGUSTUS MILVERTON"

THE GRAVESIDE SERVICE for Carly Woods, for family and close friends only, was excruciating. People cried, laughed, and sang. I didn't sing and I didn't laugh.

After we drove to the church for her memorial service, I looked at the people sitting around me. I picked out likely wife beaters, child molesters, drug users, a woman who'd poisoned her first husband, and a teenager who would eventually kill a classmate.

The decent ones seemed gullible, unaware that sitting in a church service doesn't make someone a saint. Their minds are at ease, right up to the moment the smiling usher pulls a knife and shoves it through their heart.

Cynical? I suspect people who refuse to cooperate. I suspect people too eager to cooperate. I suspect people who aren't friendly and people who are. When our new neighbor moved in and he was friendly, I ran a criminal background check on him. I just like to keep my head out of the sand. It's a good way to stay alive. I mean, only if that's important to you.

There's something ironic about a skeptic sitting in church. It's like a vegetarian at a steak house. The people around you have tastes that you just don't have…and frankly don't want.

It's especially ironic to be pondering this as you sit in the front row, guest of the bereaved family…a church family. Don't get me wrong. I was honored. But boy, was I a fish out of water.

The one consolation was Kendra coming with me. She'd met Carly and liked her, but they weren't close. She knew it meant a lot to me, so she came.

As music played and somebody sang about "The Far Country," a slide show of Carly's life played on the big screen. The little girl pictures were adorable, the troubled adolescence evident, but in the last number of years Carly's face was different. A grown woman whose face had reverted to childhood. She'd become innocent again. I remembered how she called me "Uncle Ollie." I knew she loved me. I loved her too but wasn't good at showing it. Story of my life.

Soon my face was hot and wet. I wondered why they didn't open a window or something. I felt Kendra's hand on my arm, but I couldn't look at her.

Jake stood. I've heard him preach a few dozen sermons at me, but I wasn't prepared for this. He tried to speak three times. The words started but stopped. He grabbed the sides of the podium and tried again.

"I'm not a preacher. I'm just…a father." I felt it in my throat. "And the only reason I'm up here is that I was asked to do this by someone I couldn't say no to. Carly. I told her I'd probably break down. She said, 'If you do, it's okay. They'll understand, Daddy.'"

"I said—" Jake's voice broke. "Well, I'll leave that between us. The last few months, the last years, Carly and Janet and I have found encouragement in God's Word. I want to read from 2 Timothy 4:6–8. Paul says, 'The time has come for my departure. I have fought the good fight, I have finished the race, I have kept the faith. Now there is in store for me the crown of righteousness, which the Lord, the righteous Judge, will award to me on that day.'

"Paul calls his death a departure. A relocation. It's not ceasing to exist; it's just moving from one place to another. Paul knew that the moment he died he'd be with Jesus. He wrote, 'To depart and be with Christ, which is better by far.'"

Jake gripped the podium, knuckles white.

"It's hard on us, but Carly's more alive and happier this moment than she's ever been. Death isn't a hole; it's a doorway. It's not the end of life; it's a transition to new life. The best isn't behind us if we know Jesus. The best is still ahead."

How can you say that, Jake? How can you know?

Jake glanced at his notes, then looked up. "One day Carly said to me, 'We're homesick for Eden, aren't we, Daddy?' I liked that—homesick for Eden, for its beauties and pleasures and health and relationships. The Bible says heaven's our home. It's paradoxical, isn't it? Our home's a place we've never been. We're not at home in this world because we were made for a better world. The Bible calls it the new earth."

Jake looked at people all over the congregation, then at his family members sitting next to me in the front row. But he wasn't looking at me. He didn't want me to think he was talking to me. Naturally, he was.

"God wants us to have joy…yet we end up searching for joy in all the wrong places, and instead we find addictions and hollowness and misery."

Yep.

"Janet and I and Carly have clung to God's promises in Revelation 21 and 22: 'Then I saw a new heaven and a new earth…. I saw the Holy City, the new Jerusalem, coming down out of heaven from God…. And I heard a loud voice from the throne saying, "Now the dwelling of God is with men, and he will live with them. They will be his people, and God himself will be with them and be their God.'" It says, '[God] will wipe every tear from their eyes. There will be no more death or mourning or crying or pain, for the old order of things has passed away.' And then in the next chapter it says, 'No longer will there be any curse.'

"Second Peter 3:13 says, 'In keeping with his promise we are looking forward to a new heaven and a new earth, the home of righteousness.' Well, that's what our family's been looking forward to. We know there's a reunion ahead. And we know that someday we're going to walk the new earth together.

"Maybe you're thinking this is a memorial service, so I should be talking just about Carly, not about Jesus."

You got it, Jake.

"Well, Jesus was and is the most important person in Carly's life, and she made me promise I'd tell you about Him. For all I know she may be listening right now. I'm not going to let her down. One day I'll join her…I'll see my little girl again."

He stopped. The pause was long and gut-wrenching.

"God is so holy that He can't allow sin into His presence. Romans 3:23 says, '*All* have sinned and fall short of the glory of God.' Because we're sinners, we can't enter heaven as we are. God loves us just the way we are, but He loves us too much to let us stay this way. That's why Christ came, to change us.

"So heaven is *not* our default destination. Unless our sin problem is dealt with, the only place we can go is where God isn't…and that's hell. Judging by what's said at most funerals, you'd think everyone's going to heaven. But Jesus said otherwise. The Bible says we're not good enough to go to heaven on our own."

I squirmed. Jake had a captive audience, and he knew it. Unless a murder was discovered in the next few minutes, I couldn't escape.

"How much does God love us?" Jake asked. "He went to hell for us on the cross so that we wouldn't have to. God took on our worst suffering so we could go to heaven. What more would you ask God to do than what He's done for you?

"Like any gift, forgiveness can be offered, but it isn't ours until we receive it—and we can only do that through repenting and confessing our sins and saying yes to God's offer. If you haven't done that, you can do it quietly now."

Jake the evangelist. He wasn't this way when I first met him. He's a far better man in most ways, but this part irritates me.

"I began the message by reading from Revelation 21. I'll finish with reading a few more verses: "'It is done. I am the Alpha and the Omega, the Beginning and the End. To him who is thirsty I will give to drink without cost from the spring of the water of life.'""

Weird. Right when he said those words I was thinking how thirsty I was.

↔

Afterward we had a huge dinner at Jake's church. When I was finishing my second dessert, pecan pie, Jake asked, "How was your dinner?"

"Well, I didn't drink the Kool-Aid."

He stared blankly.

"Jim Jones. Guyana. Religious cult. Poisoned Kool-Aid. Get it?"

"So, what did you think?"

"The coffee was a little weak. Great pie though."

"What did you think of the service?"

"Didn't know any of the songs except 'Amazing Grace.' You guys don't sing familiar stuff, do you?"

"What did you want, the Beach Boys? Anyway, thanks for coming, Ollie."

"I…wouldn't have missed it. I mean…it was Carly."

Jake's face collapsed, and he put his arms around me. I felt him shaking. We hugged a long time, longer than I've ever hugged a man, though I don't keep a book on that sort of thing.

When we let go, I saw Kendra looking at us. Tears were streaming down her face. I put my arm around my little girl. Now she was hugging me.

"I'm glad you have each other," Jake said to us. "Be grateful. Don't let go of each other, okay? Fathers and daughters shouldn't have regrets. Carly and I didn't have any."

Janet came up beside Jake. Now they were hugging.

Kendra and I walked out, my arm around her shoulder.

I wasn't sure how a man could feel so incredibly empty and full at the same time.

MONDAY, JANUARY 6, 9:30 A.M.

JANUARY 6 WAS MY BIRTHDAY. Like the crabby uncle in the retirement home in that Hallmark commercial, I had no intention of letting others in on it. I always put in a full day's work on my birthday, proving to myself I'm not a little girl.

On Mulch's birthday I drove east on Burnside to buy him a Dea's longburger, fries, and an orange malt—which usually gives him a brain freeze. If Mulch could drive or handle money, I knew he'd do the same for me.

Tired of looking over my shoulder at people who might have shot and hung me, I deserted my post in detective division and turned the corner for the elevator. There stood Kim Suda. I joined her for a forty-second wait, in complete silence.

There are times in detective work when you need to be subtle, and other times you need to be confrontational. But in both cases the goal is the same—to try to catch people off guard and put doubts in their minds, and to read their responses like a polygraph. I'd been subtle with Suda. This seemed like the time to go on offense.

When we got in the elevator, she pressed the ground floor button before I could.

"What would you say," I started, "if I told you that the chief claims you were the one who bugged my house? And that he told me you were covering your tracks by setting me up for Palatine's murder?"

"You're lying," Suda said.

"What if he told me you might have planted Noel's fingerprints on the gun? How easy would it be for you to have Noel's fingerprints? Your desk is eight feet from his. You could get a Black Jack wrapper out of my trash any day. What if I told you that the chief said, confidentially, you should be at the top of my suspect list?"

She stared at me, trying to keep a poker face. It wasn't working. I saw doubt in her eyes. I'd tipped her off when I'd called her a dog drugger. But now it didn't sound like a guess. Suddenly her face hardened.

"You don't scare me, Chandler. I didn't break into your house. You don't have proof, or you'd be showing your cards. You're bluffing."

"You wore your gloves, but there's something that proves you were at my house," I said. "It's going to come back to haunt you."

"Dream on," she said.

"You always have your camera with you, don't you? You think I don't know you took a picture of the professor after he was murdered? And got it to Mike Button at the *Trib*?"

"You're so lame," Suda said.

"If I'm lying, how did I know it was you? If the chief didn't tell me, who else could have?"

Right on cue, the elevator opened, and ten seconds later Kim Suda was outside the Justice Center, walking rapidly, as if she were escaping.

After a brisk two-block walk to Waterfront Park, I returned to bad news: I'd been ordered again to Shelob's Lair, the chief's office. This was my fifth summons in nine weeks. I went to the bathroom with a bag, took off my shirt, and got myself ready, just in case our conversation proved interesting.

As usual, I sat and waited. This time I brought two ESPN magazines. I read one and hid the other under a couch cushion for my next visit.

Lennox was born seventy years too late and in the wrong country. He was doing his best to compensate for having missed his chance to be commandant of a slave labor camp.

Finally he stepped out and said to Mona, "Any calls?"

"Yeah," I said under my breath. "Your proctologist called. They found your head in your—"

"Chandler!" Though he couldn't have heard me, he beckoned, and before I was through the door he asked, "Situation changed with the professor?"

"No. He's still dead."

"They did a routine security sweep of my home office this morning. Guess what they found."

"Jimmy Hoffa? D. B. Cooper? Elvis?"

"They found a bug."

"A cockroach? I know an exterminator named Jim Bob—"

"An electronic bug."

"No kidding. Did you run a check to see whose it was?"

He squeezed the shiny fountain pen in his hand. "It was issued by this department."

"You don't say."

"Don't play games with me, Chandler. I know what you did."

"Are you suggesting I planted a bug in your house?"

"Yes! My wife said she sent you to the bathroom by my office. You had opportunity."

"But you said it was issued by this department, right? If I'd requisitioned it, there'd be paperwork. They would've entered the serial number in records. They could tell you exactly who checked it out. In fact, why don't I call them right now and ask."

I reached toward the phone on his desk. The chief let loose with a string of words rivaling Nixon's Watergate tapes.

"I have good news," I said. "That bugging device didn't cost the department anything. I found it right in my living room. Somebody here at Police Headquarters tried to bug me. Can you imagine?"

"You think you know who it was?" Lennox asked, pretending ice water ran through his veins while sweat was dripping down his forehead, smearing his makeup.

"Oh yeah. We both know."

"You can't prove anything."

"Even if the detective who planted it confessed?"

"Detective?"

"What if I told you she admitted the whole thing?"

When I said "she," his face froze.

"Suppose we've got her on tape, including her middle-of-the-night meeting with you at a 7-Eleven?"

He sucked a breath and coughed.

"What would you say if I told you she left a partial print on one of the bugs? And there's a match? What would Kim Suda do?"

He sat back in his chair, considering his hand. "It looks like we have each other here, Detective."

"Actually, I have more of you than you have of me."

"I had legitimate grounds for placing a bug. You didn't."

"There's a legal process for placing a bug, cop or not. All I did was find department equipment someone placed at my house. Then I returned it to the home office of the chief of police, the one who checked it out in the first place. Okay, maybe I forgot to mention I'd returned it. And maybe I forgot to turn it off."

"You won't get away with this."

"And you won't get away with setting up some vagrant as the murderer. Tell Mona to back off on that. It's recorded. Speaking of which, if I wake up dead, Clarence and Jake and two others get a copy of the recording and documentation. I've got backups and copies. You better hope I don't die even of natural causes, because if I do, you're toast."

"You mean, you think the *chief of police* would harm you?"

"You've already broken the law. For all I know you killed the professor. I narrowed it down to the detectives—but couldn't the chief of police get his hands on everything a detective could…and more?"

I pulled from my pocket the picture of his daughter and the professor.

He snatched it.

"Got more," I said.

He stared at the picture as I stood and walked out.

I took the elevator, hoping I'd set him and Suda at odds with each other. If one didn't trust the other, somebody might sell out. Though he'd be frustrated about what I had on him, he had every reason to believe I had no knowledge of the other bugging devices in my home office or at our booth at Lou's.

Once I got in my car, I unbuttoned my shirt and checked the mini-digital recorder with the cord that ran up to my tie. I played it back.

"Jimmy Hoffa? D. B. Cooper? Elvis?"

My voice was clear.

"They found a bug."

His voice was clear.

I listened to the beginning of the profanity.

I needed to make a copy.

Sitting in my car, preferring to work out of sight from a murderer, I marked three points on a Portland map.

I made a conference call to Clarence and Ray.

"Manny's wife," I said. "That hit-and-run that nearly killed her? It happened on a direct line between the professor's home and Portland State."

"Coincidence?" Clarence asked.

"Hundreds of people, thousands, live near that line. But what if Manny learned something and he confronted Palatine about the hit-and-run?"

"You're not saying that happened?"

"I don't know what I'm saying." I told them about my meeting with the chief.

"You really told Lennox you gave us documentation in case you die?" Clarence said.

"You've watched too many movies," Ray said, laughing.

"I was winging it, okay? Somebody's made a couple of attempts on me. Figured I may as well cover my…bases."

"You mentioned us by name?" Clarence said. "Couldn't somebody come after us too?"

"No more than a one in four chance."

"I didn't know you'd found Kim Suda's fingerprints on the bug," Clarence said. "I didn't."

"You said you did."

"No. I said, 'What if I were to tell you that I found Kim Suda's fingerprints on the bug?' You made the same assumption the chief did. You both need to listen better."

After I complimented Rory on the hot pink gerbera daisies floating in a clear bowl, I explained to Jake and Clarence I'd have to cut lunch short because I had to do something back at the Justice Center, then pick up Mulch, who was going to work for me. They asked me to elaborate, but I wanted to keep it a surprise.

"Remember that article Clarence wrote," Jake said, "about investigating a murder mystery—who killed Jesus?"

"Yeah. I remember."

"I really think you should do it. Investigate who killed Jesus and why. What happened to the body? Why were His disciples willing to die for declaring that Jesus rose from the dead? Think you could handle that case?"

"I'm a homicide detective, not a priest."

"It's not a job for a priest. It's a job for a homicide detective. Apply your professional skills, your honed instincts, to the murder of Jesus."

"It'll be tough interviewing two-thousand-year-old witnesses. Might have to repeat my questions. Or do you propose time travel?"

"The historical documents are still available," Jake said. "Including extensive eye-witness testimony."

"Yeah," Clarence said. He pushed his Bible across the table.

"That's a Bible," I said.

"The historical evidence is there," Jake said. "Read it. Then make up your own mind."

"Tell you what," I said. "I'll make you a deal. If I solve the Palatine case and catch the killer, I'll pursue that investigation."

"Deal," Jake said, reaching out his hand to seal it. "But try not to die before you've investigated what's waiting for you after death."

"I'll do my best," I said.

"Seriously," Clarence said, "you don't know how much time you've got left. You've nearly been killed twice. You need to be ready, Ollie. If Daddy were here, he'd tell you, 'Can't get on board widout yo' ticket.'"

I felt like I'd been punched in the gut. "What'd you say?"

"You can't get on board without your ticket. When we were kids, Daddy was always reminding us to get on the train to heaven and that Jesus was the only ticket." He stared at me. "Something wrong?"

"You sure your daddy said that?"

"Said it all the time when I was growing up. You ever hear him say it?"

I shook my head slowly.

The lie seemed preferable to the explanation.

Clarence met me twenty minutes later at the Justice Center.

"Cover me," I told him as I started toward the opposite side of Kim Suda's workstation, behind the divider.

"What do I say if someone's coming?" he whispered.

"You'll figure it out."

"What are you doing? What's in that bag?"

"The less you know the better."

"Are you putting a bug under her desk? Are you crazy?"

I looked both ways.

"She's sitting right there," he whispered. "Wait until she leaves!"

"It's got to be now. If somebody comes, clear your throat. Loud."

While Clarence pretended to admire the map of Old Portland on the wall, I got on my knees on the back side of Suda's cubicle. I crawled underneath and looked at her shoes, no more than twelve inches from my hands. I heard her voice on the phone. I got the goods out of my bag and went to work.

Two minutes later her feet pulled back. She stood and called, "Abernathy! What are you doing? Where's Chandler?"

I froze, most of me under her cubicle, but a prominent part of me sticking out.

Clarence walked over to her quickly, cutting her off. They were standing face-to-face (actually Suda's face to Abernathy's second shirt button). This was my guess since all I could see was their feet.

"He's working on a project," Clarence said. "I was just looking at this map."

I didn't know how long this was going to last, so I crawled past their feet and over to Tommi Elam's chair. I slunk up into her chair, and just a moment later, Chris Doyle said, "What are you doing with Tommi's stuff?"

"Just leaving her a note," I said.

"I thought you said he was working on a project," Suda said to Clarence.

"I was. You'd think I was a terrorist or something." I wrote, "Tommi, give me a call. Ollie."

"You're worse than a terrorist," Doyle said. "You're a traitor."

"You going to teach me another lesson, like last time? Sarge says we've got a meeting in two hours," I said, standing up. "See you there. And next time you want to brawl, Doyle, don't bring a pawn to do a king's job."

I showed up for the special 3:00 p.m. detectives meeting five minutes late. When I walked in, every eye fell on me.

Mulch led the way, excitedly looking for some place to pee. I yanked his leash.

"What's going on?" Doyle yelled, jumping to his feet.

"I gave him permission," Sarge said.

"Somebody broke into my house and planted two police department bugs," I said. "Mulch was there. They knocked him out with a sedative. They also managed to get their scent on this towel." I held up the kitchen towel. "Mulch has been smelling it, and now he's going to see if someone in the room matches the scent."

There were howls of protest mixed with laughter from Jack Glissan and Tommi Elam, both of whom know Mulch.

I gave Mulch a whiff of the towel, then unleashed him. He ran to the center of the room, sliding on the tile. Nose in the air, he turned a sharp left toward Kim Suda. He went right for her legs, sniffing her unmercifully. She kicked him in the chops, which couldn't have felt good considering her martial arts skills. He barked at her.

"Back!" she screamed.

"He won't hurt you," Tommi said, but Suda wasn't hearing it.

"It was you, Suda," I said. "Mulch doesn't like people breaking in and giving him hamburger mickeys."

"You can't do this," Suda yelled, heading for the door. "Get him off me!"

Mulch chased her, nosing his snout into her pant leg and shoes and latching on. She gave him one last kick, and she was gone.

The detectives were all on their feet. Doyle was steaming.

"She really broke into your house and planted a bug?" Phillips asked.

"Mulch just gave her a positive ID," I said.

"You made your point," Sarge said. "Now get that mutt outta here!"

↔

"I never knew Mulch was a trained police dog," Clarence said to me fifteen minutes later in the basement of the police parking structure. He looked admiringly at Mike Hammer, who was sitting proudly in the backseat of my car.

"He isn't."

"I wrote a story on police dogs. Not every dog can isolate one human scent like that, not in a room with all those people."

I reached under my seat and pulled out the kitchen towel, then pushed it up to Clarence's face.

"It smells like…bacon."

"Yeah. When you were standing guard and I was down on my hands and knees on the other side of Suda's cubicle? I was smearing bacon grease on her shoes and pant legs."

"You mean…?"

"Mulch goes crazy at the smell of bacon. And all without special training."

I opened my stakeout Tupperware and took out four strips of cooked bacon. Three seconds later, they'd gone on to the afterlife.

46

"It is murder, refined, cold-blooded, deliberate murder. My nets are closing upon him. There is but one danger which can threaten us. It is that he should strike before we are ready to do so. Another day—two at the most—and I have my case complete, but until then guard your charge as closely as ever a fond mother watched her ailing child."

SHERLOCK HOLMES, *THE HOUND OF THE BASKERVILLES*

MONDAY, JANUARY 6, 4:00 P.M.

AFTER MULCH'S DETECTIVE DEBUT, I dropped him at Lynn Carpenter's. It was her day off and she'd agreed to dog-sit so I could get back downtown to face Kim Suda. Chris Doyle insisted on being there. Sergeant Seymour agreed, despite my objections.

"Tell us your story," Sarge said to Suda.

"I already told you—"

"Repeat yourself. Why'd you come to the professor's house that night? And why'd you lie about where you parked your car?"

"I didn't lie."

Sarge threw down Carp's photos. "This is both sides of Oak and 22nd Street, taken by the *Trib* photographer while you were still at the crime scene. Do you see your car anywhere?"

Suda chewed her lips, but inside she was chewing her brain. Finally she said, "No."

"Is your car invisible, or are you lying?" Sarge asked.

"I was on foot. I don't live that far away."

"Yeah," Doyle said, "she lives just down—"

"Shut up, Chris." Sarge's voice was a fist. He turned to Suda. "You suddenly remember you were on foot once we prove your car wasn't there? Start giving it straight—now!"

Suda looked down, then at Sarge, then Doyle. Not me.

"Here's another question not to answer," I said. "Why didn't you sign the log?"

"I told you."

"You lied. I say you didn't sign the log because you were already in the house."

She shifted, crossing and uncrossing her arms, trying to manage her body language but failing.

"When did you show up at the crime scene?" I asked. "In time to kill the professor?"

She wasn't budging. I had another card to play.

"You know that strand of hair on the professor, the one that turned out to be yours? I talked to Phil and the CSI techs. They claim that strand was bagged within fifteen minutes of when they arrived at the scene."

"So?"

"So that was thirty minutes before anybody remembers seeing you there. There's only one explanation. You were at the crime scene before any of us."

"Spill it now, or you're going to regret it," Sarge said.

"Okay, okay!" Eyes flashing, she put up her hands and pushed back her chair. "Six weeks ago, early November, somebody sent me an e-mail. Couldn't trace the source. They warned me that the professor was…a ladies' man, but worse. They said he exploited young women. Sarge, you know I worked three years as a decoy."

"If you're telling the truth," Sarge said, "whoever sent the e-mail knew this would push your button."

"It did. I hate those kinds of men. So…I followed him and bumped into him at a Starbucks. That's how we met. We went out a few times. The last one was the same night he…"

"Died?" I said.

"You *dated* him?" Chris asked.

"Well, *he* thought it was a date. To me it was a sting. I was ready for him to try something; then I was going to take him down. Teach him a lesson."

"On what legal basis?" Sarge asked.

"I was off duty. As a private citizen I have a right to defend myself against a man who's pressuring me, don't I?"

I nodded. For once, I was liking Kim Suda.

"You *dated* him?" Chris repeated.

"I met Bill—Palatine—for dinner at Salty's. He behaved okay, for a jerk."

"Bill?" Chris said.

"Yes, Bill!" Kim said. "Anyway, I followed him to his house."

"His house?" Chris said.

"One more echo, Doyle, and you're outta here," Sarge said. "Got that?"

"Soon as we're at his house, he gets a phone call. Suddenly he's upset, tells me I need to go. Says he'll call me back later that evening. He didn't."

"Maybe he just wasn't attracted to you," Doyle said.

"Thanks, Chris."

"I mean, I work with you and I wasn't attracted to you for a long time."

"Yeah, well, that was tough on me because I was always so crazy about you," Suda said. "Anyway, fast-forward to 11:20. I'm at Chris's house and I get a text message on my phone, from Bill. He says, 'I need to see you right away. Come to my house. Urgent.'"

"Those were the exact words?" I asked.

"Close enough."

"You told me you needed to get home," Chris said. "You lied to me."

"Anyway, I show up and see a broken window. Lights out. Didn't feel like a burglary. Dark and heavy. I peeked in a window and saw his right arm. No movement. I drove off, thinking I'd call 911 anonymously. But then it hit me. He'd rushed me out of there, and I'd left my coat. No ID in it, but odds and ends in the pocket. And of all things, whoever was investigating this crime would be somebody I work with, who'd recognize my maroon coat. Even men might figure that out."

"We might," I said. Or not.

"So I decided to go back for the coat. But I had to get rid of the car—couldn't let anybody see it at a murder scene. I drove to my house, then ran back and entered a gate to the backyard. Door's unlocked. I go in with a flashlight and find the body. First time I've seen a murder victim I was dating ninety minutes earlier."

"Dating," Doyle muttered. Sarge stared him down like he was squashing a bug.

"I find my coat and suddenly see lights in the driveway. I'm peeking out the broken window at patrol. I don't think I've been seen, but there's no way out. So I get in Bill's closet and push back through the clothes and stand on a plastic storage box while they search the house. They're at the far side of the place, so I call Chris on the cell, ready to cut it off if they come my direction."

"That's why you were whispering," Chris said. "You said you were with your mother. That she was sleeping."

"I lied again, okay?"

"You're the one she called to lie to," I pointed out to Doyle. "That makes you special."

"You said you called because you were sorry you had to run off," Doyle said.

"I was sorry. But also...I was trying to...well..."

"Establish an alibi," Sarge said.

"Right," I said. "Why else would you risk being heard?"

"I was scared. I needed to talk with you, Chris. Really. Anyway, I disconnect when one of the officers comes down the hallway. He enters the bedroom, turns on the lights, and looks around. He opens the closet door, bends over, sees nothing. He didn't pull back the clothes to see if someone was standing on that plastic box."

"I'll send a memo," Sarge said.

"So I stay there for what seems like an hour. At first I just hear the patrol guys. Then there's some commotion, and I hear one of them yelling out front. Then I hear someone else in the house, in the kitchen, I think. I hear a clank, like a glass or a bottle. Then someone walks in the bedroom but doesn't turn on the light.

He...or she...I don't know, stands by the window, then shines a flashlight, like he's looking for something, on the floor, the bed, everywhere."

"What did he look like?" I asked.

"No clue. I was looking through clothes, then through a door crack, into a dark room. Who was it? Do you know?"

I shook my head. I thought it was the killer, but I didn't have a name, and I wasn't going to let Suda think I didn't consider her the killer.

"What next?" Sarge asked.

"I'm wondering where the patrol guys are and why they let this other person in. I think maybe they're just standing outside, but no, I hear them again, arguing. Then people start arriving one or two at a time. Now the lights are on and they're coming in and out of Palatine's bedroom. Including you, Chandler. You were talking with Abernathy, by the window, then down on your hands and knees and taking pictures. I'm peeking at you through the crack. I shift my feet just a little, and next thing I know the plastic box under me cracks. Thought I was toast."

"I remember the noise."

"Fortunately," she said, "you checked the right side of the closet and just pointed the flashlight to my side."

Sarge glared at me. "Memo."

"Hey," I said, "there couldn't have been more than four feet between what I could see at the bottom and top of the closet."

"I scrunched down," she said. "That shrunk me a foot. It's all I needed."

"So if criminals are short enough," Sarge said to me, "you'll miss 'em?"

"You were stupid not to check," Suda said.

"You, on the other hand, were brilliant, so here we sit."

"Keep talking, Suda," Sarge said.

"So I wait and make sure no one's in the room. I back out of the closet, looking like I'd just stepped in, and start examining the floor. Phil, the criminalist, walks in and gives me a funny look. We start talking; then I work my way out to where you were."

"I was right. You didn't sign in because you were already there."

"But I didn't kill the professor."

"Sure."

"He was already dead. It's the truth."

"As opposed to the lies you told us before?"

"Give her a break," Chris said.

"I'll give Kimmy a break after I hear her next story. The one where she broke into my house, drugged my dog, and planted illegal bugs."

"I'm sure," Sarge said, "you had good reasons for doing that too?"

"I don't know what I'm supposed to tell you," Suda said.

"The truth?" Sarge said.

"Now seems like a good time to mention that when you ran from my house after planting the bug, I followed you to your car. You were parked on Albers, north side of the road facing east. You hopped in the car, did a U-turn, and headed west."

"But...if you saw me, why that drama with your dog going after me?"

"Because I couldn't prove I saw you. And Mulch deserved some payback."

"I didn't hurt him."

"You hurt his pride. He's sensitive."

"He liked the hamburger."

"He likes it better when it doesn't knock him cold."

"Suda, you've really dug a hole for yourself," Sarge said. "What made you decide to go to Chandler's?"

"Before you tell another lie," I said, "I should point out that we saw you go to the 7-Eleven on 162nd and Stark at 2:40 a.m. on December 4. And we saw the man you met."

Suda's stormy eyes looked frostbitten. Her face fell in surrender. She turned to Sarge. "I don't think I should say this in front of everybody."

"Doyle, get out," Sarge said. "Shut the door behind you."

Chris moved to the door, slothlike.

"Gives you time to make the chess team reunion," I said.

"We're not finished, Chandler," Doyle said, pointing his finger at me.

"You going to gang up on me with three other pawns?" I looked at him sympathetically. "If it makes you feel any better, Kimmy's meeting with the guy in the 7-Eleven wasn't a date."

He slammed the door. The window shook.

"Maybe I need a lawyer," Suda said, "but here it is. Lennox asked me into his office a couple of weeks ago. He said he'd been examining the Palatine case. He had me scared. I thought I'd been found out—about being at the murder scene. Anyway, he said Chandler had become the investigation's focal point, the main suspect."

"He said that?" Sarge said.

"He mentioned there was evidence, you had no alibi, and you'd been drinking and angry that night. He asked how good I was at getting into a house and planting a surveillance device. I told him I was good. I asked if it was legal. He claimed he had a court order."

"Ask to see it?" Sarge said.

"I'm supposed to ask the chief of police to prove he's not lying?"

"What you did was a felony."

"When I'm ordered to do it, in the line of duty, as part of an investigation…by the chief of police?"

"Anything else you've done I should know about?" Sarge asked.

She shook her head.

"What about photographing the dead professor and giving the picture to the *Trib*?" I asked.

"You still on that?" she said. "I didn't have my camera. And if I had, I certainly wouldn't have used it. A flash in a dark house at night? With a body on the floor?"

"Then who took that picture?"

"How should I know?"

I nearly mentioned the bugs she planted at Lou's Diner but restrained myself. That was my hole card.

"You're dismissed," Sarge said to me.

Suda stood up.

"Have plans this evening?" he asked her.

She nodded.

"Cancel them. I'm not done with you."

It was a long day, but I've seldom had a birthday present better than Mulch going after Kim Suda's pant legs.

I left downtown for the second time and picked up Mulch from Carp's house, where she'd baked him pizza snack muffins. His eyes begged me to marry her.

"Any developments on the professor's picture in the *Trib*?" Carp asked.

"Kim Suda swears she didn't take the picture and didn't give it to Mike Button. At first I assumed she was lying, but she admitted other things. Why deny that one? But if it wasn't Suda or me or you or Hatch or the patrol guys or the criminalists…"

"There's one person you're forgetting," Carp said.

"Who?"

"The killer. The killer took the picture."

"Yeah, he took the picture from the mantel. I'm talking about the photograph of the professor's body."

"So am I," Carp said. "I mean the killer was holding the camera—he removed the photograph from the mantel, laid it on the floor, then snapped that photo of the professor's body. And he's the anonymous source who got the photo to Mike Button."

I started to argue. I stopped. A minute of silence later I said, "Pizza's on me. Ice cream too."

She said she was teaching a class at Portland Community College but took a rain check. I hoped she wouldn't forget.

We stopped at WinCo. Mulch stayed in the car. Generally he's banned from public places where there's food. Once I brought him into the Fred Meyer grocery section wearing a green jacket, undercover as an in-training guide for the blind. But it was samples day. After a few incidents, one involving a roasted chicken, they asked us to leave.

I picked up a tub of Breyers cookie dough ice cream. We were going to celebrate.

I pulled up to the old brownstone and thought I saw a window blind move. Not again. I pulled my Glock and quietly moved to the front door. Mulch picked up on my mood and slunk along next to me, growling softly.

I turned the handle. When I realized it was unlocked, I whispered in Mulch's ear, "Get 'em," and pushed the door open. Mulch bounded in, growling ferociously.

As the door opened I heard a loud noise and pointed the Glock toward it. I heard screaming and flipped on the light to see the faces of two men and one woman, and someone else on the floor with Mulch on top of him. It was then I realized what I'd heard. It had been the word *surprise*.

Jake pulled Mulch off Mr. Obrist, gave him a cookie, and immediately he calmed down. (Mulch, not Mr. Obrist, who needed more than a cookie to calm him.)

As I holstered my gun, Clarence showed me the Flyin' Pie pizza and an ice cream cake from Baskin-Robbins: Jamoca Almond Fudge. I grabbed my sack from the porch and quickly buried the cookie dough in the back of the freezer, where it would remain hidden for at least a day.

Mrs. Obrist led her husband home, saying something about cardiorespiratory issues. Jake explained that when he and Clarence got in, Mr. Obrist came over, thinking the house was being invaded. So Jake and Clarence had invited them to the surprise. In retrospect, they realized it hadn't been a good plan.

Jake and Clarence sang "Happy Birthday" to me and didn't sound too bad. Maybe it's all the singing they do at church.

At nine I thanked them and told them to get home to their families. After they left, Mulch and I finished off the ice cream cake. It was my birthday, and I was determined to leave no evidence.

Fifteen minutes later I heard something on the porch. I opened the door with my right hand, holding the Glock in my left.

"Happy birthday, Daddy," Kendra said.

She held out a box that said TCBY. "It's a yogurt pie, mocha almond. It has only half the calories of ice cream."

"Yeah, ice cream'll kill you," I said. "Hey, say hi to Mulch while I take this into the kitchen. Be right back." I ran in, grabbed the Baskin-Robbins box, stuffed it in the garbage, and ran water over the four bowls.

Kendra and Mulch and I had a great time in the living room over mocha almond yogurt, which was surprisingly good.

"Since it's only half the calories," I said to Kendra, "I guess I can eat twice as much."

It was smooth sailing the whole evening. I didn't ask anything about how cows feel about yogurt. Kendra gave Mulch his own bowl. Afterward he curled up at her feet. It was my happiest birthday since Sharon died.

TUESDAY, JANUARY 7, 12:45 P.M.

It's hard to work on the detective floor when you figure the killer's within sixty feet of you and can walk by anytime and see what's on your computer screen or listen to your conversations. That's why Lou's Diner had become my honorary office. I'd had several meetings in other booths, in light of the bugs, but for today's meeting with Ray Eagle I deliberately chose our booth. I had prepped him ahead of time so we shared the same script.

"I think I'm being followed," I said to Ray.

"I've been looking over my shoulder too," Ray said. "If somebody planted a bug in your living room, there's no telling what else they're doing."

"I didn't want Clarence and Jake here. I'm going to give you some sensitive information. Once you see what it is, you'll know what to do with it."

"How sensitive?"

"It includes thirty pages of police department records."

"No joke? Where is it?"

"Couldn't bring it here. Somebody may realize the records were copied. If I was caught giving them to you, we'd be dead meat. If we're being followed, they could apprehend us on suspicion of a felony—divulging classified information. Internal Affairs would crucify me."

"So how am I going to get the papers? You come to my house? I go to yours?"

"Not with possible tails. And either of our houses could be bugged—in my case rebugged. Here's how the pros do it. We meet somewhere we've never been. We both make sure we're not tailed, or that we shake the tail. That's a lot easier after dark. Let's meet tonight, 1:30 a.m."

"Could we make it a little earlier?"

"Midnight's as early as I'll go. You know that big white building on 55th and Hawthorne, on the hill? The mansion?"

"The one they made into a seminary?"

"Yeah, that's it. Western Seminary." I pulled out my Thomas Guide and pointed. "There's a back parking lot right here on the corner of 57th and Madison. You can get in from either street. Nice hedge for privacy. Easy access but inconspicuous. Nobody's there at night. I've scoped it out. Just drive in and I'll be waiting. Shouldn't be chained, but if it is, park on 57th in front of the chain. I'll get out and hand you the documents."

"Isn't this a bit cloak-and-dagger?"

"Look, I've got lab reports, department e-mails, evidence incriminating Brandon Phillips and Kim Suda. This is hot stuff. If I was caught giving you police info, I'd lose my job in a heartbeat. And you'd lose your license."

"It's worth the risk?"

"I've done night exchanges before. Just can't let anyone know where and when. We'll be okay. Don't make copies of what I give you. After you've gone over it, burn it. Shredder's not good enough. They know you're helping me and might be sorting your trash."

"I feel like we're in a movie," Ray said with a sly smile.

"Can't use our cars. I'm borrowing a friend's black Cadillac STS, four door. You got somebody's you can use?"

"Going fancy? Well, my brother's got a silver BMW 530i, four door."

"Perfect. Midnight tonight. Whoever gets there first, stay in the car until the other arrives. I'll get out and hand you the papers; then we're gone."

"We really have to do it like this? Not a quick transfer at a public place?"

"Trust me." I winked at Ray. "I know what I'm doing."

47

"Bear in mind one of the phrases in that queer old legend and avoid the moor in those hours of darkness when the powers of evil are exalted."
SHERLOCK HOLMES, *THE HOUND OF THE BASKERVILLES*

TUESDAY, JANUARY 7, 2:00 P.M.

SERGEANT SEYMOUR told me he'd given Kim Suda a stern warning. There'd be an investigation.

"You believe her?" he asked me. "The part about the chief?"

"I saw them together. And I saw an e-mail she sent to him confirming that she'd done a job for him. That same night she planted the bugs at my place and messed with Mulch."

I handed Sarge the e-mail printout.

After rereading it a few times and bawling me out for holding it back, he said, "Why would Lennox risk his career?"

"Maybe he thinks his career is over if a police detective's guilty of murder. What's more important to him than anything else?"

"His image." Sarge scowled.

"So if the evidence makes the chief look really bad, that might explain his obsession with a cover-up. I think he's desperate to come out of this thing intact. And he's arrogant enough to think he can get away with it."

"I don't care if he's not available," I said, in the privacy of Sarge's office, which he loaned me for a half hour. "Tell him it's a call from the police department. You have caller ID? Check where I'm calling from. Portland Police."

"I'd need to give him your name," she said.

"Tell him I'm an informant. Anonymous. I've got incriminating information he'll want to have. Tell him if he doesn't get it from me tonight, I'm giving it to the newspaper. And it's not going to make him look good."

Amazing how placing an anonymous phone call from the police department can make a political VIP who was "absolutely unavailable" instantly available.

I finished the call by telling him, "I'll be driving a silver BMW 530i, four door. You come to me. I'll roll down the window. Now listen, I want you to hand me twenty sheets of blank eight-and-a-half-by-eleven paper in a plain brown envelope."

"But why—?"

"Never mind why. In exchange, I'll give you a file of information that'll show you what they've been doing under your nose. Got it?"

Five minutes later, I made a second call, finally talking my way through to the man I wanted. "Never mind who this is. I'm a police insider, and I've got a major story. Involves mishandling of the Palatine murder investigation. Ollie Chandler's a jerk, and this'll take him down."

"Why are you calling me? I can give you the names and numbers of—"

"It's you or it's nobody. You know that mansion on 55th and Hawthorne, on the hill, the one they turned into a seminary? There's a back parking lot, quiet and inconspicuous, off 57th and Madison. I'll meet you there at midnight. Come by yourself."

"Many people work for me. I'll send one of them."

"You do and he'll get nothing. If it's not important enough to show your face, I'll give it to a TV station. You can watch it on the news. I'll spread the word you turned the story down. I'll be driving a black Cadillac STS, four door. Dim your lights. Don't want faces visible."

After a long pause he said, "All right. I'll be there at midnight."

The man once known as William Palatine thought he was having a nightmare. After the disturbing phone call that had changed his evening plans, he'd been at his desk, alternating between correcting papers and playing solitaire, when he heard the knock. He shouldn't have trusted him.

He remembered the agony of his death. But why was he still conscious? He was a materialist. Nothing exists but natural phenomena. The mind was merely the brain. Man was but an animal. God was a myth. There was no life after death.

It hit him like a sledgehammer: "Nietzsche was wrong. God's not dead. He's alive, and I must answer to Him."

He saw the deceptions he'd told. He saw the faces of girls he'd seduced. He saw their shame. He saw their tears, their violated trust, their regrets. In one case, he saw her death.

He felt the full weight of guilt he'd guarded himself from. His only prayer had been answered: He didn't want God, and God wasn't here. Palatine had chosen this misery.

It turned a screw into his aching head. The hell he'd laughed at was now his residence. He knew, intuitively, that it always would be. The era of choice was past. This was the era of consequence.

Where were Hobbes and Sartre and Heidegger now? Where were Hume, Schopenhauer, and Camus? Where was Bertrand Russell? Their thoughts had been magnificent, captivating, compelling.

And, in the most important respects, wrong.

William Palatine's identity as the brilliant philosophy professor meant nothing here. The oppressive terror of utter aloneness descended on him like sharp talons.

The torment was in knowing it could have been avoided. There'd been a lifetime of opportunity to seek and knock and ask, to examine the evidence, to find the truth. But that life was over, and with it, opportunity. What he faced now was not life but mere existence, in torment.

He'd made his living speaking great ideas to students. Some of the ideas were true. Many weren't. Had he suspected it before? He'd been part of a grand scheme of deception, orchestrated by powers who'd first deceived him then used him to deceive others.

He wanted the opportunity to talk his way out of hell. He'd always been good with words. But eloquence meant nothing in a place where truth was known and unchallengeable.

In philosophy classes he had ignored or mocked—depending on his mood— the claims of Jesus. One thing he'd never done was to teach those claims, letting students investigate and draw their own conclusions. No, he'd stood between them and the truth, dealing them his prepackaged suite of conclusions. They wouldn't have to think. He'd done their thinking for them.

William Palatine had argued persuasively that God did not exist.

Bible? Myth.

Creation? Legend.

Incarnation? Fiction.

Resurrection? Invention.

Heaven and hell? Nonexistent.

The adoring looks of students, once ego-fuel, haunted him.

The judgment awaited him, he knew, but his sentence was certain. He saw a great and terrible face, twisted and hideous. The Father of Deception. Palatine cringed in fear at the thought that someone so incalculably evil had used him. He'd served a malevolent being he'd never believed in. He saw other twisted beings now. He'd been deceived by forces beyond his imagination, forces whose existence he'd denied. He caught a terrifying glimpse of hordes of these evil beings with gruesome faces. They'd hated him every moment they'd used him. Now they found pleasure in his misery.

Countless millions of poor followers of Jesus, whom he'd disdained as ignoramuses, had been right. They'd faithfully followed their Master, living lives of grace, truth, and quiet dignity. None of them were here.

How many students who'd been raised to worship Jesus had he led away from the truth? How many, under his teaching, had forever deserted their churches or felt superior to their pathetic parents who'd paid their tuition but were stupid enough to believe the Bible?

"I am Dr. William Palatine." He spoke the words but could not hear them. They evaporated into the nothingness.

He had been William Palatine. Now he was nobody.

On earth he'd rejected God while enjoying His provisions. But it was clear that God's absence meant the absence of all God gives. No God, no good. Forever.

A wave came across him. Some extension of God's presence, like a wind blowing through hell's desert. Was this the same presence that in heaven caused men to be filled with joy and awe and love? Here it was unbearable. God's love felt like wrath, His joy like torture. The consuming fire of God that was purity and goodness and comfort to those who loved the light was searing punishment to those who loved darkness. Including the once-William Palatine.

"Get away from me! Get away!"

The tedium crushed him already, though he'd been here a short time. What would a million years of this do to him? No sleep. No escape. An end without end.

"I had a choice!" he screamed in rage and horror. His scream sounded like a crazed animal, caught in a trap. The terror of hearing his own scream was exceeded only by the horror of his realization:

No one else would hear his cry.

No one would ever rescue him.

Having taken down Suda, I was on a roll. It was time to face off with Karl Baylor.

One-on-one in the conference room, I raked Baylor over the coals about his phony alibi. He refused to explain. Finally, right when I was thinking of how Jack Bauer would find some electrical wires or inject him with truth serum, Tommi Elam walked in the conference room door.

"This is private," I said.

"If it's about Karl's alibi, I have something to say."

"In that case, sit down."

"Don't do it," Karl said, standing up.

"I have no choice," Tommi said.

"If you know something about that night and why your Christian partner would lie to his wife and to me, you can speak up. Or you can be charged with obstructing justice, maybe as an accomplice to murder."

"Karl wasn't the only one who lied," Tommi said. "I did too."

"But…you said you were in bed with Peter that night. You remember Peter…your soul mate?"

"After eleven I wasn't with Peter."

"Tommi, don't—"

"Shut up, Karl," I said. "Okay, Tommi, if you weren't with Peter, where were you?"

She put her face in her hands. "I was with Karl."

48

*"My correspondence is a varied one and I am somewhat upon
my guard against any packages which reach me."*
SHERLOCK HOLMES, *THE ADVENTURE OF THE DYING
DETECTIVE*

TUESDAY, JANUARY 7, 4:00 P.M.

I'D SEEN PLENTY of affairs among cops. But I hadn't seen this one coming.

"I look forward to hearing what your wife thinks about this," I told Baylor. "And Tommi's husband."

"Peter knows all about it," Tommi said.

"He does?"

"I left the house around 10:30. He called me about midnight to see where I was."

"You answered?"

"I told him I was with Karl."

"Well, that was…honest."

"He said he was sorry."

"*He* was sorry?" I asked. "I'd have thought you'd be sorry."

She raised both arms, and her face contorted. "I didn't hit him, you idiot. He hit me!"

I'd never heard Tommi Elam call anyone names. I was her first idiot.

"But…weren't you two having an affair?"

"I'm married to him!"

"Not Peter. Karl."

"An affair? With *Karl*?" Tommi said. "You *are* an idiot. I called Karl because Peter and I had a fight. For the first and only time, he hit me. He'd been fired that day and was drinking and…anyway, I was so upset I ran out of the house and started driving. I didn't know who to turn to. I was sitting in Shari's in a corner booth with a wet washcloth and ice some poor waiter gave me. Karl and Tiffany know Peter and me, and they're always telling me God loves us. I was desperate for help, so I called him."

"Why didn't you tell your wife you went to meet Tommi?" I asked Karl.

"What makes you think I didn't?"

"Well, I…" This didn't seem the time to mention our conversation at WinCo.

"Tiffany doesn't like wakingup when I get called out or come back. As soon as we got up in the morning I told her exactly what happened. We agreed that if anyone saw me leave the hotel, we'd say I got called out on 'police business,' which it was. It was one cop calling another cop, her partner, for help. We wanted to protect Tommi's privacy."

"But," I said to Tommi, "when you gave your alibi, you said—"

"You think I'm going to tell a roomful of detectives my husband hit me?"

"Yeah, it would be a little awkward to say, 'I was sucker punched by my soul mate.'"

Tommi started bawling, and Karl said, "Was that really necessary? You trying to be cruel?"

One moment I'm certain the guy's the world's biggest jerk. Now he's suggesting I'm a bigger one.

He was right.

At 11:30 p.m. I parked my car on Salmon, off 60th, four blocks from the seminary parking lot. I'd told Ray Eagle he didn't need to come, but after the part he'd played in the setup, he couldn't stay away. He approached my passenger door window.

"I just drove by the spot," Ray said, voice sounding like a junior high boy pulling a prank. "I can't believe it's so dark. Two streetlights out, the two closest to the parking lot—who'd have thought it? And there's a chain, but it isn't across the driveway. Perfect."

"Yeah," I said, tossing a recently cut chain link in the backseat, next to my eighteen-inch bolt cutter and pellet gun.

Ray gave me a look. It reminded me of Clarence. And my mother.

The cold night worked in my favor because it was natural to have my coat collar turned up. No trench coat or fedora tonight. I had my old green ski jacket and my blue stocking cap. Ray probably wouldn't have been recognized anyway, but he wore a heavy scarf up to his mouth. We walked on opposite sides of the street, staggered so no one would think we knew each other.

Ray turned south on 58th. I walked Salmon to 57th and headed the block to Madison, leaning on a garage sale cane. I ambled, trying to time it right, looking as nonthreatening as possible, knowing there were observers. I saw three of them spread out at different locations, looking everywhere but at the corner of 57th and Madison, which meant that's what they were interested in. One young woman was talking on a cell, and a harmless looking man carried a bottle in a sack.

At 11:59, just as I hobbled twenty feet north of Madison, a black Cadillac STS rounded the corner, barely visible because two streetlights had inexplicably gone out. The car slowly turned right, then took another right into the unchained drive-way.

I crossed the street and continued south on the sidewalk across from the park-ing lot, where I could just make out the Cadillac, lights out.

Just then another car arrived from the east, turning south, then into the semi-nary parking lot. The silver BMW pulled in, rolling up close to the Cadillac, dimming his lights.

They sat for a minute while I continued to shuffle, peeking back over my shoulder as a curious bystander might. Who'd make the first move? My bet was on the Cadillac's driver. He opened his door and stepped out, too quickly to let the inside light show his face. He walked to the BMW's window, carrying a large enve-lope. The BMW window went down.

Suddenly the place exploded. Strobe lights came from both entries to the drive-way and from the back of the seminary bookstore. Eight well-armed bodies rushed the cars.

"Police! Get out…now!" a huge voice demanded through a megaphone. "You…drop what's in your hand. On the ground!"

The man from the Cadillac dropped the envelope, then dropped to the ground, saying something. No one was listening. The man in the BMW hadn't moved quickly enough. Someone yanked his door open. I heard the stress on the hinge.

"What's going on?" the man asked. "Don't you know who—?"

An officer turned the short older man and pushed him against the BMW. "Hands behind your back." I thought I recognized the cop's voice. Paul Anderson.

Someone handcuffed the tall man facedown on the ground. Neither resisted, so things started to calm down. It was then that Anderson turned around the smaller man and someone said, "Hang on, isn't that…?"

Paul Anderson, a foot from his face, finished the sentence.

"Raylon Berkley? From the *Tribune*?" His voice cracked.

"Let me up!" the man on the ground yelled. "Now!"

When he stood the light fell on his face. They didn't have to ask for his ID.

Fifty feet away, I had the perfect view of a magical moment. So did the award-winning pizza-loving *Tribune* photographer, who'd received an anonymous tip that something momentous would happen at this corner around midnight.

While cops tried to wave her off, she took a dozen photos of Garrison Branch.

The mayor of Portland.

In handcuffs.

49

"Results without causes are much more impressive."
SHERLOCK HOLMES, *THE ADVENTURE OF THE SPECKLED BAND*

WEDNESDAY, JANUARY 8, 12:05 A.M.

FORTY PEOPLE IN PAJAMAS and bathrobes were on their front porches within thirty seconds. It was the Fourth of July six months early.

After some phone calls from the arresting officers, both Raylon Berkley and Mayor Branch were released, with profuse apologies. By the time the situation was resolved, I'd walked around on the other side of the hedge, where I heard the soundtrack. The mayor promised there'd be an investigation. "Whoever was behind this will be held accountable!" Berkley promised that the *Tribune* would expose the blunders of this "so-called police department." Both men swore a lot, which I guess is a way of reclaiming your manhood when you've been emasculated.

There's plenty of injustice in their city, but these two men were not accustomed to being on the receiving end of it.

I had no ax to grind with Mayor Branch. But he and Berkley were the leverage I needed on Chief Lennox. If they were in his pocket before, they weren't now. If push came to shove, somebody might listen if Lennox transferred me to the badlands of Dakota or suspended me or tried to pull a cover-up. After this episode, Lennox's wielding of power would be under close scrutiny. He'd have to think twice before any questionable move, including pulling me off the Palatine case. That's what I wanted. Revenge for Mulch and Lou's Diner was a nice bonus.

Ray and I went to Shari's for a piece of pie. He seemed too jumpy to enjoy it. He'd hung back far enough that he didn't see all the juicy stuff but said even from a block away the lights and sound were spectacular. After Ray and I went our separate ways, about 1:15 a.m., I thought I should head home to Mulch, but I was driving right past Rosie O'Grady's. Halfway through my third beer it was time to visit the restroom, where celebrated Irish sports heroes, most of them rugby players, are featured on the walls. I made it back to my table and resumed my beer. My phone rang.

"What's up, Phillips?"

"Sorry to bug you so late, but I know you're usually up. Hear about the arrest? Raylon Berkley and the mayor. Somebody set them up."

"Bummer. Who ordered the arrest?"

"I hear it was Chief Lennox. But that's not why I called. We need to talk."

"Okeydokey."

"Not at the precinct."

"Okeydokey."

"Are you all right?"

"I'm…okeydokey."

"You're at Rosie O'Grady's, aren't you?"

"How'd you know? Tailin' me?"

"You're drunk."

"Not yet. But I'm workin' on it."

"I'll come by your house in the morning. 8:00?"

"That early?" I looked at my watch. 1:52.

"It's important. Go home and get some sleep."

"I'll finish this one. Then I'm out the door."

"You shouldn't be driving."

"Just had three drinks. Or five."

"See you in the morning. I still don't think you should drive."

"Bye, Mom."

I tried to polish off the beer, but I tipped it onto the table, drenching the left arm of my trench coat. I stood to leave. I don't lose my balance easily, but I stumbled. Needed to get out to fresh air. I walked toward my car, but wasn't seeing right.

I tried my keys in two cars that weren't mine. Needed to sit. Tried another car. It worked. Opened the door and put one arm on the hood, one on the door. All I could do to stand. Made my way into the front seat. Before driving, seemed like I should lay my head on the passenger seat.

"Hey!" Felt something on my shoulder. "I asked if you're all right. Want me to call 911?"

Bright light in my eyes. Beard and mustache, security uniform.

"You need to get out of this here parking lot, mister. Bar's closed. Somebody could mug you and steal your car. You need to go home. I'll get some coffee. Hang on."

I fell back asleep. Next thing I knew I smelled something strange, vaguely familiar. I was aware of my shirt feeling wet. Apparently I'd slopped that beer everywhere. I opened my eyes, and the guard was standing over me with a Styrofoam cup of coffee.

"You need this to drive. Drink it, then head home, okay?"

"Okeydokey."

He walked away, disappearing around the Dumpster behind Rosie O'Grady's. No other cars in the parking lot. Had to get home.

Phone rang at 3:19. Close enough to call it 3:00. I knew what that meant.

"Chandler? Sergeant Seymour. Don't hang up. This is the third time I've called."

"Huh?"

"I have to tell you something."

"Tell me?"

"I need you to understand me."

"Understand?"

"You must have been on a bender, Chandler. Listen, get up now and throw cold water on your face. Hear me? I'll wait for you. That's an order!"

"Yes, sir," I said to Captain Weber of the third armored division in Da Nang. Not sure he heard me since I hadn't seen him for thirty-seven years.

I lowered my throbbing head over the sink and repeatedly slapped my face with cold water. Didn't reach for a towel. Didn't think of that until I got back to my bed and discovered my soaked T-shirt.

"Okay, Captain."

"It's Sergeant Seymour."

"Manny and I aren't the up team again…are we?" Okay, I'm not sure that's what I actually said, but that question was attempting to make it to my tongue.

"It's one of the guys."

"Platoon?"

"Listen to me, Ollie. It's one of the detectives. It's Brandon Phillips."

"Phillips?"

"He's dead."

Sarge went on, talking gibberish. Finally I put down the phone.

I wanted to drop to the bed, but I dragged myself toward the kitchen. Somehow I shuffled to Mr. Coffee.

When I came back, I saw last night's T-shirt, lying beside the bed. It looked strange. I picked it up.

The shirt had a dark four-inch circle on the front. I pulled it to my face and smelled. I choked, pulling it back. I'd first smelled that on clothes in Vietnam. And I'd smelled it on clothes at many murders. But never on my own shirt.

I put on plastic gloves, laid my shirt on the kitchen floor and stared, trying to remember. Finally, three cups later, I went to the utility drawer, took out scissors, and started cutting.

50

*"We balance probabilities and choose the most likely.
It is the scientific use of the imagination."*
SHERLOCK HOLMES, *THE HOUND OF THE BASKERVILLES*

I SHOWED UP at the home of Brandon Phillips two hours after he'd been found.

Cimmatoni and Phillips should have been the up team. But with Phillips the victim, Sergeant Seymour had examined the workload. Manny and I were on Palatine and refused for obvious reasons to turn to detectives for assistance. Ray, Clarence, Paul Anderson, and his partner had been help I could trust. Jack and Noel were still assisting Karl and Tommi on the Frederick case, so Sarge gave the Phillips case to Kim Suda and Chris Doyle. Their last, the Hedstrom murder, was recent but had already dead-ended. I'd never seen a backup like this. And we'd just lost one of our five teams.

"Look what the cat dragged in," Suda said. "What are you doing here?"

"I was in the neighborhood. I think that's what you said when you came out of the closet at my last murder, wasn't it, Kimmy? Of course, I wasn't hiding here when you arrived."

"Where are your gloves?" she asked. "Wouldn't want you to contaminate the scene."

"What time was the murder?" I asked.

"Gunshot heard at 2:36," Doyle said, looking at Phillips. "No murder though. Offed himself."

Dr. Marsh was the ME on duty. Carlton Hatch treats the body like it's the shroud of Turin. Marsh has the deft touch of an airport baggage handler. He flipped Phillips's arms around like a rag doll.

"Apparent suicide," Marsh said.

"Based on what?" I asked.

"Gun in his hand and brains on the floor."

"Made to look like suicide," I said.

"Hence the word *apparent*."

"Where's Sheila?"

"Staying at her sister's," Doyle said. "Apparently she and Phillips had been having problems. If she needs an alibi, she's got one. It's a three-hour drive, and she was with her sister's family all evening."

"I talked with Sheila," Suda said. "She's a mess. Who wouldn't be? Wait. What's this?" Suda pointed at a dark scrap of cloth four feet from the body, two feet to my right.

Doyle bent over it. "Fabric," he said. "Blood soaked. It's been cut."

Suda gestured to one of the CSIs. "You drop this?"

"No," he said, staring at the cloth. "It wasn't there."

"Had to be," Doyle said.

"We've been here two hours," the criminalist said. "We have thirteen evidence bags, marked and ready for the lab. We picked up everything. You telling me we all missed this—including you?"

Suda gave me the evil eye. She wrote on her pad, then took three pictures of the scrap. "Bag it," she said. The criminalist picked it up with tweezers and put it in a plastic bag.

I met Sarge outside his office when he arrived at 7:00 a.m.

"I'm going to need the lab results from the Phillips investigation," I said. "We have to assume he was killed because of what he knew about Palatine. It was no suicide."

"That's a lot to assume."

"You think it's a coincidence he had something to tell me, then suddenly he was killed?"

Sarge shrugged.

"I don't trust Suda and Doyle on this investigation," I said.

"That's funny. They don't trust you on the Palatine investigation."

"Come on. Can you trust a woman hiding in a closet at a murder scene? She breaks into my house and plants illegal bugs. Abuses my dog. Now a detective dies, and she's in charge of the investigation?"

"Look, Suda's in big trouble. After the investigation she'll be suspended, at least. But that doesn't make her the killer. And right now, we're buried in murder cases. We need her. Anyway, remember, she planted the bugs under orders from the chief."

"Even he doesn't have the authority to do that."

"My point is, she wasn't winging it." Sarge shook his head. "What's happening to this department? One of our best has just died, and one of us might have killed him? It's a nightmare."

"I need those lab results as soon as they're done."

Sarge nodded. "I'll give Doyle the lab results on the Palatine case. And I'll tell him you're getting the results on this one."

"But I don't want—"

"The universe isn't about what you want, Chandler. Get used to it."

Phillips's death was too late to make the morning paper, but the arrest at the seminary dominated the front page. Oddly, pictures at the scene didn't include the faces of Berkley and Branch. If anyone else had been in the pictures, their mugs would be right there on page one, no matter how humiliating.

I called Carp's cell, which two days ago replaced Flyin' Pie on my autodial.

"I saw your pictures. Nice. But what happened to the ones with your publisher and the mayor?"

"Don't get me started," she said. "I've been yelling at people all morning, and I've left two voice mails with Berkley. I chose two great photos with Branch and Berkley. They were going in, until Berkley called and nixed them."

"Sounds like censorship," I said. "Funny how journalists don't play by their own rules."

"Stop taking shots at journalists. I'm a journalist. Berkley's an aristocrat."

"Sorry. I heard Berkley yell at you to stop taking pictures. I thought it was pretty cool you didn't stop."

"Of course I didn't stop. I do my job no matter who tells me not to."

"That's my girl."

"Got to go. Couple of heads here I haven't bitten off yet."

I looked at the newspaper again.

The front page featured two pictures of police officers, one of them with a big old guy leaning on a cane in the background. The article quoted Police Chief Lennox, who said a full investigation was being conducted to get to the bottom of the false intelligence that had been given to the police, who had acted in good faith, having every reason to believe a felony was in process in the seminary parking lot. He apologized to his "dear friend," seventy-three-year-old Raylon Berkley, and to his "close friend" Mayor Branch, and vowed that such a thing would never happen again in our great city…blah blah blah.

The article said it was a private meeting between the two. "When asked why they would meet in a seminary parking lot at midnight, both men declined to answer."

It would have been a perfect morning.

If only Brandon Phillips wasn't dead.

And my T-shirt wasn't bloodstained.

THURSDAY, JANUARY 9, 1:30 P.M.

They got a thirty-hour rush on the bloodstains in the Phillips case because the victim was a detective. By crime lab standards this was a jet on afterburners.

"Evidence is in," Sarge said. "I told the lab you'd be there along with Suda."

The criminalist, Kathy Strade, handed Suda and me identical pages at the same
time. It gave the results of fourteen pieces of evidence. Suda scanned them one at
a time, but I turned immediately to number fourteen, then went back to the top.

"That last little scrap we found on the floor?" Suda asked the criminalist.

"It was a freshly cut swatch of white fabric. Soaked with Phillips's blood, like
everything else," said the criminalist.

"How do you suppose it got there, Chandler?"

I shrugged.

"Looked like a part of somebody's T-shirt," Strade said. "It's like it was cut out
and left there deliberately. But that'd be crazy."

"Unless somebody found evidence elsewhere they didn't want to turn in," Suda
said. "By dropping it at the crime scene they'd get the state to test and see whose
blood was on it."

"Who'd do such a thing?" I asked.

"Maybe the person who arrived on the crime scene when there were only thirteen pieces of evidence and suddenly there were fourteen." Considering she'd bugged
my house and drugged my Mulch, her morally superior look wasn't convincing.

I assumed that classic "I'm just a man, so I'm stupid" pose, which usually
works. Kathy Strade seemed to buy it.

I walked out thinking that either somebody was going all-out to frame me, or
I'd done something so unthinkable I'd blocked it out. I'd need to burn my bloodstained T-shirt, with the hole in it, when I got home.

I was knocked out in that car, I told myself. Obviously I hadn't killed Phillips.
If someone was trying to frame me, they'd have left something from me at the
scene. The evidence report showed they hadn't. They were playing with me, showing me they had control.

By the time Clarence and I arrived at the morgue, on Knott Street, the forensic
pathologist, Dr. Robert Jones, had finished undressing, weighing, photographing,
and fingerprinting Brandon Phillips...or what was once Brandon Phillips. The
body had been pulled from the cooler.

I reassured Jones that Clarence was there under authority of the chief, and there
was an e-mail attachment, for heaven's sake. Once Clarence asked him to spell his

name and he sensed his fifteen minutes of fame, all was well. I nodded my approval to Clarence, who'd asked a man named Robert Jones how he spelled it.

Homicide autopsies are done in a special room, designed to limit access and protect evidence. Organs are removed and weighed, injuries photographed, measured, probed, and numbered. I figured this would be a long one, two hours, because when the victim's one of our own, we have to get it right. And when the killer's one of our own, well…

The doctor's phone rang. He pushed his Bluetooth earpiece and chatted with his son in Boston while cutting up a dead man in Portland.

Dr. Jones hit a point of disagreement with his son and paced twenty feet away. Clarence was looking green and miserable. I examined Phillips's right hand, gently moving each finger. I stopped with the index finger. The trigger finger. I wiggled it as Clarence watched.

"Please," Dr. Jones said, abandoning his son in Boston. "Hands off."

"Any suggestion this wasn't a suicide?" I asked.

"Not that I can see."

"Take a close look at that right index finger."

"It seems…unusually angled."

"Like it was broken?" I asked.

"Yes. But…it couldn't be."

"Why not?" Clarence asked.

"Because there's no swelling," I said. I asked the doctor, "But what if it was broken after he was already dead?"

"Then…" Robert Jones, spelled J-o-n-e-s, looked at me, then at Clarence, and said, "there wouldn't be any swelling."

Clarence wrote it down.

"Nice catch," I said to Jones. "Most guys would've missed that."

Jones wrapped it up in Boston, then turned to the microphone suspended over the body. He started speaking, looking at Clarence out of the corner of his eye.

"White male measuring 71 inches in length, weighing 189 pounds. Overall appearance consistent with stated age of 49, though unusually fit. Body cold with complete rigor mortis. No lacerations. All physical damage is to skull and brain. Appears to have been penetrated by a single high-velocity bullet shot from a handgun at close range. Though the bullet passed through and wasn't recovered, the wound is consistent with that of a 9 mm revolver of the sort recovered on the scene next to the body. No other abnormalities…with the exception of—" he looked at Clarence sideways "—an apparently broken index finger." He flipped a switch, shutting off the recorder.

"*Apparently* broken?" I asked.

He reversed the recorder and played "exception of" then stopped and said, "a broken index finger. I surmise, due to lack of swelling, the finger may have been broken postmortem."

"May have been?"

He rewound again and said, "The finger was probably broken postmortem." He stopped it.

"Probably? Why not certainly? Any other explanation?"

He wasn't going to change his report again, not while I was there.

Heading out the door, I turned and said, "Dr. Jones, if you find a case where a freshly broken finger of a live person doesn't swell, would you send it to me? Put it in an e-mail attachment. I'd love to see it."

Clarence and I walked around Lawndale and Chapman parks, beautiful even in winter, especially in the light snowfall. We stopped for coffee near the steps of the Multnomah County Courthouse. We walked an extra thirty feet to escape the pocket of air that smelled of wet cigarette fumes, where jury duty candidates had surfaced to smoke.

"I've been asking myself again what I would do if I were a homicide detective planning a murder in Portland to minimize the chances of me being caught. The answer came to me. Know what it is?"

He didn't.

"Think about it," I said. "The answer has the potential of landing this investigation on the runway."

"I'm still on Brandon Phillips," Clarence said. "If what you said is true, how could his finger break after he was dead?"

"If he were alone, it couldn't. But suppose somebody was trying to wrap his finger around the trigger, and it kept popping out. So he squeezed it in there real tight. Still popped out. So he squeezed it harder. If he was strong and angry or scared enough, adrenaline flowing, he could've snapped the finger. By the way, guns don't normally stay in the hand in a suicide. They drop to the floor, a couple of feet from the body."

I hated myself for not meeting with Phillips in the middle of the night. If I hadn't been drinking my life away at Rosie's, maybe he'd still be alive.

Clarence and I drove the I-205 bridge to Vancouver, Washington, and arrived at Ray Eagle's at 4:00 p.m. I found that red chair that didn't look comfortable but was, and my legs reacquainted themselves with his ottoman.

"I never heard your answer to something you asked me earlier," Clarence said, sinking into Ray's couch. "If you were a homicide detective and were going to kill somebody, how would you make sure you'd get away with it?"

"You answer first," I said to Ray.

"I'd take into account every procedure followed by the other detectives and myself and make sure I didn't do a single thing to give myself away. Obviously, I'd wear gloves and cover my face. I'd have a backup plan in which I could justify my presence even if found at the scene."

"Good answer," I said. "But I've got an even better one. It hit me the other day. If I were going to kill someone in Portland, I'd just wait until my partner and I were the up team. Then I'd commit the murder."

"So you'd be called to the scene," Ray said. "To investigate the same murder you just committed?"

"Right. So now, even if I left a strand of hair or a fingerprint at the murder scene, it's okay, because everybody knows I was there—legitimately. I could even confiscate evidence."

"Like you confiscated the Black Jack wrapper," Clarence said.

"Right. Except I didn't leave that, because I didn't kill the guy. It was planted."

"But if your theory's correct," Clarence said, "doesn't that mean that either you or Manny are the murderers? You were the up team."

"We were on call when the professor was found. But murders aren't investigated in the order they're committed."

"They're not?"

"They're investigated in the order they're discovered. By a fluke, another murder was discovered just before the professor's, the one near Lloyd Center, where the guy shot his wife's boyfriend. The up team got called to that murder instead."

"Jack and Noel," Clarence said. He clenched both my shoulders in his big mitts. "You're saying Jack or Noel killed the professor?"

*"There is a master hand here. It is no case of sawed-off
shotguns and clumsy six-shooters. You can tell an old master
by the sweep of his brush. I can tell a Moriarty when I see
one. This crime is from London, not from America."*
SHERLOCK HOLMES, *THE VALLEY OF FEAR*

FRIDAY, JANUARY 10, 11:30 A.M.

AS I STOOD JAWING with a Fourth Street vendor who cooks the best hot dogs in
Portland, Ray Eagle called.

"You know that seventh phone number I told you was a convenience store?"

"The one in the back of the Bertrand Russell book?" I said. "What about it?"

"Turns out that number's been the store's for nine years. Before that it was out
of commission for a year. But for a fifteen-year period ending ten years ago, guess
whose home number it was."

"Too tired to guess."

"Jack and Linda Glissan's."

No wonder that number rang a bell. Working on the assumption that the professor didn't consider Jack a great dating prospect, that narrowed the field to his
wife, Linda, and his daughter, Melissa, who'd been alive when the Glissans still
had that number.

I hoofed it back to the precinct and entered Sergeant Seymour's office, closing
the door. I told him about the phone number in the professor's book.

"We need to take a closer look at Jack," I said.

He nodded reluctantly.

"He's my friend," I said. "But I have to check him out."

Two hours later I was summoned to Chief Lennox's office.

I hadn't seen the chief since he'd set up the sting that took down those two
notorious felons, Raylon Berkley and Mayor Branch. He'd probably avoided me so
I wouldn't be able to gloat. I had, however, done a great deal of private gloating.

The chief couldn't accuse me of anything without revealing that he'd ordered
illegal bugs in a public establishment. I'd removed them the day after the sting.
Till then, who knows how many private conversations had been recorded at Lou's.
He couldn't expose me without incriminating himself. So he found something
else to jump on me about.

"I'm told you're going after Jack Glissan now."

Two hours and word had already reached him? Sheesh.

"First, Glissan's innocent," he said. "Second, if we had concerns about him, we could retire him early. Or if absolutely necessary, demote him. Put him back on the street."

"Yeah, that would encourage the community," I said. "Assign killers to drive our streets and protect our people."

"We wouldn't tell them. Jack would volunteer. But he's not guilty. Remember innocent until proven guilty? Doesn't that include cops? Jack is supposed to be your friend. If you had evidence, it'd be different."

"There's evidence. I'm continuing to gather it."

"Captain Swiridoff tells me you suspect Palatine was involved with Jack's daughter."

"Possibly. Plus there's the—"

"How could that account for a murder ten years later?"

"Revenge is a dish best served cold."

"That's a cliché," the chief said.

"Now that's the pot calling the kettle black."

"That's a cliché too. You're embarrassing yourself. All you're doing in this investigation is making the department look bad."

"All I'm doing is trying to keep the department from *being* bad. How it looks isn't my concern."

"You admit it!"

Like I'd confessed a murder.

"Your job's on the line, Chandler. Embarrass Jack, and I'll make sure you pay for it."

"You're still threatening me? Don't you get it? You laid the trap at the seminary parking lot based on what Ray Eagle and I said in a booth at Lou's Diner. What other conversations between my buddies and me did you listen in on? And how many other citizens sat in that booth? Can you imagine the scandal? Private citizens illegally recorded at a public establishment. And two of those recorded work for the *Tribune*! I grant you, they were probably evangelizing me—they usually are—but the point is, they're journalists, first amendment junkies, civil liberties freaks, covered under the Bill of Rights, along with car thieves and hit men. They tell the world that cops were eavesdropping…talk about a PR problem. There'd be a media feeding frenzy. After the lawsuit against this department, Lou's could be a 10-million-dollar restaurant."

"You wouldn't."

"One of them saw the bugs. He's eager to know who did it." It seemed better leverage not to mention that Clarence and Jake already knew. "They'll fill pages with this story. Can you imagine someone at Police Headquarters doing this? Zero political savvy. He'd be ruined. The man would have to be an idiot. King of the Idiots."

I went out the door, ticked not just because of his dirty tricks, but because he'd accused me of using clichés.

As I walked out I saw his daughter Jenn's sullen face in that family photo, and I found myself wishing she was more like her friend Tasha, who kept…all her stupid phone photos.

Why hadn't I thought of that before?

"Ever find those pictures with the professor?" I asked Jenn Lennox on the phone.

"Told you I didn't keep them."

"Did you ask your friend Tasha?"

"Why?"

"Because you said Tasha keeps everything. And aren't you always sending photos to her?"

"Oh." Long pause. "So if Tasha has it, do I get the Starbucks card or does she?"

"Both of you get one."

"I'll call you back."

Ten minutes later she called. "Tasha has some pictures at Palatine's. She'll send them to you, once we get the Starbucks cards. Forty dollars each."

"We agreed on thirty, just for you." Finally we settled on twenty-five each. I said, "No cards until I see the pictures."

"No pictures until I see the cards."

I swore an oath as a police officer to surrender the Starbucks cards once I got the pictures. Were it possible to strangle someone over phone lines, I'd be on death row.

Ten minutes later my phone buzzed. I went online to access pictures sent to my account. Surprisingly, the images weren't bad. In two, Palatine's mantel was visible. I sent them on to Carp. She called me back and said I should pay her a visit at the *Trib*.

I was there in twenty minutes.

"These are low resolution pictures, but the photo you're interested in is visible. I've made as many sharpness and contrast corrections as I could. The lighting's not bad. The faces aren't sharp, but not nearly as blurry as they were in those other photos I enlarged."

I looked at the first picture. It was much better. I had the sense that I recognized one of the faces. Then I looked at the silver chain around her neck…a high school graduation present from her mother.

I looked at the last picture. No doubt now who the girl was.

Kendra Chandler. My daughter.

I drove directly to Kendra's real estate office, near Parkrose High. She seemed surprised. I'd pulled into the parking lot before, to watch her through the window and make sure she was all right. One day I took out my compressor and put air in one of her tires. But this was the first time I'd shown my face inside.

"Got a few minutes?" I asked.

"I've got a break coming. We can sit in the staff room."

She introduced me, awkwardly, to a few of her coworkers. I took a good look at the three men, comparing their faces to wanted posters. I asked Kendra a few questions about her Christmas with the other family, pretending I wasn't jealous, then jumped in.

"This picture was on Dr. Palatine's mantel." I handed it to her.

"No way," she said, studying it. "Dad, I'm thirty. This would've been, what, ten years ago?"

"I was surprised to see him with you."

"Well, I happened to be in the picture, but it wasn't me he was interested in."

"The other girl?"

"You do know who that is, don't you?"

"Should I?"

"It's Melissa. Melissa Glissan. You used to work with her dad, remember?"

"I still work with him. I guess I forgot what Melissa looked like."

"Well, she'd bleached her hair blond. Maybe that threw you."

"You didn't tell me you and Melissa were in the professor's class together."

"Why should I? I didn't even remember until I saw this picture. Brings back memories."

"So Melissa knew Palatine."

"She knew him all right."

"Why'd you say it that way?"

"Well…they were just…" Her face turned red. "You know what I said. He liked the pretty girls."

I had two main memories of Melissa. One, a sunny day when she was eight years old, laughing hysterically with Kendra on our Slip 'N Slide. Two, the night I got the phone call, around 3:00 a.m. as I recall, that she'd taken her life.

It made me wonder about my Andrea, and whether she was still alive. It's hard when a man to feels powerless to take care of those he loves.

I asked myself…*Who would remove a photograph of Palatine, Kendra, and Melissa?*

I went back to the precinct and reopened Melissa Glissan's case file. I zeroed in on her roommate at Linfield College, Cherianne Takalo. I put Ray on it, and thirty minutes later he'd traced her down under her married name, in Grosse Point, Michigan. He had her home phone, work, and cell numbers.

"Ray, you scare me," I said.

I put Manny on some background research on Melissa. Anything that might be relevant. He said I was wasting his time. I told him he was paid to waste his time.

I called Cherianne. She hadn't heard the professor was dead.

"Just that name, Dr. Palatine, brings back memories," she said.

"Good ones?"

"No."

"Did you know Melissa was involved with him?"

"She talked about him all the time. He complimented her writing. She really fell for him."

"A crush?"

"She loved him. She'd read his little love notes and his sappy poetry. She showed me some. He never signed them. I wondered if he was covering his tracks so he could deny he sent them. I never met the guy, but I thought it was a big mistake getting involved with a professor."

"You knew about the drugs?"

"She only had two classes at PSU, the rest were at Linfield. She was back in our room every night. She was devastated when the professor told her not to call him anymore. She started smoking pot. I asked her not to do it in our room. I warned her it was messing her up. But that didn't help her, so she started snorting coke. She got more depressed and was sleeping more and more. Stopped doing her homework. Stopped caring."

"This was all a backlash to the professor rejecting her?"

"Melissa thought he was going to marry her. He turned out to be a jerk. I told her to just walk away. I mean, she had a decent boyfriend her own age."

"Melissa had a boyfriend?"

"She broke up with him for the professor. But he still loved her."

"What was his name?'

"It's been a long time. Ten years. Um…David? No, wait. Donald. I don't remember his last name. I only saw him twice. I think he stayed at her parents' house when he was in town."

"In town? Where did he live?"

"In the South, maybe? I remember he'd had a long flight. Wait…I remember now. It was weird. He wouldn't say where he was from. And when I asked Melissa, she wouldn't tell me. Said something about him having family problems and maybe he was going to make a break from them and start a new life."

"What was he like?"

"Nice. Maybe insecure."

"You said you saw him twice. When was the second time?"

"A few days before Melissa died."

"He was in Portland?"

"Yeah. Melissa had broken it off with him over the phone, I think. He flew in to talk her out of it. He didn't want to lose her."

"He knew there was another guy?"

"She tried not to tell him. I'm afraid I was the one who let it out."

"He knew it was the professor?"

"Melissa had told him. I felt terrible."

"How long were Donald and Melissa together?"

"They were on and off a couple of years. They got serious the summer before our junior year. When we came back to the dorm in September, she talked a lot about him. He came for a few weeks that summer and stayed at Melissa's parents' house."

"What's Donald doing now?"

"No clue. I knew Melissa's parents, and I really liked them. We kept in touch the first year after Melissa died, but I transferred to Michigan State. Just couldn't come back after my roommate died, you know? Could you do me a favor, Mr. Chandler? Do you have a photo of Melissa's parents?"

"Probably."

"Would you mind sending me one? I do scrapbooks, and I've got pictures of Melissa. But I'd like a picture of her parents. They were always nice to me."

"I could probably find something."

Cherianne gave me her address. I gave her my number. If Sharon were around, she'd know right where to look in our albums for a photo of Jack and Linda. I'd probably send her a copy of the detectives and spouses group photo, but at least she'd have Melissa's parents. Not to mention the best photo of Sharon and me. Carp would make me a copy.

Meanwhile, I shifted gears to Donald.

Where was he? And why hadn't the police reports or anyone else—especially Jack and Linda—mentioned him?

Manny chose that moment to call. "Doing the background check you wanted on Melissa Glissan."

"You got something?"

"Most of it's irrelevant, like I told you it'd be."

"But you got something, didn't you, or you wouldn't have called."

"Turns out she was an insulin-dependent diabetic."

I looked over Melissa's death report again. Toxicology reported drug use—methamphetamine and some indications she'd also snorted coke. The hanging had been the cause of death. But without the drugs would she have hung herself? Naturally her parents didn't think so. They'd said she'd never been on drugs until she'd recently become depressed.

I checked statistics. There's a much higher rate of suicide by hanging among men than women. Still, it happens.

I was just about to close Melissa's file when my eyes fell on a red scribble. It was probably just the slip of a pen, but it was enough to draw my attention to something else: the date. The report had been filed on November 21. Melissa's date of death was November 20.

I looked again at the estimated time of death. A neighbor had heard a noise, which in retrospect was probably when she hung herself. She'd died just after 11:35 p.m.

Melissa Glissan died exactly ten years before the professor.

Not just ten years to the day, but to the hour.

Likely, to the minute.

*"There are limits, you see, to our friend's intelligence.
It would have been a coup-mattre had he deduced
what I would deduce and acted accordingly."*
SHERLOCK HOLMES, *THE FINAL PROBLEM*

FRIDAY, JANUARY 10, 3:00 P.M.

I DROPPED BY JACK'S DESK, and we small talked. He mentioned Linda would be out all night at a get-together with old college roommates in Corvallis, ninety minutes away. He and Noel were going to a Winterhawks game after dinner.

Jack left at 4:30. I called Carp and asked if I could borrow her car. When I came by, I also asked if she could doctor up a couple photos for me. When I showed her what I wanted, she smiled. But didn't ask questions. I like that.

At 6:25 p.m. I sat in Carp's silver Subaru Impreza, across the street from the Nine Daggers Tavern near 39th and Belmont. My Taurus slicktop wouldn't stick out to most people, but cops notice cars. Carp's car was cleaner than most operating rooms, and since she'd seen the archaeological dig in my car, she asked me not to eat in it. Where are you supposed to eat dinner if not in a car? But I promised.

With the help of my ProStaff binoculars, I watched Jack and Noel eat dinner, looking like father and son. It took me back to when Jack was my partner, and we'd come weekly to the Nine Daggers. We had a ritual. After arresting a killer, one month later we'd down a bottle of wine, our toast to taking out the bad guy. In a few cases we celebrated annually. I still remembered Harvey Blanda, April 11, and Theda Pranke, July 27.

Jack always made it interesting. He made it seem like we were doing something that mattered. If Sharon were still alive, we'd be with Jack and Linda every week, like the old days.

I felt like a louse tailing Jack. I didn't know what I was looking for.

After dinner they got in Jack's car and drove away, I assumed to the hockey game. I headed the other direction.

When I broke into Jack Glissan's house that night, it felt creepy. I'd remembered that Jack and Linda had left Melissa's room as it was. Some visit a gravesite. Some bring the ashes into their home. They kept the room as it was. A shrine. Every day it reminded them of Melissa's life…and death.

Sharon kept Chad's favorite little gray sweatpants and white muscle shirt. Every time I saw it, it cut my heart. It also made me think about the guy who rear-ended us. If Jack and Linda blamed anyone for Melissa's death, her room might have kept that anger alive.

I shone my flashlight, close range, around Melissa's room. I recalled Jack and I coming in there with her and Kendra when they were grade-schoolers. The only time I remembered being in Melissa's room after her death was with Sharon. Linda showed us around, like a curator, making speeches about various items in the room. I thought there had been a journal or a diary and maybe a photo album.

In Melissa's top dresser drawer, I found her scrapbook. What interested me most were the last three months of her junior year of college, preceding her suicide. Three photos had been removed. Why?

I snuck into Jack's office. I went through his desk drawers, checking files with the flashlight. In the lower right drawer I found one called "Melissa's Case."

I opened it, disappointed to see only two photos, glossies that reflected too much of the flashlight. I went into the bathroom, closed the door, and turned on the light. One picture was of a man holding a hardbound book, appearing to read from it. The book was red. On the cover I saw several words, one of them "Poems."

The man was Professor William Palatine.

The other picture was of the professor with two young women. I knew instantly I'd seen it, or rather a low-quality replica of it, in Carp's office. This photo had been visible on the fireplace mantel, in the photo that cost me fifty Starbucks.

It was a clear photograph of Melissa Glissan and Kendra Chandler, but the left third of the photo had been cut off. The professor was gone.

I heard a noise. In a microsecond I switched off the light.

I stood still in the darkness, hoping no one had seen the light in the door crack. I thought of crawling into the bathtub and hiding behind the shower curtain, but I didn't want to risk the noise. Suddenly the door flew open and the light streamed on.

I was looking down the barrel of a gun.

"Who are you?" he asked.

"Detective Ollie Chandler," I said. "Jack's friend. Who are you?"

"Jack's brother."

"Warren?"

We'd met two or three times, but it had been years.

"What are you doing here?" he asked, voice edgy.

"Want to see my ID?" I said. Never reach for your pocket without permission when a nervous man is pointing a gun at your face.

"I remember," he said. "You're the dopey one."

It's good to be remembered.

"That's me."

If I was Dopey, he was Grumpy. I was hoping the other dwarves weren't with him.

"Could you lower the gun, please?"

"I asked what you're doing here."

"I have a good reason," I said. "I'll explain. What are *you* doing here?"

"Visiting from Redding. Linda's gone, and Jack's at a hockey game. I hate hockey. Had dinner with an old friend; now I'm back. What's your story?"

"We're planning a party to honor Jack for forty years on the detective force," I said, holding up three pictures.

"You stealing from Jack?"

"Not stealing. Planting." I handed him the pictures. "It's a prank. Fake photos of him arresting celebrities. Look here—he's with Lucille Ball. This one's with Frank Sinatra. See we're rubbing it in that he's been around long enough to have dealt with those people. Funny, huh? We're all going to come back to his office, and I'll pull out this stack that I was just going to hide up there in his closet. I'm a prankster. You know, the dopey one. I was just planting them when I heard a noise. Afraid it was Jack, so I hid in the bathroom. You can't let Jack know, okay? It's a surprise."

"When's the party?"

"Soon. Real soon. I'd love to invite you, but it's just the detectives. After the party's over, he'll tell you all about it. I'm not sure even Linda knows. One of the wives is pulling it off, maybe."

He put down his gun, looking at the photos. He smiled. "Where'd you get these made?"

"My friend's a professional photographer. She does miracles with Photoshop."

"There had to be a better way to do this than breaking in," Grumpy said.

"I figured if anybody caught me, it'd be Jack. We'd get a good laugh out of it."

"If he didn't shoot you first," Warren said. "You're lucky I know how to handle a gun."

We moved down the hall. "Just let me put the pictures up here." I slid them under an old Kodak slide tray on the upper closet shelf. "All right, I'm going now. Good thing I'm a cop and you know I'm his friend, huh? Don't say anything until after his party, okay?"

He nodded like an insider. "Can you get me a copy of the one with Jack and Frank Sinatra?"

"Sure," I said.

As we walked to the front door, I pointed to a family photo, Jack and Linda and Melissa. "Must be tough to lose a child like that."

"Yeah," he said, as he opened the door and stepped out behind me.

His voice was ice-cold. Under the porch light, what I saw on his face wasn't grief or hurt. It was rage.

When I got to the car, I pulled out of my coat pocket the photograph of Melissa and Kendra and put it under the flashlight.

I put myself in Jack's place. If Kendra had committed suicide and I had a few miscellaneous pictures, what would I do with them? Why put it in a file? And if I did, I wouldn't call it "Kendra's Case." Because "case" is a murder I'm investigating.

Was that what "Melissa's Case" meant to Jack? If so, why did he have this picture of Melissa and Kendra? And why was the professor cut out? Was this a huge coincidence—or was this the actual photo taken from the crime scene and now defaced? If so, did that mean Jack was the murderer?

On my way home I called Carp. "Thanks for the pictures of Jack and the celebrities. Thought it wouldn't be necessary, but they saved my bacon."

"Speaking of bacon," she said, "there's a new place on Third and Ash called McGraw's Outlaw Barbecue. Supposedly they have killer ribs wrapped in bacon. Meet me there for lunch tomorrow, 11:45?"

"Sure," I said.

What a woman.

I called Tommi and asked if she might put together a party for Jack for his years of service. I suggested she talk to Linda and see if it could be at Jack's so we could see his memorabilia.

"You're kidding me, right?" Tommi said. "Didn't you read the e-mails?"

"I'm not always good with e-mails. Especially attachments."

She laughed. "Sarge felt bad about not having a detectives New Year's party with everything that's happened. Only a few of us were at the chief's. With Brandon's death, they decided to honor him. It's not exactly a party, obviously, but it's a get-together. And it's at Jack and Linda's tomorrow night! You knew that, right? You're just kidding me. Anyway, I'm sure we could honor Jack too. That's a great idea."

"Should have read my e-mail. Could have helped in a conversation I had twenty minutes ago."

"Hey, Ollie? I think it's sweet that you're being so sensitive to Jack. How many men would be thoughtful enough to suggest we all get together and honor him like that?"

"Sometimes you women underestimate us men. We're a lot more sensitive than you give us credit for."

"You're right," Tommi said. "I really owe you an apology."

"It is a question of cubic capacity.
A man with so large a brain must have something in it."
SHERLOCK HOLMES, *THE ADVENTURE OF THE BLUE*
CARBUNCLE

SATURDAY, JANUARY 11, 7:00 P.M.

IN LIGHT OF BRANDON'S DEATH and Jack being honored, Chief Lennox came to the get-together.

Well, whoop-de-do.

Lennox invited Clarence, hoping he'd put a good spin on the camaraderie of the detectives in this tragic time. The chief came prepared, makeup and all.

We all dressed up, rare for this group. I wore my old blue sport coat. Sharon hated that coat, which was perfect because she never nagged me to wear it.

I wasn't going to ruin Jack's party. He'd served honorably forty years. Until he'd murdered a man. Apparently more than one. Including Phillips.

"As you know," Sarge said, "this gathering hasn't been on the calendar long. With Brandon's death, we considered canceling it. But it seemed like we needed another chance to connect. Brandon's funeral's Monday, and we'll honor him there, but we could…think about him now.

"Brandon was a fine cop. An outstanding detective. And a good man. We already miss him. Let's bow our heads in silence a minute, in tribute to our comrade—and to our commitment to find his killer."

That minute of silence felt like five. After some told stories about Phillips, we switched gears to honor the living, Jack Glissan, for forty years of service.

Captain Swiridoff said, "Brandon Phillips would have been the first to join us in tribute to a man he deeply respected, Jack Glissan."

Those words hit me like a harpoon through a lung.

He presented a trophy, a pretty cool-looking one. It was a pewter Sherlock Holmes, with a deerstalker cap and a drop-stem pipe.

Lieutenant Nicks said, "Jack Glissan's the finest detective I've ever known." After a long pause he added, "present company excepted." There were a few laughs.

I noticed Chief Lennox looking down through his reading glasses at notes, mouthing words.

Sarge said, "Anybody got some stories about Jack?"

Tommi told a funny stakeout story about working with Jack as a first-year detective. They even got Cimma to tell a story where Jack rescued him out of a sewer.

"Jack's been a partner and a friend, like family to me," Noel said.

Tommi teared up and Noel teared up and a couple of us made fun of him, as we men like to do to help get us through tender moments.

Abruptly, the chief strode across the front of the room and turned to address us, like he was Patton and we were his army.

"In the toughest of times, Jack Glissan has been a model Portland detective. He's a man of integrity. A champion of justice. He's a role model. He's the face not only of this department, but of our Portland Police."

Clarence was writing down every word. I wondered if the words were forming themselves into a noose, since Lennox would be quoted on the front page when Jack Glissan went down.

"When he retires, his loss will be deeply felt. I hope we'll have him several more years at least." The chief hit stride saying, "Jack Glissan is as good as gold. He does his job rain or shine. He pulls out the stops in his defense of justice. He's fit as a fiddle…"

"Hard as nails," Suda whispered.

"A force to be reckoned with," I muttered.

"White as a ghost," Clarence said.

"Up a creek without a paddle," I said, my double meaning unknown.

"He whispers sweet nothings in my ear."

I turned. It was Linda Glissan, two drinks in hand, headed back to Jack.

"Sorry," I said.

"We're on the same page," Linda said, smiling. "Jack and I are going to get some laughs out of this."

The chief droned on. "These have been the times that try men's souls. The eye of accusation has been turned upon this detective department. This is the price we pay for working on the front lines. I'm confident the reputation of this detective department, and of the Portland Police, will come out unscathed. And we can salute Jack Glissan as a man we're all proud to have represent us."

He spoke as if to thousands, as in a capitol rotunda, way too loud and emphatic for a living room. Applause was polite but restrained.

Sarge stood. "Before we eat, any more tributes to Jack?"

Eyes fell on me.

"Jack's been a great detective," I said. "I consider myself privileged to have been his friend."

"There's plenty to eat," Linda said, saving me. "The department paid for the food and drinks, so make yourselves at home. And fill your pockets when you leave."

While Jack was pumping hands, I took my drink and sat in the back hallway, leaning against the wall. I looked at the doorway to Jack's office. He used to have foosball in there. We'd spent hours battling while Linda and Sharon talked in the living room.

I considered whether to pull out those pictures of him arresting Lucille Ball and Frank Sinatra. No. It was pointless now.

A familiar voice said, "I noticed your wording. Jack's *been* a great detective. I consider myself privileged to *have been* his friend."

"I do," I said, looking up at Jack.

"But you didn't say 'I consider myself privileged to *be* his friend.'"

He had a wineglass in his hand.

"Special occasion," he said. "I told them to take every ounce of it out of the house when the party's over so Linda doesn't have to look at it." He took a gulp. "How's the investigation?"

"Now's not the time. It's a party. We're honoring you."

"May as well just say it, old buddy."

"Okay. I know the truth."

"What truth?"

"About Melissa. And Palatine. And what you did."

I pulled a replica of the sliced picture of Melissa and Kendra from my sport coat pocket and showed it to Jack. He stared at it, nodding. His face turned stormy for a moment. Then his eyes got wet.

"Know what it's like to lose your child? Sorry. I know you do. But Melissa was my only child. My little girl. At least you still have Kendra. And Andrea maybe. Every day I see Melissa's face, the color of eggplant, hanging there. I see the rope around her neck. Knowing what I knew about the professor, what would you have done?"

"I understand why it bothered you to see your daughter's picture on his mantel," I said. "I can see why you'd want to remove it. But why didn't you destroy it? You knew I was looking for it."

"Ever try to destroy your daughter's picture?"

"No."

"I didn't expect you to break into my house and steal it. Not even a warrant? We used to be friends."

"Weren't you the one who always said, 'Follow the evidence'?"

"My mistake," he said, mustering a faint smile.

"It looks like a few different fingerprints on the photo. I turned it in. Yeah, even without a warrant. This is a copy. I'm guessing we've got your prints and some of the professor's. Not like you to slip up."

He shrugged. "You do things differently when it's your daughter. Maybe part of you knows you're wrong, and you need to give fate a fair chance of catching you."

"You believe in fate?"

"I don't believe in anything. Not since Melissa died. There's no justice. There's just us."

It sounded chilling when Jack said it.

I turned to him. "Do I have to build the case, or will you admit you killed him?"

He looked like a three-legged rat in a gallon of motor oil.

"What about your alibi?" I asked. "I can see Linda lying to protect you. But Phillips? Why?"

"Phillips didn't lie for me. I lied for him."

"You lost me."

"Phillips begged me to give him an alibi."

"You're saying…he killed the professor?"

"He asked me what I'd been doing that night. I told him I was home with Linda. He was with another woman. Cheating on Sheila. He'd told her he was out working on a case. His alibi for the Palatine murder was the other woman. But he couldn't say that or Sheila would find him out. He asked if I'd say he was with me and Linda."

"So Phillips thought you were lying to give him an alibi…when he was providing one for you."

"I had Linda. He thought I was doing him this big favor." Jack shook his head and sighed.

"And then…Phillips grew a conscience? You knew he was going to tell me he'd lied? Which meant you'd lied. That's why you killed him?"

"You've got it all figured out, don't you?" he said lifelessly. "Don't be hard on Linda. She didn't know what I'd done. She goes to bed at ten, out like a light. I stay up till one. She lied about coming downstairs at 11:30 because I asked her to protect Phillips. I never told her why. Sheila's her friend."

I nodded, not feeling the usual adrenaline rush at cornering a killer.

"Have you thought about the irony that Kendra's in that picture with Melissa?" Jack asked. "We were friends then. They were friends. It could've been your daughter. What if the professor had seduced Kendra? What if she'd taken her life?"

"Then I'd have beaten the livin' tar out of him. And if I killed him, you'd be coming after me."

"Maybe I would," Jack said.

"But killing Phillips? I thought I knew you better than that."

"It's been a long time since you knew me, Ollie. When a man takes your daughter away, you can't get past it. Some sins can't be forgiven."

"It's been ten years."

"It's been simmering ten years. Finally it boiled over."

"But he didn't actually kill her."

"Sure he did. He seduced her; then he moved on and rejected her. She couldn't get over him, couldn't deal with the shame. She started taking drugs to numb the pain. Can you imagine that?"

"Yeah. I can."

"Finally she shut everybody out and killed herself. Her roommate knew about Palatine. I called around at the college assuming we could at least get him fired. I filed a complaint. They looked into it, said he denied it. No proof. No justice."

"Frederick, Hedstrom, and Phillips didn't hurt Melissa."

Jack stared into the hallway's dark shadows.

"Why play games at the crime scene?"

He slid down beside me, sitting on the floor. Our shoulders touched.

"It all meant something. The ink—love letters he wrote her. The noose—the way she killed herself. The insulin—her condition that gave her mood swings, made her more susceptible to depression."

"What triggered it? The ten-year anniversary of her death?"

"It was the *Tribune*."

"What do you mean?"

"Five or six months ago, there's this article about the professor getting an award—Teacher of the Year. There's a picture with two starry-eyed girls, students. One of them was looking at him, and I just got the feeling she was about to be another conquest, like Melissa. I couldn't handle it. Something snapped. I thought, *This guy deserves the death penalty for what he did to my daughter. And he's messing with other guys' daughters?* And he's not just getting away with it. He's getting awards. But what put me over is that this article came out on Melissa's birthday."

"June 12," I said, remembering the conversation with Carp.

"It was that picture in the *Trib* that made me want to go after him. If not for him, she'd still be alive. If not for the *Trib*, he'd still be alive. I realized the tenth anniversary of her death was only five months away. I decided to wait."

"But if the date was preset, that means you only had a one in five chance of investigating the case yourself."

"I figured if we got the case, it was destiny saying I'd get away with it. If one of the other four teams got it, I'd see what happened. I'd make it a fair fight. You got the call instead of us. Ironic since the professor died first. If someone had called 911 within an hour, or the second victim had been stabbed instead of shot and not discovered until later, Palatine would have been found first, and I'd have investigated the case. Piece of cake."

I stared at my old friend. Something he'd said kept going through my mind. *Some sins can't be forgiven.*

"I need to talk to Linda," Jack said.

"Did Noel know about it?"

"Noel? I'd never drag that boy into it. I made sure he knew nothing. This was between me and the professor. Noel's young. He's got a life in front of him. I talk to Noel about nearly everything, but never Melissa. That was private. Between me and Linda. Between me and...Palatine."

Jack picked up a drink he'd set aside. He extended his arm as if to make a toast to someone invisible.

"You're going to arrest me," he said.

"Yeah."

"Can we wait until after the party?"

I nodded. "I'm sorry, Jack."

"I know." He put his hand on my knee.

We leaned against the wall next to each other, me and my old buddy, like two little boys figuring out what to do on a rainy day. The best partner I'd ever had. Why couldn't it have been Cimmatoni or Baylor or Suda...any of them? Why did it have to be Jack?

"Tell Noel I'm sorry," Jack said. "He'll feel...left out. He'd follow me to Mars. But I didn't want him to."

"What are you guys doing on the floor?" Linda leaned down and kissed Jack.

"We need to talk," Jack said, standing.

"Slip away during the party? Sounds romantic."

"In my office."

"But...we have guests."

He took Linda's hand and led her into his office. For twenty-seven minutes I watched the door, warding off people who periodically came asking, "Where's the man of honor? Where's Linda? We're low on hors d'oeuvres."

Finally Linda walked alone out of Jack's office. She looked at me, eyes pleading. "Is it true?"

I nodded.

Just that moment Tommi came around the corner and said, "Linda, I hope you don't mind. I got out some more drinks and deli rolls and chips. You okay?"

Linda nodded, wiping her eyes. They rejoined the party.

I didn't see Jack, but the door to his office closed. I walked out and got another drink. I sat in the far corner of the living room, by myself. I turned off the lamp next to me. Karl Baylor came over to cheer me up, saying something about what a great day God had made.

Three minutes later came the explosion. The sound of a high-velocity hand-gun.

Ten pistols were drawn simultaneously. Mine wasn't one of them.

Six cops rushed down the hallway, a raging flood of law-enforcement adrenaline, into Jack's office.

I stayed seated in the dark, near the grand piano, where I turned my eyes away from the motionless profile of Linda Glissan, hanging on to a plate of vegetables and dip. Before a word came from the bedroom, while there was still only the silence of disbelief, the plate slipped out of her hands and crashed on the kitchen floor, shrapnel flying everywhere.

"I put myself in the man's place, and, having first gauged his intelligence, I try to imagine how I should myself have proceeded under the same circumstances."
SHERLOCK HOLMES, *THE ADVENTURE OF THE MUSGRAVE RITUAL*

WEDNESDAY, JANUARY 15, 2:00 P.M.

I STOOD AWKWARDLY at Jack Glissan's wake, at his sister's house, eating but tasting nothing.

The four days since Jack's suicide had been a blur of trauma, shock, and remembrance. Brandon Phillips had died Wednesday, Jack Saturday. Brandon's service had been Monday, Jack's two days later. Counting Carly's, it had been my third funeral in two weeks. The Grim Reaper was getting more than his share of people I knew. I wondered if I'd be next.

I stepped out on the back porch, wishing I smoked.

Linda walked up next to me. "He was a good man."

"I know," I said, mostly believing it.

"After I left his office, did you think he might take his life?"

"No," I lied.

"I can't believe he did this to me. Not after Melissa's suicide. He didn't just kill himself. He killed me. I'm almost as angry as I'm sad."

I'd walked away from Jack's office thinking of him, not her. I knew now I'd done her wrong. Jake and Clarence would say Jack should have faced the consequences of his sin, repented, turned to God. Maybe that would have happened to him in prison.

"He loved you," I said. "He probably thought he'd save you the agony of newspapers, trial, imprisonment."

"You think I'd rather be spared that than have him alive?"

"No."

"He wasn't thinking of me."

"He loved you."

"Would you have done that to Sharon?"

"I don't know. In the same situation? Maybe."

"Then you're as selfish as Jack was."

"I'd try to figure out how to spare Sharon the most grief. Maybe I'd make the wrong choice."

"Who else knows Jack killed that professor?"

"We felt like we could sit on it till the funeral, to do more fact-checking. We didn't want anything to cast a shadow on Jack's memory. For now. Sarge sat down with the lieutenant and captain. I'm sure the chief knows."

"You could have let Jack go."

"If things were reversed, you think Jack would have let me go?"

"No."

"Would you have advised him to?"

"Maybe not. But I can still hate you for it."

"I hate me for it. Why shouldn't you?"

I'm not a hugger, but Linda is. I felt I should take a step toward her. I did. She turned and walked away, like a robot, where the parts work but it's all stiff, as if there's no flesh, nothing human.

Some sins can't be forgiven, Jack said.

If that was true, I'd committed at least one of them.

I stayed on the wake's fringes. I was in a hallway without a bathroom, so it was low traffic. I wanted to leave but was putting in my time.

Someone stopped and looked up the hallway at me. Noel. I'd managed to stay away from him that night at Jack's. We hadn't been alone since.

He approached, his eyes red and tired. "What did you say to him?"

"I'm sorry, Noel."

He pushed me, then came at me and landed one fist on my chest, then another and another. I stood there, taking it, hoping it counted for penance. But his blows weren't that heavy. He quietly ran out of steam, then put his arms around me. He sobbed. His hug lasted five seconds. I was not born to be a man-hugger.

"I don't believe it," Noel said. "Jack wouldn't kill himself. And he would never kill anybody else."

"He admitted he did."

"But...how could he keep it from me?"

It was unthinkable to Noel that Jack could murder somebody. But it was even more unthinkable that he could leave Noel out of it if he did. I wondered what he would have done had Jack asked him. Kill the professor along with him?

"Phillips was his alibi," Noel said. "Why would Phillips lie? I don't get it."

"Wouldn't you lie if Jack asked you to?"

"Probably. But...why did he ask Phillips instead of me?"

"Because he cared more about you than Phillips," I said, choosing not to correct the details. "He told me he wouldn't do anything to hurt you."

"He could've told me."

"He didn't want you to be an accessory to murder." I sipped more Irish whiskey, which I don't even like.

"Why didn't he talk to me before he killed himself?"

"Maybe he didn't want to face you after what he did. He told me to let you know how sorry he was."

"He said that?"

"Yeah."

"Jack was no killer."

"He confessed it."

"Why should I believe you?"

"Remember when you and Jack came to the professor's house? You noticed a picture missing from the mantel?"

He nodded. "It looked fishy."

"I found it at Jack's house. It was a photo of the professor and Jack's daughter. We enlarged a picture in which that same photo was visible on the mantel."

"But…maybe Jack had his own print of the same picture."

"Got a rush on the fingerprints. The professor's prints are on the one at Jack's. Perfect wear marks on the photo matching Palatine's frame. No doubt."

"Theft isn't the same as murder."

"Come on, Noel. It places Jack at the crime scene."

"We were at the scene the next morning. *You* called Jack and asked us to come."

"You're saying he could have stolen the picture then?"

"Why not? He sees his daughter's picture and grabs it, then takes it home and cuts out the professor."

"He *admitted* to me he killed Palatine."

"You have a signed confession? Maybe you want to cover up for somebody. And Jack killed a *cop* too? No!"

"Then why did he take his life, Noel?"

He swallowed hard. "That's what I keep asking myself."

"He'd go to prison for the rest of his life. Two homicides. Three if he pushed Frederick at the apartment. Four if he killed Hedstrom."

"You believe Jack was a homicidal maniac?"

"Well…when a guy confesses and then offs himself, it's pretty convincing."

He glared at me. I raised my hands. "Sorry."

Suddenly I had Gumby legs. I slunk to the floor, back against the wall, just as I'd done at Jack's. Noel paced.

"Did he talk to you much about his daughter?" I asked.

"Melissa? One day, last summer I think, he was quiet and moody all day. He yelled at me. Then apologized. Turns out it was his daughter's birthday. Jack was ripped up about it."

I looked down the hall and caught a glimpse of Suda and Doyle. My instinct kicked in.

"Jack ever say anything about Kim Suda?"

"Why?"

"Did he?"

Noel blew out air. "Six months ago Tommi kept saying I should ask Suda out. This was before she and Chris were dating…or whatever. Anyway, I mention it to Jack and he says, 'Stay away from Kim Suda.' I ask him why. Jack says he didn't trust her, and I should just stay away. Wouldn't tell me why."

"Any guesses?"

Noel shook his head, eyes dazed, looking like one of Peter Pan's lost boys.

FRIDAY, JANUARY 17, 10:00 A.M.

Two days after Jack's funeral, I was trying to tie up loose ends. They weren't tying. Jack had killed the professor. But three innocent people, including Phillips? I couldn't buy it any more than Noel could.

I went over it again and again. Had Phillips killed the others, and Jack executed him for his crimes? But why would Phillips do it?

A thought surfaced in the gray cells. Had Jack given Phillips an alibi for a murder Phillips really committed? He'd confessed to an affair and wanted an alibi. But Jack wouldn't have asked for proof he'd been with a woman that night, would he?

Or could Phillips have been with Jack, not in the Glissan home, but at the professor's? Could they have committed the murder together?

I didn't want to face Linda Glissan again. But I had to.

The woman answering the door at Linda's looked like her skinny cousin, ten years older. But it was Linda. She'd shrunk. In just two days, she looked hollow, like a discount liposuctionist had vacuumed away her flesh, especially in her face and shoulders.

She said nothing. I sat on the couch. She didn't offer me coffee. This was Linda's ghost.

"How much did you know, Linda? About Jack and the professor?"

"Before it happened?"

I nodded.

"Jack told me I shouldn't talk about that."

She looked like she might crumble if I pressed her. I couldn't. Not now.

"Did Noel know anything?"

"Jack was protective. He would've kept Noel out of it. Don't know what Noel's going to do without him. Don't know what I'm going to do."

"I know you feel I didn't handle things well with Jack. You're probably right. But if Jack didn't kill Phillips and the others, we need to know who did. If you think of anything, would you call me?"

She said nothing. Maybe this time she'd hug me. When it was clear she wouldn't, I considered putting my arm around her. I've invested many hours at the firing range. But nobody taught me how to comfort. Skeptics aren't built to comfort.

I said an awkward good-bye, leaving Linda to her tears.

"There's so much confusion and deception there," Carly said. "Why can't they see things as they really are?"

"For the same reason that so often, when you lived there, you didn't," the Carpenter said. "There's a veil of blindness over that dark world. It goes far deeper than you realized."

"It's insanity," she said.

"They long for light, but hate it because it hurts their eyes. They prefer the comfort of darkness to the pain of sight."

Carly walked beside the Carpenter till they came to the portals, where both humans and angels stood looking at the Shadowlands.

"They complain about evil and suffering," the Carpenter said, "yet commit acts of evil and inflict suffering on others and on themselves. They ignore My warnings, then wonder why I permit what they choose."

"I'm amazed at Your patience, Lord."

"Earth under the curse is about to end. The day of judgment, and of deliverance, draws near. Justice comes as surely as sunrise—the question is which of them will be ready for it."

FRIDAY, JANUARY 17, 2:00 P.M.

As I stepped out of the car by the Nine Darts Tavern, my *24* control room phone rang.

"It's Linda. We need to talk."

"Thought we just did."

"Can you come by tonight? Around seven?"

"I can. But the last person who said they needed to talk to me was Brandon

Phillips. He died before we talked. It would have been nice if he'd told me what was on his mind when he called. Can you give me a hint?"

"Be here at seven."

"Between now and then, don't answer the door, okay?"

I sauntered up to the Nine Darts, walked to the bar for the first time in fifteen years, and showed my badge to the extra-large guy in the medium T-shirt. I figured him for the owner because no employee could get away with looking so sloppy. He seemed unimpressed by my badge.

"I'm here to ask you about two cops, regulars. Jack Glissan and Noel Barrows." I described them. "Sometimes they sit in that booth." I pointed. "You may have heard. Jack's dead."

"Offed himself," the guy said, a hint of regret at lost revenues. "What you want?"

"I need to see their receipts."

"Not without a court order. Lots of coppers come here. I don't give information."

I took out my badge again. "Take a closer look. I'm a copper too."

"I don't care if you're the Sultan of Bahrain. You get a court order, I'll talk. Otherwise, you can walk."

"You're not their attorney or their priest. There's no bartender-client privilege. Show me their receipts."

"Why should I?"

I looked around the room. "So I won't have to turn you over to my buddies at the fire department."

"Whadda ya mean?"

I looked at the ceiling then hit my fist on the wall. "You're up to code for Afghanistan, maybe. USA, you're subcode everywhere. Exposed wiring there in the corner. See those cracks outside the bathroom? Where that hairy insect just disappeared? I'm seeing half a dozen violations, and I'm not even trying. This place is a firetrap. Nothing you can't fix. With twenty thousand dollars in repairs."

"I don't have a thousand dollars."

"Then you better cough up receipts. Pronto."

"We just keep 'em six weeks, till the credit charges clear."

"I'll take what you've got."

"Don't have time to sort them out."

"I do."

"You can't take them outta here."

"Sit me down at a table with a light, and keep the roaches away."

↔

Three hours later, at 6:30, I pulled up across the street from Linda Glissan's. Since we needed dinner anyway, I decided to keep an eye on Linda's place while we ate. Mulch and I shared three Burgerville Tillamook cheeseburgers, a blackberry shake, and a large fry. I told him I was headed for the house and he should stay out of the glove box, which still smelled like Izzy's pizza. He gave me that look dogs give you, then put his snout up to the glove box.

Linda let me in. She asked why I wasn't wearing my trench coat. I told her I had my reasons. But I was relieved to see her alive and hoped she'd talk quickly. She did.

"I don't know what Jack would want me to tell you. But he left me alone, so he can't blame me for doing what I think's right. Late one night last July or August, I came to the kitchen to make tea. Jack and Noel were just around the corner, here in the living room. I heard them talking. Jack said, 'I could do it and I wouldn't get caught.'

"Naturally, I listened. Noel said something like, 'Jack, you can't. You've been a model cop.' Jack said, 'He killed our daughter, just as if he put that noose around her neck. He deserves to die.' Noel insisted Jack couldn't do it. Then Jack asked Noel if he'd turn him in if he did."

"What did Noel say?"

"He said he wouldn't turn him in, but Noel begged him not to put him in that situation. Noel refused to give him an alibi. He said he couldn't live with himself if he did that. Then Jack said he had to figure out a way to do it that didn't put himself at risk. He said he loved me too much to put me through that."

"Why didn't you tell me this before? Why that other story?"

"Because I didn't want to admit I knew about him killing the professor. I was afraid you'd consider me an accomplice. But now…I feel like I have to tell you or you'll think Noel was involved."

"So…what happened when you heard all this?"

"I scared them both to death. I stood right there, just out of sight, and said, 'I couldn't sleep that night; Jack and I stayed up after midnight watching *Air Force One*.' Then I stepped out from the kitchen and said, 'Will that alibi work?'"

"What'd they do?"

"Jack jumped up. He said, 'This is a private conversation.' I laughed at him, asking if he was actually bawling me out for eavesdropping while he was planning a murder! Then I told him I'd reread Melissa's journal. I knew how smitten she was with…that professor. Her journal documented the slide, page by page, until she was so depressed and drugged she stopped writing. I told Jack I'd thought for years the man deserved to die."

"You said that?"

"That's why I took that class with Sheila Phillips. I wanted to watch him up close, see what attracted Melissa to him. After three weeks I couldn't stomach it. The last night of class I saw him talking to one of the students. I watched the professor and the girl in the parking lot. She followed his car, and Sheila and I followed hers. He went into his house. She parked around the corner, then went through a fence to his back door. I got out and watched, in the shadows. He let her in. I saw him kiss her. That was it for me. I wanted him dead."

"You hadn't told Jack that?"

"Not till then. I didn't want him to think I was a terrible person. Truth is, when I heard him talking to Noel, I was relieved. Isn't that weird? I was relieved Jack wanted to kill him too."

"What happened next?"

"Jack asked Noel to leave, which Noel was happy to do. He kept telling Jack not to do it. He warned me not to be part of it. I suppose he thought we'd come to our senses. Jack said later he told Noel not to worry, that we'd given up on the idea."

"You're positive Noel wasn't involved?"

"Absolutely. You know that, right? Noel was in a bar with a bunch of people when the murder happened. Jack was mad at him for drinking when they were the up team. But he was relieved that Noel was off the hook. Jack said it was an airtight alibi. Isn't that true?"

"Yeah," I said. "I just need to know what Noel knew about Jack. And the murder."

"Well, Noel must have put it together once Palatine was killed, since he knew Jack had talked about it. Even I didn't know when Jack was going to do it. He kept me in the dark, to protect me I guess. He said I was never to tell anybody about anything. I'm violating that now."

"Apparently he decided he wanted Phillips for an alibi too," I said, testing her.

"No. Phillips came to Jack. He needed an alibi."

"Why?"

"Jack wouldn't tell me. But since we both knew Phillips didn't do it and it established Jack's alibi, why not?"

"You're certain Noel wasn't in on the murder?"

"Noel wanted nothing to do with it."

We talked another twenty minutes. I thanked her for her honesty. I went to the door, and this time she hugged me.

It felt good.

SATURDAY, JANUARY 18, 8:30 A.M.

I SAT AT LOU'S, in our bug-free booth. Clarence would be joining me later but said to eat without him since he'd have breakfast with Geneva.

I enjoyed my country omelet, hash browns, and the big buttermilk pancake Rory offers as a toast alternative. Admiring the yellow calla lilies, I flipped through Chris Doyle's report on Brandon Phillips. At a poignant musical moment on the Rock-Ola—"My folks were always putting him down (down, down)"—my eyes landed on two lines.

"Phillips had one outstanding financial judgement against him, but it was only for $1200… It's my judgement that Phillips could have taken his life, or could have been murdered."

It wasn't his conclusion that interested me. It was his spelling.

Clarence walked in to "…sorry I hurt you, leader of the pack." I didn't notice any tears.

"How do you spell the word *judgment*?" I asked him.

"How do Americans spell it?"

"No, how do Kuwaitis spell it?"

"The American spelling is j-u-d-g-m-e-n-t."

"Wouldn't you expect a highly educated cop to spell it right?"

"Who do you mean?"

"Chris Doyle, son of college professors."

"I'd expect Doyle to spell it with an *e* after the *g*."

"Why?"

"His mom taught him the Queen's English, remember? Judgement, with an *e* after the *g*, is the British spelling."

"How did you know that?"

"I'm a journalist. We read. We spell. We're educated."

"You've never read Nero Wolfe," I said, taking the wind out of his "I'm an intellectual" sails.

←→

I asked Ray who could do a chemical analysis on short notice. He said he knew just the man: Darrell MacKay, who formerly worked crime lab but now is a private investigator with his own lab. Ray drove us forty minutes to his place, near Battleground, northeast of Vancouver, Washington.

We parked next to an RV and entered a large split entry home, me wearing a Seahawks jacket and carrying a black garbage bag. A dark-haired guy with a winter tan, early forties, came out to meet us.

"Darrell, this is Ollie Chandler," Ray said. "And Clarence Abernathy." MacKay wore a Vikings cap, but otherwise seemed normal.

We went down a hallway past the master bedroom. He opened the door to the last room on the left. A Bunsen burner's flame licked the underside of a glass beaker. Vapor rose out of it into a tube. No kidding. I felt like I'd walked into 221b Baker Street, residence of Sherlock Holmes.

The most impressive piece, for a home lab, was the centrifuge.

"What does it do?" Clarence asked MacKay, which was akin to asking Rupert Bolin what a fountain pen does.

"The motor puts any substance in rotation around a fixed axis, so centrifugal force separates lighter and heavier components."

"I flunked chemistry," I said. "Apparently you didn't."

"Forensic toxicology is my passion. Solving crimes with science and technology. I love it. Don't spread it around, but the DA's office comes to me when they can't afford to wait for test results. They came last month because they didn't trust the chain of custody. There've been cases where detectives try to test evidence without officially turning it in."

"That's reprehensible," I said, avoiding eye contact with Ray as I swallowed my Black Jack.

"Define forensics—and toxicology," Clarence said, pen poised. "I want to get it straight so nobody whines about journalistic inaccuracies." He gave me the eye.

"Forensics is the use of science and technology to investigate and establish facts in criminal court. Toxicology is the science of adverse effects of chemicals on living organisms."

"In this case I was the living organism," I said.

"So you think someone put something in your beer?" MacKay asked.

I took my trench coat out of the garbage bag and showed him the arm that had gotten drenched in the beer that night at Rosie O'Grady's when Brandon Phillips called me. The same night he turned up dead.

MacKay put his nose to it. "Smells like beer. You sure you didn't just have a few too many?"

"I know what a few too many is. There's a firecracker; then there's a bomb. This was a bomb. That's why I didn't wash the coat. And haven't been wearing it."

MacKay took the sleeve and looked at it with a magnifying glass. "Most of it's still water repellant, but it's worn enough that the beer soaked into spots and left a residue.

He clamped something viselike on it. He collected a few flakes into a minia-ture test tube. Next he put in a drop of some long-named chemical. No reaction. He cleaned the test tube and started over with a few more residue flakes in the tube. This time the chemical turned the flakes green.

"I've narrowed it down," MacKay said.

"That quick? I'm used to waiting days."

"It's not just beer. There's a toxin. Specifically, an aldehyde or a ketone. Which narrows it down to six or seven substances."

"What substances?' Clarence asked, pen ready.

He named three of them, each at least a dozen letters, before Clarence raised his hand. "I'll pass."

MacKay said to me, "Considering the greenish stain and its effects on you and that there isn't a smell, I've got a hunch." He picked out two more bottles and put a sterile eyedropper in each. "I'm using benzidine dihydrochloride to see if there's a reaction."

Apparently there was, because he said, "Bingo."

We waited for him to redo and confirm the results.

"Yeah. Chloralhydrate. It's used as a sedative and sleep aid or as a dental anes-thetic for children. And in bigger doses, as an anesthetic for large animals." He grabbed a thick brown book off the wall.

"Why'd somebody use it on me?"

"Because you're a large animal?" Ray asked.

"It mixes easily into alcohol. Can't taste it. Induces sleep. Deep sleep."

"You got that right," I said.

He started reading aloud portions of a study of chloralhydrate done on two-year-old male mice. He read, "Russo and Levis, 1992, found chloralhydrate to be capable of inducing aneuploidy in mouse spermatocytes."

"That's more than I want to know," I said.

"If you hadn't been awakened," MacKay said, "you might have been out six hours. Even if you'd gotten a blood test, chloralhydrate decomposes internally so quickly that it's undetectable beyond four hours. Never shows up in an autopsy."

"Autopsy?"

"Yeah. It can be fatal. Finish your beer?"

"Mostly."

"We'd never have been able to prove what it was without the beer soaked into your trench coat. It paid off being a sloppy drinker."

MONDAY, JANUARY 20, 7:00 P.M.

It was two months to the day since the professor's murder. But the string included Frederick, Hedstrom, and Phillips, not to mention four unrelated deaths. Because of the high profile of the Palatine case and its apparent connection with three others, Manny and I had been given a bye when our number next came up. But Sergeant Seymour told me that next time, especially with Phillips gone, we'd have to take it. No problem now since the Palatine murder had been solved, right?

Then why did it feel wrong? Why couldn't I let it go?

It was Monday Night Football again, at Jake's. I called to say I'd be there by halftime. I thought I wanted to be alone and went to dinner at the Old Spaghetti Factory.

Sometimes I get a craving for the pasta smothered in Mizithra Cheese, which I discovered in 1969, the first year the original Old Spaghetti Factory opened on Second Street downtown. I took Sharon, and we watched the silent movies while we waited an hour to be seated, which you always did back then. When we could, we'd eat in the streetcar. It was cheap, and we went twice a month. We loved it.

The problem with the Old Spaghetti Factory in Clackamas, fifteen minutes from my house, isn't that it looks so different than the original. There's still brass headboards and wrought iron chandeliers and a streetcar. No more silent movies, not so long a wait, but the food hasn't changed much. The Mizithra's still fabulous. The menu still says of Mizithra what it's always said: "A toothsome treat for cheese lovers; legend has it that Homer lived on this while composing the *Iliad*." Still the best Thousand Island dressing in Portland. Couples still sit across from each other, lost in conversation.

What's changed is that Sharon isn't with me anymore.

Despite the toothsome treat, I walked out realizing that I craved more than Mizithra. Some places you should never eat at by yourself. I'd just been at one of them.

Twenty minutes later I was at Jake's. Early in the fourth quarter, he opened Carly's old dorm room fridge, stocked with drinks.

"Get you a pop?" Jake asked.

"Coke," I said.

Jake handed it to me. My eyes were aimed at the television, but my little gray cells were working, triggered by the word *pop*.

The sounds of cheering, announcers and Jake's voice woke me to the outside world.

"Sherlock Holmes," I said, "solved a case based on the depth parsley had sunk into the butter on a hot day."

"Did he now?" Jake said. "I've got some trivia for you—there's 3:32 left in the fourth quarter, it's tied, and the Seahawks are deep in Eagles territory."

"Why would somebody born and raised in the Pacific Northwest, never having lived elsewhere, ask, 'You want a soda?'"

Jake shrugged, looking at me like I was losing it. "I don't know."

"The answer is, he wouldn't."

56

"I suspect myself. Of coming to conclusions too rapidly."
SHERLOCK HOLMES, *THE NAVAL TREATY*

TUESDAY, JANUARY 21, 10:30 A.M.

CLARENCE AND I sat in Ray Eagle's living room. I claimed the red chair and ottoman for my tired legs, and Ray sat beside me in a low-back armchair. I handed him the page from my yellow pad on which I'd written three lines of dialogue.

Noel: *"Get you a soda?"*
Ollie: *"Sure. I'll take a Coke."*
Noel: *"Coca-Cola?"*

"Okay, but what does it mean?" Ray asked, handing the pad back to me.

"It means Noel didn't grow up in Washington."

"Yes, he did. I checked it out, remember?"

"I say he didn't."

"Why?"

"It's right here." I held up the page. "He asked me if I wanted a soda. You're from this area, right?"

"Born in southeast Portland. Moved to Detroit at twenty-one, stayed there fifteen years, and moved back here about twenty years."

"What do you call a soft drink?"

"Pop. Called it pop here and called it pop in Detroit."

"I grew up in Milwaukee, and we said soda. My cousin Lance in Madison said pop. When I was in LA, it was soda. When I moved up here to Portland thirty years ago, I thought people sounded stupid when they said pop. Swore I'd never give in. But after ten years, one day Sharon pointed out I was saying pop, just like the locals. The point is, a lifelong Northwesterner calls it pop, not soda."

"I grew up in Mississippi, before we moved to Chicago." Clarence said. "To us any soft drink was a Coke. That's what you call it. If you're drinking 7-Up, it's still a Coke."

"That's the second tip-off," I said. "When I told him I wanted a Coke, Noel asked, 'Coca-Cola?' A Northwesterner would never ask that. Of course a Coke is Coca-Cola. It couldn't be anything else."

"But I'm telling you," Ray said, "Noel grew up in Liberty Lake, Washington. I ran the background check."

"Double-check it. Find out where his parents came from. A kid could learn his words for soft drinks from parents, but his friends would be calling it pop. I don't believe he'd call it anything else if he really grew up there. Anyway, check it out."

I gave them photocopies of Jack and Noel's receipts from the Nine Darts Tavern. I explained that Linda had a class Wednesday nights, so Jack and Noel normally ate there. They usually had the same thing week to week: Jack fried chicken and Noel a burger and fries. Both would usually have two beers. The tab was the same every week, one beer more or less. But one night, the night of November 27, their tab was twenty-five dollars more than usual. Did Linda skip class and join them that night? Nope—hamburger and fried chicken, as usual. But no beers. Instead, a bottle of wine and nearly double their usual tip.

"So tell me," I said to Clarence and Ray, "why do two beer drinkers order wine?"

"Special occasion?" Clarence said. "To make a toast?"

"To celebrate," Ray said. "Graduation. Engagement. Birth of a child. Promotion. Your team wins the World Series."

"And that's when you leave a big tip, because you're happy, feeling generous," I said. "But none of those things happened November 27. Okay, it was the day before Thanksgiving, but they'd be together for Thanksgiving the next day. So what else do homicide detectives celebrate?"

"Solving a murder," Ray said.

"When I was his partner, Jack liked to celebrate one week after nailing the bad guy. Look at that date again."

"November 27," Ray said.

"What was one week earlier?"

"November 20," Clarence said. "The night of Palatine's murder. But…Jack and Noel had a murder case that same night. They were celebrating that one, right? Didn't they solve it?"

"Jack said it was easy, a no-brainer. The guy confessed within hours. Not worth celebrating. Plus, that murder was actually early morning November 21. But anyway, it's not the date of a murder you celebrate, it's the date you solve it or the killer's arrested, or brought to justice."

"What's your point?" Clarence asked.

"Well, who was brought to justice one week earlier, on November 20? Palatine. Maybe this time they were celebrating not an arrest, but an execution."

They pondered it quietly.

"There's more," I said. "Flip back a couple pages, and check the receipt. They weren't just at the Nine Darts one week after the murder. They were there the night of the murder. They didn't have beer, but they were the up team so that makes sense. But there's a second sales receipt, after the dinner, next page. They bought something for $24.99."

"A bottle of Riesling," Clarence said, reading the receipt.

"White wine. Since it's a separate transaction, not part of the dinner, the bottle of wine was to go. The Nine Darts owner confirmed that. Jack paid for it, and they took it with them."

Ray stared at me. "And that same night, two people drank white wine at Palatine's. And took the bottle with them when they left."

I came home for lunch and found the answering machine blinking.

"Who called?" I asked Mulch. When he didn't answer, I pushed New Messages.

"Detective Chandler? This is Cherianne Takalo in Michigan. I got the photo you sent. Thank you! That's just how I remember Melissa's parents. Thanks for the note saying which ones are you and your wife. But…something I don't understand. You were asking me about Donald, like you didn't know him. Anyway…call me back if you want to."

I called back. "Cherianne? Ollie Chandler. I didn't understand your message…your comment about Donald."

"I just thought it was odd that you asked me about Donald like you didn't know him."

"I don't."

"But he's standing right next to you in the picture."

"What…? Hang on." I walked over to the table by the recliner and lifted the framed picture of Portland's homicide detectives and wives. "I'm looking at it. Who are you talking about?"

"Okay, the guy on your left side, with the brown hair and silly grin, standing right next to Melissa's dad and mom."

"That's Noel Barrows, Jack's partner."

Long pause. "Are you sure?"

"Of course I'm sure."

"Wow. He looks just like Melissa's boyfriend, Donald."

Sarge let me use the phone in his office again that afternoon.

"Noel Barrows grew up in Liberty Lake," Ray Eagle insisted, "and I've got the records, transcripts, and pictures to prove it. Grade school, high school. Cub

Scouts. His parents died in a car wreck his senior year. After graduating he got a summer job in Helena, Montana, then stayed there. That's the last anyone in Liberty Lake saw him. Ended up calling a realtor and selling his parents' house without even coming back to town. Signed papers through the mail."

"You have pictures?"

"Yearbook."

"They're a perfect match to Noel?"

"I wouldn't call it perfect. He was heavy in high school. He's lost maybe thirty pounds. Hair's thinned some. I guess he looks as close to his high school picture as I do to mine—which isn't all that close. People change. But I do have something interesting. I think you should call the guy in Helena who rented him the room."

"Why?"

"I won't spoil it. Told him you'd probably call. Name's Joey Netelesky. Ask him about Noel."

"Don't recall every tenant from ten years ago," Netelesky told me ten minutes later, "but I'll never forget that boy. One day he just pulls up stakes. Leaves a buncha stuff behind. No forwarding address. Didn't say so much as 'See ya later, alligator.'"

Without warning, he violently spit some chaw. I pushed away the apple fritter in front of me.

"But he wasn't in trouble with the law. Didn't make sense. And somethin' else, by cracky. He left full payment for his rent. Cash money. Fact is, he left more than he owed."

"That's got to be unusual."

"I've rented houses and apartments twenty years, partner, had lotsa skip-outs, but this youngster's the only one ever paid more than he owed. Left the place so clean you could lick mashed banana off the floor. But he forgets some spendy stuff, like his stereo, which he listened to all the time, so why would he leave it? And he never even picks up his cleaning deposit! All told, cost hisself four hundred dollars, I reckon, plus the stuff he leaves behind. Why would a body do that?"

After hanging up, I considered it.

A body'd do that because he didn't want a blemish on his record. He didn't want police involved. He didn't want someone trying to trace him. And he might not have known the rental amount, so he leaves more than enough. Refundable cleaning deposit? He didn't know—or didn't want to show his face. Leaving a place so clean you could lick mashed banana off it? Not just to make mashed-banana-lickers happy. Maybe to eliminate forensic evidence.

Four hundred dollars and somebody else's stereo is a cheap price for a new identity, especially if you take possession of a guy's parents' assets. Then sell the house, with an easily forged signature, without ever showing your face where people might notice your face had changed.

A chill went over me. I sat there at Sarge's desk, looking out the windows to Homicide, seeing the man I knew as Noel Barrows reading a golf magazine while munching on a sandwich.

All I could think about was one thing: What happened to the body of the real Noel Barrows?

57

*"There are some trees, Watson, which grow to a certain
height, and then suddenly develop some unsightly eccentricity.
You will see it often in humans."*
SHERLOCK HOLMES, *THE ADVENTURE OF THE EMPTY
HOUSE*

ONCE A PARADIGM SHIFT OCCURS, you see everything differently. In Palatine's
living room, Clarence had commented how brothers sometimes fight. Looking
back, I could see in my mind's eye how Noel had chuckled and nodded his head,
like someone who'd experienced it. Yet he claimed to be an only child.

Was it really true that the Noel Barrows I knew was not the boy who grew up
in Liberty Lake, Washington? And if he wasn't, then who was he?

But no, I told myself. What about Linda Glissan's testimony that Noel refused
to cooperate with the murder? And what about his airtight alibi?

TUESDAY, JANUARY 21, 3:00 P.M.

I sat in Linda's living room, me in Jack's chair, her on the leather couch nearby. This
time she offered coffee, and I took it. Nice and dark. Jack and I both liked it that
way. Sometimes I add cream, but Jack always took it black, no compromise.

"I was looking through Melissa's case file," I said.

"Why?"

"I'm digging. If Jack didn't kill those other men, somebody did. Who had a
motive? I interviewed Melissa's old roommate, Cherianne Takalo."

"Cherianne? I haven't thought about her for years. Where is she?"

"Outside Detroit. She told me about the professor. And she claims Melissa
had a boyfriend named Donald, who came and stayed with you and Jack. Then
when she broke up with him, he came back to talk her out of it."

"No," Linda said. "He only came out once, when he stayed with us. Next time
he came to Portland was for the funeral."

"Where'd he live?"

"I don't remember exactly. We didn't have much of a chance to know him. I
picked him up at the airport the night before the funeral."

"What time did Noel arrive?"

"I don't know. It's been ten years. I just remember picking him up… Wait. You
called him Noel."

"Donald changed his name to Noel Barrows, didn't he?"

"How did you know?"

"Why were you hiding it?"

She stood, wringing her hands, pivoted, then fell back on the couch. "Noel…Donald, was crushed by Melissa's death. He'd stayed with us three weeks that summer. No one out here knew him. After the funeral, he didn't want to go home. He had an abusive mother and some troubles. He needed a fresh start and wanted to change his name. He even asked if he could take our name, but that seemed a little…premature." She smiled. "Jack helped him out. Noel got his name changed and entered the police academy."

"He assumed the name of a dead kid from Liberty Lake, Washington."

"He was about his age and didn't have family. Donald wasn't hurting anybody."

"Look, Linda, I've read Melissa's investigation files. There isn't anything about a boyfriend named Donald. They interviewed you and Jack. Why didn't you tell them?"

"Why? Noel had nothing to do with her being on drugs. Or the suicide. That was the professor's fault. Melissa and Noel had broken up. We were sorry because we really liked him. They were good for each other. I think sometimes how Melissa could have stayed with Noel and married him. We'd probably have grandchildren now and…" She kept swallowing but appeared to be out of tears.

"You really thought Noel wasn't in Portland until the funeral?"

"He wasn't. He stayed with us three weeks that summer. That's when we got to know him. Jack was on vacation two weeks. They played golf all the time. But like I said, he didn't come back until just before the funeral, maybe four days after Melissa died. I'm the one who called Noel to tell him. He was in…well, he wasn't in Portland."

"Cherianne Takalo says he was here before Melissa died."

"That's ridiculous."

"Why would she lie?"

"Ask Noel. He'll tell you he just came for the funeral."

"How about you call him and invite him over right now?"

Forty minutes later Noel showed up at Linda's. They hugged. She offered him a pop. Not a soda. Not a Coke.

"What are you doing here?" Noel asked me.

"When you came for Melissa's funeral, you flew to Portland straight from Pennsylvania, right?"

"Pennsylvania?" Noel looked at Linda.

"He's fishing," Linda said. "I wouldn't tell him where you're from."

"I'm from Liberty Lake, Washington," Noel said.

"No, you're not, but we'll get back to that," I said. "Melissa's funeral was Saturday, November 26, two days after Thanksgiving. When did you fly in?"

He looked at Linda. "What's going on?"

"What's going on, Noel," I said, "is that your real name is Donald."

"That's a lie." His sideglance at Linda showed he thought she'd betrayed him.

"He already knew," Linda said to him, putting her hand on his arm. "He called you Donald."

Noel paused. "It's not illegal to change your name."

"It's illegal to assume an identity."

"I had my reasons."

"Yeah, your previous girlfriend had died too." It was a shot in the dark. I watched both their faces.

"It was an accident," he said, making my bluff pay off.

"One girlfriend dies in an accident, next girlfriend commits suicide. What a coincidence."

Linda gave Noel a vacant, eerie stare.

"But you called me…back home," Noel said to her. "To tell me Melissa had died."

"That's right," Linda said, her voice lifting.

"Think back," I said. "I'll bet you got his answering machine, didn't you?"

"It's been ten years. I can't remember some things ten days ago. But it's like that terrible time is engraved in my brain. I do remember—when I left the message, I decided I couldn't say she'd died. But," she looked at Noel, "you called me back just a few hours later. I broke the news to you. You were devastated."

"I returned your call as soon as I got home from work."

"You called from Portland and checked your messages back home," I said. "It isn't hard." Okay, it was hard for *me*, but I figured it wasn't for him.

"No way."

"How could you know where he called from?" I asked Linda. "You didn't have caller ID back then, did you?"

She shook her head. She turned to Noel. "You told me you'd fly in for the funeral. You called me back and gave me details. I picked you up at the airport."

"Not where you could see him coming from the gate," I said.

"Outside baggage claim," she said to Noel. "Curbside. That's where you asked me to come."

"Right," he said. "I was there with my bags. You remember."

"Probably took a taxi to the airport," I said. "Just stood curbside with your bags, as if you'd just flown in. Piece of cake."

"You stayed with us, at our place," Linda said. "But…you were already in Portland?"

He coughed, from his waist. "I flew in Friday night, like I said. Just before you picked me up."

"Well, Donald, I have a sworn statement from Melissa's roommate that you were in Portland a few days before she died."

"My name's Noel." He looked at Linda. I saw his wheels turning, wondering if now was the time to give up part of the lie. He sighed. "Okay, I flew in early to talk with Melissa. It was private, so we didn't announce it to you and Jack. I'm sorry."

Linda's eyes sank. She didn't move, but she'd been leaning toward Noel and now leaned away.

"If your point was to visit Melissa," I said, "why wouldn't you want her parents to know? Why wouldn't you stay here like you did before, have a good time, play some golf?"

"Melissa was upset. She told me about the professor. I tried to talk her out of suicide."

"She told you she was suicidal?" Linda jumped off the couch.

"Palatine had messed up her mind."

"No one told me she was suicidal. I'm her mother. I might have been able to stop her."

"Linda…" He reached out to her, and she backed away. "Jack knew I was here. He just thought it might look awkward if…"

"*Jack* knew you were here? I don't believe you. You're lying. And *awkward*? Melissa died that night. You acted shocked when I told you on the phone. You were in Portland? You knew she was dead?"

"I heard it on the news that morning. I *was* shocked."

"You pretended you were hearing it from me."

"I thought you should be the one to tell me. I owed you that."

"You owed me that? You owed me the truth!" She slapped him. "Get out of my house!"

He looked at her sadly, apologetically. As he walked to the door, his gaze fell on me. What I saw took my breath away.

It wasn't irritation. It was murder.

58

"Improbable as it is, all other explanations are more improbable still."
SHERLOCK HOLMES, *SILVER BLAZE*

AFTER NOEL, OR DONALD, WALKED OUT, I stood in Linda Glissan's living room, in air too thick to breathe.

"Why didn't he contact Jack and me?" Linda asked, hands on her face. "Why didn't he stay with us? Why did he pretend?"

I walked around the living room, stepped into the kitchen and back out.

"What are you doing?"

"Walk me through it, Linda. That night you overheard Jack and Noel, when Jack was talking about killing the professor. You came to the kitchen to make tea?"

"Yes."

"Was that unusual?"

"I do it every night. I turn off the TV at ten and make my chamomile tea to help me sleep. I take it to the bedroom."

"So Jack would know you'd be coming to the kitchen a little after ten."

"I suppose."

"Boil water on the stove?"

"Microwave." She pointed to it at the end of the kitchen, close to the living room.

"Do me a favor and make your tea like always, okay?"

"I don't want tea."

"I'll drink it. Humor me."

She went to the cupboard, took out a mug, opened the fridge and poured water from a Brita pitcher, then put the mug in the microwave. She pressed three buttons, making three loud beeps. While the microwave heated the water, she opened the cupboard and grabbed a tea bag. I hoped chamomile wasn't like Earl Grey.

"Come here," I said, turning the corner from the kitchen to the living room.

I pointed to the recliner ten feet away, couch on one side, glider on the other. "That's Jack's favorite chair, the recliner?"

She nodded.

"Wouldn't they have to be raising their voices for you to hear them in the kitchen? I mean, knowing you were in the house, wouldn't it be strange to discuss murder in anything above a whisper?"

"They weren't raising their voices," Linda said. "They were sitting right here." She pointed to the floral patterned love seat just around the corner from the kitchen, ten feet closer than the recliner.

I sat on the love seat. The microwave sounded. I followed her the five feet into the kitchen where she put in the tea bag, dipped it and stirred, and handed me the cup. I took one sip and decided that all those years I'd gone without chamomile tea were well spent. Just give me coffee, then at bedtime knock me over the head with a mallet.

I stepped back to the living room and put the tea down on the coffee table in front of the love seat.

"These two men, cops, were sitting together here in this flowered love seat instead of over there on Jack's favorite recliner and that comfortable couch?"

"What's your point?"

"That they sat over here for one reason—so you'd overhear them."

"But…*why?*"

"Maybe Jack wanted to test you, to see how you'd feel about his plan to kill the professor."

"But…why involve Noel?"

"What if they scripted their conversation so if it came to it, you'd testify that Noel had nothing to do with the murder?"

"You think Jack would deceive me like that?"

"When a man's planning murder, is one more deception that big? He wanted to protect you and Noel both. When we were conducting interviews as partners, Jack would sometimes pretend he was angry, confused, or distracted. We'd rehearse which of us would say what and exactly when. I used to tell him he'd be a great con artist."

"He wouldn't con me."

"Unless he thought it wouldn't hurt you, maybe even help you. He knew when you came to the kitchen. He heard the beeps when you set the microwave. He knew you'd be standing there five feet from a love seat where two self-respecting men would never sit. It was rehearsed. If you stepped in and said what you did, fine. If you said nothing, fine. To Jack, your silence would be permission. If you opposed the plan, Jack could change his mind if he wanted to. No downside."

"You really think…?"

"I need to know Donald's last name."

"I can't tell you. I promised Jack I never would."

"Police academy runs a background check."

"He had a perfect background. He assumed the identity of that kid who died years ago."

"That's what he told you? Here's the truth—he assumed the identity of a guy who'd disappeared a few weeks before, and his body's never been found."

"How could he do that? People would know."

"Donald did his homework. He found someone who looked like him, whose parents had died, who wasn't close to relatives, had moved where no one knew him. No friends or neighbors or relatives to say, 'That's not him.' Who'd know it wasn't the real Noel Barrows? He could probably show up at a class reunion today and fake his way through it."

She shook her head.

"Linda, at least tell me where he came from."

"He shouldn't have lied to me, but Noel's a decent person, lovable and kind. I keep my promises. Lots of Donalds around. Good luck finding his last name."

Linda ushered me out the door, and I drove home to Mulch. My dog beside me, looking up at the computer screen, I spent the evening searching the web. After testing the number of Donalds in America and randomly reading a hundred last names to Cherianne Takalo over the phone, none of which were familiar to her, I saw this was going nowhere.

On a whim I Googled the words *soda*, *pop*, and *Coke*. My first hit was www.popvssoda.com. Within ten minutes, I was grateful to Al Gore for inventing the Internet, and for the geeks who waste their lives stocking it with generally use-less—but in this case invaluable—information.

WEDNESDAY, JANUARY 22, 9:20 A.M.

I called Clarence and Ray to my house and, trying to appear casual, sat them on both sides of me in front of my computer.

I went to the website and clicked to the county breakdowns at www.popvs-soda.com/countystats/total-county.html.

"Okay, green and yellow are where people say soda. If you ask for a soda, you're from California, Arizona, or the Northeast—New York, Jersey, or New England. Or maybe, Missouri or Nebraska. Pop's what you call your dad."

"What's all the blue?" Clarence asked.

"That's where people call soft drinks pop. Ohio, Michigan, Minnesota, most of the Midwest says pop. Everybody in Oregon and Washington calls it pop, except two small Oregon counties on the California border. But there's not a county in Washington that favors soda over pop. Soda's a cake ingredient. You grow up in Liberty Lake, you just say pop. Period."

"Okay, that confirms your theory," Ray said. "But how does it help us find which of a gazillion Donalds assumed the identity of Noel Barrows?"

"That's where it gets good. Check this out." I pointed to the red dots on the map. "Many Southerners, like Clarence when he was in Mississippi, call any soft drink a Coke. Now look at this—the map shows places where there's an even split between those who call it soda and those who call it Coke." I clicked to another page. "In Florida, 45 percent say soda, 46 percent say Coke, and less than 4 percent say pop. You've got a population that's split dead-even between soda and Coke."

"So what?" Ray asked.

"So yesterday I think back to Noel telling me how excited he was about the Miami Hurricanes playing the Florida Gators. Who gets excited about Oregon playing Oregon State? Not people in Florida, right? So I started wondering about a Northwest guy having such a passionate interest in two Florida teams. Yesterday morning, guided by this Internet map, I called a half dozen Florida police stations in areas where it's an even split between soda and Coke."

"I'm impressed with your research," Ray said.

"That's high praise coming from you. Anyway, I'm talking to Detective Gary Hunt, formerly of Tampa, now Miami-Dade County, which includes Miami and surrounding areas. Gary says he grew up calling it soda, but half the people there call every pop a Coke. Once in a while it gets confusing. If he's at the fridge and somebody requests a Coke, sometimes he clarifies by asking "Coca-cola?""

"Like Noel did," Clarence said.

"I figured maybe it wasn't a needle in a haystack now, but a needle in a bale of hay. I asked him if he knew of any cases involving a young man named Donald who may have disappeared ten years ago. I said he might have been in trouble, from a rough home, and his girlfriend died in an accident. He said it didn't ring a bell, but he'd ask around and check the records. Figured I'd never hear back from him. But last night after I came home from Linda Glissan's, as Mulch and I were eating Polish sausages and sauerkraut, guess who calls."

"Detective Hunt," Clarence said.

"Turns out there was a young man named Donald Meyer. Twelve years ago he'd been a suspect in the murder of his girlfriend. He'd been cleared, but some thought he was guilty. One day he disappears. Even his own mother claimed she didn't know where he'd gone. Since he was twenty-one and no longer a suspect, nobody searched for him."

"So you think Donald Meyer became Noel Barrows," Ray said. "But Noel doesn't have a Florida accent, does he?"

"Accents can be unlearned," I said. "Radio people and actors do it all the time. If you assume the identity of a Northwesterner, you retrain your voice."

"But if Noel changed his name, Jack must have known."

"He did. But he trusted Noel enough not to check him out. Or maybe he checked, but there was no arrest, no charge, no record. Just an investigation. He was cleared."

"Why would Jack agree to this identity change?"

"Wanted to get him into the police academy, save him the hassle of the question marks from Florida. He believed his tale of abuse."

"Was Noel's family abusive?" Clarence asked.

"I'll let you know. I fly this afternoon to Miami, to call on Donald Meyer's mother."

THURSDAY, JANUARY 23, 10:30 A.M.

MIAMI WAS WARM and humid even in January. Gary Hunt had picked me up at the airport Wednesday night and actually had me spend the night at his house, in a room with his two mastiffs, who together outweigh even me and who when we wrestled proved to be a formidable tag team. Gary's bubbly wife, who made me muffins and a killer breakfast, was very nice, but the dogs were a blast.

Considering Detective Hunt has plenty of crime of his own to deal with, I was blown away by this degree of cop cooperation, which included hospitality. I scanned their bookshelves, and wouldn't you know it, there were several Bibles and a bunch of books by C. S. Lewis. And nothing by Bertrand Russell.

Next morning Gary took me to Miami-Dade County Police Headquarters, gave me keys to the car he'd arranged for me, and handed me a MapQuest print-out pointing me to the doorstep of Brenda Meyer, 13.7 miles away.

The closer I got to the Meyer house, the more my stomach flip-flopped. I finally turned onto the designated street in a run-down neighborhood and drove the exact distance indicated on the map. Seeing no number on a weather-beaten gray house, I parked by the weed-choked yard. A half dozen side boards hung at all angles by single nails. Several were on the ground. The topsy-turvy roof needed redoing years ago.

No sign there'd been flowers, just dead grass. Front door had been white in a former life, but most of the white had peeled. What remained was a brownish gray. The house was beyond dingy—as if color had chosen to keep its distance.

The moment Donald Meyer's mother opened the front door, I smelled the house's inside. The smell pushed its way out like fresh-baked bread, but it was anything but fresh. Gagged me. I couldn't identify the smell and didn't want to.

The room was somehow misshapen and grotesque. I'm talking about the smell and the room because I don't want to speak about the woman. But I have to.

She was all teeth, bones, and gristle. I can't tell you the color of her eyes, only that they were cold and flinty. I always notice eye color, just as I notice the color of hair roots and whether a man's sideburns are equal length. But the hardness of her eyes kept their color from registering.

When she stuck out her hand, it was all rings and knuckles. She was so skeletal she appeared to have died, yet there she was, moving around. It seemed unnatural, indecent. I wanted to leave, to get fresh air. I took care not to turn my back or let down my guard, watching her as she sat on a recliner, stained with who knows what. When she reached for something under a pile of old junk mail, I reached for my Glock. She pulled out a cough drop, used, sticking to newspaper. She put it in her mouth, paper bits and all.

In the thirty-five years I've been a cop, I've been deeply afraid maybe just a few dozen times. This was one of them.

"You came about Donald."

Her voice was unnaturally deep, the raspiness suggesting she'd been smoking a few hundred years. I smelled sulfur. No sign of cigarettes or ashtrays. It smelled like garbage had been slow burning for eons.

"I wondered if he was dead," she said.

"Why?"

"Never found the body. Not that they tried." She didn't look sad. She didn't look happy. "What'd you say he calls himself?"

"Noel."

"Last name?"

"Sorry, I can't give that now. I promise to tell you later."

She shrugged. "Don't care."

Donald's mother spoke like someone who had to remind herself how to do it, as if she hadn't talked to a live human being for years. Or hadn't *been* a live human being for years.

As she spoke, I noticed a spider web connecting the left arm of her chair to the seat. A spider in the center was wrapping up an insect. The smell of the room wasn't cigarette smoke. It was death.

Speaking of spiders, when she said "they never found the body," I'd felt those spiders with wet feet again, crawling on the nape of my neck. I had the unnerving feeling that she hadn't spent much of her existence in one of these tricky little human bodies and had yet to get the hang of it.

"I was in labor thirty-five hours," she said. "Donald didn't want to come out."

Looking at her, I couldn't blame him.

"He and his brother were no good. Never should have had them."

She said it matter-of-factly.

"Donald had a brother?"

"Don't know where he is either."

"Younger or older?"

She shrugged, as if it didn't matter. "Younger."

On the walls there were no family pictures, only drab random images, including pictures from magazines that had no place in a home, one with a girl pointing a gun to her head.

"Donald was never the same after his girlfriend died."

"You knew her?"

"She came over a couple times. That was too many. Never liked her."

"What was her name?"

"Carrie." She smiled wickedly.

"He knew her in high school?"

She nodded.

"How did she die?"

"Car accident. Drove herself right off the road, hundred feet down to the rocks." She grinned. "Stupid girl."

"Did you know about a girlfriend Donald had in Oregon?"

"Don't know nothin' 'bout Oregon."

I waited, finding it hard to talk. Finally she spoke again.

"Wasn't good with girls. Couldn't keep 'em in line. Couldn't do much of anything except that stupid golf. Won a few tournaments. I never saw any money. He may as well be dead. What does it matter to me?"

"He became a cop."

"Donald?" She shook her head, in wonder or disgust. For her, the two seemed interchangeable.

"What was Carrie's last name?"

The corners of her mouth lifted slightly. "Graves."

"You said Donald had a brother. Never heard him mention a brother."

"Bet he never mentioned me neither."

He'd mentioned she was dead. Sitting there, I wasn't sure he'd lied.

"Did he mention his girlfriends?" She spit the word *girl*.

I shook my head.

"Always had bad luck with girls. Tramps."

"Did he have many girlfriends?"

"Not enough for him. Too many for me."

"You said Donald's brother was younger. How much younger?"

"Seventeen months."

"That's close."

"Too close. Shouldn't have let them be born. They was always partners in crime."

"What do you mean?"

"When they was little, it was harmless. Rodney would distract a store owner while Donald filled his pockets with candy or a radio or something. No big deal."

"Sure, no big deal," I said. Unless you're the store owner.

"Later they was always breakin' in to places. Stole a couple of cars together. Two peas in a pod." She glanced at a far wall, too dark to see.

I stood, walked to the wall, and found a small picture. I blew dust off it, took it to a window, and held it to the light. Two teenage boys. Both of them looked like Noel might have fifteen years ago.

"They could be twins."

"People couldn't tell 'em apart. Sometimes they even tricked me. Thought it was funny fooling their mother. Ungrateful punks. Their daddy beat 'em hard. Shoulda beat 'em harder. Maybe it woulda worked." She laughed.

"Mind if I borrow this picture to make a copy?"

"Keep it."

"I'll send it back. I just want—"

"Take it. Never want to see 'em again."

They peered at the tortured planet through the portal. "There's so much evil there," the young man said. "When they sense a supernatural evil, you'd think they'd turn to a supernatural good. My father is burdened not only by injustice but by malevolence. And the disappointment of his unfulfilled dreams."

The young man's mother nodded. "I wish I could have helped your father grasp the truth that one day the wicked will be judged. And one day the paralyzed will know the joy of running in a meadow and the pleasure of swimming. And many of those murdered will stand tall, never knowing dread or suffering again. And His children who seemed robbed of a childhood will know the wonders of eternal adventures on a new earth."

"My father longs for exactly what our Father promises. But above all, he longs for Elyon Himself."

"We won't give up on him, will we?" Sharon Chandler asked, putting her arm around him and pulling him to herself.

"No, Mother," Chad said, smiling. "We won't."

In the Miami airport that night, I thought I was calling Clarence, but Kendra answered the phone. I'd pressed the wrong button. "Hey," I said. "I'm in Miami."

"Miami? What're you doing there?"

"This is crazy for me to ask, and I'm sure it won't work but…I'm flying back to Portland. I'll be in at eight o'clock tonight. Any chance you could pick me up at the airport?"

"Yeah. I could do that."

"Outside Delta's baggage claim?"

"Sure."

After contemplating Donald's family during a long plane ride, when I got into Kendra's car, I told her how good it was to see her. And how grateful I was for her and her mother and her sister, wherever she is…and her little brother.

When I mentioned her mom and Andrea and Chad, Kendra cried. So did I.

It was a wet ride home.

THURSDAY, JANUARY 23, 9:45 P.M.

"You know your open-door policy?" I asked Captain Swiridoff, as I stood on his front porch.

"That's in my office. This is my house." He looked at me as if I were homeless and holding a sign: *Will solve murders for food.*

"I guess I should invite you in. What's going on, Detective?"

"I need a search warrant."

He frowned. "Can you be more specific?"

"I want to go into the home of one of our detectives and examine his shoe."

"Which one?"

"The right shoe. Maybe the left one too."

"No, I mean which detective?"

"Noel Barrows."

"I'm listening."

After telling him about the photo ID by Melissa's roommate, Cherianne, and my research into pop, soda, and Coke, he said, "I thought Barrows had a solid alibi for the professor's murder."

"He does. Better than solid."

"He couldn't have been there, right? Jack killed the professor. By himself. Jack admitted it. Jack's wife vouches for it. Jack killed himself over it. I don't see what you're going for."

I tried to explain how Jack and Noel, two grown men, sat in that love seat, how I thought they'd scripted it for Linda and Jack was protecting Noel. The captain's hand wasn't reaching toward the phone to call a judge for a search warrant.

I went back to my pop and soda angle, told him about Gary Hunt in Dade County and Noel's mother, and how Donald aka Noel had been a suspect in the murder of his girlfriend and that he was in Portland when his next girlfriend, Jack's daughter, died.

"You're certain?"

"Positive." I told him about Cherianne Takalo.

He'd been taking notes and flipped back and forth, left hand on his chin. Finally he said, "I'll get the list of judges."

The captain returned with a file and read off several names. We both kept shaking our heads until he got to Ann Sugrue.

"She's our woman," I said.

Judge Sugrue had granted search warrants when threads of evidence raised significant questions. She didn't require proof as a condition for attempting to find proof.

The captain called her. Sugrue told him she'd be in bed at eleven and wouldn't answer the door after that and said something about her Dobermans and that her husband had been a military sniper. Forty minutes later, at 10:50, we presented the judge with the search warrant draft in which we specified Noel's shoes and possible glass shards. Because I was also fishing—a term you never use with a judge—we included lots of generalities, including carpet fibers from the crime scene and "documents or photographs demonstrating the suspect's possible involvement in the murder of William Palatine." This could include notes, phone numbers, journals, handwritten letters, word processing files, e-mails, and the ever-popular e-mail attachment.

I wasn't sure Judge Sugrue would approve it, but her husband and Dobermans and she'd had a long day, so she signed quickly, which is what we look for in a judge unless it's *our* personal liberties at stake. I didn't agonize over this, since the Bill of Rights wasn't written to ensure murderers' access to more victims.

At 11:20, Manny and I and Dan Ekstrom, a uniformed officer, showed up at Noel's apartment. I couldn't bring Clarence, in case Noel went ballistic.

Noel wasn't home. The apartment manager, upon examining our IDs and getting his reading glasses to go over the warrant, finally unlocked the apartment door and asked us to lock up because he had *Sleepless in Seattle* on pause and his wife would be getting ticked.

We entered Noel's apartment and saw a card table in the middle of the living room, with playing cards faceup in multiple stacks. A completed game of solitaire. The ace of spades sat by itself, in the center.

Sitting on the table was a black plastic tray with pens, paper clips, a small notepad, and a golf ball. This was directly under a desk lamp with no shade, just a bare hundred-watt light bulb. I turned on the lamp. The light was blinding.

After wondering about the function of the golf ball, I went into the bedroom for Noel's shoes. He had eight pairs on his rack. We bagged seven, leaving his slippers and flip-flops.

Against the far wall of the bedroom was a small desk. In one of the drawers I found a love letter, undated and faded. It contained poetry about misty eyes and yellow hair and tender shoulders. I read it to Manny, which made him uncomfortable. The letter was written in a distinctive blue ink, from a fountain pen. I didn't need Rupert the Penmeister to tell me that.

"Color's royal blue," I said. "Just like what was injected into the professor. And Palatine wrote this love letter."

"The professor was in love with Noel?"

"The letter's not to Noel, smart guy. I'm betting it was to Melissa Glissan, which would make it over ten years old. It's not signed, naturally. The professor's love letters never were."

How had Noel gotten the letter? When Cherianne told Noel about the professor, had he searched Melissa's things and found it? Had he confronted her with this letter?

Had Noel gone through police academy and been groomed for detective work by Jack, anticipating that some day he'd avenge himself on William Palatine?

In the bottom desk drawer, I found several disguises, including a beard and mustache. I have a few of these myself that I've used at stakeouts and tails.

In the medicine cabinet I found an Advil bottle with a clear liquid inside. I opened it and smelled. Nothing. This needed to go to the lab.

We confiscated these and a few other items, hoping they'd stand up in court. But even if they didn't, they might convince the homicide detectives. Noel needed to be convicted by that jury of his peers.

We left the required copy of the warrant and a receipt of all items taken, a total of thirty-six, next to the lamp on the card table.

Looking over the place one last time before leaving, I noticed the edge of a file folder barely protruding under an ink blotter on the card table. I pulled it out. It was full of neatly cut newspaper clippings, all from the *Tribune*. There were a couple of cases I knew Jack and Noel had solved. But there were other cases, notably Professor Palatine, Paul Frederick, and Dr. Hedstrom. And the picture of Palatine's body and the article by Mike Button.

Though it confirmed my hypothesis, it stunned me to see them together like this. At the back of the file was one more clipping. Before pulling it out, I held my breath, expecting it to feature the story of Detective Brandon Phillips.

It didn't. Seeing it put a lump in my throat, only partly because my name was in the article.

It concerned the murder of Jimmy Ross and the arrest of Lincoln Caldwell.

60

WHAT WOULD NOEL'S REACTION be when he saw the warrant and the receipt for all the items we'd removed from his apartment? He'd be angry and scared. Maybe he'd make a drastic move. Incriminate himself.

I thought through step by step what a man might do who'd killed Palatine and perhaps three others. There was no turning back. If someone proved a serious threat to him, what would he do?

What would I do if I were a murderer like him?

I'd kill Ollie Chandler.

He'd already tried twice.

If he set his mind to it this time, what would keep him from succeeding?

FRIDAY, JANUARY 24, 10:00 A.M.

Once again I sat at the Glissans' in Jack's favorite chair.

"I can't bear to think that the only two people I've ever really loved took their lives," Linda said. "You know how that makes me feel? Death's hard enough. Suicide's unbearable."

I weighed my words. "Linda, I need to tell you some things. First, I know Donald's last name was Meyer."

"Who told you?"

"I flew to Dade County and met his mother."

"Really? What's she like?"

"There's nothing I can say to do her justice." My skin crawled. "I'll tell you about her later. Right now I need you to tell me about Noel and the relationship you and Jack had with him."

She sighed and looked at her hands, clasped together on her lap. "Jack was the father figure, but Noel usually came up with the ideas. Even when Jack didn't feel like it, Noel would talk him into golfing or fishing or a ball game…or going out to dinner, even when it messed up Jack's plans."

"I thought Jack called the shots."

"Sometimes. But when Noel wants something, which is often, he knows how to get it. He could make Jack think it was his own idea. Noel was our bridge back to Melissa since they were so close. He became our Melissa substitute. We'd lost our daughter, but now we had an adopted son. We felt we owed him something for all the grief he'd been through, and his terrible family background. It was therapy for us to take care of him."

"I have some things to say that won't be easy to hear," I said.

I told her more about Noel's girlfriend dying in Florida, how he was a major suspect. She turned so pale I came over to sit close, lest she fall off the couch.

"You brought up Melissa's suicide," I said. "I've been thinking maybe it wasn't suicide."

Her eyes pleaded, one part wanting me to be wrong, another right. "You mean you think it was Noel?"

Her eyes told me she'd been wondering the same thing.

"May I ask you something?"

He put His hand on her shoulder. "Always, Carly."

"Uncle Ollie has all these questions. He thinks You don't care, that You look the other way from evil, that You could do more to deal with suffering."

"I hear that daily. Hourly. From people scattered across the Shadowlands."

"May I ask…what's Your answer?"

"Think, my child. Did My Father look the other way and abandon His creation? Did we ignore evil and let it forever reign victorious? Did I stay off in some far corner of the universe and keep My distance? Or did I come to the dark planet to face it head on?"

She looked into His eyes, nodding.

"This is My answer—you have seen it before." He stretched out His hands, and she studied the scars and put her fingers on them. "Tell Me, My beloved. Do these look like the hands of a God who does not care?"

Innocent people don't labor to avert suspicion. It rarely occurs to the innocent that they'll look guilty. It's the guilty who think about whether they'll look guilty.

Why wouldn't Noel want Jack and Linda to know he was in town before Melissa died? Only one reason made sense to me—because he thought she was going to die. And if she did, he didn't want them to connect it to him.

Noel was covering his tracks even before he killed her.

But if Noel was the killer, why did he point out the missing picture that could ultimately incriminate him? And why plant his fingerprints on the gun? But above all, what about his ironclad alibi?

Something was still wrong.

It was time to visit the Do Drop Inn.

I sat on an uncomfortable stool at the Do Drop, legs dangling awkwardly. The bartender reminded me of Billy at Rosie's, except more amiable. This was Barry, who called seven weeks ago to confirm Noel's alibi, and who I'd bought a drink for twenty minutes ago, and since then two more. He'd already told me about his childhood growing up on the Yukon River, son of missionaries, hunting and fishing and not having to use indoor bathrooms and living the good life. If Barry the Bartender were getting married tomorrow, I was a lock for best man.

Kendra had been changing my habits, so I tried Diet Coke. For me, booze was out of the question. Not only was I on duty, but the most important meeting of my life with all the detectives was scheduled for 3:30, ninety minutes away. I had to be sharp. Barry would have to drink for the both of us. So far he was doing his job.

"Was Noel acting strange that night?" I asked.

"Sure. He'd had too much to drink. Or he was mixing booze with speed or something."

"But he wasn't supposed to be drinking at all. He was on call. You saw him drinking?"

"Well…I was just passing out pitchers. They were pouring their own. I guess I assumed he was drinking, like everybody. He's sort of an odd guy."

"How's that?"

"Like, I remember the night he first comes to the bar. He introduces himself to me. Real friendly. Tells me his name, that he's a homicide detective. Like he's trying to impress me, you know? Usually I learn about guys as time goes on, but he wanted me to know who he was right away. I figured, maybe that's just him. But from then on, he didn't talk so much. I'd just say, 'Hi, Noel,' and he'd nod and hang out on the fringes, like…" Barry's voice trailed off.

"Like what?"

"Like he was putting in time. The guys ask him about being a detective, and he tells a few good stories, but then clams up. Mostly keeps to himself."

"Where was he sitting that night of November 20?"

"If I hadn't been asked so many times back in November, I wouldn't have a clue, but now that night's carved in my brain. He was sitting right down there on the end, wearing his Dolphins jacket. Don't see many of those around here."

Dolphins jacket? A gold nugget among the mud and rocks, and Ray and Manny and I hadn't dug it up.

"Anything unusual happen that night?"

"One thing weird. Vicki, the barmaid, makes a comment to him about being careful not to trip her. He gives her a blank look."

"Why is that weird?"

"Because two weeks earlier Noel accidentally swings his leg out, and Vicki spills a pitcher of beer on him. Not something you forget. So she reminds him, and he says, 'Yeah, I forgot,' or something. I think, *How could you forget, man?* His pants got soaked with beer. Everybody has a good laugh, including him. It was just two weeks before. I figured he's so drunk he can't remember. He says he has a bad headache. Maybe that's it."

"You just noticed the strange behavior that night?"

"That's the thing. He'd been acting weird the night before too. He wasn't himself. Looked, I don't know…different. I'm here six nights a week, and he's been maybe a two- or three-nights-a-week guy since he first started. Noel's okay. Not in trouble, is he? Hope he doesn't have a brain tumor or something."

Barry the bartender had said, "He wasn't himself." Maybe literally.

Was it possible Noel had a look-alike stand in for him? Someone with the sense to say he was tired and had a headache, excusing himself for seeming out of it? They all knew Noel, but not really. No one knew him well enough to realize it wasn't him. Drinking dulls the senses. From what I'd seen of Noel's brother, Rodney, it wouldn't be easy to tell them apart.

I'd said Noel wasn't the sharpest knife in the drawer.

I'd been dead wrong.

At three I met Clarence at a bench in the plaza, to rehearse my 3:30 meeting with the detectives. I needed the fresh air. It was cold but dry and sunny.

"What will you tell them?" Clarence asked.

"What I have is persuasive cumulatively, but none of the evidence on its own is enough. No proof. I've gone over it with Sarge and Lieutenant Nicks. We can't arrest Noel. The lab tests aren't back. Anybody can clip things from newspapers. An anonymous love letter? What does that prove? Sure, ten years ago Noel assumed the name of some dead guy who disappeared. Maybe he ripped off his inheritance, but Ray's been working on it, and it's not clear. There's no proof he killed the real Noel Barrows or that he's even dead. One girlfriend died in a car crash. Another committed suicide after breaking up with him. Those aren't crimes. He even has a great alibi, the best of the whole lot, the night the professor was killed."

"But you think that was his brother at the bar."

"How can I prove it? It sounds weak, like I'm grasping at straws."

"Are you?"

"I've put together a file to draw from." I held it up on my clipboard. "He doesn't know I've met his mother."

"But remember how Noel pointed out that a picture was missing from the mantel? You said it yourself—that was a key piece of evidence. Why would he hand it to you?"

"Because he knew that's what we'd think. The murderer would never point that out—and therefore, by pointing it out, we'd know he wasn't the murderer."

"But it was important evidence."

"That bothered me until this morning. I talked to Mitzie, who types my notes from crime scenes. I dropped my notes in her inbox by 11:00 a.m. the day after the murder. I didn't get them back until late that afternoon. But guess what—her records show that Noel came to her office that day at 11:15, asking her to retrieve something from the files. He had to sign for it, so it's documented. She was in the file room at least a minute, she said. That gives him time to look through her inbox and grab my notes. Record shows he came back ten minutes later to return what he'd borrowed from the file. She walks out to refile it, and he puts my notes back in her inbox. Meanwhile he's made a photocopy. Has a detailed report. He knows my conclusion about the pictures on the mantel before he ever shows up at the scene."

"So he just mentioned out to you what he knew you'd already figured out?"

"Right. It does him no harm. In fact does him good, because how could we suspect someone who hands us critical information?"

"And you really think he planted his own fingerprints on the murder weapon?"

"When there's proof someone framed you, how could anybody believe you're guilty? It worked like a charm."

"But remember the films we watched with Ray? The detectives' meeting? When Noel was reading a golf magazine?"

"Yeah," I said. "A nervous person looks at his PDA. A bored or disinterested person looks at a golf magazine. Isn't that what I said?"

"Right. Change your mind?"

"He's sitting in a meeting of detectives being told, 'One of you is a killer.' No way you casually look through a magazine. It was a pretense. He wanted to look disinterested. I underestimated this guy. Things aren't what they appear."

"People aren't what they appear," Clarence said. "You trusted Noel more than you did Karl Baylor."

"Can't argue with you there." I latched the top button on my trench coat, sealing out the cold wind. "Let's head back."

As the Justice Center loomed in front of us, I glanced at my watch. "In ten minutes, I've got to make my case against Noel."

"Don't you think you need God's help?" Clarence asked.

"Maybe," I said.

There on Second Street, ten feet outside the entrance to the Justice Center, Clarence prayed aloud for me and the detectives and the meeting. He asked for wisdom and justice.

My stomach was so tied in knots I hardly minded it.

"Do you feel a creeping, shrinking sensation, Watson, when you stand before the serpents in the Zoo, and see the slithery, gliding, venomous creatures, with their deadly eyes and wicked, flattened faces? Well, that's how Milverton impresses me. And yet I can't get out of doing business with him."
SHERLOCK HOLMES, *THE ADVENTURE OF CHARLES AUGUSTUS MILVERTON*

FRIDAY, JANUARY 24, 3:30 P.M.

SERGEANT SEYMOUR STOOD UP in the large conference room in front of eight detectives. No Clarence, no smuggled surveillance equipment. I felt like a junior lawyer about to argue his first case before the Supreme Court.

"Look," Sarge said as the room quieted, "it's been crazy, with the plumbing problems and everything else. Backed up toilets don't make for good morale. I know it's late in the day, but there's something we've got to do if we're going to get these murders off our backs. So I'm handing the meeting over to Chandler."

I stood up, feeling like a left-wing commie addressing the John Birch Society. I'd made my plan to present the evidence and bring the charges, modeled after Nero Wolfe's practice of pulling suspects together and unveiling his deductions. Now it seemed like a whopping mistake, promising to bomb like the now legendary "where'd you grow up" meeting. But there was no turning back.

"All right," I said. "Sit back and relax. This could take an hour." Moans and groans ran their course. "But by then, I hope you'll agree we may have solved a murder…maybe four murders."

That got their attention.

"I'm going to lay it out. I'll tell you my conclusions. Some I can prove; some are educated guesses. You're the jury."

"You're a joke, Chandler," Cimmatoni said.

"I recommend this be a monologue, not a dialogue." I looked at Cimmatoni. "That means, I talk, you listen. You challenge me early, we'll be here late. Hear me out."

As I spoke, I felt the tension ratchet up.

"Is it hot in here?" I asked.

Tommi and Karl shook their heads. I wiped sweat and took off my trench coat.

"We all know Jack Glissan was a decent man. He loved his daughter Melissa, his only child. Some of you didn't know her. Melissa went to college at Linfield, but her philosophy teacher became ill midsemester, and they couldn't find a replacement. She had to have the credit, so Portland State allowed her to pick up classes there. Eventually she got depressed, turned to drugs. On November 20, she died—ruled a suicide by hanging."

Chris Doyle slapped his hand on his doughboy thigh. "What's that got to do with—"

"Shut up!" Sarge barked.

"Talking to her roommate and ex-boyfriend, Jack discovers that her philosophy professor seduced her. Within a few months he dumped her. While she fell apart, Palatine went on to his next conquest. Jack filed a complaint at the university, but since there wasn't proof, nothing happened. Ten years go by and the anger simmers on the back burner. Jack hates Palatine. Then seven months ago, on June 12 he sees this picture and article in the *Tribune*."

I held up the newspaper, compliments of Carp. "There's the heading: 'PSU philosophy prof named Teacher of the Year.' Jack sees Palatine in this picture next to a young female student, and he can't stand it any longer. Something snaps. He decides to kill the professor."

"You know this?" Karl asked.

"Eighty percent of it's straight from Jack. He confessed to me."

"So you say." Kim Suda scowled.

"Anniversaries were big with Jack. On November 4, he took me to dinner. Why? It was twenty-five years to the day after we started working as partners. Several of you have had toasts with Jack on anniversaries of solving crimes, haven't you?"

At least three heads nodded.

"You're not nodding, Noel. Why? You know it better than anyone. You know the tenth anniversary of Jack's daughter's death was huge. Did the rest of you know that Palatine was murdered, to the hour, likely to the minute, ten years after Melissa Glissan died? Of course, *you* knew that, Noel."

"Why would I?"

"Because you helped him do it."

"You're accusing *Noel* of murdering Palatine?" Tommi asked.

"And Brandon Phillips."

Cimmatoni locked his eyes, laserlike, on Noel.

"Accusing Jack is a low blow," Noel said. "I resent that more than accusing me. Okay, Jack had some issues, and he took his life. That's hard for me to accept. But kill somebody? You say he confessed to you—I say you're lying. Jack Glissan was no killer."

Doyle, Suda, and Cimmatoni all nodded their agreement.

"You going to tell us," Noel asked, "about the Black Jack wrapper you found at Palatine's and didn't turn in because it had your fingerprints on it?"

"Is that true?" Baylor asked.

"Yes, but—"

"Is it also true," Noel said, "that you'd been drunk and had a blackout the night the professor was killed? And another blackout when Phillips was killed?"

"Well, I've had a few—"

"And that you had Brandon's blood on you?" Doyle asked.

"You dropped that blood-soaked clothing fragment at our crime scene," Suda said. "Admit it."

"True?" Sarge asked.

"Not...exactly," I said. "Okay, some of it's true, but—"

"There's going to be a full investigation," Sarge said. "You're in big trouble, Chandler."

"He's fingering me to cover his guilt," I said, pointing at Noel.

"He planted his own fingerprints?" Cimmatoni asked.

I stood there with my mouth open. I skimmed the papers in my file and held up three faxed sheets.

"These are flight manifests confirming Noel made a trip from Miami to Portland. They're dated twenty years ago November 18, two days before Melissa Glissan was murdered."

"You're saying Noel also murdered Jack's daughter?" Tommi asked.

"Let me see those," Cimmatoni grabbed the papers from me. "These are alphabetized by last name. Where's Barrows?"

"You see Donald Meyer?" I asked. "I circled it."

"So? Who's Donald Meyer?" Cimmatoni asked. "What're you trying to pull, Chandler? You stand there waving these papers, pretending you have Noel's name on a ten-year-old flight manifest, which could be fake anyway. Then when I call your bluff, you pick a passenger name we've never heard of as proof that *Barrows* was on board?"

"Noel's heard of Donald Meyer, haven't you?"

"Who is he?" Noel asked.

"He's you. He's from Florida. And he has a brother."

"I'm from Washington," Noel said. "Liberty Lake. And I'm an only child." He spoke calmly, like a psychologist to a confused patient.

"A boy named Noel Barrows was from Liberty Lake. But your name was Donald Meyer, and you grew up in Dade County, Florida, outside Miami."

"I grew up in Liberty Lake. Ask my friends, Mike Clark, Bill Moon, Amy Mishima, Nancy Moore. I went to grade school and high school with them. Ask my next-door neighbors, Kevin and Alan and Jeannine Sturdy, and their mom, Carrie. Ask my teachers, Mrs. Johnson and Mr. Barber and Mr. Gradin and Mr. Holevas."

"None of them have seen Noel Barrows for thirteen years," I said, addressing the jury. "Sure, he did his homework. He knows their names. They'll all say they had Noel Barrows in class, or lived next door to him. And yeah, his age, height, and hair color generally fit. But he's not the same person."

"This is ridiculous," Doyle said, moving toward the door. "Brandon was murdered, Jack took his life, and now Chandler's trying to lynch Noel…all based on unsubstantiated accusations. I'm done."

"Sit," Sarge said. "That's not a request. All of you, calm down. Chandler's going to present some evidence…aren't you?"

"But why would this Donald assume the identity of Noel Barrows?" Baylor asked.

"Okay," I said, sighing louder than I intended. "Donald Meyer met Melissa one summer, apparently at a golf camp in California." I looked at Noel. I saw the flash in his eyes. "They exchanged numbers, talked on the phone over several months. Eventually he came out to Portland to meet Melissa's parents, Jack and Linda. He stayed with them three weeks. Hit it off with them. But later Melissa broke up with him. She didn't explain why. Enraged, Noel flew out here from Miami to reclaim his stolen property or to punish her. He didn't tell her or her parents he was coming. He found out from her roommate that Melissa was in love with her philosophy professor at PSU. He was livid. He confronted Melissa. A day or two later she was hanging from a rope."

"But if the Glissans knew him as Donald," Tommi said, "they'd know about the name change."

"After Melissa died, Jack and Linda welcomed Donald. They golfed together; he stayed with them, grieved with them supposedly. He expressed an interest in law enforcement. Jack took him under his wing. Donald had family troubles in Florida and wanted a fresh start. Maybe Jack's grief blinded him, but he went along with the name change. He gave Noel Barrows a written endorsement for the police academy. Later Jack recommended you," I was looking at Noel, "for a patrol job with Portland Police. When you made detective, Jack requested you as his partner. He mentored you. Cops talk a lot. So do golfing buddies. So what did you two talk about?"

Noel shrugged.

"Sometimes you talked about Melissa. Both of you blamed the professor for her death."

"Why not?" Suda asked. "He should've been shot."

"He was," I said, then looked at Noel. "On some of those long nights on stakeouts, I say you talked about the professor. Then when the *Tribune* published the article praising him, Jack, or maybe it was you, said, 'I wish we could get him.' And the other said, 'Why don't we?' And you figured, who better to get away with it than a couple of homicide detectives?"

"That's insane," Doyle said. "Jack's wife's positive Noel wasn't involved. Plus, he has an airtight alibi. Weren't there a half dozen guys at a tavern who say he was with them? You saying they were all that drunk, or they're all lying?"

"They believed they were with Noel. But it was somebody else."

"A clone or a shape-shifter?" Doyle asked.

"Donald Meyer's brother."

"He has a twin?" Tommi asked.

"Brother seventeen months younger. I met their mother in Dade County yesterday morning." Noel stared bullets at me. "They looked enough alike that when they were in high school they could fool their teachers. They made alibis for each other even then. Check out this picture she gave me." I handed it to Baylor.

"Which one's you?" he asked Noel. Tommi, Suda, and Cimma crowded close to see it.

"You and your photographer girlfriend do that in Photoshop?" Noel asked. "That's a phony picture. I don't have a brother and my mother's dead."

"So you believe Noel's brother sat in for him at the bar to establish his alibi?" Baylor said.

I reached in my briefcase and pulled out a yearbook. "I requisitioned this from Dr. Michael M. Krop Senior High School in Dade County. It's a genuine yearbook. No Photoshop."

"I was an only child."

"Noel Barrows was an only child. Donald Meyer had a brother named Rodney." I held up the yearbook. "I've marked a few pages. Anybody want a look?"

Cimmatoni grabbed it and flipped to the first page marked with a sticky note. Baylor and Suda hovered close for a good look.

"Donald Meyer sure looks like you." Cimmatoni flipped to the next marked page. "Rodney Meyer looks like you too."

"Check out page 84," I said. Cimmatoni flipped to the next sticky note.

"What is it?" Tommi asked.

"Golf team," Cimmatoni said.

"You're in the picture, Noel," Suda said. "Only the name underneath says Donald Meyer."

"This is just another frame. Can't you see that?"

Knowing it was time for my hole card, I flipped the lid on my laptop and said, "You want proof? Take a look at the fingerprints of Donald Meyer, in trouble with Dade County three times. On the left is Donald's fingerprint; on the right is Noel's print, on file with our department. Tell me what you see."

A crowd gathered close around the laptop, everyone but Noel and Doyle.

"Perfect match," Cimmatoni growled.

"So it's true." Tommi looked at Noel. "Donald Meyer and Noel Barrows are the same person."

62

*"In a modest way I have combated evil, but to take
on the Father of Evil himself would, perhaps,
be too ambitious a task."*
SHERLOCK HOLMES, *THE HOUND OF THE BASKERVILLES*

"STILL DENY YOU'RE DONALD MEYER?" I asked, pointing at the matching fingerprints.

Noel Barrows stood up and addressed the group. "Look, I admit I had my
problems as a kid. But I got my life together. I wanted to be a cop. I was afraid
they'd screen me out. Jack didn't think that was fair. He encouraged me to change
my name."

"You didn't just change your name," I said. "You adopted a dead man's identity."

"It gave me a fresh start. That doesn't make me a murderer!"

"I know about overcoming legal problems to become a cop," Manny said.
"But I didn't have to change my name."

"When was the last time you saw your brother?" I asked Noel.

"Haven't seen him for years. Don't even know where he lives."

"You claimed you grew up in Washington," Manny said.

"If you knew my family, you'd understand why I had to leave and start over.
When you take a new identity, you can't just announce it."

"What happened to the real Noel Barrows?" Manny asked.

"I was checking grave stones and death notices," Noel said. "Then I heard this
guy had disappeared. That's why I chose him. He was gone, but not dead apparently, so there wasn't a death certificate. It was easier to take his name as long as I
stayed at a distance."

"Missing people usually reappear," I said. "If he did, you'd be in big trouble."

"I took a chance."

"I don't think so."

"What are you suggesting?" Tommi asked.

"The real Noel Barrows was the perfect choice," I said to Donald. "He looks
enough like you that somebody who hadn't seen him for five years could think
you're him. Appearances change, memories aren't reliable. But no way you could
fool family and close friends."

"Exactly," Noel said. "I chose him because he'd moved away, didn't stay in
touch."

"I say you chose him *before* he disappeared. You shopped for the right age and appearance, someone without family. You knew he wouldn't reappear for one simple reason—you killed him and hid his body."

"You're crazy," Noel said.

"Is there anyone you're not accusing Noel of killing?" Chris Doyle said. "He's not old enough to have shot JFK, is he?"

I looked at Noel. "What would you say if I told you I could place you in Helena, Montana, ten years ago, where the real Noel Barrows had been living since he left Liberty Lake? What if I said I could put you there the same weekend he disappeared without a trace?"

"I'd say you're lying."

No, just bluffing. But I saw his lip tremble. That moment I realized I'd overlooked something.

Noel, like every detective in the room, was armed.

When you're gouging somebody with a hot poker, you generally don't want his hand twelve inches from a deadly weapon. But I hadn't won over all the detectives, so trying to take his weapon might galvanize support for him.

"I believe Jack killed Palatine," I said to Noel. "But you killed him too. And I think you—not Jack—pushed Frederick off his deck and murdered Dr. Hedstrom and Phillips. Jack wouldn't kill them. Maybe he killed himself out of guilt, thinking he led you down this path of murders, not knowing you'd killed others before the professor. Including his own daughter."

Noel shook his head emphatically.

"Was killing Palatine your idea and Jack went along?" I asked.

"That's a lie. Ask Linda Glissan. She'll tell you. Okay, maybe I should have turned Jack in when he talked about killing Palatine. But I thought I'd convinced him not to. He told me he wouldn't. My mistake was believing him. He must have lost it to kill the others. I had no reason to kill them."

"Frederick saw you at the professor's door," I said. "Hedstrom? You knew I'd interviewed him. You saw the report Mitzie typed up, didn't you? You knew that as academic dean, Hedstrom had on file every complaint about Palatine."

"I never heard of Hedstrom till he was dead."

"Jack and Linda both said that Jack went to the academic dean after Melissa died, to lodge his complaint. I requisitioned Hedstrom's files like I suggested Doyle and Suda do, but they didn't think it was worth it," I said, eyeing them. "Manny found Jack's accusation, his original letter. You knew Hedstrom, if pressed, could surrender that information. So you killed him. You knew if Jack was incriminated, you could be next."

"You're full of yourself, Chandler," Noel said, laughing.

I wondered if anyone else noticed his right hand settle unnaturally on his chest, inches from his shoulder holster. I put my hand on my heart too and saw Manny do the same. It looked like we were preparing for the Pledge of Allegiance.

"What about Phillips?" Cimmatoni asked.

I stepped just two feet from Noel. "You knew Brandon Phillips had figured something out. You knew he was about to tell me. Maybe he'd confronted you, or confronted Jack and said he was going to admit he'd lied about his alibi, which would pull the rug out from under Jack, and in turn, maybe from under you. Anyway, you killed him before he could talk."

"You're a liar and a drunk," Noel said. "And you have no proof of anything."

"You're right about me being a drunk. But I'm sober now. I don't know if there's a hell or whether you'd go there for killing Palatine. But I'm pretty sure killing the others is enough to get you there. For all I know, if he was about to talk, you'd have killed Jack too."

That pushed Noel's rage button, which I was hoping for.

"Who talked to Jack right before he took his life?" he yelled as he stood. "Who threatened him? You did. Not me!"

"I'm not the one who had two girlfriends die violently after breaking up with me."

"I admit I changed my name. The rest is a pack of lies. It's all speculation. There's no proof."

I saw a few nods. Even those who believed what I'd said knew there's a difference between belief and proof. Proving he was Donald Meyer hadn't proven he was a killer. If I had a rabbit, I'd have to pull it out of the hat.

I looked at Noel again. "The impressions on the carpet in Palatine's bedroom, by the window—your shoes match them."

"What shoes?"

"Your black size 10 Rockport World Town Classics that we confiscated with a search warrant."

"A search warrant on a fellow detective." Noel looked around the room. "How's that for teamwork and loyalty?"

"The sole of your shoes matches the impressions and dirt marks on Palatine's carpet."

"It's a common shoe," Noel said. "Or maybe somebody was framing me again. Remember those fake fingerprints?"

"Yeah. What about that, Chandler?" Cimmatoni asked.

"Ingenious. Only the innocent have evidence planted against them, right? So Noel put himself inside the circle of the innocent. Who made that 911 call, using your term *fishy*? I'm betting on your brother Rodney. You planted evidence against me and half the rest of us. We were innocent, so you joined the innocents by being framed."

Noel smiled as an artist smiles at his masterpiece. "Somebody tried to frame me from the beginning, and I think it was you, Chandler. I was cleared of the finger-prints and the 911 call, remember? I was at the Do Drop Inn. All kinds of people will testify to it."

"You were smart. But know where you messed up?"

I looked to see if he would flinch. He didn't.

"Those black Rockports we confiscated? Guess what they found just yesterday in the bottom of your right shoe?"

Noel's face held steady.

"A shard of glass the lab identified as belonging to the professor's broken win-dow. It's all the proof we need."

Noel smiled. "You're lying. There's no glass in the bottom of those shoes."

I let the words hang ut there, and looked around the room. "Cimmatoni, do you know whether you have a tiny glass shard imbedded on the bottom of your shoe? Karl, do you? Manny? Tommi? I don't. Is there anyone here who knows for sure that any particular shoe sitting in your closet at home doesn't have a piece of glass in it?"

Tommi and Karl shook their heads. The others pondered it.

"No? Then I have a question, Donald. How can you possibly know you don't have a glass shard in the bottom of your Rockports?"

He folded, then unfolded his arms.

"The only way you could know is if you went over them inch by inch to make sure there's no glass. And no one would do that in the first place…except the killer."

There were twenty seconds of eerie quiet. Then his right hand, resting on his chest, moved left. Manny and I jumped the same moment. I grabbed Noel's right hand.

"Disarm him," I said.

Cimmatoni held him, and Baylor checked his ankles. Baylor produced the gun from Noel's ankle strap two seconds after Cimmatoni held up his Smith and Wesson from the shoulder holster.

"Get off him!" Doyle yelled.

"He was going for his gun," I said.

"Let go of my hand," Noel said. I let go and he opened his fist to show a stick of gum. "I just got gum out of my shirt pocket. That's a crime too? At least it's not Black Jack."

Noel got a sympathetic look from Tommi. I got dirty looks from Suda and Doyle.

"I have to use the restroom," Noel said.

"Not without an escort," I said. "Anybody join me?"

"I'll go," Cimma said.

"Don't let him out of your sight," Sarge said. "I want him back here in five minutes. Everybody else, stay put."

As we walked out the door, I positioned myself behind and to Noel's left, Cimma walked beside him on the right. I put my hand on Noel's shoulder, and he shook it off. I put it back and clenched it.

We headed toward the detective division men's room, only to see a sign on the door: Out of Order. A pool of water had accumulated under the door crack.

"Waiting area restroom," Cimma said.

We walked through the security door into the empty waiting room, elevator on our right, restrooms on our left.

"Watch him," I said to Cimma.

I walked into the restroom, checked the garbage, pulled a paper towel, and looked under the sink. I even looked inside the toilet tank. All clear. Hey, if I can duct tape a gun under the kitchen table, somebody else can do it in a public restroom.

"All clear," I said. "Let's frisk him again."

"He's clean," Cimma said, but frisked him anyway.

Noel, trying to maintain some dignity, walked toward the restroom.

"Don't lock it," I said, "or we kick the door down, got it?"

When he closed the door, Noel's shoulders were sagging, like a man who knew he'd been beat. After he'd been in less than a minute, though the toilet hadn't flushed, he opened the door. His left arm pushed the door forward and his right arm swung up.

I was looking down the barrel of a 9 mm Beretta PXR Storm, with a magazine capacity of seventeen rounds. I knew this because it was on my wish list.

"Drop your gun," he said to Cimma, "or I blow his head off." Cimma dropped it. "Inside," he said.

When we were both inside, I saw something out of the corner of my eye, a white bottle. I heard the sound of an aerosol spray. My last memory was pain on the right side of my skull and feeling something wet on my nose and mouth, then seeing the restroom disappear.

The next voice I heard was Sarge's. "What happened?"

The left side of my head felt like it had been teed up for a Tiger Woods driver.

Sarge pulled me to my knees. I saw Cimmatoni strung out beside me, face flat, tasting the restroom floor. Karl Baylor stepped past me and knelt to check Cimma.

454R A N D Y   A L C O R N

"Smells like knockout spray," Sarge said. "Chloroform or ether. But where'd he get it?"

"Same place he got the gun," I mumbled.

"He's got a *gun*?"

Sarge stepped out and yelled at the gal by the entry window. "Call for a lock-down! Detective Noel Barrows is a fugitive, armed and dangerous. Tell the guards at the Second and Third Street entrances not to let him out!"

He ran toward her, took the phone, and gave his own message.

"Get me the Second Street door guard!" Sarge barked. "No, don't pull him away! Post two other guards pronto. Then put him on."

Sarge roared at me. "How long were you out here before he escaped?"

"Just a few minutes. I think."

"Then he's got a five-minute head start!" Sarge said. He talked into the phone. "You saw him go out the front door? Three minutes ago? You see which way he turned?" He put down the phone and yelled, "He's on the streets! Maybe to his car. Somebody call the parking garage, and get some officers there. Now!"

People scrambled to make the call.

Ten seconds later Sarge looked at me and a dazed, flat-faced Cimmatoni, supported by Karl Baylor. He confirmed that Noel hadn't stolen guns from either of us. His Beretta was enough.

They led us back to the conference room and sat us down. Three phone calls later, Sarge turned to the seven remaining homicide detectives and said, "Noel's disappeared."

"I write these few lines through the courtesy of Mr. Moriarty. He has been giving me a sketch of the methods by which he avoided the English police.... They certainly confirm the very high opinion which I had formed of his abilities.... I made every disposition of my property before leaving England and handed it to my brother Mycroft."
SHERLOCK HOLMES, *THE FINAL PROBLEM*

FRIDAY, JANUARY 24, 4:10 P.M.

MY BRAIN WAS STILL FUZZY. All I could think was, *Where did he get the gun and the knockout spray?*

Someone said they'd seen his car parked in the primo spot at the corner of Second and Madison, twenty seconds from the Justice Center's east entrance. That meant he didn't have to walk to the basement parking garage and deal with steps or elevators. He'd been prepared for a quick exit. He could have turned right and crossed the Hawthorne Bridge in a heartbeat, or headed north to the Morrison Bridge and from there could take I-5 to Seattle or Salem or wherever he wanted.

"His car," Sergeant Seymour said. "What is it? Silver...?" He snapped his fingers.

"Chrysler Sebring," Baylor said. "Two years old."

"Four door?"

"Two door," Cimmatoni said, reentering the land of the living.

"Get out the license number. APB. Top priority."

I smiled to myself. Noel wasn't the only one thinking ahead. Yesterday I'd planted a bird dog under his left rear fender. Wherever he was headed, we'd be able to trace him.

Lenny the maintenance man arrived to fix the toilets. Sarge bawled him out because if he'd come earlier, a cop-killer wouldn't have escaped. Ten minutes later Lenny emerged from the restroom.

"What was the problem?" Sarge asked.

Lenny held up a soaking wet wad of paper. "Some jerk flushed like fifty pages of paper down each of the toilets."

"Paper?"

He offered two pages to Sarge, who pulled plastic gloves from his pocket before handling the wet paper. He held it up to the light and read the smeared words.

"'I felt the heat rise off the gritty pavement. The smog was so thick you could slice it up and serve it like day-old bread.'" He looked further down the page at the next sentence he could read. "I grabbed Alfredo by the throat and said, 'You're nothin' but a two-bit pawnshop palooka.'"

"What kind of nonsense is this?" Sarge asked. "Wait, there's something at the top. It says…*The Bacon and Cheese Murders*. By…Ollie Chandler?"

An hour later, thanks to the bird dog, four patrol cars were following Noel's car up I-84 East. Three state police cars and six more officers had gathered down the interstate in Hood River, ready to take him.

Meanwhile, I needed a shower and change of clothes. Just aftr sunset I drove home to the old brownstone. Kids were shooting baskets under the streetlights as I opened the garage door to bring in the trash can. Inside, I pulled down the door and was greeted by the barrel of a pistol, a Beretta, which had grown a silencer since I'd seen it nearly two hours ago.

"Hands behind your back," said the detective formerly known as Noel Barrows. "Nose against the wall."

I felt cold metal closing on my wrists. I heard the snap and felt the ache.

"Where'd you get the Beretta?" I asked.

"Hid it in the paper towel dispenser."

"You thought ahead. Even got yourself out of a secure area by flushing my novel down the toilet."

"If it ever gets published, it won't be the last time it sees a toilet. I figured your meeting was to hammer me in front of the detectives. Getting a search warrant and confiscating my stuff was a clue."

"I left you your bedroom slippers. No hard feelings?"

"I'm taking all your pieces. Move and I blow your head off."

He reached inside my coat to the shoulder holster and got my Glock. He raided my coat pocket and took my Smith and Wesson 340 revolver.

"How many pockets in this stupid raincoat?"

"Actually, it's a trench—"

"Shut up. Sit down. Jack told me you always carry a third piece strapped to your ankle. Flail your leg, you'll never walk again."

He pulled up my right pant leg, exposing my shin.

"You need a tanning booth."

Gun pointed at my kneecap, he loosened the strap of my ankle holster and took it off, Baby Glock and all.

"Not much of a gun," he said.

I hoped for a chance to prove him wrong. Between guns and keys, he stuffed my hardware into every pocket he had.

"Why are you here?" I asked.

"Where'd you expect me to be? My apartment, with the cops? Or driving up the interstate with your bird dog?"

"I'm impressed you found it. Hope you didn't take personally anything I said at our meeting."

"We won't be staying here," Noel said, looking out the garage door window. He nodded toward the neighborhood kids still shooting baskets under the eerie glow of the streetlights. "But we'll wait till the crowd thins. Be dark in thirty minutes."

"So until then…we'll just chat in my garage?"

"We're going in your back door."

Gun pressed into my lower spine, I stepped out of the garage onto the back deck.

"Familiar territory for you, isn't it?" I said. "You and your noose and shotgun."

"Think I couldn't have gotten you with the shotgun? I was just playing with you."

"If Mulch hadn't made me duck, it would've been playing rough."

"I'm taking off your cuffs so you can grab his collar. I won't hesitate to shoot you both. This is a quality silencer. Your neighbors won't hear it."

There's only one smartest dog in the world, and every little boy has him. I love Mulch, and he's got great street smarts, but instead of something clever like waiting under the kitchen table to attack Noel, he just stood with his paws stretched up on the kitchen window and barked like crazy.

Noel handed me my keys. Beretta in his right hand, he carried a gym bag in his left. "Open the door slowly, grab his collar, and stay six feet in front of me. Lure him into a room, and close the door. Don't go in yourself, or I'll shoot you both. Dog comes at me, I kill him. Got it?"

I opened the door. Mulch was snarling now, showing his teeth, his eyes riveted on Noel behind me. I took his collar. Mulch is a great judge of character. I'd have let him go in a heartbeat if Noel didn't have the gun trained on him. I got him to my bedroom door, opened it, and pushed him in, then tried to close the door.

Mulch put it in reverse, wormed his way back out, made a quick turn, and chased Noel into the kitchen. He got his teeth on Noel's leg, and I was sure I'd hear the gun.

What happened next showed that Noel didn't trust his silencer like he claimed. I heard a thud then a yelp from Mulch as he fell to the floor. I ran to him. Noel held his gun gingerly in his hand. I cradled Mulch in my arms, wiping blood flowing out of his right ear. His teeth were showing, including a broken one, but he was as still as a piece of wood.

"He's a goner," Noel said.

I felt metal clamp on my right wrist again. He pulled it behind my back to my other wrist and snapped it in place. Both hands behind me, I put my head against Mulch's chest. I heard a heart beating. Mine.

Donald Meyer had pistol-whipped my dog. I no longer wanted to take him in. I wanted to take him down. I wanted to kill him. But I'd need to bide my time. I'd get justice for Brandon Phillips and Melissa Glissan and Paul Frederick and too many to count on one hand. Including Mulch.

Meyer pushed me down in the recliner and strapped me with duct tape he'd found in my garage.

"Don't they know how dark it is?" he asked, looking out the front window blinds at the ball players.

Though all I wanted was to get my hands on his throat, I had to calm myself. I should get any information I could, in case I survived this. I breathed deeply, and spoke calmly.

"Was it you or Jack at Palatine's front door, showing the ID?"

I was hoping he'd be proud of his work and would talk.

He opened his bag and pulled out a metal detector, then ran it over my coat. It activated. He ransacked my coat pockets until he found a metallic dot. He held it up and smiled.

"A GPS, so they can find you. Well, the problem is, you're home, recovering from your wounds, so you're not missing. We'll just leave it right here in your living room." He set it on the TV.

Next he pulled from his gym bag a TD-53 bug detector, like Ray Eagle's, then ran it over my chest. The Geiger counter effect kicked in faster and faster as he moved it toward my chest. He waved his wand over my shirt and it started beeping. Pulling back some of the duct tape holding me in the chair, he opened my shirt.

"You wired yourself." He laughed.

"In case you came after me."

He put his fingers under the white surgical tape that made an X on my chest, holding the bug in place. He ripped one of the tapes off and I winced, eyes watering. Then he ripped off the other. Next time Jack Bauer wants terrorists to give him information, I recommend pulling their chest hairs.

Donald took out the miniature recording device and looked it over. "Just a recorder, no live transmission. Good." He dropped it on my kitchen floor and ground it flat.

"You know what you could've gotten for that on eBay? I meant to say this earlier, but I'll say it now: 'I'm recording you.' Oops. Should I have mentioned it sooner?"

"You thought I wouldn't check whether you're wired. What an idiot."

It wasn't the first time I'd been called an idiot, but when the guy calling you that has a big gun with a silencer and a recent track record of at least four murders, you don't sass him. And you certainly don't make cracks about his mother.

"Like mother, like son," I said.

He slapped me with the back of his hand. Harder than the Pillsbury Doyleboy can hit, I'll tell you that.

"I hate her."

"What'd your mother do to you, Donald?"

"None of your business."

"I met her. She's something. She said your father beat you up."

"My father wasn't the problem. He left my mother because he was afraid of her."

"What'd she do?"

"Things I'd never do to anyone."

Considering what he'd done, that said it all.

"Should be dark in fifteen minutes," he said, peeking out the blinds at the ball players.

"So now you can answer my question—was it Jack or you who showed the ID at Palatine's front door?"

"Me. I'd called him in advance, told him we were conducting an investigation into a student complaint concerning him. Said we just wanted to hear his side of it and I'd be over in ten minutes. He saw my ID and let me in. I closed the blinds, then let Jack in the back door."

"You saw Frederick over at the apartments?"

"I saw somebody standing there on his deck. Since I couldn't describe him, I figured he couldn't describe me. But when I read your interview notes and found out about the binoculars, I knew he could be trouble."

"So you killed him?"

"If he identified me, I'd be dead. It was self-defense."

"Interesting definition of self-defense."

I was taped, hands behind me, in my recliner, knowing that my SIG-Sauer P226 was ten inches out of reach, taped under the chair bottom.

Donald moved Sharon's old rocking chair by the window. My wrists were on fire.

"The noose symbolized Melissa's hanging?"

"Jack's idea. He explained it to the professor as he tightened it around his neck. Said his daughter hung herself, but that as far as Jack was concerned, Palatine tied the rope. I didn't mention to Jack where I got the rope." He smiled.

"Were you really trying to frame me? Or distract me?"

"Having fun with you. When he found out later where I'd gotten the rope, and about the Black Jack wrapper, he bawled me out. I wanted people to question you, give you some serious headaches. I've never liked you."

"I'm crushed, Donald. I'll have to call my therapist."

The corners of his lips barely raised, like his mother's. The rotten apple hadn't fallen far from that tree.

"Your plan," I said, "was that you'd be investigating the murder you'd committed. The second murder that night spoiled things for you, didn't it? What were the chances that you'd be assigned to another murder before Palatine's was called in?"

"We shouldn't have counted on neighbors to call. We should've called sooner. One of those twists of fate."

"November 20 was the anniversary of Melissa's death. But you only had a one in five chance of being the up team that night, right?"

Have you ever asked a question you didn't know the answer to, and just before the last syllable comes out of your mouth you suddenly know? I said it: "You bumped yourself up the list, didn't you? By murdering people."

"Just a homeless guy and a drug dealer. No big deal."

"You killed Jimmy Ross, didn't you? And framed Lincoln Caldwell?"

"You're not as stupid as you look, Chandler. Come to think of it, nobody's as stupid as you look. Yeah, I tested my fake fingerprint skills with Lincoln Caldwell's prints. Blood sample from Lincoln's apartment to leave on Jimmy's doorknob? Easy. Needles everywhere. Getting someone with outstandings to come over in the red sweatpants? Piece of cake. Heard that guy died of an overdose a week later. Shame."

"How many people have you killed, Noel?" I deliberately addressed Noel the cop rather than Donald the serial killer in the unlikely hope they were separate personalities and the cop still had a conscience.

"None that deserved to live. You know the riffraff we deal with. They get the kids on dope. They're responsible for half the crime in this city. These lousy judges won't put them away. Even if they do, they get retirement at the state prison, compliments of the taxpayers. You know what they say—there's no justice...just us."

64

"I go into a case to help the ends of justice.... I claim the right to work in my own way and give my results at my own time—complete rather than in stages."
SHERLOCK HOLMES, *THE VALLEY OF FEAR*

FRIDAY, JANUARY 24, 6:30 P.M.

I DIDN'T KNOW where he was planning to take me. I wanted to get as much information as I could, in the unlikely hope that I'd be alive to deliver it. I twisted myself in the chair to try to look at his eyes.

"You must have been squirming that night when you got the call to the other crime scene. You couldn't turn it down."

"Right after Rodney called 911 from his old cell phone, before patrol got to Palatine's, Sarge sent us to the other murder, where the guy murdered his wife's boyfriend. After all that planning. That's when we realized you'd get our case."

"Which changed everything," I said. "Since you were sure you'd be investigating your own crime scene, you didn't have to be as careful, did you? If your prints were somewhere, it just meant you'd been careless, left your gloves off. Hair follicle on the victim? Hey, you examined him. Your shoe print by the window? You'd say, 'Sorry, my shoe covering came off.' But once you realized you wouldn't investigate your case, you must've wondered whether you left evidence. That's why you came back to the scene wasn't it? That whole episode with the ski masks."

Noel smiled. "Jack and I were a couple of blocks away. We figured we'd just sit and wait until patrol got there and called in the murder. Then we'd get our call and step in to solve the crime. When Sarge sent us to the other murder, Jack panicked."

"Why?"

Noel laughed. "That old man prided himself on how careful he was. Even after he sent me back to the scene to double-check—when I'd already gone over everything and taken the wine bottle—an hour later, at the other murder scene, he realizes he left his reading glasses right on the professor's desk!"

"Those were Jack's glasses?"

I remembered using those glasses to read the confession on the computer screen. I, and the criminalists, had assumed they were the professor's. No checks run for a stray hair or partial print? Donald was right—I *was* an idiot!

"Was it Jack or Rodney wearing the other ski mask?"

"Rodney. We had fun with it. He loved being chased. I told him they'd have to break off pursuit and get back to Palatine's. But it gave me time to get the bottle."

"Where was Jack?"

"By then, at the other crime scene. I met him there twenty minutes later. Rodney dropped me off a few blocks away."

Donald stood again, gazing through the blinds. I pictured him peering out Palatine's broken window. "When they going to stop the basketball? Maybe I should just shoot them."

"Did you plant Brandon's granola bar?"

"You ID'd that? I was hoping you would."

"The 100 cc needle—was I supposed to suspect Tommi for that, since she uses a syringe for a medical condition?"

"She does? No kidding. That's great." He laughed. "That was one of Melissa's old needles. Sentimental value. Symbolism. I kept a little collection."

"Keep a collection for the other girlfriends you murdered?"

He stared at me, looking so much like his mother that I changed the subject.

"Whose idea was the wine?"

"We always drank a glass of Riesling to celebrate bringing killers to justice. We figured, let's bring our own bottle and do it on the spot."

"Jack and I used to make a toast when we brought someone to justice," I said. "But we didn't kill them."

"Saves time. In case you haven't noticed, the other way isn't working. The professor wasn't in jail. Didn't even lose his teaching job. Got awards instead."

"Did Palatine run for his bedroom and break the window trying to get out?"

"He didn't have the guts to do anything. I dragged him in there because I knew he and Melissa had been…intimate in that room. I wanted him to know why he was going to die. He took what belonged to me."

"How did Jack feel about it?"

"He didn't like me taking the pictures. But we thought we'd be back in an hour investigating, so he wasn't that worried."

"You supplied the picture to Mike Button?"

"They printed everything I wanted them to. My own picture in the *Trib*! I saved that clipping."

"Did you know Melissa's picture was in that photo?"

"Of course. Facedown. Didn't think you'd figure that out, but congratulations. Too bad nobody'll mention it at your funeral."

The funeral reference reinforced my need to buy extra time. Fortunately Noel enjoyed talking. He'd put a lot of work into this murder and wanted some credit.

He gazed, face tense, at the basketball players.

"What about Rosie O'Grady's? While I was in the bathroom, you put chloral-hydrate in my beer?"

He grinned. "That was Rodney. He was sitting in a corner and knew you'd have to make a pit stop. So when you did, he walked by and dumped it in your beer. Easy. But it shouldn't have lasted in your system. How'd they identify it as chloralhydrate?"

"I took a sample." Okay, I spilled it on my sleeve. "Got it tested."

"You were heads up enough to take a sample? How…maybe you're not a complete moron. Not that it matters. They can't trace it back to us anyway. Rodney had a gallon container of the stuff. Always buys in bulk. He poured it into the Columbia River and said five minutes later fish were floating." He laughed loudly.

"The security guard who woke me in Rosie's parking lot…your brother?"

"Yeah. He loves disguises. I collected some blood from the scene, to incriminate somebody, and when I called Rodney, he said you were passed out in your car. So we figured, perfect, why not put Phillips's blood on your shirt? So I dropped by and gave it to him, and he poured it on you before he woke you up."

"Why'd he wake me and give me coffee?"

"We didn't want anybody finding you and giving you an alibi, swearing you were too far from the scene or too drunk to have done it."

"But why kill Phillips?"

"I overheard him talking with Jack by our workstation. He said he was going to admit to you that he'd lied about his alibi. Jack said it was okay. Well, it wasn't okay with me. You'd be asking why Jack was so willing to lie and maybe figure he wanted more alibi than Linda could give him. But then you'd ask, Why would Jack need it? Pretty soon you'd be thinking about me. I couldn't let that happen."

He peered out the window again. "Come on, goofballs, give it up. We gotta go."

"Where you so eager to take me?"

"I could kill you right here. Maybe I want to keep you alive. But remember, as we go to the car, I've got this gun with a silencer in my coat pocket and this knife." He held it up, sharp and shiny. "You try anything, I won't hesitate to kill you where you stand. If you cooperate, you may live. Choice is yours."

I didn't think he was bluffing. I twisted my head around, trying to see Mulch.

"Can I look at my dog?"

"Say please."

"Please."

"No, you can't."

If the recliner were half its weight, I could jump to my feet and swing the chair around and sideswipe him. I wanted to stomp him. After a minute's silence, I composed myself.

"I still don't understand how Palatine's window broke."

"We thought somebody'd call 911 when they heard the shots. But we were listening to police radio. Nothing. Jack said the insulation was too good. Maybe people just thought it was a backfire. He suggested I break the bedroom window. Soon as I did, lights go on in the neighborhood. But a few minutes later they go out. I'm standing there, lights out in the room so no one could see me, and I'm looking out this broken window at these witnesses. Left my shoe impression, huh? Thought of that later and removed a little glass, like you figured out. Think you're pretty smart, don't you? Anyway, I was assuming somebody'd call 911. Nobody did! It's sad. Two gunshots and a broken window? It's like people don't watch out for their neighbors anymore."

"That must really bother a community-minded guy like you."

"We left through the back door. Jack's car was three blocks away, by Wally's Donuts." He smiled.

"We sat and listened to the scanner. Nobody was calling. Finally Jack said to have Rodney make the anonymous 911 call. When he used the word *fishy*, that wasn't planned. Just a word we grew up using."

It had been so dark so long I couldn't believe they were still shooting baskets.

"Five minutes, boys, and I swear I'm going to start shootin'."

Just when I feared Donald's fuse was going to break, he smirked and said, "How'd you like my spelling of *judgement*?"

"You did that to point us to Doyle?"

"Yeah. Adjusted the chair to point to Suda. Put the mouse on the left side since she's left-handed. And Phillips is ambidextrous. Did you know that? And the Bible verse about the millstone? Made you think of Karl Baylor, didn't I?"

"Not really," I lied, thinking he was too proud of himself. "But you don't strike me as a Bible scholar."

"I went to Sunday school when my father was around. Hated it. Hated him. Sunday school never took for me."

"No kidding?"

We'd been there thirty-five minutes. Twice he made calls on his cell phone, whispering.

Donald had dumped the bird dog by now, probably smashed it. Presumably, he'd parked close enough to get to the old brownstone on foot. My cell phone had rung three times without an answer, Donald looking at it each time. Maybe somebody'd put two and two together and realize he'd come after me.

Just then my cell rang again. Donald leaned to look at it. "Kendra? Your daughter? Maybe she'll be the one to find your body."

An assault team could be in position outside. If so, they'd wait for the ball players to stop. If there was a shoot-out, they couldn't risk innocents in the line of fire. But the delay had been in my favor. They'd had time to set up.

Finally, the game stopped. A minute later it was completely quiet.

Donald uncuffed me. I was tempted to try something, but I felt the muzzle pushing on the center of my back, heart level.

"Put on your stupid raincoat. We're going in your car."

I walked in front of him out the front door, ready to hit the ground to give the snipers a clean shot. I looked for signs of an assault team. As it should be, I couldn't see them.

He led me to the passenger seat and helped me in, looking at the vacant street. I was in the car. They'd get him as he walked to the driver's side.

Donald got in and pulled out of my driveway. Nothing.

As we turned off 150th, he said, "Thought they'd jump me, didn't you? You don't know beans, Chandler. After I left the precinct, I took off your bird dog, went to a truck stop, and planted it on an eighteen-wheeler headed to Idaho. Talked to the driver myself. They're tracing the bird dog, but they're looking for my car, so they'll think somehow I snuck by them in traffic. By the time they realize it's on a truck, I figure it'll be a couple more hours. They just think you're home napping after a tough day. Too bad for you."

I thought now would be a good time for a dying alien to show up and offer me a chance to be Green Lantern.

If no one was coming to the rescue, I'd have to wing it. If I waited too long, I'd be dead. But if I moved too soon, at the wrong time, I'd be dead too. I had to either create a distraction or wait for one. My options were limited. I needed at least one second of uncertainty.

Donald put on a Bluetooth earpiece and punched a number on his cell phone, on his lap. His gun stayed in his left hand, butt sidled against his stomach, pointing at my left side.

"On my way," he said to someone. "You took care of him? Perfect. He's checking in? Okay. Be there in ten."

65

"I was forced to confess that I had at last met an antagonist who was my intellectual equal. My horror at his crimes was lost in my admiration of his skill."
SHERLOCK HOLMES, *THE FINAL PROBLEM*

FRIDAY, JANUARY 24, 7:45 P.M.

I SAT THERE IN THE FRONT SEAT of my own car, wrists bent like pretzels, contemplating my Baby Glock under the Kleenex in the glove box. I've got three Baby Glocks, the triplets, and I love them all. Now I wished I'd hidden one in the crack in the passenger side seat upholstery, the one place my hands could access. A guy could be handcuffed behind his back, in the passenger seat of his car. Why hadn't I anticipated that?

If only Baby was within reach, I could grab it, turn sideways toward the window, point it behind my back at Donald, and spray him with slugs. Preferably at a stoplight.

Donald pulled into Dr. Alexander's podiatry clinic, adjacent to his apartment complex. He didn't know I'd put a bird dog on my car too. Just in case. Sergeant Seymour had rolled his eyes at me when I'd told him. Given that I was out of contact and my car was moving now, would it get their attention? If they traced it here, I hoped they'd realize we'd gone to Donald's apartment.

But why were we here? Donald was a fugitive. A cop or two would be posted at his apartment despite the decoy moving up the highway. He had to know that.

"I'm going to uncuff you again. We'll walk naturally to the apartments. There's an inside hallway. We'll pass people. Act like we're old friends. Hey, we *are* old friends. Don't forget I've got the gun and the knife if I need to keep it quiet. You say or do anything fishy, I won't just kill you, I'll kill them. Got it?"

I was willing to risk my life, already up for grabs. But was I willing to risk the lives of bystanders? In conflicts like these, men without consciences have certain advantages.

One step behind me, Donald talked cheerily when someone appeared in the hallway. "Hi, Jessica. How's Stuart doing in school?"

We walked toward his apartment, third on the right.

Where were the cops? Who'd been on the other end of that phone call?

If he hadn't been a cop, I would have tried something right as we went through his door. But he was too focused, too alert. Maybe if I behaved, he wouldn't put the cuffs back on. Maybe I'd get a chance.

Donald shoved a chair in the center of his studio apartment. He told me to sit by the card table. I looked at the ace of spades lying there. I felt compelled to nudge it with my finger. Underneath it was a piece of scratch paper with one name: Ollie Chandler.

I'd been compliant for the last half hour at my house and for the car ride and the walk into the apartment. Now that we were here, on his turf, Donald's comfort level was instinctively higher. If I could maintain my low threat level, that would work to my advantage. The fact that he hadn't handcuffed me was promising. I asked myself what Jack Bauer would do. I wished I had Chloe out there helping me with a notebook computer and a satellite.

Donald produced two big duffel bags. One appeared already packed. He started packing the other. He spoke aloud as he went from closet to drawers. "Heavy jacket. Light jacket. Ammo. Candles. Matches. Scissors."

He must have further use for me. Not for ransom. The chief wouldn't trade a bar of hotel soap for me. But as a hostage, I might have value. Or, and this seemed more likely, he had just the right burial place planned for me and wanted me to get there on my own two feet, making it a lot easier for him. Likely it was a favorite spot, where others were already buried, including the real Noel Barrows.

I felt those wet-footed spiders on my neck.

I'd been close to death before. This time I could taste it. My conversations with Jake and Clarence came back to me. Whatever they had that I didn't, it made them ready to die in a way I wasn't. This was no time for soul-searching…but maybe it was the only time left.

Donald opened every drawer, then looked around the room. He'd stuffed the duffel bag with warm waterproof clothes, a sleeping bag, even a small propane stove. He took a gigantic black trash bag from the closet and crammed it in the duffel. I hoped its function wasn't what I thought it might be. He also had a white trash bag stuffed with something light. He opened the first duffel and stuffed it in.

Donald spoke now, excitedly. "I've scoped out a half dozen places in the mountains where I could live for a year without being found. Once I grow a beard and put on glasses, when I come out for groceries nobody'll notice. I worked in vice. I've seen a hundred fake IDs, and I've made three different ones, two for fallback."

He couldn't stand not bragging about it.

"Eventually I'll come out of the woods and watch myself on *America's Most Wanted*. By then my hair'll be red. I'll either be lean or bulked up, maybe as fat as you. Haven't decided. Fat sounds more fun."

"What will you do, run Ferris wheels at carnivals?"

Okay, it was random, but when you're buying minutes of life, you take what little the gray cells give you.

"I have a plan for that too. I've got this bag of cash, taken here and there on the street." He pointed at the white bag. "Twenty-three thousand dollars, from drug dealers, pimps, and lowlifes. That'll tide me over. Maybe someday I'll set up an office, hang a shingle: Private Investigator."

"Why'd you call my house from Palatine's?"

"A little joke while waiting for the professor to die. I witnessed Melissa's death. I didn't want to miss his death. It was ten years to the minute. Not almost. Exactly."

He opened his fridge and began pulling stuff out.

"Oh, yeah, the Budweiser bottles at Palatine's. If they ever run the DNA tests, guess whose saliva's on the bottles?"

"Whose?"

"Yours. Took them right from your garage. Got 'em when I got the rope."

"But it's your saliva on the wineglasses."

"Jack's. Not mine. While Jack looked the place over, I said I'd wash the glasses. I washed mine with soap and water, and I wiped off Jack's prints, but didn't touch the rim of his glass and left wine residue in it. I'm sure his saliva traces are there. It'll look like Jack celebrated with wine and you with Budweiser. True to form. Surprised they haven't found your prints on the bottles yet. They will."

He looked at the food in front of him, doing inventory. "Beef, mustard, onion, bread, butter, soda."

"For the record, people from the Pacific Northwest don't say soda. We say pop."

"Thanks for pointing that out. It could trip me up."

"It already did."

"Yeah, and here we are, me with the gun and you looking up its barrel." He pointed it at my face. "Who was it that tripped up?"

Donald's cell rang. He listened, then said, "Good. See you then."

He moved quickly now.

It's a strange thing to be in a situation where your adrenaline is flowing like water through a fire hose but you have to appear relaxed.

Why hadn't he killed me yet? Did he still think there was reasonable doubt on the other murders? I had to admit that the circumstantial evidence against him wasn't absolute. He hadn't confessed to the detectives. Sure, he bolted from the precinct, but innocent people have run when they believed they were being framed. His attorney could argue that in court. The planted fingerprints and 911 call made to sound like him could lead to reasonable doubt. Not to mention that I'd held out evidence against myself, which contaminated all evidence I'd presented against him. He hadn't harmed me or Cimmatoni, though he could have. He didn't even take our weapons. Girlfriends dying? It happens. Taking the identity of Noel Barrows would get him a hand slap, but it wasn't that serious given his subsequent service to society.

Think like he's thinking, I told myself. He wants it to be like the other murders. No proof that he did it. He just needs me to disappear. To get me to where he'll dispose of my body. Then, in his worst-case scenario, if they find him someday, there'd be no proof he'd killed me or anyone else. He ran because he was framed. Yeah, that's what he must be thinking. Which meant once we got in the car again, away from civilization, every mile would mean less hope of survival.

I turned slightly so he couldn't see my left hand. I reached to my belt, where my pocketknife hung on the inside from its thin metal wire.

My cooperation had relaxed Donald's guard. If I talked, maybe he wouldn't realize I was doing something else.

"I remember when I first met Jack. He taught me how to…"

While I talked, I took the knife in my right hand and cut my left palm, deep. I cupped my hand to contain the pool of blood so it wasn't dripping on the carpet yet. I walked toward the couch. A few drops landed on the carpet, but he didn't notice. I sat on the couch, talking about Jack, my left hand still blocked from his view. I let the blood flow behind the cushion. I hung my hand over the side of the couch and wiped it into the fabric, then let it spill freely onto the carpet. Blood flowed to the end of my index finger and thumb, and I flicked it onto wall and curtain. All this time I droned on and on, keeping my body between him and my left hand.

While that hundred-watt bulb was blinding, it left the corners of the room shadowed, allowing me to make DNA deposits all over without being noticed.

While Noel finished packing food into plastic bags, I continued to talk about Jack. I walked toward the window.

"The blinds are down, Chandler. Nobody's seeing you."

I talked about a particular stakeout on a case that involved an orangutan. By now my blood had marked a chair, a bookcase, and several CD covers.

"They're going to find your brother," I said.

"He stuck around too long. When you said you saw me at Starbucks, I realized he had to get out of town, or we'd get tripped up. Fortunately you're too stupid to figure out that it wasn't me you saw."

He stared, and I stood still. "You still don't know why there's no cop here, do you, Chandler? I called Rodney back to town when you searched my apartment. Ten minutes before we got here, he posed as the assistant manager and visited the officer right at my door." Noel smiled. "He took the officer for a ride. He's checking in with his sergeant regularly and saying everything's okay."

"And if he stops cooperating?"

"He'll die."

"Your brother's a killer too?"

Noel laughed. "I'm the nice brother."

Left hand behind me, smearing the wall by the stereo, I said, "Ask yourself what Jack would want you to do. Don't you think you should turn yourself in?"

Picking up the two duffel bags, he froze. "What are you doing?"

He turned on a second light, then a third. He looked around the room at the bloodstains.

"Show me your hand. Your left hand!"

I squeezed it tight, then held it up, letting a nice bloody dribble fall on his cream-colored carpet. He grabbed a kitchen towel and threw it at me. "Wrap it up."

"You can kill me, but they still have the case I built against you. And now my blood's all over. You'll never get it clean. It's a killer's worst nightmare—physical evidence everywhere, in your own home."

He stared at the carpet, not seeing my right hand, which I raised at that moment and swiped across his left arm with my knife. It was a clean cut, good and bloody, though I missed the inside of his wrist, which I was going for. His blood hit the floor within seconds.

As he stepped back and grabbed his arm, clutching the gun awkwardly, I threw the knife at his face. It hit his cheek, the blade piercing his skin before it fell. I reached in my pocket then threw his golf ball at him. It bounced off his forehead with a loud thud. These things all happened with a couple of seconds, and now I charged him. But he backed up, his gun's muzzle pointed at me, then suddenly stepped forward and I knew he would shoot. The gun was now six inches from the bridge of my nose.

"That's two blood sources in the carpet, yours and mine," I said. "Your house is going to scream, 'Killer.' And your face is going to have a nice scar. And a big bruise on your forehead."

Granted, if he made it to the woods, it might just be squirrels and deer taking a second look at him. But it was a long way to the woods.

He pushed the gun to my forehead, pressing muzzle against thin flesh. As I stepped back, he kept coming, pushing it harder.

"I'll kill you right here, right now."

My cell phone, in his pocket, rang. He pulled it out, dropped it on the ground, and stomped on it.

"You make a good point, Chandler. Now that I know I'd have to face murder charges if I'm ever discovered—which I don't plan to be—why should I risk taking you somewhere else to kill you? Who cares where your body ends up? Why not leave it right here? You just took away my only reason for not killing you here and now."

It was a good point.

One I maybe should have thought of sooner.

66

"Yes, the setting is a worthy one.
If the devil did desire to have a hand in
the affairs of men…"
SHERLOCK HOLMES, *THE HOUND OF THE BASKERVILLES*

HE PUSHED THE MUZZLE into my right temple. "Say your prayers."

I started to, wishing I had more time.

Five seconds later he pulled the gun back, pushed me to the bathroom, and ordered me to clean up. Waving his Beretta at the medicine cabinet, he told me to wrap a bandage and athletic tape around my hand.

"I've decided I'm not done with you," he said in a voice like his mother's. "I've got a place all picked out for you. Others are waiting for you to join them, and I don't want to disappoint them."

He stood in the bathroom doorway and never took his eye off me. After ordering me out, he gave one last sweeping gaze of the apartment. I stood six feet from the front door, and he was two feet behind me. He gestured for me to move to the door.

I walked wide to the right, pretending not to notice a stereo wire, and tripped on it, landing on my face in front of the door. It was hard not to take an athletic roll, but it had to look like an accident.

"Get up, idiot."

I positioned myself with my bandaged left hand pushing up on the floor. I pulled up my left pant leg with my right hand and grabbed the Baby Glock, then shot Donald Meyer in the right shoulder. He screamed. His Beretta dropped to the floor.

I punched his wounded shoulder twice with my bandaged left hand and backed him against the wall. I took the knife out of his pocket and searched him for other weapons while he moaned and groaned like a sissy.

"I took that gun from your ankle holster," he said, like I'd treated him unfairly.

"I have *two* ankles, dunderhead. You only saw one of my white shins, remember? Speaking of which, in prison they don't tan much. And the golfing's seriously limited."

"You were carrying *four* guns? Nobody carries four guns." He was writhing, but he wouldn't let it go. "Who could possibly need four guns?"

"Me. Today."

He grasped his shoulder moaning, tears coming to his eyes.

"Baby Glock's not much of a gun, huh? Enough to make you into a crybaby, you little sissy. Messin' with me's like wearin' cheese underwear down rat alley."

I punched his right shoulder. "Don't forget it, numskull." I punched it again. "That one's for pistol-whipping my dog."

I cuffed Donald extra tight, and we headed down the hallway. "Get ready to walk the Green Mile, scumbag." One of the neighbors came out her door, and I nodded and smiled.

"Help me," Donald said to her. "This man assaulted me."

I flipped open my badge. "I'm a police officer, ma'am. He's under arrest."

"I'm the police officer," Donald said. "You know me."

"He is a police officer," she said to me, pointing at Donald. "I know he is." She pulled out her cell phone.

"Yes, ma'am, but he's the police officer in handcuffs, and I'm the police officer with the big gun." I pulled Donald's Beretta from my pocket.

She nodded and started to put away her cell phone.

"May I use that, ma'am?" I'd confiscated Donald's phone and his earpiece, but didn't want to contaminate evidence by using it.

I reached out my bloody left hand and took it, then called Jake and asked him to go immediately to my house. I told him to call Megan Wood, the vet who'd come to Mulch's rescue earlier.

I called 911, then Sergeant Seymour. Before I could say anything he said, "You been napping? They're still tracing Noel's car up I-84. Set up two roadblocks, but somehow he got away."

"Actually, Sarge, Donald's right here with me. Want to talk to the little whiner?"

Sarge insisted I not leave the building until backup arrived. While I was waiting by the front door, I was deliberately a little lax, hoping Donald would try something. He decided to kick me where it hurts in the hopes that he could make a run for it. After he took his best shot, a little high, I pocketed the Beretta, stepped toward him, grabbed his jacket with both hands, and yanked his head toward mine. My head met him halfway. It sounded like two coconuts fired from cannons, colliding with each other. My coconut is harder, so he was unconscious before hitting the floor.

When Sarge showed up with backup, he hugged me This was uncomfortable enough, but then I had to explain Donald's condition. Sarge said Donald's attorney would accuse me of brutality, but I didn't care. It was worth it.

The EMTs focused on Donald, who finally regained consciousness. Despite everyone's urging, I insisted I didn't need another hospital visit. I told the paramedics I was on a first name basis with a nurse named Angela at Adventist Medical Center, and she would vouch for me. They settled for bandaging my hand and treating my forehead, which had been a skin donor to Donald's forehead. The rest was bumps and bruises, the worst from falling on my face as part of my act of clumsiness. At least it was the opposite side of my face from when I'd fallen from the knockout spray. I like to spread out the damage.

I insisted on going home to see Mulch. If I wouldn't go to the hospital, Sarge insisted I go to precinct. I called home and Jake answered.

"I've got somebody here who wants to talk to you," he said.

I heard a grunt, a nuzzle, a sneeze, and a familiar little growl.

"Hi, Clarence," I said.

"It's Mulch," Jake said. "He's got a headache. Megan says it's a concussion, and she's taking him in to the clinic. But she's optimistic. She knows him pretty well by now."

"To the right of the microwave, the upper cupboard has five pounds of the best beef jerky money can buy. The sky's the limit for Mulch. Have some yourself. Take a handful home for Champ. Tell Megan to fill her pockets."

"She'll be thrilled."

I entered the Justice Center, carrying a box from my car. Clarence was waiting in detective division when I arrived. He came straight to me, put his arm around me, and asked if I was okay. Every detective was there, seven of us now, without Brandon Phillips, Jack Glissan, and Noel Barrows, aka Donald Meyer. Sergeant Seymour joined us minutes later.

They wanted to hear my story and led me into the conference room. We'd all been in this same room just six hours ago. They kept interrupting with questions, which was okay because Karl brought in three boxes of Krispy Kremes and Tommi two gallons of milk. I felt like royalty.

As I told the story there were lots of smart comments, but I felt part of the team for the first time in two months.

"Okay, I believe you about Noel," Chris Doyle said. "But where's evidence that's beyond reasonable doubt?"

"In fact," Kim Suda said to me, "for Palatine's murder, and Brandon's too, there's more physical evidence against you than against him, right?"

I nodded.

"What's to keep Noel from saying he ran from us because you framed him?" Sarge said. "He wanted to escape to prove he was innocent. He's still got the alibi in the tavern, unless you can produce his brother."

"I can't," I said.

"So it sounds like a wild guess," Suda said. "But that's not all. Noel's attorney calls a criminalist to the stand, maybe Phil Oref, and he has to testify that you tampered with evidence, right? Chris and I have to testify that bloody fabric appeared at the scene after you showed up. Put that with Noel's fake fingerprints and the Black Jack gum and if your DNA's really on the beer bottle…that's plenty of reasonable doubt."

"But look at what just happened," Clarence said. "This guy assaulted Ollie at his house, knocked out Mulch, handcuffed Ollie and abducted him to his place, where Ollie's blood's everywhere."

"But he could reverse everything," Cimmatoni said, looking at me. "He could claim you caught him, took him to your place, and brained your dog yourself."

"That wouldn't hold up with a jury of dog owners," Tommi said.

"It was your car that went to his place," Sarge said. "It looks like you drove him there."

"And cutting your palm, your blood all over his apartment?" Doyle said. "They could see that as you trying to corroborate your made-up story. You admit you cut your own hand. What actual harm did he inflict on you, some bruises? You're the one who shot him. You tried to frame him with fake prints, he'll say. You tried to frame him again by cutting your hand with your own knife."

"It's not like you'd be convicted of anything," Baylor said. "We all know now he's guilty. But sometimes you can't prove what you know. This is way more than enough reasonable doubt to get him acquitted."

"We've got plenty of dead people," Sarge said, sighing. "I say he walks unless we find irrefutable evidence, something that couldn't have been falsified, that's not just our gut feelings or your word against his."

After another big gulp of milk, washing down the last bite of a glazed raspberry-filled Krispy Kreme, I said, "Would a recording of Noel's confession help?"

They all stared at me. If he'd been there, the chief would have said you could hear a pin drop.

"But…you don't have that," Suda said. "You told us he found the wire and pulled it."

"When people suspect you're wired, what do they do?" I asked.

"Search for it," Suda said.

"When do they stop searching?"

"After they look and don't find it."

"Or?"

"After they do find it," Tommi said.

"Right. When they find a wire, they stop looking for a wire. Just like when they find the gun on your right ankle, they don't look for a gun on your left ankle."

"What are you saying, Chandler?" Cimmatoni asked.

"You're all making the same assumption Donald did. That there was only one wire."

I stood, asked the ladies to excuse me, reached back under my boxer shorts, and pulled out the tiny device taped there, with a thin wire that came out by my belt buckle, where the miniature microphone was. I held the device, retrieved from my boxers, in my palm.

"Gross," Suda said.

"I turned on this little gadget with my index finger since my hands were conveniently cuffed right there. It sent a signal to a device in the trunk of my car, with a six-hour recording capacity. Since Donald commandeered my car, it was in signal range at his apartment." I picked up the box I'd carried in and showed them the recorder from my car.

They insisted we play it right then. I'd tell them when to fast-forward, to find the relevant parts. They ordered pizza delivery, and somebody brought in pop (not soda). It was like the Waltons settling into the living room to listen to FDR on the radio. They listened intently for a couple of hours, until Sarge's voice came on the recording, and Donald was in custody.

"Well, it's good enough for me, but it won't hold up in court," Cimmatoni said.

"Might depend on the judge," I said. "I did inform Donald he was being taped, remember? He destroyed the other device, but I was referring to this one. And I used the present tense—I said 'I'm recording you.' Present tense, not past. It's all right there. I can't help it if he didn't understand plain English. If I were a judge, I'd equate that with informing Donald he was being recorded."

"If you were a judge," Sarge said, "you'd equate saying, 'Talk or I'll shoot you,' with reading someone their Miranda rights."

FRIDAY, JANUARY 24, 9:40 P.M.

After hearing the recording, Manny, Sarge, and Lieutenant Nicks interrogated Donald Meyer. Captain Swiridoff was already in touch with the DA about reopening the Melissa Glissan case as a possible murder by her boyfriend, Donald Meyer.

Precinct electronics experts would be working all night on duplicating and gleaning highlights from the recordings of my adventures with Donald.

The captain told me to go home and get a good night's sleep because there'd be a 10:00 a.m. press conference, and we'd have to be coached by Chief Lennox's press secretary about what to say and what not to say. Swiridoff instructed me to find something to wear that looked respectable, "even if you have to borrow it."

Clarence was having a ball, in a Clarence sort of way, which shows itself in a look of sober intensity as he scratches down notes.

↔

I took off to join Mulch at home. He was back from the vet and being babysat by Jake and Janet. She was caressing Mulch's ears and feeding him snacks. Mike Hammer was milking it. When he saw me, he jumped and nearly knocked me over. We wrestled carefully since he had tape and bandages between his ear and jaw.

Before Jake and Janet left, Jake said to me, "Okay if I tell God thanks for protecting you like He did?"

I nodded.

"Thank You, Father, for answering our prayers and keeping Ollie safe."

That was all.

"You want to thank Him, Ollie?" Jake asked.

I shut my eyes tight, like praying people do. "God…if You're there, I guess I owe You one. And…especially, thanks that Mulch made it."

Janet hugged me, and it felt good. Jake hugged me, and I didn't hurl. It had been a record day for man-hugs, including Sarge's. I hoped I wouldn't get used to it.

Mulch and I stayed up late. After watching Jack Bauer and Chuck Norris, I picked up Sharon's old Bible, which Janet had not-very-inconspicuously left on my recliner. I started reading parts she'd underlined.

The phone rang at 11:30.

"Daddy? It's Kendra."

"Hi, honey."

"Jake called me a few hours ago, but I just got his message. Are you okay? I'm coming over now!"

"It's late. You need your sleep."

It was nearly midnight when she got here and 2:45 when she left. The three hours seemed like thirty minutes. She played on the floor with Mulch and let him lick her face, and not once did she mention salads, meat, wetlands, or gun control. She even said she was grateful I was carrying that fourth gun. I introduced her to each of my Baby Glocks, the triplets. She said they were cute. When she was leaving, while we stood at the door, she wrapped her arms around me and hugged me.

My little girl hugging me. It doesn't get any better than that.

I'm not going to tell you much of what we said to each other, not because it would embarrass me, but because the telling couldn't capture the magic, and it would leave you thinking it was less than it was.

But we did talk about the woman we loved more than anyone, who we'd lost, the boy we never had much opportunity to know, and the girl we missed so much. And when Kendra told me how angry she was that her mom had been taken, I said I understood and felt the same way. But maybe, I said, we couldn't own her any more than you can own a comet or a sunset or fresh rain on a dry dusty day. You're glad to experience them, they make you happy, but when they're gone, instead of being mad, maybe you should just be grateful they were there for you in the first place.

Okay, I maybe didn't say it that poetically, but that's how I wrote it down later.

I said that if Jake and Clarence were right, maybe one day we could actually see Sharon again and be with her. Maybe Chad too, who knows? Kendra asked me if I really believed that. I said I didn't know, but I was beginning to think it's possible.

Instead of arguing, Kendra hugged me. I hugged her back, on this Guinness day of hugs. We held on to each other. And for the first time I could remember, I felt hope.

That night I was grateful for the sand in the top half of my hourglass. Still, I knew much less remained on top than had already fallen. And it seemed like the more gravity drained the top half, the faster the sand was falling.

*"My name figures in no newspaper. The work itself,
the pleasure of finding a field for my peculiar powers,
is my highest reward."*
SHERLOCK HOLMES, *THE SIGN OF FOUR*

SATURDAY, JANUARY 25, 10:00 A.M.

AN ARMY OF REPORTERS marched past Chief Lennox's office, its door wide open, with the chief's honors displayed like bowling trophies.

Detectives rarely talk with the press. Jack Glissan and Brandon Phillips were our golden boys, but now they're gone. As Obadiah Abernathy said, "We's here, then we's gone, like a warm breath on a cold day."

Sixty of us crammed in a media room made for thirty. I was surprised to see Jake.

"This is big stuff," he said. "I'll get a few columns out of it myself. Couldn't miss your moment of glory."

Lennox's press secretary introduced the chief like he was a rock star, saying he'd been *magna cum something* at some university back east with a lousy football team, which probably hadn't produced many good cops either. If Mulch hadn't had a toothache and a migraine, I'd have wished he were there to reacquaint himself with Lennox's pant leg.

"We have news this morning that is both good and bad," Lennox said, riding the room's aura of excitement. "For our police force and our city stand or fall together. The bad news is that Detective Noel Barrows has been arrested for the murder of William Palatine. He's a suspect in another case being investigated as I speak."

Try five other cases, I thought.

"The good news is that this man has been arrested, charged, and if found guilty, will be punished. From the beginning I told our people, we must chase down the killer, no matter who he is, no matter what the consequences. When we first suspected it could be one of our own, I insisted we do our jobs no matter how bad it might look for us. We pulled out the stops, chased down every lead. We left no stone unturned."

We came out like gangbusters.

"I'm proud of our detective department. And I assure you that one bad apple has *not* spoiled the barrel."

Lennox droned on, alluding to his critical behind-the-scenes role in this case. Someone interrupted, "What about the suicide of Jack Glissan, Barrows's partner? Was he involved in any of the murders?"

"We're investigating the extent to which Detective Glissan might have become aware of his partner's crimes."

No reason to sully the reputation of an exemplary cop and hurt his widow, and the department, and the chief. Damage control. Deception. All for a good cause.

Though Clarence was in the second row, raising his hand continually, somehow the chief managed not to notice him, the equivalent of not noticing a Humvee in your dining room.

"I will personally oversee the investigation of Noel Barrows," the chief said, "making sure every *t* is crossed and every *i* is dotted. Time for just one more question."

Clarence stood and started talking even though the chief was pointing to a reporter three rows back on the other side, a reporter known for throwing softballs at the chief and playing poker with him Saturday nights.

"As you know," Clarence said in his 'Luke, I am your father' voice, "I was assigned to cover this case."

"Yes, since our police department has nothing to hide," Lennox said, "I invited a *Tribune* reporter to cover this investigation from the beginning."

"I worked daily alongside Detective Ollie Chandler, observing his handling of this case," Clarence said. "In my opinion, he did an outstanding job. Do you have any comments on Detective Chandler's performance?"

"Yes, I have commended him for his comportment."

I don't know what comportment means, but I'd have thought commending someone would include some actual communication with that person—some nice words, a greeting card, a box of chocolates, or tickets to a Seahawks game. Apparently not.

Clarence wasn't satisfied. "Ollie Chandler put his life on the line and was in mortal danger three times. Without his tireless efforts, Noel Barrows wouldn't have been caught. Do you agree, Chief Lennox?"

"Well…he had a significant role, as did our entire team. As general of this army, I'm proud of all my soldiers."

"You sound as if you played some role in solving this crime."

"As chief of police, I play a role in everything this department does."

Clarence's face hardened. "While I was involved in this case, I was never aware of you doing anything to help solve it."

"You're here to ask questions, not to make statements," Lennox said, squeezing the podium, makeup running. "But I assure you that my role in this, while behind the scenes, was substantial. I supervised the detectives involved. Nothing happens in this department without my being part of it."

"Including multiple murders?"

Man, I *love* that Clarence Abernathy. Score one for the journalists.

The chief halted, stumbled, and explained something about the best-laid plans of mice and men and when the going gets tough, the tough get going.

When the chief thanked everyone for coming and stepped away, waving like a candidate, one of the television reporters asked, "Clarence, would you answer some questions?"

Abernathy nodded. For the next twenty minutes he repeatedly gave me credit, using words like *brilliant*, *brave*, and *pit-bull determination*. He only mentioned my "idiosyncrasies" a couple of times and Krispy Kremes once. Clarence also gave high praise to Manny, who sat quietly but took notice. He paid tribute to Ray Eagle, doing everything short of passing out his business phone number.

I made a mental note to commend him for his comportment.

After three more questions Clarence pointed to me and said, "The man you really should talk to is Detective Ollie Chandler."

The smiling Lynn Carpenter winked as she turned her camera toward me, in my blue sport coat. A dozen other cameras, still and video, followed. The questions came, none hostile. For the first time I could remember, it was fun to look into the faces of the media.

I answered questions for forty minutes. Afterward, several journalists introduced themselves to me and shook my hand. Two actually thanked me for doing my job. They seemed almost human. But, I reminded myself, things often aren't what they appear.

When the others had left, Carp took a few more pictures, then kissed her finger and put it on one of my half dozen facial owies. She said she was glad I was okay. As she went out the door, she mouthed words that touched me in ways hard for a man to express: "double cheese, double pepperoni."

SATURDAY, JANUARY 25, 12:20 P.M.

It was noon when the press conference finally ended, sixty minutes after the chief stepped out, meaning three-fourths of it took place without him. Jake said he was buying at Lou's. Rory knocked himself out with a display of yellow pansies, which despite the name were pretty cool.

Jake said the tunes were on him, and a minute later Jan and Dean joined us in the booth, singing "Little Deuce Coupe." They were followed by Buddy Holly and the Crickets performing "Peggy Sue." I nodded at Rory, who looked up at the picture of him and his dad with Buddy and the gang.

"Did you see Lennox peeking in the door?" Jake asked, laughing. "He couldn't stand it that the press conference was still going after he left."

"There's still a lot I don't get," Clarence said. "Why would Glissan and Barrows take those chances? Why leave the wineglasses, use the noose, the insulin bottles, and leave Melissa's chain on the professor?"

"For Jack, maybe it was trying to play fair, give us a chance to catch him if somehow he didn't work the case. For Noel, it was arrogance. Criminal masterminds think they're invincible. Jack often consulted me on cases, and it might look suspicious if he didn't on this one. Noel figured from the beginning I'd probably visit the scene, see some evidence, maybe recognize the rope, learn about the Black Jack and the phone call. He wanted to play with me, unnerve me. It backfired."

"I understand Jack never suspected that Noel killed Melissa," Jake said. "But he had to figure out Noel had killed those other people, right?"

"Once Frederick and Hedstrom died, Jack had to know," I said. "But he had a blind loyalty to Noel. If Jack confronted him, we'll probably never know what was said."

"What's going to happen in court?" Clarence asked. "If they don't allow your recording, is there enough evidence to convict him?"

"Noel's a master of deception. He'll convince his attorney he's innocent. Maybe a jury too. Jack wouldn't betray Noel, but Noel made sure evidence pointed to Jack. Melissa's chain, the insulin bottles, the unwashed wineglass with Jack's DNA, if the lab ever comes up with it. I can hear Noel suggesting to Jack it would honor Melissa to use her needle, insulin, and chain. But those could point to Jack, not Noel. Nobody but Jack and Linda would realize Noel's connection to Melissa. He never thought he'd be exposed as Donald Meyer."

"Noel really took Jack in, didn't he?" Jake asked.

"Talk about irony," I said. "They bonded by their grief at Melissa's death, but the guy the Glissans bonded with, the one they wish had fathered their grandchildren, was their daughter's killer. Jack befriends him, does stakeouts with him, golfs with him, drinks a toast to him in honor of Melissa, never suspecting this guy murdered his little girl."

Jake shook his head. "And what jury would believe a man would plant his own fingerprints at the scene of a crime? He eliminated himself as a suspect by making himself a suspect, then proving he'd been framed. Wow."

"By planting evidence against you," Clarence asked.

"The gun wasn't found until seven hours after the murder. He probably put it there after he knew we were investigating. Noel had practice producing fake prints—from what Phil told us, he could probably do it in two hours. In this case, he wouldn't even have to find someone's print. He plants his own prints, then puts the gun in the Dumpster. Manny finds it. It's that simple."

"Talk about things not being as they seem," Clarence said. "His alibi. I know he looks like his brother, but wouldn't you think one of those guys could tell the difference?"

"That bugged me too until I found out Noel had been going to the Do Drop Inn two or three times a week for just five weeks and always when they were watching a ball game. Eyes were on the television. He has the same build, same hair as his brother, voice almost identical. Maybe women sit around and study each other's faces. These guys were staring at TV, beer, peanuts, lotto results, or pool balls, not at each other. He was hanging out with men who'd only seen him in a bar, say four times each, and always when they were drinking. He'd been there just enough for them to know his name and general appearance. Perfect alibi. They'd swear it was him, but a close facsimile would be good enough to fool them."

"Speaking of Rodney Meyer, do you think they'll find him?" Clarence asked.

"Who knows? I'm just grateful he let the officer go. Maybe he's waiting for Noel in his hideout in the woods."

"You said Noel had duplicated fingerprints before," Jake said. "When was that?"

"Remember the Jimmy Ross murder? Killed by Lincoln Caldwell? You'll read about this in the next few days when it's official. Heck, maybe you'll write about it. I called Phil and asked him to take a closer look at Lincoln Caldwell's fingerprints. He said sure enough, same thing. Definite traces of glycerin. Fake prints."

"You're saying Noel killed Jimmy Ross?"

"And framed Lincoln Caldwell. Two for the price of one."

"Where's Caldwell?"

"In jail awaiting trial. So he thinks. Soon as the paperwork's done—Manny's on it now—Caldwell will be released. I'm going over to see him myself. Bringing him a box of chocolates."

"Chocolates?"

"Flowers seemed inappropriate. I got those See's chocolates. Classy. I had a couple to make sure they're okay. Caldwell won't notice."

Rory brought three hot fudge sundaes. Clarence said he couldn't, but after hearing us groan with ecstasy, he shot some insulin and dug in.

"I keep thinking about Rodney," I said. "Donald claimed his brother's the mean one. If that's true, one of these days I might wake up dead."

"One of these days we'll each wake up dead," Jake said. "The question is what we'll wake up to. And whether we'll be ready for it."

"You know my favorite part?" Clarence asked. "What linked the professor to Melissa Glissan, before you saw her in the picture, was the phone number in the back of a book called *Why I Am Not a Christian*. The Lord sovereignly used that book, written as an argument against Him, to accomplish His purposes. In fact, if Jake hadn't read through that book to the final page, you might not have solved this murder. So how about you follow through with your commitment and read *Mere Christianity*—or, better yet, the Bible?"

"Maybe I will," I said. "But right now, I want to present you two with a gift."

I pulled out a classy little bag, with two identical gifts in fancy wrapping paper. Clarence opened the perfectly tied ribbon while Jake ripped into his.

At the same time they said, "A fountain pen?"

"Rupert Bolin called this morning and had these sent over. I won a drawing." I pulled another fountain pen from my pocket, same design and different color from theirs. "He reminded me that in an age of encroaching illiteracy, fountain pens are tools of articulation and civility. And since you write for a living, and I'm a budding novelist, I figure we can be the three literary amigos. Plus, Rupert says you can use them to write saucy letters to your wives."

"I have something for you too, Ollie," Clarence said.

He handed me an envelope. I opened it. My heart nearly stopped.

"A fifty-dollar gift certificate to Krispy Kreme?"

"The manager of the Krispy Kreme on 82nd sent it as thanks for mentioning them three times in my articles."

I stood up and threw my arms around Abernathy. "It's like winning the lottery. I think I'm gonna cry."

Jake laughed. Clarence wasn't so sure.

See, Clarence has an agenda for me—to find Jesus. And I've got one for him. If he's so happy about Jesus, I think he should let his face know about it. Like his daddy did.

Sure enough, next moment a big smile spread across Clarence's kisser. I was looking at Obadiah Abernathy.

"Any final thoughts, gentlemen," I said, "before we lay this case to rest?"

"Noel didn't look like a murderer," Clarence said.

"Murderers seldom do."

"To quote a brilliant detective, things often aren't as they appear," Clarence said. "You'd made up your mind about Jack, Noel, Karl, and Lincoln Caldwell. But you were dead wrong about all of them. You had to follow the evidence before you could uncover the deception."

I nodded. "Jake?"

"Well, you've told us that you don't believe God will bring justice. Or that Jesus is who He claimed to be—the only way to God. So if you were wrong about Noel, Jack, Karl, and Caldwell, could you be wrong about God too? Could you be wrong about Jesus?"

"I suppose."

"Is Jesus important enough to justify you conducting an investigation?" Clarence asked.

"Follow the evidence wherever it leads," Jake said. "That's all we're asking you to do."

Clarence nodded.

Apparently, it was unanimous.

Epilogue

IT'S BEEN THREE MONTHS since I solved the Palatine murder and Donald Meyer was taken into custody. Rodney Meyer hasn't been found.

I've been hanging out a lot with Kendra. We've been to the Old Spaghetti Factory three times. We went April 3, Sharon's and my anniversary. I told her stories about her mother and me in the original Spaghetti Factory thirty-five years ago. Kendra said she remembers us taking her there as a little kid and sitting in the streetcar. So on April 3 we waited for seating in the streetcar. I talked her into trying the Mizithra since no cows are killed to make it. She loved it. It was one of the best nights of my life.

I'm back to one day a week with Jake and Clarence at Lou's. We're reading together—I forget what. Jake talked me into going with him to a recovery group thingie at his church. It wasn't as lame as I expected.

Lynn Carpenter and I made a list of fifteen pizza places in the greater Portland area. Last night we hit number seven, DiCianni's, a new place in Gresham, with outdoor seating by a stand of honeysuckles, beautiful in the unusually warm spring weather.

This morning the phone rang at 3:00 a.m. on the dot, according to those big red digits. I groped for the phone in the darkness.

"Who died?" I groaned.

"Daddy? It's me."

"Kendra? Sweetheart? You okay?"

"I went into a quick labor four hours ago."

"What? Need a police escort?"

"Relax, make some coffee. I'm in the hospital, safe and sound. Things went superfast, one in a hundred the doctor said. Anyway, the bottom line—you have a grandson."

"The baby's born?"

"Yeah. And he's adorable. He's right here with me."

"He's born?"

"Yeah. Otherwise he wouldn't be in my arms."

"No kidding?"

"No kidding. Drink that coffee and it'll all make sense."

"Wow. I'll be there soon."

"And Daddy?"

"Yeah."

"Guess what I named the baby."

"Baby Glock?" I thought that was pretty good for 3:00 a.m.

She giggled. "No. Justice Oliver Chandler."

"No kidding?"

"I can see Mom in him. You too."

I jumped up, switched on the French roast, hugged Mulch, gave him a Tender Tbonz Sizzlin' Steak snack, and told him he had a nephew. Then I looked at my smiling mug in the bathroom mirror.

Justice Oliver? Wow. That beat Jack Bauer or Nero Wolfe. It even beat Baby Glock. And I liked the initials: My grandson was a JOC.

I'm driving to the hospital right now. Tonight I'll round up my guns, unload them, and store them high, out of my grandson's reach. And then I'll get him a Seahawks jacket and pick out a couple dozen children's books I can read to the little Sam-I-am.

I've been waiting all my life to get good news from a 3:00 a.m. phone call. Well, this morning it finally happened.

Maybe there's a God after all.

And maybe there really is a two thousand-year-old murder mystery worth investigating.

Justice Oliver Chandler?

No kidding.

"And will not God bring about justice for his chosen ones,
who cry out to him day and night?
Will he keep putting them off?
I tell you, he will see that they get justice, and quickly."
JESUS
LUKE 18:7-8

"Stop judging by mere appearances, and make a right judgment."
JESUS
JOHN 7:24

"Who are you?" they asked.
"Just what I have been claiming all along," Jesus replied.
JOHN 8:25-26

Man is destined to die once, and after that to face judgment.
HEBREWS 9:27

DISCUSSION QUESTIONS

Warning: Contains spoilers. Read only after you finish the book!

1. Can you relate to Ollie Chandler? If so, in what ways? (Besides a fondness for pastry.) How are you different than Ollie? What do you like and dislike about him?

2. What are some of your favorite scenes in *Deception* and why? Who are some of your favorite characters? (If you read the prequels *Deadline* or *Dominion*, in what ways is this book similar, and in what ways is it different?)

3. What are your overall impressions of the book, positive or negative? What did you take away from it that might stick with you awhile?

4. Why do you think Randy Alcorn named the book *Deception*? What forms did deception take in this book? What forms has it taken in your life or someone close to you?

5. Ollie often feels like he's on the outside looking in when he views the hope and faith in Jake, Clarence, Little Finn, and others. Has there been a time in your life when you experienced this feeling? Explain.

6. Ollie hesitates to believe in a good God because he sees injustice all around him. Read Matthew 5:6 and Luke 18:7–8. What does Jesus tell us about those who long for justice, like Ollie, and the God who loves them?

7. Ollie had a number of difficult questions for God such as, why do people suffer, why did He let Sharon die, and if He can make things right quickly, why doesn't He? There are no easy answers, but what would you say to Ollie—or the Ollies you know? What hidden purposes might God have for the heartbreaking troubles people often face? (See an article by the author, "How Could a Good God Allow Evil and Suffering?" at www.epm.org/articles/allowevil.html.)

8. Ollie drinks excessively to try to relieve the pain caused by his wife's death and his struggling relationships with his daughters. What things do you find yourself doing to avoid feeling pain in your life? What other pain-relieving activities are common in our culture?

9. When you read about Carly entering heaven, what touched you the most? How does your view of heaven compare with this scene in *Deception*? What do you think about the allusions to a future New Earth? Have you been taught to look forward to a New Earth, as 2 Peter 3:13 says we should be doing? (See the author's book *Heaven* for more information on the New Earth.)

10. Does reading about Professor Palatine's after-death experience affect your views about hell? What struck you about it?

11. When Sharon was sick and later died, well-meaning Christians made some unintentionally hurtful remarks to Ollie. Why do you think this sometimes happens? What do you say or do when someone you are close to is really hurting like Ollie was? What do you say to people who are without faith in Christ? Do you believe Romans 8:28 is true? Why or why not? Is there a right time and a right way to share what's true, and a wrong time and a wrong way to do it?

12. Jake and Clarence are loyal friends to Ollie. They're usually sensitive to Ollie's skepticism, yet they seem unapologetic for talking about Christ. What does this teach you about friendships with unbelievers? Also, Jake told Ollie the hard truth when he needed to. Do you think this was right? How do your friendships compare to Ollie's with Jake and Clarence?

13. If you're not a Christian, what did you learn about Christians in *Deception*? If you are a believer, what did you learn about non-Christians, including how they view Christians? What misperceptions do Christians and non-Christians sometimes have about each other? How can we improve our relationships with each other? (What do you learn from Ollie's respect for Obadiah Abernathy, whom he met in *Dominion*? Why was Ollie so touched by this old man?)

14. Do you relate to Ollie's heartache and struggles related to his children—one whom he lost, one who has chosen to cut off contact with him, and one,

Kendra, with whom he doesn't get along? Admitting that he wasn't the best father, Ollie finally started working hard at his relationship with Kendra. Is it possible for difficult relationships with family members to improve over time? Why or why not?

15. How do the following verses describe God? Deuteronomy 1:31, Psalm 68:5, Isaiah 49:15–16, Matthew 6:8–9, and Luke 13:34. How do they change or enhance your view of God as our Father or parent?

16. In a scene with Sharon, the Lord tells her that we humans long for the light, but hate it because it hurts our eyes; that we sometimes prefer the comfort of darkness to the pain of sight. Are there situations in the world around you, or in your own life, that this describes? Explain.

17. Jake told Ollie that death is not a hole but a doorway, but Ollie doesn't know what to think. Read John 5:24. What are your own beliefs about life after death? On what do you base these beliefs? What do people in our society commonly believe about the afterlife, and on what do they base their beliefs?

18. Seeing Jake's and Clarence's hope and faith, something in Ollie wants to believe, but his deeply ingrained belief system is that you can only put faith in what you can see. Whether you're a Christian or not, what holds you back from fully believing the claims of Jesus Christ?

19. A theme running throughout *Deception* is that many things are not as they first appear. What situations or people in the book ended up not being what they first seemed to be?

20. "Examine the evidence. Then follow wherever it leads." This quote was taped to Ollie's fridge. At the end of *Deception*, Ollie decided to examine the two-thousand-year-old murder of Jesus mystery. Where do you think his investigation might lead? Have you undertaken that investigation? If so, where has it led you? If not, what's keeping you from it?

ABOUT THE AUTHOR

Randy Alcorn is the founder and director of Eternal Perspective Ministries (EPM), www.epm.org. Prior to 1990, when he started EPM, he served as a pastor for fourteen years. He has spoken around the world and has taught on the adjunct faculties of Multnomah Bible College and Western Seminary in Portland, Oregon.

Randy is the bestselling author of twenty-five books (over 3 million in print), including the novels *Deadline* and *Dominion* (prequels to *Deception*), *Lord Foulgrin's Letters*, *The Ishbane Conspiracy*, *Edge of Eternity*, the Gold Medallion winner *Safely Home*, and his 2007 children's picture book *Wait Until Then*.

His nonfiction works include *Money, Possessions, and Eternity*; *Pro-Life Answers to Pro-Choice Arguments*; *In Light of Eternity*; *The Treasure Principle*; *The Grace and Truth Paradox*; *The Purity Principle*; *The Law of Rewards*; *Why Pro-Life?*; *Heaven*; *50 Days of Heaven*; and *Heaven for Kids*.

Randy has written for many magazines and produces the popular complimentary periodical Eternal Perspectives. He's been a guest on over six hundred radio and television programs, including *Focus on the Family*, *Family Life Today*, *The Bible Answer Man*, *Revive Our Hearts*, *Truths That Transform*, and *Faith Under Fire*.

The father of Karina (married to Dan Franklin) and Angela (married to Dan Stump), Randy lives in Gresham, Oregon, with Nanci, his wife and best friend. They have three delightful grandsons, Jake, Matt, and Ty. Randy enjoys hanging out with his family, playing tennis, biking, conducting research, and reading.

RANDY ALCORN
FICTION

DEADLINE

When tragedy strikes those closest to him, award-winning journalist Jake Woods must draw upon all his resources to uncover the truth about their suspicious accident. Soon he finds himself swept up in a murder investigation that is both complex and dangerous. Unaware of the threat to his own life, Jake is drawn in deeper and deeper as he desperately searches for the answers to the immediate mystery at hand and—ultimately—the deeper meaning of his own existence.

DOMINION

When two senseless killings hit close to home, columnist Clarence Abernathy seeks revenge for the murders—and, ultimately, answers to his own struggles regarding race and faith. After being dragged into the world of inner-city gangs and racial conflict, Clarence is encouraged by fellow columnist Jake Woods (from the bestseller *Deadline*) to forge an unlikely partnership with a redneck homicide detective. Soon the two find themselves facing the powers of darkness that threaten the dominion of earth, while unseen eyes watch from above.

RANDY ALCORN
MORE GREAT FICTION

LORD FOULGRIN'S LETTERS

Foulgrin, a high-ranking demon, instructs his subordinate on how to deceive and destroy Jordan Fletcher and his family. It's like placing a bugging device in hell's war room, where we overhear our enemies assessing our weaknesses and strategizing attacks. *Lord Foulgrin's Letters* is a *Screwtape Letters* for our day, equally fascinating yet distinctly different—a dramatic story with earthly characters, setting, and plot. A creative, insightful, and biblical depiction of spiritual warfare, this book will guide readers to Christ-honoring counterstrategies for putting on the full armor of God and resisting the devil.

THE ISHBANE CONSPIRACY

Jillian is picture perfect on the outside, but terrified of getting hurt on the inside. Brittany is a tough girl who trusts almost no one. Ian is a successful athlete who dabbles in the occult. And Rob is a former gangbanger who struggles with guilt, pain, and a newfound faith in God. These four college students will face the ultimate battle between good and evil in a single year. As spiritual warfare rages around them, a dramatic demonic correspondence takes place. Readers can eavesdrop on the enemy, and learn to stave off their own defeat, by reading *The Ishbane Conspiracy*.

Nonfiction titles from **RANDY ALCORN**

THE TREASURE PRINCIPLE:
Unlocking the Secret of Joyful Giving
Bestselling author Randy Alcorn uncovers the revolutionary key to spiritual transformation: joyful giving! Jesus gave his followers this life-changing formula that guarantees not only kingdom impact, but immediate pleasure and eternal rewards.

THE PURITY PRINCIPLE:
God's Safeguards for Life's Dangerous Trails
God has placed warning signs and guardrails to keep us from plunging off the cliff. Find straight talk about sexual purity in Randy Alcorn's one-stop handbook for you, your family, and your church.

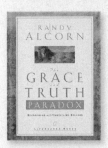

THE GRACE AND TRUTH PARADOX:
Responding with Christlike Balance
Living like Christ is a lot to ask! Discover Randy Alcorn's two-point checklist of Christlikeness—and begin to measure everything by the simple test of grace and truth.

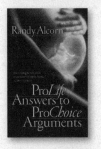

PROLIFE ANSWERS TO PROCHOICE ARGUMENTS
This revised and updated guide offers timely information and inspiration from a "sanctity of life" perspective. Real answers to real questions appear in logical and concise form. More than 85,000 copies sold!

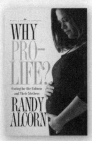

WHY PRO-LIFE?
Caring for the Unborn and Their Mothers
Bumpersticker slogans prevail, but you want the facts. Pro-choicers, pro-lifers, and fence-straddlers alike will appreciate the answers given here in a concise, straightforward, and nonabrasive manner.